THE TREASON OF ISENGARD

THE HISTORY OF THE LORD OF THE RINGS, PART TWO

THE HISTORY OF MIDDLE-EARTH

J.R.R. TOLKIEN

THE TREASON
OF ISENGARD

The History of
The Lord of the Rings
Part Two

Christopher Tolkien

HOUGHTON MIFFLIN COMPANY
Boston   New York

First Houghton Mifflin paperback edition 2000

Visit our Web site: www.hmco.com/trade.

Library of Congress Cataloging-in-Publication Data

Tolkien, J.R.R. (John Ronald Reuel), 1892–1973. The
treason of Isengard. (The history of Middle-earth ; 7)
ISBN 0-395-51562-9
ISBN 0-618-08358-8 (pbk.)

1. Tolkien, J.R.R. (John Ronald Reuel), 1892–1973. Lord of the
rings — Criticism, Textual. 2. Fantastic fiction, English — History and
criticism. 3. Middle Earth (Imaginary place) 4. Fantastic fiction, English.
I. Tolkien, Christopher. II. Title. III. Series: Tolkien, J.R.R. (John
Ronald Reul), 1892–1973. History of Middle-earth ; 7.
PR6039.032L6375 1989
823'.912 89-20093

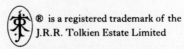
Printed in the United States of America

QUM 10 9 8 7 6 5 4 3 2

CONTENTS

ILLUSTRATIONS

FOREWORD

In 'The History of Middle-earth' I have tried to make each book as much an independent entity as possible, and not merely a section cut off when the book had reached a certain size; but in the history of the writing of *The Lord of the Rings* this has proved difficult. In *The Return of the Shadow* I was able to bring the story to the point where my father, as he said, 'halted for a long while' while the Company of the Ring stood before the tomb of Balin in the mines of Khazad-dûm; but this meant leaving till later the further complex restructurings of earlier parts of *The Fellowship of the Ring* that belong to that period.

In this volume my hope and intention was to reach the second major halt in the writing of *The Lord of the Rings*. In the Foreword to the Second Edition my father said that in 1942 he 'wrote the first drafts of the matter that now stands as Book III [the story from 'The Departure of Boromir' to 'The Palantír'], and the beginnings of Chapters 1 and 3 of Book V ['Minas Tirith' and 'The Muster of Rohan']; and there as the beacons flared in Anórien and Théoden came to Harrowdale I stopped. Foresight had failed and there was no time for thought.' It seems to have been around the end of 1942 that he stopped, and he began again ('I forced myself to tackle the journey of Frodo to Mordor') at the beginning of April 1944, after an interval of well over a year.

For this reason I chose as a title for this book *The Treason of Isengard*, that being a title my father had proposed for Book III (the first Book of *The Two Towers*) in a letter to Rayner Unwin of March 1953 (*The Letters of J. R. R. Tolkien* no. 136). But I have found repeatedly that a history of the writing of *The Lord of the Rings* tends to set its own pace and scale, and that there comes a sort of critical point beyond which condensation of the intricacies of the evolving structure is not possible, without changing the nature of the enterprise. Finding that the story was not moving rapidly enough to reach the great ride of Gandalf with Pippin on Shadowfax before I ran out of space, I rewrote a great part of the book in an attempt to shorten it; but I found that if I rejected material as being less essential or of less interest I was always confronted at a later point with the need for explanations that destroyed my gains. Finally I decided that 'The King of the Golden Hall' does in fact provide a very suitable stopping-place, not in terms of the movement of composition but in terms of the movement of the story; and I have retained the title *The Treason of Isengard*, because that was the central new element in this part of *The Lord of the Rings*, even though in this book the account of the destruction of Isengard and the reward of Saruman's betrayal is only reached in a preliminary outline.

Of course it would be possible to shorten my account very considerably by treating such matters as the chronology and geography far more superficially, but as I know well there are some who find these often exceedingly complex questions of great interest, and those who do not can easily pass them by. Or I might have omitted some passages of original writing where it is not very distinctively different from the published work; but it has been my intention throughout this 'History' that the author's own voice should be largely heard.

The way in which *The Return of the Shadow* was constructed has meant that the first part of *The Treason of Isengard* must deal at some length with further developments in *The Fellowship of the Ring* up to the point reached in the first book, and this part is of necessity a continuation of the account in *The Return of the Shadow* and stands in very close relation to it – though most of the many page-references made to it are no more than references and need not be looked up in order to follow the discussion.

This book is again very largely descriptive in intent; and in general I have thought it more useful to explain why I believe the narrative to have evolved as I describe it than to enlarge on my own views of the significance of particular features.

As the writing of *The Lord of the Rings* proceeds the initial draftings become more and more difficult to read; but for obvious reasons I have not hesitated to try to present even the most formidable examples, such as the original description of Frodo's vision on Amon Hen (pp. 372–3), though the result must be peppered all over with dots and queries.

In the preparation of this book I have again been greatly indebted to the help of Mr Taum Santoski generously and unfailingly given, and to that of Mr John D. Rateliff who has assisted in the analysis of manuscripts in the possession of Marquette University. I thank also Mr Charles B. Elston, the Archivist of the Memorial Library at Marquette, for providing photographs of the designs on the West Gate of Moria and the inscription on Balin's Tomb, and Miss Tracy Muench, who has been responsible for the photocopying of many manuscripts.

Mr Charles Noad very kindly undertook an additional and independent reading of the proofs, together with a meticulous checking of all references and citations from published works. In this connection I must explain, what I should have explained in *The Return of the Shadow*, a perhaps rather misleading device that I have employed in these books: when relating an earlier text to the published form I often treat passages as identical although the wording actually differs in unimportant ways. Thus for example (p. 370) 'Sam broke in on the discussion... with "Begging your pardons, but I don't think you understand Mr Frodo at all" (FR p. 419)' is not a misquotation of *The Fellowship of the Ring* (which has ' "Begging your pardon," said Sam. "I don't think you understand my master at all" '), but a 'shorthand' by which I indicate the precise point in *The Fellowship of the Ring* but also cite accurately the reading of the earlier text. I do this also when relating successive early versions to each other.

The illustration of Orthanc in the Ring of Isengard reproduced as the frontispiece is the earliest of successive conceptions of the tower, and may be taken to represent my father's image of it at the time when the texts in this book were written. It was done on the back of an examination script in 1942, and was found, together with other drawings, among the original drafts of 'The Road to Isengard'. The evolution of Orthanc will be described in Volume VIII, but it seemed suitable to use this picture as the frontispiece to *The Treason of Isengard*.

As in *The Return of the Shadow*, when citing texts I follow my father's representation of names, which was very inconsistent, especially in the use of capital letters. I abbreviate *The Fellowship of the Ring* as FR, *The Two Towers* as TT, and *The Lord of the Rings* as LR; and I refer to the previous volumes in this 'History', listed on the title-page, as (e.g.) 'II.189, V.226'.

I take this opportunity to explain an error in *The Return of the Shadow* (not present in the first American printing). After correction of the second proofs, lines 11–12 on page 32 of that book came to be repeated in lines 15–16 in place of the correct text, which should read:

Bingo's last words, 'I am leaving after dinner', were corrected on the manuscript to 'I am leaving now.'

I

GANDALF'S DELAY

In *The Return of the Shadow*, after citing and discussing the remark-able notes and plot-outlines bearing the date August 1939 (Chapter XXII: 'New Uncertainties and New Projections'), I turned to the continuation of the story at Rivendell and after, as far as Moria. But at this time (towards the end of 1939) my father was also engaged in substantial further revision to what ultimately became Book I of *The Fellowship of the Ring* (FR), arising primarily from a changed story of Gandalf's movements, and an explanation of his delay. I doubt that it would be possible to deduce a perfectly clear and coherent, step-by-step chronology of this period in the narrative evolution, or to relate precisely the development of the early chapters of what became Book II to the new work on Book I; for my father moved back and forth, trying out new conceptions and then perhaps abandoning them, and producing such a tangle of change as cannot always be untied: and even if it could be, it would require a vast amount of space to make it all remotely comprehensible without the manuscripts. However, granting that many uncertainties remain, I do not think that they constitute a real impediment to understanding the development in all essentials.

Most of this new work on the story as far as Rivendell can be treated in terms of the individual chapters, but some outlines, time-schemes, and notes are best collected together, though I cannot certainly determine the order in which they were set down. These are the subject of this chapter.

(1) This slip of paper begins 'State of Plot assumed after XI. (Much of explanation in XII and of incident in Bree chapter will have to be rewritten.)' The reference is clearly to Chapter XII 'The Council of Elrond', which at this stage included the narrative afterwards separ-ated off as 'Many Meetings' (see VI.399–400). Then follows:

> Bilbo gives Party and goes off. At that time he does not know anything about the ring's powers or origin (other than invisibility). Motive writing book (bring in his wry expression about 'living happily to end of [his] days') – and a restlessness: desire to see either Sea or Mountains while his days last. Confesses to a slight re-luctance to leave the ring, mixed with an oddly opposite feeling. Says to Gandalf he sometimes feels it is like an eye looking at [him].

These two things give Gandalf food for thought. He helps Bilbo therefore with his preparations – but keeps an eye on the Ring.

(Cut out a lot of the genealogical stuff and most of the Sackville-Baggins stuff.)

Then Gandalf goes off and is absent for 3 and 7 years. At the end of the last absence (14–15 years after Bilbo's disappearance) Gandalf returns and actually stays with Frodo. Then he explains what he has discovered. But he does *not* advise Frodo yet to go off, though he does mention the Cracks of Doom and the Fiery Mountain.

He departs again; and Frodo becomes restless. As Gandalf does not come back for a year and more Frodo forms the idea of going *perhaps* to the Cracks of Doom, but at any rate to Rivendell. There he will get advice. He finally makes his plans with his friends Merry and [Folco >] Faramond[1] (no Odo) and Sam. They go off just as the Black Riders come to Hobbiton.

Gandalf finds out about the Black Riders but is delayed, because the Dark Lord is hunting him (or because of Treebeard). He is alarmed at finding Frodo gone and immediately rides off to Buckland, but is again too late. He loses their trail owing to the Old Forest escapade, and actually gets ahead. He falls in with Trotter. Who is Trotter?

At the end of this sketch my father for a moment contemplated an entirely novel answer to this question: that Trotter was 'a disguised elf – friend of Bilbo's in Rivendell.' He was one of the Rivendell scouts, of whom many were sent out, and he 'pretends to be a ranger'. This was struck out, probably as soon as written.

If this is compared with the note dated August 1939 given in VI.374 it will be seen that a passage in the latter bears a distinct similarity to what is said here:

Gandalf does *not* tell Frodo to leave Shire ... The plan for leaving was entirely Frodo's. Dreams or some other cause [*added:* restlessness] have made him decide to go journeying (to find Cracks of Doom? after seeking counsel of Elrond). Gandalf simply vanishes for years. ... Gandalf is simply trying to *find* them, and is desperately upset when he discovers Frodo has left Hobbiton.

That Treebeard was a hostile being, and that he held Gandalf in captivity during the crucial time, appeared in the 'third phase' Chapter XII (VI.363); cf. also VI.384, 397.

(2) In another undated scrap is seen the actual emergence of 'Trotter's' true name – as a Man: *Aragorn*.

Trotter is a man of Elrond's race descendant of [*struck out at once:* Túrin][2] the ancient men of the North, and one of Elrond's household. He was a hunter and wanderer. He became a friend of Bilbo. He knew Gandalf. He was intrigued by Bilbo's story, and found Gollum.[3] When Gandalf went off on the last perilous quest – really to find out about Black Riders and whether the Dark Lord would attack the Shire – he [> Gandalf and Bilbo] arranged with Trotter (real name [*other unfinished names struck out in the act of writing:* Bara / Rho / Dam] Aragorn son of Aramir) to go towards the Shire and keep a lookout on the road from East (Gandalf was going South). He gives Aragorn a letter to Frodo. Aragorn pretends he is a Ranger and hangs about Bree. (He also warns Tom Bombadil.)

Reason of wooden shoes – no need in this case because Aragorn is a man.[4] Hence there is no need for Gandalf...[5] The cache of food at Weathertop is Aragorn's. Aragorn steers them to Weathertop as a good lookout.

But how could Trotter miss Gandalf?

What delayed Gandalf? Black Riders or other hunters. Treebeard. Aragorn did not miss Gandalf and arranged tryst on Weathertop.

At the end is written very emphatically and twice underlined: NO ODO.

The likeness of what is said of Trotter/Aragorn here (he was a man of Elrond's race and household, he became a friend of Bilbo's, and he 'pretends he is a Ranger') to the proposal at the end of §1 (Trotter was 'a disguised elf', one of the Rivendell scouts, a friend of Bilbo's in Rivendell, and he 'pretends to be a ranger') may suggest that the one arose directly from the other. On the other hand, my father had still not finally decided the question; for on the reverse of this piece of paper and undoubtedly at the same time he wrote:

Alternative function for Trotter. Trotter is Peregrin Boffin that Bilbo took away with him or who ran off with Bilbo – but this rather duplicates things – unless you cut out all Frodo's friends.[6]

If Trotter is Peregrin Boffin then Bilbo must go off quietly and Peregrin simply vanish *about the same time*.

This is followed by a brief passage sketching a rough narrative on these lines:

There was peace in Hobbiton for many years. Gandalf came seldom and then very quietly and mainly to visit Bilbo. He seemed to have given up trying to persuade even [?young] Tooks to go off on mad adventures out of the Shire. Then suddenly things began to happen. Bilbo Baggins disappeared again – that is hardly exact: he walked off without saying a word except to Gandalf (and to his nephews Peregrin and Frodo,[7] it may be supposed). It was a great blow to Frodo. He found Bilbo had left everything he possessed to himself and Peregrin. But Peregrin also disappeared, leaving a will in which his share

Here these notes end, the idea abandoned. Perhaps it was here that Trotter ceased finally to be a hobbit, Peregrin Boffin.

(3) A page of clear notes in ink, agreeing in part with features of §1 and §2, is headed optimistically *Final decisions. Oct. 8 1939.* This was subsequently emended in pencil, but I give it first as it was written.

> (1) General plot as at present. Bilbo vanishes at party (but all that chapter will have to be reduced, especially the Sackville-Baggins business). (Begin with a conversation between Bilbo and Frodo?)[8]
> (2) Gandalf *not* expected by Frodo. Gandalf had not been seen for 2/3 *years.* Frodo grew restless and went off – although Gandalf had really not wished him to go till he returned.
> (3) When Bilbo went Gandalf *not* sure of nature of Ring. Bilbo's longevity had made him suspicious – and he induced Bilbo *not* to take Ring with him. Bilbo had no idea that Ring was dangerous – hence simplify all Bilbo's motives, and remove the difficulty of his burdening Frodo with it.
> (4) Frodo's friends are Meriadoc Brandybuck and Peregrin Boffin called Merry and Perry (only; no Odo). Peregrin drops off at Crickhollow. Merry at Rivendell. Sam only goes on to end.
> (5) Trotter is not a hobbit but a real *ranger* who had gone to live in Rivendell after much wandering. Cut out shoes.

In (4) it is seen that despite the decision – which was indeed final – that Trotter was a Man, 'Peregrin Boffin' survived the loss of his *alter ego,* remaining an intimate of the owner of Bag End in a later generation; and for a brief moment may be said to step into the shoes of Odo Bolger – since he 'drops off at Crickhollow'.

Pencilled emendations were made to (4) and (5). To (4) was first added: 'Peregrin stays at Hobbiton and tells Gandalf.' This was struck out, and the first sentence of the note was changed to read: 'Frodo's friends are Meriadoc Brandybuck and Ham [ilcar] Bolger and Faramond Took, called Merry, Ham, and Far', with the further addition: 'Ham drops off at Crickhollow, but is picked up by Gandalf and used as a decoy. ?' (On this see under §6 below, p. 13.) Thus once more 'Odo Bolger' will bounce back, but now under the name of Hamilcar of that ilk. 'Hamilcar' has appeared hitherto only in a note dated August 1939, where it is proposed that 'Odo' be changed to 'Hamilcar' or 'Fredegar' (VI.373). 'Peregrin Boffin' disappears again – but only temporarily.

To (5) was added in pencil, after 'a real *ranger*': 'descendant of Elendil. Tarkil.' The name *Tarkil* appears in the *Etymologies* in V.364 (stem KHIL 'follow'): **tāra-khil*, in which the second element evidently bears the sense 'mortal man' (*Hildi* 'the Followers', an Elvish name for Men, V.245).

(4) A page of very rough notes in pencil, covered with emendations

and additions, is dated 'Autumn 1939' and headed *New Plot*. There now enters a very important development: a far more explicit account of what had caused Gandalf's delay than anything that has been said hitherto; and the evil figure of 'Giant Treebeard', his captor, disappears – though not for good (see p. 72).

Time Scheme won't work out for Gandalf to be ahead.

(1) Crickhollow scene – only Hamilcar [*struck out:* or Folco][9] there. He blows horn and startles the Riders' horses, which bolt. They run out of the house, and find a way[10] as the hue and cry wakes.

(2) Gandalf is *behind* at Bree. He knows Trotter (real name Aragorn). Trotter helped him track Gollum. He brings Trotter back in April 1418 to keep watch especially S.E. of Shire. It was a message of Trotter's in July (?) that took Gandalf away[11] – fearing Black Riders. He meets Trotter at Sarn Ford.[12] He then tells him of Frodo's intended departure on Sept. 22. Begs him to watch East Road in case anything happens to Gandalf himself. He visits Bree on way back to Shire on Sept. [*date illegible*]. But is pursued and tries to get round to west of Shire.

Black Riders pursue them [*read* him] – Gandalf has insufficient magic to cope with Black Riders unaided, whose king is a wizard. They pursue him over Sarn Ford and he cannot (or dare not) go back to Shire.

Eventually he is besieged in the *Western Tower*. He cannot get away while they guard it with five Riders. But when Black Riders have located Frodo and found that he has gone off without Gandalf they ride away. Three are ahead. Three follow Frodo, but miss him and get ahead at Bree. Three come behind.[13] Gandalf follows after – meets Peregrin [*written above*: news from Gaffer].

The remainder of this outline is a very rough and much corrected chronology of Gandalf's subsequent movements, which is best considered together with other chronologies of this time (§6).

A remarkable feature of this 'New Plot' is the date April 1418, for this is the first appearance of any 'exterior' chronology; moreover 1418 is the year in LR, Appendix B – according to the Shire Reckoning, i.e. 3018 of the Third Age. At the present time, at any rate, I am unable to cast any light on the chronology underlying this date, or to make any suggestion as to the process by which it had arisen.

(5) On the reverse of the page bearing this 'New Plot' is a series of notes on unconnected topics.

(1) Some mention of Bill Ferney's pony. Does this remain at Rivendell? [The question is answered 'Yes'.]

(2) Real name of Trotter? [Pencilled against this: 'Aragorn'. See §§ 2, 4.]

(3) Elrond should tell more of Gilgalad?

(4) New name of Dimrilldale (now transferred to South). River
     Hoarwell flowing out of ? Hoardale. Nen fimred. Wolfdale
     [*written above:* Entishdale]. The region west of the Misty
     Mountains north of Rivendell is called the Entishlands – home
     of Trolls.[14]

(5) Gandalf says Tom Bombadil never leaves his own ground.
     How then known to Butterbur? Tom's boundaries are from
     Bree to High Hay?[15] [Against the words 'How then known to
     Butterbur?' my father pencilled 'Not'.]

(6) Trotter is a Ranger – descendant of Elendil? – he is known to
     Bilbo, and Gandalf. He has previously been to Mordor and
     been tormented (caught in Moria). Gandalf brought him back
     towards borders of Shire in April. It was a message from
     Trotter that fetched Gandalf away in summer before Frodo left.

(7) Note Frodo's red sword is broken. Hence he accepts Sting.[16]

A final note was added in pencil: '(8) Not *Barnabas* Butterbur.' – In
the remarks about Trotter here the only point that has not appeared in
notes already given is that Trotter was captured in Moria: cf. the
original story of the Council of Elrond (VI.401): 'Trotter had tracked
Gollum as he wandered southwards, through Fangorn Forest, and
past the Dead Marshes, until he had himself been caught and
imprisoned by the Dark Lord.' It is seen here that the story of Trotter's
capture and torturing survived his change from hobbit to man.

Since Trotter's real name is not yet known these notes evidently
preceded those in §2 and §4; but no doubt they all come from the
same time.

(6) *Time-schemes.* In this section I attempt to present four chronologies of Gandalf's movements, which I label A, B, C, D. A is the
conclusion of the 'New Plot' given in §4 above, and was probably the
first to be set down. The schemes vary among themselves, each one
giving slightly different chronologies; and it is hard to be sure to what
extent the story differed in each, since my father was more explicit and
less explicit at different points in the different schemes. They were
working chronologies, much confused by alternatives and additions,
and they cannot be usefully reproduced as they stand, but in the table
on p. 12 I set out comparatively the (final) dates in each, with
statements in the original wording or closely based on it. The dates of
Frodo's journey from Hobbiton to Weathertop remain of course
unchanged, but I repeat them here for convenience:

Thurs. Sept. 22   Frodo's party
Fri.   23   Frodo and his friends leave Hobbiton
Sat.   24   Night with the Elves
Sun.   25   Farmer Maggot; reach Crickhollow
Mon.   26   Old Forest; first night with Bombadil

Tues.		27	Second night with Bombadil
Wed.		28	Leave Bombadil; Barrow-downs
Thurs.		29	Reach Bree
Fri.		30	Leave Bree; in Chetwood
Sat.	Oct.	1	In Chetwood
Sun.		2	In the Midgewater Marshes
Mon.		3	Second day in the Marshes
Tues.		4	Camp by stream under alders
Wed.		5	Camp at feet of the hills
Thurs.		6	Reach Weathertop; attack at night

Notes on the Time-schemes (table on p. 12).

The relative chronology of Gandalf's movements is much the same in all four, though the actual dates differ; but in C he takes longer from Hobbiton to Crickhollow, and in D he takes a day less from Bree to Weathertop. In A and B the date of Gandalf's escape from the Tower was first given as 24 September, the night that Frodo and his companions passed with the Elves in the Woody End, and in B there is a suggestion, struck out, that Frodo 'dreamt his dream at night with the Elves'; as is seen from the other schemes, he dreamed of Gandalf in the Western Tower. In C it is said that Frodo dreamt of the Tower when 'with the Elves near Woodhall', but against this my father wrote: 'No – at Crickhollow'; he also noted here that the attack on Crickhollow should be told on the night of *The Prancing Pony* (whence the 'doubled' opening of FR Chapter 11, 'A Knife in the Dark'). In D the placing of Frodo's 'vision of Gandalf' or 'Dream of the Tower' hesitates between the night he spent with the Elves, the night at Crickhollow, and the first night at Bombadil's house. – For the remarkable history of the dream see pp. 33–6.

The mention in A and B of Gandalf's meeting with Peregrin Boffin (Perry) at Hobbiton after his escape belongs with the addition made to the 'final decisions' given in §3 above: 'Peregrin stays at Hobbiton and tells Gandalf.' This was a short-lived idea – indeed already in the 'New Plot' (§4) my father scribbled in here 'news from Gaffer': a reference to the story that will appear in the next phase of work on 'The Council of Elrond' (p. 135; FR p. 276).

Scheme A makes no mention of what happened at Crickhollow, but the 'New Plot' that precedes it begins with the statement that only Hamilcar Bolger was there, and that the horses of the Riders bolted when he blew a horn: which presumably means that the attack took place before Gandalf arrived. An addition to B (contradicting the chronology of that scheme) says that

The Black Riders creep into Buckland, but too late to see Frodo depart. They track him to Crickhollow and guard it, and see Gandalf enter. But Gandalf (and Ham pretending to be Frodo) burst out on night of Sept. 29.

Journeys of Gandalf

	A	B	C	D
Sun. Sept. 25	Escapes from Tower	Escapes from Tower at dawn	Leaves White Tower at dawn	
Tues. Sept. 27	Reaches Hobbiton; sees Perry Boffin	Reaches Hobbiton; sees Perry Boffin (morning)	Reaches Hobbiton	
Wed. Sept. 28		Reaches Crickhollow late		Returns to Shire
Thurs. Sept. 29	Crickhollow	Leaves Crickhollow early, goes to Bombadil	Reaches Crickhollow via Bridge, evening, Riders attack at night	Riders attack Crickhollow; carry off Ham, pursued by Gandalf (midnight)
Fri. Sept. 30	Leaves Crickhollow, goes to Bombadil	Leaves Bombadil, reaches Bree late, 'very tired'	Dawn: breaks out with Ham and 'rides off' to Bombadil	Early morning: rescues Ham, goes to Bombadil
Sat. Oct. 1	Leaves Bombadil; reaches Bree	Leaves Bree early	Reaches Bree in evening	Leaves Bombadil early, reaches Bree
Sun. Oct. 2	Leaves Bree in morning		Leaves Bree	Leaves Bree with Ham early
Mon. Oct. 3		Reaches Weathertop late		Reaches Weathertop in evening. Holds out during night
Tues. Oct. 4	Breaks through Riders and reaches Weathertop	Pursued by Riders leaves Weathertop early	Reaches Weathertop in evening. Leaves during night	Flies from Weathertop pursued by Riders

With this cf. the addition to §3 above: 'Ham drops off at Crickhollow, but is picked up by Gandalf and used as a decoy.' Scheme C says that it was at dawn on the 30th (the morning on which the hobbits left Bree with Trotter after the attack on the inn) that 'Gandalf broke out with Ham'; he then 'rode off to Tom' (which way did he go?).

A different story is seen in D, in which it is told that at midnight on the 29th/30th Black Riders crossed the Brandywine by the Ferry, attacked the house at Crickhollow, and *carried off* Ham, 'pursued by Gandalf'; and that in the early morning of the 30th Gandalf *rescued* Ham, the Black Riders fled in terror to their King, and Gandalf went on to visit Tom.

For narrative drafts reflecting these versions of the events at Crickhollow see pp. 53–6, 68–70.

All the schemes agree that Gandalf went from Buckland to visit Tom Bombadil; cf. the original version of 'The Council of Elrond', VI.401, where Gandalf says that 'when I had chased the Riders from Crickhollow I turned back to visit him.'

Scheme D has a note that 'Trotter reaches the Shire border Sept. 14 and hears ill news on morning of 25th from Elves.' This scheme also provides an account of the movements of the individual Riders, who are identified by the letters A to I. It was D who came to Hobbiton on 23 September, the night on which Frodo left, and it was D and E who trailed the hobbits in the Shire, while GHI were on the East Road and F was to the southward. On the 25th, the day that Frodo reached Crickhollow, DEGHI assembled at the Brandywine Bridge; G waited there while H and I passed through Bree on Monday the 26th. On the 27th D and E 'got into Buckland and looked for Baggins'; on the 28th they 'located' him and went to get the help of G. On the night of the 29th DEG crossed the River by the Ferry; and on the same night H and I returned and attacked *The Prancing Pony*. Pursued by Gandalf from Crickhollow DEG fled to the King. ABCDEFG 'rode East after Gandalf and the supposed Baggins' on 1 October; F and G were sent direct to Weathertop, and the other five, together with H and I, rode through Bree at night, throwing down the gates, and from the inn (where Gandalf was) the noise of their passage was heard like a wind. F and G reached Weathertop on the 2nd; Gandalf was pursued North from Weathertop by CDE, while ABFGHI patrolled the East Road.

Of these four time-schemes only D treats fully the chronology from Weathertop to the Ford. A mentions that Gandalf went North 'via Entish Lands' and reached Rivendell on 14 October; two Riders pursued him 'towards Entish Dale; these are they that came from the flank at the Ford.'[17] B also has Gandalf reach Rivendell on the 14th, and says:

But messages from the Elves of the Shire have travelled swiftly since Sept. 24. Already Elrond has heard in Rivendell that the Ring had set out alone, and that Gandalf is missing, and the Ringwraiths are out. He sends out scouts North, South, and West. These scouts are Elves of power. Glorfindel goes along the Road. He reaches the Bridge of *Mitheithel*[18] at dawn on Oct. 12 and drives off the Black Riders and pursues them West till they escape. On Oct. 14 he turns and searches for traces of Frodo's party for several days (2/3), finds them, and then comes after them, catching them up on the evening of Oct. 18.

In Scheme D the final chronology for this part of the story, agreeing (except in one point) with that in LR Appendix B though fuller, was attained. For earlier phases of the development see VI.219, 360.

October

Wed.	5	Camp near hills	
Thurs.	6	Attack on camp at Weathertop	
Fri.	7	Frodo leaves Weathertop	
Sat.	8		News reaches Elrond
Sun.	9	Frodo in the Cheerless Lands	Glorfindel leaves Rivendell
Mon.	10		
Tues.	11		Gandalf at Hoarwell (Mitheithel) Rain. Glorfindel at Bridge of Mitheithel
Wed.	12	Frodo and Trotter see Road and rivers	
Thurs.	13	Frodo crosses Last Bridge	
Fri.	14	Frodo in hills	Glorfindel finds tracks
Sat.	15	Hills (wet)	
Sun.	16	Hills (shelf) [See FR p. 214: 'a stony shelf']	
Mon.	17	Troll-ridge	
Tues.	18	Trolls	Gandalf and Ham reach Rivendell Glorfindel finds Trotter etc.
Wed.	19	Bend [See FR p. 224: 'the Road bent right']	
Thurs.	20	Battle at Ford of Bruinen[19]	
Fri.	21		
Sat.	22	Frodo unconscious	
Sun.	23		
Mon.	24	Frodo wakes	
Tues.	25		
Wed.	26	Council of Elrond	

The only point in which this differs from the final chronology is that a whole day passes between Frodo's waking and the Council of Elrond, which thus takes place here on the 26th of October, not on the 25th.

But this is not a slip, for the same appears in other closely related chronologies of this period.

NOTES

1 *Faramond Took* replaced *Folco Took* in the original version of 'The Council of Elrond', VI.406 and subsequently.
2 Túrin of course had no descendants. Possibly *Túrin* was a slip for *Tuor*, grandfather of Elrond.
3 That it was Trotter who found Gollum appears in the original version of 'The Council of Elrond' (VI.401 and note 20).
4 The meaning of this very elliptical remark is possibly that when Trotter was a hobbit the injury to his feet caused him to wear shoes, which for a hobbit was highly unusual; but if he was a man that would not be the case.
5 From its appearance the illegible word could well be *otiose*, but that does not seem likely. If however this is what it is, 'Hence there is no need for' must be a sentence left in the air, followed by 'Gandalf otiose' – i.e. Gandalf need have nothing to do with Weathertop: Aragorn 'steered them to Weathertop' simply because it was 'a good lookout'. But the whole passage is very obscure.
6 I.e., if Bilbo went off with Peregrin Boffin there would be a duplication when Frodo in his turn went off with younger companions.
7 Cf. the story of Peregrin Boffin in VI.385–6: there Peregrin and Frodo stood in the same relationship (first cousins once removed) to Bilbo.
8 The bracketed sentence was struck out, with the note: 'No, because that would give away suspense.' On the same piece of paper as these 'final decisions' there is a sketch of such a conversation, although in this there is no suggestion of a party:
    'I am going for a holiday, a long holiday!' said Bilbo Baggins to his young 'nephew' Frodo. 'What is more, I am going tomorrow. It will be April 30th, my anniversary and a good day to start on. Also the weather is fine!'
    Bilbo had made this announcement a great many times before; but each time he made it, and it became plainer that he really meant it, Frodo's heart sank lower. He had lived with Bilbo for nearly 12 years and known him longer, and he was devoted to him. 'Where are you going?' he asked, but he did not expect any answer, as he had also asked this question often before and got no satisfactory reply.
    'I would tell you if I knew myself for certain – or perhaps I would,' answered Bilbo as usual. 'To the Sea maybe, or the

Mountains. Mountains, I think; yes, Mountains,' he said, as if to himself.

'Could I come with you?' asked Frodo. He had never said that before; and he had not really any desire to leave Bag-End or the Shire that he loved; but that night with Bilbo's departure so near

Here this fragment ends.

9   or Folco: cf. §3 (4): 'Peregrin [Boffin] drops off at Crickhollow.'

10   find a way is clear, but my father possibly intended ride away, or flee away, or something similar.

11   In the 'third phase' version Gandalf still left Bag End 'one wet dark evening in May' (VI.323). In FR (p. 76) he left at the end of June.

12   The name Sarn Ford is here met for the first time. It is found on the most original part of the original LR map (pp. 299, 305).

13   The numbers were first written two ahead, four following Frodo, three behind. The passage was bracketed with a note: 'No, see Black Riders' movements': this is a reference to the full account in Scheme D (see p. 13).

14   For the transference of Dimrill-dale to the South and the other side of the Misty Mountains and its replacement by Hoardale see VI.432–3, notes 3 and 13. The present note is very probably where the River Hoarwell (see VI.192, 360) rising in Hoardale, and the Entish Lands, first emerged. No doubt it was at this time that Hoardale was written on the manuscript of the first version of 'The Ring Goes South' (VI.432, note 3); but Entish Dale evidently soon replaced it – it is found in one of the Time-schemes (p. 13) and was written in on the present note. On Ent as used in these names, in the sense of Old English ent 'giant', the Ents of Fangorn not having yet arisen, see VI.205.

15   In the 'third phase' narrative Tom Bombadil was still thought of as visiting The Prancing Pony (VI.334), but in the first version of 'The Council of Elrond' (VI.402) Gandalf says that 'the mastery of Tom Bombadil is seen only on his own ground – from which he has never stepped within my memory.'

16   Bilbo's gift to Frodo of Sting is first mentioned in the initial draft for 'The Council of Elrond' (VI.397), and Frodo's possession of it in the sketch for the Moria story (VI.443). – Why is Frodo's sword called 'red'? In another isolated note, written much later, this reappears: 'What happened to the red sword[s] of the Barrows? In Frodo's case it is broken at the Ford and he has Sting.' In the 'third phase' version of 'Fog on the Barrow-downs' they were 'bronze swords, short, leaf-shaped and keen' (VI.128, 329); at some later time the reading of FR (p. 157), according to which they were 'damasked with serpent-forms in red and gold', was entered on that manuscript.

17 On *Entish Dale* see note 14. – In the 'third phase' version of the story there were six Riders in ambush at the Ford (VI.361); in FR there were four (cf. p. 62).

18 This is the first appearance in the texts of the Elvish name *Mitheithel* of the River Hoarwell (see note 14) and of the Last Bridge, by which the East Road crossed the river (but they are found on the sketch-maps redrawn in Vol. VI, p. 201).

19 This is the first occurrence of the name *Bruinen*, other than on one of the sketch-maps mentioned in note 18.

II

THE FOURTH PHASE (1):
FROM HOBBITON TO BREE

The rethinking and rewriting of this period led to an extremely complex situation in the actual constituent chapter-manuscripts of the book as it stood. Some of the manuscripts of the 'third phase' were now in their turn covered with corrections and deletions and interspersed with inserted riders, so that they became chaotic (cf. VI.309). In this case, however, since substantial parts of those manuscripts were in no need of correction, or of very little, my father wrote out fair only those parts of the chapters that had been much affected by revision, and added to these the unaffected portions of the original 'third phase' texts. For this 'fourth' phase, therefore, some of the manuscripts are textually hybrids, while others remain common to both 'phases' (no doubt a somewhat artificial conception).

The rejected parts of the 'third phase' manuscripts were separated and set aside and in a sense 'lost', so that when the 'fourth phase' series was sent to Marquette University some eighteen years later these superseded pages – and a good deal of preliminary draft writing for their replacement – remained in England. To put it all together again, and to work out the intricacies of the whole complex become so widely separated, has been far from easy; but I have no doubt that in the result the history of these texts has been correctly ascertained.[1]

Where necessary to distinguish rough revision in draft and the fair copy manuscript based on it I shall call the former 'A' and the latter 'B' for the purpose of this chapter.

The revision of this period came very near to attaining the text of FR Book I through a great part of its length, though with certain major and notable exceptions; and in what follows a host of minor changes is to be presupposed, since there would be little purpose in spelling them out. It is indeed remarkable to see that by the end of 1939 the story as far as Rivendell had been brought, after so many and such meticulous revisions, to a point where one could read the greater part of it and scarcely suspect any difference from FR without careful comparison; yet at this time my father was without any clear conception of what lay before him.

In my account chapter by chapter of the 'fourth phase' I shall concentrate on the major elements of reconstruction that belong to this time.

Chapter I: 'A Long-expected Party'

The sixth or 'third phase' version of this chapter (VI.314–15) was heavily reworked in certain passages, bringing the story at almost all points virtually to the form in FR. The substantial rider added at the beginning, introducing the story of the youth of Peregrin Boffin or Trotter (see VI.384–6), was rejected when the decision was finally taken that Trotter was a Man, and does not appear in the fair copy B.

Many changes reflect suggestions in the notes dated August 1939 given in VI.370 ff., and some new features derive from the notes and outlines given in Chapter I of this book. Thus Bilbo took with him 'a bundle wrapped in old cloths': his 'elf-armour' (see VI.371–2). Now, just as in FR (p. 40), he put the envelope on the mantlepiece (but suddenly took it down and stuck it in his pocket), and Gandalf entered at that moment (changing the previous story, in which Gandalf met Bilbo at the bottom of the hill, VI.315). Their conversation (for the form of it before this revision see VI.238–40) becomes exactly as in FR, as far as 'It's time he was his own master now' (p. 41), and this clearly derives from the 'August 1939' note given in VI.374: 'Neither Bilbo nor Gandalf must know much about the Ring, when Bilbo departs. Bilbo's motive is simply *tiredness*, an unexplained restlessness...' Bilbo's words about his book, which Gandalf says nobody will read, are taken up from the note given in VI.371.[2] But here this 'fourth phase' version shows a significant difference from FR: for there is *no quarrel* between them as yet, though it hovers on the verge of being devised (on the first germ of the quarrel see VI.378–9). I give the passage in the form of the fair copy B (which the draft A approaches very closely):

'Everything?' said Gandalf. 'The ring as well?'

'Well, or yes I suppose so,' stammered Bilbo.

'Where is it?'

'I put it in an envelope for him, and put it on the mantle – well no! Isn't that odd now! Here it is in my pocket!'

Gandalf looked again very hard at Bilbo, and his eyes glinted. 'I think, Bilbo,' he said quietly, 'I should leave it with him. Don't you want to?'

'Well yes – and yet it seems very difficult to part with it somehow. Why do you want me to leave it behind?' he asked, and a curious note of suspicion came into his voice. 'You are always worrying about it lately, but you have never bothered me about the other things I got on my journey.'

'Magic rings are – well, *magic*,' answered Gandalf; 'and they are not, nowadays, very common. Let's say that I am professionally interested in your ring, and would like to know where it is. Also I think *you* have had it long enough. You won't want it any more, Bilbo, unless I am quite mistaken.'

'Oh, very well,' said Bilbo. 'It would be a relief, in a way, not to be bothered with it. It has been rather growing on my mind lately. Sometimes I have felt that it was like an eye looking at me;[3] and I am always wanting to put it on and disappear, don't you know, or wondering if it is safe and pulling it out to make sure. I tried leaving it locked up, but I found I couldn't rest without it in my pocket. I don't know why. Well! Now I must be starting, or somebody else will catch me. I have said good-bye, and I couldn't bear to do it all over again.' He picked up his bag and moved towards the door.

'You have still got the ring in your pocket,' said the wizard.

'So I have, and my will and all the other documents too!' cried Bilbo. 'I had better give them to you to deliver to Frodo. That will be safest.' He held out the envelope, but just as Gandalf was about to take it, Bilbo's hand jerked and the envelope fell on the floor. Quick as lightning the wizard stooped and seized it, before Bilbo could pick it up. An odd look passed over the hobbit's face, almost like anger. Suddenly it gave way to a look of relief and a smile.

'Well, that's that!' he said. 'Now I'm off!'

From this point the revision brings the narrative almost to the final form. The dwarves, now three and no longer named, play only the same rôle as in FR; and when Frodo returns to Bag End he finds Gandalf sitting in the dark, whereupon the conversation between them in FR (pp. 44–5) follows. A minute but characteristically subtle difference remaining is that it is not said, in the passage just cited, that when the envelope fell to the floor Gandalf 'set it in its place' on the mantlepiece; and now Gandalf says to Frodo: 'He left a packet with me to give to you. Here it is!' Then Frodo took the envelope from the wizard. In FR Gandalf pointed to it on the mantelpiece; he would not sit waiting for Frodo with the envelope containing the Ring in his hand.

Once again the list of Bilbo's labelled legacies changes (see VI.247), in that Uffo Took now receives the final name Adelard, while the somnolent Rollo Bolger, recipient of the feather-bed, makes his last appearance, his first name changed to Odovacar, in A; in B he has gone.

The conversation between Gandalf and Frodo at Bag End on the following day (see VI.242–3) now becomes precisely as in FR with, of course, the one major difference that there is no reference to the variant stories which Bilbo had told concerning his acquisition of the

Ring (p. 49). The rewriting of this conversation again clearly springs from the note of August 1939 (VI.374) referred to above, to the effect that Gandalf still did not know very much about the Ring at this time; for Gandalf now knows less about it than he had done. He no longer warns Frodo against allowing it to gain power over him, nor is there now any mention in their conversation of Bilbo's state of 'preservation', and his restlessness, as concomitants of his possession of the Ring.

The revision got rid of the Dwarf Lofar, who had previously remained at Bag End after Bilbo's departure with the other Dwarves, but at first provided no clear substitute for Frodo's aide-de-camp whose task (as it turned out) was to receive the Sackville-Bagginses. In the fair copy B this is Merry, as in FR; but in the draft revision A my father replaced Lofar by one scribbled name after another: 'Merry' > 'Peregrin Boffin' > 'Folco Took'; at subsequent occurrences in this episode 'Peregrin Boffin' > 'Folco', and once 'Peregrin' retained. 'Peregrin Boffin' had been moved from the rôle of Trotter in his youth, but survived as one of Frodo's intimates: as such we have already met him (pp. 8, 11). See further pp. 30–2.

Chapter II: 'Ancient History'

This chapter (ultimately one of the most worked upon in all *The Lord of the Rings*) underwent very substantial rewriting at this time in certain passages, but remained still in important respects far different from 'The Shadow of the Past' in FR. The 'third phase' manuscript (VI.318 ff.), not much changed in substance from the second version (VI.250 ff.), was reduced to a wreck in the process; and here again my father made a new text (B) of the chapter, taking up all this rough correction and new writing (A), but incorporated into the new manuscript those parts of the old that were retained more or less intact, so that the new version is again textually a hybrid.

In draft revision of the beginning of the chapter Frodo's 'closest companions were Folco Took [*pencilled above*: Faramond] and Meriadoc Brandybuck (usually called Merry), both a few years younger than himself' (cf. VI.318); in B his companions become Faramond Took, Peregrin Boffin, and Hamilcar Bolger, while his closest friend was Merry Brandybuck. With this cf. the notes given on p. 8. In the drafts (A) the names Folco, Faramond, Peregrin, shift and replace each other at every occurrence, and it is scarcely possible to say whether characters or merely names are in question.

Otherwise, the new version reaches the final form in most respects for a long stretch. The chronology of Gandalf's visits to Bag End, from the Party to the time of this chapter, becomes precisely that of FR (p. 55); but the passage (FR pp. 52–3) concerning the 'rumours of strange things happening in the world outside' was at this stage left virtually unchanged – which means that it still essentially took the form it had in the second version, VI.253.

The first part of the conversation between Gandalf and Frodo now takes a great step towards that in FR (pp. 55–6; cf. VI.319), but Gandalf as yet says nothing of the making of rings 'in Eregion long ago', nor does he speak here of the Great Rings, the Rings of Power. Though his words are the same as in FR, they apply only to the ring in Frodo's possession: thus he says 'Those who keep this ring do not die,' &c. His account of Bilbo's knowledge of and feeling about his ring are very much as in FR, but he says here that Bilbo 'knew, of course, that it made one invisible, if it encircled any part of the body.' In rejected drafts for this passage occur the following:

He certainly had not yet begun to connect his long life and 'good preservation' with the ring – but he had begun to feel the restlessness that is the first symptom of the stretching of the days.

On that last evening I saw plainly that the ring was trying to keep hold of him and prevent his parting with it. But he was not yet conscious of it himself. And certainly he had no idea that it would have made him permanently invisible, nor that his long life and 'good preservation' – how the expression annoyed him! – had anything to do with it.

From Frodo's question at the end of Gandalf's remarks about Bilbo, the new version retains the existing text (VI.319) concerning Gandalf's memories, but is then developed quite differently, though still far from that of FR (p. 57):

'How long have you known?' asked Frodo again.
'I knew very little of these things at first,' answered Gandalf slowly, as if searching back in memory. The days of Bilbo's journey and the Dragon and the Battle of Five Armies seemed dim and far off, and many other dark and strange adventures had befallen him since. 'Let me see – it was after the White Council in the South that I first began to give serious thought to Bilbo's ring. There was much talk of rings at the Council: even wizards have much to learn as long as they live, however long that may be. There are many sorts of ring, of course. Some are no more than toys (though dangerous ones to my mind), and not difficult to contrive if you go in for such things – they are not in my line. But what I heard made me think a good deal, though I said nothing to Bilbo. All seemed well with him. I thought he was safe enough from any evil of that sort. I was nearly right but not quite right. Perhaps I should have been

more suspicious, and have found out the truth sooner than I did
– yet if I had, I don't know what else could have been done.

'Then, of course, I noticed that he did not seem to grow older.
But the whole thing seemed so unlikely that I did not get
seriously alarmed, never until the night he left this house. He
said and did things then that were unmistakeable signs of
something wrong.[4] From that moment my chief anxiety was to
get him to go and give up the ring. And I have spent most of the
years since in finding out the truth about it.'

'There wasn't any permanent harm done, was there?' asked
Frodo anxiously. 'He would get right in time, wouldn't he – be
able to rest in peace, I mean?'

'That I don't know for certain,' said Gandalf. 'There is only
one [added: Power] in this world who knows all about the ring
and its effects. But I don't think you need fear for him. Of
course, if anyone possessed the ring for many years, it would
probably take a long while for the effects to wear off. How long
is not really known. He might live for ages. But not wearily, I
think. He would, I now believe, just stop as he was when he
parted with the ring; and would be happy, if he parted with it of
his own accord and with good intent. Though as far as I know
that has only happened once. I was not troubled about dear
Bilbo any more, once he had let the ring go. It is for *you* that I
feel responsible...'[5]

There is of course no reference here to Bilbo's 'two stories' of how
he came by the Ring; nor does Saruman appear. Yet Gandalf's
mention of the discussion of Rings at the White Council, and his
suggestion that there are wizards who, unlike himself, 'go in for such
things', prepares the place that Saruman would fill when he had arisen
– although, characteristically, he did not arise in order to fill that
place.

The new version introduced no changes into Gandalf's account of
the Ruling Ring and its history (for the text as it had developed
through the three preceding versions see VI.78, 258–61, 319–20):
indeed almost all of this part of the chapter is constituted from pages
taken out of the 'third phase' manuscript (see p. 18). Before the new
version of the chapter was completed, however (see note 12), my
father changed Gollum's original name from *Dígol* (through *Déagol*)
to *Sméagol*, and introduced a rider telling the story of Deagol and his
murder:

He had a friend called Deagol, of similar short, sharper-eyed
but not so quick and strong. They were roaming together, when

in the mud of a river-bank, under the twisted roots of an ancient thorn-tree,[6] Deagol found the Ring. Smeagol came up behind him, just as he was washing the mud off, and the Ring gleamed yellow.

'Give us that, Deagol my love,' said Smeagol over his friend's shoulder.

'Why?' said Deagol.

'Because it's my birthday . . .

The remainder of the inserted text is virtually word for word as in FR (p. 62). On this new story see pp. 27–8.

Very substantial rewriting begins again with Gandalf's discussion of Gollum's motives (FR pp. 63–6; for the previous versions see VI.79–80, 261–2, 320–1). Here there is more than one draft preceding the new manuscript B, and the relations between these texts are not entirely clear, though they differ chiefly only in the placing of certain elements. I give this passge in the form of B, with some variants from the drafts A recorded in the notes.

'Gollum!' said Frodo. 'Do you mean the very Gollum-creature that Bilbo met? Is that his history? How loathsome!'

'I think it is a sad story,' said the wizard, 'and it might have happened to others, even to some hobbits I have known.'

'I can't believe Gollum was connected with hobbits, however distantly,' said Frodo with some heat. 'What an abominable idea!'

'It is true all the same,' replied Gandalf. 'It is suggested even by Bilbo's own account; and partly explains the very curious events. There was a lot in the background of their minds and memories that was very similar: Bilbo and Gollum understood one another (if you think of it) better than hobbits have ever understood dwarves or goblins, or even elves. Think of the riddles they both knew, for one thing!'

'But why did Gollum start the Riddle-game, or think of giving up the Ring at all?' asked Frodo.[7]

'Because he was altogether miserable, and yet could not make up his wretched mind. Don't you realize that he had possessed the Ring for ages, and the torment was becoming unendurable? He was so wretched that he knew he was wretched, and had at last understood what caused it. There was nothing more to find out, nothing left but darkness, nothing to do but furtive eating and regretful remembering. Half his mind wanted above all to be rid of the Ring, even if the loss killed him. But he hated parting with it as much as keeping it. He wanted to hand it on to someone else, and to make him wretched too.'

'Then why didn't he give it to the Goblins?'

'Gollum would not have found that amusing! The Goblins were already beastly and miserable. And anyway he was afraid of them: naturally he had no fancy for an invisible goblin in the tunnels. But when Bilbo turned up half his mind saw that he had a marvellous chance; and the other half was angry and frightened, and was thinking how to trap and eat Bilbo. So he tried the Riddle-game, which might serve either purpose: it would decide the question for him, like tossing up. Very hobbit-like, I call that. But of course, if it had really come to the point of handing the Ring over, he would have immediately desired it terribly, and have hated Bilbo fiercely. It was lucky for Bilbo that things were arranged otherwise.'[8]

'But how was it that Gollum did not realize that he had got rid of it, if Bilbo had the Ring already?'

'Simply because he had only lost it for a few hours: not nearly long enough for him to feel any change in himself. And also he had not given it away of his own free will: that is an important point. All the same I have always thought that the strangest thing about Bilbo's whole adventure was his finding the Ring like that: just putting his hand on it in the dark. There was something mysterious in that; I think more than one power was at work. The Ring was trying to get back to its master. It had ruined Gollum, and could make no further use of him; he was too small and mean. It had already slipped from one owner's hand and betrayed him to death. It now left Gollum: and that would probably have proved Gollum's death, if the finder had not been the most unlikely creature imaginable: a Baggins all the way from the Shire! But behind all that there was something at work beyond any design of the Ringmaker. I can put it no plainer than by saying that *Bilbo was meant* to find the Ring, and *not* by its maker. In which case *you* were also meant to have it, and that may be an encouraging thought, or it may not.'

'It isn't,' said Frodo, 'though I am not sure that I understand you. But how have you learned all this about the Ring, and about Gollum? Do you really know it all, or are you guessing?'

'I have learned some things, and guessed others,' answered Gandalf. 'But I am not going to give you an account of the last few years just now. The story of Gilgalad and Isildur and the

One Ring is well known to the learned in Lore. I knew it myself, of course, but I have consulted many other Lore-masters. Your ring is shown to be that One Ring by the fire-writing, quite apart from other evidence.'

'And when did you discover that?' asked Frodo interrupting.

'Just now in this room, of course,' answered Gandalf sharply. 'But I expected to find it. I have come back from many dark journeys to make that final test. It is the last proof, and all is now clear. Making out Gollum's part, and fitting it into the gap in the history, required some thought; but I guessed very near the truth. I know more of the minds and histories of the creatures of Middle-earth than you imagine, Frodo.'

'But your account does not quite agree with Bilbo's, as far as I can remember it.'

'Naturally. Bilbo had no idea of the nature of the Ring, and so could not guess what was behind Gollum's peculiar behaviour. But though I started from hints and guesses, I no longer need them. I am no longer guessing about Gollum. I know. I know because I have seen him.'[9]

'You have seen Gollum!' exclaimed Frodo in amazement.

'The obvious thing to try and do, surely,' said Gandalf.

'Then what happened after Bilbo escaped from him?' asked Frodo. 'Do you know that?'

'Not so clearly. What I have told you is what Gollum was willing to tell – though not, of course, in the way I have reported it. Gollum is a liar, and you have to sift his words. For instance, you may remember that he told Bilbo that he had been given the Ring as a birthday present long ago when such rings were less uncommon.[10] Very unlikely on the face of it: no kind of magic ring was ever common in his part of the world. Quite incredible, when one suspects what ring this one really was.[11] It was a lie, though with a grain of truth. I fancy he had made up his mind what to say, if necessary, so that the stranger would accept the Ring without suspicion, and think the gift natural. And that is another hobbit-like thought! Birthday present! It would have worked well with any hobbit. There was no need to tell the lie, of course, when he found the Ring had gone; but he had told that lie to himself so many times in the darkness, trying to forget Deagol,[12] that it slipped out, whenever he spoke of the Ring. He repeated it to me, but I laughed at him. He then told me more or less the true story, but with a lot of snivelling and snarling. He thought he was misunderstood and ill-treated...

In the third version of this chapter Gandalf had said (VI.321): 'Very unlikely on the face of it: incredible when one suspects what kind of ring it really was. It was said merely to make Bilbo willing to accept it as a harmless kind of toy' (i.e., Gollum, speaking – according to Gandalf's elaborate theory – from that part of his mind that wished to get rid of the Ring, said off the top of his head that it had been a birthday present in order to get Bilbo to accept it more readily). While drafting a new version of this passage, my father was struck by a perturbing thought. He stopped, and across the manuscript he wrote: 'It must be [i.e. It must have been] a birthday present, as the birthday present is not mentioned by Gollum until after he finds the ring is *lost*'.[13] In other words, if the story of its being a birthday present was a fabrication pure and simple, why should Gollum only trot it out when there was no longer any use for it? Apparently in order to counter this, Gandalf's words were changed:

It was a lie, though with a grain of truth. But how hobbit-like, all that talk of birthday-presents! I fancy he had made up his mind what to say, if it came to the point of giving, so that Bilbo would accept the Ring without suspicion, and think it just a harmless toy. He repeated this nonsense to me, but I laughed at him.

The implication of this seems to be that Gollum brought out this story of the Ring having been a birthday present to him long ago only when he found that he had it no longer, because it had 'a grain of truth'; and it was because it had 'a grain of truth' that he had decided on this story. But there is no suggestion in the draft of what this grain of truth might be. Only with the fair copy B does it appear – and there only by implication: 'There was no need to tell the lie, of course, when he found the Ring had gone; but he had told that lie to himself so many times in the darkness, *trying to forget Deagol*, that it slipped out, whenever he spoke of the Ring.' This shows of course that the Deagol story (pp. 23–4) had already entered; but my father made the point clearer by pencilling on the fair copy after the words 'though with a grain of truth': *He murdered Deagol on his birthday.*

He was being driven to more and more intricate shifts to get round what had been said in *The Hobbit*. But it seems to me very likely that it was precisely while he was pondering this problem that the story of the murder of Deagol (and incidentally the changing of Gollum's true name to Smeagol) arose. That Gollum had *lied* about its being a birthday present was an obvious necessity, from the story of the Ring that had come into being; but Gandalf's theory in the third version that Gollum told this lie to Bilbo in order to get him to accept the Ring had a serious weakness: why did Gollum only do so (as the story was told in *The Hobbit*) *after* he found that he had lost it? The answer to this was that it was an invention of Gollum's that he had come partly to believe, quite independently of Bilbo's arrival; but why was that?

And this story of the murder of Deagol on Smeagol's birthday, the ground of Smeagol's 'lie with a grain of truth', became a permanent element in the tale of Gollum; surviving when, years later, the story of 'Riddles in the Dark' was recast and the very difficulty that (if I am right) had brought it into being was eliminated.

From 'He thought he was misunderstood and ill-treated' (p. 26) this fourth version of 'Ancient History' scarcely differs for a long stretch from the third, whose pages were largely retained;[14] and since the third version closely followed the second, this part of the conversation of Gandalf and Frodo preserves, apart from detail of expression, the text given in VI.263–5. But from 'The Wood-elves have him in prison, if he is still alive, as I expect; but they treat him with such kindness as they can find in their wise hearts' the new version reaches the form in FR (p. 69) with almost no difference to the end of the chapter. Gandalf's words about the fire that could melt and consume the Rings of Power (FR p. 70) remain however nearer to the earlier form:

It has been said that only dragon-fire can melt any of the Twenty Rings of Power; but there is not now any Dragon left on earth in whom the old Fire is hot enough to harm the Ruling Ring. I can think of only one way: one would have to find the Cracks of Doom in the depths of Orodruin, the Fire-Mountain, and cast the Ring in there, if he really wished to destroy it, or put it beyond all reach until the End.

The name *Orodruin* is met here for the first time.[15] In another point also the former version is retained: Gandalf still says when he goes to the window and draws aside the curtain (VI.322):

'In any case it is now too late. You would come to hate me and call me a thief; and our friendship would cease. Such is the power of the Ring. Keep it, and together we will shoulder the burden that is laid on us.'

Lastly, Gandalf does not in this version give Frodo a 'travelling name' ('When you go, go as Mr. Underhill', FR p. 72).

The subsequent history of this chapter, traced in detail, would itself almost constitute a book, for apart from the marvellous intricacies of the route by which the story of Gollum and the 'birthday present' was ultimately resolved, Gandalf's conversation with Frodo became the vehicle for the developing history of the Rings of Power, afterwards removed from this place, and the chapter could not be treated separately from 'The Council of Elrond'. But the great mass of this work, and probably all of it, belongs to a later time than we have reached; and in any case the attempt to trace in 'linear' fashion the history of the writing of *The Lord of the Rings* cannot at the same time take full account of the great constructions that were rising behind the onward movement of the tale. So far as the story of Bilbo and Gollum is concerned it seems that this fourth version of 'Ancient History', in which my father was still constrained within the words of the original story told in *The Hobbit*, remained for some time as the accepted form.

Chapter III: 'Three is Company'

The third version of this chapter, described in VI.323–5, was also revised at this time. The title was now changed from 'Delays are Dangerous' to 'Three is Company' (cf. the original title, 'Three's Company and Four's More', VI.49 and note 2); and the order of the opening passages was reversed, so that the chapter now begins as in FR with ' "You ought to go *quietly*, and you ought to go *soon*," said Gandalf', and his conversation with Frodo precedes the speculations in the *Ivy Bush* and *Green Dragon* (see VI.274 and note 1). This reorganisation and rewriting was very roughly done on the pages of the third phase manuscript and on inserted riders ('A'); the revised opening was then written out fair ('B'), as far as Gaffer Gamgee's conversation with the Black Rider in Bagshot Row, and the remainder of the existing text added to it, to form textually speaking a hybrid, just as in the case of the first two chapters.

The draft revision A of Gandalf's departure from Bag End takes this form:

Gandalf stayed at Bag-End for over two months. But one evening, soon after Frodo's plan had been arranged, he suddenly announced that he was going off again next morning. 'I need to stretch my legs a bit, before our journey begins,' he said. 'Besides, I think I ought to go and look round, and see what news I can pick up down south on the borders, before we start.'

He spoke lightly, but it seemed to Frodo that he looked rather grave and thoughtful. 'Has anything happened? Have you heard something?' he asked.

'Well, yes, to tell you the truth,' said the wizard, 'I did hear something today that made me a bit anxious. But I won't say anything, unless I find out more for certain. If I think it necessary for you to get off at once, I shall come back immediately. In the meanwhile stick to your plan...'

The remainder of his farewell words are as in FR (p. 76), except that he says 'I think you will need my company on the Road', not that 'after all' Frodo 'may' need it. As written in the fair copy B the passage is the same as this, except that Gandalf no longer refers to 'our journey' – he says: 'I need to stretch my legs a bit. There are one or two things I must see to: I have been idle longer than I should'; and his last words are: 'I think after all you will need my company on the Road.'

Frodo's friends, who came to stay with him to help in the packing up of Bag End, are now (as also in the contemporary rewriting of 'Ancient History', p. 21) Hamilcar Bolger, Faramond Took,[16] and his closest friends Peregrin Boffin and Merry Brandybuck. It is now Hamilcar Bolger who goes off to Buckland with Merry in the third cart.[17] In the draft revision A 'Peregrin Boffin went back home to Overhill after lunch', whereas in B 'Faramond Took went home after lunch, but Peregrin and Sam remained behind', and Frodo 'took his own tea with Peregrin and Sam in the kitchen.' At the end of the meal 'Peregrin and Sam strapped up their three packs and piled them in the porch. Peregrin went out for a last stroll in the garden. Sam disappeared.'

Throughout these manuscripts 'Pippin' appears as a later correction of 'Folco'; and in the passage referred to above, naming Frodo's four friends who stayed at Bag End, 'Faramond Took' was changed subsequently to 'Folco Boffin', 'Peregrin Boffin' to 'Pippin Took', and 'Hamilcar Bolger' to 'Fredegar Bolger'. These, with Merry Brandybuck, are the four who are present on this occasion in FR (p. 76). But such corrections as these prove nothing as to date: they could have been entered on the manuscript at any subsequent time.

Nonetheless, it must have been at this stage, I think, that 'Peregrin Took' or 'Pippin' at last entered. Under Chapter V 'A Conspiracy Unmasked' below, it will be seen that in a rewritten section of the manuscript from this time (as distinct from mere emendation to the existing 'third phase' text) not only does 'Hamilcar' appear, as is to be expected, but 'Pippin' appears for the first time *as the text was written*. This rewritten section of 'A Conspiracy Unmasked' certainly belongs to the same time as the rewritten ('fourth phase') parts of 'Ancient History'·and 'Three is Company'. The correction of 'Folco (Took)' to 'Pippin' in these manuscripts therefore does in fact belong to the same period; though they are carefully written texts, the final stage in the evolution of the 'younger hobbits' was taking place as my father wrote them; and though at the beginning of the B text of 'Three is Company' Frodo's friend was Peregrin Boffin, he may have already been Peregrin Took by the time he took his last stroll in the Bag End garden.

The question is not perhaps worth spending very long on, since it is now very largely one of name simply, but I have followed the tortuous trail too long to leave it without an attempt at analysis at the end. What happened, I think, was as follows. Folco Took of the 'third phase' (who had an interesting and complex genesis out of the original 'young hobbits', Frodo (Took) and Odo, see VI.323–4) was renamed Faramond Took (p. 15, note 1). At this time 'Peregrin Boffin', who had first entered as the 'explanation' of Trotter, became one of Frodo's younger friends. This is the situation in the rewritten or 'fourth phase' portions of Chapters II and III (pp. 21, 30). In Chapter III Faramond Took 'went home after lunch', and he is then out of the story. 'Peregrin' and Sam stayed on at Bag End, and it is clear that they are going to be Frodo's companions on the walk to Buckland.

'Peregrin' (Boffin) is thus stepping into the narrative place of Folco (briefly renamed Faramond) Took; or rather – since the narrative was now in a finished form – this *name* takes over the character. Just why Folco/Faramond Took would not do I cannot say for certain. It may have been simply a preference of names. But if Faramond Took is got rid of and Peregrin Boffin made the third member of the party walking to Buckland, there would be no Took at all: my father would have left himself with a Baggins, a Boffin, a Brandybuck, and a Gamgee. Perhaps this is why the Boffin was changed into a Took, and the Took into a Boffin: Peregrin Boffin became Peregrin (or Pippin) Took, and Faramond Took, reverting to his former name Folco, became Folco Boffin (who 'went home after lunch' in FR, p. 77). These corrections to the new text of Chapter III were evidently made before my father rewrote the ending of Chapter V, where 'Pippin' first appears in a text as written and not by later correction.

Thus it is that Peregrin Took of LR occupies the same *genealogical* place as did Frodo Took of the earliest phases (see VI.267, note 4): and thus 'Folco' of the 'third phase' manuscripts is corrected every-where to 'Pippin'.

It would be legitimate, I think, to see in all this a single or particular hobbit-character, who appears under an array of names: Odo, Frodo, Folco, Faramond, Peregrin, Hamilcar, Fredegar, and the very ephemeral Olo (VI.299) – Tooks, Boffins, and Bolgers. Though no doubt a very 'typical' hobbit of the Shire, this 'character' is in relation to his companions very distinct: cheerful, nonchalant, irrepressible, commonsensical, limited, and extremely fond of his creature comforts. I will call this character 'X'. He begins as Odo Took, but becomes Odo Bolger. My father gets rid of him from the first journey (to Buckland), and as a result Frodo Took (Merry Brandybuck's first cousin), who had been potentially a very different character (see VI.70), becomes 'X', while retaining the name Frodo Took. Odo, however, reappears, because he has gone on ahead to Buckland with Merry Brandybuck while the others are walking; he may be called 'XX'. He will have a separate adventure, riding with Gandalf to Weathertop and ultimately turning up again at Rivendell, where (for a very brief time in the development of the narrative) he will rejoin 'X', now renamed 'Folco Took' (since Bingo Baggins has taken over the name Frodo).

In the 'third phase' of the narrative, then, 'X' is Folco Took, Merry's cousin; and 'XX' is Odo Bolger. But now 'X' is renamed Faramond Took, and 'XX' is renamed Hamilcar Bolger. A new character called Peregrin Boffin appears: beginning as a much older figure, originally a hobbit of the Shire who became through his experiences a most unusual person, known as 'Trotter', he, or rather his name, survives to become one of Frodo's younger friends. 'Faramond Took' is pushed aside and left with scarcely any rôle at all, becoming the shadowy Folco Boffin; and 'Peregrin Boffin', becoming 'Peregrin Took' or 'Pippin', becomes 'X' – and Merry's first cousin.

Looking back to the beginning, therefore, 'Pippin' of LR will largely take over 'Odo's' remarks; but as I said (VI.70), 'the way in which this came about was strangely tortuous, and was by no means a simple substitution of one name for another.' For Pippin is Merry's first cousin, and is derived through Folco/Faramond from the original Frodo Took: he is not derived from Odo, who was moved sideways, so to speak, becoming Hamilcar (Fredegar). But Pippin *is* derived from Odo, in the sense that he like Odo is 'X'.

For the rest, Lobelia Sackville-Baggins' son, while keeping his name Cosimo, loses his pimples and gains 'sandy-haired' as his defining epithet. Gaffer Gamgee's observation on the subject of having Lobelia as his neighbour is recorded: ' "I can't abide changes at my time of life," said he (he was 99),[18] "and anyhow not changes for the worst." ' In FR the Gaffer's complaint was reported by Gandalf to the Council of Elrond (p. 276).

From the point where my father merely retained the manuscript of the 'third phase', and in subsequent chapters, 'Folco' was corrected to 'Pippin'.

Chapter IV: 'A Short Cut to Mushrooms'

In this case the third phase manuscript was retained intact (apart from 'Peregrin' or 'Pippin' for 'Folco' throughout), the final form having already been attained (see VI.325).

Chapter V: 'A Conspiracy Unmasked'
(with 'The Dream of the Tower')

A rough draft of a rewriting of the end of this chapter survives (for the previous forms of the passage see VI.104–5, 301–2, 326). Odo has become Hamilcar, and the conversation proceeds now almost exactly as in FR p. 118: that Hamilcar should stay behind was part of the original plan. Frodo no longer gives a letter to Odo/Hamilcar (VI.326), but says: 'It would not have been safe to leave a written message: the Riders might get here first, and search the house.' The only elements in FR that are still lacking are that Hamilcar's family came from Budgeford in Bridgefields,[19] and that 'he had even brought along some old clothes of Frodo's to help him in playing the part.' This rewriting stops before the account of Frodo's dream that night, of a sea of tangled trees and something snuffling among the roots (VI.302), but it is clear that at this stage it remained unchanged.

It is necessary here to turn aside for a moment from the end of 'A Conspiracy Unmasked' and to bring in a remarkable brief narrative of this time, extant in several texts, which may be called 'The Dream of the Tower'. In the narrative outline dated 'Autumn 1939' given on p. 9 Gandalf is 'besieged in the *Western Tower*. He cannot get away while they guard it with five Riders. But when Black Riders have located Frodo and found that he has gone off without Gandalf they ride away.' This is what Frodo saw in his dream.

My father was much exercised about the placing of it (see p. 11). In the Time-schemes A and B the date of Gandalf's escape from the Western Tower was first given as 24 September, and there is a suggestion that Frodo dreamt his dream of the event that night, when with the Elves in the Woody End. The date was then changed to the 25th, when Frodo was at Crickhollow, and so appears in schemes A, B, and C. Scheme D gives no date for Gandalf's escape, and places the 'Dream of the Tower' variously on the 24th, 25th, or 26th. For some reason, however, my father decided to place it after the event, on the night of the 29th, when Frodo was at Bree, and Gandalf was at Crickhollow.

The text of Frodo's dream at Bree is found in three forms, two preparatory drafts and a finished manuscript.[20] I give it here in the third form, since the only significant difference from the drafts is that in them the figure who summons the watchers from the Tower is seen by the dreamer ('another dark-robed figure appeared over the brow of the hill: it beckoned and gave a shrill call in a strange tongue').

The narrative begins almost exactly as in FR p. 189, with Frodo waking suddenly in the room at *The Prancing Pony*, seeing Trotter sitting alert in his chair, and falling asleep again.

Frodo soon went to sleep again; but now he passed at once into a dream. He found himself on a dark heath. Looking up, he saw before him a tall white tower, standing alone upon a high ridge. Beyond it the sky was pale, and far off there came a murmur like the voices of the Great Sea which he had never heard nor beheld, save in other dreams. In the topmost chamber of the tower there shone dimly a blue light.

Suddenly he found that he had drawn near and the tower loomed high above him. About its feet there was a wall of faintly shining stones, and outside the wall sat silent watchers:

black-robed figures on black horses, gazing at the gate of the tower without moving, as if they had sat there for ever.

There came at last the soft fall of hoofs, climbing up the hill. The watchers all stirred and turned slowly towards the sound. They were looking towards Frodo. He did not dare to turn, but he knew that behind him another dark figure, taller and more terrible, had appeared: it beckoned, and called out in a strange tongue. The horsemen leaped to life. They raised their dark heads towards the lofty chamber, and their mocking laughter rang out cruel and cold; then they turned from the white wall and rode down the hill like the wind. The blue light went out.

It seemed to Frodo that the riders came straight towards him; but even as they passed over him and beat him to the ground, he thought in his heart: 'I am not here; they cannot hurt me. There is something that I must see.' He lifted his head and saw a white horse leap the wall and stride towards him. On it rode a grey-mantled figure: his white hair was streaming, and his cloak flew like wings behind him. As the grey rider bore down upon him he strove to see his face. The light grew in the sky, and suddenly there was a noise of thunder.

Frodo opened his eyes. Trotter had drawn the curtains and had pushed back the shutters with a clang. The first grey light of day was in the room. The vision of his dream faded quickly, but its mingled fear and hope remained with him all the day; and for long the far sound of the Sea came back to him whenever great danger was at hand.

As soon as Trotter had roused them all he led the way to their bedrooms.

The manuscript continues a little further, almost word for word as in FR, and ends with Butterbur's 'Guests unable to sleep in their beds, and good bolsters ruined and all! What are we coming to?'

Taking into account the words of the outline given on p. 9 that Gandalf, pursued by the Riders, tried to get round to the west of the Shire, and the mention of the sound of the Sea in the text, it is seen that Gandalf had fled to the Elf-towers[21] on the Tower Hills beyond the west marches of the Shire – those towers which, at the very beginning of the writing of The Lord of the Rings, Bingo said that he had once seen, shining white in the Moon: 'the tallest was furthest away, standing alone on a hill' (VI.93; cf. VI.312 and FR p. 16).

Turning back to 'A Conspiracy Unmasked': my father now rewrote the ending again, on the basis of the draft already referred to, and added it to the 'third phase' manuscript, rejecting the existing conclusion of the chapter.[22] In this new text he still kept the original dream, but now combined with it the 'Dream of the Tower', transferring it back from Frodo's night at Bree to his night at Crickhollow (see p. 33). Thus Frodo has the vision of Gandalf's escape from the Western Tower on the night of the event itself, the 25th of September. The new version reads thus, in part:

When at last he got to bed, Frodo could not sleep for some time. His legs ached. He was glad that he was riding in the morning. Eventually he fell into a vague dream, in which he seemed to be looking out of a high window over a dark sea of tangled trees. Down below among the roots there was the sound of creatures crawling and snuffling. He felt sure they would smell him out sooner or later.

Then he heard a noise in the distance. At first he thought it was a great wind coming over the leaves of the forest. Then he knew that it was not leaves, but the sound of the Sea far-off: a sound he had never heard in waking life, though it had often troubled other dreams. Suddenly he found he was out in the open. There were no trees after all. He was on a dark heath, and there was a strange salt smell in the air. Looking up he saw before him a tall white tower, standing alone on a high ridge. In its topmost chamber a blue light shone dimly.

As he drew nearer the tower loomed high above him. About its feet there was a wall of faintly gleaming stones, and outside the wall sat silent watchers: there seemed to be four blackrobed figures seated on black horses, gazing at the tower without moving, as if they had sat there for ever.

He heard the soft fall of hoofs climbing up the hill behind him. The watchers all stirred...

From this point the vision is told in practically the same words as in the previous text, and ends in the same way: 'A light grew in the sky, and there was a noise of thunder.' When Frodo had dreamt the dream at Bree, the light in the sky and the noise of thunder were associated with Trotter's opening the shutters with a clang and the light of morning entering the room.

In this text 'Pippin' is the name that was first written, not a subsequent correction of 'Folco'; see p. 30.

Later (see p. 139, note 36), when the story of Gandalf had been further changed, the description of the Western Tower and the siege of the Riders was largely, but not entirely, struck out on this manuscript: the opening was retained, as far as 'Looking up he saw before him a tall white tower, standing alone on a high ridge.' At the same time a brief new conclusion was added:

A great desire came over him to climb the tower and see the Sea. He started to struggle up the ridge towards the tower; but suddenly a light came in the sky, and there was a noise of thunder.

Thus altered, this is the text of FR, pp. 118–19. And so the tall white tower of Frodo's dream at Crickhollow in the final tale remains from what was the precursor of Orthanc; and the thunder that he heard goes back to the interruption of his dream by Trotter's thrusting back the shutters at *The Prancing Pony*. But Frodo would still dream of Gandalf imprisoned in a tower: for as he slept in the house of Tom Bombadil he would see him standing on the pinnacle of Isengard.

Chapter VI: 'The Old Forest'

The existing 'third phase' manuscript of this chapter was retained, but with a good deal of correction, evidently deriving from different times. To this period belong the alteration of 'Odo' to 'Hamilcar' at the beginning of the chapter, and 'Folco' to 'Pippin'; I would ascribe to it also the attainment of the final form of the hobbits' descent out of the forest to the Withywindle (see VI.327), and the final ascription of the parts in the encounter with Old Man Willow, with Merry exchanging rôles with Frodo as the one trapped in the tree and the one pushed into the river (*ibid.*).

Chapter VII: 'In the House of Tom Bombadil'

In this chapter as in the last, the existing manuscript was retained intact. As the story stood in that text, Gandalf came to Crickhollow and routed the Riders on the night of Monday 26 September, the first night spent by the hobbits in the house of Tom Bombadil, and the account of the attack on Crickhollow was introduced as a short separate narrative in the body of Chapter VII (see VI.303–4, 328). But this had now been changed, and the attack by the Riders delayed by three days, with the postponement of Gandalf's coming to Bree. My father therefore wrote on the manuscript at this point: 'This did not occur till Sept. 29', i.e. the night passed by the hobbits at Bree (see the time-schemes tabulated on p. 12). The episode was now in the wrong chapter, and was struck from the text here.

It is often difficult or impossible to say with certainty when changes to the manuscripts that are unrelated to movements in the narrative structure (or to movements in names) were made. Thus the introduction of Frodo's dream of Gandalf on Orthanc is obviously later; but the striking out of 'I am Ab-Origine, that's what I am' (and the substitution of Tom's words in FR, p. 142: 'Don't you know my name yet?...'), and of 'He saw the Sun rise in the West and the Moon following, before the new order of days was made' (see VI.329) may well belong to this time.

Chapter VIII: 'Fog on the Barrow-downs'

The original manuscript was again retained, and most of the changes that were made to it were from a later time (notably those introducing Carn Dûm and Angmar, FR pp. 154, 157). The final page of the 'third phase' manuscript was however rejected and replaced by a new ending to the chapter, most of which is found also in a preparatory draft, marked 'Revised ending of VIII to fit revised plot (concerning Gandalf's delay and Trotter's knowledge of the name Baggins)'. Now Frodo says, 'Please note – all of you – that the name Baggins must *not* be mentioned again. I am Mr *Green*, if any name must be given.' In the narrative of the third phase, as in that of the second, Frodo took the name of 'Mr Hill of Faraway' (VI.280, 334). 'Green' as a pseudonym (for Odo) goes back to the original version (VI.135 etc.).

At this time Tom's words (VI.329) 'he [Butterbur] knows Tom Bombadil, and Tom's name will help you. Say "Tom sent us here", and he will treat you kindly' were rejected, and Tom's parting words in FR appear: 'Tom's country ends here: he will not pass the borders.' In this connection see the note given on p. 10 concerning the boundaries of Tom's domain: there my father was thinking of harmonising Gandalf's remark at the Council of Elrond that Bombadil never left his own ground with the story that he was known to Butterbur by supposing that Tom's 'boundaries' extended to Bree. But he concluded that Tom Bombadil was not in fact known to Butterbur, and the changes here reflect that decision.

NOTES

1 The texts in such a situation are often very tricky to interpret, for there are these possible ingredients or components: (1) a page from the 'third phase' manuscript corrected but retained; (2) a page from the 'third phase' manuscript rejected and replaced; (3) draft version(s) for replacement of rejected 'third phase' manuscript; (4) fair copy replacement of rejected 'third phase' manuscript (with or without preceding draft). A correction, say of a name, made in a case of (1) will stand on the same footing in the textual history as the name first written in a case of (3) or (4), but the latter provide more certain indication of the relative dating.

2 With Bilbo's remark 'I have thought of a nice ending for it: *and he lived happily ever after to the end of his days*' (FR p. 41) cf. the outline §1 on p. 5. With the passage that follows, in which Bilbo says of Frodo

He would come with me, of course, if I asked him. In fact he offered to once, just before the party. But he does not really want to, yet. I want to see the wild country again before I die, and the Mountains; but he is still in love with the Shire...

cf. the fragment of narrative given in note 8 to the preceding chapter (p. 15).

3   Cf. the outline §1 on p. 5: 'Says to Gandalf he sometimes feels it is like an eye looking at him.'

4   Gandalf's words 'He said and did things then that were unmistakeable signs of something wrong' refer of course to his parting conversation with Bilbo in this 'phase', given on pp. 19–20, where Bilbo's behaviour was still not violently out of character as it afterwards became.

5   This is the form of the text in B. The draft A has no reference to the discussion of Rings at the White Council.

6   At this stage the old story of how the Ring was found 'in the mud of the river-bank under the roots of a thorn tree' (VI.78) was retained.

7   In the later form of 'Riddles in the Dark' in The Hobbit there was no question of Gollum's giving up the Ring, of course: Bilbo's prize if he won the competition was to be shown the way out, and Gollum only went back to his island in the lake to get the Ring so that he might attack Bilbo invisibly.

8   This passage, from 'But of course...', was added to the text, but it takes up a draft passage against which my father had written 'Omit?':

Yet I wonder what would have happened in the end, if he had been obliged to hand it over. I don't think he would have dared to cheat openly; but I am sure he would have tried to get the Ring back. He would have immediately desired it terribly, and have hated Bilbo fiercely. He would have tried to kill him. He would have followed him, visible or invisible, by sight or smell, till he got a chance.'

9   The draft text still retained the curious passage, going back through the third to the second version of the chapter (VI.263), in which Gandalf has Frodo quote the first riddle that Gollum asked, and then says, in this version: 'Roots and mountains: there's a good deal of Gollum's mind and history in that.'

10 This was said in the original story of Gollum in the first edition of The Hobbit: 'in the end Bilbo gathered that Gollum had had a ring – a wonderful, beautiful ring, a ring that he had been given for a birthday present, ages and ages before when such rings were less uncommon.'

11 Draft texts still retain the wording of the third version (VI.321): 'what kind of ring it really was.'

12 The words trying to forget Deagol are a part of the text B as

written, and show that the passage (pp. 23–4) concerning the murder of Deagol was inserted before this version was completed.

13   In the original story in *The Hobbit* it was only when Gollum came back from his island in the lake, where he had gone to get the 'present', that Bilbo learnt – from Gollum's 'tremendous spluttering and whispering and croaking' – about the ring and that it had been a birthday present; see note 10.

14   The change noted in VI.320, whereby Gandalf ceases to be the one who actually tracked Gollum down, belongs to this 'fourth phase'.

15   Above -*ruin* was pencilled -*naur*, sc. *Orodnaur*.

16   In the draft revision A of this passage Faramond is called 'Faramond II and the heir apparent'; cf. VI.251, where Faramond's precursor Frodo Took is called 'Frodo the Second ... the heir and rather desperate hope of the Hole of Took, as the clan was called.'

17   In the draft revision A at this point 'Ham (that is Hamilcar)' was replaced by 'Freddy (that is Fredegar)', but Ham/Hamilcar was then restored. Cf. the note dated August 1939 given in VI.373: 'Odo > Fredegar Hamilcar Bolger'.

18   In the genealogy in LR, Appendix C, Gaffer Gamgee was 92, and he died at the age of 102.

19   Neither Budgeford nor Bridgefields appear on my father's original map of the Shire (frontispiece to Vol. VI). On my large map of the Shire made in 1943 (VI.107) both names were lightly pencilled in by him, Budgeford being the crossing of the Water by the road (pencilled in at the same time) to Scary. See note 22.

20   The second version stands as the opening of a chapter, numbered 'X' and without title (corresponding to the 'second opening' of Chapter XI 'A Knife in the Dark' in FR, after the 'Crickhollow episode'); the third likewise, but numbered 'XI' (because by then the 'Bree' chapter had been divided, see p. 40), and with an erased title 'The Way to Weathertop'.

21   In some rough chronological workings there is a reference to Gandalf's being besieged in 'the West Towers', which is what Trotter called the Elf-towers in VI.155, 159.

22   Hamilcar's family now comes from Bridgefields in the Eastfarthing. Budgeford was written in later, perhaps much later. See note 19.

III

THE FOURTH PHASE (2):
FROM BREE TO THE FORD OF RIVENDELL

Chapter IX: 'At the Sign of the Prancing Pony (i)
The Cow Jumped over the Moon'

The 'third phase' version of this chapter (VI.331 ff.) had been developed in two forms, in the first of which the story of the coming of Gandalf and Odo to Bree was told by Butterbur, while in the second (the 'red version' as my father called it) it was told by the narrator (VI.344–7); and in the second the coming of the four Riders to the west gate of Bree on the evening of Wednesday 28 September was described (VI.347–8). The already complex manuscript was then used for a rough, drastic recasting of the narrative, the 'blue version' (see VI.343): this belongs with the new plot, and all reference to a visit of Gandalf to Bree in the days immediately preceding Frodo's arrival is cut out. A 'blue' rider to the original 'third phase' manuscript is written on the back of a calendar page for September 1939.

So far as it went, this was effectively a draft ('A') for a new version of this always crucial chapter; and in this case my father set aside the now chaotic 'third phase' manuscript entirely (though taking from it the pages containing the text of *The Cat and the Fiddle*), and it got left behind in England many years later; the 'fourth phase' version is a new manuscript ('B'), and this went to Marquette. Notably, this bears a date on the first page: 'Revised Version Oct. 1939'.

It remained at this time a single, very long chapter, extending through FR Chapter 10 'Strider'; but my father decided (doubtless on account of its length) to divide it into two chapters, 'IX' and 'X', both called 'At the Sign of the Prancing Pony', but with sub-titles; and these names remained for a long time. This arrangement was apparently made soon after the new text was completed, and it is convenient to follow it here.

The new version, to the point where the hobbits returned from the common room of the inn after Frodo's 'accident', now reaches, except in a few features, the final form, and variation even from the precise wording of FR is infrequent. The most notable respect in which it differs is that at this stage my father preserved the account of the black horsemen who spoke to Harry Goatleaf the gatekeeper on the evening of the 28th of September:

The fog that enveloped the Downs on Wednesday afternoon lay deep about Bree-hill. The four hobbits were just waking from their sleep beside the Standing Stone, when out of the mist four horsemen rode from the West and passed through the gates at dusk. ...

The episode closely follows that in the 'red version' of the 'third phase' (VI.347–8), but of course Harry Goatleaf no longer refers to 'a hobbit riding behind an old man on a white horse, last night', and his conversation with the Rider takes this form:

'We want news!' hissed a cold voice through the key-hole.

'What of?' he answered, shaking in his boots.

'News of hobbits, riding on ponies out of the Shire. Have they passed?'

Harry wished they had, for it might have satisfied these riders if he could have said *yes*. There was a threat in the cold voice; but he dared not risk a *yes* that was not true. 'No sir!' he said in a quavering voice. 'There's been no Shire-hobbits on ponies through Bree, and there isn't likely to be any.'

A hiss came through the key-hole, and Harry started back, feeling as if something icy cold had touched him. 'Yes, it is likely!' said the voice fiercely. 'Three, perhaps four. You will watch. We want Baggins. He is with them. You will watch. You will tell us and not lie! We shall come back.'[1]

This episode was struck from the text, but I cannot say when this was done.

The conversation between Frodo and Merry and the gatekeeper is as in FR. The gatekeeper still however calls out to 'Ned' (his brother, presumptively) to watch the gate a while, since he has 'business up at *The Pony*' (as in VI.349); then follows: 'He had been gone only a moment, and Ned had not yet come out, when a dark figure climbed in quickly over the gate and vanished in the dark in the direction of the inn.' The reference to Harry Goatleaf's visit to the inn was afterwards struck out, and does not appear in FR (see below).

There is now, as is to be expected, no reference to Tom Bombadil when the hobbits arrive at *The Prancing Pony*, and Frodo's pseudonym is 'Mr Green' (see p. 37); the reference in FR (p. 167) to the Underhills of Staddle is of course absent. Folco is still Folco, corrected to Pippin, which shows that this text was written before the revised ending of Chapter V (pp. 30, 35).[2] Frodo still noticed the gatekeeper among the company in the common room of the inn, wondering whether it was his night off duty, but this was struck out, and does not appear in FR. Folco/Pippin now tells the story of the collapse of the 'Town Burrow' in Michel Delving, though the fat

Mayor is unnamed. Trotter is of course a Man, but the description of him is that of the old versions (VI.137, 334): he is still, as he was when he was a hobbit, 'queer-looking, brown-faced', with a short-stemmed pipe under his long nose, and nothing is said of his boots (FR p. 168).

When Bill Ferney and the Southerner left the common room, 'Harry the gatekeeper went out just behind them.' This, like the other references to the gatekeeper's presence at the inn noted above, was struck out. An isolated note of this time proposes: 'Cut out Harry – he is unnecessary': clearly referring to his visit to the inn after the arrival of the hobbits and his vaguely sinister association with Bill Ferney, not to his function as gatekeeper, which is certainly necessary. It is curious therefore that in the typescript that followed the present manuscript this last reference, though very clearly crossed out in the manuscript, was reinstated, and so appears in FR (p. 172), but quite anomalously, since all the references to his presence at the inn up to this point had been removed.

Chapter X: 'At the Sign of the Prancing Pony (ii)
All that is gold does not glitter'

In the 'blue version' recasting of the 'third phase' narrative, or 'A', the story of Trotter's 'eavesdropping' beside the Road reaches the final form, in association with the new ending to Chapter VIII (p. 37): he hears the hobbits talking with Bombadil, and Frodo declaring that he is to be called 'Mr Green' (for the previous story, in which Trotter overheard Gandalf and Odo talking, see VI.337). After Trotter's 'I should advise him and his friends to be more careful what they say and do' (FR p. 176) there follows in A:

'I have not "left my name behind", as you put it,' said Frodo stiffly. 'My reason for taking another here is my own affair. I do not see why my real name should interest anyone in Bree; and I have still to learn why it interests *you*. Mr Trotter may have an honest reason for spying and eavesdropping; but if so I should advise him to explain it!'

'That's the line to take!' laughed Trotter. 'But you wait till old Butterbur has had his private word with you – you'll soon find out how your real name could be guessed, and why it may be interesting in Bree. As for myself: I was looking for Mr Frodo Baggins, *because I had been told to look for him*. And I have already given you hints, which you have understood well enough, that I know about the secret you are carrying.'

'Don't be alarmed!' he cried, as Frodo half rose from his seat, and Sam scowled. 'I shall take more care of the secret than you do. But now I had better tell you some more about myself.'

At that moment he was interrupted by a knock at the door. Mr Butterbur was there with a tray of candles...

Butterbur now has only news of the Black Riders to communicate. The story he tells is as before (VI.338–40), but the first Rider passed through Bree on the Tuesday, not the Monday, preceding, three not four of them came to the inn-door, and of course he does not refer to Gandalf and 'Baggins' (Odo) having gone off eastwards. The conversation continues:

' "Baggins!" said I. "If you are looking for hobbits of that name, you'd best look in the Shire. There are none in Bree. The last time one of that name came here was nigh on a score of years back.[3] Mr Bilbo Baggins he was, as disappeared out of Hobbiton: he went off East long enough ago."

'At that name he drew in his breath and sat up. Then he stooped at me again. "But there is also Frodo Baggins," said he,[4] in a whisper like a knife. "Is he here? Has he been? Do not lie to us!"

'I was all of a twitter, I can tell you; but I was angry as well. "*No* is the answer," said I; "and you'll get no lies here, so you'd best be civil. If you have any message for any party, you may leave it, and I'll look out for them." "The message is *wait*," said he. "We may return." And with that the three of them turned their horses and rode off into the fog. Now, Mr Green, what do you say to that?'

'But they asked for Baggins, you say, not Green,' said Frodo warily.

'Ah!' said the landlord with a knowing wink. 'But they wanted news of hobbits out of the Shire, and such a party doesn't come here often. It would be queer, if there were two different parties. And as for *Baggins*: I've heard that name before. Mr Bilbo was here more than once, in my dad's time and mine; and some funny tales have come out of the Shire since he went off: vanished with a bang while he was speaking, they say. Not that I believe all the tales that come out of the West – but here you go vanishing in the middle of a song by all accounts, right in my house. And when I have time to scratch my head and think, I remember noticing your friends call you Frodo, and I begin to wonder if Baggins should not come next. "Maybe those black men were right," I says to myself. Now the question is, what shall I say, if they come back? Maybe you want to see them, and more likely not. They mean no good to anyone, I'll wager. Now you and your friends *seem* all right in spite of your pranks, so I thought I had best tell you and find out what you wish.'

'They mean no good at all,' said Frodo. 'I did not know they had passed through Bree, or I should have stayed quiet in this room, and I wish I had. I ought to have guessed it, from the way the gatekeeper greeted us – and you, Mr Butterbur; but I hoped perhaps Gandalf had been here asking for us. I expect you know who I mean, the old wizard. We hoped to find him here or have news of him.'

'Gandalf!' said the landlord. 'Know him! I should think I do. He was here not so long back, in the summer. A good friend of mine is Gandalf, and many a good turn he has done me. If you had asked after him sooner I should have been happier. I will do what I can for any friends of his.'

'I am very grateful,' said Frodo, 'and so will he be. I am sorry I can't tell you the whole story, but I assure you we are up to no mischief. I *am* Frodo Baggins, as you guess, and these – er – Black Riders are hunting for me, and we are in danger. I should be thankful for any sort of help, though I don't want you to get into trouble on my account. I only hope these Riders won't come back.'

'I hope not indeed,' said the landlord with a shiver. 'But spooks or no spooks, they'll have to mend their manners at my door.'

The latter part of this version is in hasty pencil, and soon after this point it peters out without further significant development. Obviously Gandalf's letter will still come from Trotter, not from Butterbur.

As I have said, this revision belongs with the new conception of Gandalf's movements: he only got ahead of Frodo and his friends by racing on horseback to Weathertop while they were toiling through the Midgewater Marshes. In the outline given on p. 9 there is mention of a visit of Gandalf to Bree before Frodo set out, and before his captivity in the Western Tower; and Butterbur says in this draft that he saw him 'not so long back, in the summer' (cf. also note 1). This led, I think, to the bringing back of the story (present in one of the alternative versions of the original 'Bree' chapter, VI.156) that it was Butterbur and not Trotter who had the letter from Gandalf; and this in turn led to refinement of the scene at the inn where Trotter proves that he is a friend.

As in the draft A above (p. 42), in the new or 'fourth phase' manuscript B Trotter says: 'I was looking for Mr Frodo Baggins, *because I had been told to look for him.*' But an important change in the structure now enters. In A Trotter has just said 'But now I had better tell you some more about myself' when he is interrupted by Mr Butterbur's knock on the door – an interruption at this point that goes back through the earlier versions: see VI.338 ('third phase'), VI.150 (original text). In the new account, Trotter is not interrupted at this point. After saying that he will take more care of the secret than they do, the story now proceeds thus:

'...But now I had better tell you some more.' He leaned forward and looked at them. 'Black horsemen have passed through Bree,' he said in a low voice. 'On Tuesday morning one came up the Greenway; and two more appeared later. Yesterday evening in the fog three more rode through the West-gate just before it was closed. They questioned Harry the gatekeeper and frightened him badly. I heard them. They also went eastward.'

There follows a passage quite closely approaching that in FR (pp. 176–7, from 'There was a silence'), with Frodo's regret that he had gone to the common room of the inn, and Trotter's recounting that the landlord had prevented him from seeing the hobbits until it was too late. But to Frodo's remark that the Riders 'seem to have missed me for the present, and to have gone on ahead' Trotter replies:

'I should not be too sure of that. They are cunning, and they divide their forces. I have been watching them. Only six have passed through Bree. There may be others. There are others. I know them, and their proper number.' Trotter paused and shivered. 'Those that have passed on will probably return,' he went on. 'They have questioned folk in the village and outlying houses, as far as Combe [> Archet], trying to get news by bribes and threats – of a hobbit called Baggins. There were others beside Harry Goatleaf in the room tonight who were there for a purpose. There was Bill Ferney. He has a bad name in the Bree-land, and queer folk call at his house sometimes. You must have noticed him among the company: a swarthy sneering fellow. He was very close with one of the southern strangers, and they slipped out together just after your "accident". Harry is an old curmudgeon, and he is frightened; but he won't do anything, unless they go to him.[5] Ferney is a different matter – he would sell anything to anybody; or make mischief for the fun of it.'

From this point (Frodo's 'What will Ferney sell?') the text of FR is largely achieved, as far as Trotter's question: 'Will you have him?' Then follows:

Frodo made no answer. He looked at Trotter: grim and wild and rough-clad. It was hard to know what to do, or to feel sure of his good will. He had been successful in one thing at any rate: he had made Frodo suspect everybody, even Mr Butterbur. And all his warnings could so well apply to himself. Bill Ferney, Trotter: which was the most likely to betray them? What if Trotter led them into the wild, to 'some dark place far from help'? Everything he had said was curiously double-edged. He had a dark look, and yet there was something in his face that was strangely attractive.

The silence grew, and still Frodo found no answer. 'There is one obvious question you have not put,' said Trotter quietly. 'You have not asked me: "Who told you to look out for us?" You might ask that before you decide to class me with Bill Ferney.'

'I am sorry,' stammered Frodo; but at that moment there came a knock at the door. Mr Butterbur was there with candles...

The interruption by Mr Butterbur takes place at structurally the same point as in FR (p. 178), though the conversation he interrupts is quite different. Trotter now withdrew into a dark corner of the room, and when Nob had gone off with the hot water to the bedrooms, the landlord began thus:

'I've been asked to look out for a party of hobbits, and for one by the name of Baggins in particular.'

'What has that got to do with me, then?' asked Frodo warily.

'Ah!' said the landlord with a knowing wink. 'You know best; but old Barnabas can add up two and two, if you give him time. Parties out of the Shire don't come here often nowadays, but I was told to look out for one at just about this time. It would be queer, if there was no connexion, if you follow me. And as for Baggins, I've heard that name before. Mr Bilbo was in this house more than once, and some funny stories have come out of the Shire since he went off: vanished with a bang, while he was speaking, they say. Not that I believe all the tales that come from the West – but here you go vanishing in the middle of a song by all accounts, right in my house. Maybe you did, and maybe there was some mistake, but it set me thinking. And when I have time to scratch my head, I remember noticing how your friends call you *Frodo*; so I begin to wonder if Baggins should not come after it.[6] For it was Frodo Baggins I was told to look for; and I was given a description that fits well enough, if I may say so.'

'Indeed! Let's hear it then!' said Frodo, a little impatient with the slow unravelling of Mr Butterbur's thoughts.

'*A round-bellied little fellow with red cheeks,*' answered the landlord with a grin. 'Begging your pardon; but he said it, not me.' Folco [> Pippin] chuckled, but Sam looked angry.

'*He* said it? And who was he?' asked Frodo quickly.

'Oh, that was old Gandalf, if you know who I mean. A wizard they say he is, but he is a right good friend of mine, whether or no. Many a good turn has he done me. "Barney," he says to me, it would be a matter of a month and more ago, in August,[7] if I recollect rightly, when he came in late one evening. Very tired he was, and uncommon thirsty. "Barney," he says, "I want you to do something for me." "You've only to name it," said I. "I want you to look out for some hobbits out of the Shire," said he. "There may be a couple, and there may be more. Nigh the end of September[8] it will be, if they come. I hope I shall be with them, and then you'll have no more to do than draw some of your best ale for us. But if I'm not with them, they may need help. One of them will be Frodo Baggins, if it is the right party: a great friend of mine, a round-bellied..." '

'All right!' said Frodo, laughing in spite of his impatience. 'Go on! We've heard that already.'

Mr Butterbur paused, put out of his stride. 'Where was I?' he said. 'Ah yes. "If this Frodo Baggins comes," said he, "give him this"; and he handed me a letter. "Keep it safe and secret, and keep it in your mind, if your head will hold anything so long," says he. "And don't you mention all this to anybody." I've kept that letter by me night and day, since he gave it to me.'

'A letter for me from Gandalf!' interrupted Frodo eagerly. 'Where is it?'

'There now!' cried Mr Butterbur triumphantly. 'You don't deny the name! Old Barney can put two and two together. But it's a pity you did not trust me from the beginning.' Out of an inner pocket he brought a sealed letter and handed it to Frodo.[9] On the outside it was inscribed: TO F.B. FROM G. ⚒

'There's another thing I ought to say,' Mr Butterbur began again. 'I guess you may be in trouble, seeing how Gandalf isn't here, and *they* have come, as he warned me.'

'What do you mean?' said Frodo.

'The black horsemen,' said Butterbur. ' "If you see horsemen in black," says Gandalf to me, "look out for trouble! And my friends will need all the help you can give." And they have come, sure enough: yesterday and the day before.[10] The dogs all yammered, and the geese screamed at them. Uncanny, I call it. They've been asking for news of a hobbit called Baggins, I hear. And that Ranger, Trotter, he has been asking questions, too. Tried to get in here, before you had had bite or sup, he did.'

'He did!' said Trotter suddenly, coming forward into the light. 'And a lot of trouble would have been saved, if you had let him in, Barnabas.'

The landlord jumped with surprise. 'You!' he cried. 'You're always popping up. What do *you* want?'

'He's here with my leave,' said Frodo. 'He's offering us his help.'

'Well, you know best, maybe,' said Mr Butterbur, looking doubtfully at Trotter. 'Of course, I don't know what's going on, or what these black fellows want with you. But they mean no good to you, I'll swear.'

'They mean no good to anyone,' answered Frodo. 'I am sorry I can't explain it all. I am tired and very worried, and it is a long tale. But tell Gandalf everything, if he turns up, and he will be very grateful, and he may tell you more than I can. But I ought at least to warn you what you are doing in helping me. The Black Riders are hunting me, and they are perilous. They are servants of the Necromancer.'

'Save us!' cried Mr Butterbur, turning pale. 'Uncanny I knew they were; but that is the worst bit of news that has come to Bree in my time!'

This version now attains the form in FR (p. 181) as far as Butterbur's departure to send Nob out to look for Merry with scarcely any deviation. Trotter speaks of 'the Shadow in the South', not 'in the East', and refers of course to 'Mr Green', not 'Mr Underhill'; and after Butterbur's remark that there are others in Bree quicker in the uptake than Nob is, he adds: 'Bill Ferney was here tonight, and he's an ugly customer.' – It will be seen that with the structural change in the ordering of the chapter (bringing the landlord to the hobbits' room at a later point) the information about the Black Riders (itself very brief) is now given by Trotter, while Butterbur himself is left with only a few words on the subject.[11] In previous versions his account of the coming of the Riders to the inn door was a chief element in the conversation; now there is no mention of it (though it reappears briefly in FR, p. 180).

In this version, the landlord before leaving the room asks if Trotter is going to stay there, to which Trotter replies: 'I am. You may need me before the morning.' 'All right, then,' said the landlord, 'if Mr Green is willing.' When Butterbur has gone:

'Well, now you ought to guess the answer to the question I spoke of before he came in,' said Trotter. 'But aren't you going to open the letter?'

Frodo looked carefully at the seal before he broke it. It seemed certainly to be Gandalf's. Inside, written in the wizard's thin long-legged script,[12] was the following message. Frodo read it aloud.[13]

The Prancing Pony, Bree; Tuesday, September 12th.[14] *Dear F. I am starting back tomorrow, & should reach you in a day or two. But things have become very dangerous, and I may not get through in time. (He has found the Shire: the borders are watched, and so am I.) If I fail to come, I hope that will be sufficient warning to you, & you will have sense to leave Shire at once. If so, there is just a chance you will get through as far as Bree. Look out for horsemen in black. They are your worst enemies (save one): they are Ringwraiths. Do not use It again: not for any reason at all. Do not move in the dark. Try and find Trotter the ranger. He will be looking out for you: a lean, dark, weatherbeaten fellow, but one of my greatest friends. He knows our business. He will see you through, if any one can. Make for Rivendell as fast as possible. There I hope we may meet again. If not, Elrond will advise you. Yours* ᚷᚫᚾᛞᚫᛚᚠ ⋅⊗⋅

PS. You can trust Barnabas Butterbur and Trotter. But make sure it is really Trotter. The real Trotter will have a sealed letter from me with these words in it

> *All that is gold does not glitter,*
> *all that is long does not last,*
> *All that is old does not wither,*
> *not all that is over is past.*

PPS. It would be worse than useless to try and go beyond Bree on your own. If Trotter does not turn up, you must try and get Butterbur to hide you somewhere, and hope that I shall come.

PPPS. I hope B. does not forget this! If he remembers to give it to you, tell him I am very grateful, & still more surprised. Fare well wherever you fare. ⊗

'Well, that is from Gandalf all right, quite apart from the

hand and the signature,' said Frodo as he finished. 'What about your letter, Trotter?'

'Do you need it? I thought you had made up your mind about me already! If not, you ought not to have let me stay; and you certainly ought not to have read that aloud to me.'

'I haven't made up *my* mind,' said Sam suddenly. 'And I am not going to see Mr Frodo made fun of and put upon. Let's see that letter, or Sam Gamgee'll take a hand!'

'My good Sam,' said Trotter. 'I've got a weapon under my cloak, as well as you! And I don't mind telling you that if I was not the real Trotter, you would not have a chance, not all three of you together. But steady there!' he said, as Sam sprang up. 'I *have* got a letter, and here it is!'

Onto the table he tossed another sealed letter, outwardly exactly like the other. Sam and Folco [> Pippin] looked at it, as Frodo opened it. Inside there was a small paper in Gandalf's hand. It said:

> All that is gold does not glitter;
> all that is long does not last;
> All that is old does not wither;
> not all that is over is past.

This is to certify that the bearer is Aragorn son of Celegorn,[15] *of the line of Isildur Elendil's son, known in Bree as Trotter; enemy of the Nine, and friend of Gandalf.* ᛉ ᚠ ᛏ ᛗ ᚠ ᚱ ᚤ ⦂ ⊗ ⦂

Frodo stared at the words in amazement. 'Of the line of Elendil!' he said, looking with awe at Trotter. 'Then It belongs to you as much as to me, or more!'

'It does not belong to either of us,' said Trotter; 'but you are to keep it for a while. For so it is ordained.'[16]

'Why didn't you show this to us sooner? It would have saved time, and prevented me, and Sam, from behaving absurdly.'

'Absurdly! Not at all. Sam is very sensible: he doubted me to the last, and I think he still does. Quite right, too! If you'd had more experience of your Enemy, you would not trust your own hands, except in broad daylight, once you knew that he was on your track. I had to make sure of *you*, too. That was one reason why I delayed. The Enemy has set snares for me before now. But I must admit that I tried to persuade you to take me as a friend, for my own sake without proofs. A hunted wanderer wearies sometimes of distrust, even while he is preaching it.[17] But there, I fear my looks are against me.'

There follows the ill-judged intervention of Folco/Pippin – '*Handsome is as handsome does* we say in the Shire', which had remained unchanged from Odo's original remark in VI.155; then follows:

Folco [> Pippin] subsided; but Sam was not daunted, and he still eyed Trotter dubiously. 'You could make yourself look like you do, if you were play-acting,' he said. 'What *proof* have we had that you are the real article, I should like to know?'

Trotter laughed. 'Don't forget Butterbur's letter, Sam!' he said. 'Think it out! Butterbur is certainly the real Butterbur, unless the whole of Bree is bewitched. How could the words *all that is gold* appear in Butterbur's letter and in mine, unless Gandalf wrote them both? You may be sure Gandalf did not give a spy a chance of knowing that Butterbur's letter existed. Even if he did, a spy could not know the key-words, without reading the letter. How could that have been done without Butterbur's knowledge?'

Sam scratched his head long and thoughtfully. 'Ah!' he said at last. 'I dessay it would have been difficult. But how about this: you could have done in the real Trotter and stolen his letter, and then popped it out, like you did, after hearing Butterbur's and seeing how the land lay? You seem mighty unwilling to show it. What have you got to say to that?'

'I say you are a splendid fellow,' said Trotter. 'I see why Gandalf chose you to go with your master. You hang on tight. I am afraid my only answer to you, Sam, is this: if I had killed the real Trotter, I could kill you, and I should have killed you already without so much talk. If I was after the Ring, I could have it – now!' He stood up, and seemed suddenly to grow taller. In his face there gleamed a light, keen and commanding. They did not move. Even Sam sat still, staring dumbly at him.

'But I am the real Trotter, fortunately,' he said, looking down at them with a sudden kindly smile. 'I am Aragorn son of Celegorn, and if by life or death I can save you, I will.' There was a long silence.

At last Frodo spoke hesitatingly. 'Did those verses of Gandalf's apply to you, then?' he asked. 'I thought at first they were just nonsense.'

'Nonsense, if you will,' answered Trotter. 'Don't worry about them. They have served their turn.'

'If you want to know,' said Frodo, 'I believed in you before Butterbur came in. I was not trying to trust you, but struggling not to trust you, to follow your own teaching. You have frightened me several times tonight, but never in the way that servants of the Enemy would, or so I imagine. I think one of those would ... would, well, seem fairer and feel fouler. You ... well, it is the other way round with you.'

'I look foul and feel fair, is it?' laughed Trotter. 'We'll leave it at that, and say no more about round bellies!'

'I am glad you are to be our guide,' said Folco [> Pippin]. 'Now that we are beginning to understand the danger, we should be in despair without you. But somehow I feel more hopeful than ever.'

Sam said nothing.

Afterwards my father abandoned this spider's web of argumentation, arising from there being two letters from Gandalf, and handled the question of the verse of recognition *All that is gold does not glitter* and Aragorn's knowledge of it extremely adroitly by making Aragorn use the words himself (not having seen or heard Gandalf's one letter) à propos Frodo's remark (already present in this version) about 'foul and fair' (FR p. 184). But the complication of the two letters survived the crucial decision that Gandalf's letter to Frodo was written to be received by him before he left Bag End and failed in delivery through Butterbur's forgetfulness.

After 'Sam said nothing' this version is the same as FR (p. 184), with Trotter's words about the leaving of Bree and the making for Weathertop. But his answer to Frodo's question about Gandalf is much slighter:

Trotter looked grave. 'I don't know,' he said. 'To tell you the truth, I am very troubled about him – for the first time since I have known him. He meant to arrive here with you two days sooner than this. We should at least have had messages. Something has happened. I think it is something that he feared, or he would not have taken all these precautions with letters.'

From Frodo's question 'Do you think the Black Riders have anything to do with it?' the remainder of FR Chapter 10 was now attained except in a few minor particulars, the chief of which occurs in Merry's account of his experience. This story now returns to the original version (VI.161–2), according to which the Rider went eastwards through the village and stopped at Bill Ferney's house (whereas in the 'third phase' version, VI.353–4, it went in the other direction to the West-gate); but it differs from FR (p. 185) in that when Merry was about to bolt back to the inn 'another black shape rose up before me – coming down the Road from the other gate – and ... and I fell over.' In this version Trotter says: 'They may after all try some attack before

we leave Bree. But it will be dark. In the light they need their horses.'[18]
For the subsequent history of this chapter see pp. 76–8.

Chapter XI: 'A Knife in the Dark'

This chapter was another of those that my father at this time
reconstituted partly from the existing 'third phase' text (the latter part
of Chapter X and the first part of Chapter XI, see VI.359) and partly
from new manuscript pages, and as with the previous chapters in this
form some rejected pages of the older version became separated and
did not go to Marquette.

The new text opens with the attack on Crickhollow, which with the
change in its date had been moved from its original place in Chapter
VII (see p. 36). For the previous form of the episode see VI.328; this
was almost identical to the original text, VI.303–4. To both of these
my father pencilled in glimpses of the story that Odo left with Gandalf
as he rode after the Black Riders – a story that seems only to have
entered the 'third phase' narrative when the 'Bree' chapter was
reached: see VI.336. But in the second version Crickhollow was not
empty: a curtain moved in a window – for Odo had stayed behind.

I give first a preliminary draft of the attack on Crickhollow written
for its new place in the story.

As they slept there in the inn of Bree, darkness lay on
Buckland. Mist strayed in the dells and along the river-bank.
The house at Crickhollow stood silent. Not long before, when
evening had just fallen, there had been a light in a window. A
horse came quickly up the lane, and halted. Up the path in haste
a figure walked, wrapped in a great cloak, leading a white horse.
He tapped on the door, and at once the light went out. The
curtain at the window stirred, and soon after the door was
opened and he passed quickly in. Even as the door closed a
black shadow seemed to move under the trees and pass out
through the gate without a sound.[19] Then darkness slowly
deepened into night, a dead and misty night: no stars shone over
Buckland.

There came the soft fall of hoofs, horses were drawing near,
led slow and cautiously. The gate in the hedge opened, and up
the path filed three shapes, hooded, swathed in black, and
stooping low towards the ground. One went to the door, one to
each corner of the house-end on either side; and there they
stood, silent as the black shadows of stones, while time went
slowly on, and the house and the trees about it seemed to be
waiting breathlessly.

There was a faint stir in the leaves, and a cock crowed. The cold hour before dawn had come.[20] Suddenly the figure by the door moved. In the dark, without star or moon, the blade that was drawn gleamed, as if a chill light had been unsheathed. There was a blow, soft but heavy, and the door shuddered.

'Open in the name of Sauron!' said a voice, cold and menacing. At a second blow the door yielded, and fell back with its lock broken and timbers burst. The black figures passed swiftly in.

At that moment, nearby among the trees a horn rang out. It rent the night like fire on a hill-top, echoing over the land. *Awake! Fear! Fire! Foes! Awake!* Someone was blowing the Horn-call of Buckland, which had not been sounded for a hundred years, not since the white wolves came in the Fell Winter when the Brandywine was frozen. Far away[21] answering horns were heard. Distant sounds of waking and alarm came through the night. The whole of Buckland was aroused.

The black shapes slipped swiftly from the house. In the lane the sound of hoofs broke out, and gathering to a gallop went racing into the darkness. Behind them a white horse ran. On it sat an old man clad in grey, with long silver hair and flowing beard. His horn still sounded over hill and dale. In his right hand a wand flared and flickered like a sheaf of lightning.[22] Behind him, clinging to his cloak, sat a hobbit. Gandalf and Hamilcar were riding to the North Gate, and the Black Riders fled before them. But they had found out what they wished to know: Crickhollow was empty and the Ring had gone.

The story here must be that Gandalf and Hamilcar left the house by the back door, as Fredegar Bolger did in FR (p. 188), but then waited among the trees surrounding the open space in which the house stood. A note added to the time-scheme B (p. 11) seems to fit this version: 'The Black Riders creep into Buckland, but too late to see Frodo depart. They track him to Crickhollow and guard it, and see Gandalf enter. But Gandalf (and Ham pretending to be Frodo) burst out on night of Sept. 29.'

Another short text, written on the same slip of paper and obviously at the same time as that just given, provided only the end of the episode; and in this text, which was later struck through, there is no mention of Gandalf:

Ham Bolger was blowing the Horn-call of Buckland, which had not been sounded for a hundred years... [*&c. as before*] The black shapes slipped swiftly from the house.

In the lane the sound of hoofs broke out and gathering to a gallop raced off madly northwards into the dark. The black riders had fled, for their concern was not yet with the little folk of the Shire, but only with the Ring. And they had discovered what they wished to know: Crickhollow was empty and the Ring had gone.

This perhaps goes with the outline §4 on p. 9: 'Crickhollow scene – only Hamilcar there. He blows horn . . .'

The version of the story that appears in the 'fourth phase' manuscript changes again. It begins thus:

As they slept there in the inn at Bree, darkness lay on Buckland: mist strayed in the dells and along the river-bank. The house at Crickhollow stood silent. A curtain stirred in a window and for a moment a light gleamed out. At once a black shadow moved under the trees and passed out through the gate without a sound. The night deepened. There came the soft fall of hoofs . . .

The draft text given on p. 53 is then followed closely; but from 'The black figures passed swiftly in' there is a new story:

The black figures passed swiftly in. In a moment they came out again; one was carrying a small bundled figure in an old cloak: it did not struggle. Now they leaped upon their horses without caution; in the lane the noise of hoofs broke out, and gathering to a gallop went hammering away into the darkness.

At the same moment, [*struck out:* from the direction of the Ferry,] another horse came thundering along the lane. As it passed the gate a horn rang out.[23] It rent the night like fire on a hill-top . . . [*&c. as before*] Far away answering horns were heard; the alarm was spreading. Buckland was aroused.

But the Black Riders rode like a gale to the North Gate. Let the little people blow! Sauron would deal with them later. In the meanwhile they had earned his thanks: Baggins was caught like a fox in a hole. They rode down the watchmen, leaped the gate, and vanished.

And that is how Hamilcar Bolger first crossed the Brandywine Bridge.

This version evidently belongs with the story in the time-scheme D (p. 12), where on September 29 'the Riders attack Crickhollow and carry off Ham, pursued by Gandalf' – although there this took place at midnight, whereas here it was 'the cold hour before dawn'. Gandalf arrived just too late, and (and as will appear later) thought that it was

Frodo who had been taken; but the further story of Hamilcar Bolger must be briefly postponed (see pp. 68 ff.).

Frodo's 'dream of the tower' had been removed from the night at Bree to the night at Crickhollow (see pp. 33–6), and his sleep at Bree is now described as it is in FR: 'his dreams were again troubled with the noise of wind and of galloping hoofs ... far off he heard a horn blowing wildly.'

New writing (i.e. replacement of the 'third phase' manuscript) continues as far as the departure of the hobbits with Trotter from Bree and their coming into open country. At this stage Folco was still Folco, not Pippin; but the text of FR (pp. 189–93) was reached in all but trifling details.[24] The later story of Merry's ponies now appears, changed from the earlier (VI.164) in which Tom Bombadil, when he found them, went to the inn at Bree to find out what had happened to the hobbits, and paid Mr Butterbur for the ponies; the relationship between Bombadil and Butterbur had been abandoned (pp. 10, 37).

From the point where the companions saw the houses and hobbit-holes of Staddle on their left (FR p. 193) the 'third phase' manuscript was retained, and lightly corrected, as far as the arrival of Trotter, Frodo, and Merry on the summit of Weathertop. As the manuscript stood at this stage the text of FR was very nearly attained, but some additions were later: such as the lights in the eastward sky seen from the Midgewater Marshes, the burnt turf and blackened stones on the summit of Weathertop, and the ring of ancient stonework about it; apparently the alteration of Trotter's remark that 'not all the rangers are to be trusted, nor all the birds and beasts', which goes back to the original form of the story (VI.167), to 'not all the birds are to be trusted, and there are other spies more evil than they are' was also a much later change. Strider's account in FR (p. 197) of the great watchtower on Weathertop and its ruin is not entered on the manuscript at all, and the text remains here unchanged from its earliest form (VI.169, 355). Sam's song of Gil-galad was written at this time, and entered into the manuscript.[25]

On the summit of Weathertop the old story underwent an important change. Gandalf's message on a paper that fluttered from the cairn of stones (VI.170, 355) has gone, and the text of FR (p. 199) is reached (without, as already noted, any mention of a fire: the stone on which the marks were found was not 'flatter than the others, and whiter, as if it had escaped the fire', but 'smaller than the others, and of different colour, as if it had been rubbed clean'). The scratches on the stone were X : IIII (the Old English G-rune still being used), interpreted to mean that Gandalf had been there on 4 October. The marks were however changed to read X : I.III, and a new passage was inserted (and subsequently rejected):

'But there's a dot between the first 1 and the next three,' said

Sam poring over the stone. 'It doesn't say G.4, but G.1.3.'

'Quite right!' agreed Trotter. 'Then if Gandalf made these marks, it might mean that he was here from the first to the third; or perhaps that he and another were here on the third.'

This is odd, because Sam stayed down in the dell and did not go up to the summit of Weathertop; moreover this inserted discussion takes place at the summit, so that it is no help to suppose that Trotter brought the stone down with him to the dell. – Later, the marks were changed again to X:III.

To Frodo's 'It would be a great comfort to know that he was on the way to Rivendell' Trotter replies simply: 'It would indeed! But in any case, as he is not here himself, we must look after ourselves, and make our own way to Rivendell as best we can.' In answer to Merry's question 'How far is Rivendell?' Trotter at first replied very much as in the original version (VI.171), but distinguished between three weeks in fair weather and a month in foul weather from Brandywine Bridge to the Ford, and concludes: 'So we have at least twelve days' journey before us,[26] and very likely a fortnight or more.' This was rejected in the act of writing and the text of FR substituted, in which Trotter states the time it took from Weathertop to the Ford without computing it so elaborately: 'twelve days from here to the Ford of Bruinen, where the Road crosses the Loudwater[27] that runs out of Rivendell.'

In the 'third phase' the chapter ended with Trotter, Frodo, and Merry slipping down from the summit, and the next chapter began with 'Sam and Folco had not been idle' (in the dell). In the new version the chapter continues, and as in FR includes the attack by the Black Riders. The passage opens exactly as in FR (p. 201), and Gandalf's supplies of *cram*, bacon, and dried fruits (VI.357) have gone,[28] but Trotter has different things to report from his examination of the tracks in the dell, and he does not assert that Rangers had been there recently, and that it was they who had left the firewood.

'It is just as I feared,' he said when he came back. 'Sam and Folco [> Pippin] have trampled the soft ground, and the marks are spoilt or confused. There has been somebody here in *boots* lately, which means somebody who is not a Ranger, but that is all I can say for certain. But I don't quite like it: it looks as if there had been more than one pair of boots.' To each of the hobbits there came the thought of the cloaked and booted riders. If they had already found the dell, the sooner Trotter took them somewhere else the better. But Trotter was still considering the meaning of the footprints.

'There was also something even more strange,' he went on: 'I think there are hobbit-tracks, too: only I can't now be sure that there is a third set, different from Folco's [> Pippin's] and Sam's.'

'But there aren't any hobbits in this part of the world, are there?' said Merry.

'There are four here now,' answered Trotter, 'and one more can't be called impossible; but I have no idea what that would mean.'

'It might mean that these black fellows have got the poor wretch as a prisoner,' said Sam. He viewed the bare dell with great dislike...

Sam's remark is of course a mere surmise, and he speaks without any particular reference: boots and hobbit-tracks merely suggest the possibility that the Riders might have a hobbit with them. But though Trotter's remarks are inconclusive, and within the narrative intentionally so, it is obvious that the story of Hamilcar Bolger's ride with Gandalf is present here.

Merry's question to Trotter beginning 'Can the Riders *see?*' now takes the same form as in FR (p. 202), and Trotter's reply is similar but less elaborate.[29]

In this text, as noted above, Trotter does not say anything about its being a Rangers' camp in the dell, and the firewood is left unexplained. Where in FR he says simply: 'Let us take this wood that is set ready for the fire as a sign', here he adds: 'Whoever left it, brought it and put it here for a purpose; for there are no trees near. Either he meant to return, or thought that friends in need might follow him. There is little shelter or defence here, but fire will make up for both. Fire is our friend in the wilderness.'[30]

The passage in the previous version (VI.358) describing Trotter's tales as they sat by the fire in the dell was changed, presumably at this time, to its reduced form in FR (p. 203); and his story of Beren and Lúthien now appears in the form that it has in FR (pp. 205–6). The song itself is missing; but the final form was apparently achieved at this time, since it is found written out roughly but in finished composition among draft papers of this period.[31]

Chapter XII: 'Flight to the Ford'

This chapter was constituted from the existing text, with replacement of some pages; but in this case the whole manuscript was kept together. Folco is still Folco in the passages of new writing, but was corrected to Pippin or Peregrin throughout.

The River Hoarwell or Mitheithel, and the Last Bridge, have now emerged, and the Ettenmoors and Ettendales[32] of FR (the Dimrill-dale(s) of the 'third phase') are now the Entish Lands and Entish Dales (see p. 10 and note 14, and p. 14 and note 18). The 'Riven River' or 'Rivendell River' of the 'third phase' (VI.360) is now the Loudwater or Bruinen (note 27); and Trotter tells his companions that the Hoarwell joins the Loudwater away in the South: 'Some call it the Greyflood after that' (FR p. 212).

Trotter finds the elf-stone in the mud on the Last Bridge; but the passage in which he speaks of the country to the north of the Road remains virtually as it was in the earliest form of the story (VI.192–3; cf. FR p. 214): he does not say that he once dwelt in Rivendell, and the history of Angmar and the North Kingdom had not emerged (cf. pp. 37, 56).

The removal of the names 'Bert' and 'William' from the Stone Trolls was also a later decision; but it was now that Sam's 'Troll Song' was introduced (after some hesitation). My father's original intention had been to have Bingo sing it at *The Prancing Pony* (see VI.142, notes 11 and 12), and he had made a rough, uncompleted version for that occasion, developed and much changed from the original Leeds song *The Root of the Boot* of the 1920s (given in Vol.VI, see pp. 142–4).[33]

The 'Troll Song' is found here in three distinct and carefully written versions, beside much rough working; the third version was taken up into the manuscript. The 'Bree' version, which I did not print in Vol.VI, was already much closer to the first of these than to *The Root of the Boot*, from which my father rejected all such references as 'churchyard', 'aureole', 'wore black on a Sunday', etc. I give the first text here, in the form in which it was written out fair in ink; there are many pencilled variants, here ignored. For the development of the second and third versions see note 35.

In *The Root of the Boot* the Troll's opponent was named Tom, and his uncle John; in the 'Bree' version he was John, and his uncle Jim, with John changed back to Tom while the text was being worked on. In all three of the present texts the names are John and Jim, as they still were when my father sang the song to Mr and Mrs George Sayer at Malvern in 1952;[34] in FR they are Tom and his uncle Tim.

> *A troll sat alone on his seat of stone,*
> *And munched and mumbled a bare old bone;*
> *   For many a year he had gnawed it near,*
> *   And sat there hard and hungry.*
> *   Tongue dry! Wrung dry!*
> *   For many a year he had gnawed it near*
> *   And sat there hard and hungry.*
>
> *Then up came John with his big boots on.*
> *Said he to the troll: 'Pray, what is yon?*
> *   For it looks like the shin o' my nuncle Jim,*
> *   As went to walk on the mountain.*
> *   Huntin'! Countin'!*

    It looks like the shin o' my nuncle Jim,
      As went to walk on the mountain.'

'My lad,' said the troll, 'this bone I stole;
But what be bones that lie in a hole?
    Thy nuncle were dead as a lump o' lead,
      Before I found his carkis.
         Hark'ee! Mark'ee!
    Thy nuncle were dead as a lump o' lead,
      Before I found his carkis.'

Said John: 'I doan't see why the likes o' thee
Without axin' leave should go makin' free
    With the leg or the shin o' my kith and my kin,
      So hand the old bone over!
         Rover! Trover!
    So give me the shin o' my kith and my kin,
      And hand the old bone over!'

'For a couple o' pins,' says the troll, and grins,
'I'll eat thee too, and gnaw thy shins.
    A bit o' fresh meat will go down sweet,
      And thee shall join thy nuncle!
         Sunk well! Drunk well!
    A bit o' fresh meat will go down sweet,
      And thee shall join thy nuncle.'

But just as he thought his dinner was caught,
He found his hands had hold of naught;
    But he caught a kick both hard and quick,
      For John had slipped behind him.
         Mind him! Blind him!
    He caught a kick both hard and quick,
      For John had slipped behind him.

The troll tumbled down, and he cracked his crown;
But John went hobbling back to town,
    For that stony seat was too hard for feet,
      And boot and toe were broken.
         Token! Spoken!
    That stony seat was too hard for feet,
      And boot and toe were broken.

There the troll lies, no more to rise,
With his nose to earth and his seat to the skies;
    But under the stone is a bare old bone
      That was stole by a troll from its owner.
         Donor! Boner!

Under the stone lies a broken bone
That was stole by a troll from its owner.[35]

At the end of the recital Frodo says of Sam: 'First he was a conspirator, now he's a jester. He'll end up by becoming a wizard – or a toad!' – The stone that marked the place where the trolls' gold was hidden is still marked with Old English G and B runes in a circle, and the text remains as in the 'third phase' (VI.360).

Glorfindel now hails Trotter, not as in the previous version with *Ai, Du-finnion!* but with *Ai, dennad Torfir!* A short preparatory draft for the passage beginning with Glorfindel's greeting to Frodo (VI.361, FR p. 222) is found, as follows:

'Hail, and well met at last!' said the elf-lord to Frodo. 'I was sent from Rivendell to look for your coming. Gandalf feared that you might follow the Road to the Ford.'

'Gandalf has reached Rivendell then?' cried Frodo joyfully.

'More than five days ago,' answered Glorfindel. 'He rode out of the Entish Dales over the Hoarwell springs.'

'Out of the Entish Dales!' exclaimed Trotter.

'Yes,' said Glorfindel, 'and we thought you might come that way to avoid the peril of the Road. Some are seeking you in that region. I alone have come this way. I rode as far as the Bridge of

Here the text breaks off. That Glorfindel should have set out after Gandalf reached Rivendell is at variance with the time-schemes (p. 14) and this brief draft must have preceded them. Abandoned in mid-sentence, it was replaced by another very close to what Glorfindel says in FR: he had left Rivendell nine days before; Gandalf had not then come; and Elrond had sent out from Rivendell not on account of Gandalf but because he had had news from Gildor's people – 'some of our kindred journeying beyond the Branduin (which you turned into Brandywine)'. This was taken up into the manuscript of the chapter (without the reference to the hobbits' name for the river: the moment was too urgent for such reflections).[36] It may be that this change in the story came about from the consideration that too little time was allowed for Gandalf's great detour northward through the Entish Dales.

In any case, the time-scheme D reflects the revised text: Glorfindel left Rivendell on 9 October and found Trotter and the hobbits nine days later, on the 18th, while Gandalf and Ham Bolger only reached Rivendell on that same day, having taken a full fortnight from Weathertop.

In the new version, Sam's protective fierceness when Frodo was attacked by pain and swayed is more bitterly expressed: ' "My master is sick and wounded, though perhaps Mr Trotter has not told you that," said Sam angrily.' Much later, the latter part of this was struck out.

At the end of the chapter the three Riders who came out of the tree-hung cutting become, by correction to the existing manuscript, five, and the six who came from ambush away to the left become four. This change goes of course with the change of three Riders to five in the attack on Weathertop (see note 31).

NOTES

1 In the draft A there is also a rejected version of the words between the Rider and the gatekeeper:
    'Have you seen Gandalf?' said the voice after a pause.
    'No sir, not since midsummer,' said Harry.
    'You will watch for him,' said the voice slowly. 'You will watch for hobbits. We want Baggins. He is with them....'

2 In the fair copy B of the end of Chapter V (pp. 34–5); in the draft A (p. 32) the name is still Folco.

3 'nigh on a score of years back' refers to Bilbo's passage through Bree after his Farewell Party, on his way to Rivendell. Butterbur had therefore seen Bilbo since he 'vanished with a bang while he was speaking', as the landlord goes on to say. See p. 83.

4 This development, showing the Riders to be well informed about the Bagginses of Bag End, was not retained.

5 On Trotter's references to Harry Goatleaf see pp. 41–2.

6 This speech of Butterbur's is largely derived from the draft text A (p. 43), where however it stands in a different context: there, it was on account of the questions of the Black Riders at the inn door, whereas here Butterbur has not mentioned the Riders.

7 'a month' was corrected to 'a fortnight', and at the same time 'in August' was struck out. The date on Gandalf's letter (p. 49) is 12 September, showing that these changes were made while the chapter was in progress.

8 'September' was corrected to 'this month'; see note 7.

9 The relations between the versions in respect of Gandalf's letter are:

    'Third phase' of the 'Bree' chapter:
    Butterbur tells Frodo of Gandalf's visit two days before, and of his message to hurry on after him (VI.338–9)
    Trotter has the letter from Gandalf (VI.343)

    Draft revision A of the 'third phase' version:
    Butterbur has nothing to communicate from Gandalf, who has not recently been in Bree (p. 43)
    Trotter has the letter from Gandalf (p. 44)

    The present text:
    Butterbur tells Frodo of Gandalf's visit to Bree (in August >) on 12 September (p. 47 and note 7)

Butterbur has the letter from Gandalf (p. 47)

The Fellowship of the Ring:
Butterbur tells Frodo of Gandalf's visit at the end of June, leaving with the landlord a letter to be taken to the Shire, which was not done (p. 179).

10 'yesterday and the day before': i.e. Tuesday and Wednesday, 27 and 28 September. Similarly in A the first Rider passed through Bree on the Tuesday (p. 43), not as in the previous versions on the Monday (VI.151, 339). In FR (pp. 176, 180) the first appearance of the Black Riders in Bree was again on Monday the 26th.

11 This is in fact a reversion to the alternative text 'B' of the original 'Bree' chapter (see VI.159), where Butterbur does not encounter the Riders and has nothing to say about them.

12 'thin long-legged script': 'strong but graceful script' FR. In the earlier versions Gandalf's handwriting is 'trailing' (VI.154, 352).

13 There are two very rough draft versions of the letter. The first reads:

> *The Prancing Pony* Aug. 30. Tuesday. Dear F. I hope you will not need this. If you get this (I hope old Butterbur will not forget) things will be far from well. I hope to get back in time, but things have happened which make it doubtful. This is to say: look out for horsemen in black. Avoid them: they are our worst enemies (save one). Don't use It again, *not for any reason whatever.* Make for Rivendell as fast as you possibly can; but *don't move in the dark.* I hope, if you reach Bree, you will meet Trotter the Ranger: a dark rather lean weather-beaten fellow, but my great friend, and enemy of our enemies. He knows all our business. He has been watching the east borders of the Shire since April, but for the moment has disappeared. You can trust him: he will see you through if it can be done. I hope we may meet in Rivendell. If not Elrond will advise you. If I don't come I can only hope that will be sufficient warning for you, and that you (and Sam, too, at least) will leave the Shire as soon as possible.

The other draft is the very close forerunner of the letter in the present manuscript, and scarcely differs from it, but it bears no date. – For previous forms of the letter see VI.154, 158, 352.

14 On the date 12 September (beside 30 August in the draft, note 13) see notes 7 and 8.

15 'Aragorn son of Celegorn' is certainly later than 'Aragorn son of Aramir' (p. 7). – The original form of the name of the third son of Fëanor was *Celegorm*, but this was changed to *Celegorn* in the course of the writing of the *Quenta Silmarillion* (V.226, 289). Later it became *Celegorm* again.

16 These words of Frodo and Aragorn were afterwards used in 'The Council of Elrond' (see p. 105, note 3).

17   There is much initial drafting in exceedingly rough form for this
     part of the chapter. The first form of this passage was:
         The Enemy has set snares for me before now. Of course I did
     not really doubt you after seeing you with Tom Bombadil, and
     certainly not after hearing Frodo's song. Bilbo wrote that, and I
     don't see how servants of the Enemy could possibly have
     known it. But I had to teach you caution and convince you that
     I was personally to be trusted all the same – so that you should
     have no doubts or regrets later. Also a wanderer, an old ranger,
     had a desire to be taken as a friend for his own sake for once,
     and without proofs.
     For the origin of this speech of Trotter's see VI.155.
18   With 'In the light they need their horses' cf. Strider's words on
     Weathertop (FR p. 202): 'the black horses can see, and the Riders
     can use men and other creatures as spies'; for earlier forms of this
     see VI.178, 357, and p. 58 and note 29.
19   I take the significance of this to be that the one Rider who had
     stood sentinel under the trees went to fetch the other two.
20   These two sentences replaced, soon after the time of writing, 'A
     curtain in one of the windows moved' (cf. VI.328).
21   'Far away answering horns were heard': in all the variant forms
     of the 'Crickhollow episode' the reading is 'Far away' (adverbial).
     The reading of FR (p. 189), 'Far-away answering horns' (adjec-
     tival), which appears already in the first impression of the first
     edition, is I think an early error.
22   The expression *a sheaf of lightning*, going back to the earliest
     form of the episode (VI.304), seems not to be recorded. The
     Oxford English Dictionary gives a meaning of *sheaf* 'a cluster of
     jets of fire or water darting up together', with quotations from the
     nineteenth century, but I doubt that this is relevant. Conceivably
     my father had in mind a 'cluster' or 'bundle' of lightnings', like a
     'sheaf of arrows'.
23   These sentences (from 'At the same moment...') were a replace-
     ment, made as I think at or very soon after the time of
     composition, of 'Nearby among the trees a horn rang out.'
24   Some corrections made to attain it were put in subsequently, as is
     seen at once from the fact that in one of them 'Pippin' is the name
     written, not changed from 'Folco'; but I doubt that they were
     much later, and the question has here no importance.
25   The original workings of Sam's song of Gil-galad are extant, with
     the original form of the dialogue that followed his recital:
         The others turned in amazement, for the voice was Sam's.
     'Don't stop!' said Folco.
         'That's all I know, sir,' stammered Sam blushing. 'I learned it
     out of an old book up at Mr. Bilbo's, when I was a lad. I always
     was as one for elves: but I never knew what that bit was about,

until I heard Gandalf talking. Mr. Frodo'll remember that day.'
  'I do,' said Frodo; 'and I know the book. I often wondered
where it came from, though I never read it carefully.'
  'It came from Rivendell,' said Trotter. 'That is part of
Here the text breaks up into a mass of rough variants, including
'It comes from "The Fall of Gilgalad", which is in an old tongue.
Bilbo must have been translating it', and 'I know the book you
mean (said Frodo). Bilbo wrote his poems in it. But I never
thought of them as true.'

26 'at least twelve days' journey before us': i.e. 21 less 9 (2 from the
Brandywine Bridge to Bree, 7 from Bree to Weathertop).

27 *Bruinen* occurs in the time-scheme D, p. 14; *Loudwater* is first
met here (but is found also on one of the sketch-maps redrawn in
VI.201).

28 In draft fragments there are many versions of the passage
concerning the problem of provisions that now beset the
travellers, and in these there are still several mentions of 'the
additional supplies left by Gandalf.'

29 The passage in the final form 'but our shapes cast shadows in
their minds ... they smell the blood of living things, desiring and
hating it' is lacking. The final text is found in this manuscript, but
whether added at this time or later I cannot say.

30 Aragorn's remark in FR about the Riders and fire ('Sauron can
put fire to his evil uses...') was added to the manuscript. – In a
draft for the earlier passage where he examines the traces in the
dell he says:
    'The wood is interesting. It is beech. There are no trees of
    that sort for many miles from this place, so the wood was
    brought from a distance. It must have been hidden here for a
    purpose: that is, either the campers meant to stay or to return,
    or they thought friends were likely to follow.'

31 Two differences from FR that remained in the 'third phase' were
corrected on this manuscript: 'three tall figures' to 'five', and
Frodo's cry to O *Elbereth! Gilthoniel!* (see VI.358).

32 The *Ettenmoors* and *Ettendales* of FR (pp. 212, 215) were
written into this manuscript, but certainly at some later time –
replacing *Entish Lands* and *Entish Dales* when the word *Ent* had
acquired its special meaning. It may be that *Etten-* from Old
English *eoten* 'giant, troll' (Grendel in *Beowulf* was an *eoten*),
Middle English *eten*, was first devised on this manuscript, in the
passage where Trotter says 'If we keep on as we are going we
shall get up into the Entish Dales far north of Rivendell' (FR
p. 215), for my father wrote here *Thirs* before he wrote *Ettendales*. He must have been thinking of using the Old English word
þyrs, of the same general meaning as *ent*, *eoten*, Middle English
thirs (and other forms). On the other hand a note on the First

Map (see p. 306) seems also to show *Etten-* at the moment of its emergence.

33   There was also a fleeting idea that it would be Bilbo's song at Rivendell (see VI.412, note 6).

34   See Humphrey Carpenter, *Biography*, p. 213; *Letters of J. R. R. Tolkien* no. 134 (29 August 1952). The tape-recording of the 'Troll Song' made by Mr. Sayer on that occasion is heard on the Caedmon record (TC 1477) issued in 1975. The version sung by my father was the third of the present texts.

35   The second text is much closer to that in FR, but still distinct: in the first verse *And sat there hard and hungry* stands in place of *For meat was hard to come by*, in the third *Before I found his carkis* for *Afore I found his shin-bone*, and in the fifth *Thee'll be a nice change from thy nuncle!* for *I'll try my teeth on thee now*. In this text the fifth, sixth, and seventh lines of each verse were omitted, but were pencilled in later, mostly as they appear in FR.

The third text changed *And sat there hard and hungry* in the first verse to *And seen no man nor mortal* (with rhyming words *Ortal! Portal!*), which goes back to *The Root of the Boot* in *Songs for the Philologists* (VI.143), but this was corrected on the manuscript to the final line *For meat was hard to come by* (and was so sung by my father in 1952, see note 34). The third verse preserved *Afore I found his carkis* (with the last line *He's got no use for his carkis*), and the fifth preserved *Thee'll be a nice change from thy nuncle!*

36   But the information that the Baranduin was the Brandywine survived as a footnote at this point in FR (p. 222). – This is no doubt the first occurrence of *B(a)randuin* in the narrative, origin of the 'popular etymology' *Brandywine* among the hobbits. Both *Branduin* and *Baranduin* are given in an added entry in the *Etymologies* in Vol. V (stem BARÁN, p. 351). – As the passage appears in the manuscript, the name of the river was written *Branduin*, corrected to *Baranduin*, and (much later) to *Malevarn*.

IV

OF HAMILCAR, GANDALF, AND SARUMAN

On 5 August 1940 the Registrar of Oxford University wrote to my father enclosing examination scripts that had been received from an American candidate in the Honour School of English. These provided a good quantity of paper, and my father used it for the continuation of the interrupted story of the Mines of Moria and for revisions of the story already in existence; he was still using it when he came to the departure of the Company from Lothlórien.[1] In the Foreword to the Second Edition of *The Lord of the Rings* he said that he 'halted for a long while' by Balin's tomb in Moria; and that 'it was almost a year later' when he went on 'and so came to Lothlórien and the Great River late in 1941.' I have argued (VI.461) that in saying this he erred in his recollection, and that it was towards the end of 1939, not of 1940, that he reached Balin's tomb; and the use of this paper, received in August 1940, for the renewed advance in the narrative seems to support this view.[2] Of course it may be that he did not begin using it until significantly later, though that does not seem particularly likely.

At any rate, for the attempt to deduce a consecutive account of the writing of *The Lord of the Rings* this was a most fortunate chance, since the use of a readily recognisable paper the supply of which was limited makes it possible to gain a much clearer idea of the development that took place at this time than would otherwise be the case. I shall refer to this paper as 'the August 1940 examination script'.

It is not, to be sure, clear whether my father meant that he put the whole thing away for the better part of a year, or whether he distinguished between 'new narrative' – the onward movement of the story from the Chamber of Mazarbul – and the rewriting of existing chapters. Dates in the latter part of 1939 have appeared in the preceding chapters: the 'final decisions' of 8 October 1939 (p. 8), the 'New Plot' of Autumn 1939 (p. 9), and the date October 1939 of the 'fourth phase' version of the long 'Bree' chapter (p. 40). A 'New Plot', given in the present chapter, is dated August 1940. It may be much oversimplified to suppose that nothing at all was done between the last months of 1939 and the late summer of 1940, but at least it is convenient to present the material in this way, and in this chapter I collect together various texts that certainly belong to the latter time.

In the 'fourth phase' version of 'A Knife in the Dark' the story of the attack on Crickhollow took this form (p. 55): the Black Riders carried Hamilcar Bolger out of the house as an inert bundle, and as they rode away 'another horse came thundering along the lane. As it passed the gate a horn rang out.' I noted that this story belongs with what is said in the time-scheme D (p. 12: Thursday 29 September: 'Riders attack Crickhollow and carry off Ham, pursued by Gandalf').

A very rough manuscript written on the August 1940 examination script described above gives a version of the event as recounted later at Rivendell by Gandalf and Hamilcar Bolger. This text takes up at the point where Frodo, leaving his bedroom at Rivendell, goes down and finds his friends in the porch (for the previous state of this part of the story see VI.365); but I do not think that anything has been lost before this point – it was a particular passage of the 'Many Meetings' chapter rewritten to introduce the new story.

There seemed to be three hobbits sitting there with Gandalf. 'Hurray!' cried one of them, springing up. 'Here comes our noble cousin!' It was Hamilcar Bolger.

'Ham!' cried Frodo, astounded. 'How did you come here? And why?'

'On horseback; and representing Mr. F. Baggins of Crick-hollow, and late of Hobbiton,' answered Ham.

Merry laughed. 'Yes,' he said. 'We told him so, but he didn't believe it: we left poor old Ham in a dangerous post. As soon as the Black Riders had found Crickhollow, where Mr. Baggins was popularly supposed to be residing, they attacked it.'

'When did that happen?' asked Frodo.

'Before dawn on Friday morning,[3] four days nearly after you left,' said Ham. 'They got me' – he paused and shuddered – 'but Gandalf came in the nick of time.'

'Not quite the nick,' said Gandalf. 'A notch or two behind, I am afraid. Two of the Riders must have crept into Buckland secretly, while a third took the horses down the other side of the River inside the Shire. They stole the ferryboat from the Buckland shore on Thursday night, and got their horses over. I arrived too late, just as they reached the other side. Galeroc had to swim the river. Then I had a hard chase: but I caught them ten miles beyond the Bridge. I have one advantage: there is no horse in Mordor or in Rohan that is as swift as Galeroc.[4] When they heard his feet behind them they were terrified: they thought I was somewhere else, far away. I was terrified too, I may say: I thought it was Frodo they had got.'

'Yes!' said Hamilcar with a laugh. 'He did not know whether

he was relieved or disgusted when he found it was only poor old
Ham Bolger. I was too crushed to mind at the time: he bowled
the Rider that was carrying me clean over; but I feel rather hurt
now.'

'You are perfectly well now,' said Gandalf; 'and you have had
a free ride all the way to Rivendell, which you would never have
seen, if you had been left to your own sluggishness. Still, you
have been useful in your way.' He turned to Frodo: 'It was from
Ham that I heard you had gone into the Old Forest,' he said;
'and that filled me with fresh anxiety. I turned off the Road at
once, and went immediately to visit Bombadil. That seems to
have proved lucky; for I believe the three Riders reported that
Gandalf and "Baggins" had ridden East. Their chieftain was at
Amrath, far down the Greenway in the south, and the news
must have reached him late on Friday. I fancy the Chief Rider
was sorely puzzled when the advance guard reported that
Baggins and the Ring had been in Bree the very night when they
thought they had caught him in Crickhollow! Some Riders seem
to have been sent straight across country to Weathertop. Five[5]
came roaring along the Road. I was safe back at the *Pony* when
they passed through Bree on Saturday night. They leaped the
gates and went through like a howling wind. The Breelanders
are still shivering and wondering what is happening to the
world. I left Bree next morning, and rode day and night behind
them, and we reached Weathertop on the evening of the third.'

'So Sam was right!' said Frodo. 'Yes, sir, seemingly,' said
Sam, feeling rather pleased;[6] but Gandalf frowned at the
interruption.

'We found two Riders already watching Weathertop,' he
went on. 'Others soon gathered round, returning from the
pursuit further east along the Road. Ham and I passed a very
bad night besieged on the top of Weathertop. But they dared
not attack me in the daylight. In the morning we slipped away
northwards into the wilds. Several pursued us; two followed us
right up the Hoarwell into the Entishlands. That is why they
were not in full force when you arrived, and did not observe you
at once.'

Here the text ends, but it is followed by another version of the last
part, following on from 'we slipped away northwards into the wilds':

...not too secretly – I wanted to draw them off. But the Chief
Rider was too cunning: only four came after us, and only two

pursued us far; and they turned aside when we reached the
Entishlands and went back towards the Ford, I fancy. Still, that
is why they were not in full force when you arrived, and why
they did not at once pursue [you] in the wild / Still, that is why
they did not immediately hunt for you in the wilderness, or
observe your arrival at Weathertop; and why they were not in
full force for the attack on you.

Comparison of this account with the time-scheme D (pp. 12–13) will
show that the narrative fits the scheme closely. In both, the Riders
crossed the Brandywine by the Ferry on the night of Thursday 29
September; Gandalf rescued Ham from the Riders on Friday morning;
two Riders (as the narrative was first written, see note 5) were sent
direct to Weathertop, and (again as first written) seven rode through
Bree, throwing down or leaping the gates, on the night of Saturday 1
October, while Gandalf and Ham were at *The Prancing Pony*; two
Riders were already at Weathertop when Gandalf and Ham got there
in the evening of Monday 3 October, after riding day and night; and
Gandalf and Ham left Weathertop on the following morning.

Gandalf's horse is now named *Galeroc*, replacing earlier *Narothal*
(VI.345); and the name *Amrath* appears, of the place where the chief
of the Riders remained, 'far down the Greenway in the south.'[7]

This narrative seems to belong also with the 'fourth phase' version
of 'A Knife in the Dark' (p. 55): the horse that came racing up the lane
as the Riders rode off with Ham Bolger was bearing Gandalf from the
Ferry, 'a notch or two behind' the nick of time, as he said at Rivendell.
Yet there is a difficulty, or at any rate a difference; for the story of the
attack on Crickhollow in this version, as in all those preceding it,
described a long period ('time went slowly on') between the coming of
the Riders into the garden of Crickhollow and the breaking into the
house. If Gandalf came to Bucklebury Ferry just as the Riders with
their horses reached the other side, and he at once put Galeroc to swim
the river, he cannot have been more than a matter of minutes behind
them.

A new narrative outline, written roughly and rapidly on two sides of
a single sheet, is headed: '*New Plot*. Aug. 26–27, 1940'. This outline
was subsequently altered and added to, but I give it here as first
written. I have expanded contractions and in other small ways slightly
edited the text to make it easier to follow.

The wizard Saramond the White [*written above at the same time:*
Saramund the Grey] or Grey Saruman sends out a message that
there is important news: Trotter hears that Black Riders are *out* and
moving towards the Shire (for which they are asking). He sends
word to Gandalf, who leaves Hobbiton at the end of June. He goes

S.E. (leaving Trotter to keep an eye on the Shire-borders) towards Rohan (or Horserland).

Gandalf knows that 9 Black Riders (and especially their king) are too much for him alone. He wants the help of Saramund. So he goes to him where he lived on the borders of Rohan at Angrobel (or Irongarth).

Saramund betrays him – having fallen and gone over to Sauron: (*either*) he tells Gandalf false news of the Black Riders, and they pursue him to the top of a mountain; there he is left standing alone with a guard (wolves, orcs, etc. all about) while they ride off with mocking laugh; (*or else*) he is handed over to a giant Fangorn (Treebeard) who imprisons him?

Meanwhile the Black Riders attack the Shire, coming up the Greenway and driving a crowd of fugitives among which are one or two evil men, Sauronites.[8] The King of the Black Riders encamps at Amrath to guard Sarn Ford and Bridge.

6 Riders (DEFGHI) go ahead and invade the Shire. The vanguard Rider (D) reaches Bag-End on Sept. 23 (night). Two (DE) then trail Frodo etc. to the Ferry (Sept. 25). FGHI are on the main road. DE, foiled at the Ferry (Sept. 25), ride off to Brandywine Bridge and join FGHI (dawn on Sept. 26).

HI then ride along scouring both sides of the Road and reach Bree up and down Greenway [*sic*] on Tuesday Sept. 27.[9]

On night (cockcrow) of Sept. 26–27 DEF attack Crickhollow. There they carry off Ham. G was left guarding the Bridge but now comes with them.

HI go on through Bree asking for news, to make sure 'Baggins' has not escaped and got ahead. They get in touch with Bill Ferney.

DEFG with poor Ham now ride to Greenway (does Harry see them? Probably not). At Amrath they meet the King (A) and BC, on Wednesday 28th, leaving for the moment the Road deserted. The King is angry at this. He is suspicious of a plot since Ham has no Ring. DE are sent back to Bree, arriving late on Thursday 29th. (Meanwhile the hobbits have got to the Inn.) FG go back to the Shire.

DE get in touch with Bill Ferney, and hear of news at the Inn. [*Struck out at once:* They attack the Inn but fail (and get the idea that 'Green'[10] has gone off?)] They fear 'Trotter', but get Bill Ferney and the Southerner to burgle the Inn and try and get more news, especially of the Ring. (They are puzzled by two Bagginses.) The burglary fails; but they drive off all the ponies.

FG bring news to the King that Gandalf has escaped and is in the Shire (which he reached on Wednesday 28th [> Thursday 29th night], and visited Bag-End and the Gaffer).

DE return to the King and report (Sept. 30): he is puzzled by 'Green' and the Ring, by Baggins and Ham, and troubled by news of

Gandalf behind. He does not kill Ham because he wants to find out more, and Sauron has ordered him to bring 'Baggins' to Mordor. H I return (Oct. 1) reporting nothing on the Road as far as Weathertop, and that Green and Trotter have left Bree and vanished. The King decides to pursue Green with all his forces, carrying Ham with him.

Gandalf goes to Crickhollow late on Thursday 29th and finds it deserted. Old cloak of Frodo dropped. Gandalf is terrified lest Frodo is captive. (? Does he visit Tom – if so make him arrive in the Shire on the 28th and visit Buckland on the 29th; if not, arrive in the Shire on the 29th, visit Buckland on the 30th.) Either visiting Tom or not, Gandalf reaches Bree on Saturday Oct. 1 (after the hobbits have gone). He rides after them. The Black Riders meanwhile have left Amrath and revisited Bree to get news of Green, and gone off along the Road on both sides. Gandalf crashes into D E who are carrying Ham and rescues him. He gallops to Weathertop, reaching it on Oct. 3. He sees Black Riders gather and goes off North (three Riders, D E F, pursue him). The rest patrol round and watch Weathertop.

Here we have the story of the capture of Hamilcar Bolger again, but with a significant difference. In Time-scheme D (p. 12), and in the story told by Gandalf at Rivendell (p. 68), the attack on Crickhollow took place on the night of Thursday–Friday 29–30 September; and the story there was that Gandalf arrived just as the Riders left, and he was able to catch them up ten miles east of the Brandywine Bridge. In the present outline, the attack on Crickhollow took place three nights earlier, on that of Monday–Tuesday 26–27 September (Frodo and the others having left on the Monday morning), and since Gandalf still arrives there late on the 29th (or the 30th) he finds the trail cold; but he also finds Frodo's cloak dropped on the step. He still rescues Ham, but not till his captors have passed Bree. It is curious therefore that (though he was uncertain about it) my father had not decisively rejected the visit to Tom Bombadil, since with this plot Gandalf could have had no notion that the hobbits had entered the Old Forest.

This is very probably the first appearance of Saruman (Saramond, Saramund), who steps into the narrative quite unheralded – but he enters at once as a Wizard whose aid Gandalf seeks, and who has 'fallen and gone over to Sauron'; moreover he dwells at *Angrobel* or 'Irongarth' (cf. *Isengard*) 'on the borders of Rohan'. But my father was still quite uncertain what happened to Gandalf, having rejected the story of the Western Tower: the possibilities suggested here show that the imprisonment in a tower had been for the moment abandoned. Giant Fangorn or Treebeard again appears as a hostile being (cf. p. 9).

I suspect that the primary question that my father was pondering here was that of the emergence of the Ringwraiths from Mordor, Gandalf's knowledge of this in the summer before Frodo left Bag End, and Trotter's message. It has been said already (p. 9) that 'It was a message of Trotter's in July (?) that took Gandalf away – fearing Black Riders', and again (p. 10) 'It was a message from Trotter that fetched Gandalf away in summer before Frodo left'. These notes indicate that Gandalf already had reason, when he left Hobbiton, to suspect the emergence of the Ringwraiths; but it is now told, at the beginning of the present outline, that the message from Trotter (itself emanating from Saruman) was an actual report that the Nine had left Mordor and were moving towards the Shire. This would raise the question: why, in that case, did Gandalf, before he went off, not urge Frodo to leave for Rivendell as soon as he could? Scribblings on the manuscript of this outline show my father concerned with the question: 'Both Gandalf and Trotter must go away *together* and not fear to be captured, or else Gandalf would have sent a message to Frodo to start, or Trotter would have.' Then follows a suggestion that Trotter 'got cut off from Gandalf, only arriving in Bree hard on the tracks of the Black Riders.' But this does not seem entirely to meet the difficulty. Later my father noted here: 'Leaves Butterbur a letter which he *forgets* to send to Frodo', and this is clearly where that essential idea arose.

In FR (p. 269) the problem is resolved by reverting to the story that when Gandalf left Hobbiton he had no definite knowledge, and by the introduction of Radagast. 'At the end of June I was in the Shire, but a cloud of anxiety was on my mind, and I rode to the southern borders of the little land; for I had a foreboding of some danger, still hidden from me but drawing near.' It was Radagast who told Gandalf that the Nine were abroad, whereupon Gandalf, at Bree, wrote the letter to Frodo which Butterbur forgot to send.

Another brief but distinctive narrative passage is clearly associated with this 'August 1940' outline. It was substituted in the manuscript of the 'fourth phase' version of Chapter IX ('At the Sign of the Prancing Pony (i)') for that in which the Black Riders spoke to Harry Goatleaf, the gatekeeper at Bree, on the evening of Wednesday the 28th of September (pp. 40–1), and was itself subsequently rejected.

The rain that swept over the Forest and the Downs on Tuesday was still falling long and grey on Bree when evening came. The lights were just being lit in Tom's house,[11] when the noise of horses approaching came down the Road from the west. Harry Goatleaf the gatekeeper peered out of his door and scowled at the rain. He had been thinking of going out to close the gate, when he caught the sound of the horsemen. Reluctantly he waited, wishing now that he had shut the gate earlier: he did not like the sound. Two horsemen had appeared in Bree late the day before[12] and wild stories were going about. People had been scared; some said the riders were uncanny: dogs yammered, and geese screamed at them. Yet they were asking for news of hobbits out of the Shire, especially for one called Baggins. Very queer.

Harry thought it even queerer a minute later. He went out, grumbling at the rain, and looking up the Road he thought he saw dark figures approaching swiftly, three or maybe four. But suddenly they turned left at the Cross Roads[13] just beyond the gate, and went off southwards and down the Greenway; all sound of their horses' feet died away on the grass-grown track.

'Queerer and queerer!' he thought. 'That way leads nowhere. Who would turn off on a wet night just in sight of the Inn at Bree?' He shivered suddenly all down his back. Locking the gate he hurried into his house and bolted the door.

Wednesday turned foggy after midday; but still the queer events went on. Out of the mists up the Greenway there straggled such a company as had not been seen in Bree for many a year: strange men from the South, haggard and wayworn, and bearing heavy burdens. Most of them had a hunted look and seemed too tired and scared to talk; but some were ill-favoured and rough-spoken. They made quite a stir in Bree.

The next day, Thursday, was clear and fine again, with a warm sun and a wind that veered from East towards the South. No traveller passed the western gate all day, but Harry kept on going to the gate, even after nightfall.

This would then join on to the next part of the text, 'It was dark, and white stars were shining, when Frodo and his companions came at last to the Greenway-crossing and drew near the village' (cf. VI.348).

With this compare the 'August 1940' outline (p. 71): 'DEFG with poor Ham now ride to Greenway (does Harry see them? Probably not).' I think it is clear that when Harry Goatleaf saw the dark figures mysteriously turn off down the Greenway at the crossroads in the rain at dusk, they had Hamilcar Bolger with them, bearing him to the King at Amrath. And with the description of the company that came up the Greenway on the Wednesday cf. an earlier passage in the same outline: 'Meanwhile the Black Riders attack the Shire, coming up the Greenway and driving a crowd of fugitives among which are one or two evil men, Sauronites.'

In the margin of the 'fourth phase' version of the attack on Crickhollow (p. 55) my father later noted:

Omit, or bring into line with old version (in middle of Chapter VII). Ham cannot be captured (Black Riders would obviously kill him). It probably spoils surprise to show what Gandalf is up to at this point. Gandalf can briefly explain that [? he was at] Crickhollow.

There is a definitive tone about this that suggests that this is where the 'Odo-Hamilcar' adventure was finally abandoned; and if this is so it must be placed, of course, after the outline dated 'Aug. 26–27, 1940'. Presumably it was at this time that the 'fourth phase' version of the 'Crickhollow episode' was struck through.

Labelling this rejected form 'A', my father seems now to have tried out a version (labelled 'B') which follows his direction to 'bring (the story) into line with the old version (in middle of Chapter VII)' – i.e. the original form of the episode, which was inserted in the course of the 'second phase' into Chapter VII 'In the House of Tom Bombadil' (VI.303–4), at which stage the story was that the house at Crickhollow was empty when the Riders came, for no hobbit had been left behind there. In version 'B' there is no mention of Hamilcar Bolger at all. The 'man in grey', leading a white horse, comes up the path, looks in at the windows, and disappears round the corner of the house; then the Black Riders come; at first cockcrow they break in the door; and at that moment the horn call rings out, the Riders flee, with 'a cry like the cry of hunting beasts stricken unawares' (cf. VI.304), and Gandalf appears wielding horn and wand and thunders after them.

A page of notes is associated with these attempts to find the right form for the opening of 'A Knife in the Dark'. These begin:

> It will improve matters to cut out Ham Bolger. Version B will provide for that. (Gandalf arrives, takes Ham Bolger out of the house, and chases off the Black Riders.)

This is obscure, since there is no mention in the version labelled 'B' of Gandalf's entering the house, no mention of a light in the window, nor any suggestion that it was inhabited. But in any case it was clearly not my father's meaning when he wrote 'It will improve matters to cut out Ham Bolger' that he intended to cut him out of the narrative altogether: he meant only that Ham was to be excluded from further adventures after the 'Crickhollow episode' was ended. Conceivably, he had here a passing notion that Gandalf came to Crickhollow, entered secretly, told Ham Bolger to clear out, and proceeded to look after the Black Riders himself. Whatever the meaning, these notes continue:

> But better would be this:
> Gandalf is captured by [Saramund >] Saruman.
> Elves send word that he is missing, which reaches Rivendell Sat. 8th.[14] Glorfindel is sent out, and messengers sent to Eagles. The Eagles are told about Oct. 11. They fly all over the lands, and find Gandalf about Sat. 15. Bring ... to Rivendell Wed. 19th.
> The XIII and wood are Sam's discovery. Trotter says it is *a rangers' camp*.
> Weakness of this is that Black Riders are sure to make *some* attempt on Crickhollow. How was it foiled?

Ham flies as shown overleaf.

Then Gandalf can come and find house deserted and only old cloak of Frodo's. He thinks Frodo [*struck out:* is capt(ured)]. He follows like thunder.

'Ham flies as shown overleaf' refers to a third version, labelled 'C', which (though at first differently ordered in the articulation of the narrative) scarcely differs from that in FR (with Ham opening the door of the house, seeing a black shape in the garden, and fleeing out of the back door and over the fields), apart of course from the fact that this is Hamilcar and not Fredegar, and apart from the notable words, afterwards lost, following 'Ham Bolger had not been idle': 'Terror will drive even a Bolger to action'. The hobbit-cloak let fall by one of the Riders as he fled reappears from the 'August 1940' outline (p. 72). At the head of this version my father noted:

> Gandalf *does not follow* [i.e. he does not follow the Black Riders from Crickhollow]. Either he comes later, Saturday Oct. 1 or [Sunday Oct.] 2 (and finds cloak), or else he is taken by eagles ... to Rivendell.

This no doubt preceded the notes given above. These are certainly the first references to Gandalf's escape from captivity by the aid of the Eagles; and the entry of Radagast is now on the threshold.[15]

The apparently irrelevant mention of Trotter's saying that 'it is a rangers' camp' is presumably associated with the idea that the Eagles found Gandalf and carried him to Rivendell – so that, with this story, he would never go to Weathertop at all. But what the significance of 'The XIII and wood are Sam's discovery' may be I cannot say. Sam's *interpretation* of the 'X:IIII' has appeared, but that was only a refinement of Trotter's view that they were marks made by Gandalf on the stone found on the summit of Weathertop and referred to the date: see pp. 56–7. I have noticed there that Sam's intervention does not fit the story, since there is never any suggestion that he was among those who went up to the high place where the stone was found; and also that 'X:IIII' was subsequently changed to 'X:III'. Conceivably, the passing idea here was that the 'X III', retained but given a different significance (a Rangers' mark?), was not found on the stone on the cairn, but on the firewood in the dell.

At this time Chapter X, 'At the Sign of the Prancing Pony (ii)', was once more heavily overhauled.[16] This revision was carried out in two stages, clearly not long separated. The completion of the revision was written on pages of the August 1940 examination script; and with this the chapter as it stands in FR was achieved in all points, save for a few minor additions and alterations that were certainly later.

By this time 'Pippin' was firmly established. In the first stage of revision Frodo's assumed name at Bree was still 'Green', but became

'Underhill' in the second. Mr Butterbur is still Barnabas, not Barliman. His account of Frodo's distinguishing marks as received from Gandalf (in addition to his bring 'a round-bellied little fellow with red cheeks') at first gave him 'a white lock of hair by his left ear and a wart on his chin.' The second version made him 'broader than most and fairer than some', and still with a wart on his chin. The final description came in later.

The scribbled suggestion on the manuscript of the 'New Plot' (p. 73), 'Leaves Butterbur a letter which he *forgets* to send to Frodo', was now taken up, but it was not until the second stage of revision that the form of the episode in FR was reached. At first the preceding version was more largely retained, notably in the story of the two letters (pp. 49 ff.). The substance of Gandalf's letter to Frodo reaches the form in FR (with the date now Friday July 2nd), but there are differences in the postscripts:

> *PS. Look out for horsemen in black. Deadly enemies, especially after dark. Do not move by night. Do not use IT again, not for any reason whatever.*
>
> *PPS. Make sure it is the real Trotter. His true name is Aragorn son of Celegorn.*[17]
>> *All that is gold does not glitter,*
>> *not all those that wander are lost;*
>> *All that is old does not wither,*
>> *and fire may burn bright in the frost;*
>> *Not all that have fallen are vanquished,*
>> *not only the crowned is a king;*
>> *Let blade that was broken be brandished,*
>> *and Fire be the Doom of the Ring!*[18]
>
> *Aragorn would know that rhyme. Ask him what follows after All that is gold does not glitter.*
>
> *PPPS. I hope Butterbur sends this promptly. A worthy man, but his mind is like a lumber-room: things wanted always buried. If he forgets, I shall have words with him one day.*
>
> *The real Trotter will have a sealed letter (addressed to you) with these words inside: All that is gold does not glitter etc.*

At this stage Frodo still read Gandalf's letter aloud; and Trotter produced the second letter, which after the verse reads:

> *This is to witness that the bearer is Aragorn son of Celegorn [> Kelegorn] known as the Trotter. Who trusts Gandalf may trust him.*

As there is now no mention of Elendil, the passage that followed in the former version ('Then It belongs to you as much as to me, or more' etc., p. 50) was removed (see p. 105, note 3); and Trotter now says, after 'The Enemy has set traps for me before now', 'I was puzzled –

because you did not produce your letter or ask for the pass-words. It was not till old Barnabas confessed that I understood.'

I do not think that it was long before my father abandoned the story of the second letter, and on pages of the August 1940 script the FR text was reached – with Gandalf's letter read silently, Trotter using the words *All that is gold does not glitter* quite independently, and drawing out the Sword that was Broken (see p. 116). The date of Gandalf's letter now becomes Wednesday June 30th, and (probably at this time) the verse was changed again:

> *All that is gold does not glitter,*
> *not all those that wander are lost;*
> *All that is old does not wither,*
> *and bright may be fire in the frost.*
> *The fire that was low may be woken;*
> *and sharp in the sheath is the sting;*
> *Forged may be blade that was broken;*
> *the crownless again may be king.*[19]

Gandalf's signature remains still in Old English runes.

Aragorn's account of his last meeting with Gandalf at Sarn Ford on the first of May (FR p. 184) now appears, and in the same words.[20] The story in the 'New Plot' (p. 70) that 'Trotter hears that Black Riders are *out* and moving towards the Shire.... He sends word to Gandalf, who leaves Hobbiton at the end of June' had presumably been abandoned, and the rôle of Radagast in telling Gandalf of the emergence of the Ringwraiths introduced (see pp. 82, 131).

The now chaotic text of the chapter, a mass of emendations, rejected pages, and inserted riders, was later replaced by a typescript fair copy: how much later I cannot say. Near the end of the chapter (FR p. 184) Trotter says (in the manuscript): 'Well, with Sam's permission we'll call that settled. Trotter shall be your guide. *And now I think it is time you went to bed and took what rest you can.* We shall have a rough road tomorrow....' In the typescript text that followed (the latter part of which was not typed by my father) the italicised words were omitted; but there is no suggestion in the manuscript that they should be, and indeed the words 'We shall have a rough road tomorrow' clearly depend on them. But the omission was never picked up, and the sentence does not appear in FR.

The series of rewritings of the beginning of Chapter XI, 'A Knife in the Dark', leading to the final elimination of Ham Bolger's ride with Gandalf, have been considered already (pp. 74–6). An associated revision belonging to this time removed the passage (pp. 57–8) in which Trotter thought that he found hobbit footprints in the dell below Weathertop that might be distinct from those of Pippin and Sam, and replaced it by a form very close to that in FR p. 201 (beginning

'Rangers have been here lately. It is they who left the firewood behind'; cf. 'Trotter says it is *a rangers' camp*', p. 75).

NOTES

1   The candidate's name was Richard Creswell Rowland. The scripts had been sent from the United States. At first my father received only the scripts in the subjects that personally concerned him as an examiner, but subsequently most or all of the candidate's writing came to him. He used not only the blank verso sides of the paper, but also the blue covers of each booklet, where his writing becomes peculiarly hard to decipher.

2   A further argument in favour of this dating can now be adduced. In notes dated Autumn 1939 and October 8 1939 (pp. 8–9) Trotter has definitively ceased to be a hobbit and has become a man, Aragorn; but in the original 'Moria' chapter he was still a hobbit (or at any rate he certainly was in the original version of 'The Ring Goes South', with which 'The Mines of Moria' was continuous). See further p. 379.

3   'Before dawn on Friday morning' was an immediate change from 'Thursday night'; cf. p. 55.

4   I do not think that there is any suggestion here that Galeroc was a horse from Rohan: he is simply Gandalf's horse, and it is essential that he be extraordinarily swift.

5   In the preceding sentence 'Some Riders' (those sent to Weathertop) was first written 'Two Riders', and 'Five' here (those who rode along the Road to Bree) was written 'Seven', agreeing with the scheme D (p. 13). 'Two' was then changed to 'Four' and 'Seven' to 'Five'; finally 'Four' to 'Some'. – By *roaring along the Road* my father meant going at wild speed, with also a suggestion of the great noise of their passage.

6   This refers to the markings on the stone at Weathertop, which (by a change introduced into the 'fourth phase' version of 'A Knife in the Dark') Sam realised were to be read, not as G.4, but as G.1.3, and which Trotter in his turn thought might mean that Gandalf and another were at Weathertop on 3 October; see pp. 56–7.

7   With this cf. *Unfinished Tales* p. 348: 'The Black Captain established a camp at Andrath, where the Greenway passed in a defile between the Barrow-downs and the South Downs.' On the First Map (p. 305) *Andrath* (very probably first written *Amrath*, p. 298) is marked as a point beside the Greenway a little nearer to Bree than to Tharbad.

8   Cf. the end of the short text given on pp. 73–4.

9   The date Tuesday Sept. 27 was subsequently altered to 'late Monday 26th'; see p. 63, note 10, and note 12 to this chapter.

10   Frodo's assumed name 'Green' (replacing 'Hill') has already appeared (pp. 37, 41, etc.).

11   Tuesday 27 September was the second night spent by the hobbits in the house of Tom Bombadil.

12   The riders H and I, according to the outline (p. 71), where their arrival in Bree was altered from Tuesday 27 September to Monday the 26th (note 9).

13   'turned *left* at the Cross Roads': i.e. from the point of view of the gatekeeper, who was looking out westwards.

14   Word reaches Rivendell that Gandalf is missing on Saturday 8 October: cf. the time-scheme D, p. 14.

15   Radagast has been named, but no more, in previous texts (VI.379, 397), and with no indication of what part my father was envisaging for him.

16   A development from this time in Chapter IX, 'At the Sign of the Prancing Pony (i)', has been given on pp. 73–4.

17   *Aragorn* was later changed here to *Elfstone, Erkenbrand*, again *Elfstone, Ingold*, and finally back to *Aragorn*, and in the passage 'I am Aragorn son of Kelegorn, and if by life or death I can save you, I will' the name was changed to *Elfstone son of Elfhelm*. But these changes were made after the second stage of revision had been completed. The renaming of Aragorn and its implications are discussed on pp. 277–8.

18   An earlier stage in the evolution of the verse, following from the original form in the 'fourth phase' version of the chapter (pp. 49–50), was:

> *All that is gold does not glitter;*
> *not all those that wander are lost.*
> *All that grows old does not wither;*
> *not every leaf falls in the frost.*
> *Not all that have fallen are vanquished;*
> *a king may yet be without crown,*
> *A blade that was broken be brandished;*
> *and towers that were strong may fall down.*

19   In all these versions of *All that is gold does not glitter*, including the original form on pp. 49–50, the verses are written in the manuscript as long lines (i.e. four lines not eight).

20   In FR Gandalf arrived at Bag End after his long absence on an evening of early April (pp. 54–5); 'two or three weeks' later he advised Frodo that he ought to leave soon (p. 74); and he 'stayed in the Shire for over two months' (p. 76) before he left at the end of June. There is no reference to his having left Hobbiton during this time.

V

BILBO'S SONG AT RIVENDELL:
ERRANTRY AND EÄRENDILLINWË

We come now again to Rivendell, and to Book II of *The Fellowship of the Ring*. In the 'third phase' the chapter which afterwards became 'Many Meetings' was numbered XII and entitled 'The Council of Elrond' (VI.362) – because at that stage my father thought that it would include not only Frodo's conversation with Gandalf when he awoke at Rivendell, the feast, and his meeting with Bilbo, but the deliberations of the Council also. Trotter was still at that time, of course, a hobbit. I have argued (VI.369) that this chapter (and the 'third phase' of writing) ended abruptly in the middle of Glóin's conversation with Frodo at the feast – at precisely the same point as did the original form of the story in the 'first phase'; and that the remainder of the chapter in this manuscript was added in later – when Trotter had become Aragorn. Simply for the purpose of this discussion I will call the first or 'third phase' part of the manuscript (VI.362–6) 'I', and the second part 'II'. Behind 'II' lie the rough draftings given in VI.391–4 (in which Trotter was still the hobbit Peregrin Boffin).

I have not been able to determine when 'II' was written, but it perhaps comes from the period of work represented by the notes and rewritings of the 'fourth phase' in the first three chapters of this book. Both 'I' and 'II' were subjected to emendation at different times: for one substantial passage of rewriting the August 1940 examination script was used, but many other minor alterations may be earlier or later. In view of these uncertainties I shall do no more here than look briefly through the chapter (now numbered XIII, since the 'Bree' chapter had been divided into two, IX and X) and show what seems to have been its form at the stage of development we have now reached.

Looking first at changes made to section 'I' of the manuscript, the passage in the third phase version (VI.362–3) beginning 'It is no small feat to have come so far and through such dangers, still bearing the Ring', in which Gandalf told of his captivity at the hands of Giant Treebeard and teased Frodo's curiosity about Trotter, was entirely rewritten. It now begins:

'We should never have done it without Trotter,' said Frodo.

'But we needed you. I did not know what to do without you.'

'I was delayed,' said Gandalf; 'and that nearly proved our ruin. And yet I am not sure: it may have been better so. Knowing the peril I should not have dared to take such risks, and we might either have been trapped in the Shire, or if I had tried some long way round we might have been hunted down in some wild place far from all help. As it is we have escaped the pursuit – for the moment.'

To Frodo's astonished 'You?' when Gandalf said that he was held captive his reply now takes this form:

'Yes, I, Gandalf the Grey,' said the wizard solemnly. 'There are many powers greater than mine, for good or evil, in the world. I cannot stand alone against all the Black Riders.'[1]

'Then you knew of the Riders already – before I met them?'

The text is then as in FR, including Gandalf's words 'But I did not know that they had arisen again or I should have fled with you at once. I heard news of them only after I left you in June' (see p. 78). He says: 'There are few left in Middle-earth like Aragorn son of Kelegorn.[2] The race of the Kings from over the Sea is nearly at an end', and Frodo in reply says: 'Do you really mean that Trotter is of the race of Númenor?'[3] To Frodo's 'I thought he was only a Ranger' Gandalf replies 'indignantly':

'Only a Ranger! Many of the Rangers are of the same race, and the followers of Aragorn: all that he has left of the realm of his fathers. We may need his help before all is over. We have reached Rivendell; but the Ring is not yet at rest.'

From this point to the end of section 'I' of the manuscript the 'third phase' text was little changed, and the differences from FR noted in VI.363–6 were mostly still present. Gandalf's words 'And the Elves of Rivendell are descendants of his chief foes' (VI.364) were changed to 'And among the Elves of Rivendell are some descendants of his chief foes', and 'the Wise say that he [the Dark Lord] is doomed in the End, though that is far away' (*ibid.*) was removed. Also removed of course were the references to Odo's arrival, and when Frodo goes down with Sam to find his friends in the porch Odo's remarks are given to Pippin. The sentence describing Elrond's smile and laughter (VI.365) was struck out, and Glóin's wink (VI.366) also disappears: his reply to Frodo's question concerning his errand from the Lonely Mountain now takes the form it has in FR (p. 240).

In section 'II' of the manuscript (see p. 81), beginning at Frodo's question 'And what has become of Balin and Ori and Oin?', the text of

FR (pp. 241 ff.) was very largely reached (apart from the absence of Arwen), and there are only a few particular points to notice.

When in the first draft (VI. 392) Bilbo said 'I shall have to get that fellow *Peregrin* to help me', he now says the same of *Aragorn*, changed in the act of writing to *Tarkil* (in FR, *the Dúnadan*). At this stage Aragorn's absence from the feast was still explained by his being much in demand in the kitchens.

I noted that in the original draft 'the entire passage (FR pp. 243–4) in which Bilbo tells [Frodo] of his journey to Dale, of his life in Rivendell, and his interest in the Ring – and the distressing incident when he asks to see it – is absent.' In this version Bilbo does give an account of his journey, but it was at first different from what he says in FR:

When he had left Hobbiton he had wandered off aimlessly along the Road, but somehow he had steered all the time for Rivendell.

'I got here in a month or two without much adventure,' he said, 'and I stayed at *The Pony* in Bree for a bit;[4] somehow I have never gone any further. I have almost finished my book. And I make up a few songs which they sing occasionally...'

This was changed, probably soon, to the text of FR, in which Bilbo tells of his journey to Dale. The rest of the passage, in which Bilbo speaks of Gandalf and the Ring, was present in this version from the start, the only differences being that Bilbo names the Necromancer, not the Enemy, and where in FR he says that he could get little out of Gandalf concerning the Ring but that 'the Dúnadan has told me more', here he calls him *Tarkil*, and adds 'He was in the Gollum-hunt' (this being afterwards struck out).

The episode of Bilbo's asking to see the Ring is present as in FR, the only difference here being that where FR has 'When he had dressed, Frodo found that while he slept the Ring had been hung about his neck on a new chain, light but strong', this version has 'When he dressed Frodo had hung the Ring upon a chain about his neck under his tunic.'

When Aragorn joins Bilbo and Frodo, the conversation is as in FR, with *Tarkil* for *Dúnadan, the Dúnadan*; but Bilbo's reply to Frodo's 'What do you call him *Tarkil* for?' is different:

'Lots of us do here,' answered Bilbo, 'just to show off our knowledge of the old tongue, and to show our deep respect. It means Man of the West, out of Númenor, you know, or perhaps you don't. But that is another story. He can tell it you some other time. Just now I want his help. Look here, friend Tarkil, Elrond says this song of mine is to be finished before the end of the evening...'

This was changed to:

'He is often called that here,' answered Bilbo. 'It is a title of honour. The Elder Tongue is remembered in Rivendell; and I thought you knew enough at least to know *tarkil*: Man of Westernesse, Númenórean. But this isn't the time for lessons. Just now I want your Trotter's help in something urgent. Look here, friend Tarkil...'[5]

The passage leading up to Bilbo's song is much as in FR (pp. 245–6), but the sentence beginning 'Almost it seemed that the words took shape...' is absent, and where FR has 'the interwoven words in elven-tongues' ('in the Elven-tongue', First Edition) this text has 'the interwoven words in the high elven-tongue'.

The reception of the song moves close to the text of FR (p. 249), but with some differences. No Elf is individually named (*Lindir* in FR). From Bilbo's words about Men and Hobbits – 'They're as different as peas and apples' – this version has:

'No! – little peas and large peas!' said some. 'Their languages all taste much the same to us, anyway,' said others.

'I won't argue with you,' said Bilbo. 'I am sleepy after so much music and singing. I'll leave you to guess, if you want to.'

'Well, we guess that you thought of the first two lines, and Tarkil did all the rest for you,' they cried.

'Wrong! Not even warm; stone cold, in fact!' said Bilbo with a laugh. He got up and came towards Frodo.

'Well, that's over!' he said in a low voice. 'It went off better than I expected. I don't often get asked for a second hearing, for any reason. As a matter of fact quite a lot of it was Tarkil's.'

'I'm not going to try and guess,' said Frodo, smiling. 'I was half asleep when you began – it seemed to follow on from something I was dreaming about, and I didn't realize it was really you who were speaking until near the end.'

The chapter ends now as it does in FR, except that the old form of the chant to Elbereth remains (VI.394), and the passage following it, concerning Aragorn and Arwen, is of course absent.

★

No poem of my father's had so long and complex a history as that which he named *Errantry*. It issued ultimately in two entirely distinct poems, one of which was the song that Bilbo chanted at Rivendell; and this is a convenient place to set out fairly fully the nature of this divergence, this extraordinary shape-changing.

My father described the origin and nature of *Erranty* in a letter written to Donald Swann on 14 October 1966. (*Errantry* had been published in *The Adventures of Tom Bombadil* in 1962, and it was set to music by Donald Swann in *The Road Goes Ever On*, 1967: see his remarks on the poem in his foreword to that book.) In this letter my father said:

> With regard to *Errantry*: I am most interested in your suggestion. I wonder if it is not too long for such an arrangement? I looked to see if it could be abbreviated; but its metrical scheme, with its trisyllabic near-rhymes, makes this very difficult. It is of course a piece of verbal acrobatics and metrical high-jinks; and was intended for recitation with great variations of speed. It needs a reciter or chanter capable of producing the words with great clarity, but in places with great rapidity. The 'stanzas' as printed indicate the speed-groups. In general these were meant to begin at speed and slow down. Except the last group, which was to begin slowly, and pick up at *errand too!* and end at high speed to match the beginning.[6] Also of course the reciter was supposed at once to begin repeating (at even higher speed) the beginning, unless somebody cried 'Once is enough'.[7]
>
> The piece has had a curious history. It was begun very many years ago, in an attempt to go on with the model that came unbidden into my mind: the first six lines, in which, I guess, *D'ye ken the rhyme to porringer* had a part.[8] Later I read it to an undergraduate club that used to hear its members read unpublished poems or short tales, and voted some of them into the minute book. They invented the name *Inklings*, and not I or Lewis, though we were among the few 'senior' members. (The club lasted the usual year or two of undergraduate societies; and the name became transferred to the circle of C. S. Lewis when only he and I were left of it.)[9] It was at this point that *Errantry* began its travels, starting with a typed copy, and continuing by oral memory and transmission, as I later discovered.

The earliest version that my father retained is a rough pencilled manuscript without title: there were certainly preliminary workings behind it, now lost, since this text was set down without hesitations or corrections, but it seems very probable that it was in fact the first complete text of the poem, possibly that from which he read it to the original 'Inklings' in the early 1930s. The page has many alterations and suggestions leading to the second version, but I give it here as it was first set down.

> There was a merry passenger,
> a messenger, an errander;
> he took a tiny porringer
> and oranges for provender;

he took a little grasshopper
and harnessed her to carry him;
he chased a little butterfly
that fluttered by, to marry him.
He made him wings of taffeta
to laugh at her and catch her with;
he made her shoes of beetle-skin
with needles in to latch them with.
They fell to bitter quarrelling,
and sorrowing he fled away;
and long he studied sorcery
in Ossory a many day.
He made a shield and morion
of coral and of ivory;
he made a spear of emerald
and glimmered all in bravery;
a sword he made of malachite
and stalactite, and brandished it,
he went and fought the dragon-fly
called wag-on-high and vanquished it.
He battled with the Dumbledores,
and bumbles all, and honeybees,
and won the golden honey-comb,
and running home on sunny seas,
in ship of leaves and gossamer
with blossom for a canopy,
he polished up and burnished up
and furbished up his panoply.
He tarried for a little while
in little isles, and plundered them;
and webs of all the attercops
he shattered, cut, and sundered them.
And coming home with honey-comb
and money none – remembered it,
his message and his errand too!
His derring-do had hindered it.[10]

Among my father's papers are five further texts, all titled *Errantry*, before the poem's publication in *The Oxford Magazine*, Vol. LII no. 5, 9 November 1933, which I give here. In fact, the form published in 1933 was virtually achieved already in the second version, apart only from the beginning, which went through several stages of development: these are given at the end of the *Oxford Magazine* version.

There was a merry passenger
a messenger, a mariner:
he built a gilded gondola

to wander in, and had in her
a load of yellow oranges
and porridge for his provender;
he perfumed her with marjoram
and cardamom and lavender.

He called the winds of argosies
with cargoes in to carry him
across the rivers seventeen
that lay between to tarry him.

He landed all in loneliness
where stonily the pebbles on
the running river Derrilyn
goes merrily for ever on.
He wandered over meadow-land
to shadow-land and dreariness,
and under hill and over hill,
a rover still to weariness.

He sat and sang a melody
his errantry a-tarrying;
he begged a pretty butterfly
that fluttered by to marry him.
She laughed at him, deluded him,
eluded him unpitying;
so long he studied wizardry
and sigaldry and smithying.

He wove a tissue airy-thin
to snare her in; to follow in
he made a beetle-leather wing
and feather wing and swallow-wing.
He caught her in bewilderment
in filament of spider-thread;
he built a little bower-house,
a flower house, to hide her head;
he made her shoes of diamond
on fire and a-shimmering;
a boat he built her marvellous,
a carvel all a-glimmering;
he threaded gems in necklaces –
and recklessly she squandered them,
as fluttering, and wavering,
and quavering, they wandered on.

They fell to bitter quarrelling;
and sorrowing he sped away,

on windy weather wearily
and drearily he fled away.

He passed the archipelagoes
where yellow grows the marigold,
where countless silver fountains are,
and mountains are of fairy-gold.
He took to war and foraying
a-harrying beyond the sea,
a-roaming over Belmarie
and Thellamie and Fantasie.

He made a shield and morion
of coral and of ivory,
a sword he made of emerald,
and terrible his rivalry
with all the knights of Aerie
and Faërie and Thellamie.
Of crystal was his habergeon,
his scabbard of chalcedony,
his javelins were of malachite
and stalactite – he brandished them,
and went and fought the dragon-flies
of Paradise, and vanquished them.

He battled with the Dumbledores,
the Bumbles, and the Honeybees,
and won the Golden Honeycomb;
and running home on sunny seas
in ship of leaves and gossamer
with blossom for a canopy,
he polished up, and furbished up,
and burnished up his panoply.

He tarried for a little while
in little isles, and plundered them;
and webs of all the Attercops
he shattered them and sundered them –
Then, coming home with honeycomb
and money none, to memory
his message came and errand too!
In derring-do and glamoury
he had forgot them, journeying,
and tourneying, a wanderer.

So now he must depart again
and start again his gondola,
for ever still a messenger,

> a passenger, a tarrier,
> a-roving as a feather does,
> a weather-driven mariner.[11]

In the second version the poem began thus:

> There was a merry messenger,
> a passenger, an errander;
> he gathered yellow oranges
> in porringer for provender;
> he built a gilded gondola
> a-wandering to carry him
> across the rivers seventeen
> that lay between to tarry him.
>
> He landed there in loneliness
> in stoniness on shingle steep,
> and ventured into meadow-land
> and shadow-land, and dingle deep.
>
> He sat and sang a melody, &c.

The poem otherwise, as I have said, scarcely differs from the *Oxford Magazine* version; but the last four lines were:

> for ever still a-tarrying,
> a mariner, a messenger,
> a-roving as a feather does,
> a weather-driven passenger.[12]

The third version reached the opening of the published form, except that it began 'There was a merry *messenger*, a *passenger*, a mariner', and retained the lines

> He landed all in loneliness
> in stoniness on shingle steep,
> and wandered off to meadowland,
> to shadowland, to dingle deep.

The fourth version reached the published form except in this third verse, which now read:

> He landed all in loneliness
> where stonily on shingle go
> the running rivers Lerion
> and Derion in dingle low.
> He wandered over meadow-land
> to shadow-land and dreariness, &c.

Rayner Unwin mentioned in a letter to my father of 20 June 1952 that he had received an enquiry from someone unnamed about a poem called *Errantry*, 'which made such a deep impression on him that he is most anxious to trace it again.' To this my father replied (22 June 1952, *Letters* no. 133):

As for 'Errantry': it is a most odd coincidence that you should ask about that. For only a few weeks ago I had a letter from a lady unknown to me making a similar enquiry. She said that a friend had recently written out for her from memory some verses that had so taken her fancy that she was determined to discover their origin. He had picked them up from his son-in-law who had learned them in Washington D.C. (!); but nothing was known about their source save a vague idea that they were connected with English universities. Being a determined person she apparently applied to various Vice-Chancellors, and Bowra[13] directed her to my door. I must say that I was interested in becoming 'folk-lore'. Also it was intriguing to get an oral version – which bore out my views on oral tradition (at any rate in early stages): sc. that the 'hard words' are well preserved,[14] and the more common words altered, but the metre is often disturbed.

In this letter he referred to two versions of *Errantry*, an 'A.V.' ('Authorised Version'), this being the *Oxford Magazine* text, and an 'R.V.' ('Revised Version'). The 'R.V.', in which substantial alterations were made to the 'A.V.', is the text published in *The Adventures of Tom Bombadil* ten years later. – He also said in this letter that the poem was

in a metre I invented (depending on trisyllabic assonances or near-assonances, which is so difficult that except in this one example I have never been able to use it again – it just blew out in a single impulse).

On this Humphrey Carpenter remarked (*Letters* p. 443):

It may appear at a first glance that Tolkien did write another poem in this metre, 'Eärendil was a mariner', which appears in Book II Chapter 1 of *The Lord of the Rings*. But this poem is arguably a development of 'Errantry' rather than a separate composition.

That this is true will be seen from the earlier forms of Bilbo's song at Rivendell.

*

There are no less than fifteen manuscript and typescript texts of the 'Rivendell version', and these may be divided into two groups: an earlier, in which the poem begins with the line *There was a merry messenger* (or in one case a variant of it), and a later, in which the poem begins *Earendel was a mariner* (the name being spelt thus in all texts). The textual history of the first group is very complex in detail, and difficult to unravel with certainty owing to the fact that my father hesitated back and forth between competing readings in successive texts.

In the earliest text of all the poem was still in the process of emergence. The opening lines are here particularly interesting, for they remain so close to the first verse of *Errantry* as to be scarcely more than a variant:

> There was a merry messenger
> a passenger a mariner:
> he built a boat and gilded her,
> and silver oars he fashioned her;
> he perfumed her with marjoram
> and cardamon[15] and lavender,
> and laded her with oranges
> and porridge for his provender.

Eärendel is hardly present here! Yet this initial text at once moves away from *Errantry*, and the new poem in its first 'phase' was already quite largely achieved in this manuscript. It was followed, no doubt immediately, by the version that I print below. It is indeed extremely difficult and even unreal to delimit 'versions' in such cases, where my father was refining and enlarging the poem in a continuous process; but this second text was originally set down as if in a finished and final form, and in this form I give it here.[16]

> There was a gallant passenger
> a messenger, a mariner:
> he built a boat and gilded her
> and silver oars he fashioned her;
> her sails he wove of gossamer
> and blossom of the cherry-tree,
> and lightly as a feather
> in the weather went she merrily.   8
>
> He floated from a haven fair
> of maiden-hair and everfern;
> the waterfalls he proudly rode
> where loudly flowed the Merryburn;
> and dancing on the foam he went
> on roving bent for ever on,
> from Evermorning journeying,
> while murmuring the River on   16
> to valleys in the gloaming ran;
> and slowly then on pillow cool
> he laid his head, and fast asleep
> he passed the Weepingwillow Pool.

The windy reeds were whispering,
and mists were in the meadow-land,
and down the River hurried him
and carried him to Shadowland.   24

The Sea beside a stony shore
there lonely roared, and under Moon
a wind arose and wafted him
a castaway beyond the Moon.

He woke again forlorn afar
by shores that are without a name,
and by the Shrouded Island o'er
the Silent Water floating came.   32

He passed the archipelagoes
where yellow grows the marigold,
and landed on the Elven-strands
of silver sand and fallow gold,
beneath the Hill of Ilmarin
where glimmer in a valley sheer
the lights of Elven Tirion,
the city on the Shadowmere.   40

He tarried there his errantry,
and melodies they taught to him,
and lays of old, and marvels told,
and harps of gold they brought to him.
Of glamoury he tidings heard,
and binding words of sigaldry;
of wars they spoke with Enemies
that venom used and wizardry.   48

In panoply of Elvenkings,
in silver rings they armoured him;
his shield they writ with elven-runes,
that never wound did harm to him.
His bow was made of dragon-horn,
his arrows shorn of ebony,
of woven steel his habergeon,
his scabbard of chalcedony.   56
His sword was hewn of adamant,
and valiant the might of it;
his helm a shining emerald,
and terrible the light of it.

His boat anew for him they built
of timber felled in Elvenhome;
upon the mast a star was set,

its spars were wet with silver foam;   64
and wings of swans they made for it,
and laid on it a mighty doom
to sail the seas of wind and come
where glimmering runs the gliding moon.[17]

From Evereven's lofty hills,
where softly spill the fountains tall,
he passed away, a wandering light
beyond the mighty Mountain-wall;   72
and unto Evernight he came,
and like a flaming star he fell:
his javelins of diamond
as fire into the darkness fell.
Ungoliant abiding there
in Spider-lair her thread entwined;
for endless years a gloom she spun
the Sun and Moon in web to wind.[18]   80

His sword was like a flashing light
as flashing bright he smote with it;
he shore away her poisoned neb, '
her noisome webs he broke with it.
Then shining as a risen star
from prison bars he sped away,
and borne upon a blowing wind
on flowing wings he fled away.   88

To Evernoon at last he came,
and passed the flame-encircled hill,
where wells of gold for Melineth
her never-resting workers build.
His eyes with fire ablaze were set,
his face was lit with levin-light;
and turning to his home afar,
a roaming star at even-light   96
on high above the mists he came,
a distant flame, a marineer
on winds unearthly swiftly borne,
uplifted o'er the Shadowmere.
He passed o'er Carakilian,
where Tirion the Hallowed stands;
the sea far under loudly roared
on cloudy shores in Shadowland.   104

And over Evermorn he passed,
and saw at last the haven fair,
far under by the Merry-burn

in everfern and maidenhair.
But on him mighty doom was laid,
till moon should fade and all the stars,
to pass, and tarry never more
on hither shore where mortals are,   112
for ever still a passenger,
a messenger, to never rest,
to bear his burning lamp afar,
the Flammifer of Westernesse.

The chief changes introduced on this manuscript were in lines 14–17, altered to read:

on roving bent from hitherland,
from Evermorning journeying,
while murmuring the River ran
to valleys in the Gloaming fields

and in lines 93–6, which were rewritten and extended thus:

The seven-branchéd Levin-tree
on Heavenfield he shining saw
upflowering from its writhen root;
a living fruit of fire it bore.
The lightning in his face was lit,
ablaze were set his tresses wan,
his eyes with levin-beams were bright,
and gleaming white his vessel shone.

From World's End then he turned away
and yearned again to seek afar
his land beneath the morning light
and burning like a beacon star
(on high above the mists he came, &c.)

The *seven-branchéd Levin-tree* was first *everbranching*, and it bore *a living fruit of light*.

The third version was that in the text of 'Many Meetings' described at the beginning of this chapter. The pages in that manuscript (at Marquette) bearing the poem have been lost, but Taum Santoski has provided me with a transcription of the pages that he made before the loss occurred. This text was remarkably close to the second version (as emended) printed above. The opening now returns to *There was a merry messenger*;[19] *from Evermorning* in line 15 becomes *through Evermorning*; *the Weepingwillow Pool* in line 20 becomes *Pools* (a return to the earliest workings); and lines 67–8 become:

to sail the windy skies and come
behind the Sun and light of Moon.

This, then, was the form at the time we have reached. It will be seen that in this poem the Merry Messenger, the Passenger, the Mariner, 'changes shape' and emerges as the figure of Eärendel (though he is not named). At the beginning he *dances on the foam* in his boat with *sails of gossamer and blossom of the cherry-tree*, and he still *passed the archipelagoes where yellow grows the marigold*, but he is drawn into the gravity of the myth and *mighty doom* is laid on him; the dance dies out of the verse, and he ends as the *Flammifer of Westernesse*. There is no question now of returning to the beginning, even though the fate of Eärendel remains that of the Merry Messenger: *for ever still a passenger, a messenger, to never rest...*

Many years later my father ingeniously related the two poems thus, in the Preface to *The Adventures of Tom Bombadil* – when the Eärendel version was of course that given in FR:

[Errantry] was evidently made by Bilbo. This is indicated by its obvious relationship to the long poem recited by Bilbo, as his own composition, in the house of Elrond. In origin a 'nonsense rhyme', it is in the Rivendell version found transformed and applied, somewhat incongruously, to the High-elvish and Númenorean legends of Eärendil. Probably because Bilbo invented its metrical devices and was proud of them. They do not appear in other pieces in the Red Book. The older form, here given, must belong to the early days after Bilbo's return from his journey. Though the influence of Elvish traditions is seen, they are not seriously treated, and the names used (*Derrilyn, Thellamie, Belmarie, Aerie*) are mere inventions in the Elvish style, and are not in fact Elvish at all.

Yet the places of Eärendel's journey in this first phase of the Rivendell version are not by any means entirely identifiable in terms of *The Silmarillion*. Was his journey to the Sea a journey down Sirion? Are *the Weepingwillow Pools* Nan-tathren, the Land of Willows? Or are they still 'mere inventions in the *Silmarillion* style'? And what of *the seven-branchéd Levin-tree on Heavenfield*, and *the wells of gold for Melineth* that *her never-resting workers build*? These certainly do not suggest 'mere invention' like *Thellamie* or *Derrilyn*.

Some names are in any case clear in their reference: as *Tirion* (in the *Quenta Silmarillion* still named *Tûn* or *Túna*, upon the hill of Kôr), *Carakilian* (in the *Quenta Silmarillion* in the form *Kalakilya*, the Pass of Light). *The Hill of Ilmarin* (a name not met before) is Taniquetil, and *the mighty Mountain-wall* is the Pelóri, the Mountains of Valinor. *The Shadowmere* perhaps looks back to the 'shadowy arm of water', the 'slender water fringed with white', which is described in the old tale of *The Coming of the Elves* (I.122). *The Shrouded Island* is perhaps the Lonely Isle: it was subsequently changed to *the Shrouded Islands*, but then became *the Lonely Island* before the line was lost. That Eärendel slew Ungoliant 'in the South' is recorded in the *Sketch of the Mythology* (IV.38), and in the *Quenta Noldorinwa* (IV.149, 152); cf. also the very early notes on Eärendel's voyages, II.254, 261.[20]

But the legend of Eärendel as found in the existing sources is not present here.[21] Indeed, it seems as if he arose unbidden and unlooked for as my father wrote this new version of the poem: for how could Eärendel be called *a merry messenger?* Years later, in the Preface to *The Adventures of Tom Bombadil* just cited, my father described the transformation as 'somewhat incongruous' – and he was then referring of course to the form of the poem in FR, where the transformation had gone far deeper than in the present version. Yet there was a 'congruity' that made this original transformation possible, and even natural. Behind both figures lay the sustaining idea of the wanderer, a restless spirit who seeks back to the places of his origin, but cannot escape the necessity of passing on. At this stage therefore we should not, I believe, try to determine where was Evernoon, or to give any other name to

> the haven fair,
> far under by the Merry-burn
> in everfern and maidenhair.

They belong to the same geography as *the archipelagoes where yellow grows the marigold.*

Following the third version, lost but happily not unknown, there are six further texts in the 'Merry Messenger' phase. Five of these are typescripts that can be readily placed in order. The sixth is a beautiful small manuscript, written on four slips of paper the last of which is the back of a letter addressed to my father and dated 13 December 1944. Precisely where the manuscript comes in this series is not perfectly clear, but it seems most likely to have preceded the first typescript.[22] Thus there was an interval of several years between the first three and the next six texts. Progressive emendation of these gave a final version in this 'phase':

> There was a merry messenger,
> a passenger, a mariner:
> he built a boat and gilded her,
> and silver oars he fashioned her;
> her sails he wove of gossamer
> and blossom of the cherry-tree
> and lightly as a feather in
> the weather went she merrily.   8
>
> He floated from a haven fair
> of maidenhair and ladyfern;
> the waterfalls he proudly rode
> where loudly flowed the Merryburn;
> and dancing on the foam he went

on roving bent from Hitherland
through Evermorning journeying,
while murmuring the river ran   16
to valleys in the Gloaming-fields;
then slowly he on pillow cool
let fall his head, and fast asleep
he passed the Weeping-willow Pools.

The windy reeds were whispering,
and mists were in the meadowland,
and down the river hurried him,
and carried him to Shadowland.   24
He heard there moan in stony caves
the lonely waves; there roaring blows
the mighty wind of Tarmenel.
By paths that seldom mortal goes
his boat it wafted pitiless
with bitter breath across the grey
and long-forsaken seas distressed;
from East to West he passed away.   32

Through Evernight then borne afar
by waters dark beyond the Day
he saw the Lonely Island rise
where twilight lies upon the Bay
of Valinor, of Elvenhome,
and ever-foaming billows roll;
he landed on the elven-strands
of silver sand and yellow gold   40
beneath the Hill of Ilmarin,
where glimmer in a valley sheer
the lights of towering Tirion,
the city on the Shadowmere.

He tarried there from errantry,
and melodies they taught to him,
and lays of old and marvels told,
and harps of gold they brought to him.   48
Of glamoury he tidings heard,
and binding words of wizardry;
they spoke of wars with Enemies
that venom used and sigaldry.

In panoply of Elven-kings,
in silver rings they armoured him;
his shield they writ with elven-runes
that never wound did harm to him.   56
His bow was made of dragon-horn,

his arrows shorn of ebony,
of mithril was his habergeon,
his scabbard of chalcedony.
His sword of steel was valiant;
of adamant his helm was wrought,
an argent wing of swan his crest;
upon his breast an emerald.   64

His boat anew they built for him
of timber felled in Elvenhome;
upon the mast a star was set,
her spars were wet with driven foam;
and eagle-wings they made for her,
and laid on her a mighty doom,
to sail the windy skies and come
behind the Sun and light of Moon.   72

From Evereven's lofty hills,
where softly silver fountains fall,
he passed away a wandering light
beyond the mighty Mountain Wall.
From World's End then he turned away,
and yearned again to seek afar
his land beneath the morning-light;
and burning like a beacon-star   80
on high above the mists he came,
a distant flame, a marineer,
on winds unearthly swiftly borne,
uplifted o'er the Shadowmere.

He passed o'er Calacirian,
where Tirion the hallowed stands;
the Sea below him loudly roared
on cloudy shores in Shadowland;   88
and over Evermorn he passed
and saw at last the haven fair
far under by the Merryburn
in ladyfern and maidenhair.

But on him mighty doom was laid,
till Moon should fade, an orbéd star
to pass and tarry never more
on Hither Shores where mortals are;   96
for ever still a passenger,
a messenger, to never rest,
to bear the burning lamp afar,
the Flammifer of Westernesse.

The major change in the poem, rendering it substantially shorter than before, had come about in two stages. By emendation to the second of these typescripts the original lines 25–8 (p. 92) became:

> The Sea beside a stony shore
> there lonely roared; and wrathful rose
> a wind on high in Tarmenel,
> by paths that seldom mortal goes
> on flying wings it passed away,
> and wafted him beyond the grey
> and long-forsaken seas distressed
> from East or West that sombre lay.

In this text the remainder of the poem was unaffected by any important changes, and remained close to the original form (with of course the alterations given on p. 94). In the last two of these typescripts, however, a new form of lines 25 ff. entered, as given above: *He heard there moan in stony caves*, &c.[23] Now *Evernight* is named at this point, and at the same time the entire section of the poem in the existing text from line 73 *and unto Evernight he came* to *From World's End then he turned away* (pp. 93–4) was eliminated, with the disappearance of Ungoliant and the mysterious scenes of Evernoon, the 'Tree of Lightning' with its seven branches and the *wells of gold for Melineth* in *the flame-encircled hill.*

*

While I certainly do not know this as a fact, I think that there is a strong presumption that there was a further long interval between the 'Merry Messenger' versions and the second group beginning *Eärendel was a mariner.*

The first text of this group, which I will for convenience call A, I give in full. It will be seen that while it advances far towards the poem in FR, much is retained from the preceding version, and notably the arming of Eärendel (*In panoply of Elven-kings...*, p. 97 lines 53 ff.) stands in its former place, during his sojourn in Tirion, and not as in FR at the beginning of his great voyage.

> Eärendel was a mariner
> that tarried in Arvernien;
> he built a boat of timber felled
> in Nimbrethil to journey in;
> her sails he wove of silver fair
> of silver were her lanterns made,
> her prow he fashioned like a swan,
> and light upon her banners laid.   8
>
> Beneath the moon and under star
> he wandered far from northern strands,

bewildered on enchanted ways
beyond the days of mortal lands.
From gnashing of the Narrow Ice
where shadow lies on frozen hills,
from nether heat and burning waste
he turned in haste, and roving still   16
on starless waters far astray
at last he came to night of Naught,
and passed, and never sight he saw
of shining shore nor light he sought.
The winds of wrath came driving him,
and blindly in the foam he fled
from West to East, and errandless,
unheralded he homeward sped.   24

As bird then Elwing came to him,
and flame was in her carcanet,
more bright than light of diamond
was fire that on her heart was set.
The Silmaril she bound on him
and crowned him with a living light,
and dauntless then with burning brow
he turned his prow, and in the night   32
from otherworld beyond the Sea
there strong and free a storm arose,
a wind of power in Tarmenel;
by paths that seldom mortal goes
his boat it bore with mighty breath
as driving death across the grey
and long-forsaken seas distressed;
from East to West he passed away.   40

Through Evernight then borne afar
by waters dark beyond the Day,
he saw the Lonely Island rise,
where twilight lies upon the Bay
of Valinor, of Elvenhome,
and ever-foaming billows roll.
He landed on forbidden strands
of silver sand and yellow gold;   48
beneath the Hill of Ilmarin
a-glimmer in a valley sheer
the lamps of towering Tirion
were mirrored on the Shadowmere.

He tarried there from errantry
and melodies they taught to him,

and lays of old and marvels told,
and harps of gold they brought to him.   56
In panoply of Elven-kings,
in serried rings they armoured him;
his shield they writ with elven-runes
that never wound did harm to him,
his bow was made of dragon-horn,
his arrows shorn of ebony,
of silver was his habergeon,
his scabbard of chalcedony;   64
his sword of steel was valiant,
of adamant his helmet tall,
an argent flame upon his crest,
upon his breast an emerald.

His boat anew they built for him
of mithril and of elven-glass;
the Silmaril was hanging bright
as lantern light on slender mast;   72
and eagle-wings they made for her,
and laid on her a mighty doom,
to sail the shoreless skies and come
behind the Sun and light of Moon.

From Evereven's lofty hills,
where softly silver fountains fall,
he rose on high, a wandering light
beyond the mighty Mountain Wall.   80
From World's End then he turned away,
and yearned again to seek afar
his land beneath the morning-light,
and burning like a beacon-star
on high above the mists he came,
a distant flame, a marineer,
on winds unearthly swiftly borne,
uplifted o'er the Shadowmere.   88

He passed o'er Calacirian
where Tirion the hallowed stands;
the sea below him loudly roared
on cloudy shores in Shadowland;
and over Middle-earth he passed,
and heard at last the weeping sore
of women and of Elven-maids
in Elder Days, in years of yore.   96

But on him mighty doom was laid,
till Moon should fade, an orbéd star,

to pass, and tarry never more
on Hither Shores where mortals are;
for ever still on errand, as
a herald that should never rest,
to bear his shining lamp afar,
the Flammifer of Westernesse.   104

The next text (B) is a typescript of A, but introduces some minor changes that were retained in the FR version (*his boat it bore with biting breath / as might of death* 37–8, *the lamplit towers of Tirion* 51), and line 25 is here *Bird-Elwing thither came to him.* My father then used this typescript B as the vehicle for massive rewriting, including the movement of the 'arming of Eärendel' to its later place as the second stanza. A new typescript (C)[24] was made incorporating all this, and the form of the poem in FR was now virtually achieved; a very few further minor changes were made, and entered on this text.[25] Careful examination of these texts shows the development from A to the published form with perfect clarity.

But the history of this, perhaps the most protean, in its scale, of all my father's works, does not end here. It ends, in fact, in the most extraordinary way.

This text C was not the last, although the published form of the poem was achieved in it. Another typescript (D) was made, doubtless at the same time as C, and given the title *The Short Lay of Eärendel.* In this, a new element entered at the beginning of the fourth stanza (*There flying Elwing came to him*): the attack of the four surviving sons of Fëanor on the Havens of Sirion, Elwing's casting herself into the sea, bearing the Silmaril, and her transformation into a seabird, in which guise she flew to meet Eärendel returning (IV.152–3).

In wrath the Fëanorians
that swore the unforgotten oath
brought war into Arvernien
with burning and with broken troth;
and Elwing from her fastness dim
then cast her in the roaring seas,
but like a bird was swiftly borne,
uplifted o'er the roaring wave.
Through hopeless night she came to him
and flame was in the darkness lit,
more bright than light of diamond
the fire upon her carcanet.
The Silmaril she bound on him (&c.)

There then followed a fine manuscript (E), with elaborate initials to the stanzas, and this was entitled *The Short Lay of Eärendel:*

Eärendillinwë. In this text a rewriting of lines 5–8, which had been entered in the margin of D, appears:

> Her woven sails were white as snow,
> as flying foam her banner flowed;
> her prow was fashioned like a swan
> that white upon the Falas goes.

But my father abandoned E at the foot of the first page, the end of the third stanza, and the reason why he abandoned it was that he had already begun to rewrite in the margin both the lines just given and also the second stanza (*In panoply of ancient kings*). So he began once again, with a very similar and equally beautiful manuscript (F), bearing the same title; and this was completed. The revisions made to D and to E (so far as that went) were taken up; and this manuscript remained intact, without the smallest further change.

It was in fact the last, the ultimate development of the poem. The history I have attempted to convey is schematically thus:

A – B $\begin{cases} - \text{C (the form in FR achieved)} \\ - \text{D – E – F (the ultimate form of the poem)} \end{cases}$

I have studied all these texts at length and at different times, and it had always seemed strange to me that the chain of development led at last to a superb manuscript (F) without any disfigurement through later changes, but which was *not* the form found in FR. The solution was at last provided by the text C at Marquette, which showed that there were *two lines of development* from B.

What actually happened one can only surmise. I believe the most likely explanation to be that the texts D, E, F were mislaid, and that at the crucial time the version represented by C went to the publishers, as it should not have done. It looks also as if these lost texts did not turn up again until many years had passed, by which time my father no longer remembered the history. In what are obviously very late notes he went so far as to analyse their readings in relation to the published form, and was evidently as puzzled as I was: his analysis at that time contains demonstrably incorrect conclusions – because he assumed, as I did, that all these texts must have *preceded* the 'final form' in FR.

I give finally the *Eärendillinwë* in the form in which it should have been published.[26]

Stanza 1   Eärendil was a mariner
              that tarried in Arvernien:
              he built a boat of timber felled
              in Nimbrethil to journey in.
              Her sails he wove of silver fair,
              with silver were her banners sewn;
              her prow he fashioned like the swans
              that white upon the Falas roam.

Stanza 2   His coat that came from ancient kings
of chainéd rings was forged of old;
his shining shield all wounds defied,
with runes entwined of dwarven gold.
His bow was made of dragon-horn,
his arrows shorn of ebony,
of triple steel his habergeon,
his scabbard of chalcedony;
his sword was like a flame in sheath,
with gems was wreathed his helmet tall,
an eagle-plume upon his crest,
upon his breast an emerald.

Stanza 3   As in FR, but with *winds of fear* for *winds of wrath* in line
13 of the stanza.

Stanza 4   In might the Fëanorians
that swore the unforgotten oath
brought war into Arvernien
with burning and with broken troth;
and Elwing from her fastness dim
then cast her in the waters wide,
but like a mew was swiftly borne,
uplifted o'er the roaring tide.
Through hopeless night she came to him,
and flame was in the darkness lit,
more bright than light of diamond
the fire upon her carcanet.
The Silmaril she bound on him,
and crowned him with the living light,
and dauntless then with burning brow
he turned his prow at middle-night.
Beyond the world, beyond the Sea,
then strong and free a storm arose,
a wind of power in Tarmenel;
by paths that seldom mortal goes
from Middle-earth on mighty breath
as flying wraith across the grey
and long-forsaken seas distressed
from East to West he passed away.

Stanza 5   As in FR.

Stanza 6   As in FR, but with a difference in the twelfth line:[27]

for ever king on mountain sheer;

Stanza 7   A ship then new they built for him
of mithril and of elvenglass

with crystal keel; no shaven oar
nor sail she bore, on silver mast
the Silmaril as lantern light
and banner bright with living flame
of fire unstained by Elbereth
herself was set, who thither came (&c. as in FR)

Stanza 8   As in FR.

Stanza 9   As in FR except at the end:

till end of Days on errand high,
a herald bright that never rests,
to bear his burning lamp afar,
the Flammifer of Westernesse.

Only one line survived now from *Errantry* (as published in 1933): *his scabbard of chalcedony.*

NOTES

1   This suggests that the story of Gandalf's captivity found in the 'New Plot' of August 1940 was present (p. 71): 'Saramund betrays him ... he tells Gandalf false news of the Black Riders, and they pursue him to the top of a mountain...' The final story of what had happened to Gandalf (set to stand on the pinnacle of Orthanc) first appears in this period of the work (pp. 131 ff.).

2   Changed in pencil later to *Elfstone son of Elfhelm*; see p. 80 note 17. At one occurrence of Trotter in this passage, where Gandalf names him, this too was changed to *Elfstone*; at the other two *Trotter* was retained, since it is Frodo who is speaking.

3   In a preliminary draft for this passage Frodo says 'in wonder': 'Is he of that race?' Then follows:

'Didn't he tell you, and didn't you guess?' said Gandalf. 'He could have told you even more: he is Aragorn son of Kelegorn, descended through many fathers from Isildur the son of Elendil.'

'Then It belongs to him as much as to me or more!' said Frodo.

'It does not belong to either of you,' said Gandalf; 'but you, my good hobbit, are to keep it for a while. For so it is ordained.'

This was the second time that this dialogue had been used; it first occurred at Bree between Trotter and Frodo (p. 50), when Gandalf named Aragorn as a descendant of Elendil in his letter, but this had now been removed (p. 77). It was finally used in 'The Council of Elrond'.

4   See p. 43 and note 3. The words 'I stayed at *The Pony* in Bree for
    a bit' were crossed out before the rest of the passage was changed,
    perhaps at the time of writing.
5   On *Tarkil* see p. 8. *Westernesse*: Númenor.
6   In the version of *Errantry* published in 1962 the last stanza began
    not as in the 1933 *Oxford Magazine* version but at *He tarried for
    a little while* (p. 88).
7   One of the early texts has the head-note: 'Elaboration of the
    well-known pastime of the never-ending Tale'; and at the end,
    after the last line *a weather-driven mariner*, returns to *He called
    the winds of argosies* in the second verse (p. 87), with the note: *da
    capo, ad lib, et ad naus.*
8   I cannot explain this reference.
9   See Humphrey Carpenter, *The Inklings*, pp. 56–7; also *Letters*
    no. 133 (to Rayner Unwin, 22 June 1952) and no. 298 (to W. L.
    White, 11 September 1967).
10 *morion*: helmet. *bravery*: splendour, finery. *dumbledore*:
    bumble-bee. *panoply*: suit of armour. *attercop*: spider (Old
    English *attor* 'poison'; cf. *cobweb*, 'cop-web'). Bilbo called the
    spiders in Mirkwood *Attercop*.

On the back of the page, with every appearance of having been
written at the same time, is a section of a dramatic dialogue in
rhyming verse that preceded by more than twenty years the
publication of *The Homecoming of Beorhtnoth Beorhthelm's
Son* in *Essays and Studies*, 1953. The Englishmen who took the
body of Beorhtnoth from the battlefield at Maldon are here called
Pudda and Tibba. – *Panta* (Old English) is the river Blackwater.

Pudda   Come, hurry. There may be more. Let's get away
        Or have the pirate pack on us.
Tibba   Nay, nay.
        These are no Northmen. What should such come for?
        They are all in Ipswich drinking to Thor.
        These have got what they deserved, not what they
        sought.
Pudda   God help us, when Englishmen can be brought
        By any need to prowl like carrion-bird
        And plunder their own.
Tibba   There goes a third
        In the shadows yonder. He will not wait,
        That sort fight no odds, early or late,
        But sneak in when all's over. Up again!
        Steady once more.
Pudda   Say, Tibba, where's the wain?
        I wish we were at it! By the bridge you say –
        Well, we're nearer the bank. 'Tis more this way,
        If we're not to walk in Panta, and the tide's in.

Tibba   Right! here we are.

Pudda   How did they win
Over the bridge, think you? There's little sign
Here of bitter fight. And yet here the brine
Should have been choked with 'em, but on the planks
There's only one lying.

Tibba   Well, God have thanks.
We're over! Gently! Up now, up! That's right.
Get up beside. There's a cloth; none too white,
But cover him over, and think of a prayer. I'll drive.

Pudda   Heaven grant us good journey, and that we arrive!
Where do we take him? How these wheels creak!

Tibba   To Ely! Where else?

Pudda   A long road!

Tibba   For the weak.
A short road for the dead – and you can sleep.

This text is extremely rough, one would say in the first stage of composition, were there not another text still rougher, but in very much the same words (though with no ascription of the speeches to speakers), in the Bodleian Library, where it is preserved (I believe) with my father's pictures. This begins at *In the shadows yonder* and continues a few lines further. On it my father wrote: 'early version in rhyme of Beorhtnoth'.

11   *sigaldry*: sorcery (see note 14). *glamoury*: magic.

12   Preliminary lines of a new ending were written on the manuscript of the first version:

> So now he must depart again
> and start again his gondola,
> a silly merry passenger,
> a messenger, an errander,
> a jolly, merry featherbrain,
> a weathervane, a mariner.

Other differences in the second version from that published in 1933 were:

> he wrought her raiment marvellous
> and garments all a-glimmering

in the fifth verse; and 'He made a *sword* and morion' in the eighth (with *spear* for *sword* in the third line).

13   Maurice Bowra, at that time Vice-Chancellor of Oxford University.

14   In the letter to Donald Swann cited on p. 85 my father gave an example of this (Swann had himself known the poem by 'independent tradition' for many years before its publication in *The Adventures of Tom Bombadil*): 'A curious feature was the preservation of the word *sigaldry*, which I got from a 13th century text (and is last recorded in the Chester Play of the

Crucifixion).' The word goes back to the second version of *Errantry*; it was used also in the *Lay of Leithian* line 2072, written in 1928 (*The Lays of Beleriand*, p. 228).

15 *cardamon* is so spelt, but *cardamom* in preliminary rough workings, as in the *Oxford Magazine* version of *Errantry*.

16 I ignore all variants (though a few, as *merry* written above *gallant* in line 1, *ladyfern* above *everfern* in line 10) may belong to the time of writing. A few inconsistencies of hyphenation are preserved. In the latter part of the poem the stanza-divisions are not perfectly clear. Line-numbers at intervals of 8 are marked on the original.

17 This verse is absent from the first text, but a space was left for it, with the note: 'They enchant his boat and give it wings'.

18 A four-line stanza follows here:

> She caught him in her stranglehold
> entangled all in ebon thread,
> and seven times with sting she smote
> his ringéd coat with venom dread.

But this was struck out, apparently at once, since the line-numbering does not take account of it. – *ebon*: old form for *ebony*; here meaning 'black, dark'.

19 In the second version (that printed here) *merry* was written as a variant to *gallant*; in the third *gallant* is a variant to *merry*.

20 The encounter of the Messenger with the Attercops in *Errantry* was a point of contact with the Eärendel legend.

21 The texts are found in II.252–77; IV.37–8, 41, 148–54; V.324–9.

22 The manuscript was perhaps a development from the third version parallel to the first typescript, for it takes up certain variants from the former (as *everfern* in line 10, *Gloaming-bree* (bree 'hill') in line 17), where the first typescript takes up others (*ladyfern*, *Gloaming-fields*).

23 An intermediate version of these lines was:

> He heard there moan in stony caves
> the lonely waves of Orfalas;
> the winds he heard of Tarmenel:
> by paths that seldom mortals pass
> they wafted him on flying wings
> a dying thing across the grey
> and long-forsaken seas distressed;
> from East to West he passed away.

24 This is the typescript of 'Many Meetings' that followed the version described at the beginning of this chapter.

25 These were made on B also, and so appear in the other line of development as well.

26 It could be argued of course that my father actually *rejected* all

the subsequent development after the text C, deciding that that was the version desirable at all points; but this would seem to me to be wholly improbable and far-fetched.

27 This case is slightly different, in that it is the only point where text C does not reach the form in FR (*in Ilmarin on mountain sheer*), but has the line found also in D (followed by E and F), *for ever king on mountain sheer*. This must have been a final emendation in the 'first line' of development, and might of course have been made to the 'second line' as well if that had been available.

VI

THE COUNCIL OF ELROND (1)

The Second Version

A new version of this part of the narrative[1] is a characteristic 'fair copy': too close to the preceding text (VI.399 ff.) to justify the space needed to set it out, but constantly differing in the expression chosen. The chapter is numbered XIV (see p. 81), but has no title.

The story was still that Bilbo and Gandalf came to Frodo's room in the morning (VI.395); and those present at the Council were in no way changed (VI.400). Boromir still comes from 'the Land of Ond, far in the South'.[2] The first important change comes after Gandalf's speech, in which he 'made clear to those who did not already know it the tale of the Ring, and the reasons why the Dark Lord so greatly desired it.' Here, in the original version, Bilbo's story followed; but in this text the following passage enters:

When he told of Elendil and Gilgalad and of their march into the East, Elrond sighed. 'I remember well their array,' he said. 'It reminded me of the Great Wars and victories of Beleriand, so many fair captains and princes were there, and yet not so many or so fair as when Thangorodrim was broken [> taken].'

'You remember?' said Frodo, breaking silence in his astonishment, and gazing in wonder at Elrond. 'But I thought the fall of Gilgalad was many ages ago.'

'So it was,' said Elrond, looking gravely at Frodo; 'but my memory reaches back many ages. I was the minstrel and counsellor of Gilgalad. My father was Eärendel, who was born in Gondolin, seven years before it fell; and my mother was Elwing, daughter of [Dior, son of] Luthien, daughter of Thingol, King of Doriath; and I have seen many ages in the West of the World. I knew Beleriand before it was broken in the great wars.'

This is the origin of the passage in FR p. 256; but it goes back to and follows quite closely part of an earlier and isolated writing, given in VI.215–16,[3] in which the story of Gil-galad and Elendil was told at much greater length by Elrond to Bingo, apparently in a personal conversation between them; and that text was in turn closely related to the conclusion of the second version of *The Fall of Númenor* (V.28–9).

The new text continues:

They passed then from the winning and losing of the Ring to Bilbo's story; and once more he told how he had found it in the cave of the Misty Mountains. Then Aragorn took up the tale, and spoke of the hunt for Gollum, in which he had aided Gandalf, and of his [> their] perilous journey through southern Mirkwood, and into Fangorn Forest, and over the Dead Marshes to the very borders of the land of Mordor. In this way the history was brought slowly down to the spring morning ... (&c. as VI.401).

In the first version Trotter was still the hobbit Peregrin, with his wooden shoes (VI.401 and note 20).

Gandalf in his reply to Elrond's question about Bombadil 'Do you know him, Gandalf?' now says:

'Yes. And I went to him at once, naturally, as soon as I found that the hobbits had gone into the Old Forest. I dare say he would have kept them longer in his house, if he had known that I was so near. But I am not sure – not sure that he did not know, and not sure that he would have behaved differently in any case. He is a very strange creature, and follows his own counsels: and they are not easy to fathom.'

It seems that when my father wrote this he cannot have had in mind the outline dated August 26–27 1940, in which Gandalf arrived at Crickhollow and found it deserted (p. 72), since Gandalf could only have learnt from Hamilcar Bolger that the other hobbits had gone into the Old Forest. On the other hand my father was still uncertain (p. 72), in that outline and with that plot, whether Gandalf had visited Bombadil or not. At any rate, by what looks to be an almost immediate change, the wizard's remarks were rewritten:

'I know of him, though we seldom meet. I am a rolling stone, and he is a gatherer of moss. Both have a work to do, but they do not help one another often. It might have been wiser to have sought his aid, but I do not think I should have gained much. He is a strange creature...'

It must have been at this point that my father finally decided that there had been no visit to Bombadil, and the story reverted to its earlier form (see VI.413 note 23).

The sentence in Gandalf's reply to Erestor 'I doubt whether Tom

Bombadil alone, even on his own ground, could withstand that Power'[4] (VI.402) was soon rewritten thus (anticipating in part both Gandalf and Glorfindel in FR p. 279): 'Whether Bombadil alone, even on his own ground, could withstand that Power is beyond all guessing. I think not; and in the end, if all else is conquered, Tom will fall: last as he was first, and the Night will come. He would likely enough throw the Ring away, for such things have no part in his mind.'

Glóin's answer to Boromir's question concerning the Seven Rings remains almost exactly as it was (VI.403–4),[5] but Elrond's reply to the question about the Three Rings has certain changes: notably, he now states as a fact known to him what Gandalf (in 'Ancient History', VI.320) had asserted only as his belief: 'The Three Rings remain still. But wisely they have been taken over the Sea, and are not now in Middle-earth.' He continues:

From them the Elvenkings have derived much power, but they have not availed them in their strife with Sauron. For they can give no skill or knowledge that he did not himself already possess at their making. To each race the rings of the Lord bring such power as each desires and can best wield. The Elves desired not strength, or domination, or hoarded wealth, but subtlety of craft and lore and knowledge of the secrets of the world's being. These things they have gained, yet with sorrow. But all in their mind and heart which is derived from the rings will turn to their undoing, and become revealed to Sauron, if he regains the Ruling Ring, as was his purpose.'

The omission here of the words in the original text 'For they came from Sauron himself' does not, I think, show that the conception of the independence of the Three Rings of the Elves from Sauron had arisen, in view of the following words which were retained: 'For they can give no skill or knowledge that he did not himself already possess at their making'; moreover Boromir still in his question concerning them says that 'these too were made by Sauron in the elder days', and he is not contradicted. See further pp. 155–6.

The next text then follows the old very closely indeed (VI.404–7), until the point where Gandalf, in the afternoon following the Council, overtakes Frodo, Merry, and Faramond (still so called, with Peregrin written in later) walking in the woods; and here the new version diverges for a stretch, Gandalf's remarks about the composition of the Company being quite different – and not only because Trotter is now Aragorn: a doubt here appears about the inclusion of the two younger hobbits.

'... So be careful! You can't be too careful. As for the rest of the party, it is too soon to discuss that. But whether any of you go with Frodo or not, I shall make other arrangements for the supply of intelligence.'

'Ah! Now we know who really is important,' laughed Merry. 'Gandalf is never in doubt about that, and does not let anyone else forget it. So you are already making arrangements, are you?'

'Of course,' said Gandalf. 'There is a lot to do and think of. But in this matter both Elrond and Trotter will have much to say. And indeed Boromir, and Glóin, and Glorfindel, too. It concerns all the free folk left in the world.'

'Will Trotter come?' asked Frodo hopefully. 'Though he is only a Man, he would add to the brains of the expedition.'

'"Only a Man" is no way to speak of a *tarkil*, and least of all Aragorn son of Celegorn,' said Gandalf. 'He would add wit and valour to any expedition. But as I said, this is not the time and not the place to discuss it. Yet I will say just this in your ears.' His voice sank to a whisper. 'I think *I* shall have to come with you.'

So great was Frodo's delight at this announcement that Gandalf took off his hat and bowed. 'But I only said: I *think* I shall have to go, and perhaps for part of the way only. Don't count on anything,' he added. 'And now, if you want to talk about such things, you had better come back indoors.'

They walked back with him in silence; but as soon as they were over the threshold Frodo put the question that had been in his mind ever since the Council. 'How long shall I have here, Gandalf?' he asked.

'I don't know,' answered the wizard. 'But we shan't be able to make our plans and preparations very quickly. Scouts have already been sent out, and some may be away a long while. It is essential to find out as much as we can about the Black Riders.'

The new version then returns to the first and follows it very closely to the end of that text ('... waiting for him to set out', VI.409). But it then continues into 'The Ring Goes South' (VI.415) without break or heading, and again follows the old pretty closely for some distance – as far as Gandalf's words 'And the hunters will have to come all the way back to the Ford to pick up the trail – if we are careful, and lucky' (VI.416). There are a few differences to be noted. This version begins: 'When the hobbits had been some three weeks in the house of Elrond, and November was passing' (see VI.415 and note 2); the scouts who had gone north had been 'almost as far as Hoardale' (later > 'as far as the Hoardales'), where in the original text they had reached 'the

Dimrill-dales' (see p. 10 and note 14); and it is said of the High Pass: 'where formerly the Goblins' door had been'. Very faint pencillings at the foot of the page give Elvish names of the places mentioned in the text, just as are found in the preceding version (see VI.432 note 4), but these are not the same. The note reads:

In Elvish *Annerchion* = Goblin Gate   *Ruinnel* = Redway
          Nenvithim = Hoardales   *Palath-ledin* = Gladden
                                                              Field[s]
                                              Palath = Iris

But where in the first version Gandalf says: 'We had better get off as soon as possible now – and as quietly', and the story then passes almost at once to the day of departure, this text diverges to the first full and clear account of the selection of the Company of the Ring – who are still to be seven (see VI.409–10); and the selection now takes place at the same point in the narrative as it does in FR (pp. 288–9).

'... It is time we began to make preparations in earnest, and the first thing to do is to decide who is going. I have my own ideas, but I must consult Elrond.'

Both Elrond and the wizard were agreed that the party must not be too large, for their hope lay in speed and secrecy. 'Seven and no more should there be,' said Elrond. 'If Frodo is still willing, then Frodo as ring-bearer must be the first choice. And if Frodo goes, then Sam Gamgee must go too, because that was promised, and my heart tells me that their fates are woven together.'

'And if two hobbits go, then I must go,' said Gandalf, 'for my wits tell me that I shall be needed; and indeed *my* fate seems much entangled with hobbits.'

'That is three then,' said Elrond. 'If there are others, they should represent the other free folk of the world.'

'I will go on behalf of Men,' said Trotter. 'I claim some right to share in the adventures of the Ring; but I wish also to go out of friendship for Frodo, and therefore I will ask his leave to be his companion.'

'I could choose no one more gladly,' said Frodo. 'I had thought of begging what is freely offered.' He took Trotter's hand.

'Boromir will also come,' said Gandalf. 'He is resolved to return as soon as he can to his own land, to the siege and war[6] that he has told of. His way goes with ours. He is a valiant man.'

'For the Elves I will choose Galdor of Mirkwood,' said Elrond, 'and for the Dwarves Gimli son of Glóin. If they are willing to go with you, even as far as Moria, they will be a help to you. That is seven and the full tale.'

'What about Meriadoc and Faramond [> Peregrin]?' said Frodo, suddenly realizing that his friends were not included. 'Merry has come far with me, and it will grieve him to be left behind now.'

'Faramond [> Peregrin] would go with you out of love for you, if he were bidden,' said Gandalf; 'but his heart is not in such perilous adventures, much though he loves you. Merry will be grieved, it is true, but Elrond's decision is wise. He is merry in name, and merry in heart, but this quest is not for him, nor for any hobbit, unless fate and duty chooses him. But do not be distressed: I think there may be other work for him to do, and that he will not be left long idle.'

When the names and number of the adventurers had thus been decided, it was agreed that the day of departure should be the following Thursday, November the seventeenth. The next few days were busy with preparations, but Frodo spent as much time as he could alone with Bilbo. The weather had grown cold, and was now cheerless and grey, and they sat often together in Bilbo's own small room. Then Bilbo would read passages from his book (which seemed still very incomplete), or scraps of his verses, and take notes of Frodo's adventures.

On the morning of the last day, Bilbo pulled out from under his bed a wooden box, and lifted the lid, and fumbled inside. 'You have got a good sword of your own, I believe,' he said hesitatingly to Frodo; 'but I thought, perhaps, you would care to have this as well, or instead, don't you know.'

From this point the new text reaches virtually the final form in FR pp. 290–1,[7] as far as 'I should like to write the second book, if I am spared.' This was evidently where the chapter ended at this stage.

For a brief while my father evidently suspected that Meriadoc and Faramond/Peregrin would be superfluous in what he conceived to be the last stage of the Quest. – It is curious that Elrond, when declaring his choice of Galdor of Mirkwood and Gimli son of Glóin, here refers to Moria as if the passage of the Mines were already determined; but this cannot have been intentional.

Later pencilled changes made to the name *Ond* in this manuscript may be mentioned here. At the first occurrence *the Land of Ond* was struck out, and in the margin my father wrote *Minas-tir Minas-ond Minas-berel*, finally putting *the City of Minas-tirith*. This may be the place where *Minas Tirith* (which already existed in the *Quenta*

Silmarillion, V.264, 269) first emerged in this application. At a subsequent occurrence *Ond* was changed to *Minas-berel* and then to *Minas Tirith*.

*

A very rough pencilled outline, written on the 'August 1940' examination script described on p. 67, brings in entirely new aspects of the discussion at the Council. At the head of the page stand these names:

   Minas Giliath   Minas rhain[8] *Othrain* = ... city[9] *Minas tirith*
Then follows:

> At Council.
>   Aragorn's ancestry.
>   Glóin's quest – to ask after Bilbo. ? News of Balin. ??
>   Boromir. Prophecies had been spoken. The Broken Sword should be reforged. Our wise men said the Broken Sword was in Rivendell.
>   I have the Broken Sword, said Tarkil. My fathers were driven out of your city when Sauron raised a rebellion, and he that is now the Chief of the Nine drove us out.
>   Minas Morgol.
>   War between Ond and Wizard King.
>   There Tarkil's sires had been King. Tarkil will come and help Ond. Tarkil's fathers had been driven out by the wizard that is now Chief of the Nine.
>   Gandalf's story of Saruman and the eagle. Elrond explains that Eagles had been sent to look. This only if Gandalf goes straight to Rivendell. Otherwise how could the eagles find Gandalf?

The Broken Sword appears in the last revisions to the 'Prancing Pony' story (written on the same paper as this outline), where Trotter draws it out in the inn (p. 78).[10] – The meaning of the last two sentences of the outline is presumably that Gandalf went straight to Rivendell when he left Hobbiton in June, and there told Elrond that he intended to visit Saruman. Compare the notes given on p. 75: 'Gandalf is captured by Saruman. Elves send word that he is missing . . . Glorfindel is sent out, and messengers sent to Eagles. . . . They fly all over the lands, and find Gandalf . . .'

The Third Version

More is told of this story of 'Tarkil's sires' and Ond in a manuscript written on the same paper, which I give next, and which despite its being so rough and incomplete I will call 'the Third Version'. This text develops Glóin's story, and is followed by the account given by Galdor of Mirkwood of Gollum's escape, which here first enters.[11] In these parts of the text there is a great advance towards FR (pp. 253–5, 268–9), where however the ordering of the speeches made at the Council is quite different. Finally we reach the story of the Númenórean kingdoms in Middle-earth, still in an extremely primitive form, and written in a fearsome scrawl; most unhappily a portion of this is lost.

There are a fair number of alterations in pencil, but I think that these belong to much the same time as the writing of the manuscript (which ends in pencil). I take these up silently where they are of slight significance, but in many cases I show them as such in the text.

Much was said of events in the world outside, especially in the South, and in the wide lands east of the Mountains. Of these things Frodo had already heard many rumours. But the tales of Glóin and of Boromir were new to him, and he listened attentively. It appeared that the hearts of the Dwarves of the Mountain were troubled.

'It is now many years ago,' said Glóin, 'that a shadow of disquiet fell upon our folk. Whence it came we did not at first know. Whispered words began to be spoken: it was said that we were hemmed in a narrow place, and that greater wealth and splendour were to be found in the wider world. Some spoke of Moria – the mighty works of our fathers of old, that we called in our ancient tongue Khazaddûm – and they said that we now had the power and numbers to return and there re-establish our halls in glory and command the lands both West and East of the Mountains. At the last, some score of years ago, Balin departed, though Dáin did not give leave willingly, and he took with him Óin and Ori and many of our folk, and they went away south. For a while we heard news, and it seemed good: messages reported that Moria had been re-entered, and great work begun there. Then all fell silent. There was peace under the Mountain again for a space, until rumour of the rings began to be heard.

'Messages came a year ago from Mordor far away; and they offered us rings of power such as the lord of Mordor could make – on condition of our friendship and aid. And they asked urgently concerning one Bilbo, whom it seemed they had learned was once our friend. They commanded us to obtain from him if we could, willing or unwilling, a certain ring that he had possessed. In exchange for this we were offered three such rings as our fathers had of old. Even for news of where he might be found we were promised lasting friendship and great reward.

'We knew well that the friendship of such messages was

feigned and concealed a threat, for by that time many rumours of evil also reached us concerning Mordor. We have returned yet no answer; and I have come first from Dáin, to warn Bilbo that he is sought by the Dark Lord, and to learn (if may be) why this is so. Also we crave the counsel of Elrond, for the shadow grows. We perceive that messages have also been sent to King Brand in Dale, and that he is afraid to resist. Already there is war gathering on his southern borders. If we make no answer the Dark Lord will move other men to assail him and us.'

'You have done well to come,' said Elrond. 'You will hear today all that is necessary for the understanding of the Enemy's purposes, and why he seeks Bilbo. There is nought you can do other than to resist, whether with hope or without it. But as you will hear, your trouble is only part of ours [> the troubles of others]; and your hope will rise and fall with the fortunes of the Ring. Let us now hear the words of Galdor of Mirkwood, for they are yet known to few.'

Galdor spoke. 'I do not come,' he said, 'to add to all the accounts of gathering war and unrest, though Mirkwood is not spared, and the dark things that fled from it for a while are returning in such number that my people are hard put to it. But I am sent to bear tidings: they are not good, I fear; but how ill, others must judge. Smeagol that is now called Gollum has escaped.'

'What!' cried Trotter in surprise. 'I judge that to be ill news, and you may mark my words: we shall regret this. How came the Wood-elves to fail in their trust?'

'Not through lack of vigilance,' said Galdor; 'but perhaps through overmuch kindness, and certainly through aid from elsewhither. He was guarded day and night; but hoping for his cure we had not the heart to keep him ever in dungeons beneath the ground.'

'You were less tender to me,' said Glóin with a flash of his eye, as ancient memories of his prison in the halls of the Elven-king were aroused.

'Now, now!' said Gandalf. 'Don't interrupt! That was a regrettable misunderstanding.'

'In days of fair weather we led him through the woods,' Galdor went on; 'and there was a high tree, standing alone far from others, which he liked to climb. Often we let him climb in it till he felt the free wind; but we set a guard at the foot. One day he would not descend, and the guards having no mind to climb after him (he could cling to branches with his feet as well as with his hands) sat by the tree into the twilight. It was on that very evening in summer under a clear moon that the Orcs came down upon us. We drove them off after some time; but when the battle was over, we found Gollum was gone, and the guards had vanished also. It seems clear that the attack was arranged for the rescue of Gollum, and that he knew of it beforehand; but in what way we cannot guess. We failed to recapture him. We came on his trail and that of some Orcs, and it seemed to plunge deep into Mirkwood going south and west; but ere long it escaped even our skill, nor dare we continue the hunt, for we were drawing near the Mountains of Mirkwood in the midst of the forest, and they are become evil, and we do not go that way.'

'Well, well!' said Gandalf. 'He has got away, and we have no time or chance now to go after him again. Evidently the Enemy wants him. What for, we may discover in good time, or in bad time.[12] I still had some hopes of curing him; but evidently he did not wish to be cured.'

'But now our tale goes far away and long ago,' said Elrond [> Gandalf]. [*Direction here for insertion of a rider which is not extant; but see p. 126.*] 'In the days that followed the Elder Days after the fall of Númenor the men of Westernesse came to the shores of the Great Lands, as is recorded still in history and legend [> in lore]. Of their kings Elendil was the chief, and his ships sailed up the great river which flows out of Wilderland [*in margin, struck out in pencil:* This river they name *Sirvinya*, New Sirion.] and finds the Western Sea in the Bay of [Ramathor Ramathir >] Belfalas. In the land about they made a realm [> In the land about its lower course he established a realm]; and the [> his] chief city was Osgiliath the Fort of Stars, through which the river flowed. But other strong places were set upon hills upon either side: Minas Ithil the Tower of the Moon in the West, and Minas Anor the Tower of the Sun in the East [> Minas Ithil the Tower of the Rising Moon in the East, and Minas Anor the Tower of the Setting Sun in the West].

'And these cities were governed by the sons of Elendil: Ilmandur [*struck out in pencil*], Isildur, and Anárion. But the sons of Elendil did not return from the war with Sauron, and only in Minas Ithil [> Anor] was the lordship of the West maintained. There ruled the son of Isildur [> Anárion] and his sons after him. But as the world worsened and decayed Osgiliath fell into ruin, and the servants of Sauron took Minas

Anor [*not changed to* Ithil], and it became a place of dread, and was called Minas Morgol, the

The whole of the last paragraph was struck through in pencil. The last words stand at the foot of a page, and the following page is lost. This is a misfortune, since a part of the earliest form of the history is lost with it. The text when it takes up again is complex, and it is clearest to number it in sections from (i) to (iii). We are now in the middle of a speech by Boromir.

(i)

'... But of these words none of us could understand anything, until we learnt after seeking far and wide that *Imlad-ril* [> *Imlad-rist*] was the name of a far northern dale, called by men [> men in the North] Rivendell, where Elrond the Half-elven dwelt.'

'But the rest shall now be made clear to you,' said Trotter, standing up. He drew forth his sword, and cast it upon a table before Boromir: in two pieces. 'Here is the Sword that was Broken, and I am the bearer.'

'But who are you, and what have you or it to do with Minas Tirith?' asked Boromir.

'He is Aragorn son of Celegorn, descended in right line [*added:* through many fathers] from Isildur of Minas Ithil, son of Elendil,' said Elrond. 'He is *tarkil* and one of the few now left of that people.'

(At this point there is a mark of insertion for another passage, here identified as (iii), which is to replace what now follows, the continuation of passage (i).)

(ii)

'And the Men of Minas Tirith drove out my fathers,' said Aragorn. 'Is not that remembered, Boromir? The men of that town have never ceased to wage war on Sauron, but they have listened not seldom to counsels that came from him. In the days of Valandur they murmured against the Men of the West, and rose against them, and when they came back from battle with Sauron they refused them entry into the city.[13] Then Valandur broke his sword before the city gates and went away north; and for long the heirs of Elendil dwelt at Osforod the Northburg in slowly waning glory and darkening days. But all the Northland has now long been waste; and all that are left of Elendil's folk few.

'What do the men of Minas Tirith want with me – to return to aid [them] in the war and then reject me at the gates again?'

This passage (ii) was struck through in pencil. Hurled onto the page, this narrative is only one stage advanced from the highly provisional outlines which my father made at various points as the work proceeded. I think that this obscure story, with its notable suggestion of a subject population that was not Númenórean (although the cities were founded by Elendil), was rejected almost as soon as written; it may be that it was the earliest form of the history of the Númenórean realms in exile that my father conceived.

The passage to replace (ii) was scribbled very rapidly and in pencil; it was not struck out.

(iii)

'Then it belongs to you as much as me, or more!' cried Frodo, looking at Trotter in amazement.

'It does not belong to either of us,' said Trotter, 'but it is ordained that you should keep it for a while.[14] Yes, I am the heir of Elendil,' said he, turning again to Boromir; [*all the following struck out at the time of writing:* 'for I have heard it said that long ago you drove out the Men of the West from Minas Anor. You have ever fought against Sauron, but not seldom you have hearkened to counsels that came from him. Do you wish that I should return to Minas Morgol or to Minas Tirith? For Valandil son of Elendil was taken [?as child] For the Men of Minas Ithil] 'For Valandil son of Isildur remained among the Elves, and was saved, and he went at last with such of his father's men as remained, and dwelt in the North in Osforod, the Northburg, which is now waste, so that its very foundations can scarce be seen beneath the turf. And our days have ever waned and darkened through the years. But ever we have wandered far and wide, yes, even to the borders of Mordor, making secret war upon the Enemy. But the sword has never been reforged. For it was Elendil's and broke under him as he fell, and was brought away by his esquire and treasured. And Elendil said: "This sword shall not be brandished again for many years; but when a cry is heard in Minas Anor, and the power of Sauron grows great in the Middle-earth, then let it be whetted."'

Finally, (ii) continues in pencil from the point reached ('... and then reject me at the gates again?'), and this was not struck out:

'They did not bid me to make any request,' said Boromir, 'and asked only for the meaning of the words. Yet we are sorely pressed, and if Minas Tirith falls and the land of Ond, a great region will fall under the Shadow.'

'I will come,' said Trotter. 'For the half-high have indeed set forth, and the spoken days are near.' Boromir looked at Frodo and nodded with sudden understanding.

The text ends here. In these earliest workings it is interesting to see that the Sword that was Broken existed before the story that it was broken beneath Elendil as he fell: indeed it is not clear that at first it was indeed Elendil's sword, nor how Valandur (whose sword it was) was related to him (though it seems plain that he was a direct descendant of Elendil: very possibly he was to be Isildur's son).

In the passage (iii) the final story of the Broken Sword is seen at the moment of its emergence. Valandil appears as the son of Isildur, and there is a glimpse of the later story that Valandil, the youngest son, remained on account of his youth in Imladris at the time of the War of the Last Alliance, that he received the sword of Elendil, and that he dwelt in Elendil's city of Annúminas.

As my father first wrote the present text he evidently meant (p. 119) that Ilmandur (probably the eldest son of Elendil) ruled Osgiliath, the name of his city being appropriate to his own name (*Ilmen*, region of the stars), as were the cities which they ruled to his brothers' names; but Ilmandur was removed and Osgiliath became Elendil's city – for in this text Elendil sailed up the Great River (which receives ephemerally the name *Sirvinya* 'New Sirion', displacing *Beleghir* 'Great River', VI.410) and established a realm in the land about its lower course. This is entirely at variance with the story found much earlier in Elrond's conversation with Bingo (see p. 110; VI.215–16), where Elrond told that Elendil was 'a king in Beleriand', that 'he made an alliance with the Elf-king of those lands, whose name is Gilgalad', and that their joined armies 'marched eastward, and crossed the Misty Mountains, and passed into the inner lands far from the memory of the Sea.'

That text was very closely related to the end of the second version of *The Fall of Númenor* (V.28–9), and used many of the same phrases. Subsequently a new ending to *The Fall of Númenor* was substituted; this has been given in V.33, but I cite it again here.

But there remains a legend of Beleriand. Now that land had been broken in the Great Battle with Morgoth; and at the fall of Númenor and the change of the fashion of the world it perished; for the sea covered all that was left save some of the mountains that remained as islands, even up to the feet of Eredlindon. But that land where Lúthien had dwelt remained, and was called Lindon. A gulf of the sea came through it, and a gap was made in the Mountains through which the River Lhûn flowed out. But in the land that was left north and south of the gulf the Elves remained, and Gil-galad son of Felagund son of Finrod was their king. And they made Havens in the Gulf of Lhûn whence any of their people, or any other of the Elves that fled from the darkness and sorrow of Middle-earth, could sail into the True West and return no more. In Lindon Sauron had as yet no dominion. And it is said that the brethren Elendil and Valandil escaping from the fall of Númenor came at last to the mouths of the rivers that flowed into the Western Sea. And Elendil (that is Elf-friend), who had aforetime loved the folk of Eressëa, came to Lindon and dwelt there a while, and passed into Middle-earth and established a realm in the North. But Valandil sailed up the Great River Anduin and established another realm far to the South. But Sauron dwelt in Mordor the Black Country, and that was not very distant from Ondor the realm of Valandil; and Sauron made war against all Elves and all Men of Westernesse or others that aided them, and Valandil was hard pressed. Therefore Elendil and Gil-galad seeing that unless some stand were made Sauron would become lord of [?all] Middle-earth they took counsel together, and they made a great league. And Gil-galad and Elendil marched into the Middle-earth [?and gathered force of Men and Elves, and they assembled at Imladrist].

These three accounts can only be placed in this sequence:

(I)   Elrond's account to Bingo (together with the original ending of the second version of *The Fall of Númenor*): Elendil in Beleriand.

(II) The present text (the 'third version' of 'The Council of Elrond'): Elendil comes up the Great River and founds a realm in the South.

(III) The revised ending of *The Fall of Númenor*, cited above: Elendil comes to Lindon; Valandil his brother comes up the Great River and founds the realm of Ondor in the South.

That (I) is the earliest is shown of course by the name Bingo; that (III) followed (II) is shown by the names *Anduin* and *Ondor*. But this is hard to understand: for the story seen emerging in (II), pp. 119–21 above – Isildur and Anárion the rulers of Minas Ithil and Minas Anor, and Valandil Isildur's son surviving and dwelling in the North – is the story that endured into *The Lord of the Rings*.

A single sheet of manuscript found in isolation bears on this question without aiding its solution; it is also of great interest in other respects.

After the 'breaking of the North' in the Great Battle, the shape of the North-west of Middle-earth was changed. Nearly all Beleriand was drowned in the Sea. Taur na Fuin became an Island. The mountains of Eredwethion &c. became small isles (so also Himling). Eredlindon was now near the Sea (at widest 200 miles away). A great gulf of the Sea came in through Ossiriand and a gap made in the Mountains through which [the Branduinen flowed (later corrupted to Brandywine) >] the Lhûn flowed. In what was left between the Mountains and the Sea the Elves of Beleriand remained in North and South Lindon; and Havens of Escape were made in the Gulf. The lord was Gilgalad (son of [*struck out:* Fin...] Inglor?). Many of his people were Gnomes; some Doriath-Danians.

Between Eredlindon and Eredhithui [*written above:* Hith-dilias] (Misty Mountains) many Elves dwelt, and especially at Imladrist (Rivendell) and Eregion (Hollin). In Hollin there was a colony of Gnomes, who would not depart. Down in Harfalas (or Falas) ...[15] the Black Mountains [Ered Myrn >] Eredvyrn (Mornvenniath) dwelt a powerful assembly of Ilkorins.

Elendil and Valandil kings of Númenórë sailed to the Middle-earth and came into the mouths of the Anduin (Great River) and the Branduinen and the Lhûn (Blue River).

Here the name *Anduin* shows that this text followed (II), the present version of 'The Council of Elrond'. Here, as in (III), Elendil has a brother Valandil (and they are called 'kings of Númenórë'),[16] and the meaning of the last sentence is presumably that, again as in (III), they came separately to Middle-earth and sailed up different rivers.

The simplest conclusion, indeed the only conclusion that seems available, is that my father for some time held different views of the coming of the Númenóreans, and pursued them independently.

Other features of this text must be briefly noticed. That it preceded (III) seems clear from its being at first the Branduinen (Brandywine), subsequently changed to the Lhûn, that flowed through the great gap in Eredlindon (the Blue Mountains), whereas in (III) Lhûn was written from the first. This indicates also that the text preceded that portion of the original map (Map I, p. 302) which shows these regions. On the other hand the statement that Eredlindon was now at no point further than 200 miles from the Sea agrees well with that map;[17] and we meet here an apparently unique reference to the isles of *Tol Fuin* and *Himling*, which are shown on it.[18]

The Misty Mountains receive for the first time Elvish names (*Eredhithui, Hithdilias*), as do the Black Mountains in the South, afterwards the White Mountains, (*Eredvyrn, Mornvenniath*); and the name *Eregion* of Hollin appears. The name of Gil-galad's father as first written cannot be interpreted; the fourth letter seems to be an *r*, but the name is certainly not *Finrod*. *Inglor*, though here marked with a query, agrees with (III), which has *Felagund*; in the texts that I have called (I) above he was a descendant of Fëanor.

I return now to the 'third version' of 'The Council of Elrond'.

The verse (if it was already a verse) that brought Boromir to Rivendell is lost in its earliest form with the lost page (p. 120), but from what follows it is plain that it referred to the Sword that was Broken, which was in *Imlad-ril*, and to 'the half-high', who will 'set forth' (cf. FR p. 259).

There are several interesting names in this text.

Khazaddûm (p. 117) is here first used – in the narrative – of Moria (see V.274, VI.466), but it appears in the original sketch of a page from the Book of Mazarbul: see VI.467 and the Appendix to this book, p. 458.

The city of *Osgiliath* on the Great River appears, with the fortresses of *Minas Anor* and *Minas Ithil* on either side of the river valley, though their positions were originally reversed, with Minas Ithil in the west becoming *Minas Tirith* and Minas Anor in the east becoming *Minas Morgol*.

The *Bay of Belfalas* (replacing at the time of writing *Ramathor*, *Ramathir*) here first appears (see VI.438–9). On the name *Sirvinya* 'New Sirion' of the Great River see p. 122.

Imlad-ril is no doubt the earliest form and first appearance of the Elvish name of Rivendell; *Imlad-rist* which here replaced it is the form found in the texts given on pp. 123–4. *Imladris* is found in the *Etymologies* (V.384, stem RIS).

With *Osforod* 'the Northburg' cf. the later *Fornost (Erain)*, 'Norbury (of the Kings)'.

At the end of the manuscript there are a few lines concerning Bombadil: ' "I knew of him," answered Gandalf. "Bombadil's one name. He has called himself by others, suiting himself to the times. Tombombadil's for the Shire-folk. We have seldom met." '

Pencilled scribbles beneath this, difficult to interpret, give other names of Bombadil: *Forn for the Dwarves*[19] (as in FR p. 278); *Yárë for the Elves*, and *Iaur* (see the *Etymologies*, V.399, stem YA); *Erion* for the Gnomes; *Eldest for m[en]* (cf. FR p. 142: 'Eldest, that's what I am').

The Fourth Version

The next complete manuscript of the chapter is a formidably difficult document. It contains pages 'cannibalised' from the second version, with just such elements retained from them as were still suitable, and it also contains later writing at more than one stage in the evolution of the Council, with further emendation on top of that clearly deriving from different times. It is difficult to determine how this complex evolved; but I think a good case can be made for the account of the evolution that I give here, in which a 'fourth' and a 'fifth' version are separated out.

On this view, my father now decided that the extremely difficult and incomplete 'third version', introducing so much new material, called for an ordered text in clear manuscript. The chapter (XIV) was now titled 'The Council of Elrond', and it begins (on the 'August 1940' examination script) with a revised version of the opening (see p. 110): Frodo and Sam now meet Gandalf and Bilbo sitting 'on a seat cut in the stone beside a turn in the path', as in FR (p. 252). But there is no further development at this stage in the membership of the Council: the Elf of Mirkwood is still Galdor. Boromir is now 'from the city of Minas Tirith in the South'.

From the start of the Council itself, the 'third version', taking up at the words 'Much was said of events in the world outside' (p. 117), was for the most part closely followed, though with movement in detail towards the expression in FR. Glóin is still followed by Galdor's news of Gollum's escape and Gandalf's resigned observations on the matter. But after 'And now our tale goes far away and long ago' Elrond here adds:

'for all here should learn in full the tale of the Ring. I know,' he added with a glance at Boromir, who seemed about to speak. 'You think that you should speak now in turn after Galdor. But wait, and you will see that your words will come in more fitly later.'

This passage may very well represent what was contained in the missing rider referred to on p. 119.

Elrond's brief account of the foundation of the realm of Ond is not changed from the 'third version' (as emended: see p. 119). Elendil still established it, about the lower course of the Great River (here not given any other name), and 'his chief city was Osgiliath, the Fortress of Stars', while Isildur and Anárion governed Minas Ithil and Minas Anor. But where the previous text has (as emended) 'But the sons of Elendil did not return from the war with Sauron, and only in Minas Anor was the lordship of the West maintained. There ruled the son of Anárion and his sons after him' this fourth version greatly expands Elrond's speech:

'...But Isildur, the elder, went with his father to the aid of Gilgalad in the Last Alliance. Very mighty was that host.' Elrond paused for a while, and sighed. 'I remember well the splendour of their banners,' he said...

Elrond's recollection of the mustering of the hosts of the Last Alliance, and Frodo's astonished interjection, now reach the form in FR (p. 256; for the earlier forms of the passage see p. 110); but after 'I have seen many ages in the West of the World, and many defeats, and many fruitless victories' the new text proceeds:

'... Such proved indeed the alliance of Gilgalad and Elendil.'

And thereupon Elrond passed to the tale of the assault upon Mordor that Frodo had heard already from Gandalf / yet not so fully or so clearly; and he spoke of the winning of the Ring [*changed perhaps at this time to:* But now all was set forth in full, and memories were unlocked that had long lain hidden. Great forces were gathered together, even of beasts and of birds; and of all living things some were in either host, save only the Elves. They alone were undivided, and followed Gilgalad.[20] Then Elrond spoke of the winning of the Ring], and the flight of Sauron, and the peace that came to the West of Middle-earth for a time.

'Yet,' said Elrond, 'Isildur, who took the Ring, and greatly diminished the power of Sauron, was slain, and he came never back to Minas Ithil, in the Land of Ond, nor did any of his folk return. Only in Minas Anor was the race of Westernesse maintained for a while.[21] But Gilgalad was lost, and Elendil was dead; and in spite of their victory, Sauron was not wholly destroyed, and the evil creatures that he had made or tamed were abroad, and they multiplied. And Men increased, and Elves were estranged from them; for the people of Númenor decayed, or turned to dark thoughts, and destroyed one another; and the world worsened. Osgiliath fell into ruin; and evil men took Minas Ithil, and it became a place of dread, and was called Minas-Morgol, the

It is at this point that the previous manuscript breaks off, through the loss of a leaf, and does not take up again till after Boromir has declared the 'dream-verse' of Minas Tirith, concerning which he came to Rivendell (p. 120).

Tower of Sorcery, and Minas Anor was renamed Minas Tirith the Tower of Guard. And these two cities stood opposed to one another, and were ever at war; and in the ruins of Osgiliath shadows walked. So it has been for many lives of men. For the men of Minas Tirith fight on, though the race of Elendil has long failed among them. But listen now to Boromir, who is come from Minas Tirith in the Land of Ond.'

'Truly in that land,' said Boromir proudly, taking up the tale, 'we have never ceased to defend ourselves, and to dispute the passage of the River with all enemies from the East. By our valour some peace and freedom has been kept in the lands to the West behind us. But now we are pressed back, and are near to despair, for we are beset and the crossing of the River has been taken.[22] And those whom we defend shelter behind us, and give us much praise and little help.

'Now I am come on an errand over many dangerous leagues to Elrond. But I do not seek allies in war; for the might of Elrond is not in numbers, nor do the High-elves put forth their strength in armies. I come rather to ask for counsel and the unravelling of hard words. A dream came many months ago to the Lord of Minas Tirith in the midst of a troubled sleep; and afterward a like dream came to many others in the City, and even to me. Always in this dream there was the noise of running water upon one hand, and of a blowing fire upon the other; and in the midst was heard a voice, saying:

> Seek for the Sword that was broken:
>   in Imlad-rist it dwells,
> and there shall words be spoken
>   stronger than Morgol-spells.
> And this shall be your token:
>   when the half-high leave their land,
> then many bonds shall be broken,
>   and Days of Fire at hand.

Of these words none of us could understand anything,[23] until after long seeking we learned that *Imlad-rist* was the elvish name of a far northern dale, called by Men in the North *Rivendell*, where Elrond Halfelven dwelt.

The third version is then followed closely (pp. 120–1, passages (i) and (iii)) as far as 'but it has been ordained that you should have it for a while'; then follows in this fourth version:

'Yes, it is true,' he said, turning to Boromir with a smile. 'I do not look the part, maybe: I have had a hard life and a long, and the leagues that lie between here and Ond would go for little in the count of my wanderings. I have been in Minas Tirith, and walked in Osgiliath by night, and even to Minas Morgol I have been, and beyond.' He shuddered. 'But my home, such as I have, has been in the North; for Valandil son of Isildur was harboured by the Elves in this region after the death of his father;

and he went at last with such of his folk as remained, and dwelt in Osforod the North-burg. But that is now waste, so that its very foundations can scarce be seen beneath the turf. And our days have ever waned and darkened through the years; and we are become a wandering folk, few and secret and sundered, pursued ever by the Enemy, and pursuing him. And the sword has never been reforged. For it was Elendil's, and broke beneath him in his fall; and it was brought away by his esquire and treasured. For Elendil said in his last hour: "This blade shall not be brandished again for many ages. And when a voice is heard in Minas Anor, and the shadow of Sauron grows great again in Middle-earth, let it then be remade." '

It seems to me extremely probable that it was here, very near the point where the draft third version ended, that my father abandoned in its turn this fourth version, or more accurately went back over what he had written, changing the sequence of the speeches at the Council and introducing much new material. He then continued to the end of the chapter; and this is the fifth version.

In the third and fourth versions, ending (on this view) at much the same place, the sequence had been the same:

(1) Glóin's account of the return to Moria and the messages from Mordor;

(2) Galdor's news of Gollum's escape;

(3) Elrond's story ('But now our tale goes far away and long ago...');

(4) Boromir and the 'dream-verse' of Minas Tirith;

(5) Aragorn produces the Sword of Elendil, and Elrond proclaims his ancestry; Frodo says 'Then it belongs to you as much as me, or more!'

(6) Aragorn speaks of Valandil son of Isildur and the life of his descendants in the North.

The differences between this structure and that of FR are essentially that in the final form the story of (Galdor) Legolas comes in much later, and that after Frodo's exclamation in (5) and Aragorn's reply Gandalf calls on Frodo to bring forth the Ring – whereupon Elrond says 'Behold Isildur's Bane!'; this in turn leads to Aragorn's account of himself, Aragorn being followed by Bilbo's story and then Frodo's.

A single page of rough drafting shows both developments: Frodo's bringing forth the Ring at this juncture and Elrond's naming it 'Isildur's Bane' (which would lead to the insertion of the name into the 'dream-verse', from which it was at first absent, p. 128), and also a scheme for a new sequence. In this, after Aragorn's explanation to Boromir of the Broken Sword (FR p. 260), there follows:

(1) Bilbo's story;

(2) Gandalf's account of the Rings, and of the identification of
   Bilbo's Ring with Isildur's Bane;
(3) The story of the hunt for Gollum;
(4) Galdor's tidings of Gollum's escape;
(5) Frodo's story;
(6) 'Gandalf's captivity';
(7) 'Question about Tom Bombadil'.

Although in FR (2) was very greatly enlarged, and embraces Aragorn's
story (3), this is essentially the final sequence, with the exception of
(5): in FR Frodo follows Bilbo. An intervention, following Frodo's
story, by the Elf from the Grey Havens (Galdor, not yet present) leads
in FR to Gandalf's two long accounts (2) and (6), into which (4) comes
as an interruption.

The sequence given above is found in the fifth version, to be given
(in part) shortly; and the way in which the speeches at the Council
were relinked to achieve the final sequence can be understood from a
comparison of FR with the material presented here.

Gandalf's Tale

I think it very likely, indeed almost certain, that it was at this
juncture, before he began on the fifth version of 'The Council of
Elrond', that my father finally set down the full story of why Gandalf
failed to return to Hobbiton before Frodo's departure. Only a few
hints towards this had been put in writing. Saruman appeared for the
first time in the outline dated 26–27 August 1940 (pp. 70–1), where
the earliest ideas concerning him and his rôle emerge. He dwells at
Angrobel or Irongarth, on the borders of Rohan; he 'sends out a
message that there is important news' (that the Ringwraiths had come
forth from Mordor); Gandalf wants his help against them; but
Saruman has 'fallen and gone over to Sauron'. At that stage my father
was still entirely uncertain what in fact happened to Gandalf –
whether he was pursued by the Riders to the top of a mountain from
which he could not escape, or whether he was handed over to
Treebeard and imprisoned by him; and in that outline there is no
mention of his escape from whatever durance he suffered. In the brief
scheme given on p. 116, however, there is mention of 'Gandalf's story
of Saruman and the eagle'; and the question is touched on there, how
did the Eagles know where to seek for Gandalf? – unless he had gone
at once to Rivendell when he left the Shire in June, and had told
Elrond of his intention.

Now at last the final story emerges; and the earlier conception of the
Western Tower, an Elf-tower of Emyn Beraid, in which Gandalf stood
guarded by the Ringwraiths sitting motionless on their horses, as
Frodo saw them in his dream (see pp. 33–6), changes into Orthanc,

Saruman's tower within the circuit of the 'Irongarth'; and Saruman is his captor.

This first draft, for which my father used the blue booklet-covers of the 'August 1940' examination script, was written in his most rapid handwriting, in which words were often reduced to mere marks or lines with slight undulations, and I have not been able to interpret it at every point. But this original text of Gandalf's story is of much interest, and I give it here in full so well as I can. It will be seen that while the texture of the narrative is thinner than in the final form (FR pp. 269 ff.), many essential features were already present. The pages of the manuscript are lettered from 'b' onwards, showing that the first page is lost.

'It has', said Gandalf, 'and I was about to give an account.[24] At the end of June a cloud of anxiety came upon my mind and I went through the Shire to its southern borders. I had long felt a foreboding of some danger that was still hidden from me. I passed down the Baranduin as far as Sarn Ford, and there I met a messenger. I found I knew him well, for he leapt from his horse when he saw me and hailed me: it was Radagast who dwelt once upon a time near the southern borders of Mirkwood.

Here my father broke off, and without striking out what he had written began again in the course of the second sentence.

and rode round the borders of the Shire, for I felt a foreboding of some danger that was still hidden from me. I found nothing, though I came upon many fugitives, and it seemed to me that on many a fear sat of which they could not speak. I came up from the South and along the Greenway, and not far from Bree I came upon a man sitting by the roadside. His [?dappled grey] horse was standing by. When he saw me he leaped to his feet and hailed me. It was Radagast my cousin,[25] who dwelt once upon a time near the southern borders of Mirkwood. I had lost sight of him for many years. "I am seeking you," he said. "But I am a stranger in these parts, and I heard a rumour that you were in a land called by a strange name: the Shire." "I was," said I, "and you are near. ... [?River] but [?far] to East. What do you want with me so urgently?" For he is never a great traveller.

'He then told me dread news and revealed to me what I had feared without knowing it. This is what he said. "The Nine Wraiths are released," he said. "The Enemy must have some great and urgent need, but what it is that should make him

look to these desolate ... parts where men and wealth are scanty
I do not know." "What do you mean?" said I. "The Nine are
coming this way," he said. "Men and beasts are flying before
them. [*Added in pencil:* They have taken the guise of horsemen
clad in black as of old.]"

'Then my heart failed for a moment; for the Chief of the Nine
was of old the greatest of all the wizards of Men, and I have no
power to withstand the Nine Riders when he leads them.

'"Who sent you?" I asked. "It was Saruman the [Grey >]
White,"[26] he said, [*added in pencil:* "and he bids me say that
though the matter is too great for you he will help, but you must
seek his help at once, and this seemed good to me"] and then I
had a light of hope. For Saruman the [Grey >] White is as you
know the greatest among us, and was chief of the White
Council. Radagast the Grey [*in pencil* > Brown] is of course a
master of shapes and changes of hue,[27] and has much lore of
beast, bird, and herb; but Saruman has long studied the works
of the Enemy to defeat him, and the lore of rings was his
especial knowledge. The last of the 19 rings he had. . . .[28]

'"I will go to Saruman," I said. "Then you must go now,"
said Radagast; "for the time is very short, and even if you set
out this hour you will hardly come to him before the Nine cross
the Seven Rivers.[29] I myself shall take my horse and ride away
now, since my errand is at an end." And with that he mounted
and rode off without another word – and that seemed to me
very strange. [*Marginal addition:* and would have ridden off
there and then. "Stay a moment, Radagast," I said. "We need
help of many kinds. Send out messages to all the birds and
beasts that are your friends. Tell them to bring news to Saruman
and Gandalf. Let any message go to Orthanc."][30] But I could
not follow him. I had ridden far and Galeroc[31] was weary. I
stayed the night in Bree and departed at dawn – and if I ever see
the [?innkeeper] again there will be no Butter left in Butterbur. I
will melt the fat from him. . . .[32] But bless him, he is a worthy
man and seems to have shown a stout heart. I shall probably
relent. However, being in great need I trusted him to send the
message to Frodo, and went off at dawn; and I came at last to
the dwelling of Saruman the White. And that is in Isengard, in
the north of the Black Mountains in the South.[33] There there is
a circle of sheer-sided hills that enclose a vale, and in the midst
of the vale is a tower of stone that is called Orthanc. I came to
the great gate in the wall of rock and they said that Saruman

expected me;[34] and I rode in, and the gate closed behind, and a sudden fear came on me.

'Saruman was there but he had changed. He wore a ring on his finger. "So you have come, Gandalf," he said to me, and I seemed to see a deadly laughter in his eyes. "Yes, I have come for your aid, Saruman the White." But that title seemed to fill him with anger. "For aid?" he said coldly. "It is seldom heard that Gandalf the *Grey* sought for aid, one so cunning and so wise, wandering about the lands, and concerning himself in every business, be it his own or others".'

'"But now matters are afoot," I said, "that need all our strengths [?in union]. The Chief of the Nine is guised as a Rider in Black and his companions likewise. This Radagast told me."

'"Radagast the Brown," he said, and shook with laughter. "Radagast the Simple, Radagast the Fool. [*Added in pencil:* Yet he had just the wits to play the part that I set him.] He must have played his part well nonetheless. For here you are [*added in pencil:* and that is the purpose of the message]. And, Gandalf the Grey, here you will stay. For I am Saruman: Saruman the Wise, Saruman of many colours. For white cloth may be dyed, and the white page overwritten, and the white light broken." [*Pencilled in margin without direction for insertion:* And I looked then and saw that his robes were not white as had been his custom, but were of many hues, and with every movement he changed hue.]

'"In which case it is no longer white," I said. "For white may be blended of many colours, but many colours are not white." "You need not speak to me as to one of the fools that you make your friends," he said. "I have not brought you here to be instructed, but to give you a choice. A new power has arisen. Against it there is no hope. With it there is such hope as we never had before. The power is going to win. [*Added in margin without direction for insertion:* We fight against it in vain – and in any case foolishly; for we have looked always at it from the outside with hatred, and have not considered what are its further purposes. We have seen only the things done, often under necessity, or caused by resistance and foolish rebellion.] I shall grow as it grows, until all things are ours. In the end, I – or *we*, if you will join me – may in the end come to control that Power. Indeed why not? Could not we by this means accomplish all, and more than all, that we have striven for before with the help of the weak Men and fugitive Elves?"

' "Be brief!" I said. "Name your choice! It is this, is it not? To submit as you have to Sauron [*alternative reading:* To submit to you and to Sauron], or what?"

' "To stay here till the end," said he.

' "Till what end?"

' "Till the Lord has time to consider what fate for you would give him most pleasure."

'They took me,' said Gandalf, 'and placed me on the pinnacle of Orthanc, in the place where Saruman of old was wont to watch the stars. There is no descent but by a narrow stair. And the vale that was once fair was filled with wolves and orcs, for Saruman was there mustering a great force for the service of his new master.[35] I had no chance of escape, and my days were bitter. For I had but little room in which to walk to and fro, and brood on the coming of the Riders to the North. But there was always a hope that Frodo had set forth as I had bidden, and would reach Rivendell ere the inescapable pursuit began. But both my fear and my hope were cheated. For I made the mistake that others have made. I did not yet understand that in the Shire the power of Sauron would halt and fumble, and the hunt be at a loss. And my hope was founded on an innkeeper: one of the best in the world, but not made to be a tool in high matters.'

'Who sent the eagles?' said Frodo eagerly, for suddenly the strange dream that he had had came back to him.

Gandalf looked at him in surprise. 'I thought you asked what had happened to me,' he said. 'But you seem to know, and don't need ... the telling of my tale ...'

'Your words have recalled a dream,' said Frodo, 'that I thought only a dream and had forgotten.'

'Well,' said Gandalf, 'your dream was true.[36] Gandalf was caught like a fly in a spider's web; yet he is an old fly that has known many spiders. I was not content to send a message only to the Shire. At first I feared, as Saruman wished that I should, that Radagast had also fallen. But it is not so: he trusted Saruman, who had not revealed his purposes to him. And the very fact that Saruman had so successfully deceived Radagast proved the undoing of his scheme. For Radagast did as I bid.[37] And the Eagles of the Misty Mountains kept watch and they saw the mustering of orcs, and got news of the escape of Gollum, and they sent word to Orthanc of this to me. And so it was when the moon was still young on a night of autumn that Gwaewar the Windlord[38] chief of the eagles came to me; and I spoke to him and he bore me away before Saruman was aware, and the orcs and wolves that he released found me not.

'"How far can you bear me?" said I to Gwaewar.

'"Many leagues," he said; "but not to the ends of the earth. Had I known that you wished to fly I would have brought helpers. I was sent as the swiftest and as a bearer of [?tidings]."

'"Then I must have a steed," I said, "and a steed of surpassing swiftness; for I have never had such a need."

'"Then I will take you to Rohan," he said, "for that is not far off. For in Rohan [*added:* the ?Riddermark] the Rohiroth[39] the horse-masters dwell still, and there are no horses like the horses of that land."

'"But are they yet to be trusted?" "They pay tribute ... yearly in horses to Mordor," said Gwaewar, "but they are not yet under the yoke;[40] yet their doom is not far off, if Saruman is fallen."

'I reached Rohan ere dawn, and there I got a horse the like of which I have never seen.'

'He is indeed a fine steed,' said [Elrond >] Aragorn; 'and it grieves me that Sauron should have such tribute. For in the steeds of Rohan there is a strain that ... descended from the Elder Days.'

'One at least is saved,' said Gandalf; 'for there I got my grey horse, and I name him Greyfax. Not even the Chief of the Nine could go with such tireless speed; and by day his coat glistens like silver, and at night it is as unseen as a shadow. So swift was my going from Rohan that I reached the Shire within a week of the appointed day, and I came to his[41] home and found he was gone. I found in fact the Sackville-Bagginses there and was [?ordered off]. I went to the Gaffer's and he was hard to comfort; but l had need of comfort myself, for amidst his confused talk I gathered that the Riders had come even as you left; and I rode to Buckland and all was in uproar; but I found Crickhollow broken and empty, and on the threshold I picked up a cloak that was Frodo's.

'That was my worst moment. I rode then on the trail of the Black Riders like the wind, and I came behind them as they rode through Bree. They threw down the gates ... and passed by like a wind. The Breelanders I guess are quaking still, and expect the end of the world. This was on the night after you had left, I now know. Next day I rode on, and in two days I reached Weathertop, and there I found two of the Enemy already, but they drew off before my [?wrath]. But that night … gathered, and I was besieged on the top, but I perceived they had not got you.

The text ends with the words: 'Fled at sunrise'. – With only slight prevision (as it appears), a massive new element and dimension had entered the history. There were of course certain essential features lacking. Most important, Saruman was not acting independently of the Dark Tower (see note 35); and while Gandalf's great ride from Rohan on 'Greyfax' now enters, there is no suggestion that the relations of Rohan with Mordor will have any especial significance in the story (though those relations are now differently conceived: see note 40) – and Gandalf's remark 'In Rohan I found evil already at work' (FR p. 275) is absent.

The story of Hamilcar Bolger's ride with Gandalf has finally gone (see p. 75), as has that of Gandalf's visit to Tom Bombadil (see p. 111).

A notable feature is the evolution of the 'colours' of the wizards, Gandalf, Saruman, and Radagast, which came to the final form in the course of the writing of this draft. Saruman is at first 'the Grey',[42] becoming at once 'the White', and Radagast immediately takes on the epithet 'Grey' (p. 132). But Gandalf then becomes 'the Grey',[43] and Saruman calls Radagast 'the Brown' in the text as written on p. 133.

NOTES

1   This text has been put together from pages used in a subsequent version that went to Marquette University and others that were left behind. Many changes were made to it afterwards, but in the citations that I make from it here I take account only of those that were made in ink and at or very near to the time of composition.

2   Elrond still says of Boromir that he 'brings tidings that must be considered', but as in the original version (VI.409) we are again not told what they were, and no explanation is given of his journey to Rivendell. Subsequently in this version, however, Gandalf says that Boromir 'is resolved to return as soon as he can to his own land, to the siege and war that he has told of.'

3   That my father had the earlier text before him is shown by the recurrence here of the casual error (which I did not observe in Vol. VI) 'Elwing daughter of Lúthien': Elwing was the daughter of Dior, son of Lúthien.

4   In the preceding sentence, 'In time the Lord of the Ring would find out its hiding-place', just as in the first version (VI.402 and note 25) Lord of the Rings was first written but changed at once to Lord of the Ring.

5   'Thráin father of Thrór' (VI.403 and note 28), contradicting The Hobbit, was repeated. See pp. 159–60.

6   See note 2.

7   That Bilbo gave Frodo Sting and his mailcoat appears in the original outline for 'The Council of Elrond', VI.397. Bilbo does not here, as he does in FR, produce the pieces of Frodo's sword, nor indeed refer to the fact of its having been broken, though the story of its being broken at the Ford of Bruinen goes back to the beginning (VI.197). – The coat of mail (which Bilbo still calls his 'elf-mail') is described as 'studded with pale pearls' ('white gems', FR); cf. the original text of *The Hobbit*, before it was changed to introduce 'mithril': 'It was of silvered steel, and ornamented with pearls' (VI.465, note 35).

8   See p. 287 note 3.

9   The illegible word probably begins with F and might be 'Fire'.

10 It is possible that the Sword that was Broken actually emerged from the verse 'All that is gold does not glitter': on this view, in the earliest form of the verse in which the Broken Sword is referred to (p. 80, note 18) the words *a king may yet be without crown, A blade that was broken be brandished* were no more than a further exemplification of the general moral.

11 Gollum's escape, though only now emerging, had been a necessity of the story ever since Gandalf told Bingo (VI.265) that 'the Wood-elves have him in prison', if Gollum was to reappear at the end, as had long been foreseen (see VI.380–1).

12 Afterwards it is Treebeard who says this (*The Two Towers* III.4, p. 75): 'There is something very big going on, that I can see, and what it is maybe I shall learn in good time, or in bad time.'

13 Cf. the outline given on p. 116: 'My [i.e. Aragorn's] fathers were driven out of your city when Sauron raised a rebellion', and 'There Tarkil's sires had been King'.

14 For previous uses of this dialogue in other contexts see pp. 50 and 105 note 3.

15 The illegible word is an abbreviation, perhaps 'bet.', which my father used elsewhere for 'between'; if this is what it is, he may have intended (the manuscript is very hasty) to write 'between the Black Mountains and the Sea'. *Harfalas* is not named here on the First Map (p. 309, map III).

16 Cf. p. 119: 'Of their kings [i.e. of the Men of Westernesse] Elendil was the chief'.

17 Text (III), the revised ending to *The Fall of Númenor*, says that 'the sea covered all that was left ... *even up to the feet of Eredlindon*' (pp. 122–3), but this can be accommodated to the map by supposing that it refers to the northern extent of the range (where it bent North-east).

18 In the Introduction to *Unfinished Tales* (p. 14) I said that 'though the fact is nowhere referred to it is clear that Himring's top rose above the waters that covered drowned Beleriand. Some way to

the west of it was a larger island named *Tol Fuin*, which must be the highest part of *Taur-nu-Fuin*.' When I wrote that I did not know of the existence of this text. – The later form *Himring* had appeared already in the second text of the *Lhammas* (V.177, 189), and in the *Quenta Silmarillion* (V.263, 268); *Himling* here and on the map are surprising, but can have no significance for dating.

19   This is Old Norse *forn* 'ancient'.

20   Cf. *Of the Rings of Power*, in *The Silmarillion* p. 294: 'All living things were divided in that day, and some of every kind, even of beasts and birds, were found in either host, save the Elves only. They alone were undivided and followed Gil-galad.'

21   In this text there is no reference to the death of Anárion. It is made clear that he did not go to the War of the Last Alliance.

22   Contrast FR: 'But if the passages of the River should be won, what then?' In FR (pp. 258–9) Boromir describes the assault on Osgiliath: 'A power was there that we have not felt before. Some said that it could be seen, like a great black horseman, a dark shadow under the moon'; but 'still we fight on, holding all the west shores of Anduin'. An addition to the present text may belong to this time or later: 'Nine horsemen in black led the host of Minas Morgol that day and we could not withstand them.' See p. 151.

23   Here the 'third version' draft takes up again after the missing page (p. 120).

24   Cf. the next version (p. 149): ' "It has much to do with it," said Gandalf, "and if Elrond is willing I will give my account now." '

25   Cf. *The Hobbit*, Chapter VII 'Queer Lodgings': ' "I am a wizard," continued Gandalf. "I have heard of you, if you have not heard of me; but perhaps you have heard of my good cousin Radagast who lives near the Southern borders of Mirkwood?" ' – On Radagast's appearance in the story see p. 76 and note 15.

26   The change of *Grey* to *White* followed the same change in the next sentence, which was made in the act of writing; a little further on *Saruman the White* was written thus from the first.

27   Can this have been suggested by Beorn's acquaintance with Radagast? (see note 25).

28   I cannot make out the two concluding words, though the first might be 'gathered'. But whatever the words are, the meaning is clearly that Saruman had acquired the last of the Rings – and wore it on his finger, as appears subsequently in this text (cf. FR p. 271). – In the last text of 'Ancient History' that has been given Gandalf refers to the discussion of the Rings at the White Council, and to those who 'go in for such things'; see p. 22.

29   The *Seven Rivers*: see pp. 310–12.

30   It is seen subsequently (see note 37) that this addition was made

while the writing of this text was in progress; and it is seen from the addition that Radagast first entered the story as the means by which Gandalf was lured to Saruman's dwelling. The abrupt haste of Radagast's departure seemed to Gandalf 'very strange', and it is possible that when first drafting the story my father supposed that Radagast's part was not simply that of innocent emissary: later, at Isengard, Saruman says (p. 133) 'He must have played his part well nonetheless'. This is not in FR. When the addition here was made, Radagast became also the means by which the Eagles knew where to find Gandalf (see p. 130); and this development necessarily disposed of the idea that Radagast had been corrupted — but Gandalf's fear that he had been remains: 'At first I feared, as Saruman wished that I should, that Radagast had also fallen' (p. 134; this is preserved in FR, p. 274). — This is the first appearance of the name *Orthanc*, though its first actual use in the narrative is probably in the description of Isengard that immediately follows.

31   *Galeroc*: see pp. 68 and note 4, 70.

32   The illegible words are perhaps 'fingers and all' ('butterfingers').

33   The name *Isengard* first occurs here (cf. *Angrobel* or *Irongarth*, p. 71), and it is placed, not at the southern end of the Misty Mountains, but in the north of the Black Mountains.

34   This is the first description of Isengard. — There is a faint pencilled addition at this point: 'But something strange in their look and voices struck me; and I dismounted from my horse and left him without. And that was well, for' (here the addition breaks off). This was perhaps a thought, abandoned as soon as written, for some other story of Gandalf's escape, and his need for a horse to take him back to the Shire. The great speed of Galeroc had been emphasised earlier (p. 68: 'there is no horse in Mordor or in Rohan that is as swift as Galeroc').

35   Cf. FR pp. 273–4: 'for Saruman was mustering a great force on his own account, in rivalry of Sauron and not in his service yet.'

36   Before writing this passage about Frodo's dream ('"Who sent the eagles?"...) my father first put '"And how did you get away?" said Frodo.' It was thus probably at this very point that he decided to introduce Frodo's vision of Gandalf on the pinnacle of Orthanc into his dream in the house of Tom Bombadil (FR p. 138; for previous narratives of his dream on that night see VI.118–20, 328). His vision of Gandalf imprisoned in the Western Tower had also of course to be removed (see p. 35).

37   It is seen from this passage that the addition discussed in note 30 was put in while the draft was in course of composition.

38   On the form *Gwaewar* (*Gwaihir* in LR) see V.301.

39   The name following *Rohan* is very unclear, but can scarcely be other than the first occurrence of *Riddermark. Rohiroth, Rochi-*

roth is found on the earliest rough map of the region, VI.439–40.

40   Cf. VI.422 (the earliest text of 'The Ring Goes South'): 'The Horse-kings have long been in the service of Sauron.'

41   'his', though Frodo has not been mentioned, because 'the appointed day' replaced 'Frodo's departure'.

42   In the plot dated 26–27 August 1940 (p. 70), where Saruman first appears, he was 'Saramond the White or Grey Saruman'.

43   He calls himself 'Gandalf the Grey' in the version of his conversation with Frodo at Rivendell cited on p. 82, but that is not earlier than the present text.

VII

THE COUNCIL OF ELROND (2)

The Fifth Version

A fifth version of 'The Council of Elrond' followed, and is conveniently placed here, though it is not necessarily the case that these revisions
proceeded in unbroken sequence while other writing remained at a
standstill. This version incorporated the changed sequence of speakers
(pp. 129–30) and Gandalf's story, and changed the history of Elendil
and his sons; but for this rewriting and reconstruction my father made
use of existing material, whence arises the extraordinarily complicated
state of the manuscript. Many emendations were made to this version
at different times. In this case they can be readily separated into two
groups, on the basis of a typescript that was made of the fifth version
after a certain amount of change had been carried out.

This typescript was very carefully and accurately made, with a
remarkably small number of errors, seeing that the typist seems not to
have been well acquainted with the story: the name *Saruman* was
typed *Samman* throughout (*ru* and *m* being very similar or identical in
my father's handwriting). Where my father missed a needed change (as
Galdor > Legolas) the typist dutifully set down the manuscript form.
These characteristics make the typescript a mirror of the state of the
manuscript when it was made. This is to be sure of only limited value
without knowledge of when that was; but I think that it belongs
clearly to this period.

In those parts of the fifth version that are cited here, I indicate only
those subsequent emendations to the manuscript (and only if of
significance) that appear in the typescript as typed.

Glóin's story was altered in the following way. In the third version,
retained in the fourth, he had said: 'At the last, some score of years
ago, Balin departed, though Dáin did not give leave willingly, and he
took with him Óin and Ori and many of our folk, and they went away
south' (p. 117). This was now replaced by the following, written on a
page of the 'August 1940' examination script.

'... For Moria was of old one of the wonders of the Northern
world. It is said that it was begun when the Elder Days were
young,[1] and Durin, father of my folk, was king; and with the
passing of the years and the labour of countless hands its mighty

halls and streets, its shafts and endless galleries, pierced the mountains from east to west and delved immeasurably deep. But under the foundations of the hills things long buried were waked at last from sleep, as the world darkened, and days of dread and evil came. Long ago the dwarves fled from Moria and forsook there wealth uncounted; and my folk wandered over the earth until far in the North they made new homes. But we have ever remembered Moria with fear and hope; and it is said in our songs that it shall be re-opened and re-named ere the world ends. When again we were driven from the Lonely Mountain, Erebor,[2] in the days of the Dragon, Thrór returned thither. But he was slain by an Orc, and though that was revenged by Thorin and Dáin, and many goblins were slain in war, none of Thrór's folk, neither Thráin, nor Thorin his son, nor Dáin his sister-son, dared to pass its gates; until at last Balin listened to the whispers that I have spoken of, and resolved to depart. Though Dáin did not give leave willingly, he took with him Óin and Ori and many of our people, and they went away south. That was two score years ago.

This passage, of which only a trace remains in FR (pp. 253–4), reveals the development of new conceptions in the history of the Dwarves. In the original text of 'The Ring Goes South' (VI.429) Gandalf said that *the Goblins drove the Dwarves from Moria*, and most of those that escaped removed into the North. This must have been based on what was told in *The Hobbit*: in Chapter III Elrond had said that 'there are still forgotten treasures to be found in the deserted caverns of the mines of Moria, since the dwarf and goblin war', and in Chapter IV there was a reference to the goblins having 'spread in secret after the sack of the mines of Moria'. Presumably therefore what my father said in the first version of 'The Ring Goes South' was what he actually had in mind when he wrote those passages in *The Hobbit*: the Goblins drove the Dwarves out of Moria.

If this is so, it was only now that a new story emerged, in which the Dwarves left Moria for an entirely different reason. In the present passage the cause of their flight is indeed only hinted at most obliquely: 'they delved immeasurably deep', and 'under the founda-tions of the hills things long buried were waked at last from sleep' With this compare LR Appendix A (III):

The Dwarves delved deep at that time.... Thus they roused from sleep a thing of terror that, flying from Thangorodrim, had lain hidden at the foundations of the earth since the coming of the Host of the West: a Balrog of Morgoth. Durin was slain by it, and the year after Náin I, his son; and then the glory of Moria passed, and its people were destroyed or fled far away.

On this question see further pp. 185–6.

Concomitantly with this, the 'dwarf and goblin war' took on a new interpretation and history (and this was why the word 'sack' in the sentence quoted from Chapter IV of *The Hobbit* above was changed in the third edition (1966) to 'battle'). It was the savage murder of Thrór, Thorin's grandfather, on his return to Moria, that led to the war of the Dwarves and the Orcs, ending in the fearsome victory of the Dwarves in the battle of Azanulbizar (Dimrill Dale), described in LR Appendix A (III). The passage in the present text, telling that Thrór 'was slain by an Orc, and though that was revenged by Thorin and Dáin, and many goblins were slain in war, none of Thrór's folk, neither Thráin, nor Thorin his son, nor Dáin his sister-son, dared to pass [Moria's] gates', suggests that the essentials of the later story were now already present. In the story told in LR Appendix A (III) Thorin played an important part in the battle, and from his prowess derived his name 'Oaken-shield'; and Dáin slew Azog, the slayer of Thrór, before the East Gate of Moria. This latter event was indeed derived from *The Hobbit*, where in Chapter XVII Gandalf said of Dáin that he slew the father of Bolg (leader of the Goblins in the Battle of Five Armies) in Moria.[3] It is further told in Appendix A (III) that after the death of Azog Dáin came down from the Gate 'grey in the face, as one who has felt great fear'; and that he said to Thráin, Thorin's father:

> 'You are the father of our Folk, and we have bled for you, and will again. But we will not enter Khazad-dûm. You will not enter Khazad-dûm. Only I have looked through the shadow of the Gate. Beyond the shadow it waits for you still: Durin's Bane. The world must change and some other power than ours must come before Durin's Folk walk again in Moria.'

It appears from *The Hobbit* Chapter XV that Dáin of the Iron Hills was Thorin Oakenshield's cousin (and from Chapter XVII that his father was called Náin). In the present text Dáin is called Thráin's sister-son. In the table given in LR Appendix A (III), however, he is not Thráin's sister-son: his father Náin was Thráin's first cousin, and thus Thorin Oakenshield and Dáin Ironfoot were second cousins.

After Elrond's words to Glóin 'You will learn that your trouble is only part of the trouble that we are here met to consider' (cf. p. 118), Galdor of Mirkwood no longer follows (see pp. 129–30), and the fifth version reads here:[4]

'For hearken all!' said Elrond in a clear voice. 'I have called you together to listen to the tale of the Ring. Some part of that tale is known to all, but the full tale to few. Other matters may be spoken of, but ere all is ended, it will be seen that all are bound up with the Ring, and all our plans and courses must wait upon our decision in this great matter. For, what shall we do with the Ring? That is the doom that we must deem ere we depart.

'Behold, the tale begins far away and long ago. In the Black Years that followed the Elder Days, after the fall of Númenor the Men of Westernesse returned to the shores of Middle-earth, as is recorded still in lore. Of their kings Elendil the Tall was their chief, and his sons were Isildur and Anárion, mighty lords of ships. They sailed first into the Gulf of Lindon, where the Elf-havens were and still are, and they were befriended by Gilgalad, King of the High-elves of that land. Elendil passed on into Middle-earth and established a realm in the North, about the rivers Lhûn and Branduin, and his chief city was called Tarkilmar [> Torfirion] (or Westermanton), that now is long desolate. But Isildur and Anárion sailed on southwards, and brought their ships up the Great River, Anduin,[5] that flows out of Wilderland and finds the Western Sea in the Bay of Belfalas. In the lands about its lower courses they established a realm where are now the countries of Rohan and Ondor.[6] Their chief city was Osgiliath, the Fortress of Stars, through the midst of which the river flowed. Other strong places they made: Minas Ithil, the Tower of the Rising Moon, to the eastward upon a spur of the Mountains of Shadow; and Minas Anor, the Tower of the Setting Sun, westward at the feet of the Black Mountains. But Sauron dwelt in Mordor, the Black Country, beyond the Mountains of Shadow, and his great fortress, the Dark Tower, was built above the valley of Gorgoroth; and he made war upon the Elves and the Men of Westernesse; and Minas Ithil was taken. Then Isildur sailed away and sought Elendil in the North; and Elendil and Gilgalad took counsel together, seeing that Sauron would soon become master of them all, if they did not unite. And they made a league, the Last Alliance, and marched into Middle-earth gathering great force of Elves and Men. Very mighty was that host.

It will be found that in this passage are the bones of a part of the narrative of the separate work *Of the Rings of Power and the Third Age*, which was published in *The Silmarillion* (see pp. 290–3). In the later development of 'The Council of Elrond' the chapter became the vehicle of a far fuller account of the early Númenórean kingdoms in

Middle-earth, and much of this is now found not in *The Lord of the Rings* but in *Of the Rings of Power and the Third Age*.

Here the later story of Elendil enters (see pp. 122–4), in which Elendil remained in the North, whereas his sons sailed south down the coasts of Middle-earth and brought their ships up the Great River. Elendil's city in the North emerges, afterwards *Annúminas*, but here bearing the names *Tarkilmar* or *Westermanton*: on the western portion of the First Map (pp. 304–5) the Elvish name is *Torfirion*, to which *Tarkilmar* was changed on the present manuscript. In Mordor the valley of *Gorgoroth* appears, the name deriving from the *Ered Orgoroth (Gorgoroth)*, the Mountains of Terror south of Taur-na-Fuin in the Elder Days; and the *Mountains of Shadow* are the first mention of the later-named *Ephel Dúath*, the great chain fencing Mordor on the West and South.

From 'Very mighty was that host' my father returned to and retained the pages of the preceding (fourth) version, pp. 126–8. The result of this combination of the new passage just given with the text of the fourth version was to *repeat the taking of Minas Ithil*. In the original account (pp. 119–20) Elrond told that *after* the war with Sauron 'as the world worsened and decayed Osgiliath fell into ruin', and the servants of Sauron took the eastern city, so that 'it became a place of dread, and was called Minas Morgol'. In the fourth version (pp. 126–7) this was repeated more fully and plainly; and the structure of Elrond's story here can be summarised thus:

– Isildur went to the War of the Last Alliance
– Elrond recalls the mustering of the hosts
– He tells of the war
– Isildur's death; 'he came never back to Minas Ithil, nor did any of his folk return. Only in Minas Anor was the race of Westernesse maintained for a while'
– Despite the victory over Sauron, the world worsened; the Númenóreans decayed and were corrupted, 'Osgiliath fell into ruin; *and evil men took Minas Ithil*, and it became a place of dread, and was called Minas-Morgol'

But in the fifth version the structure of Elrond's story becomes:

– *Sauron captured Minas Ithil*. Thereupon Isildur departed and went north, *and there followed the War of the Last Alliance* (The story returns to the fourth version)
– Elrond recalls the mustering of the hosts (&c. as in the fourth version)

This is the form of the story in the typescript made from the fifth version. It is not clear to me whether my father fully intended this result. As the fifth version stands, Minas Ithil was captured by Sauron *before* the War of the Last Alliance, and indeed its capture was a prime cause of the making of the league; yet it is still said that Isildur 'came never back to Minas Ithil', and it is still told that *long after the war* 'evil men took Minas Ithil'. This is of course perfectly explicable: when Sauron was cast down Minas Ithil was retaken from his servants, and only much later did the 'evil men' repossess it. But one might expect this to have been made explicit; and the impression remains of a 'doubled' account arising from the use of the fourth version material at this point.

However this may be, it is curious that the history of Minas Ithil never was made entirely explicit. In *Of the Rings of Power and the Third Age* nothing is said of its retaking after the war, nor indeed of its history until the time of the great plague that came upon Gondor in the seventeenth century of the Third Age, when 'Minas Ithil was emptied of its people' (*The Silmarillion* p. 296).

Various changes were made to the manuscript, which is common to both fourth and fifth versions, in this part of the chapter (extending as far as 'it has been ordained that you should have it for a while', p. 128). These changes were apparently made at different times; those that were taken up into the typescript (see p. 141) are given here.

Elrond now says that 'It was even at Imladris, here in Rivendell, that they were mustered'. *Ond* becomes *Ondor* (see note 6), and *Minas-Morgol* becomes *Minas-Morghul*. The sentence 'Only in Minas Anor was the race of Westernesse maintained for a while' was cut out, and the following inserted at this point: 'And Anárion was slain in battle in the valley of Gorgoroth' (see p. 127 and note 21). In the 'dream-verse' of Minas Tirith *Imlad-rist* was altered to *Imlad-ris*, and the second half of the verse was changed to read:

> *This sign shall there be then*
> *that Doom is near at hand:*
> *The Halfhigh shall you see then*
> *with Isildur's bane in hand.*

On *Isildur's bane* see pp. 129–30. At every occurrence of *Trotter* or *Aragorn* in this passage, and throughout the manuscript, the name *Elfstone* was written in, and is the name found in the typescript, and *Aragorn son of Kelegorn* becomes *Elfstone son of Elfhelm* (cf. p. 80 note 17, and for discussion of this question see pp. 277–8).

But at Aragorn's words 'it has been ordained that you should have it for a while' the new structure enters, with '"Bring out the Ring, Frodo!" said Gandalf solemnly' (see pp. 129–30), and the text that follows in FR (pp. 260–1) is all but achieved. It is (significantly) not said that 'Boromir's eyes glinted as he gazed at the golden thing'; but Aragorn's explanation to him of the meaning of the 'Sword that was broken' in the 'dream-verse' is as in FR, with his reference to the prophecy that it should be re-made when Isildur's Bane was found, and he ends 'Do you wish for the house of Elendil to return to the land of Ond [> Ondor]?'[7] Bilbo in irritation at Boromir's doubtfulness of Aragorn 'bursts out' with the verse *All that is gold does not glitter*[8]

(" "I made that up for Tarkil [> Elfstone]," he whispered to Frodo with a grin, "when he first told me his long tale" "). But Aragorn's speech to Boromir (cf. pp. 121, 128) is still substantially different from that in FR, and lacks much that he afterwards said.

Aragorn [> Elfstone] smiled; then he turned again to Boromir. 'I do not look the part, truly,' he said; 'and I am but the heir of Elendil, not Elendil himself. I have had a hard life and a long; and the leagues that lie between here and Ond [> Ondor] are a small part in the count of my journeys. I have crossed many mountains, and many rivers, and trodden many plains, even into far regions where the stars are strange. I have been in Minas Tirith unknown,[9] and have walked in Osgiliath by night; and I have passed the gates of Minas-Morgol [> Minas-Morghul]; further have I dared even to the Dark Borders, and beyond. But my home, such as I have, is in the North. For Valandil, Isildur's son, was harboured by the Elves in this region when his father was lost; and he went at last with such of his folk as remained to him, and dwelt in Osforod [> Fornobel],[10] the North Burg. But that is now waste, and the foundations of its walls can scarce be seen beneath the turf.

'Our days have ever waned and darkened through the years, and we are dwindled to a wandering folk, few and secret and sundered, pursued ever by the Enemy. And the sword has never yet been re-forged, for Isildur's Bane was lost. But now it is found and the hour has come. I will return to Minas-Tirith.'

At the end of Aragorn's speech the fourth version of 'The Council of Elrond' ended (p. 129). The fifth version continues:

'And now,' said Elrond, 'the tale of the Ring comes down the years. It fell from Isildur's hand and was lost. And it shall now be told in how strange a manner it was found. Speak Bilbo! And if you have not yet cast your story into verse,' he added with a smile, 'you may tell it in plain words.'

To some of those present Bilbo's tale was new, and they listened with amazement while the old hobbit (not at all displeased) retold the story of his adventure with Gollum, not omitting a single riddle.

Then Gandalf spoke, and told of the White Council that had been held in that same year, and of the efforts that had been made to drive the Necromancer from Mirkwood, and how that had failed to check the growth of his power. For he had taken again his ancient name, and established a dominion over many

men, and had re-entered Mordor. 'It was in that year,' said
Gandalf, 'that rumour first came to us that he was seeking
everywhere for the lost Ring; and we[11] gathered such lore as we
could from far and wide concerning its fashion and properties,
but we never thought that it would be found again to our great
peril.' Gandalf spoke then of the nature and powers of the One
Ring; and how it had at last become clear that the ring of
Gollum was indeed Isildur's Bane, the Ruling Ring.

He told how he had searched for Gollum; and then the story
was taken up first by Galdor [> Legolas] of the Wood-elves,[12]
and in the end by Aragorn [> Elfstone]. For in that chase he had
made a perilous journey following the trail from the deep places
of Mirkwood through Fangorn Forest and the Riddermark,
Rohan the land of Horsemen, and over the Dead Marsh
[> Marshes] to the very borders of the land of Mordor.

'And there I lost the trail,' he said, 'but after a long search I
came upon it again, returning again northwards. It was lurking by
a stagnant pool, upon the edge of the Dead Marsh [> Marshes],
that I caught Gollum; and he was covered with green slime.
I made him walk before me, for I would not touch him; and
I drove him towards Mirkwood. There I gave him over to
Gandalf and to the care of the Elves, and was glad to be rid of
his company, for he stank. But it is as well that he is in
safekeeping. We do not doubt that he has done great harm, and
that from him the Enemy has learned that the Ring is found; but
he might well do further ill. He did not return, I am sure, of his
own will from Mordor, but was sent forth from there to aid in
the design of Sauron.'

'Alas!' said Galdor [> Legolas] interrupting, 'but I have news
that must now be told. It is not good, I fear; but how ill, others
must judge. All that I have heard warns me that you may take it
amiss. Smeagol, who is now called Gollum, has escaped.'

'What!' cried Aragorn [> Elfstone] in angry surprise. 'Then
all my pains are brought to nothing! I judge that to be evil news
indeed. You may mark my words: we shall all rue this bitterly.
How came the Wood-elves to fail in their trust?'

Galdor's story, which was already close (see pp. 118–19) to that in
FR, now moves still closer in detail of expression. Gandalf's rather
resigned comments on Gollum's escape remain as they were; now
however he ends by saying: 'But now it is time that the tale came to
Frodo' (on the sequence here see p. 130). Frodo's story, and Bilbo's
remarks about it, are very much as in FR, where they come in at a

different point, pp. 262–3: here his brief conversation with Bilbo forms the link to Gandalf's story, which is given a heading in the manuscript,

Gandalf's tale

'There are whole chapters of stuff before you ever got here!'

'Yes, it made quite a long tale,' answered Frodo; 'but the story doesn't seem complete to me. I still want to know a good deal.'

'And what question would you ask?' said Elrond, overhearing him.

'I should like to know what happened to Gandalf after he left me, if he is willing to tell me now. But perhaps it has nothing to do with our present business.'

'It has much to do with it,' said Gandalf, 'and if Elrond is willing I will give my account now. At the end of June a cloud of anxiety came upon my mind ...

Gandalf's story in this version is still fairly close to the preliminary draft (pp. 131–5), but the writing is much developed towards the form in FR. A detailed comparison of the three would take a great deal of space, but I notice here all the chief features of difference.

Gandalf now calls Radagast his 'kinsman', not his 'cousin', and his dwelling is named (but by an addition to the manuscript: see p. 164) *Rhosgobel*; he still says that the Nine Wraiths 'have taken the guise of Riders in black, *as of old*' (this was a pencilled addition to the draft, p. 132); he does not name them *Nazgûl*. Gandalf says of the 'fell captain of the Nine' that he was 'a great king of old'; and of Saruman he says:

... For Saruman the White is, as some of you know, the greatest of my craft, and was the leader in the White Council. ... But Saruman long studied the arts of the Enemy, and was thus often able to defeat him; and the lore of rings was one of his chief studies. He knew much of the history [of the rings of power >] of the Nine Rings and the Seven, and somewhat even of the Three and the One; and it was at one time rumoured that he had come near the secret of their making.

Radagast tells Gandalf that 'even if you set out from this spot you will hardly reach him before the Nine have crossed the seventh river' (cf. p. 132). Gandalf's horse, formerly Galeroc, is not now named.

Isengard is still in the Black Mountains, but is now defined as being 'not far from the great vale that lies between them and the last hills of the Misty Mountains, in that region which is known to some as the

Gap of Rohan' (which is here first named); and of Orthanc Gandalf now says that in the midst of the valley of Isengard 'is the tower of stone called Orthanc, for it was made by Saruman, and it is very great, and has many secrets, but it looks not to be a work of craft. It cannot be reached save by passing the circle of Isengard, and in that there is only one gate.' The implication of the word *for* in 'for it was made by Saruman' is that the tower was called *Orthanc* (Old English *orþanc* 'artifice, device, work of craft') because it was such (it was made by Saruman); yet it did not look to be.

Saruman says nothing of Gandalf's having concealed from him 'a matter of greatest import' (FR p. 272); and Gandalf still says as in the draft (p. 133): 'For white may be blended of many colours, but many colours are not white', not 'And he that breaks a thing to find out what it is has left the path of wisdom'.

Saruman's declamatory and visionary speech to Gandalf at this stage may be cited in full:

'He stood up then, and began to declaim as if he were speaking to many: "A new Power has arisen. Against it, there is no hope. With it, there is such hope as we never had before. None can now doubt its victory, which is near at hand. We fought it in vain – and foolishly. We knew much but not enough. We looked always at it from the outside and through a mist of old falsehood and hate; and we did not consider its high and ultimate purpose. We saw not the reasons, but only the things done, and some of those seemed evil; but they were done under necessity. There has been a conspiracy to hinder and frustrate knowledge, wisdom, and government. The Elder Days are gone. The Middle Days are passing. The Younger Days are beginning. The day of the Elves is over. But Our Days are begun! The Power grows, and I shall grow as it grows, until all things are ours. And listen, Gandalf my old friend," he said, coming near and speaking now suddenly in a soft voice. "In the end, I – or *we*, if you will join with me – we may come to control that Power. We can bide our time. We can keep our thoughts in our hearts. There need not be any real change of purpose – only of method. Why not use this new strength? By it we may well accomplish all and more than all that we have striven to do with the help of the weak and foolish. And we shall have time, more time. Of that I can assure you."[13]

'"I have heard this before, but in other places," I said. "I do not wish to hear it again. All that I wish to hear is the choice that I am offered. One half at least is already clear. I am to submit to you and to Sauron, or – what?"

' "To stay here till the end," he said.

' "Till what end?"

' "Till the Power is complete, and the Lord has time to turn to lighter matters: such as the pleasure of devising a fitting end for Gandalf the Grey."

' "There is a chance that I may not prove one of the lighter matters," said I. I am not given to idle boasting; but I came near it then.'

At this point, separate from the text but I think belonging to the same time, my father wrote: 'I don't suppose my fate would have been much different if I had welcomed his advance; but I have no doubt that Saruman will prove a faithless ally; and less doubt that the Dark Lord knows it, well.' This was marked with a query; and it does not appear in the typescript text (see note 16). – Saruman is of course still 'mustering a great force for the service of his new master', as in the draft (p. 134 and note 35).

Frodo's interruption concerning his dream is now given in two forms, marked as alternatives. The first reads:

'I saw you!' said Frodo, 'walking backwards and forwards: the moon shone in your hair.'

Gandalf looked at him in amazement. 'Wake up, Frodo,' he said, 'you are dreaming.'

'I *was* dreaming,' said Frodo. 'Your words suddenly recalled a dream I had. I thought it was only a dream and had forgotten it. I think it was in Bombadil's house. I saw a shadow –'

'That's enough!' laughed Gandalf. 'It was a dream, but a true one, it seems. However, the story is mine, and you need not spoil the telling of it.'

This was rejected in favour of the second version, which begins in the same way and follows with the dialogue preserved in FR (p. 274).

The Eagles of the Misty Mountains are now said by Gandalf to have seen, not 'the Nine Riders going hither and thither in the lands', as in FR, but 'the Nine Riders driving back the men of Minas Tirith'. This goes with the addition to Boromir's speech given on p. 138, note 22, where he speaks of the nine horsemen in black who led the host of Minas Morgol when the crossing of the Anduin was taken. The Eagle who came to Orthanc is still *Gwaewar* (and also *Gwaiwar*), not *Gwaihir*, but he is now called 'swiftest of the Great Eagles', not 'chief of the eagles' as in the draft. In Gandalf's conversation with Gwaewar as they flew from Isengard Rohan was first called *the Horsermark*, changed at once to *the Riddermark*; the men of Rohan are still the *Rohiroth*. Gandalf still makes no reference to his having found 'evil already at work' in Rohan (see p. 136). Aragorn says of the horses of

Rohan that 'in them is a strain that is descended from the days of Elendil', not 'from the Elder Days'; and of the horse that he got in Rohan Gandalf says: 'One at least is saved. He is a grey horse and was named Halbarad,[14] but I have called him [Greyfax *changed at once to*] Shadowfax. Not even the horses of the Nine are so tireless and swift. ....'

When Gandalf came to Crickhollow 'hope left me; till I found Hamilcar Bolger. He was still shaking like a leaf, but he had the wits to rouse all the Brandybucks.' This was changed at the time of writing to the reading of FR (p. 276): 'and I did not wait to gather news, or I might have been comforted.' His thought of Butterbur is expressed thus: ' "Butterbur they call him," thought I; "but he will be plain Bur when I leave him, or nothing at all: I will melt all the butter in him..."' His account of his visit to Bree and his ride to Weathertop, and the siege of him there by the Riders, reached almost the final form (FR p. 277): his defence by fire ('such light and flame cannot have been seen on Weathertop since the war-beacons of old') now at last appears (see p. 56).

Lastly, Gandalf's journey from Weathertop to Rivendell, 'up the Hoarwell and through the Entish lands', took him ten days – 'I was only three days ahead of you at the end of the chase';[15] and he makes no further mention of Shadowfax (in FR he 'sent him back to his master', since he could not ride him on that journey).

At the end of Gandalf's tale there follows:

There was a silence. At last Elrond spoke again. 'This is grave news concerning Saruman,' he said. 'All trust is shaken in these days. But such falls and betrayals, alas! have happened before.[16] Of all the tales the tale of Frodo was most strange to me. I have known few hobbits save Bilbo here; and it seems to me now that he is perhaps not so alone and singular as I had thought. The world has changed much since I was last in the West. The Barrow-wights we knew of by many names;[17] and of the Old Forest, that was once both ancient and very great, many tales have been told; but never before have I heard tell of this strange Bombadil. Is that his only name? I would like to know more of him. Do you know him, Gandalf?'

'I knew *of* him,' answered the wizard. 'Bombadil is one name. He has called himself others, suiting himself to times and tongues. Tom-bombadil's for the Shirefolk; Erion is for Elves, Forn for the dwarves, and many names for men.[18] We have seldom met. I am a rolling-stone and he is a moss-gatherer. There is work for both, but they seldom help one another. It might have been wise to have sought his aid, but I do not think I should have gained much.[19] He is a strange creature, and follows his own counsels – if he has any: chance serves him better.'

'Could we not now send messages to him, and obtain his help?' asked Erestor. 'It seems that he has a power even over the Ring.'

'That is not quite the way of it,' said Gandalf. 'The Ring has no power over him, or for him: it cannot either cheat or serve him. He is his own master. But he has no power *over* it, and he cannot alter the Ring itself, nor break its power over others. And I think that the mastery of Bombadil is seen only on his own ground, from which he has never stepped within my memory.'[20]

The discussion of what to do with the Ring is much developed from the original form (VI.402–3), which had been little changed in the second version; but it remains far from the debate in FR (pp. 279–80). It is still Gandalf, not as in FR Glorfindel, who expounds the ultimate futility of entrusting the Ring to Bombadil, since he could not withstand the assault of the Dark Lord (cf. p. 112); but then follows in the new version:

'In any case,' said Glorfindel, 'his ground is far away; and the Ring has come from his house hither only at great hazard. It would have to pass through far greater peril to return. If the Ring is to be hidden, it is here in Rivendell that we must hide it – if Elrond has the might to withstand the coming of Sauron at the last, when all else is conquered.'

'I have not the might,' said Elrond.

'In that case,' said Glorfindel, 'there are but two things for us to attempt: we may send the Ring West over Sea; or we may destroy it.'[21]

'There is great peril in either course, but more hope in the former,' said Erestor: 'we must send the Ring West. For we cannot, as Gandalf has revealed, destroy it by our own skill; to destroy it we must send it to the Fire. But of all journeys that journey is the most perilous, and leads straight to the jaws of the Enemy.'

'I judge otherwise,' said Glorfindel. 'The peril of the road of flight is now the greater; for my heart tells me that Sauron will expect us to take the western way, when he hears what has befallen. Too often have we fled, and too seldom gone forward against him. As soon as news reached him that any from Rivendell were journeying westwards, he would pursue them swiftly, and he would send before us and destroy the Havens to prevent us. Let us hope, indeed, that he does not assail the Towers and the Havens in any case, so that hereafter the Elves may have no way of escape from the shadows of Middle-earth.'

'Then there are two courses,' said Erestor, 'and both are without hope. Who will read this riddle for us?'

'None here can do so,' said Elrond gravely. 'None can foretell what will betide if we take this road or that, whether good or ill – if that is what is meant. But it is not hard to choose which is now the right road. The Ring must be sent to the Fire. All else is but postponement of our task. In the One Ring is hidden much of the ancient power of Sauron before it was first broken. Even though he himself has not yet regained it, that power still lives [*struck out:* and works for him and towards him]. As long as the Ring remains on land or in the sea, he will not be overcome. He will have hope; and he will grow, and all men will be turned to him; and the fear lest the Ring come into his hand again will weigh on all hearts, and war will·never cease.

'Yet it is even as Glorfindel says: the way of flight is now the more perilous. But on the other road, with speed and care travellers might go far unperceived. I do not say that there is great hope in this course; but there is in other courses less hope, and no lasting good.'

'I do not understand all this,' said Boromir. 'Though Saruman is a traitor, did he not have some glimpse of wisdom? Why should not the Elves and their friends use the Great Ring to defeat the Enemy? And I say that all men will *not* turn to him. The Men of Minas Tirith are valiant and they will *never* submit.'

'*Never* is a long word, Boromir,' replied Elrond.

From this point the conclusion of the chapter remains little changed from the second version, whose pages my father retained here, which is to say that it is little changed from the original text, VI.403 ff. Glóin's reply to Boromir's question about the Rings of the Dwarves now however takes this form (and appears thus in the typescript):

'I do not know,' answered Glóin. 'It was said in secret that Thrór, father of Thráin, father of Thorin who fell in battle, possessed one that had descended from his sires. Some said it was the last. But where it now is no dwarf knows. We think maybe it was taken from him, ere Gandalf found him in the dungeons of the Necromancer long ago, or maybe it was lost in the mines of Moria. We guess that it was partly in hope to find the ring of Thráin that Balin went to Moria. For the messages of Sauron aroused old memories. But it is long since we heard any news: it is unlikely that he found any Ring.'

'It is indeed unlikely,' said Gandalf. 'Those who say that the last ring was taken from Thrór by the Necromancer speak truly.'

This passage was the product of emendation on the manuscript of the second version at different times, and in the result a strange confusion was produced.

In the earliest sketch for 'The Council of Elrond' (VI.398) Glóin said: 'Thráin of old had one that descended from his sires. We do not now know where it is. We think it was taken from him, ere you found him in the dungeons long ago (or maybe it was lost in Moria).' The same is said in the first full form of the chapter (VI.403), where however Glóin's words begin: 'It was said in secret that Thráin (father of Thrór father of Thorin who fell in battle) possessed one that had descended from his sires.' This was a contradiction of the text of *The Hobbit*, where Thrór was the father of Thráin, not his son; but it was repeated in the second version of 'The Council of Elrond' (p. 136 note 5). On this question see the Note at the end of this chapter, pp. 159–60.

In the present text the genealogy is corrected (Thrór – Thráin – Thorin), but it now becomes *Thrór* who was found in the dungeons of the Necromancer, and Gandalf says that the ring was taken there from *Thrór*; whereas in *The Hobbit* it was explicit that Thrór was killed by a goblin in Moria, and his son Thráin was captured by the Necromancer. On the other hand Glóin says here that the Dwarves believe that it was partly in hope to find the ring of *Thráin* that Balin went to Moria.[22]

In the original version of the chapter Elrond had said (VI.404) that 'The Three Rings remain still', and he continued:

'They have conferred great power on the Elves, but they have never yet availed them in their strife with Sauron. For they came from Sauron himself, and can give no skill or knowledge that he did not already possess at their making. And to each race the rings of the Lord bring such powers as each desires and is capable of wielding. The Elves desired not strength of domination or riches, but subtlety of craft and lore, and knowledge of the secrets of the world's being. These things they have gained, yet with sorrow. But they will turn to evil if Sauron regains the Ruling Ring; for then all that the Elves have devised or learned with the power of the rings will become his, as was his purpose.'

This was largely retained in the second version (p. 112), with the difference that Elrond now declared that the Three Rings had been taken over the Sea. In the fifth version he says:

'The Three Rings remain. But of them I am not permitted to speak. Certainly they cannot be used by us. From them the Elvenkings have derived much power, but they have not been used for war, either good or evil. For the Elves desire not strength, or domination, or hoarded wealth, but subtlety of craft and lore...'

and continues as in the second version. Thus, while in the second version the original words 'For they came from Sauron himself' were removed but 'they can give no skill or knowledge that he did not himself already possess at their making' were retained, in this text the latter words are also lost. Yet *Certainly they cannot be used by us* in the new version seems to me to imply that they were made by Sauron; and the argument that I suggested (p. 112) in connection with the second version, that when Boromir says that they were made by Sauron he is not contradicted, holds here with equal force.

There were no further changes of any moment[23] from the original text of the chapter (VI.405–7, scarcely altered in the second version); but the chapter now ends at virtually the same point as in FR ('A nice pickle we have landed ourselves in, Mr. Frodo!'), continuing only with the brief further passage that goes back to the original version (VI.407):

'When must I start, Master Elrond?' asked Frodo.

'First you shall rest and recover full strength,' answered Elrond, guessing his mind. 'Rivendell is a fair place, and we will not send you away until you know it better. And meanwhile we will make plans for your guidance, and do what we can to mislead the Enemy and discover what he is about.'

NOTES

1   Cf. VI.429 (the original text of 'The Ring Goes South'), where Gandalf said that the Mines of Moria 'were made by the Dwarves, of Durin's clan many hundreds of years ago, when elves dwelt in Hollin'.

2   The first occurrence of the name *Erebor*, which in the narrative of LR is not found before Book V, Chapter IX of *The Return of the King*.

3   In the original edition of *The Hobbit* the goblin who slew Thrór in Moria was not named, as he is not in the present passage ('he was slain by an Orc'). In the third edition of 1966 the name *Azog* was introduced (from LR) in Chapter I as that of the slayer of

Thrór, and a footnote was added in Chapter XVII stating that Bolg, leader of the Goblins in the Battle of Five Armies, was the son of Azog.

4   The new passage was written in ink over pencil, but the underlying text, which has been deciphered by Taum Santoski, was little changed. The name *Anduin* was not present, though *Ond* was already *Ondor* (see notes 6 and 7); and the translated name of Elendil's city Tarkilmar was both *Westermanton* and *Aldemanton* (*Alde* probably signifying 'old', sc. 'the "town" of the ancient Men (of the West)').

5   This is the first occurrence of the name *Anduin*, as originally written, in the narrative texts of LR – as they are here presented, but it is not in the over-written pencilled text of the passage (note 4).

6   This is the first occurrence of *Ondor* for *Ond*, and is so written in both pencilled text and ink overlay (note 4).

7   It is curious that here, in a passage of new manuscript, and again a few lines below, the form should have been first written *Ond*, whereas on p. 144 it is *Ondor* (note 6).

8   The verse remains in the latest form that has been given (p. 78).

9   Aragorn had said in the fourth version (p. 128) that he had been in Minas Tirith, but the word 'unknown' here is possibly the first hint of the story of Aragorn's service in Minas Tirith under the name Thorongil (LR Appendix A (I, iv, *The Stewards*), Appendix B (years 2957–80)).

10 *Fornobel* is the name on the First Map (Map II, pp. 304–5).

11 Written above 'we' and probably at once, but struck out: 'Saruman our chief'.

12 It is not clear why Galdor/Legolas should have contributed to the story of Gollum at this point, but cf. 'Ancient History' (VI.320), where Gandalf says 'it was friends of mine who actually tracked him down, *with the help of the Wood-elves*'.

13 Various minor changes (mostly expansions) were made to the manuscript in Saruman's speech, and since these appear in the typescript (p. 141) I have included them in the text. – In speaking of 'more time' Saruman was referring to possession of the Ring. In a later change to the typescript he adds after 'more time': 'longer [> lasting] life'.

14 Afterwards *Halbarad* became the name of the Ranger who bore Aragorn's standard and died in the Battle of the Pelennor Fields.

15 That Gandalf should have taken only ten days from Weathertop to Rivendell does not agree with the dating. He left Weathertop early on 4 October, and if he reached Rivendell three days before Frodo he arrived on the 17th, i.e. just under a fortnight from Weathertop, not ten days. This is in fact what he says in the same passage in FR (p. 278): 'It took me nearly fourteen days from

Weathertop ... I came to Rivendell only three days before the Ring.' But this does not agree with LR Appendix B (nor with the Time-scheme D on p. 14), where he arrived on the 18th, only two days before Frodo.

16   Struck out here: 'Sauron it would seem has gained an ally already faithless to himself; yet I do not doubt that he knows it and laughs'. This is very similar to the sentence doubtfully given to Gandalf on p. 151.

17   In a rejected draft of this passage Elrond goes on: 'There are others elsewhere, wherever the men of Númenor sought dark knowledge under the shadow of death in Middle-earth, and they are akin to the' [Ringwraiths]. Cf. VI.118–20, 401.

18   See p. 125. The reading given is the product of much changing on the manuscript. At first my father wrote: *Yárë's for the Elves, Erion is for Gnomes, Forn for the dwarves*; and names of Bombadil among Men, all struck out, were *Oreald, Orold* (Old English: 'very old'), and *Frumbarn* (Old English: 'first-born'). In FR (p. 278) Bombadil was called *Orald* 'by Northern Men'.

19   This passage in which Gandalf contrasts his nature with Bombadil's entered in the second version, p. 111, replacing the earlier story that Gandalf had visited him as a matter of course. Much further back, however, in an isolated draft for a passage in Gandalf's conversation with Bingo at Rivendell on his first waking (VI.213–14), he spoke of Bombadil in a way not unlike his words here (though his conclusion then was entirely different):

   We have never had much to do with one another up till now. I don't think he quite approves of me somehow. He belongs to a much older generation, and my ways are not his. He keeps himself to himself and does not believe in travel. But I fancy somehow that we shall all need his help in the end – and that he may have to take an interest in things outside his own country.

20   Gandalf's account of Bombadil's power and its limitations goes back almost word for word to the original text of 'The Council of Elrond', VI.402.

21   This speech was first given to Erestor, as in the original version (VI.402). When my father gave it to Glorfindel instead, he followed it at first with the remainder of Erestor's original speech, in which he defined the opposing perils, and ended 'Who can read this riddle for us?' This speech was struck out as soon as written, and in its place Erestor was given the speech that follows in the text ('There is great peril in either course...'), in which he argues that the Ring must be sent to the Grey Havens and thence over the Sea.

22   The following seems a plausible explanation of this strange situation. My father added Glóin's surmise that Balin had hoped

to find the ring of *Thráin* in Moria to the existing (second) version while the statement 'It was said in secret that Thráin, father of Thrór, father of Thorin who fell in battle, possessed one' still stood. Subsequently he added in Gandalf's assurance that the last ring had indeed been taken from the captive dwarf in the dungeons of the Necromancer. Now since according to the story in *The Hobbit* it was the son (Thorin's father) whom Gandalf found in the dungeon, and the son had received the map of the Lonely Mountain from *his* father (Thorin's grandfather), he made it *Thrór* who was captured by the Necromancer – for the erroneous genealogy Thráin – Thrór – Thorin was still present. Finally he realised the error in relation to *The Hobbit*, and roughly changed Glóin's opening words to 'It was said in secret that *Thrór*, father of *Thráin* ... possessed one', without observing the effect on the rest of the passage; and in this form it was handed over to the typist.

In Glóin's story at the beginning of the chapter, p. 142, the correct genealogy is present.

23   A correction to the manuscript which is also found in the typescript as typed altered Elrond's reply to Boromir's question 'What then would happen, if the Ruling Ring were destroyed?' Instead of 'The Elves would not lose what they have already won; but the Three Rings would lose all power thereafter' his answer becomes: 'The Elves would not lose that knowledge which they have already won; but the Three Rings would lose all power thereafter, and many fair things would fade.'

Note on Thrór and Thráin

There is no question that the genealogy as first devised in *The Hobbit* was Thorin Oakenshield – Thrain – Thror (always without accents). At one point, however, Thror and Thrain were reversed in my father's typescript, and this survived into the first proof. Taum Santoski and John Rateliff have minutely examined the proofs and shown conclusively that instead of correcting this one error my father decided to extend Thorin – Thror – Thrain right through the book; but that having done so he then changed all the occurrences back to Thorin – Thrain – Thror. It is hard to believe that this extraordinary concern was unconnected with the words on 'Thror's Map' in *The Hobbit*: 'Here of old was *Thrain* King under the Mountain'; but the solution of this conundrum, if it can be found, belongs with the textual history of *The Hobbit*, and I shall not pursue it further. I mention it, of course, because in early manuscripts of *The Lord of the Rings* the genealogy reverts to Thorin – Thror – Thrain despite the publication of Thorin – Thrain – Thror in *The Hobbit*. The only solution I can propose for this is that having, for whatever reason, hesitated so long between the alternatives, when my father was drafting 'The Council of Elrond' Thorin – Thror – Thrain seemed as 'right' as Thorin – Thrain – Thror, and he did not check it with *The Hobbit*.

Years later, my father remarked in the prefatory note that appeared in the second (1951) edition:

A final note may be added, on a point raised by several students of the lore of the period. On Thror's Map is written *Here of old was Thrain King under the Mountain*; yet Thrain was the son of Thror, the last King under the Mountain before the coming of the dragon. The Map, however, is not in error. Names are often repeated in dynasties, and the genealogies show that a distant ancestor of Thror was referred to, Thrain I, a fugitive from Moria, who first discovered the Lonely Mountain, Erebor, and ruled there for a while, before his people moved on to the remoter mountains of the North.

In the third edition of 1966 the opening of Thorin's story in Chapter I was changed to introduce Thrain I into the text. Until then it had read:

'Long ago in my grandfather's time some dwarves were driven out of the far North, and came with all their wealth and their tools to this Mountain on the map. There they mined and they tunnelled and they made huge halls and great workshops...'

The present text of *The Hobbit* reads here:

'Long ago in my grandfather Thror's time our family was driven out of the far North, and came back with all their wealth and their tools to this Mountain on the map. It had been discovered by my far ancestor, Thrain the Old, but now they mined and they tunnelled and they made huger halls and greater workshops...'

At the same time, in the next sentence, 'my grandfather was King under the Mountain' was changed to 'my grandfather was King under the Mountain again.'

The history of Thráin the First, fugitive from Moria, first King under the Mountain, and discoverer of the Arkenstone, was given in *The Lord of the Rings*, Appendix A (III), *Durin's Folk*; and doubtless the prefatory note in the 1951 edition and the passage in Appendix A were closely related. But this was the product of development in the history of the Dwarves that came in with *The Lord of the Rings* (and indeed the need to explain the words on the map 'Here of old was Thrain King under the Mountain' evidently played a part in that development). When *The Hobbit* was first published it was Thrain son of Thror – the only Thrain at that time conceived of – who discovered the Arkenstone.

VIII

THE RING GOES SOUTH

The intractable problems that had beset *The Lord of the Rings* thus far were now at last resolved. The identity of Trotter had been decisively established, and with the work done in successive versions of 'The Council of Elrond' his place and significance in the history of Middle-earth was already made firm – meagre though that history still was by comparison with the great structure that would afterwards be raised on these foundations. The hobbits were equally secure in number and in name, and the only Bolger who ever roved far afield would rove no more. Bombadil is to play no further part in the history of the Ring. Most intractable of all, the question of what had happened to Gandalf was now conclusively answered; and with that answer had arisen (as it would turn out) a new focal point in the history of the War of the Ring: the Treason of Isengard.

There still remained of older narrative writing the journey of the Company of the Ring from Rivendell to the Red Pass beneath Caradras, and the passage of the Mines of Moria as far as Balin's tomb. One major question remained, however, and a final decision must imperatively be made: who were the members of the Company to be?

Notes and drafts written on the 'August 1940' examination script show my father pondering this further. One manuscript page reads as follows:

Chapter XV. Cut out converse in garden.[1]
Begin by saying hobbits were displeased with Sam.
Tell them of the scouts going out.
Elrond then says *union of forces* is impossible. We cannot send or
  summon great force to aid Frodo. We must send out messages to
  all free folk to resist as long as possible, and that a new hope,
  though faint, is born. But with Frodo must go helpers, and they
  should represent all the Free Folk. Nine should be the number to
  set against the Nine Evil Servants. But we should support the war
  in Minas Tirith.
  Galdor Legolas[2]

Hobbits	{ Frodo	1
	{ Sam (promised)	2
Wizard	Gandalf	3

| Elf | Legolas | 4 |
| Half-elf | Erestor | 5 |

The road *should go to Minas Tirith*, therefore so far at least should go:

Men	{ Aragorn	6
	{ Boromir	7
Dwarf	Gimli son of Glóin	8

Merry, Pippin. They insist on going. [*Struck out:* Pippin only if Erestor does not go.] Elrond says there may be work in the Shire, and it may prove ill if they all go.
Shall Pippin return to the Shire?
Then come preparations, and the scene with Bilbo and Frodo and giving of Sting &c.

Here the number of Nine members of the Company, expressly corresponding to the Nine Ringwraiths, is reached;[3] but even so there remains a doubt as to its composition where the hobbits are concerned (see p. 115), and my father's lingering feeling that one at least should return to the Shire at this stage was still a factor, especially since the inclusion of Erestor 'Half-elf'[4] took the number to eight. But this was the last moment of indecision. A short draft, written hastily in ink on the same paper, introduces the final complement of the Company of the Ring. On it my father pencilled: 'Sketch of reduction of the choosing of the Company'.[5]

In the end after the matter had been much debated by Elrond and Gandalf it was decided that the Nine of the Company of the Ring should be the four hobbits, aided by Gandalf; and that Legolas should represent the Elves, and Gimli son of Glóin the Dwarves. On behalf of Men Aragorn should go, and Boromir. For they were going to Minas Tirith, and Aragorn counselled that the Company should go that way, and even maybe go first to that city. Elrond was reluctant to send Merry and Pippin, but Gandalf [?supported].

My father now proceeded to a new text of 'The Ring Goes South'; and of preliminary work nothing survives, if any existed, apart from a few passages in rough drafting from the beginning of the chapter. The new version is a good clear manuscript in ink, using in part the 'August 1940' script that had been used for the drafting of major developments in 'The Council of Elrond'. The story now advanced confidently, and for long stretches scarcely differs from that in FR in the actual wording of the narrative and the speeches of the characters. There are a number of later emendations, a good many of which can be shown to come from a little later in the same period of composition. As written, the chapter had no title, various possibilities being pencilled in afterwards: although in the original text, when the chapter was continuous with 'The Council of Elrond', there was a sub-heading

'The Ring Goes South' (VI.415), my father now tried also 'The Company of the Ring Departs' and 'The Ring Sets Out'.

Since the previous chapter now ended where it ends in FR, at the conclusion of the Council, the ensuing conversation among the hobbits, interrupted by Gandalf, was moved to the beginning of 'The Ring Goes South'. My father now took up his direction to 'cut out converse in garden' (see note 1), and the chapter begins exactly as in FR, with the hobbits talking in Bilbo's room later on the same day, and Gandalf looking in through the window. The new conversation almost reaches the form in FR (pp. 285–7), and only the following differences need be mentioned. Gandalf speaks of 'the Elves of Mirkwood', not of 'Thranduil's folk in Mirkwood', and he does not say that 'Aragorn has gone with Elrond's sons' (who had not yet emerged); and Bilbo's remarks about the season of their departure were first written:

> '... you can't wait now till Spring, and you can't go till the scouts come back. So off you go nice and comfortable just when winter's beginning to bite.'
> 'Quite in the Gandalf manner,' said Pippin.
> 'Exactly,' said Gandalf.

This was replaced at once by Bilbo's verse (*When winter first begins to bite*) that he speaks here in FR. Lastly, Gandalf says: 'In this matter Elrond will have [the decision >] much to say, and your friend Trotter, Aragorn the tarkil, too' (FR: 'and your friend the Strider').

While still writing the opening of the chapter, my father hesitated about the structure. One possibility seems to have been to keep the new conversation in Bilbo's room but to put it back into the end of 'The Council of Elrond', ending at Sam's remark 'And where will they live? That's what I often wonder'; another, to cut out the conversation among the hobbits, and Gandalf's intervention at the window, almost in its entirety. He went so far as to provide a brief substitute passage; but decided against it.[6]

The chronology in FR, according to which the Company stayed more than two months in Rivendell and left on 25 December, had not yet entered. In the second version of 'The Council of Elrond', which continued for some distance into the narrative of 'The Ring Goes South', 'the hobbits had been some three weeks in the house of Elrond, and November was passing' when the scouts began to return; and at the Choosing of the Company the date of departure was settled for 'the following Thursday, November the seventeenth' (pp. 113, 115).[7] In the new text the same was said ('some three weeks ... November was passing'), but this was changed, probably at once, to 'The hobbits had been nearly a month in the house of Elrond, and November was half over, when the scouts began to return'; and subsequently (as in FR p. 290) Elrond says: 'In seven days the Company must depart.' No actual date for the leaving of Rivendell is now mentioned, but it had been postponed to nearer the end of the month (actually to 24 November, see p. 169).

The account of the journeys of the scouts moves on from the previous versions (VI.415–16 and VII.113–14), and largely attains the text in FR, apart from there being, as at the beginning of the chapter, no mention of Aragorn's having left Rivendell, nor of the sons of Elrond. Those scouts who went north had gone 'beyond the Hoarwell into the Entishlands', and those who went west had 'searched the lands far down the Greyflood, as far as Tharbad where the old North Road crossed the river by the ruined town'. This is where *Tharbad* first appears.[8] Those who had climbed the pass at the sources of the Gladden[9] had 'reached the old home of Radagast at Rhosgobel': this is where *Rhosgobel* is first named, and in the margin my father wrote 'Brownhay'.[10]

These last 'had returned up the Redway[11] and over the high pass that was called the Dimrill Stair'. The name 'Dimrill Stair' for the pass beneath Caradras has appeared in later emendations to the original version of 'The Ring Goes South' (VI.433–4, notes 14 and 21). In the present passage the name was not emended at any stage; but further on in the chapter, where in this text Gandalf says 'If we climb *the pass that is called the Dimrill Stair* ... we shall come down into the deep dale of the Dwarves', my father (much later) emended the manuscript to the reading of FR (p. 296): 'If we climb *the pass that is called the Redhorn Gate* ... we shall come down *by the Dimrill Stair* into the deep vale of the Dwarves' (and thus Robert Foster, in *The Complete Guide to Middle-earth*, defines *Dimrill Stair* as 'Path leading from Azanulbizar to the Redhorn Pass'). The name of the pass (called in this text the 'Dimrill Pass' as well as the 'Dimrill Stair') was changed also at other occurrences in this chapter, but at this place my father having missed it in the manuscript it was retained in the typescript that soon followed (note 6), and so survived into FR, p. 287: 'over the high pass that was called the Dimrill Stair' – an error that was never picked up.

The Choosing of the Company is found in this manuscript in two alternative versions. Though the essential content is the same in both, and both end with the inclusion of Merry and Pippin after Gandalf's advocacy, the one written first is rather nearer to the preceding version (pp. 113–15): the chief difference between them being that in the first the formation of the Company is seen as it takes place, whereas in the second (which is almost identical to the form in FR) the deliberations have been largely completed and Elrond announces the decision to the hobbits.[12]

There are several differences worth noticing in the first of these versions. After Gandalf's remark that his fate 'seems much entangled with hobbits' Elrond says: 'You will be needed many times before the journey's end, Gandalf; but maybe when there is most need you will

not be there. This is your greatest peril, and I shall not have peace till I
see you again.' The loss of Gandalf was of course foreseen (VI.443,
462). Aragorn, after saying to Frodo that since he himself is going to
Minas Tirith their roads lie together for many hundreds of leagues,
adds: 'Indeed it is my counsel that you should go first to that city'. And
after saying that for the two unfilled places needed to make nine he
may be able to find some 'of my own kindred and household' Elrond
continues (but the passage was at once deleted): 'The elf-lords I may
not send, for though their power is great it is not great enough. They
cannot walk unhidden from wrath and spirit of evil, and news of the
Company would reach Mordor by day or night.'

In these passages, and throughout the rest of the chapter (in
intention), *Aragorn* was again changed to *Elfstone*, and *son of
Kelegorn* to *son of Elfhelm* (see pp. 277–8), as also was *Trotter*,
except where he is directly addressed thus by one of the hobbits.

The reforging of the Sword of Elendil now enters, and the description of it is at once precisely as in FR (p. 290), with the 'device of seven
stars set between the crescent moon and the rayed sun', save that the
reforged sword is given no name. This was added in somewhat later:
'And Elfstone gave it a new name and called it *Branding*' (see p. 274
and note 19).

For the next part of the chapter (Bilbo and Frodo during the last
days at Rivendell) my father simply took over the actual manuscript
pages of the second version of 'The Council of Elrond', from 'The
weather had grown cold ... ' (p. 115); this passage was already close
to the form in FR.[13] After 'I should like to write the second book, if I
am spared' (which is where the second version of 'The Council of
Elrond' ended) my father wrote on the manuscript 'Verses?', but
Bilbo's song *I sit beside the fire and think* is not found in this
manuscript. The original workings for the song are extant, however,
and certainly belong to this time.[14]

The day of departure was 'a cold grey day near the end of
November' (see p. 164). At first there were two ponies, as in the
original version (VI.416), but 'Bill' bought in Bree, and greatly
invigorated by his stay in Rivendell, was substituted as my father
wrote.[15] The departure was at this time much more briefly treated
than it is in FR: there is no blowing of Boromir's war-horn, no account
of the arms borne by each member of the Company or of the clothing
provided by Elrond, and no mention of Sam's checking through his
belongings – so that the important minor element of his discovery that
he has no rope is absent (cf. pp. 183, 280).

The story of the journey from Rivendell to Hollin is now very close
to FR, but there are differences in geography and geographical names,
which were evolving as the new version progressed. The journey had
still taken 'some ten days' to the point where the weather changed
(VI.418), whereas in FR it took a fortnight; and there was only one

great peak, not three. An Elvish name for Hollin: '*Nan-eregdos* in the elfspeech' was added, apparently at the time of writing.[16] Gandalf estimates that they have come 'fifty leagues as the crow flies' ('five-and-forty leagues as the crow flies' FR, 'eighty leagues' in the original version). And where in the first version, in reply to the observation of Faramond (Pippin) that since the mountains are ahead they must have turned east, Gandalf said 'No, it is the mountains that have turned', he now replies, 'No, it is the mountains that have bent west' (FR: 'Beyond those peaks the range bends round south-west'). On this difficult question of geography see VI.440–1.

Gimli's speech about the Mountains is present, almost word for word as in FR, except that the three peaks not yet being devised his words 'we have wrought the image of those mountains into many works of metal and of stone, and into many songs and tales' seem to have a more general bearing. But he continues (as in FR): 'Only once before have I seen them from afar in waking life, but I know them and their names, for under them lies Khazad-dûm, the Dwarrowdelf, that is now called the Black [Gulf >] Pit,[17] Moria in the elvish tongue', and it seems that he is here speaking of certain notable and outstanding peaks, distinctive in the chain of the Misty Mountains, beneath which lay Moria. (The three great Mountains of Moria were in any case just about to enter, in Gimli's next speech.) Here he says, as in FR, 'Yonder stands Barazinbar, the Redhorn, cruel Caradhras', 'cruel' being altered at the moment of writing from 'the windy', and that from 'the tall', as also was *Caradhras* from *Caradras*.[18] And he speaks also of 'Azanul-bizâr, the Dimrill-dale that elves call Nanduhirion'.[19]

Gandalf's reply, and Gimli's further words about the Mirrormere, are a difficult complex of rapid changes in the manuscript, when new elements are seen at the moment of emergence. With some slight doubt as to the precise sequence of correction, the passage seems to have developed thus:

'It is for Dimrill-dale that we are making,' said Gandalf. 'If we climb the pass that is called the Dimrill Stair under the red side of Caradhras, we shall come down into the deep dale of the Dwarves.[20] There the River [Redway rises in the black wat(er) Morthond Blackroot >] Morthond the cold rises in the Mirror-mere.'

'Dark is the water of Kheledzâram,' said Gimli, 'and mirrors only the far sky and three white peaks; and cold is the water of Buzundush. My heart trembles at the thought that I may see them soon.'

Obviously, it was as my father began to write the words he intended: 'the River Redway rises in the black wat[er of the Mirrormere]' that he changed the name of the river to *Morthond*, 'Blackroot'; and I think that it was here also that the three peaks above Moria entered, mirrored in the water.[21] He then wrote a new passage, no doubt intended to supersede part of that just given, but struck it out, probably immediately:

There lies Kheledzâram, the Mirror-mere, deep and dark, in which can be seen only the far sky and three white peaks. From it issues Buzundush, the Blackroot River, Morthond cold and swift. My heart trembles at the thought that I may see them soon.'[22]

Gandalf replying said: '... we at least cannot stay in that valley. We must go down the Morthond into the woods of Lothlórien...' (FR: 'into the secret woods'). This is where, as it seems, the name *Lothlórien* first appears. And when Merry asked: 'Yes, and where then?' the wizard answered: 'To the end of the journey – in the end. It may be that you will pass through Fangorn, which some call the Topless Forest. But we must not look too far ahead. ...' The reference to Fangorn was deleted.

Several versions of Legolas' words about the forgotten Elves of Hollin were written before the final form was achieved: the first reads:

'That is true,' said Legolas. 'But the Elves of this land were of a strange race, and the spirit that dwells here is alien to me, who am of the woodland folk. Here dwelt Noldor, the Elven-wise, and all the stones about cry to me with many voices: they built high towers to heaven, and delved deep to earth, and they are gone. They are gone. They sought the Havens long ago.'

The story of the great silence over all the land of Hollin, the flights of black crows, Pippin's disappointment at the news and Sam's failure to comprehend the geography, the mysterious passage of something against the stars, and the sight of Caradhras close before them on the third morning from Hollin, all this is told in words that remained virtually unchanged in FR, save for a few details. Trotter says that the crows are 'not natives to this place', but does not add that 'they are *crebain* out of Fangorn and Dunland'; and after saying that he has glimpsed many hawks flying high up, he says 'That would account for the silence of all the birds', this being struck out immediately (see VI.420 and note 17). Sam calls Caradhras 'this Ruddyhorn, or whatever its name is', as he did in the original version (VI.421), but *Ruddyhorn* was then to be its accepted English name (VI.419 and note 11).

As the Company walked on the ancient road from Hollin to the Pass, the moon rose over the mountains 'almost at the full'; as in the original version it is said that the light was unwelcome to Trotter and

Gandalf, and 'they were relieved when at last late in the night the moon set and left them to the stars'. In the original text it was a crescent moon (VI.421 and note 19), and 'it stayed but a little while'; in FR the moon was full, and still low in the western sky when the shadow passed across the stars.

In the original version it was Trotter who favoured the passage of Moria, Gandalf who favoured the Pass, and what they said was coloured by their opinions. This was still the case when my father came to the new version, although what is said is virtually what is said in FR (p. 300):

'Winter is behind,' [Gandalf] said quietly to Trotter. 'The peaks away north are whiter than they were; snow is lying far down their shoulders.'

'And tonight,' said Trotter, 'we shall be on our way high up the Dimrill Stair. If we are not seen by watchers on that narrow path, and waylaid by some evil, the weather may prove as deadly an enemy as any. What do you think of our course now?'

Frodo overheard these words [&c. as in FR]

'I think no good of any part of our course from beginning to end, as you know well, Aragorn', answered Gandalf, his tone sharpened by anxiety. 'But we must go on. It is no good our delaying the passage of the mountains. Further south there are no passes, till one comes to the Gap of Rohan. I do not trust that way, since the fall of Saruman. Who knows which side now the marshals of the Horse-lords serve?'

'Who knows indeed!' said Trotter. 'But there is another way, and not by the pass beneath Caradhras: the dark and secret way that we have spoken of.'

'And I will not speak of it again. Not yet. Say nothing to the others, I beg. Nor you, Frodo,' said Gandalf, turning suddenly towards him. 'You have listened to our words, as is your right as Ring-bearer. But I will not say any more until it is plain that there is no other course.'

'We must decide before we go further,' said Gandalf.

'Then let us weigh the matter in our minds, while the others rest and sleep,' answered Trotter.

Since the speakers of the last two speeches are out of order with the preceding conversation, it was at this point that my father 'realised' that it was Trotter and not Gandalf who especially feared Moria, and at once changed the text of the passage accordingly.

Gandalf's words to the Company at the end of his discussion with Trotter, and the whole account of the snowstorm, are very much as in

FR (pp. 300–2), though in the latter part of this chapter the actual wording underwent more development later to reach the FR text than had been the case till now. Boromir says that he was born in the Black Mountains (see VI.436, note 31); and the reference to Bilbo alone of hobbits remembering the Fell Winter of the year 1311 is absent. Another use of names from the legends of the Elder Days, immediately rejected, appears in Boromir's words about the snowstorm: 'I wonder if the Enemy has anything to do with it? They say in my land that he can govern the storms in [*struck out:* Mountains of Shadow Daedeloth Deldúath] the Mountains of Shadow that lie on the confines of Mordor.'[23]

In Frodo's dream, as he fell into a snow-sleep, Bilbo's voice said: *Snowstorm on December the ninth* (in the original version 2 December, VI.424; in FR 12 January). The journey from Rivendell to Hollin had taken 'some ten days' (p. 165); and a chronological scheme that seems clearly to derive from this time and to fit this narrative gives the date of departure from Rivendell as the evening of Thursday 24 November. According to this scheme the Company reached Hollin on 6 December, the journey from Rivendell having thus taken eleven days (and twelve nights), and 'Snow on Caradras' is dated 9 December.

The liquor that Gandalf gives to the Company from his flask is still called 'one of Elrond's cordials', as in VI.424, and the name *miruvor* does not appear. Gandalf, as the flame sprang up from the wood, said: 'I have written *Gandalf is here* in signs that even the blind rocks could read', but he does not say, as he thrusts his staff into the faggot, *naur an edraith ammen!*[24]

The account of the descent remains distinctively different from the story in FR, and closer to the original (VI.426–7), despite the fact that Trotter was there still a hobbit, and Gimli and Legolas not present.

'The sooner we make a move and get down again the better,' said Gandalf. 'There is more snow still to come up here.'

Much as they all desired to get down again, it was easier said than done. Beyond their refuge the snow was already some feet deep, and in places was piled into great wind-drifts; and it was wet and soft. Gandalf could only get forward with great labour, and had only gone a few yards on the downward path when he was floundering in snow above his waist. Their plight looked desperate.

Boromir was the tallest of the Company, being above six feet and very broad-shouldered as well. 'I am going on down, if I can,' he said. 'As far as I can make out our course of last night, the path turns right round that shoulder of rock down there. And if I remember rightly, a furlong or so beyond the turn there was a flat space at the top of a long steep slope – very heavy going it was as we came up. From that point I might be able to get a view, and some idea of how the snow lies further down.'

He struggled slowly forward, plunging in snow that was everywhere above his knees, and in places rose almost shoulder-high. Often he seemed to be swimming or burrowing with his great arms rather than walking. At last he vanished from sight and passed round the turn. He was long gone, and they began to be anxious, fearing that he had been engulfed in some drift or snow-filled hollow, or had fallen over the hidden brink into the ravine.

When more than an hour had passed they heard him call. He had reappeared round the bend in the path and was labouring back towards them, 'I am weary,' he said; 'but I have brought back some hope. There is a deep wind-drift just round the turn, and I was nearly buried in it, but fortunately it is not wide. Beyond it the snow suddenly gets less. At the top of the slope it is barely a foot deep, and further down, white though it looks, it seems to be but a light coverlet: only a sprinkling in places.'

'It is the ill will of Caradras,' muttered Gimli. 'He does not love dwarves, or elves. He has cast his snow at us with special intent. That drift was devised to cut off our descent.'

'Then Caradras happily has forgotten that we have with us a mountaineer who knows his far kindred, the peaks of the Black Mountains,' said Gandalf. 'It was a good fortune that gave us Boromir as a member of our Company.'

'But how are *we* to get through this drift, even if we ever get as far as the turn?' asked Pippin, voicing the thoughts of all the hobbits.

'It is a pity,' said Legolas, 'that Gandalf cannot go before us with a bright flame, and melt us a path.'

'It is a pity that Elves cannot fly over mountains, and fetch the Sun to save them,' answered Gandalf. 'Even I need something to work on. I cannot burn snow. But I could turn Legolas into a flaming torch, if that will serve: he would burn bright while he lasted.'

'Spare me!' cried Legolas. 'I fear that a dragon is concealed in the shape of our wizard. Yet a tame dragon would be useful at this hour.'

'It will be a wild dragon, if you say any more,' said Gandalf.

'Well, well! *When heads are at a loss, bodies must serve*, as they say in my country,' said Boromir. 'I have some strength still left; and so has Aragorn. We must use that, while it lasts. I will carry one of the Little Folk, and he another. Two shall be set on the pony, and led by Gandalf.'

At once he set about unlading Bill. 'Aragorn and I will come back when we have got the Little Folk through,' he said. 'You, Legolas and Gimli, can wait here, or follow behind in our track, if you can.' He picked up Merry and set him on his shoulders. Trotter took Pippin. Frodo was mounted on the pony, with Sam clinging behind. They ploughed forward.

At last they reached and passed the turn, and came to the edge of the drift. Frodo marvelled at the strength of Boromir, seeing the passage that he had already forced through it with no better tool than his sword and his great arms.[25] Even now, burdened as he was with Merry clinging on his back, he was thrusting the snow forward and aside, and widening the passage for those who followed. Behind him Trotter was labouring. They were in the midst of the drift, and Boromir and Merry were almost through, when a rumbling stone fell from the slope above and, hurtling close to Frodo's head, thudded deep into the snow. But with the casting of that last stone the malice of the mountain seemed to be expended, as if it were satisfied that the invaders were in retreat and would not dare to return. There was no further mishap.

On the flat shelf above the steep slope they found, as Boromir had reported, that the snow was only shallow. There they waited, while Trotter and Boromir returned with the pony to fetch the packs and burdens and give some help to Legolas and the dwarf.

By the time they were all gathered together again morning was far advanced.

It was Gandalf's reply here ('It is a pity that Elves cannot fly over mountains, and fetch the Sun to save them') to Legolas' remark (originally Boromir's, VI.426) about melting a path that led to Legolas' saying in FR 'I go to find the Sun!', and was very probably (as I think) the source of the idea that the Elf, so far from being as helplessly marooned as Gimli, Gandalf, and the hobbits, could run upon the snow. It is noticeable that Gandalf's real ill-humour in the original version is here diminished, while in FR it has probably disappeared.

The remainder of the chapter is as in FR, but it ends thus:

The wind was blowing stiffly again over the pass that was hidden in cloud behind them; already a few flakes of snow were curling and drifting down. Caradras had defeated them. They turned their backs on the Dimrill Stair, and stumbled wearily down the slope.

NOTES

1 This refers to the story, first appearing in the original version of 'The Council of Elrond' (VI.407) and retained in the second (p. 112), that Gandalf came upon the hobbits walking in the woods in the afternoon following the Council.

2 This is probably the point at which my father determined on the change of *Galdor* to *Legolas* (see p. 141). Legolas Greenleaf the keen-eyed thus reappears after many years from the old tale of *The Fall of Gondolin* (II.189, etc.); he was of the House of the Tree in Gondolin, of which Galdor was the lord.

3 In fact, nine had been the original number, in the first sketch for 'The Council of Elrond' (VI.397): Frodo, Sam; Gandalf; Glorfindel; Trotter; Burin son of Balin; Merry, Folco, Odo. It is curious to see how close in its conception the complement of the Company was at the very beginning to the final form, though it was at once rejected.

4 On Erestor 'Half-elf' see VI.400 and note 17.

5 The word 'reduction' may however imply that the first of two alternative versions of the final 'Choosing of the Company' had already been written; see note 12.

6 This latter option survived into a typescript text made not long after (probably by myself), where the long and short openings of the chapter are set out one after the other as variants.

7 On the days of the week in relation to the dates see p. 14. Frodo's escape over the Ford of Bruinen took place on Thursday 20 October. If precisely three weeks are counted from that day we are brought to Thursday 10 November.

8 *Tharbad*: see the *Etymologies*, V.392, stem THAR; and see Map II on p. 305.

9 In the original form of the passage (VI.416) and in that in the second version of 'The Council of Elrond', as well as in the present text, my father wrote 'the *sources* of the Gladden'. This was obviously based on the Map of Wilderland in *The Hobbit*, where the Gladden, there of course unnamed, rises in several streams falling from the Misty Mountains (these are not shown on the First Map (Map II, p. 305), but the scale there is much smaller). In the typescript that followed the present text the typist put *source*, and my father corrected it to *sources*. I suspect therefore that *source* in FR is an error.

10 *Rhosgobel* has appeared previously, but as a subsequent addition

to the fifth version of 'The Council of Elrond' (p. 149); the present passage is clearly where the name was devised. In *Brownhay* 'Brown' is evidently to be associated with Radagast 'the Brown', and 'hay' is the old word meaning 'hedge', as in the *High Hay, Ringhay* (= Crickhollow, VI.299). For the etymology of *Rhosgobel* see V.385, Noldorin *rhosc* 'brown' (stem RUSKĀ), and V.380, Noldorin *gobel* 'fenced homestead', as in *Tavrobel* (stem PEL(ES)).

11 *Redway*: original name of the Silverlode.

12 The brief account of the 'Choosing' given on p. 162 may be compared: 'In the end *after the matter had been much debated by Elrond and Gandalf* it was decided ... ' It is possible that this text followed the first and preceded the second of the alternative versions: my father referred to the second as the 'short version' (though it is not markedly shorter than the other), which may explain why he noted on the brief draft text that it was a sketch of a 'reduction' of the choosing of the Company. – As with the variant openings of the chapter (note 6) both alternatives were retained in the typescript.

13 A few minor changes were introduced (but not the mention of the lay of Beren and Lúthien heard by the hobbits in the Hall of Fire); Bilbo now refers to the fact that Frodo's sword had been broken (see p. 136, note 7), but does not produce the pieces (and the mailcoat remains 'elf-mail', not 'dwarf-mail').

14 In these workings the last verse (for which there is a preparatory note: 'He ends: but all the while he will think of Frodo') reads:

> *But all the while I sit and think*
> > *I listen for the door,*
> *and hope to hear the voices come*
> > *I used to hear before.*

This is the form of the verse in the typescript text, where the song first appears in the chapter.

15 A halfway stage is found in a draft for the passage: here there were still two pack-ponies, but one of them was the beast bought in Bree; this Sam addresses as 'Ferny', though it is also called 'Bill'. Cf. the note about Bill Ferny's pony given on p. 9: 'Does this remain at Rivendell? – Yes.'

16 *Eregion* was written in subsequently (this name appears in the isolated text given on p. 124). No Elvish name is given in the typescript.

17 This is the first occurrence of the name *Dwarrowdelf*. Cf. my father's letter to Stanley Unwin, 15 October 1937 (*Letters* no. 17): 'The real "historical" plural of *dwarf* ... is *dwarrows*, anyway: rather a nice word, but a bit too archaic. Still I rather wish I had used the word *dwarrow*.' – 'Black Gulf' as a translation of *Moria* is found several times in the original text of

'The Ring Goes South', once as a correction of 'Black Pit' (VI.435, note 24).

18   This is the first occurrence of the Dwarvish name *Barazinbar*, concerning which my father wrote long after (in the notes referred to in VI.466, notes 36, 39) that Khuzdul *baraz* (BRZ) probably = 'red, or ruddy', and *inbar* (MBR) a horn, Sindarin *Caradhras* < *caran-rass* being a translation of the Dwarvish name. – Subsequently both *Caradhras* and *Caradras* occur as the manuscript was originally written, but the latter far more frequently.

19   On *Azanulbizâr* see VI.465, note 36. *Nanduhirion* here first occurs, but the form *Nanduhiriath* is found as an emendation to the text of the original version of the chapter, VI.433, note 13.

20   On *Dimrill Stair* as the name of the Redhorn Pass see p. 164.

21   The names of the other Mountains of Moria were not devised at once, however, since though entered on the manuscript they are still absent from the typescript, where my father inserted them in the same form. As first devised, the names of the other peaks were *Silverhorn, Celebras (Kelebras) the White* (in FR *Silvertine, Celebdil*), and *the Horn of Cloud, Fanuiras the Grey* (in FR *Cloudyhead, Fanuidhol*); the Dwarvish names were as in FR, *Baraz, Zirak, Shathûr* (but *Zirak* was momentarily *Zirik*). In the later notes referred to in note 18 my father said that since *Shathûr* was the basic Dwarvish name the element probably refers to 'cloud', and was probably a plural 'clouds'; *Bund(u)* in the fuller name *Bundu-shathûr* 'must therefore mean "head" or something similar. Possibly *bund* (BND) – *u* – *Shathûr* "head in/of clouds".' On *Zirak* and the longer form *Zirakzigil* see note 22.

22   When *Silverlode* superseded *Blackroot*, as it did before the original text of the 'Lothlórien' story was completed, the passage was changed to its form in FR: ' "Dark is the water of Kheledzâram," said Gimli, "and cold are the springs of Kibil-nâla." ' The name *Kheledzâram* first appears in these variant passages; see VI.466, note 39, where I cited my father's much later note explaining the name as meaning 'glass-pool'. In the same notes he discussed the Dwarvish word for 'silver':

> *Zirak-zigil* should mean 'Silver-spike' (cf. 'Silvertine', and *Celebdil* < Sindarin *celeb* 'silver' + *till* 'tine, spike, point'). But 'silver' is evidently KBL in *Kibil-nâla* – KBL seems to have some connexion with Quenya *telep-* 'silver'. But all these peoples seem to have possessed various words for the precious metals, some referring to the material and its properties, some to their colour and other associations. So that *zirak* (ZRK) is probably another name for 'silver', or for its grey colour. *Zigil* is evidently a word for 'spike' (smaller and more slender than a 'horn'). Caradhras seems to have been a great mountain

tapering upwards (like the Matterhorn), while Celebdil was simply crowned by a smaller pinnacle.

Still later pencilled notes reversed this explanation, suggesting that *zigil* (ZGL) meant 'silver' and *zirak* meant 'spike'. – Of *Kibil-nâla* my father noted that 'the meaning of *nâla* is not known. If it corresponds to *rant* [in *Celebrant*] and *lode* [in *Silverlode*], it should mean "path, course, rivercourse or bed".' He added later: 'It is probable that the Dwarves actually found silver in the river.'

23 *Deldúath*: 'Deadly Nightshade', Taur-na-Fuin; *Dor-Daedeloth*: 'Land of the Shadow of Dread', the realm of Morgoth. See references in the Index to Vol. V, entries *Deldúwath*, *Dor-Daideloth*.

24 Literally: 'fire be for saving of us'.

25 The passage that follows here must have been rejected as soon as written:

As he stepped forward Boromir suddenly stumbled on some hidden point of stone, and fell headlong. Trotter, who was just behind, was taken unawares and fell on top of him. Merry and Pippin were flung from their shoulders and vanished deep into the snow.

This, though changed to suit the altered story of the descent, was derived from the old version, VI.427.

IX

THE MINES OF MORIA (1):
THE LORD OF MORIA

It seems very probable, if not actually demonstrable, that a new version of the first part of the Moria story (corresponding to FR II Chapter 4, 'A Journey in the Dark') preceded the first draft of its continuation, and I therefore give the texts in their narrative sequence. The original draft of 'The Mines of Moria' (VI.445–60) had come to an end as the Company stood before the tomb of Balin, and at this time the narrative of *The Lord of the Rings* went no further – apart from a preliminary sketch of the further events in Moria, VI.442–3 and 462. This therefore is the last chapter for which formed narrative from an earlier phase of work existed.

In a manuscript that bears a distinct resemblance in style to that of the new version of 'The Ring Goes South' described in the last chapter, my father now rewrote the first part of the story of the journey through the Mines. As in the last chapter, there are a few pages of rough initial drafting for particular passages, but (unless more have been lost) the development of the new version was very largely achieved in the actual writing of this manuscript, which is a mass of (mostly small) corrections made at the time of composition. Of subsequent pencilled emendation there is not a great deal, for the text of FR II.4 was effectively reached here: for most of its length the only differences from the final form are extremely minor points of sentence structure and choice of words, with no significance for the narrative, and for substantial stretches the two texts are identical. There are however certain features where this is not the case.

The chapter, numbered XVI, was given a title, 'The Mines of Moria (i)'. Pencilled titles were written in beside this: 'The Lord of Moria' and 'The Tomb'; the latter was struck through, and the typescript that followed this manuscript was titled: 'The Mines of Moria (1): The Lord of Moria'. The original version had included the debate of the Company after the descent from the Pass of Cris-caron and the discussion of Moria in 'The Ring Goes South' (VI.428–30), and 'The Mines of Moria' had begun at 'Next day the weather changed again' (VI.445; FR p. 313). Now, of course, the new chapter XVI follows on from the end of the new chapter XV, and the division is as in FR.

Aragorn is called *Trotter* throughout, and throughout *Trotter* was changed later in pencil to *Elfstone* (see pp. 277–8).

In the debate of the Company Boromir's references to the geography of the southern lands are very curious (cf. FR p. 309):

'It is a name of ill-omen,' said Boromir. 'Nor do I see the need to go there. If we cannot cross the mountains, let us take the road to my land that I followed on my way hither: through Rohan and the country of Seven Streams. Or we could go on far into the South and come at length round the Black Mountains, and crossing the rivers Isen and Silverlode[1] enter Ond from the regions nigh the sea.'

'Things have changed since you came north, Boromir,' said Gandalf. 'Did you not hear what I told of Saruman? We must not come near Isengard or the Gap of Rohan. As for the even longer road, we cannot afford the time....'

The remainder of Gandalf's reply is very much as in FR, except that he tells Boromir that 'you are free to leave us and return to Minas Tirith by any road you choose.'

The 'Seven Rivers' have been referred to in the first version of Gandalf's story to the Council of Elrond, where he reported Radagast's words to him (p. 132): 'even if you set out this hour you will hardly come to him [Saruman] before the Nine cross the Seven Rivers' (in the next version this becomes 'before the Nine have crossed the seventh river', p. 149).

Features of the geography much further to the South were already in being. Before the story had got very much further it is made plain that 'the Land of Seven Streams' lay 'between the mountains [i.e. the Black Mountains, the later White Mountains] and the sea' (see p. 272); yet Boromir's words here seem only to allow of a quite contrary interpretation of 'the country of Seven Streams'. The choices he proposes are essentially as in FR: through Rohan from the West (i.e. passing through the Gap of Rohan) and so to Minas Tirith, or going on South, crossing the Isen, and coming to Minas Tirith through the lands between the mountains and the sea; but they will traverse 'the country of Seven Streams' if they choose the *first* option, and pass north of the mountains. I cannot explain this, except on the assumption that it was a mere slip, or else on the assumption that the geography of these regions was still in a more fluid state than one would otherwise suppose.

The river Isen first appears here in the narrative,[2] and the 'Silverlode', which was afterwards the 'Blackroot', the two names being transposed (see p. 235). In this passage also are the first occurrences of an Elvish name for Sauron's dwelling in Southern Mirkwood, and of the name *Barad-dûr*:

'I alone of you have ever been in the dungeons of the Dark Lord;

and only in his older and lesser dwelling at Dol-Dúgol in Southern Mirkwood. Those who pass the gates of Barad-dûr, the Dark Tower in the Land of Shadow, do not return.'

The confusion over Thrór and Thráin is no longer present: 'Yet it will not be the first time that I have been to Moria: I sought there long for Thráin son of Thrór after he was lost.' And Trotter utters his warning to Gandalf (on the change of rôles between Gandalf and Trotter in their willingness to consider the passage of Moria see p. 168).

The episode of the attack by the Wargs enters in this text, and reached virtually the final form outright, with relatively little correction in the course of composition;[3] and the account of the journey of the Company from the little hill where the attack took place to the arrival of Gandalf, Gimli, and Frodo at the top of the steps by the Stair Falls reaches the FR text in almost every point.[4] But Gandalf's words when they saw what had happened to the Gate-stream were much changed. At first he made no reference to the Door(s); then the following was substituted:

'That is where the Door stood once upon a time,' said Gandalf pointing across the water to the cliff opposite. But Frodo could see nothing that marked the spot, unless it was some bushes at the foot of the wall, and some rotting stems and branches that stood up from the water near its further side.

This was in turn rejected and replaced by:

'That is where the Doors stood once upon a time,' said Gandalf pointing across the water. 'There was the Elven-door at the end of the road from Hollin by which we have come, [*struck out:* and the Dwarven-door further south]. We must get across [*struck out:* to the Elven-door] as quickly as we can. This way is blocked....'

The idea that there were two distinct western entrances to Moria had appeared in the original version, where Gandalf said (VI.429): 'There were two secret gates on the western side, though the chief entrance was on the East.' Gandalf's words in the present passage in FR (p. 315): 'And there the Gate stood once upon a time, *the Elven Door* at the end of the road from Hollin by which we have come' derive from this, although in the context of FR, where there is no 'Dwarven Door', the 'Elven Door' is understood in relation to what Gandalf said subsequently: 'the West-door was made chiefly for [the Elves'] use in their traffic with the Lords of Moria' (an idea which in fact goes back to the original version, VI.448: 'the westgates were

made chiefly for their use in their traffic with the dwarves'). See further
p. 191 and note 3.

The many references to the Moon in this part of the chapter were
almost all removed by emendation to the typescript that followed this
manuscript, and do not appear in FR. All references to the time of day,
and the sunset, are here precisely as in FR to this point in the story, but
after the words 'The day was drawing to its end' (FR p. 315) my father
wrote: 'and the moon was already shining on the edge of the sunset',
where FR has 'and cold stars were glinting in the sky high above the
sunset'. As Pippin, the last in the Company (in FR Sam), stepped onto
the dry ground after wading through the 'green and stagnant pool'
(following the old version: in FR 'a narrow creek') at the north-
ernmost end of the lake, and there was 'a swish, followed by a plop' in
the distant water, 'at that moment shadows came over the last gleams
of the sunset, and the rising moon was veiled in a passing cloud.'
'Rising' can only be a slip without significance; but here FR has: 'The
dusk deepened, and the last gleams of the sunset were veiled in cloud.'
The two great holly-trees beneath the cliff stood 'stiff, dark, and silent,
throwing deep shadows in the moon', where FR has 'throwing deep
night-shadows about their feet'. Thus in FR there is no reference to the
moon until Gandalf passed his hands over the smooth space on the
cliff-wall and 'The Moon now shone upon the grey face of the rock'.
     After this point, other references to the Moon were similarly
removed. When Gandalf's spells had no effect, it is said here that 'the
moon shone pale, the wind blew cold, and the doors stood fast'; in FR
'the countless stars were kindled,' etc. When the doors at last opened,
'a shadowy stair could be seen climbing steeply up. The moonlight fell
upon the lower steps, but beyond the darkness was deeper than night';
in FR the reference to the moonlight on the steps is absent. The
tentacles of the Watcher in the Water 'came wriggling over the
threshold, glistening in the moon', where FR (p. 322) has 'glistening in
the starlight'. But inside Moria, when Gandalf stood in doubt before
the archway opening into three passages, and said in the present text
'It is all night inside here; but outside the moon has long sunk and the
night is getting old [> the moon is sinking and the dark hours are
passing]', in FR he said 'outside the late Moon is riding westward and
the middle-night has passed.'
     My father had said that six nights before, the first night march of the
Company from Hollin (p. 167), the Moon was 'almost at the full' ('at
the full', FR); and on the previous night, when the Wargs attacked
again, 'the night was old, and westward the waning moon was setting'
(so also in FR). My father had forgotten this, and as he wrote the
present version he evidently saw a young moon in the West ('shining
on the edge of the sunset'). When he realised that the moon must now
be almost into its last quarter and rising late he changed the text as

described above; but surely the reference to the moon shining on the cliff-face should have been removed with all the others?[5]

A narrative element that came to nothing is seen in some rejected passages. While Gandalf was 'gazing at the blank wall of the cliff' (FR p. 317) it is said that Legolas (who in FR was 'pressed against the rock, as if listening') 'exploring southward along the lake-side was lost in the twilight'; and when the ripples on the water came closer to the shore 'the voice of Legolas was calling; his feet were running in haste towards them.' As Bill the pony dashed away into the darkness 'Legolas ran up breathless with his drawn knife in his hand; he was talking wildly in the elvish tongue' – but this was evidently rejected as soon as written in view of what is said subsequently, when Gandalf drove the Company into the doorway: 'Legolas at last came running up, gasping for breath' and sprang over the tentacles that were already fingering the cliff-wall; 'Gimli grasped him by the hand and dragged him inside.' It was at this point that my father abandoned the idea.[6]

As first written, the description of the design that Gandalf brought to light was scarcely developed from the original account (VI.449). Beneath the arch of interlacing letters 'in the elvish character' there were 'the outlines of an anvil and hammer surmounted by a crown and crescent moon. More clearly than all else there shone forth three stars with many rays.' It is now Gimli, not Gandalf, who says 'There are the emblems of Durin!', and Legolas says 'And there are the star-tokens of the High-elves!' Gandalf still says that 'they are made of some silver substance that is seen only when touched by one who knows certain words', but he adds: 'and I guess too that they shine only in the moonlight' (in the original text, when the story was that the sun was shining on the cliff-wall, he said 'at night under the moon they shine most bright'). His words were changed, apparently at once, to the text of FR: 'They are made of *ithildin*[7] that mirrors only the starlight and the moonlight, and sleeps until it is touched by one who speaks words now long forgotten in Middle-earth.'
    The description of the design itself was changed to read:

... the outlines of an anvil and hammer surmounted by a crown with seven stars. Below were two trees bearing a crescent moon. More clearly than all else there shone forth in the middle of the door a single star with many rays.
    'There are the emblems of Durin!' cried Gimli.
    'And there is the Tree of the High-elves!' said Legolas.
    'They are made of *ithildin*,' said Gandalf ...

Gandalf's reference in FR to 'the Star of the House of Fëanor' is thus absent.
    There is found in this manuscript, as an integral part of the text, the

earliest drawing of the arch and the signs beneath (reproduced on p. 182).[8] It will be seen that this drawing fits the *revised* description, in that the crown is accompanied by seven stars, there are two trees surmounted by crescent moons, and there is only one star in the centre, not three as in the first description. The natural assumption would be that the alteration of the description in the text, which stands on the page preceding the drawing, was made immediately; but in that case it is very puzzling that a little later in this version, when Gandalf uttered the word *Mellon*, 'the *three stars* shone out briefly, and faded again' (which was not corrected).

Taum Santoski has provided the explanation of this characteristic textual impasse. The fuzziness at the top of the trees is caused by heavy erasures; and he suggests that in the drawing as it was originally made, accompanying the first description in the text, there were three stars: the one in the centre was retained, but the two to either side were erased and replaced by trees. I have no doubt whatever that this is the correct solution. The revised description in the text thus fits the revised drawing; and at that time my further merely failed to notice the subsequent reference to the three stars when Gandalf spoke the word *Mellon*.

An erasure above the crown shows that there was originally a crescent moon here, as in the first form of the description. Taum Santoski has also been able to see that in a preliminary stage of the introduction of the two trees they were larger, and each had both a circle (whether a sun or a full moon) and a crescent above it.[9]

When Gandalf was striving to find the spell that would open the doors he said that he once knew 'every spell in all the tongues of Elf, Dwarf, or Goblin' (FR 'of Elves or Men or Orcs') that was ever so used; he did not say 'I shall not have to call on Gimli for words of the secret dwarf-tongue that they teach to none'; and he declared that 'the opening word was Elvish' (FR 'the opening words were Elvish') – anticipating the solution of the riddle. The words of the first spell that Gandalf tried remain exactly as in the original version (VI.451); but as already indicated the opening word is now *Mellon* as in FR, not the plural *Mellyn* as formerly.

When Frodo asked Gandalf what he thought of the monster in the water of the lake (FR p. 323) Gandalf at first replied: 'I do not know. I have never before seen or heard tell of such a creature'. This was struck out and replaced by the words in FR, 'but the arms were all guided by one purpose'. Possibly in relation to this, there is a pencilled note at this point in the manuscript: '? Insert words of Gimli saying that there were traditions among the Dwarves about strangling fingers in the dark.' – 'Goblins' appear again, as in the old version, where FR has 'Orcs', in Gandalf's 'There are older and fouler things than goblins in the deep places of the world.'

In the account of the two long marches through Moria there are

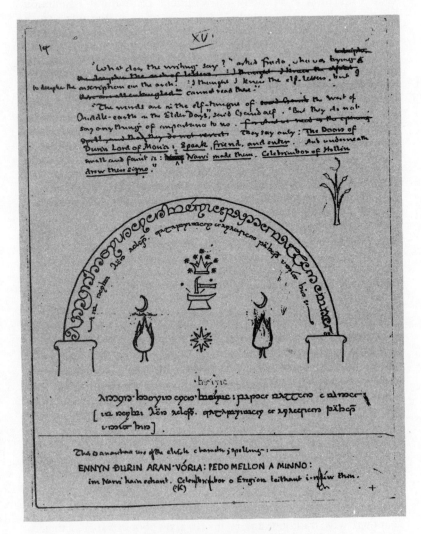

The West Gate of Moria:
the earliest drawing of the inscription and signs.

scarcely any differences to be remarked. It is 'the hobbits' (not Pippin) who dared not make the leap over the great fissure (FR p. 325); and Sam's mention of rope ('I knew I'd want it, if I hadn't got it!') is absent – just as the passage in which he goes through his belongings before leaving Rivendell and discovers that he has no rope ('Well, I'll want it. I can't get it now', FR p. 294) is absent from the preceding chapter (p. 165).[10]

When the Company came to the great hall in which they passed the second night (and which Gandalf declared, as in FR, was a good deal higher than 'the Dimrill Gate'), Gimli replied thus to Sam's question 'They didn't live down in these nasty darksome holes, surely?':

'They were not nasty holes, and even now they are not so, unless others than the dwarves here made them so. How would you have passed through, and breathed and lived, if it were not for the skill of the builders long ago? Though many shafts, I doubt not, are blocked and broken with the years, the air still flows and is for the most part good. And of old the halls and mines were not darksome

Here the text breaks off, all of Gimli's speech being struck through and replaced by his words in FR: 'These are not holes. This is the great realm and city of the Dwarrowdelf. And of old it was not darksome but full of light and splendour, as [I will sing you a song >] is still remembered in our songs.' There is an isolated draft for this rejected speech of Gimli's, in which it is completed: 'And of old they were not darksome: they were lit with many lights and sparkled with polished metals and with gems.'

Gimli's song here appears (in a rider to the manuscript) written out clear in its final form (but with *countless lamps* for *shining lamps* in the third verse, and *There ruby, beryl, opal pale* for *There beryl, pearl, and opal pale* in the fourth). A few pages of rough drafting are found (one of which begins with the draft of Gimli's words in praise of Moria just mentioned), but these do not carry the development of the song very far; more workings must have been lost. Only the verse beginning *The world was fair, the mountains tall* was achieved here, and there is little else save fragmentary and rejected lines. There is also drafting (no doubt the earliest) for a form in four-line stanzas with a rhyme scheme *aaba* and internal rhyme in the third line; of this three quatrains were completed:

> The world was young, the mountains green,
> No mark upon the moon was seen,
> When Durin came and gave their name
> To lands where none before had been.
> > nameless lands had been.

> *The world was fair, the mountains tall,*
> *With gold and silver gleamed his hall,*
> *When Durin's throne of carven stone*
> *Yet stood behind the guarded wall.*

> *The world is dark, the mountains old,*
> *In shadow lies the heapéd gold;*
> *In Durin's halls no hammer falls,*
> *The forges' fires are grey and cold.*

Among many other half-formed lines or couplets are:

> *When Durin woke and gave to gold*
> *its first and secret name of old*

> *When Durin came to Azanûl*
> *and found and named the nameless pool*[11]

There are also the isolated words *Where Nenechui cold* > *Where cold Echuinen spills. Nen Echui* has occurred as the Noldorin name for *Cuiviénen*, the Waters of Awakening (V.366, 406); here my father was pondering its application to Mirrormere (for the much later Elvish name *Nen Cenedril* 'Lake Looking-glass' see VI.466, note 39).

On one of the pages of drafting for Gimli's song my father wrote: 'Gandalf on *Ithil Thilevril*[12] *Mithril*' (i.e. Gandalf is to speak on this subject). This is the first appearance of the name *Mithril*, replacing the passing *Thilevril, Ithil*, and the original *Erceleb* (see VI.458 and notes 34–5); and an isolated page of drafting shows my father developing Gandalf's account of it. This text begins with various forms of Gandalf's reply to Sam's question 'Are there piles of jewels and gold lying about here then?' Several answers to this question were tried. In one Gandalf said: 'There may be. . . . For the wealth of Durin was very great: not only in such things as were found in the Mines themselves. There was a great traffic to his gates from East and West.' In another he said: 'No. The dwarves carried much away; and though the dread of its dark mazes has protected Moria from Men and Elves it has not defended it from the goblins, who have often invaded it and plundered it.' Against these my father wrote: 'Mithril is now nearly all lost. Orcs plunder it and pay tribute to Sauron who is collecting it – we don't know why – for some secret purpose of his weapons not for beauty.'[13]

The final version here, written in a rapid scrawl with pencilled additions and alterations, is as follows:

'No one knows,' said Gandalf. 'None have dared to seek for the armouries and treasure chambers down in the deep places since the dwarves fled. Unless it be plundering orcs. It is said that they were laid under spells and curses, when the dwarves fled.'

'They were,' said Gimli, 'but orcs have plundered often inside Moria nonetheless [added: and nought is left in the upper halls].'

'They came here because of Mithril,' said Gandalf. 'It was for that that Moria was of old chiefly renowned, and it was the foundation of the wealth and power of Durin: only in Moria was mithril found save rarely and scantily. Moria-silver or true-silver some have called it. Mithril was the Elvish name: the dwarves have a name which they will not tell. Its value was thrice that of gold, and now is beyond price. It was nearly as heavy as lead, malleable as copper, but the dwarves could by some secret of theirs make it as hard as [> harder than] steel. It surpassed common silver in all save beauty, and even in that it is its equal. [Added: It was used by the Elves who dearly loved it – among many other things they [?wrought] it to make ithildin. Also perhaps to be placed here: ... the dwarflords of Khazad-dûm were wealthier than any of the Kings of Men, and the traffic to the Gates brought them jewels and treasure from many lands of East and West.] Bilbo had a corslet of mithril-rings that Thorin gave him. I wonder what he did with it. I never told him, but its worth was greater than the value of the Shire and everything in it.'[14]

[Added: Frodo laid his hand under his tunic, and felt the rings of the mail-shirt, and felt somewhat staggered to think he was walking about with the price [of the] Shire ...]

The text of the passage that appears in the completed manuscript is very close to FR. It is still said that mithril was not found only in Moria: 'Here alone in the world, save rarely and scantily in far eastern mountains, was found Moria-silver.' The reference to Bilbo's having given his mailcoat to 'Michel Delving Museum' (not 'Mathom-house') appears.

But there is one important difference. It is said in this text: 'The dwarves tell no tale, but even as mithril was the foundation of their wealth so also it was their destruction: they delved too greedily and too deep, and disturbed that from which they fled.'[15] This is exactly as in FR, but without the last two words: Durin's Bane. In this connection also, where Gandalf says in FR: 'And since the dwarves fled, no one dares to seek the shafts and treasuries down in the deep places: they are drowned in water – or in a shadow of fear', my father first wrote in this manuscript: '... some are drowned in water, and some are full of the evil from which the dwarves fled and of which they will not speak.' This was changed to: '... they are drowned in water – or in shadow.'

The absence of the words 'Durin's Bane' does not of course prove that the conception of 'Durin's Bane' had not yet arisen; while a feeling that the words 'some are *full of the evil* from which the dwarves fled' are not really appropriate to the Balrog is too slight to build on. That there was a Balrog in Moria appears in the original sketch for the story given in VI.462. Even so, I think it probable that at this stage it was not the Balrog that had caused the flight of the Dwarves from the great Dwarrowdelf long before. The strongest evidence for this comes from the original version of the Lothlórien story, where it is at least strongly suggested (being represented as the opinion of the Lord and Lady of Lothlórien) that the Balrog had been sent from Mordor not long since (see further on this question p. 247 and note 11). Moreover, in the texts of the story of the Bridge of Khazad-dûm from this time Gimli does not cry out 'Durin's Bane!' (pp. 197, 202–3).

I think also that Gandalf is represented as not knowing himself what was the evil from which the Dwarves fled (it cannot be said, of course, what my father knew).[16]

There is nothing else to note in the remainder of the chapter except the Runic inscription on the tomb of Balin (on which see the Appendix on Runes, pp. 456–7). Gandalf's words about the inscription differ from what he says in FR: 'These are dwarf-runes, such as they use in the North. Here is written in the old tongue and the new: *Balin son of Fundin, Lord of Moria.*' In FR he says: 'These are Daeron's Runes, such as were used of old in Moria. Here is written in the tongues of Men and Dwarves...'

The inscription is written on a strip of blue paper,[17] and since that could not be reproduced in black and white there is here reproduced instead the version from the typescript that followed the manuscript, this being very closely similar to the first in its design and identical in all its forms.

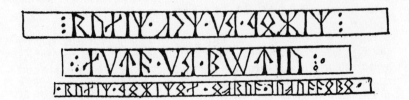

The inscription reads:

BALIN SON OF FUNDIN
LORD OF MORIA
Balin Fundinul Uzbad Khazaddûmu

NOTES

1 *Silverlode* was changed in pencil to *Blackroot*; see p. 235. At the same time *Ond* was changed to *Ondor*.

2 On the First Map the name was first *Iren*, changed to *Isen*; see p. 298.

3 Gandalf's cry as he tossed the blazing brand into the air (FR p. 312) here takes the form: *Naur ad i gaurhoth!*

4 The references to the 'power that wished now to have a clear light in which things that moved in the wild could be seen from far away', and Gandalf's remark that 'here Aragorn cannot guide us; he has seldom walked in this country', are lacking; while a comment is made in this text on the fact of the land in which Gandalf sought for the Sirannon, the Gate-stream, being 'bleak and dry': 'not a flake of snow seemed to have fallen there.'

5 The change in the present text of 'outside the moon has long sunk' to 'outside the moon is sinking' implies the corrected view of the moon's phase, but none of the previous references were emended on the manuscript.

6 This is a convenient place to mention a textual detail. Gimli says that Dwarf-doors are invisible when shut, 'and their own makers cannot find them or open them, if their secret is forgotten.' *Makers* is certain (but could be misread), and seems altogether more appropriate and likely than *masters*. This, appearing in the first typescript of the chapter, was clearly an error, perpetuated in FR (p. 317).

7 The name *ithildin* was devised here. My father first wrote *starmoon* or *thilevril* (on *thilevril* see p. 184 and note 12).

8 This has been previously reproduced by Humphrey Carpenter, *Biography*, facing p. 179. – The writing on the arch, but nothing more, appears in the original version of the chapter, VI.450.

9 The trees in the design reproduced on p. 182 are of a highly stylized form seen frequently in my father's pictures (for example, the tree in the drawing of Lake-town in *The Hobbit*). These trees might be further formalized into geometrical shapes, or their surfaces cut into planes (so that they appear like rocks rising from trunks). The tree pencilled in above the arch, with distinct branches, single large leaves, and a crescent moon as its topmost growth, was the model for a second version of the design (also at Marquette University), which differs from the first only in the form of the trees. It may be that it was to this that the corrected text in the manuscript refers, since the trees are said to *bear* crecent moons. In a third version (in the Bodleian Library) the trees, much larger, still bear a crescent moon at the summit, but the branches also curl over into crescents (as in the final form). A fourth version (also in the Bodleian) differs from the final form

only in that the branches pass behind and do not entwine the pillars.

It can be seen in the narrative passage above the first version of the design that the name *Narvi* was first spelt *Narf[i]*, as in the original text (VI.449). The stroke through the first *m* of *Celebrimbor* in the transcription of the *tengwar* at the bottom of the page removes an erroneous *m*; the stroke through the second removes a necessary *m*. – The second *tengwa* in the penultimate word of the inscription, transliterated as *i·ndíw*, is used in the words *ennyn* and *minno* to represent *nn*, not *nd*. Perhaps to be connected with this is the form of the eighth *tengwa* in *Celebrimbor*, which would naturally be interpreted as *mm*, not *mb*.

10 The origin of Gandalf's sword Glamdring is still referred to here, as in VI.454, since the passage where it occurs in FR (p. 293), the account of the arms borne by the members of the Company, had not yet been added to the previous chapter.

11 Cf. VI.466, note 36.

12 *Thilevril* was thus a rejected possibility for both *ithildin* and *mithril* (see note 7).

13 Another draft puts this slightly more fully: 'They give it in tribute to Sauron, who has long been gathering and hoarding all that he can find. It is not known why: not for beauty, but for some secret purpose in the making of weapons of war.'

14 This is the point (at least in terms of actual record) at which the connection was made between *mithril* or 'Moria-silver' and Bilbo's mailcoat, ultimately leading to an alteration in the text of *The Hobbit*, Chapter XIII: see VI.465–6, notes 35, 38. The mailcoat will no longer be called 'elf-mail' (see p. 173, note 13).

15 A final draft for this passage ends illegibly: 'The dwarves will not say what happened; but mithril is rich only far down and northward towards the roots of Caradras, and some ... [?think] they disturbed some [?guarding]'. – *Caradras* is spelt thus also in the text of the passage in the completed manuscript; see p. 174, note 18.

16 In the fifth version of 'The Council of Elrond' (p. 142) Glóin says that the Dwarves of Moria 'delved immeasurably deep', and 'under the foundations of the hills things long buried were waked at last from sleep'.

In FR there seems to be some ambiguity on the question of what Gandalf knew. He says that the Dwarves fled from Durin's Bane; but when the Balrog appeared, and Gimli cried out 'Durin's Bane!', he muttered: 'A Balrog! Now I understand.' (These words, like Gimli's cry, are lacking in the versions of the scene from this time, pp. 197, 202–3). What did Gandalf mean? That he understood now that the being that had entered the Chamber of Mazarbul and striven with him for the mastery through the closed door was a Balrog? Or that he understood at last what it was that had destroyed Durin? Perhaps he meant both; for if he had known what Durin's Bane was, would he not have surmised, with horror, what was on the other side of the door? – 'I have never felt such a challenge', 'I have met my match, and have nearly been destroyed.'

17 The blue paper is from the cover of one of the booklets of the 'August 1940' examination script, which my father was still using for drafting. The strip was pasted onto the manuscript page, covering an earlier form of the Runic inscription; for this see the Appendix on Runes, p. 457.

X

THE MINES OF MORIA (2):
THE BRIDGE

We come at last to the point where my father took up the narrative again beside Balin's tomb in Moria. A sketch for the fight in the Chamber of Mazarbul was in existence (VI.443), going back to the time when he wrote the original text of 'Moria (i)', and this sketch he now for the most part followed closely. There was also a sketch from the same time (VI.462) of Gandalf's encounter on the bridge and his fall, when his opponent was to be a Black Rider.

The new chapter, numbered XVII, was entitled 'The Mines of Moria (ii)', and corresponds to Book II Chapter 5 in FR, 'The Bridge of Khazad-dûm'. The original manuscript is in pencil, ink, and ink over pencil, and was written on the same 'August 1940' examination script as was used for so much of the preceding work. It is a very rough draft indeed: parts of it would be quite beyond the limits of legibility were it not for clues provided by later texts. Some very minor editorial alteration is made here in respect of punctuation and the breaking of sentences, increasing the readability and comprehensibility of the text though disguising the furious haste in which it was written.

That this manuscript followed the new text of 'The Ring Goes South' is seen at once from the occurrence of the name *Blackroot* (the later *Silverlode*) in the Book of Mazarbul; for *Blackroot* replaced *Redway* as that text was being written (p. 166). For evidence that it followed the second version of 'Moria (i)' see note 3.

Two notes are written at the head of the first page: '2 West Gates' (see note 3), and 'No dates in Book'.

THE MINES OF MORIA (ii)

The Company of the Ring stood some time in silence beside the tomb of Balin. Frodo thought of Bilbo and his friendship with the dwarf, and Balin's visit to Bilbo long ago.

After a while they looked about the chamber to see if they could discover any tidings or signs of Balin's people. There was another door on the other side, under the shaft. By both doors they now saw that in the dust were lying many bones, and among them broken swords, and axe-heads, cloven shields and helms. Some of the swords were crooked: orc-weapons with black blades.

There were recesses and shelves cut in the wall, and in them were large iron-bound chests: all had been broken open and plundered; but beside the broken lid of one lay the tattered fragments of a book. It had been hewn with a sword and stabbed, and was so stained with dark marks like old blood that only little of it could be read. It only a cover [sic][1] and much was missing or in small pieces. Gandalf laid it carefully on the slab and pored over it; it was written in dwarvish and elvish script by many different hands.

'It is a record of the fortunes of Balin's folk,' said the wizard, 'and seems to begin with their coming to the Great Gate 20 years ago. Listen!

'*We drove out Orcs from ... first hall. We slew many under the bright sun in the Dale. Flói was killed by an arrow. He slew... We have occupied [> taken] the Twenty-first Hall of North-end [added: to dwell in]. There is there ... shaft is... Balin has set up his seat in the Chamber of Mazarbul ... gold ... Durin's axe. Balin is Lord of Moria ... We found true-silver ... Well-forged ... (To)morrow Óin is ... seek [> Óin to seek] for the upper armouries and treasury of the Third Deep ... mithril.*

'There are one or two more rather ill-written and much-damaged pages of that sort. Then there must be a number missing, and some I cannot read. Let me see. No, it is burned and cut and stained. I can't read that. Wait! Ah, here is one more recent, well-written. Fifth year of their colony. Look – a large hasty hand and using *elvish* character!

'*Balin Lord of Moria fell in Dimrill Dale. He went alone to look in Mirror-mere. an orc shot him from behind a stone. We slew the orc, but many ... up from East up Blackroot...* Now two lines are gone. *We have barred the Gates.* No more is clear on that page. What is this? The last written page – rest seems blank [> stuck to the cover]. *We cannot get out. We cannot get out. The Pool is up to the Wall in the West. There lies the Watcher in the Water. It took Óin. We cannot get out.*

'*They have taken the Gates. Frár and Lóni and Náli*[2] *fell there ... noise in the Deeps.* Poor things. They could not get out by either Gate. It was perhaps well for us that the water had sunk somewhat, and that the Watcher was guarding the Dwarf-door not the Elfdoor we came by.[3] The last thing written,' said Gandalf, 'is a hasty scrawl in elf-letters. *They are coming.*'

He looked round. 'They seem to have made a last stand by both the doors of this chamber,' he said. 'But there were not many left by that time. So ended the attempt to re-take Moria. It was brave but foolish. The time is not yet. Their end must have been desperate. But I fear we must now say farewell to Balin son of Fundin: he was a noble dwarf. Here may he lie in the halls of his fathers. We will take this book, and look at it more carefully later. You had better keep it, Frodo, and give it to Bilbo. It will interest him though I fear it will grieve him.[4] I think I know where we are now. This must be the Chamber of Mazarbul and that hall the 21st Hall of the North-end. Then we ought to leave either by the south or the east arch in the hall, or possibly by this other eastward door here. I think we will return to the Hall. Come, let us go! The morning is passing.'

At that very moment there was a great sound, a great rolling *boom* that seemed to come from far below and to tremble in the stone at their feet. They sprang to the door in alarm. But even as they did so there was an echoing blast; a great horn was being blown in the hall, and answering horns and harsh cries were heard in the corridors; there was a hurrying sound of many feet.

'Fool that I have been!' cried Gandalf, 'to delay here. We are nicely trapped just as they were before. But I was not here then: we will see what –'

Boom came the shuddering noise again, and the walls shook.

'Slam the doors and wedge them!' shouted Trotter. 'And keep your packs on: we may get a chance to cut a way out.'

'No!' said Gandalf. 'Wedge them but keep them just ajar. We must not get shut in. We'll go by the further door if we get a chance.'

There was another harsh horn-call and shrill cries coming down the corridor. There was a ring and clatter as the Company drew their weapons. [*Added:* Glamdring and Sting were shining with whitish flames, glinting at the edges.] Boromir thrust wedges of broken blades and splinters of wooden chest under the bottom of the western door by which they had entered. Then Gandalf went and stood behind it. 'Who comes here to disturb the rest of Balin Lord of Moria?' he cried in a loud voice.

There was a rush of hoarse laughter like the fall of a slide of stones into a pit, but amid the clamour there was one deep voice. *Boom boom boom* went the noises in the deep. Swiftly

Gandalf went to the opening and thrust forward his staff. There was a blinding flash that lit the chamber and the passage beyond. For an instant Gandalf looked out. Arrows whined and whistled down the corridor as he sprang back.

'There are goblins: very many of them,' he said. 'Evil they look and large: black Orcs.[5] They are for the moment hanging back, but there is something else there. A troll, I think, or more than one. There is no hope of escape that way.'

'And no hope at all if they come at the other door as well,' said Boromir.

'But there is no sound outside,' said Trotter, who was standing by the eastern entrance listening. 'The passage here goes down steps: it [?prob(ably)] does not give on to the hall at all. Our only chance is to gather here. Do what damage we can to the attackers and then fly down these steps. If only we could block the door as we went: but they both open inwards.'

Heavy feet were heard in the corridor. Boromir kicked the wedges away from the west door and heaved it to.[6] They retreated toward the still open eastern door, first Pippin and Merry, then Legolas, then Frodo with Sam at his side, then Boromir, Trotter, and last Gandalf. But they had no chance to fly yet. There was a heavy blow at the door, and it quivered; and immediately it began to move inwards grinding at the wedges and thrusting them back. An enormous arm and shoulder with dark green scaly skin (or clad in some horrible mesh) thrust through the widening gap. Then a great three-toed foot was thrust in also. There was dead silence outside.

Boromir leaped forward and hewed the arm with his sword[7] but it glanced aside and fell from his shaken hand: the blade was notched.

Frodo suddenly, and very unexpectedly, felt a great wrath leap up in his heart. 'The Shire,' he cried, and ran forward with Sting stabbing at the hideous foot. There was a bellow and the foot jerked back, nearly wrenching the blade from his hand: drops dripped from it and smoked on the stone.

'One for the Shire!' cried Trotter delightedly. 'You have a good blade, Frodo son of Drogo.' Sam looked as if for the first time he really liked Trotter. There was a crash and another crash: rocks were being heaved with huge strength against the door. It staggered back and the opening widened. Arrows came whistling in, but struck the north wall and fell to the ground. The horns rang again, there was a rush of feet, and orcs one after another leaped in. Then Legolas loosed his bow. Two fell pierced through the throat. The sword of Elendil struck down others.[8] Boromir laid about him and the orcs [?feared] his sword. One that dived under his arm was cloven ... by Gimli's axe. Thirteen orcs they slew and the others fled. 'Now is the time if ever,' said [Trotter >] Gandalf, '– before that Troll-chief or more of them return. Let us go!'

But even as they retreated once more a huge orc-chief, almost man-high, clad in black mail from head to foot, leaped through the door. Behind him but not yet daring to advance stood many followers. His eyes were like coals of fire. He wielded a great spear. Boromir who was at the rear turned, but with a thrust of his shield the orc put aside his stroke and with huge strength bore him back and flung him down. Then leaping with the speed of a snake he charged and smote with his spear straight at Frodo. The blow caught him on the right side. Frodo was hurled against the wall and pinned. Sam with a cry hewed at the spear and it broke. ... but even as the orc cast the shaft aside and drew his scimitar the sword of Elendil drove down upon his helm. There was a flash like flame and the helm burst. The orc-chieftain fell with cloven head. His followers who were ... by the now nearly open door yelled and fled in dismay. *Boom, boom* went the noises in the Deep. The great voice rolled out again.

'Now!' said Gandalf. 'Now is the last chance!' He picked up Frodo and sprang through the eastern door. The others followed. Trotter the last to leave pulled the door behind him. It had a great iron ring on either side, but no lock to be seen.

'I am all right,' gasped Frodo. 'Put me down!'

Gandalf nearly dropped him in amazement.

Without striking out this last passage my father at once went on to rewrite it:

'Now!' cried Gandalf. 'Now is the last chance!' Trotter picked up Frodo and sprang through the eastern door. Even in the heat of battle Gimli bowed to Balin's tomb. Boromir heaved the door to: it had a great iron ring on each side but the key was gone and the lock broken.

'I am all right,' gasped Frodo. 'Put me down!'

Trotter nearly dropped him in amazement. 'I thought you were dead,' he cried. 'Not yet,' said Gandalf turning round. 'But there is no time [*struck out:* to count (*sc.* wounds)].[9] Get away down these stairs, and look out! Wait a moment for me and then run: bear right and south.'

As they went down the dark stairs they saw the pale light gleam from the wizard's staff. He was still standing by the closed door. Frodo leaning on Sam halted a moment and peered back. Gandalf seemed to be thrusting the tip of his staff into the ancient keyhole.

Suddenly there was a flash more dazzling ... [than] any that they had ever conceived of. They all turned. There was a deafening crash. The swords in their hands leaped and wrenched in their fingers, and they stumbled and fell to their knees as the great blast passed down the stairway. Into the midst of them fell Gandalf.

'Well, that's that,' he said. 'It was all I could do. I expect I have buried Balin. But alas for my staff: we shall have to go by guess in the dark. Gimli and I will lead.'

They followed in amazement, and as they stumbled behind he gasped out some information. 'I have lost my staff, part of my beard, and an inch of eyebrows,' he said. 'But I have blasted the door and felled the roof against it, and if the Chamber of Mazarbul is not a heap of ruins behind it, then I am no wizard. All the power of my staff was expended [?in a flash]: it was shattered to bits.'

Here the text in ink stops for the moment. My father at once heavily rewrote the passage beginning 'Suddenly there was a flash...' in pencil and then continued on in pencil from the point he had reached (cf. note 4). There is of course no question that the story was coming into being in these pages, and the handwriting is so fast as to be practically a code, while words are missed out or misrepresented, so that one must try to puzzle out not merely what my father did write, but what he intended.

Suddenly they heard him cry out strange words in tones of thunder, and there was a flash more dazzling ... [than] any that they had ever conceived of: it was as if lightning had passed just before their eyes and seared them. The swords in their hands leapt and wrenched in their fingers. There was a deafening crash, and they fell or stumbled to their knees as a rush of wind passed down the stairway. Into the midst of them fell Gandalf.

'Well, that's that,' he said. 'I have buried poor old Balin. It was all I could do. I nearly killed myself. [*Struck out as soon as written:* It will take me years to recover my strength and wizardry.] Go on, go on! Gimli, come in front with me. We must go in the dark. Haste now!'

They followed in amazement feeling the walls, and as they stumbled behind him he gasped out some information. 'I have lost part of my beard and an inch of my eyebrows', he said. 'But I have blasted the door and felled the roof against it, and if the Chamber of Mazarbul is not a heap of ruins behind it, then I am no wizard. But I have expended all my strength for the moment. I can give you no more light.'

The echoes of Gandalf's blast seemed to run to and fro, . . . ing in the hollow places of stone above them. From behind they heard *boom, boom*, like the beating and throbbing of a drum. But there was no sound of feet. For an hour they [?hurried on guided by Gandalf's nose]; and still there was no sound of pursuit. Almost they began to hope that they would escape.

'But what about you, Frodo?' asked Gandalf, as they halted to take a gasping breath. 'That is really important.'

'I am bruised and in pain, but I am whole,' said Frodo, 'if that is what you mean.'

'I do indeed,' said Gandalf. 'I thought it was a heroic but dead hobbit that Aragorn picked up.'

'. . . it seems that hobbits or this hobbit is made of a stuff so tough that I have never met the like,' said Trotter. 'Had I known I would have spoken softer in the Inn at Bree. That spear thrust would have pierced through a boar.'

'Well, it has not pierced through me,' said Frodo, 'though I feel as if I had been caught between a hammer and anvil.' He said no more. His breath was difficult, and he thought explanations could wait.

From this point ('They now went on again', FR p. 342) the original text is very largely lost for some distance, because my father overwrote it (and largely erased it first) as part of a revised version, but something can be read at the end of this section:

There was no time to lose. Away beyond the pillars in the deep [?gloom] at the west end of the hall to the right there came cries and horn calls. And far off again they heard *boom, boom* and the ground trembled [?to the dreadful drum taps]. 'Now for the last race!' said Gandalf. 'Follow me!'

The remainder of the original text is in ink and is at first fairly legible, but towards the end becomes in places impossible to decipher, being written at great speed, with small words indicated by mere marks, word-endings omitted, and scarcely any punctuation.

He turned to the left and darted across the floor of the hall. It was longer than it looked. As they ran they heard behind the beat and echo of many feet running on the floor.[10] A shrill yell went up: they had been seen. There was a ring and clash of steel: an arrow whistled over Frodo's head.

Trotter laughed. 'They did not expect this,' he said. 'The fire has cut them off for the moment. We are on the wrong side!'

'Look out for the bridge!' cried Gandalf over his shoulder. 'It is dangerous and narrow.'

Suddenly Frodo saw before him a black gulf. Just before the end of the hall the floor vanished and fell into an abyss. The exit door could not be reached save by a narrow railless bridge of stone that spanned the chasm with a single curving leap of some fifty feet. Across it they could only pass in single file. They reached the chasm in a pack and halted at the bridge-end for a moment. More arrows whistled over them. One pierced Gandalf's hat and stuck there like a black feather. They looked back. Away beyond the fiery fissure Frodo saw the swarming black figures of many orcs. They brandished spears and scimitars which shone red as blood. *Boom, boom* rolled the drum-beats now advancing louder and louder and more and more menacing. Two great dark troll-figures could be seen [?towering] among the orcs. They strode forward to the fiery brink.

Legolas bent his bow. Then he let it fall. He gave a cry of dismay and terror. Two great dark troll-shapes had appeared; but it was not these that caused his cry.[11] The orc-ranks had opened as if they themselves were afraid. A figure strode to the fissure, no more than man-high yet terror seemed to go before it. They could see the furnace-fire of its yellow eyes from afar; its arms were very long; it had a red [?tongue]. Through the air it sprang over the fiery fissure. The flames leaped up to greet it and wreathed about it. Its streaming hair seemed to catch fire, and the sword that it held turned to flame. In its other hand it held a whip of many thongs.

'Ai, ai,' wailed Legolas. '[The Balrogs are >] A Balrog is come.'

'A Balrog,' said Gandalf. 'What evil fortune – and my power is nearly spent.'

The fiery figure ran across the floor. The orcs yelled and shot many arrows.

'Over the Bridge,' cried Gandalf. 'Go on! Go on! This is a foe beyond any of you. I will hold the Bridge. Go on!'

When they gained the door they turned, in spite of his command. The troll-figures strode across the fire carrying orcs across. The Balrog rushed to the Bridge-foot. Legolas [?raised] his bow, and [an] arrow pierced his shoulder. The bow fell useless. Gandalf stood in the midst of the bridge. In his hand Glamdring gleamed. In his left he held up his staff. The Balrog advanced and stood gazing at him.

Suddenly with a spout of flame it sprang on the Bridge, but Gandalf stood firm. 'You cannot pass,' he said. 'Go back [*struck out probably as soon as written:* into the fiery depths. It is forbidden for any Balrog to come beneath the sky since Fionwë son of Manwë overthrew Thangorodrim]. I am the master of the White Fire. The red flame cannot come this way.' The creature made no reply, but standing up tall so that it loomed above the wizard it strode forward and smote him. A sheet of white flame sprang before him [?like a shield], and the Balrog fell backward, its sword shivered into molten pieces and flew, but Gandalf's staff snapped and fell from his hand. With a gasping hiss the Balrog sprang up; it seemed to be [?half blind], but it came on and grasped at the wizard. Glamdring shore off its empty right hand, but in that instant as he [?delivered the stroke] the Balrog [?struck with] its whip. The thongs lashed round the wizard's knees and he staggered.

Seizing Legolas' bow Gimli shot, [but] the arrow fell ... Trotter sprang back along the bridge with his sword. But at that moment a great troll came up from the other side and leaped on the bridge. There was a terrible crack and the bridge broke. All the western end fell. With a terrible cry the troll fell after it, and the Balrog [?tumbled] sideways with a yell and fell into the chasm. Before Trotter could reach the wizard the bridge broke before his feet, and with a great cry Gandalf fell into the darkness.[12]

Trotter [?recoiled]. The others were rooted with horror. He recalled them. 'At least we can obey his last command,' he said. They [?passed] by the door and stumbled wildly up the great stair beyond, and beyond [?up there] was a wide echoing passage. They stumbled along it. Frodo heard Sam at his side weeping as he ran, and then he [?realized] that he too was weeping. *Boom, boom, boom* rang the echo of ... behind them.

On they ran. The light grew. It shone through great shafts.

They passed into a wide hall, clear-lit with high windows in the east. [?Through that] they ran, and suddenly before them the Great Gates with carven posts and mighty doors – cast back.

There were orcs at the door, but amazed to see that it was not friends that ran they fled in dismay, and the Company took no heed of them.

The original draft of the chapter ends here, and does not recount the coming of the Company into Dimrill Dale. There is a pencilled note written on the manuscript against the description of the Balrog: 'Alter description of Balrog. It seemed to be of man's shape, but its form could not be plainly discerned. It *felt* larger than it looked.' After the words 'Through the air it sprang over the fiery fissure' my father added: 'and a great shadow seemed to black out the light.' And at the end of the text – before he had finished it, for the concluding passage is written around the words – he wrote: 'No – Gandalf breaks the bridge and Balrog falls – but lassoos him.'

It will be seen that for much of its length this chapter was very fully formed from its first emergence; while scarcely a sentence remained unchanged into FR, and while many details of speech and event would be altered, there really was not very far to go. But in certain passages this earliest draft underwent substantial development in the narrative.

The first of these is the account of Gandalf's blocking of the east door out of the Chamber of Mazarbul (FR pp. 340–1), where there was as yet no suggestion that some greater power than any orc or troll had entered the chamber, and where the blasting of the door and felling of the roof was not caused by competing spells of great power, but was a deliberate act on Gandalf's part to preserve the Company from pursuit down the stair.

It cannot be said precisely how the story stood in the lost passage (p. 196), though from a word still decipherable here and there it can be seen that Gimli saw a red light ahead of them, and that Gandalf told them that they had reached the First Deep below the Gates and were come to the Second Hall. Clearly then the essential elements of the final narrative were already present.

The second passage in which the original draft would undergo major development is the narrative of the final attack on the fugitives and the battle on the Bridge of Khazad–dûm (FR pp. 343–5). That there was a bridge in Moria, that Gandalf would hold it alone against a single adversary of great power, and that both would fall into an abyss when the bridge broke beneath them, had been foreseen in the original sketch (VI.462); but the final form of the famous scene was not achieved at a stroke. Here, the trolls do not bring great slabs to serve as gangways over the fiery fissure, but carry orcs across (it may be noted incidentally that 'orcs', rather than 'goblins', becomes pervasive in this text: see note 5); the form of the Balrog is clearly perceived; there is no blast of Boromir's horn; Legolas is pierced in the shoulder by an arrow as he attempts to shoot; and Aragorn and Boromir do not remain with Gandalf at the end of the bridge. The physical contest between Gandalf and the Balrog is differently conceived: Gandalf's staff breaks at the moment when the Balrog's sword shivers into molten fragments in the 'sheet of white flame', and though the whip catches Gandalf round his knees it is not the cause of his fall. Here, it is the great troll leaping onto the bridge that causes it to break, carrying with it troll, Balrog, and wizard together. But even before he had finished the initial draft of the chapter my father saw 'what really happened': 'Gandalf breaks the bridge and the Balrog falls – but lassoos him'. He thereupon moved the 'sheet of white flame' and the snapping of Gandalf's staff from the initial clash between the adversaries to the point where Gandalf broke the bridge.

It is clear that my father turned at once to the making of a fair copy of the original draft text – that he did so at once, before continuing the story, is seen from the fact that Sam's wound in the affray in the Chamber of Mazarbul only appears in the new version but is present at the beginning of 'Lothlórien'.

The new version (a good clear manuscript in ink, with little hesitation in the course of composition and without a great deal of subsequent pencilled alteration) was still called 'The Mines of Moria, 2'; a subtitle was added in pencil, 'The Bridge'. For some distance the text proceeds as a characteristic polishing and slight elaboration of the draft, bringing it very close to FR, which I take here as the basis with which the present text is compared.

The Book of Mazarbul is not described as 'partly burned', and its pages are said to have been written 'in both dwarf-runes and elvish script', where in FR a distinction is made between the runes of Moria and of Dale. The text of the first page that Gandalf read out runs thus:

'*We drove out Orcs ... from guard* something *and first hall. We slew many under the bright sun in the Dale. Flói was killed by an arrow. He slew* ... then I can only read stray words for many lines. Then comes *We have taken the Twenty-first Hall of North-end to dwell in. There is* ... I cannot read what: a *shaft* is mentioned. Then *Balin has set up his seat in the Chamber of Mazarbul.*'

'The Chamber of Records,' said Gimli. 'I guess that is where we now stand.'

'Well, I can read no more for a long way, except the word *gold,*' said Gandalf; 'and, yes, *Durin's axe* and something *helm*. Then *Balin is Lord of Moria*. After some stars there comes *We found true-silver* and later the word *well-forged*; then something, I have it! *Óin to seek for the upper armouries and treasury of the Third Deep and* ... but I can make out no more on the page but *mithril, west,* and *Balin.*'

This text corresponds almost exactly to the third drawing of the page (see the Appendix, p. 459).

The text of the second page that Gandalf read out, in 'a large bold hand writing in elvish script', now identified by Gimli as Ori's, scarcely differs from the text given on p. 191, except that after *We have barred the Gates* Gandalf can doubtfully read *horrible* and *suffer: all is.* Thus the passage giving the date (10 November) of Balin's death in Dimrill Dale is still absent. The earliest, or earliest extant, drawing of Ori's page was done at the same time as the third drawing of the first page (see the Appendix, p. 459), and obviously accompanies the present version of the narrative.

The text of the last page of the book remains exactly the same as that given on p. 191; and the earliest extant drawing (accompanying the third of the first page and the first of Ori's page) fits it exactly.

In this version Gandalf no longer makes any mention of the Watcher in the Water and the two Doors, but Gimli says: 'It was well for us that the pool had sunk a little, and that *we came to the Elven-door that was closed.* The Watcher was sleeping, or so it seems, down at the southern end of the pool.' The italicized words were struck out, probably at once, and so the conception of the two separate entrances into Moria from the West was finally abandoned. Gandalf still gives the Book of Mazarbul to Frodo, for him to give to Bilbo 'if you get a chance.'

In his last words before the attack on the Chamber of Mazarbul began Gandalf says that 'the Twenty-first Hall should be on the seventh level, that is five above the Gate level' (six in FR). He still says 'There are goblins... They are evil and large: black Orcs', but the troll becomes 'a great cave-troll' as in FR, and its three-toed foot was changed on the manuscript to a toeless foot.[13] Sam now gets a wound in the affray, 'a cut on the arm', which as mentioned above appears in the original draft of 'Lothlórien' ('The cut in his arm was paining him', p. 220). A rider to the present text changed this to 'a glancing cut in his shoulder'. 'The sword of Elendil' still has no other name, *Branding* being substituted later in pencil (see p. 165, and p. 274 and note 19).

In the story of the flight of the Company from the Chamber of Mazarbul the new version followed the original draft fairly closely. As Frodo and Sam peered up the steps they heard Gandalf muttering, and the sound, they thought, of his staff tapping. The searing flash like lightning, the wrenching of their swords in their hands, and the great rush of wind down the stairs forcing them to their knees, were still present (the blasting of the Chamber remaining a deliberate act); and Gandalf still says 'I have lost part of my beard and an inch of my eyebrows'. The long descent in the dark down flights of stairs now enters, Gandalf feeling the ground with his staff 'like a blind man'; but at the words 'Almost they began to hope against hope that they would escape' (FR p. 341) this new version stops, and all this part of the story, from the killing of the orc-chieftain in the Chamber, was rejected.[14]

The development of the chapter from this point took much unravelling, but it seems clear that my father decided at this juncture that further drafting was required before the fair copy on which he was engaged could be continued. He therefore wrote now a new rough draft carrying the story from the flight of the Company from the Chamber of Mazarbul to their final escape out of Moria; and having done this, he returned to the fair copy and went on with it again, following the draft quite closely. I believe that all this was continuous work, that it can be shown that the story of the chapter 'The Bridge of Khazad-dûm' was brought almost to its final form before the story of Lothlórien was begun (see p. 204 and note 20). For clarity, in the remainder of this chapter I will call the new draft 'B' and the fair copy manuscript 'C', the original draft, which has been given in full, being 'A'.[15]

This new draft B for the latter part of the chapter was written very fast, mostly in soft pencil, and is hard to read, but for much of its length the final narrative was now almost achieved, with scarcely any differences of substance. Gandalf still says 'I nearly killed myself', and he does not say 'I have met my match, and have nearly been destroyed'; he knows 'one or two (shutting-spells) that will hold, though they don't stop the door being smashed if great strength comes'; and he says that the Orcs on the other side of the door 'seemed to be talking their horrible secret language, which I never knew more than a word or two of.' In the fair copy C these become: 'I ran up against something unexpected I haven't met before'; 'I know several that will hold'; and 'talking their hideous secret language.'

The overwriting of the erased passage in the primary text A (p. 196) forms a part of the new draft, and the new text (from 'They now went on again' to ' "Now for the last race!" cried Gandalf') is so close to the final form in FR (pp. 342–3) as to need no commentary.

In the last part of the chapter (from 'He turned left and sped across the smooth floor of the hall') the drafting of the new version is as rough as was the original text A that it replaced in this part, the language unpolished and the conclusion scarcely legible. The actual narrative of FR pp. 344–6 is present, however, except in these points. The Balrog when first seen beyond the fiery fissure is described as 'of man-shape maybe, and not much larger' (cf. pp. 197, 199). The fair copy C has here likewise 'and not much greater' (FR: 'of man-shape maybe, yet greater').[16] Gimli's cry of 'Durin's Bane!' and Gandalf's words 'Now I understand' were still absent from both B and C,

Gimli's words (only) being added in pencil to the latter; on this matter see pp. 185–6 and note 16 to the last chapter.

Following Legolas' cry 'Ai! Ai! A Balrog is come!' it is told in B that 'he turned to fly and an arrow struck him in the shoulder. He stumbled and began to crawl on all fours along the Bridge.' That an arrow pierced Legolas in the shoulder is told in the original version of the story (p. 198). In B my father struck out the incident, then ticked it for retention; but it is absent from C. Boromir's horncall is absent from both texts, though my father added it in pencil to C, at first placing it after 'A Balrog is come!' but then deciding to put it in earlier, before 'Legolas turned and set an arrow to the string', so that it was the Orcs who were momentarily halted by the blast of the horn and not the Balrog. In neither text do Aragorn and Boromir remain at the bridge-foot, and thus it is said subsequently that Trotter 'ran back out to the bridge' and 'ran out onto the Bridge', i.e. from the doorway where he had been standing with the others.

In B it is said only that the Balrog 'stood facing him': in C 'the Balrog halted facing him, and the shadow about him reached out like great wings'.[17] Immediately afterwards, where in FR the Balrog 'drew itelf up to a great height, and its wings were spread from wall to wall', neither B nor C has the words 'to a great height' nor speaks of the 'wings'. Gandalf's words to the Balrog remain in B very close to the original draft (p. 198), with 'White Fire' for 'the White Fire'; in C this was changed in the act of writing: 'You cannot pass. I am the master of White Flame. [Neither Red Fire nor Black Shadow can >] The Red Fire cannot come this way. Go back to the Shadow!'

Both B and C continued a little way beyond the point where 'The Bridge of Khazad–dûm' ends in FR, the former giving first a description of Dimrill Dale and Mirrormere, which was omitted in C.

Northward it ran up into a glen of shadows between two great arms of the mountains, over which towered three white peaks. Before them (west) [*read* east][18] the mountains marched to a sudden end. To their right (south) they receded endlessly into the distance. Less than a mile away (and below them where they stood on the skirts of the mountains) lay a mere – just clear of the shadow, under the sunny sky. But its waters looked dark, a deep blue such as the night sky seen through a lighted window. Its surface was utterly still. About it lay a smooth sward, sloping swiftly down on all sides towards its bare unbroken brink. There lay the Mirror Mere. High on the shores above stood a rough broken column. Durin's Stone.

This passage was an overwriting in ink, but the pencilled text beneath, visible here and there, was written continuously with what precedes (the Company looking back at Moria Gate), and is certainly the most original form of the description of Mirrormere. Against it my father wrote *Not yet used*. He used it in fact in the original draft of 'Lothlórien' (p. 219): a clear demonstration that the new draft B of the latter part of the present chapter preceded work on 'Lothlórien' (see note 20).

B then continues to its conclusion thus:

'So we have passed through Moria,' said Trotter at last, passing his hand over his eyes. 'I know not what put the words into my mouth, but did I not say to Gandalf: If you pass the Gates of Moria, beware![19] Alas that I should have spoken true. No fortune could have been so ill as this: hardly ... had all perished. But now we must do as we can without our friend and guide. At least we may yet avenge him. Let us gird ourselves. It is better for us to strike hard than to mourn long.'

With slightly altered wording this was used as the conclusion of the chapter in the fair copy C also.[20]

Throughout C, *Trotter* (as he is named at every occurrence save once where Gandalf names him) was subsequently changed to *Elf-stone* (see pp. 277–8).

NOTES

1 Though the words 'it only a cover' seem clear, my father cannot have intended 'it only had a cover', as the following text shows.

2 A dwarf *Frár*, companion of Glóin, appeared in the earliest drafts of 'The Council of Elrond' (VI.397, 412), where he was replaced by Burin son of Balin. The three Dwarf-names *Frár, Lóni, Náli*, retained in FR, were again taken from the Old Norse *Elder Edda* – whereas *Flói* (slain in the Dimrill Dale) was not.

3 On the conception of two distinct entrances to Moria from the West, which goes back to the original version of 'The Ring Goes South', see p. 178. The striking out (probably at once) of the reference in the previous chapter (*ibid.*) to 'The Dwarven-door further south' (i.e. south of the Elven-door at the end of the road from Hollin) could be taken as an indication that the present text in fact preceded the new version of 'Moria (i)'. On the other hand, if this were so, it is hard to see why my father should have put in the direction '2 West Gates' at the beginning of the present text (p. 190), seeing that the two entrances were already present in the oldest version of the story of Moria. It seems to me most probable that he wrote '2 West Gates' precisely because he had now changed his mind again; this detail being therefore actually evidence that the first writing of 'Moria (ii)' did follow the new

version of 'Moria (i)'. – Further, in the fair copy text of the present chapter Gimli says (p. 201) that 'it was well for us that ... we came to the Elven-door that was closed', though this was at once or soon rejected.

4   In FR Gandalf entrusted the book to Gimli, to give to Dáin. – The first page of the manuscript, which ends at approximately this point, was written in pencil, but from the beginning of Gandalf's reading from the book my father overwrote it in ink – and then, from this point, carried on the initial text in ink. Thus the original drafting of the words and phrases which Gandalf could interpret in the Book of Mazarbul is partly obliterated; but most of the underlying pencil can be made out, and it can be seen that the text given here (itself emended) did not greatly differ from what it superseded.

5   My father first wrote here: 'veritable Orcs'. Cf. the original sketch for the chapter given in VI.443: 'Gandalf says there are goblins – of very evil kind, larger than usual, real orcs', and my discussion of 'goblins' and 'orcs' in VI.437 note 35. In FR at this point Gandalf says: 'There are Orcs, very many of them. And some are large and evil: black Uruks of Mordor.'

6   In FR it was at this point that Boromir, closing the west door of the chamber, wedged it with broken sword-blades and splinters of wood. It is odd that in the present text it is said here that Boromir kicked the wedges away from the door and heaved it to, and yet immediately afterwards the door 'began to move inwards grinding at the wedges and thrusting them back.'

7   This sentence replaced: 'Gandalf leaped forward and hewed the arm with Glamdring.'

8   The reforging of the Sword of Elendil has been told in the new version of 'The Ring Goes South' (p. 165).

9   In a subsequent version of the passage Gandalf says 'There is no time for counting wounds.'

10 This sentence was first written: 'As they ran cries and the noise of many feet entered the far end behind them.'

11 This passage, with the two references to the appearance of the Trolls, is confused. Though all was written at the same time, phrases were added and rejected phrases were left standing, and my father's intention is in places impossible to determine.

12 Written in the margin at the time of composition: 'Go on ... Do I fight in vain? Fly!' Cf. Trotter's words 'At least we can obey his last command' in the text immediately following.

13 The oddity of the original story (see p. 193 and note 6) in the matter of the wedging of the western door is now removed, for when Boromir had kicked away the wedges and heaved it to he then re-wedged it. All the passages concerned were corrected, probably at once, to give the story as it is in FR.

14   The rejected part of the manuscript (a single sheet written on both sides) was found among my father's papers, the rest of it having gone to Marquette.

15   The sequence of development in this chapter can be expressed thus:

   A → C (C interrupted); B → C (C continued).

16   In a pencilled addition in C to the scene of the Balrog's fall from the Bridge my father changed 'the stone upon which it stood' (the text of FR) to 'the stone upon which *the vast form* stood'.

17   The second *him* is Gandalf, not only from the syntax, but also because the Balrog is always referred to as *it*. FR has 'the shadow about it'.

18   See p. 237 note 5.

19   Aragorn's words to Gandalf *If you pass the doors of Moria, beware!* had entered in 'Moria (i)', p. 178.

20   With this revised wording the passage is found at the beginning of the first draft of 'Lothlórien' (p. 219). In the fair copy C of the present chapter my father subsequently struck it out, and wrote at the end of the text that precedes it: *End of Chapter*. It is clear from this that not only the draft B but also the fair copy of 'The Mines of Moria (ii): The Bridge' were completed before 'Lothlórien' was begun.

XI

THE STORY FORESEEN FROM MORIA

At about this time, and still using the reverse pages and blue covers of the same invaluable examination script, my father wrote a much more elaborate outline of the story to come than any he had yet done. When this was written in relation to the narrative that had been achieved cannot be precisely demonstrated, but far the most likely time, to judge from the beginning of the outline, would be when 'The Mines of Moria (ii)' was at least initially drafted (and probably actually completed in the fair copy) and 'Lothlórien' was immediately contemplated; and therefore I give it in this place.

It is particularly interesting to observe what elements in this new plot derive from earlier sketches, and how those ideas had evolved by this time, as the actual writing of the narrative drew nearer. These are: (1) an isolated page which I have tentatively dated to August 1939 (VI.380); (2) a page actually dated August 1939 (VI.381); (3) an outline set down at the time of the first drafting of 'The Council of Elrond' (VI.410–11).

The new text was written very quickly and roughly, mostly in pencil, and is in places hard to make out. I have expanded contractions and made a few other very small editorial clarifications. It will be seen that despite its fullness it does not at all represent a clearly defined, step-by-step sequence: ideas were emerging and evolving as my father wrote it.

Sketch of Plot

Reach Lothlórien Dec. 15.[1] Take refuge up Trees. Elves befriend them. Dec. 15, 16, 17 they journey to Angle between Anduin and Blackroot.[2] There they remain long. (While they are up trees orcs go by – also Gollum.)

At Angle they debate what is to be done. Frodo feels it is his duty to go straight to Fire Mountain. But Aragorn and Boromir wish to go to Minas Tirith, and if possible gather force. Frodo sees that that will not help. As Minas Tirith is still a long way from Fire Mountain and Sauron will only be the more warned. (Boromir is secretly planning to use the Ring, *since Gandalf is gone*.)

Boromir takes Frodo apart and talks to him. Begs to see Ring again. Evil enters into his heart and he tries to daunt Frodo and then to take it by force. Frodo is obliged to slip it on to escape him. (What does he see then – cloud all round him getting nearer and many fell voices in air?)

Frodo seeing that evil has entered into the Company dare not stay and does not want to imperil hobbits or others. He flies. His loss is not discovered for some time because of Boromir's lies. (Boromir says he has climbed a tree and will be coming back soon?) The hunt eventually fails because Frodo went a long way invisible.

The search. Sam is lost. He tries to track Frodo and comes on Gollum. He follows Gollum and Gollum leads him to Frodo.

Frodo hears following feet. And flies. But Sam comes up too to his surprise. The two are too much for Gollum. Gollum is *daunted* by Frodo – who has a power over him as Ringbearer. (But use of Ring proves bad since it re-establishes power of Ring over Frodo after his cure. At end he cannot willingly part with it.)

Gollum pleads for forgiveness and feigns reform. They make him lead them through the Dead Marshes. (Green faces in the pools.) Lithlad Plain of Ash. The Searching Eye of Barad-dur (a single light in a high window).

★ At point where Sam, Frodo and Gollum meet return to others – for whose adventures see later. *But they should be told at this point.*

The Gap of Gorgoroth not far from Fire Mountain. There are Orc guard-towers on either side of Gorgoroth.[3] They see a host of evil led by Black Riders. Gollum betrays Frodo. He is beaten off, but escapes shrieking to the Black Riders. The Black Riders now have taken form of demonic eagles and fly before host, or [?take eagle-like] vulture birds as steeds.

Frodo toils up Mountain to find Crack.

Rumour of Battle had already reached Frodo, Sam and Gollum. (That is why the host of Mordor was riding out.)

While Frodo is toiling up Mountain he looks back and sees Battle gathering. He hears faint sound of horns in the hills. A great dust where the Horsemen are coming. Thunder from Baraddur and a black storm comes up on an East wind. Frodo wonders what is happening but has no hope that he himself can be saved. The Ringwraiths swoop back. They have heard Gollum's cries.

Orodruin [*written above:* Mount Doom] has three great fissures North, West, South [> West, South, East] in its sides. They are very deep and at an unguessable depth a glow of fire is seen. Every now and again fire rolls out of mountain's heart down the terrific channels. The mountain towers above Frodo. He comes to a flat place on the mountain-side where the fissure is full of fire – Sauron's well of fire. The Vultures are coming. He *cannot* throw Ring in. The Vultures are coming. All goes dark in his eyes and he falls to his knees. At that moment Gollum comes up and wrestles with him, and takes Ring. Frodo falls flat.

Here perhaps Sam comes up, beats off a vulture and hurls himself and Gollum into the gulf?

Function for Sam? Is he to die? (He said there is something I have to do before [I die >] the end.)[4]

Sam could get hold of the Ring. Frodo betrayed by Gollum and taken by orcs (?) to Minas Morgol.[5] They take his ring and find it is no good; they put him in a dungeon, and threaten to send him to Baraddur.

How can Sam get hold of Ring? He keeps watch at night and hears Gollum muttering to himself, words of hatred for Frodo. He draws his sword and leaps on Gollum, [?dragging] him off. He tries to [*insert* utter] horrible words over Frodo – incantation of sleep. A spider charm, or does Gollum get spiders' help? There is a ravine, a spiders' glen, they have to pass at entrance to Gorgoroth. Gollum gets spiders to put spell of sleep on Frodo. Sam drives them off. But cannot wake him. He then gets idea of taking Ring. He sits beside Frodo. Gollum betrays Frodo to the Orc-guard. They are overwhelmed and Sam knocked silly with a club. He puts on Ring and follows Frodo. (A ring from Mazarbul would be useful.)[6]

Sam comes and *uses* Ring. Passes into Morgol and finds Frodo. Frodo feels hatred of Sam and sees him as an orc. But suddenly the orc speaks and holds out Ring and says: Take it. Then Frodo sees it is Sam. They creep out. Frodo is unable.... Sam dresses up like an orc.

They escape but *Gollum follows.*

It is *Sam* that wrestles with Gollum and [?throws] him finally in the gulf.

How are Sam and Frodo saved from the eruption?[7]

An additional passage, but contemporary with the rest, is marked for insertion to this part of the outline.

When Ring *melts* Dark Tower falls or is buried in ash. A great

black cloud and shadow floats away east on a *rising west wind*.
(The smell and sound of the Sea?)

Eruption. The forces of Mordor flee and Horsemen of Rohan
pursue.

Frodo standing on side of Fire Mountain holds up sword. He
now commands Ringwraiths and bids them be gone. They fall
to earth and vanish like wisps of smoke with a terrible wail.

How is Frodo (and Sam) saved from Eruption?

Story turns for a while – after first meeting of Sam, Frodo and
Gollum – to others.

Owing to Boromir's treachery and Frodo's use of Ring the
hunt fails. Merry and Pippin are distracted by loss of Sam and
Frodo. They themselves get lost following echoes. They come to
Entwash and the Topless Forest,[8] and fall in with Treebeard
and his Three Giants.

Legolas and Gimli also get lost and get captured by Saruman.?

Boromir and Aragorn (who notes a change in Boromir – who
is keen to break off the chase and go home) reach Minas Tirith,
which is besieged by Sauron except at back. ? Siege is briefly
told from point of view of watchers on battlements. Evil has
now hold of Boromir who is jealous of Aragorn. The Lord of
Minas Tirith is slain[9] and they choose Aragorn. Boromir deserts
and sneaks off to Saruman, to get his help in becoming Lord of
Minas Tirith.

How does Gandalf reappear?

All this section, concerned with the 'western story', was struck out
and replaced, immediately, by a fuller and altered version, in which
the idea that Legolas and Gimli were captured by Saruman is rejected
and their new story is linked to the reappearance of Gandalf.

Story turns for a while to the others – ? after first meeting of
Sam, Frodo and Gollum.

(*one chapter*) Owing to Boromir's treachery and Frodo's use of
Ring the hunt fails. Aragorn is overwhelmed with grief, thinking
he has failed trust as Gandalf's successor. Merry and Pippin are
distracted by losing Sam and Frodo, and wandering far (deluded
by echoes) they also get lost. Merry and Pippin come up
Entwash into Fangorn and have adventure with Treebeard.
Treebeard turns out a decent giant. They tell him their tale. He
is very perturbed by news of Saruman, and more so by the fall of
Gandalf. He won't go near Mordor. He offers to carry them to
Rohan and perhaps Minas Tirith. They set off.

(one chapter)   Boromir, Aragorn, and Legolas and Gimli.

Legolas feels the Company is broken up, and Gimli has no more heart. The four part. Aragorn and Boromir to Minas Tirith, Legolas and Gimli north. Legolas means to join Elves of Lothlórien for a while. Gimli means to go back up Anduin to Mirkwood and so home. They journey together. Legolas and Gimli both sing laments. Suddenly they meet Gandalf!

Gandalf's story. Overcame Balrog. The gulf was not deep (only a kind of moat and was full of silent water). He followed the channel and got down into the Deeps. ?? Clad himself in Mithril-mail and fought his way out slaying many trolls.

[?Does] Gandalf *shine* in the sun. He has a new power after overcoming of Balrog? *He is now clad in white.*

Gandalf is dreadfully downcast at the news of the loss of Frodo. He hastens south again with Legolas and Gimli.

(one chapter)   Inside Minas Tirith. Aragorn began to suspect Boromir at the time of the loss of Frodo. A sudden change seems to come over Boromir. He is anxious to go away home at once and not look for Frodo.

Minas Tirith is besieged by Sauron's forces that have crossed Anduin at Osgiliath, and by Saruman who is come up in rear. There seems no hope. Evil has now got complete hold of Boromir. The Lord of Minas Tirith is slain. They choose Aragorn as chief. Boromir is jealous and enraged – he deserts and sneaks off to Saruman, seeking his aid in getting lordship.

At this point the siege must be broken by Gandalf with Legolas and Gimli and by Treebeard. (But not too much fighting or it will spoil last battle of Gorgoroth.) Gandalf might simply walk through lines, or else have a contest with Saruman. Treebeard walks through. They see a huge tree walking over plain.

Saruman shuts himself up in Isengard.

Sally from Minas Tirith. Gandalf drives Black Riders back and takes crossing of Anduin at Osgiliath. Horsemen ride behind him to Gorgoroth. Hear a great wind and see flames out of Fire Mountain.

Somehow or other Frodo and Sam must be found in Gorgoroth. Possibly by Merry and Pippin. (If any one of the hobbits is *slain* it must be the cowardly Pippin doing something brave. For instance –

Here the outline breaks off, but after a large space continues again lower down on the same page, and now with numbered chapters, beginning at 'XXVI'. Since 'Moria (ii)' was XVII, my father envisaged eight further chapters to this point.

After fall of Mordor. They return to Minas Tirith. Feast. Aragorn comes to meet them. Moon rises [?on] Minas Morgol.

XXVI   Aragorn looks out and sees moon rise over Minas Morgol. He remains behind – and becomes Lord of Minas *Ithil*. What about Boromir? Does he repent? [*Written later in margin*: No – slain by Aragorn.]

Gandalf calls at Isengard (see addition). [*This addition is found on a separate slip*: On way home: they ride horses from Rohan. The[y] call at Isengard. Gandalf knocks. Saruman comes out very affable. 'Ah, my dear Gandalf. What a mess the world is in. Really we must consult together – such men as we are needed. Now what about our spheres of influence?'

Gandalf looks at him. 'I am the White Wizard now,' he said – 'look at your many colours.' Saruman is [?clad] in a filthy mud colour. 'They seem to have run.' Gandalf takes his staff and breaks it over his knee. [?He gives a thin shriek.] 'Go, Saruman,' he said, 'and beg from the charitable for a day's digging.'

Isengard is given to the Dwarves. Or to Radagast?]

They ride home to Rivendell.

XXVII   Song of the Banished Shadow.

Rivendell.   Meeting with Bilbo.

XXVIII   What happens to Shire?

Last scene. *Sailing away of Elves* [*added faintly*: Bilbo with them] and the [*sic*]

XXIX   Sam and Frodo go into a green land by the Sea?

Certain of these narrative ideas had appeared before, in the earlier plot-sketches referred to on p. 207, such as the siege of Minas Tirith, Frodo's separation from the Company and Sam's seeking for him, Gollum's seeming reform and guidance to the Mountain of Fire, the Searching Eye, the 'host of evil' led by Black Riders, Gollum's treachery, Frodo's inability to cast the Ring into the Fire, and the eruption of the Mountain. But now the structure becomes more solid and secure.

To look through this new outline in sequence: the fact that nothing is told here about Lothlórien (though its people are mentioned – 'Elves befriend them', and later it is told that it was Legolas' intention 'to join Elves of Lothlórien for a while') suggests, not that the Lothlórien story had been written, but that my father was on the verge of writing it and had no need to set down much about it. If it had been written he would surely not have included it in the outline at all; and the words

'While they are up trees orcs go by – also Gollum' look like the first written emergence of this element in the story. But the actual name *Lothlórien* has already made its appearance in the LR papers, in the new version of 'The Ring Goes South', p. 167.

The 'angle' between the river flowing down from Dimrill Dale (Redway, Blackroot, Silverlode) and the Great River (see the original rough sketch-map given in VI.439) is now called *Angle*. Here the Company 'remained long', but there is no indication whether Elves of Lothlórien were present. It is at Angle that a major feature of the structure of LR first enters. In an earlier outline (VI.410) Frodo becomes separated from the Company, involuntarily as it seems, through fear of Gollum; but now (being already determined to go directly to Mordor rather than by way of Minas Tirith) he is brought to the point of fleeing away alone through Boromir, who desires to appropriate the Ring for the purposes of Minas Tirith. Already my father foresaw that Boromir, speaking to Frodo apart, would ask to see the Ring again, that (as is implied) Frodo would refuse, and that Boromir would then try to take it by force and oblige Frodo to put it on in order to escape from him – explaining how it was that Frodo got clear away and could not be found despite the hunt for him. On the other hand, since all this takes place at Angle, there is *no journey down Anduin*, boats are never mentioned – and there is no mention even of Frodo's need to cross the river. The whole story of how Sam would come to accompany Frodo on his journey to the Fiery Mountain would be entirely changed (though not before it had been further developed from its form in this outline).

In the account of that journey several new names appear. *Lithlad* the Plain of Ash appears once in LR (*The Two Towers* IV.3, 'the mournful plains of Lithlad and of Gorgoroth'), though for some reason the name was not entered on either of the maps published in LR; it is found however on the First Map (p. 309) and subsequently. The plain of Lithlad lay south of Ered Lithui, the Ash Mountains, away to the east of Barad–dûr; there would thus seem no reason for Frodo and Sam ever to have come to it, as seems to be implied in this outline. The valley of Gorgoroth, above which was built the Dark Tower, appears in the fifth version of 'The Council of Elrond' (p. 144), and the Gap of Gorgoroth ('with Orc guard-towers on either side') in this outline is the first intimation of a pass between the mountain-walls fencing Mordor on north and west (afterwards Udûn, between the Morannon and the Isenmouthe).

The winged Nazgûl – Black Riders horsed now upon vultures – appear, but here in the rôle of leaders of the host of Mordor as it rides out to battle. Sam's part in the final events was still very shadowy and speculative, but already the idea enters that Gollum (whose inner motives seem to have been far less complex in respect of Frodo than they afterwards became) would betray Sam and Frodo to spiders in a ravine or glen 'at the entrance to Gorgoroth'. At this stage, as will be seen later, the entry into Mordor by way of the Stairs of Cirith Ungol did not exist, and when that name appears it will bear a different geographical sense. The spiders seem to have arisen in the context of explaining how Sam came to take the Ring from Frodo; and features of the later story begin to take shape: Sam's rout of the spider(s), Gollum's betrayal of the unconscious Frodo to the orcs, his capture and imprisonment (but here in Minas Morgol), Sam's entry into the fortress wearing the Ring, Frodo's sudden hatred of Sam whom he sees as an orc, and their escape.

The Breaking of the Fellowship imposed on my father the need to follow two distinct narrative paths, but he would still follow the fortunes of Frodo and Sam somewhat further before returning to the others (since the reunion of Sam and Frodo, involving Sam's first falling in with Gollum, was much less swiftly achieved than it is in FR).

The second narrative again takes a huge step forward here, but there was still a great way to go. Most important, Merry and Pippin now move into a central position in the story, and it is they (not as in a former outline Frodo, VI.410) who encounter Treebeard – although the entire narrative of the attack by Orcs on the camp beneath Amon Hen, Boromir's death, the forced march across Rohan, and the battle between the Rohirrim and the Orcs on the eaves of Fangorn is absent. Merry and Pippin merely become lost as they seek for Frodo and Sam, and wandering along the river Entwash (which here first appears) come to the Forest of Fangorn without any relation to the larger story; but through them Treebeard (now finally established as a 'decent' sort of person, cf. p. 71) comes to play a part in the breaking of the siege of Minas Tirith.

On the other hand, for Aragorn and Boromir my father had at this time a plan almost wholly different from what would soon emerge. Departing together to Minas Tirith, the original Company will be still further fragmented, for Legolas and Gimli (escaping the fate of capture by Saruman momentarily projected for them, p. 210) set off north together. It is indeed Legolas and Gimli who fall in with Gandalf returned, now clad in white and possessed of new powers, and with him they turn back and hasten south; but there is no indication of where they met him (save that it was south of Lothlórien), and in fact no indication of geography for any of these events. Rohan plays no part in the story at all (beyond the several mentions of the Horsemen riding against Mordor), and the Siege of Minas Tirith is (mysteriously) to be 'broken by Gandalf with Legolas and Gimli and by Treebeard.' Boromir would play a shameful part, treacherously fleeing to Saruman (a faint adumbration of Wormtongue?) in his hatred for Aragorn, chosen to be successor to the slain lord of Minas Tirith. Isengard remains inviolate, and the Ents do not appear[10] – yet the visit of

Gandalf to Saruman in his fortress, and his humiliation, is present, placed here on the homeward journey.

Much of the narrative 'material', it may be said, was now assembled. But the structure of that narrative in the lands west of Anduin as my father now foresaw it would be wholly changed, and changed above all by the emergence of the Kingdom of Rohan into the full light of the story, and of its relations with Gondor and with Isengard.[11]

NOTES

1   'Reach Lothlórien Dec. 15': this date does not agree with the chronology, which is surprising. The time-scheme referred to on p. 169, which clearly accompanied this state of the narrative, continues on from 'December 9   Snow on Caradras' (a date that actually appears in the text) thus:

Dec. 10   Retreat. Wolves at night.

     11   Start for Moria. Reach Doors at sundown. Travel in Mines till midnight (15 miles).

     12   Well-chamber. All day in Moria (20 miles). Night in 21st Hall.

     13   *Mazarbul*. Battle of Bridge. Escape to Lothlórien.

This scheme was made when the 'Lothlórien' story was at any rate in progress, but the earliest sketch of the march of the Company from Dimrill Dale (p. 218) demands the date 13 December.

2   The name *Anduin*, thus written and not the result of subsequent correction, occurs in the fifth version of 'The Council of Elrond' (p. 157 note 5). The name *Blackroot* shows that this outline was written after the new version of 'The Ring Goes South' (see p. 166).

3   This sentence was put in as an afterthought at a different point in the manuscript, but it seems appropriate to insert it here.

4   Sam said this to Frodo after the night spent with the Elves in the Woody End (FR p. 96).

5   This part of the text was written in pencil, but these few lines were overwritten in ink later (apparently simply for clarity's sake), and the form as overwritten is actually *Morgul*; elsewhere in the outline, however, the form is *Morgol*.

6   The 'ring from Mazarbul' evidently refers back to what is said earlier: 'They take [Frodo's] ring and find it is no good.'

7   A scrap of torn paper found in isolation bears the following pencilled notes dashed down in haste:

    Could Sam *steal the Ring* to save Frodo from danger?

    The Black Riders capture Frodo and he is taken to Mordor – but he has no Ring and is put in prison.

Sam flees – but is pursued by Gollum.
It is Sam and Gollum that wrestle on the Mountain.
Frodo is saved by the fall of the Tower.

It seems very probable that these notes belong to the same time as the present outline. On the same scrap are notes referring to the Shire at the end of the story, when Frodo and Sam returning find that 'Cosimo [Sackville-Baggins] has industrialised it. Factories and smoke. The Sandymans have a biscuit factory. Iron is found.' The last words are: 'They go west and set sail to Greenland.' *Greenland* is clear, however improbable it may seem; but cf. the last words of the present outline (p. 212): 'Sam and Frodo go into a *green land* by the Sea'.

8   Fangorn is called 'the Topless Forest' in a rejected sentence in the new version of 'The Ring Goes South', p. 167.

9   In the outline given in VI.411 the King of Ond was Boromir's father.

10 Since in the sketch-plot given in VI.410 the 'tree-giants' assailed the besiegers of Ond, it may be that their presence was understood in this outline also; but this is not in any way suggested.

11 Looked at in terms of the movements of the principal persons, it seems that a crucial idea, though at once rejected, would turn out to have been the capture of Legolas and Gimli by Saruman (p. 210). My father remained convinced, perhaps, that Saruman did nonetheless play a part in the fragmentation of the Company of the Ring; and the aimless wanderings of Merry and Pippin along the Entwash that brought them to Treebeard's domain were transformed into the forced march of captives to Isengard – for Isengard was close to the Forest of Fangorn. Thus entered also the death of Boromir, and the withdrawal of Aragorn from immediate departure to Minas Tirith.

XII

LOTHLÓRIEN

In the first fully-written narrative, the two chapters 6 and 7 in Book II of FR ('Lothlórien' and 'The Mirror of Galadriel') are one, though here treated separately. This text is extremely complex in that, while it constitutes a nearly complete narrative, the form in which it exists is not the result of writing in a simple sequence; parts of it are later, with later names, and were written over a partly or wholly erased earlier form. Other parts were not rewritten and earlier names appear, sometimes corrected, sometimes not; and the original text was much emended throughout.

In fact, it seems to me certain that the whole text, including some scraps of initial drafting and outlining on isolated pages, belongs to the same time and the same impulse. The 'August 1940' examination script was once again used for the entire complex of papers. The manuscript varies greatly in difficulty, some sections being fairly clear and legible, others very much the reverse. In places words are so reduced and letter-shapes so transformed that one might well hit upon the right word but not know it, if there are insufficient clues from the context or from the later text. Word-endings are miswritten or omitted, successive forms of a sentence are left standing side by side, and punctuation is constantly lacking. This is a case where the actual appearance of the manuscript is exceedingly different from the printed interpretation of it.

No satisfactory presentation of such a text as this is really possible. If the earliest form of the story is given, and the later alterations ignored, then difficulties such as the following are encountered. In the passage where Legolas reports to the others his conversation with the Elves in the mallorn-tree (FR p. 357) the original narrative (in ink) had:

Now they bid us to climb up, three in each of these trees that stand here near together. I will go first.

This was corrected (in pencil) to a form close to that of FR:

Now they bid me to climb up with Frodo, of whom they seem to have heard. The rest they ask to wait a little, and to keep watch at the foot of the tree.

But the primary narrative then continues (in pencil) on the next sheet with this revised story, in which Legolas and Frodo are the first to ascend (with Sam behind). On the other hand, if all later alteration (which is in any case far from achieving an overall consistency) is admitted, the FR form is closely approached and the earlier stages ignored. I have adopted therefore the former method, and attempt to clarify complexities as they arise. The notes to this chapter form a commentary on the text and are integral to its presentation.

A few brief notes about the sojourn of the Company in Lothlórien begin the long preparatory synopsis given in the last chapter (p. 207). There is there no suggestion of Galadriel and Celeborn; and it is 'at Angle', between Blackroot and Anduin, that Boromir accosts Frodo and attempts to take the Ring. The first march from Moria is more fully sketched in the following notes.

> They pass into Dimrill Dale. It is a golden afternoon, but dark in the Dale.
> Mirrormere. Smooth sward. Deep blue like night sky.
> [*Notes scribbled in later:* Orcs won't come out by day. Frodo's wounds dressed by Trotter, so they discover the mithril-mail.]
> No time to stay. Gimli's regret. See the black springs of Morthond;[1] follow it.
> Make for Lothlórien. Legolas' description. The wood is in winter but still bears leaves that have turned golden. They do not fall till spring, when the green comes, and great yellow flowers. It was a garden of the Wood-elves long ago – before the dwarves disturbed the evils beneath the mountains, he said (Gimli does not like that). They lived in houses in trees before the darkening world drove them underground.[2]
> In dusk Frodo again hears feet but cannot see anything following. They march on into the dusk.
> They take refuge in trees, and see Orcs march by beneath.
> Frodo long after sees a sloping back[ed] figure moving swiftly. It sniffs under the tree, stares up, and then disappears.

The passage of the Orcs beneath, and the coming of Gollum, were first referred to in the outline given on p. 207.

I turn now to the narrative. The chapter is numbered XVIII, and paginated continuously (with one gap), but it has no title. As I have said, I give (so far as possible) the most original form of the text, and do not, as a rule, indicate small subsequent emendations bringing it nearer to FR, though many or all of them may well belong to the same time.

'Alas, I fear we cannot wait here longer!' said Aragorn. He looked towards the mountains, and held up his sword. 'Farewell, Gandalf,' he cried. 'Did I not say to you: *if you pass*

the doors of Moria, beware? I know not what put the words
into my mouth, but alas! that I spoke true. No fortune could
have been more grievous. What hope have we without you?' He
turned to the Company. 'We must do without hope!' he said.
'At least we may yet be avenged. Let us gird ourselves and weep
no more. It is better to strike hard than to mourn long!³ Come!
We have a long road and much to do!'

They rose and looked about them. Northward the Dale ran
up into a glen of shadows between two great arms of the
mountains, above which three tall white peaks towered.⁴ Many
torrents fell white over the steep sides into the valley. A mist of
foam hung in the air.

To the west [*read* east]⁵ the mountains marched to a sudden
end, and far lands could be descried beyond them vague and
wide. To the south the mountains receded endlessly as far as
sight could reach. Less than a mile away, and below them a little
(for they stood still on the skirts of the mountains) lay a mere: it
was long and oval, shaped like a great spear-head that thrust up
deep into the northern glen. Its southern end was beyond the
edge of the shadow, under the sunny sky. But its waters were
dark: a deep blue like the night sky seen through a lighted
window. Its face was still and unruffled. About it lay a smooth
sward shelving on all sides down to its bare unbroken rim.⁶

'There lies Kheledzâram,⁷ the Mirror-mere!' said Gimli sadly.
'I hoped to look on it in joy and linger here a while. I remember
that he said: "May you have joy of the sight, but whatever you
may do I cannot stay." Now it is I that must hasten away, and
he that must stay.'

The Company went down the road, fading and broken, but
still showing that here a great paved way had once wound up
from the lowlands to the gate. It passed hard by the sward of
Mirror-mere, and there not far from the road by the brink of the
water there stood a single column, now broken at the top.

'That is Durin's Stone,' said Gimli. '[We >] I cannot pass
without pausing there a minute, to look upon the wonder of the
Dale.'

'Be swift then,' said Trotter, looking back towards the Gate.
'The sun sinks early. Orcs will not come out till it is dusk, but
we must be far away ere night comes. The moon will appear for
the last time tonight and it will be dark.'

'Come with me, Frodo,' said the dwarf, 'and any else who
wish.' But only Sam and Legolas followed.⁸ He ran down the

sward and looked at the pillar. The runes upon it were worn away. 'This stone marks the spot where Durin first looked in the Mirror-mere,' said the dwarf. 'Let us look.' They stooped over the water.

For a while they could see nothing. No shadow of themselves fell on the mere. Slowly at the edges they saw the forms of the encircling mountains revealed, mirrored in a profound blue, and amidst it a space of sky. There like jewels in the deep shone glinting stars, though the sunlight was in the sky above. No shadow of themselves was seen.

'Fair Kheledzâram,' said Gimli. 'There lies the crown of Durin till he wakes. Farewell.' He bowed and turned away, and hastened back up the sward to the road again.

It wound now quickly down running away southwest [read southeast][9] out from between the arms of the mountains. A little below the Mere they came upon a deep well of dark water almost black; from it a freshet fell over a stone lip and ran gurgling away in a stony channel. 'This is the spring whence the Blackroot rises,' said Gimli. 'Do not drink from it: it is icy cold.'

'Soon,' said Trotter, 'it will become a swift river, fed by many other torrents from [?all the land]. Our road leads beside it. And we must go swifter than it runs. There is our way.' Out on before them they could see the Blackroot winding away in the lower land, until it was lost in a distance that glowed like pale gold on the edge of sight.

'There lie the woods of Lothlórien,' said Trotter. 'Their eaves are yet many miles away (four leagues or more), but we must reach them before night.'

[Now they went on silently][10] for some time, but every step grew more painful for Frodo. In spite of the bright [?winter] sun the air seemed biting after the warm dark of Moria. Sam at [his] side was also failing. The cut in his arm was paining him.[11] They lagged behind together. Trotter looked back anxiously. 'So much has happened,' he said, 'that I had forgotten you, Frodo, and Sam. I am sorry: you are both hurt, and we have done nothing to ease you or to find out how serious are your hurts. What shall we do? There is nothing we can do in this empty region, with the gate and our foes so near behind.'

'How far is there still to go?' said Frodo.

They have a first meal 2½ hours after noon. Beside a beautiful little fall in the Blackroot, where another torrent coming from west flowed out and they both fell over some green stone. Trotter dresses Sam's wound. 'The cut is looking ill – but luckily is not (as orc-cuts may be) poisoned.' Trotter bathes it in the water and lays a leaf of *athelas* against it.

Then he turns attention to Frodo. Reluctantly he strips off his jacket and tunic, and suddenly the mithril-corslet shines and flashes in the sun. Trotter strips it from him and holds it up. Description of its radiance.

'This is a pretty hobbit-skin!' said Trotter. 'If it were known they wore such a hide, all the hunters of the world would be crowding to the Shire.'

'And all the hunters of the world [would] shoot in vain,' said Gimli, staring in amazement. 'Bilbo saved your life – it was a generous and timely gift.'

There was a great dark bruise on Frodo's side and breast, the rings driven through shirt into flesh... His left side also was bruised against the wall.

'Nothing is broken,' said Trotter.

The text now becomes for a space very ragged, the story being in its most primitive form of composition, and soon passes into a rough sketch of the narrative to come.

Kindle fire warm water bathed in *athelas*. Pads fastened under the mail, which is put on again.

They hurry on again. Sun sinks behind mountains. Shadows creep out down mountain side and over the land. Dusk is about them, but there is a glow on the land to the East. ... pale yellow in dusk.[12] They have come 12–14 miles from Gate and are nearly done. Legolas describes Lothlórien.

Near forest gate another small river comes in from right (west) across the path. The bridge is no longer there. They wade across and halt on other side with water as defence. Climb trees.

Orcs ... at night. But a pleasant [?adventure] with Wood-elves next day. They are escorted to Wood-elves' houses in trees in angle of Blackroot and Anduin by light marches (no orc comes). Several (2–3) pleasant days. 40 miles. Sorrow of whole world for news of fall of Gandalf. They are now nearly 100 leagues (300 miles) south of Rivendell.[13]

An isolated page of very rough drafting takes up with Frodo's reply to Gimli's question (' "What is it?" said the dwarf', FR p. 351):

'I don't know,' said Frodo. 'I thought I heard feet, and I thought I saw light – like eyes. I have done so often since we entered Moria.'

Gimli paused and stooped to the ground. 'I can hear nothing but the night-speech of plant and stone,' he said. 'Come, let us hurry! The others are out of sight already.'

The night wind blew chill up the valley to meet them. They passed many scattered trees, tall with pale stems. In front a great shadow loomed, and the endless rustle of leaves like poplars in the breeze.

'Lothlórien,' said Legolas. 'Lothlórien. We are come to the [?gates] of the golden wood. Alas that it is winter.'

Here the formed narrative takes up again.[14]

Under the night the trees stood tall before them, arched over the stream and road that ran suddenly beneath their spreading boughs. In the dim light of the stars their stems were grey, and their quivering leaves a hint of fallow gold.

'Lothlórien!' said Aragorn. 'Glad I am to hear the leaves! We are barely five leagues from the Gates, but we can go no further. Let us hope that there is some virtue of the Elves that will protect us this night – if Elves indeed dwell here still in the darkening world.'[15]

'It is long since any of my folk returned hither,' said Legolas; 'for we dwell now very far away; yet it is told that though some have gone for ever some abide still in Lothlórien, but they dwell deep in the wood many leagues from here.'[16]

'Then we must fend for ourselves tonight,' said Aragorn. 'Let us go on yet a little way until the wood is all about us, and then will turn aside from the road.'

A mile within the wood they came upon another stream flowing down swiftly from the tree-clad slopes that climbed back towards the Mountains. They heard it splashing over a fall away among the shadows on their right. Its dark hurrying waters ran across the path before them and joined the [Blackroot >] Morthond in a swirl of dim pools among the roots of trees.

'Here is the [Taiglin >] Linglor,' said Legolas. 'Of it the wood-elves made many songs, remembering the rainbow upon its singing falls and the golden flowers that floated in its foam. All is dark now, and the Bridge of Linglor that the elves made is broken down. But it is not deep. Let us wade across. There is healing in its [cold >] cool waters / But I will bathe my feet in it – for it is said that its waters are healing. On the further bank we can rest, and the sound of running water may bring us sleep.'[17]

They followed the elf, and one by one climbed down the steep bank and bathed their [feet][18] in the stream. For a moment

Frodo stood near the bank and let the cold water flow about his
tired feet. It was cold but its very touch was clean, and as it
mounted to his knees he felt that the stain of travel and the
weariness of his limbs was washed away.

When all the Company had crossed they sat and rested and
ate a little food, while Legolas told them tales of Lothlórien
before the world was grey.

Here there is a space in the manuscript, with the words *insert song*.
There are many pages of rough working for Legolas' song of Amroth
and Nimrodel, leading to a version that (while certainly belonging to
this time) is for much of its length very close to the form in FR (pp.
354–5). The name of the maiden is *Linglorel* (once *Inglorel*), becoming *Nimladel*, *Nimlorel* (see note 17), and in the final version found
here *Nimlothel* (corrected to *Nimrodel*). Her lover was *Ammalas* (as
he appears in the narrative that follows), and the form *Amroth* can be
seen emerging as my father wrote the first line of the ninth verse:
'When Ammalas beheld the shore', with a rejected name *Amaldor*
momentarily appearing before the line became 'When *Amroth* saw the
fading shore'.

Associated with the texts of the song is a version of the words of
Legolas that preceded it (FR p. 353):

> 'I will sing you a song,' he said. 'It is a fair song in the woodland
> tongue: but this is how it runs in the common speech, as some in
> Rivendell have turned it.' In a soft voice hardly to be heard amid the
> rustle of the leaves above he began.

This is apparently the first appearance of the term *Common Speech*. –
The final version found here is virtually as that in FR through the first
six verses (but with the name *Nimlothel*); then follows:

> *A wind awoke in Northern lands*
> *and loud it blew and free,*
> *and bore the ship from Elven-strands*
> *across the shining sea.*
>
> *Beyond the waves the shores were grey,*
> *the mountains sinking low;*
> *as salt as tears the driving spray*
> *the wind a cry of woe.*
>
> *When Amroth saw the fading shore*
> *beyond the heaving swell*
> *he cursed the faithless ship that bore*
> *him far from Nimlothel.*
>
> *An Elven-lord he was of old*
> *before the birth of men*

> *when first the boughs were hung with gold*
> *in fair Lothlórien.*

A variant of this verse is given:

> *An Elven-lord he was of old*
> *when all the woods were young*
> *and in Lothlórien with gold*
> *the boughs of trees were hung.*

The eleventh verse, and the last verse, are as in FR, but the twelfth reads here:

> *The foam was in his flowing hair,*
> *a light about him shone;*
> *afar they saw the waves him bear*
> *as floats the northern swan.*

Pencilled suggestions in the margins, no doubt of this same time, move the verses a little further towards the final form; and at the end of the song my father noted: 'If all this is included, Legolas will have to say that it represents only a few of the verses of the original (e.g. the departure from Lórien is omitted).'

An outline for the next part of the story may be given here. It is very roughly written indeed, and I have made one or two obvious corrections.

> Legolas sings song of Linglorel.
> Legolas describes the houses of the Galadrim.
> Gimli says trees would be safer.
> Aragorn decides to climb for night.
> They find a group of great trees near the falls (to right). Legolas is about to climb one with many low boughs when a voice in elven-speech comes from above. He fears arrows. But after a converse in elven-speech reports that all is well. Warnings of things afoot have reached folk of Lórien from the Gladden Fields, when Elrond's messengers came East. They have set guards. (Saw many orcs passing west of Lórien towards Moria: put this in later, when Elves talk to Company.) [See pp. 227–8.]
> They did not challenge or shoot because they heard Legolas' voice – and after the sound of his song. They have a great platform in 2 trees by the falls.
> Legolas, Sam and Frodo go on platform with 3 elves. Others on another platform and Aragorn and Boromir in crotch of a large tree.
> Orcs come to Linglorel in night. The Elves do not shoot because they are in too great number: but one slips away to warn folk in wood and prepare an ambush.

After all is quiet again Frodo sees Gollum creep into wood. He looks up and begins to climb, but just as the Elves fit arrows to bow Frodo stays them. Gollum has a sense of danger and fades away.

Next day the Elves lead them to Angle.

After the song of Legolas the narrative continues:

His voice faltered and fell silent. 'I do not remember all the words,' he said. 'It is a fair song, and that is but the beginning; for it is long and sad. It tells how sorrow came upon Lothlórien, Lórien of the flowers, when the world darkened, and the dwarves awakened evil in the Mountains.'

'But the dwarves did not make the evil,' said Gimli.

'I said not so,' said Legolas sadly. 'Yet evil came. And it was told that Linglorel[19] was lost. For such was the name of that maiden, and they gave the same name to the mountain-stream that she loved: she sang beside the waterfalls playing upon a harp. There in spring when the wind is in the new leaves the echo of her voice may still be heard, they say. But the elves of her kindred departed, and she was lost in the passes of the mountains,[20] and none know where she now may be. It is said in the song that the elven ship waited in the havens long for her, but a wind arose in the night and bore him into the West; and when Ammalas[21] her lover saw that the land was far away he leaped into the sea, but whether he came ever back to the Hither Shores and found Linglorel is not told.

'It is said that Linglorel had a house built in branches of a tree; for that was the manner of the Elves of Lórien, and may be yet; and for that reason they are called Galadrim, the Tree-people.[22] Deep in the wood the trees are very tall and strong. And our people did not delve in the ground or build fastnesses before the Shadows [read Shadow] came.'

'Yet even so, in these latter days, a dwelling in the trees might be thought safer than sitting on the ground,' said Gimli. He looked across the water to the road that led back to Dimrill Dale, and then up into the roof of dark boughs above them.

'Your words bring good counsel, Gimli,' said Aragorn.[23] 'We have no time to build, but tonight we will become Galadrim and seek refuge in the tree-tops, if we can. We have sat here beside the road longer already than was wise.'

The Company now turned aside from the path, and went into the shadows of the deeper woods westward, away from the Blackroot. Not far from the falls of Linglorel they found a cluster of tall strong trees, some of which overhung the stream.[24]

'I will climb up,' said Legolas, 'for I am at home among trees, or in their branches; though these trees are of a kind strange to me. *Mallorn* is their name, those that bear the yellow blossom, but I have never climbed in one. I will see now what is their shape and growth.' He sprang lightly upward from the ground and caught a branch that grew from the tree-bole high above his head. Even as he swung a voice spoke from the shadows above them.

'*Daro!*'[25] it said, and Legolas dropped back again in surprise and fear. He shrank against the tree-bole. 'Stand still,' he whispered to the others, 'and do not speak!'

There was a sound of laughter above their heads and another clear voice spoke in the Elven-tongue. Frodo could catch little that was said, for the speech of the silvan folk east of the mountains, such as they used among themselves, was strange.[26] Legolas looked up and answered in the same tongue.

'Who are they and what do they say?' said [Pippin >] Merry.

'They're elves,' said Sam. 'Can't you hear the voices?'

'They say,' said Legolas, 'that you breathe so loud that they could shoot you in the dark. But that you need have no fear. They have been watching us for a long time. They heard my voice across the Linglorel and knew of what people I came, so that they did not oppose our crossing. And they have heard my song and heard the names of Linglorel and Ammalas. Now they bid us to climb up, three in each of these trees that stand here near together. I will go first.'

The last part of Legolas' remarks was changed in pencil to the text of FR: 'Now they bid me to climb up with Frodo, of whom they seem to have heard. The rest they ask to wait a little, and to keep watch at the foot of the tree.' The manuscript then continues for a short stretch in pencil, and clearly belongs with this alteration, since Legolas and Frodo are the first to ascend.

Out of the shadows there was let down a ladder of silver rope – very slender it looked, but proved strong enough to bear many men. Legolas climbed swiftly followed more slowly by Frodo, and behind came Sam trying not to breathe loud. The tree was very tall [*written above:* a mallorn], and its large bole was fair and round with a smooth silken bark. The branches grew out nearly straight at first and then swept upwards; but near the top of the main stem dwindled into a crown, and there they found a wooden platform [*added:* or 'flet' as such things were called in those days: the elves called it *talan*. It was] made of grey close-grained wood – the wood of the mallorn.

Three elves were seated on it. They were clad in grey, and could not be seen against the tree-stems unless they moved. One of them uncovered a small lamp that gave out a slender silver beam and held it up, looking at their faces. Then he shut out the light and spoke words of welcome in the Elven tongue. Frodo spoke haltingly in return.

'Welcome,' they said again in ordinary speech. Then one spoke slowly. 'We speak seldom any tongue but our own,' he said; 'for we dwell now in the heart of the woods and do not willingly have dealings with any other folk. Some only of us go abroad for the gathering of tidings and our protection. I am one. Hathaldir is my name. My brothers Orfin and Rhimbron speak your tongue but little. We have heard of your coming, for the messengers of Elrond passed through Lothlórien on their way home by the Dimrill Stair.[27] We had not heard of hobbits before, nor even seen one until now. You do not look evil, and you come with Legolas, who is of our northern kindred. We are willing to do as Elrond asked and befriend you. Though it is not our custom we will lead you through our land. But you must stay here tonight. How many are you?'[28]

'Eight,' said Legolas. 'Myself, four hobbits, two men (one is Aragorn, an elf-friend, beloved of Elrond), and a dwarf. [And we are yet weighed with sorrow, for our leader is lost. Gandalf the wizard was lost in Moria.]'[29]

'A dwarf!' said Hathaldir. 'I do not like that. We do not have dealings with dwarves since the evil days. We cannot allow him to pass.'

'But he is an elf-friend and known to Elrond,' said Frodo. 'Elrond chose him to be of our company; and he has been valiant and faithful.'

The Elves spoke together in soft voices, and questioned Legolas in their own tongue. 'Well then,' said Hathaldir. 'We will do this though it is against our liking. If Aragorn and Legolas will guard him and answer for him he shall go blindfold through Lothlórien.

'But now there is need of haste. Your company must not remain longer on the ground. We have been keeping watch on the rivers, ever since we saw a great troop of orcs going north along the skirts of the mountains towards Moria many days ago. Wolves were howling on the wood's border. If you have indeed come from Moria the peril cannot be far behind. Tomorrow you must go far. The hobbits shall climb up here and stay with us – we do not fear them! There is another [guard's nest > flet >] *talan* in the next tree. There the others must go. You Legolas must be our security. And call to us if aught is amiss. Have an eye on that dwarf!'

Legolas went down again bringing Hathaldir's message; and soon afterwards Merry and Pippin climbed up onto the high [?platform]. 'There,' said Merry, 'we have brought up your blankets for you. The rest of our baggage Aragorn has hidden in a deep drift of old leaves.'

'There was no need,' said Hathaldir. 'It is chill in the tree tops in winter, though the wind is southward; but we have drink and food to give you that will keep out night chills, and there are skins and wraps to spare with us.'

The hobbits accepted the second supper gladly, and soon, wrapped as warmly as they could, they tried to get to sleep. Weary as they were it was not easy for them, for hobbits do not like heights and do not sleep upstairs (even when they have any upstairs, which is rare). The flet was not at all to their liking. It had no kerb or rail, and only a wind screen on one side which could be moved and fixed in different places. 'I hope if I do get to sleep I shan't roll off,' said Pippin. 'Once I get to sleep, Mr Pippin,' said Sam, 'I shall go on sleeping whether I roll off or no.'

Frodo lay for a while and looked at the stars that glinted now and again through the thin roof of pale rustling leaves above him. Sam was snoring at his side before he himself, lulled by the wind in the leaves above and the sweet murmur of the falls of Nimrodel[30] below, fell into a sleep with the song of Legolas still running in his mind. Two of the elves sat with arms about their knees speaking in whispers; one had gone down to take up his post on one of the lower boughs.

Late in the night Frodo woke. The other hobbits were asleep. The elves were gone. The last thin rind of the waning moon was gleaming dimly in the leaves. The wind was still. A little way off he heard a harsh laugh and the tread of many feet. Then a ring of metal. The sounds died away southward going deeper into the wood.

The grey hood of one of the elves appeared suddenly above

the edge of the flet. He looked at the hobbits. 'What is it?' said Frodo, sitting up.

'Yrch!' said the Elf in a hissing whisper, and cast onto the flet the rope-ladder rolled up.

'Orcs,' said Frodo, 'what are they doing?' But the Elf was gone.

There was no more sound; even the leaves were silent. Frodo could not sleep. Thankful as he was that they had not been caught upon the ground, he knew that the trees offered little protection save concealment, if orcs discovered where they were, and they have a scent keen as hounds. He drew out Sting and saw it glow like a blue flame, and slowly fade.

[Before long Hathaldir came back to the flet and sat near the edge with drawn bow and arrow in the string. Frodo rose and crawled to the edge of the flet and peered over.]³¹ Nonetheless the sense of immediate danger did not leave him. Rather it deepened. He crawled to the edge of the flet and peered over. He was almost sure he heard the soft sound of stealthy movement in the leaves at the tree's foot far below. Not the elves, he feared, for the woodland folk were altogether noiseless in their movements (so quiet and deft as to excite the admiration even of hobbits). And there seemed to be a sniffing noise. Something was scrabbling on the bark of the tree. He lay looking down holding his breath. Something was climbing, and breathing with a soft hissing sound. Then coming up close to the stem he saw two pale eyes. They stopped and gazed upwards unwinking. Suddenly they turned away and a shadowy figure slipped round the trunk and vanished on the further side. Shortly afterwards Hathaldir climbed up.

'There was something in this tree that I have never seen before,' he said. 'Not an orch [sic]. But I did [not] shoot because I was not sure, and we dare not risk battle. It fled as soon as I touched the tree-stem. There was a strong company of orcs. They crossed the Nimrodel (curse them for defiling our water) and went on – though they seemed to pick up some scent, and halted for a while searching on both sides of the path where you sat last evening. We dare not risk a battle, three against a hundred, and we did not shoot, but Orfin has gone back by secret ways to our folk, and we shall not let them return out of Lórien if we can help it. There will be many elves hidden [?beside] Nimrodel ere another night is gone. But now we too must take the road as soon as it is light.'

Dawn came pale from the East. As the light grew it filtered through the golden leaves of the mallorn, and chill though the dawn-wind blew it seemed to be sunshine of an early summer morning. The pale blue sky peeped between the moving leaves. Climbing a slender branch up from the flet Frodo looked out and saw all the valley southward, eastward of the dark shadow of the mountains, lying like a sea of fallow gold tossing gently in the breeze.

[When they had eaten the sweet food of the elves, sparing their own dwindling store,] The morning was still young and cold when / the Company set out again, guided by Hathaldir. Rhimbron remained on guard on the flet. Frodo looked back and caught a gleam of white among the grey tree-stems. 'Farewell Nimrodel!' said Legolas. 'Farewell,' said Frodo. It seemed to him that he had never heard a running water so musical: ever changing its note and yet playing ever the same endless music.

They went some way along the path on the east [*read* west][32] of the Blackroot, but soon Hathaldir turned aside into the trees and halted on the bank under their shadow. 'There is one of my people over there on the other side,' he said, 'though you may not see him. But I see the gleam of his hair in the shadow.' He gave a call like the low whistle of a bird, and from the tree-stems an elf stepped out, clad in grey, but with his hood thrown back. Skilfully Hathaldir flung over the stream to him a coil of stout grey rope. He caught it and fastened it to a tree-stem near the bank.

'The river has already a strong stream here,' said Hathaldir. 'It is not wide; but it is too deep to wade. And it is very cold. We do not set foot in Morthond unless we are compelled. This is how we cross! Follow me!' Securing his end of the rope to another tree, he stepped onto it and ran lightly across, as if he was on a firm path.

'I can walk this path,' said Legolas, 'but only with care, for we have not this skill in Mirkwood; but the rest cannot. Must they swim?'

'No,' said Hathaldir. 'We will cast two more ropes. Fasten them to the tree man-high and half-high, and then with care they can cross.' The Elves drew the strong grey ropes taut across the stream. Then first Aragorn crossed slowly, holding the upper rope. When it came to the hobbits' turn Pippin went first. He was light of foot and went across with fair speed, holding only with one hand on the lower rope. Merry trying to rival him slipped for a moment and hung over the water. Sam shuffled across slowly and cautiously behind Frodo, looking down at the dark eddying water below his feet as if it was a chasm of many fathoms deep. Gimli and Boromir came last.

When they had all crossed Rhimbron[33] untied the ends of the ropes and cast two back. Then coiling up the other he returned to Nimrodel to keep watch in his post.

'Now,' said Hathaldir, 'you have entered the Gore, Nelen[34] we call it, which lies in the angle between Blackroot and Anduin the Great River. We do not allow strangers to walk here if we can prevent it, nor to go deep into the angle where [our dwellings are >] we live. As was agreed I shall here blindfold the eyes of Gimli the dwarf; the others shall walk free for a while until we get nearer to our hidden dwellings.'

This was not at all to Gimli's liking. 'The agreement was made without my consent,' he said. 'I will not walk blindfold like a prisoner or traitor. My folk have ever resisted the Enemy, nor had dealings with orcs or any of his servants. Neither have we done harm to the Elves. I am no more likely to betray your secrets than Legolas or any others of the Company.'

'You speak truly, I do not doubt,' said Hathaldir. 'Yet such is our law. I am not master of the law, and cannot set it aside at my own judgement. I have done all that I dared in letting you set foot in [Nelen >] the Gore.'

But Gimli was obstinate. He set his feet firmly apart and laid his hand upon the haft of his axe. 'I will go forward free, or I will go back north alone, though it be to perish in the wilderness,' he said.

'You cannot depart,' said Hathaldir grimly. 'You cannot cross Morthond, and behind you north are hidden defences and guards across the open arms of the Angle between the rivers. You will be slain before you get nigh them.' The other elf fitted an arrow to his bow as Gimli drew his axe from his belt.

'A plague on dwarves and their stiff necks!' muttered Legolas.

'Come!' said Aragorn. 'If I am to lead the Company you must all do as I bid. We will all be blindfold, even Legolas. That will be best, though it will make the journey slow and dull.'

Gimli laughed suddenly. 'A merry troop of fools we shall look!' he said. 'But I will be content, if only Legolas shares my blindness.'

This was little to Legolas' liking.

'Come!' said Aragorn. 'Let us not cry "plague on your stiff neck" also. But you shall not be our hostage. We will all share the necessity alike.'

'I shall claim full amends for every fall and stubbed toe, if you do not lead us well,' said Gimli as they bound a cloth about his eyes.

'You will not have need,' said Halthadir. 'We shall lead you well, and our paths are smooth and green.'

'Alas! for the folly of these days,' said Legolas in his turn. 'Here all are enemies of the one Enemy, and yet I must walk blind, while the sun is shining in the woodland under leaves of gold!'

'Folly it may seem,' said Hathaldir. 'And in truth in nothing is the evil of the Enemy seen more clear than in the estrangements that divide us all. Yet so little faith and trust is left that we dare not endanger our dwellings. We live now in ever-growing peril, and our hands are more often set to bowstring than to harp. The rivers have long defended us, [but] they are no longer a sure guard. For the Shadow has crept northward all about our land. Some speak [?already] of departing, yet for that maybe it is already too late. The mountains to the west have an evil name for us. To the east the land is waste. It is rumoured that we cannot with safety go south of the mountains through Rohan, and that even if we did pass into the western lands the shores of the sea are no longer secure. It is still said that there are havens in the north beyond the land of the half-high,[35] but where that lies we do not know.'

'You might at least guess now,' said Pippin. 'The havens lie west of my land, the Shire.'

The elf looked at him with interest. 'Happy folk are hobbits,' he said, 'to dwell near Havens of Escape. Tell me about them, and what the sea is like, of which we sing, but scarce remember.'

'I do not know,' said Pippin. 'I have never seen it. I have never been out of my land before. And had I known what the world was like outside, I do not think I should have had the heart to leave it.'

'Yes, the word is full of peril, and dark places,' said Hathaldir. 'But still there is much that is very fair, and though love is now mingled with grief it is not the less deep. And some there are among us who sing that the Shadow will draw back again and peace shall be. Yet I do not believe that the world will be again as of old, or the light of the sun as it was before. For the

Elves I fear it will mean only a peace in which they may pass to the Sea unhindered and leave the middle-earth for ever. Alas! for Lothlórien. It would be a life far from the *mellyrn*. But if there are mallorn-trees beyond the Sea none have reported it.'

As they spoke thus the Company went slowly along paths in the wood. Hathaldir led them and the other elf walked behind. Even as Hathaldir had said they found the ground beneath their feet smooth and soft, and they walked slowly but without fear of hurt or fall.[36] Before long they met many grey-clad elves going northward to the outposts.[37] They brought news, some of which Legolas interpreted. The orcs had been waylaid, and many destroyed; the remainder had fled westward towards the mountains, and were being pursued as far as the sources of Nimrodel. The elves were hastening now to guard the north borders against any new attack.

I interrupt the text here to introduce a page of fearsomely rough notes which show my father thinking about the further course of the story from approximately this point. They begin with references to *Cerin Amroth* and to 'a green snowdrop', with the Elvish words *nifred* and *nifredil*. It may well be that this is where the name *nifredil* arose (both *nifred* 'pallor' and *nifredil* 'snowdrop' are given under the stem NIK-W in the *Etymologies*, V.378). Then follows:

> News. H[athaldir] says he has spoken much of Elves. What of Men? The message spoke of 9. Gandalf. Consternation at news.

With this cf. p. 227 and note 29. My father was thinking of postponing the revelation of Gandalf's fall to the halt at Cerin Amroth, before he finally decided that it should not be spoken of until they came to Caras Galadon.

There is then a sentence, placed within brackets, which is unhappily – since it is probably the first reference my father ever made to Galadriel – only in part decipherable: '[?Lord] of Galadrim [?and ?a] Lady and . . . . . . [?went] to White Council.' The remaining notes are as follows:

> They climb Cerin Amroth. Frodo says [*read* sees] Anduin far away a glimpse of Dol Dúgol.[38] H[athaldir] says it is reoccupied and a cloud lowers there.
>
> They journey to Nelennas.[39]
>
> Lord and Lady clad in white, with *white hair*. Piercing eyes like a lance in starlight.[40] Lord says he knows their quest but won't speak of it.
>
> They speak [of] Gandalf. Song of Elves.
>
> Of the [?harbour] to Legolas and aid to Gimli. Beornings.[41]
>
> Leave Lothlórien. Parting of ways at Stonehills.

I return now to the draft text.

'Also,' said Hathaldir, 'they bring me a message from the Lord of the Galadrim. You may all walk free. He has received messages from Elrond, who begs for help and friendship to you each and all.' He removed the bandage from Gimli's eyes. 'Your pardon,' he said bowing. 'But now look on us nonetheless with friendly eyes. Look and be glad, for you are the first dwarf to behold the sun upon the trees of Nelen-Lórien since Durin's day!'

As the bandage dropped from his eyes Frodo looked up. They were standing in an open space. To the left stood a great mound covered with a sward of grass, as green as if it were springtime. Upon it as a double crown grew two circles of trees: the outer had a bark of snowy white and were leafless but beautiful in their slender and shapely nakedness; the inner were mallorn-trees of great height, still arrayed in gold. High amid their branches was a white flet. At their feet and all about the sides of the hill the grass was studded with small golden starshaped flowers, and among them nodding on slender stalks flowers of a green so pale[42] that it gleamed white against the rich green of the grass. Over all the sky was blue and the sun of afternoon slanted among the tree-stems.

'You are come to Coron [*written above:* Kerin] Amroth.[43] For this is the mound of Amroth, and here in happier days his house was built. Here bloom the winter flowers in the unfading grass: the yellow *elanor*[44] and the pale *nifredil*. Here we will rest a while, and come to the houses of the Galadrim[45] at dusk.'

They cast themselves on the soft grass at the mound's foot;[46] but after a while Hathaldir took Frodo and they went to the hill top, and climbed up to the high flet. Frodo looked out East and saw not far away the gleam of the Great River which was the border of Lórien. Beyond the land seemed flat and empty, until in the distance it rose again dark and drear. The sun that lay upon all the lands between seemed not to lie upon it.

'There lies the fastness of Southern Mirkwood,' said Hathaldir. 'For the most part it is a forest of dark pine and close fir – but amidst it stands the black hill Dol-Dúgol, where for long the Necromancer had his [?fort]. We fear it is now rehabited and threatens, for his power is now sevenfold. A dark cloud lies often above it. [?? Fear of the time is] war upon our eastern borders.'

The draft text continues ('The sun had sunk behind the mountains') without a break, whereas in FR a new chapter, 'The Mirror of Galadriel', now begins; and I also pause in the narrative here (it was not long before my father introduced this division). It will be noticed that towards the end of the earliest 'Lothlórien' material given thus far the narrative is less advanced towards the final form, and notably absent is Frodo's sight southward from Cerin Amroth of 'a hill of many mighty trees, or a city of green towers', Caras Galad(h)on (FR p. 366).

The next text of 'Lothlórien' is a good clear manuscript, thus titled, with a fair amount of alteration in the process of composition; but it cannot be entirely separated off from the initial drafting as a distinct 'phase' in the writing of the story, for it seems certain that at the beginning of the chapter the draft and the fair copy overlapped (see note 14). There seems nothing to show, however, that the rest of the new text actually overlapped with the drafts, and it is in any case most convenient to treat it separately.

The text of 'Lothlórien' in FR was now for the most part very closely approached, the chief differences of substance being the absence of all passages referring to or implying Aragorn's previous knowledge of Lothlórien,[47] and the meeting of the Company with the Elves coming up from the south shortly after their rest at noon on the first day of their journey from Nimrodel (see note 37). The original story was still followed in various minor points, as in its being Pippin and not Merry who speaks to Haldir (replacing Hathaldir of the draft text, see note 28) of the Havens (p. 232); Sam does not refer to his uncle Andy (FR p. 361), and it was still in his arm that he was wounded in Moria (p. 201).[48]

By an addition to the text that looks as if it belongs with the first writing of the manuscript the *Dimrill Stair* acquires its later meaning (see p. 164): ' "Yonder is the Dimrill Stair," said Aragorn pointing to the falls. "Down the deep-cloven way that climbs beside the torrent we should have come, if fortune had been kinder" ' (FR p. 347).

The Silverlode was at first named Blackroot or Morthond, but in the course of the writing of the manuscript the name became Silverlode (the Elvish name *Kelebrant* being added afterwards). The Company 'kept to the old path on the west side of the Blackroot' (FR p. 360; cf. note 32); but ten lines later Haldir says, in the text as written, 'Silverlode is already a strong stream here'. It was presumably at this juncture that my father decided on the transposition of the names of the northern and southern rivers (see note 36), a transposition that had already taken place in the initial drafting of 'Farewell to Lórien' (p. 279).

One of Haldir's brothers is still called *Orfin* as in the original draft; at one occurrence only, he is changed to *Orofin*, and in the drafting of

'Farewell to Lórien' he is *Orofin* (p. 279; FR *Orophin*). The other, in the draft text *Rhimbron*, is now *Romrin*, becoming *Rhomrin* in the course of the writing of the manuscript.

The Elvish name for 'the Gore' is here *Narthas*, where the original text (p. 231) has *Nelen* (replacing *Nelennas*): 'you have entered Narthas or the Gore as you would say, for it is the land that lies like a spear-head[49] between the arms of Silverlode and Anduin the Great', and 'I have done much in letting you set foot in Narthas'. But Haldir here says also: 'The others may walk free for a while until we come nearer to *the Angle, Nelen, where we dwell*', where the original draft has 'until we get nearer to our hidden dwellings'; and when they come to Kerin Amroth (as it is now written) he tells Gimli that he is 'the first dwarf to behold the trees of *Nelen-Lórien* since Durin's Day!' – where the original draft has *Nelen-Lórien* likewise (p. 234).

This seems to show that in the first stage my father intended *Nelen*, *Nelen-Lórien*, 'the Gore', 'the Gore of Lórien', as the name for Lórien between the rivers, without devising an Elvish name for the southward region where the Elves of Lórien actually dwelt; while in the stage represented here *Narthas* 'the Gore' is the larger region, and *Nelen* 'the Angle' the smaller, the point of the triangle or tip of the spearhead. If this is so, when Hathaldir/Haldir first spoke of 'the trees of Nelen-Lórien' the name bore a different sense from what he intended by the same words in the present manuscript.[50]

In the first sentence of this chapter in this manuscript *Trotter* is so named, as he was throughout the preceding one (p. 204); this was changed at once to *Aragorn*, and he is *Aragorn* as far as the Company's coming to the eaves of the Golden Wood, where he becomes *Elfstone* in the text as written.[51] Subsequently *Aragorn*, so far as it went, was changed to *Ingold*, and *Elfstone* was likewise changed to *Ingold*; then *Ingold* was changed back to *Elfstone*.[52]

There remain to notice some remarkable pencilled notes that occur on pages of this manuscript. The first is written on the back of the page (which is marked as being an insertion into the text) that bears the Song of Nimrodel, and reads:

Could not Balrog be Saruman? Make battle on Bridge be between Gandalf and Saruman? Then Gandalf ... clad in white.

The illegible words might conceivably be *comes out*. This was struck through; it had no further significance or repercussion, but remains as an extraordinary glimpse into reflections that lie beneath the written evidence of the history of *The Lord of the Rings* (and the thought, equally baldly expressed, would reappear: p. 422).

A second rejected note was written at some later time against Haldir's words 'they bring me a message from the Lord and Lady of the Galadrim':

Lord? If Galadriel is alone and is wife of Elrond.

A third note, again struck through, is written on the back of the inserted page that carries the preliminary draft of Frodo's perceptions of Lothlórien (note 46):

Elf-rings

.... [*illegible word or name*]

The power of the Elf-rings must *fade* if One Ring is *destroyed*.

NOTES

1 On 'the black springs of Morthond' see p. 166.

2 At this point, then, my father conceived of the Elves of Lothlórien as dwelling underground, like the Elves of Mirkwood. Cf. Legolas' later words on p. 225: 'It is said that Linglorel had a house built in branches of a tree; for that was the manner of the Elves of Lórien, and may be yet... And our people [i.e. the Elves of Mirkwood] did not delve in the ground or build fastnesses before the Shadow came.'

3 This passage was first used at the end of the preceding chapter, 'Moria (ii)': see p. 204 and note 20.

4 On the emergence of the three peaks (the Mountains of Moria) in the new version of 'The Ring Goes South' see p. 166.

5 The word *west* is perfectly clear, but can only be a slip; FR has of course *east*. The same slip occurs in the first emergence of this passage at the end of 'Moria (ii)' (p. 203), and it occurs again in the fair copy of 'Lothlórien'.

6 This passage, from 'Northward the Dale ran up into a glen of shadows', was first used at the end of 'Moria (ii)': see pp. 203–4.

7 For the first appearance of *Kheledzâram* see p. 166.

8 In FR Legolas did not go down with Gimli to look in Mirrormere.

9 The word *southwest* is clear (and occurs again in the fair copy of 'Lothlórien'), yet is obviously a slip; cf. note 5.

10 The words *Now they went on silently* were struck out emphatically, but they are obviously necessary.

11 It is not told in the original text of 'Moria (ii)' (p. 194) that Sam received any wound in the Chamber of Mazarbul; this story first appears in the fair copy of that chapter (see p. 201).

12 The text becomes illegible for a couple of lines, but elements of a description of the wood can be made out.

13 This passage possibly suggests that at this stage the Company did not encounter Elves on the first night. The 'several (2–3) pleasant days' are clearly the days of their journey through Lothlórien, not the days they spent at 'Angle' (cf. the plot outline, p. 207: 'Dec. 15, 16, 17 they journey to Angle between Anduin and Blackroot. There they remain long').

That they were now nearly 300 miles south of Rivendell
accords precisely with the First Map: see Map II on p. 305, where
the distance from Rivendell to the confluence of Silverlode and
Anduin on the original scale (squares of 2 cm. side, 2 cm. = 100
miles) is just under six centimetres measured in a straight line.
Aragorn's reckoning, when they came to the eaves of the Golden
Wood, that they had come 'barely five leagues from the Gates',
does not accord with the First Map, but that map can scarcely be
used as a check on such small distances.

14 It seems that my father began making a fair copy of the chapter
when the draft narrative had gone no further than the point
where Frodo and Sam began to lag behind as the Company went
down from Dimrill Dale. When he came to this point he stopped
writing out the new manuscript in ink, but continued on in pencil
on the same paper, as far as Legolas' words 'Alas that it is
winter!' He then overwrote this further passage in ink and erased
the pencil; and then went back to further drafting on rough paper
– which is why there is this gap in the initial narrative, and why it
takes up again at the words 'Under the night the trees stood tall
before them...' Overlapping of draft and fair copy, often writing
the preliminary draft in pencil on the fair copy manuscript and
then erasing it or overwriting it in ink, becomes a very frequent
mode of composition in later chapters.

15 In FR these last words are given to Gimli, for Aragorn in the later
story had of course good reason to know that Elves did indeed
still dwell in Lothlórien.

16 In a preliminary draft of Legolas' words here they take this form:
     So it is said amongst us in Mirkwood, though it is long since we
     came so far. But if so they dwell deep in the woods down in
     Angle, *Bennas* between Blackroot and Anduin.
The name *Bennas* occurs only here in narrative, but it is found in
the *Etymologies*, V.352, under the root BEN 'corner, angle':
Noldorin *bennas* 'angle'. The second element is Noldorin *nass*
'point; angle' (V.374–5).

17 The passage beginning 'A mile within the wood...' (of which the
first germ is found on p. 221) appears also in a superseded draft:
     A mile within the wood they came upon another stream
     flowing down swiftly from the tree-clad slopes that climbed
     back towards the Mountains to join the Blackroot (on their
     left), and over its dark hurrying waters there was now no
     bridge.
     'Here is the Taiglin,' said Legolas. 'Let us wade over if we
     can. Then we shall have water behind us and on the east, and
     only on the west towards the Mountains shall we have much to
     fear.'
In the consecutive narrative at this point the name *Taiglin* (from

The Silmarillion: tributary of Sirion in Beleriand) underwent many changes, but it is clear that all these forms belong to the same time – i.e., the final name had been achieved before the first complete draft of the chapter was done (see note 30). *Taiglin* was at once replaced by *Linglor*, and then *Linglor* was changed to *Linglorel*, the form as first written shortly afterwards in the manuscript and as found in the rough workings for Legolas' song. This was succeeded by *Nimladel*, *Nimlorel*, and finally *Nimrodel*.

18 The word actually written was *waters*.

19 *Linglorel* was altered in pencil, first to *Nimlorel* and then to *Nimrodel* (see note 17). I do not further notice the changes in this case, but give the name in the form as it was first written.

20 *the mountains* changed to *the Black Mountains* (*the White Mountains* FR).

21 *Ammalas* changed in pencil to *Amroth*; see p. 223.

22 In a separate draft for this passage the reading here is: 'Hence the folk of Lórien were called *Galadrim*, the Tree-folk (*Ornelië*)'.

23 *Aragorn* was here changed later to *Elfstone*, and at some of the subsequent occurrences; see p. 236 and note 52.

24 Written in the margin here: 'Name of the tree is *mallorn*'. This is where my father first wrote the name; and it enters the narrative immediately below.

25 On *daro!* 'stop, halt' see the *Etymologies*, V.353, stem D A R.

26 A detached (earlier) draft describes the event differently:

> Turning aside from the road they went into the shadows of the deeper wood westward of the river, and there not far from the falls of Linglorel they found a group of tall strong trees. Their lowest boughs were above the reach of Boromir's arms; but they had rope with them. Cast[ing] an end about a bough of the greatest of the trees Legolas . . . up and climbed into the darkness.
>
> He was not long aloft. 'The tree-branches form a great crown near the top,' he said, 'and there is a hollow where even Boromir might find some rest. But in the next tree I think I saw a sheltered platform. Maybe elves still come here.'
>
> At that moment a clear voice above them spoke in the elven-tongue, but Legolas drew himself hastily [?close] to the tree-bole. 'Stand still', he said, 'and do not speak or move.' Then he called back into the shadows above, [?answering] in his [?own] tongue.
>
> Frodo did not understand the words, for [the speech of the wood-elves east of the mountains differed much from] the language was the old tongue of the woods and not that of the western elves which was in those days used as a common speech among many folk.

There is a marginal direction to alter the story to a form in which the voice from the tree speaks as Legolas jumps up. The passage which I have bracketed is not marked in any way in the manuscript, but is an example of my father's common practice when writing at speed of abandoning a sentence and rephrasing it without striking out the first version.

For a previous reference to the 'Common Speech' see p. 223; now it is further said that the Common Speech was the tongue of 'the western elves'.

27   The words *by the Dimrill Stair* still refer to the pass (later the Redhorn Pass or Redhorn Gate): see p. 164. FR has here (p. 357) *up the Dimrill Stair*.

28   In a rejected draft for this passage, in content otherwise very much the same as that given, none of the three Elves of Lórien speak any language but their own, and Legolas has to translate. The three Elves are here called *Rhimbron*, [*Rhimlath* >] *Rhimdir*, and *Haldir*: when this last name replaced *Hathaldir* it was thus a reversion. – *Hathaldir the Young* was the name of one of Barahir's companions on Dorthonion (V.282).

29   This passage was enclosed in square brackets in the manuscript, and subsequently struck out. It is explicit later (p. 247) that the loss of Gandalf was not spoken of at this time.

30   The name *Nimrodel* now appears in the text as written; see notes 17 and 19.

31   These two sentences are not marked off in any way in the manuscript, but were nonetheless obviously rejected at once. In the narrative that follows Hathaldir did not climb up to the flet until Gollum had disappeared (as in FR, p. 360); Frodo's peering over the edge is repeated; and 'Nonetheless the sense of immediate danger did not leave him' must follow on the fading of Sting at the end of the previous paragraph.

32   'They went back to the old path on the west side of the Silverlode', FR p. 360 (second edition: 'to the path that still went on along the west side of the Silverlode'). Since the Nimrodel flowed in from the right, and they had to cross it, the road or path from Moria was on the right (or west) of the Blackroot (Silverlode), which was on their left, as is expressly stated (see note 17); the word *east* here, though perfectly clear, is therefore a mere slip (cf. notes 5 and 9).

33   Earlier (p. 230) Rhimbron has remained at the flet, and the Company is guided by Hathaldir alone; now Rhimbron, like Rúmil in FR (pp. 360–1), comes with Hathaldir as far as the crossing of the river and then returns. It is seen from the manuscript that my father perceived here the need for Rhimbron's presence at the crossing.

34 A rejected form here was *Nelennas*; cf. *Bennas* 'Angle' in note 16, and stem NEL 'three' in the *Etymologies*, V.376. On *Nelennas* see note 39.

35 Contrast Hathaldir's words earlier (p. 227): 'We had not heard of hobbits before' (i.e. before they received tidings of the Company from the messengers of Elrond). At the corresponding point in FR (p. 357) Haldir said: 'We had not heard of – hobbits, of halflings, for many a long year, and did not know that any yet dwelt in Middle-earth.'

36 An isolated passage, dashed down on a sheet of the same paper as that used throughout and clearly belonging to the same time, shows the first beginning of the passage in FR p. 364, 'As soon as he set foot upon the far bank of Silverlode a strange feeling had come upon him...':

> As soon as they pass Silverlode into Angle Frodo has a curious sense of walking in an older world – unshadowed. Even though 'wolves howled on the wood's border' they had not entered. Evil had been heard of, Orcs had even set foot in the woods, but it had not yet stained or dimmed the air. There was some secret power of cleanness and beauty in Lórien. It was winter, but nothing was dead, only in a phase of beauty. He saw never a broken twig or disease or fungus. The fallen leaves faded to silver and there was no smell of decay.

A part of this appears a little later in FR, p. 365, where however the 'undecaying' nature of Lothlórien is expressed in terms less immediate: 'In winter here no heart could mourn for summer or for spring. No blemish or sickness or deformity could be seen in anything that grew upon the earth.' Cf. note 46.

Silverlode has here replaced *Blackroot*: see p. 235. On the same page as this passage are the following notes:

> Transpose names *Blackroot* and *Silverlode*. *Silverlode* dwarfish *Kibilnâla* elvish *Celeb(rind)rath*.

The meaning of this is seen from Boromir's words in the new version of 'Moria (i)', p. 177: 'Or we could go on far into the South and come at length round the Black Mountains, and crossing the rivers Isen and *Silverlode* enter Ond from the regions nigh the sea.' The two river-names being transposed, *Silverlode* in this speech of Boromir's in the earlier chapter was changed at this time to *Blackroot* (p. 187 note 1); and in the new version of 'The Ring Goes South' the Dwarvish name of the northern river was changed from *Buzundush* to *Kibil-nâla* (p. 167 and note 22).

In the original text of 'The Ring Goes South' occurs by later substitution the form *Celebrin* (VI.434 note 15). For *rath* in *Celeb(rind)rath* (and also *rant* in the later name *Celebrant*) see the *Etymologies*, V.383, stem RAT.

37   The following passage was rewritten several times. In the original
     form this dialogue occurs:
          'What is this?' said one of the Elves, looking in wonder at
       Legolas. 'By his raiment of green and brown [?he is an] Elf of
       the North. Since when have we taken our kindred prisoner,
       Hathaldir?'
          'I am not a prisoner,' said Legolas. 'I am only showing the
       dwarf how to walk straight without the help of eyes.'
     Later, a passage was inserted making the blindfold march longer:
          All that day they marched on by gentle stages. Frodo could
       hear the wind rustling in the leaves and the river away to the
       right murmuring at times. He had felt the sun on his face when
       they passed across a glade, as he guessed. After a rest and food
       at noon, they went on again, turning it seemed away from the
       river. After a little while they heard voices about them. A great
       company of elves had come up silently, and were now speaking
       to Hathaldir.
     In the corresponding passage in FR (p. 364) they had passed a
     day and a night blindfold, and it was at noon on the second day
     that they met the Elves coming from the south and were released
     from their blindfolds.
38   *Dol Dúgol* occurs in 'Moria (i)', p. 178.
39   'They journey to Nelennas': at an earlier occurrence of *Nelennas*
     (see p. 231 and note 34) it was changed to *Nelen*, 'the Gore'.
     Since they are now deep in 'the Gore', *Nelennas* perhaps refers
     here to the city (Caras Galadon); see p. 261 note 1.
40   It is notable that the Lady of Lothlórien at first had white hair;
     this was still the case in the first actual narratives of the sojourn of
     the Company in Caras Galadon (pp. 246, 256).
41   For explanation of these references see p. 248 and note 15.
42   The actual text here is extremely confused, and I set it out as a
     characteristic, if extreme, example of my father's way of writing
     when actually composing new narrative (nothing is struck out
     except as indicated):
          ... the grass was studded with small golden [*struck out:*
       flowers] starshaped and slanting [?leaved] and starshaped and
       among them on slender nodding on slender stalks flowers of a
       green so pale...
43   In the *Etymologies*, V.365, stem KOR, both *coron* and *cerin*
     appear as Noldorin words, the latter being the equivalent of
     Quenya *korin* 'circular enclosure' (cf. the *korin* of elms in which
     Meril-i-Turinqi dwelt in *The Book of Lost Tales*, where the word
     is defined (I.16) as 'a great circular hedge, be it of stone or of
     thorn or even of trees, that encloses a green sward'). But the
     meaning of *cerin* in *Cerin Amroth* is certainly 'mound', and
     indeed long afterwards my father translated the word as 'circular

mound or artificial hill'. – *Amroth* has now replaced *Ammalas* in the text as written; see note 21.

44 This is the first appearance of the name *elanor*, which replaced at the time of writing another name, *yri* (see note 45).

45 After 'the houses of the Galadrim' my father wrote *Bair am Yru* (see note 44), but struck it out.

46 A page inserted into the manuscript (but obviously closely associated in time with the surrounding text) gives the primitive drafting for the passage in FR p. 365 beginning 'The others cast themselves down upon the fragrant grass' and continuing to Sam's words about the 'elvishness' of Lórien. The latter part of this is of an extreme roughness, but I give the rider in full as a further exemplification of the actual nature of much preliminary drafting:

The others cast themselves down on the fragrant grass, but Frodo stood for a while lost in wonder. Again it seemed to him as if he had stepped through a high window that looked on a vanished world. It was a winter that did not mourn for summer or for spring, but reigned in its own season beautiful and eternal and perennial. He saw no sign of blemish or disease, sickness or deformity, in anything that grew upon the earth, nor did he see any such thing in [Nelen >] the heart of Lórien.

Sam too stood by him with a puzzled expression rubbing his eyes as if he was not sure that he was awake. 'It's sunlight and bright day,' he muttered. 'I thought Elves were all for moon and stars, but this is more Elvish than anything in any tale.'

and caught his breath for the sight was fair in itself but it had a quality different to any that he felt before [*variant:* had beside a beauty that the common speech could not name]. The shapes of all that he saw All that he saw was shapely but its shapes seemed at once clearcut and as if it had been but newly conceived and drawn with swift skill swift and [?living] and ancient as if [it] had endured for ever. The hues were green, gold and blue white but fresh as if he but that moment perceived them and gave them names.

47 Thus the entire passage (FR pp. 352–3) in which Boromir demurs at entering the Golden Wood and is rebuked by Aragorn is absent, as also is the conclusion of the chapter in FR, from 'At the hill's foot Frodo found Aragorn, standing still and silent...' (pp. 366–7).

This is a convenient point to mention a small textual corruption in the published form of this chapter (FR p. 359). In the fair copy manuscript Pippin says: 'I hope, if I do get to sleep in this bird-loft, that I shan't roll off'; but in the typescript that followed, not made by my father, *bird-loft* became *bed-loft*, and so remains.

48   A few other details worth recording are collected here:

      wood-elves (p. 222) remains, where FR (p. 353) has *Silvan Elves*.

      the common speech (p. 223) remains, where FR (p. 353) has *the Westron Speech*.

      in ordinary speech (p. 227) becomes *in ordinary language*, changed later to *in the Common Tongue* (*in the Common Language* FR p. 357).

      Hathaldir's words about hobbits (p. 227) are scarcely changed: *We had not heard of – hobbits before, and never until now have we seen one*; see note 35.

      and that even if we did pass into the western lands the shores of the sea are no longer secure in the original draft (p. 232) becomes *and the mouths of the Great River are held by the Enemy* (*are watched by the Enemy*, FR p. 363).

      there are still havens to be found, far north and west, beyond the land of the half-high (cf. p. 232 and note 35), where FR (p. 363) has *havens of the High Elves ... beyond the land of the Halflings*.

      near Havens of Escape (p. 232) was at first retained, but changed at once to *near the shores of the Sea*, as in FR.

49   'Narthas or the Gore as you would say, *for* it is the land that lies like a spear-head': the word *for* (preserved in FR p. 361) is used because *gore*, Old English *gāra* (in modern use meaning a wedge-shaped piece of cloth, but in Old English an angular point of land) was related to *gār* 'spear', the connection lying in the shape of the spear-head.

50   Later, *Narthas* and *Nelen-Lórien* were changed to *the Naith* (*of Lórien*), though in 'the Angle, Nelen, where we dwell' *Nelen* was left to stand. – *Dol Dúgol*, retained from the original draft, with the reference to the Necromancer (p. 234), was later changed to *Dol Dûghul*.

51   This is to be connnected with the interruption in the writing of the fair copy manuscript (note 14).

52   In fact, there is a good deal of variation, since when making these name-changes my father worked through the manuscripts rapidly and missed occurrences. Thus in this manuscript, in addition to *Aragorn > Ingold > Elfstone* and *Elfstone > Ingold > Elfstone*, there is found also: *Aragorn > Elfstone*; *Elfstone > Ingold*; *Elfstone > Ingold > Aragorn*; *Elfstone > Aragorn*. This apparently patternless confusion can be explained: see pp. 277–8. The name *Ingold* for Aragorn has been met before, in later emendation to the text of Gandalf's letter at Bree (p. 80 and note 17).

XIII

GALADRIEL

I have divided the draft manuscript of the 'Lothlórien' story into two parts, although at this stage my father continued without break to the end of FR Book II Chapter 7, 'The Mirror of Galadriel'; and I return now to the point where I left it on p. 234. From the coming of the Company to Cerin Amroth the draft is in thick, soft pencil, and very difficult.

The sun had sunk behind the mountains, and the shadows were falling in the wood, when they went on again. Now their paths went deep into dense wood where already a grey dusk had gathered. It was nearly night under the trees when they came out suddenly under a pale evening sky pierced by a few early stars. There was a wide treeless space running in a vast circle before them. Beyond that was a deep grass-clad dike, and a high green wall beyond. [?Rising] ground inside the circle was [??thick with] mallorn-trees, the tallest they had yet seen in that land. The highest must have been nearly 200 feet high, and of great girth. They had no branches lower than 3 fathoms above their roots. In the upper branches amid the leaves hundreds of lights gold and white and pale green were shining.

'Welcome to Caras Galadon,' he said, 'the city of Nelennas which [?mayhap] in your tongue is called Angle.[1] But we must go round; the gates do not look north.'

There was a white paved road running round the circuit of the walls. On the south side there was a bridge over the dike leading to great gates set on the side where the ends of the wall overlapped. They passed within into deep shadow where the two green walls ended [?in a] lane. They saw no folk on guard,[2] but there were many soft voices overhead, and in the distance he [sc Frodo] heard a voice falling clear out of the air above them.

The original pencilled text continues for some distance from this point, but my father partly overwrote it in ink, and (more largely) erased it wholly before the new text was set down in its place. Here and there bits of the original text were retained, and where it was not erased but overwritten a name or a phrase can be made out. There was no long interval between the two forms of the text; my father may in any case have rewritten this section mainly because it was so nearly illegible.

They passed along many paths and climbed many flights of steps, until they saw before them amid a wide lawn a fountain. It sprang high in the air and fell in a wide basin of silver, from which a white stream ran away down the hill. Hard by stood a great tree. At its foot stood three tall elves. They were clad in grey mail and from their shoulders hung long white cloaks. 'Here dwell Keleborn and Galadriel,[3] the Lord and Lady of the Galadrim,' said Halldir.[4] 'It is their wish that you should go up and speak to them.'

One of the elf-wardens then blew a clear note on a small horn, and a ladder was let down. 'I will go first,' said Haldir. 'Let the chief hobbit go next, and with him Legolas. The others may follow as they wish. It is a long climb, but you may rest upon the way.'

As he passed upwards Frodo saw many smaller flets to this side or that, some with rooms built on them; but about a hundred feet above the ground they came to a flet that was very wide – like the deck of a great ship. On it was built a house so large that almost it might have been a hall of men upon the earth. He entered behind Haldir, and saw that he was in a chamber of oval shape, through the midst of which passed the bole of the great tree. It was filled with a soft golden light. Many elves were seated there. The roof was a pale gold, the walls of green and silver. On two seats at the further end sat side by side the Lord and Lady of Lothlórien. They looked tall even as they sat, and their hair was white and long.[5] They said no word and moved not, but their eyes were shining.

Haldir led Frodo and Legolas before them, and the Lord bade them welcome, but the Lady Galadriel said no word, and looked long into their faces.

'Sit now, Frodo of the Shire,' said Keleborn. 'We will await the others.' Each of the companions he greeted courteously by name as they entered. 'Welcome, Ingold son of Ingrim!'[6] he said. 'Your name is known to me, though never in all your wanderings have you sought my house. Welcome, Gimli son of Glóin! It is almost out of mind since we saw one of Durin's folk in Calas Galadon. But today our long law is broken: let it be a sign that though the world is dark, better things shall come, and friendship shall grow again between our peoples.'

When all the Company had come in and were seated before him, the Lord looked at them again. 'Is this all?' he asked. 'Your number should be nine. For so the secret messages from Rivendell have said. There is one absent whom I miss, and had hoped much to see. Tell me, where is Gandalf the grey?'[7]

'Alas!' said Ingold. 'Gandalf the grey went down into the shadows. He remains in Moria, for he fell there from the Bridge.'

At these words all the Elves cried aloud with grief and amazement. 'This is indeed evil tidings,' said Keleborn, 'the most evil that have here been spoken for years uncounted. Why has nothing been said to us of this before?' he asked, turning to Haldir.

'We did not speak of it to [your people >] Haldir,' said Frodo. 'We were weary and danger was too nigh, and afterwards we were overcome with wonder.[8] Almost we forgot our grief and dismay as we walked on the fair paths of Lothlórien. But it is true that Gandalf has perished. He was our guide, and led us through Moria; and when our escape seemed beyond hope he saved us, and fell.'

'Tell me the full tale,' said Keleborn.

Ingold then recounted all that had happened upon the pass of Caradras and afterwards; and he spoke of Balin and his book and the fight in the Chamber of Mazarbul, and the fire, and the narrow bridge, and the coming of the Balrog.

'A Balrog!' said Keleborn.[9] 'Not since the Elder Days have I heard that a Balrog was loose upon the world. Some we have thought are perhaps hidden in Mordor [?or] near the Mountain of Fire, but naught has been seen of them since the Great Battle and the fall of Thangorodrim.[10] I doubt much if this Balrog has lain hid in the Misty Mountains – and I fear rather that he was sent by Sauron from Orodruin, the Mountain of Fire.'

'None know,' said Galadriel, 'what may lie hid at the roots of the ancient hills. The dwarves had re-entered Moria and were searching again in dark places, and they may have stirred some evil.'[11]

There was a silence. At length Keleborn spoke again. 'I did not know,' he said, 'that your plight was so evil. I will do what I can to aid you, each according to his need, but especially that one of the little folk that bears the burden.'

'Your quest is known to me,' said Galadriel, [?seeing] Frodo's look, 'though we will not here speak more openly of it. I was at the White Council, and of all those there gathered none did I love more than Gandalf the Grey. Often have we met since and spoken of many things and purposes. The lord and lady of Lothlórien are accounted wise beyond the measure of the Elves of Middle-earth, and of all who have not passed beyond the Seas. For we have dwelt here since the Mountains were reared and the Sun was young.[12]

'Now we will give you counsel.[13] For not in doing or contriving nor in choosing this course or that is my skill, but in knowledge of what was and is, and in part of what shall be. And I say that your case is not yet without hope; yet but a little this way or that and it will fail miserably. But there is yet hope, if all the Company remains true.' She looked at each in turn, but none blenched. Only Sam blushed and hung his head before the Lady's glance left him. 'I felt as if I hadn't got nothing on,' he explained afterwards. 'I didn't like it – she seemed to be looking inside me, and asking me whether I would like to fly back to the Shire.' Each of them had had a similar experience, and had felt as if he had been presented with a choice between death and something which he desired greatly, peace, ease [*written above:* freedom], wealth, or lordship.

'I suppose it was just a test,' said Boromir. 'It felt almost like a temptation. Of course I put it away at once. The men of Minas Tirith at any rate are true.'[14] What he had been offered he did not say.

'Now is the time for any to depart or turn back who feels that he has done enough, and aided the Quest as much as he has the will or power to do. Legolas may abide here with my folk, as long as he desires, or he may return home if chance allows. Even Gimli the dwarf may stay here, though I think he would not long be content in my city in what will seem to him a life of idleness. If he wishes to go to his home, we will help him as much as we can; as far as the Gladden Fields and beyond. He might hope thus to find the country of the Beornings, where Grimbeorn Beorn's son the Old is a lord of many sturdy men. As yet no wolf or orc make headway in that land.'

'That I know well,' said Gimli. 'Were it not for the Beornings the passage from Dale to Rivendell would not be possible.[15] My father and I had the aid of Grimbeorn on our way west in the autumn.'

'You, Frodo,' said Keleborn, 'I cannot aid or counsel. But if you go on, do not despair – but beware even of your right hand

and of your left. There is also a danger that pursues you, which I do not see clearly or understand. You others of the little folk I could wish had never come so far. For now unless you will dwell here in exile while outside in the world many years run by, I see not what you can do save go forward. It would be vain to attempt to return home or to Rivendell alone.'

The whole of this passage, from 'Now is the time for any to depart', is marked off with directions 'To come in later' and 'At beginning of next chapter before they go'. At the top of the page, and no doubt written in after this decision was made, is the following:

'Now we have spoken long, and yet you have toiled and suffered much, and have travelled far,' said Keleborn. 'Even if your quest did not concern all free lands deeply, you should here have refuge for a while. In this city you may abide until you are healed and rested. We will not yet think of your further road.'

The character of the manuscript now changes again. Very roughly written in ink, it is evidently the continuation of the original pencilled text that was over-written or erased in the preceding section (see p. 245). At the top of the first page of this part are notes on the names of the Lord and Lady of Lothlórien. In pencilled text visible in the last section their original names *Tar* and *Finduilas* had changed to *Aran* and *Rhien* (note 3), and then to *Galadaran* and *Galdri(e)n* (note 9) – *Galadriel* on p. 246 belongs with the later, overwritten text. Their names now change further:

Galathir = *Galað-hîr* tree-lord
Galadhrien = *Galað-rhien* tree-lady

The name of the Lord does not appear in the concluding part of this chapter, but the name of the Lady is *Galadrien* (at the first occurrence only, *Galdrien*), with pencilled correction in some cases to *Galadriel*.

This is a convenient place to set out my father's original scheme for the next part of the story. This was written at furious speed but has fortunately proved almost entirely decipherable.

They dwell 15 days in Caras Galadon.

Elves sing for Gandalf. They watch weaving and making of the silver rope of the fibre under mallorn bark. The [?trimming] of arrows.

King Galadaran's mirror shown to Frodo. Mirror is of silver filled with fountain water in sun.

Sees Shire far away. Trees being felled and a tall building being made where the old mill was.[16] Gaffer Gamgee turned out. Open trouble, almost war, between Marish and Buckland on one hand – and the West. Cosimo Sackville-Baggins very rich, buying up land. (All / Some of this is future.)

King Galdaran says the mirror shows past, present, and future, and skill needed to decide which.

Sees a grey figure like Gandalf [?going along] in twilight but it seems to be clad in white. Perhaps it is *Saruman*.

Sees a mountain spouting flame. Sees Gollum?

They depart. At departure Elves give them travel food. They describe the Stone hills, and bid them beware of Fangorn Forest upon the *Ogodrûth* or Entwash. He is an Ent or great giant.

It is seen that it was while my father was writing the 'Lothlórien' story *ab initio* that the Lady of Lothlórien emerged (p. 233); and it is also seen that the figure of Galadriel (Rhien, Galadrien) as a great power in Middle-earth was deepened and extended as he wrote. In this sketch of his ideas, written down after the story had reached Caras Galadon, as the name *Galdaran* shows (note 9), the Mirror belongs to the Lord (here called King).

It is also interesting to observe that the images of the violated Shire seen in the Mirror were to be Frodo's. The Stone hills mentioned at the end of this outline are mentioned also in the plot-notes given on p. 233, where the 'parting of the ways' is to take place 'at Stonehills'. The Entwash (though not the Elvish name *Ogodrûth*) has been named in the elaborate outline that followed the conclusion of the story of Moria (p. 210): 'Merry and Pippin come up Entwash into Fangorn and have adventure with Treebeard.' Here the name *Entwash* clearly implies that Treebeard is an *Ent*, and he is specifically so called (for the first time) in the outline just given; but since Treebeard was still only waiting in the wings as a potential ingredient in the narrative this may be only a slight shift in the development of the word. The Troll-lands north of Rivendell were the *Entish Lands* and *Entish Dales* (Old English *ent* 'giant'); and only when Treebeard and the other 'Ents' had been fully realised would the Troll-lands be renamed *Ettendales* and *Ettenmoors* (see p. 65 note 32).

I return now to the narrative, which as I have said recommences here in its primary form (and thus we meet again here the names *Gal(a)drien*, *Hathaldir*, and *Elfstone*, which had been superseded in the rewritten section of the draft text).

'Yet let not your hearts be troubled,' said the Lady Galdrien. 'Here you shall rest tonight and other nights to follow.'

That night they slept upon the ground, for they were safe within the walls of Caras Galadon. The Elves spread them a pavilion among the trees not far from the fountain, and there they slept until the light of day was broad.

All the while they remained in Lothlórien the sun shone and the weather was clear and cool like early spring rather than mid-winter. They did little but rest and walk among the trees,

and eat and drink the good things that the Elves set before them.
They had little speech with any for few spoke any but the
woodland tongue. Hathaldir had departed to the defences of the
North. Legolas was away all day among the Elves. [*Marginal
addition of the same time as the text:* Only Frodo and Elfstone
went much among the Elves. They watched them at work
weaving the ropes of silver fibre of mallorn bark, the [?trim-
ming] of arrows, their broidery and carpentry.]

They spoke much of Gandalf, and ever as they themselves
were healed of hurt and weariness the grief of their loss seemed
more bitter. Even the Elves of Lothlórien seemed to feel the
shadow of that fall. Often they heard near them the elves
singing, and knew that they made songs and laments for the
grey wanderer [*written above:* pilgrim], as they called him,
Mithrandir.[17] But if Legolas was by he would not interpret,
saying that it passed his skill. Very sweet and sad the voices
sounded, and having words spoke of sorrow to their hearts
though their minds understood them not.[18]

On the evening of the third day Frodo was walking in the cool
twilight apart from the others. Suddenly he saw coming towards
him the Lady Galadrien gleaming in white among the stems. She
spoke no word but beckoned to him. Turning back she led him
to the south side of the city, and passing through a gate in a
green wall they came into an enclosure like a garden. No trees
grew there and it was open to the sky, which was now pricked
with many stars.[19] Down a flight of white steps they went into a
green hollow through which ran a silver stream, flowing down
from the fountain on the hill. There stood upon a pedestal
carved like a tree a shallow bowl of silver and beside it a ewer.
With water from the stream she filled the bowl, and breathed on
it, and when the water was again still she spoke.

'Here is the mirror of Galadrien,' she said. 'Look therein!'

Sudden awe and fear came over Frodo. The air was still and
the hollow dark, and the Elf-lady beside him tall and pale.
'What shall I look for, and what shall I see?' he asked.

'None can say,' she answered, 'who does not know all that is
in your heart, in your memory, and your hope. For this mirror
shows both the past and the present, and that which is called the
future, in so far as it can be seen by any in Middle-earth.[20] But
those are wise who can discern [to] which of [these] three [the]
things that they see belong.'

Frodo at last stooped over the bowl. The water looked hard

and black. Stars were shining in it. Then they went out. The
dark veil was partly withdrawn, and a grey light shone;
mountains were in the distance, a long road wound back out of
sight. Far away a figure came slowly: very small at first, but
slowly it drew near. Suddenly Frodo saw that it was like the
figure of Gandalf. So clear was the vision that he almost called
aloud the wizard's name. Then he saw that the figure was all
clothed in white, not in grey, and had a white staff. It turned
aside and went away round a turn of the road with head so
bowed that he could see no face. Doubt came over him: was it a
sight of Gandalf on one of his many journeys long ago, or was it
Saruman?[21]

Many other visions passed over the water one after another.
A city with high stone walls and seven towers, a great river
flowing through a city of ruins, and then breathtaking and
strange and yet known at once: a stony shore, and a dark sea
into which a bloodred sun was sinking among black clouds, a
ship darkly outlined was near the sun. He heard the faint sigh of
waves upon the shore. Then ... nearly dark and he saw a small
figure running – he knew that it was himself, and behind him
[?stooped to the ground] came another black figure with long
arms moving swiftly like a hunting dog.[22] He turned away in
fear and would look no more.

'Judge not these visions,' said Galadrien, 'until they are
shown true or false. But think not that by singing under the trees
[?and alone], nor even by slender arrows from [?many] bows,
do we defend Lothlórien from our encircling foes. I say to you,
Frodo, that even as I speak I perceive the Dark Lord and know
part of his mind – and ever he is groping to see my thought: but
the door is closed.' She spread out her hands and held them as in
denial towards the East.[23] A ray of the Evening Star shone clear
in the sky, so clear that the pillar beneath the basin cast a faint
shadow. Its ray lit the ring upon her finger and flashed. Frodo
gazed at it stricken suddenly with awe. 'Yes,' she said, divining
his thought. 'It is not permitted to speak of it, and Elrond [?said
nought]. But verily it is in Lothlórien that one remains: the Ring
of Earth, and I am its keeper.[24] He suspects but he knows not.
See you not now why your coming is to us as the coming of
Doom? For if you fail then we are laid bare to the Enemy. But if
you succeed, then our power is minished and slowly Lothlórien
will fade.'[25]

Frodo bent his head. 'And what do you wish?' he said at last.

'That what should[26] be shall be,' she said. 'And that you should do with all your might that which is your task. For the fate of Lothlórien you are not answerable; but only for the doing of your own task.'

Here the narrative ends (and on the last page of the manuscript my father wrote 'Chapter ends with Lady's words to Frodo' – meaning of course the whole story from Dimrill Dale), but the text continues at once with Sam's vision in the Mirror (see note 19), which my father did not at this stage integrate with what he had just written. What Sam saw in the water appeared already in the preliminary outline (p. 249), though there given to Frodo.

(Put in *Sam's* vision of the Shire before the ring scene.)

Sam saw trees being felled in the Shire. 'There's that Ted Sandyman,' he said, 'a-cutting down trees that .shouldn't be. Bless me, if he's not felling them on the avenue by the road to Bywater where they serve only for shade. I wish I could get at him. I'd fell *him*.' Then Sam saw a great red building with a tall [?smoke] chimney going up where the old mill had been. 'There's some devilry at work in the Shire,' he said. 'Elrond knew what was what, when he said Mr Brandybuck and Pippin should go back.'[27]

Suddenly Sam gave a cry and sprang away. 'I can't stay here,' he said wildly. 'I must go home. They're digging up Bagshot Row and there is the poor old gaffer going down the hill with his bits of stuff in a barrow. I must go home!'

'You cannot go home,' said the Lady. 'Your path lies before you. You should not have looked if you would let anything that you see turn you from your task. But I will say this for your hope: remember that the mirror shows many things, and not all that you see have yet been. Some of the things it shows come never to pass, unless one forsakes the path [?and] turns aside to prevent them.'

Sam sat on the grass and muttered. 'I wish I had never come here.'

'Will you now look, Frodo? said the Lady, 'or have you heard enough?'

'I will look,' said Frodo ... Fear was mingled with desire.

Here the manuscript ends, with the following notes scribbled at the foot of the page: 'Chapter ends with Lady's words to Frodo. Next Chapter begins with departure from Lothlórien on New Year's Day, midwinter day, just before the sun turned to the New Year and just after New Moon.'[28]

On a separate slip, certainly of this time, is written (in ink over pencil) the passage in which Frodo sees the searching Eye in the Mirror (see note 23). This is almost word for word the same as in FR (pp. 379–80), except for these sentences: 'the black slit of its pupil opened on a pit of malice and despair. It was not still, but was roving in perpetual search. Frodo knew with certainty and horror...'

On the back of this slip is scribbled the original draft of the speeches of Galadriel and Frodo beside the Mirror in FR pp. 381–2:

Frodo offers Galadriel the Ring. She *laughs*. Says he is revenged for her temptation. Confesses that the thought had occurred to her. But she will only retain the unsullied Ring. Too much evil lay in the Ruling Ring. It is not permitted to use anything that Sauron has made.

Frodo asks why he cannot *see* the other rings. Have you tried? You can see a little already. You have penetrated my thought deeper than many of my own folk. Also you penetrated the disguise of the Ringwraiths. And did you not see the ring on my hand? Can you see my ring? she said, turning to Sam. No, Lady, he said. I have been wondering much at all your talk.

In this passage there emerges at last and clearly the fundamental conception that the Three Rings of the Elves were not made by Sauron: 'She will only retain the unsullied Ring. Too much evil lay in the Ruling Ring. It is not permitted to use anything that Sauron has made.'

With this compare the passage from the original version of 'The Council of Elrond' (VI.404) cited on p. 155: 'The Three Rings remain still. They have conferred great power on the Elves, but they have never yet availed them in their strife with Sauron. For they came from Sauron himself, and can give no skill or knowledge that he did not already possess at their making.' In the fifth version of that chapter (p. 156) Elrond's words become: 'The Three Rings remain. But of them I am not permitted to speak. Certainly they cannot be used by us. From them the Elvenkings have derived much power, but they have not been used for war, either good or evil.' I have argued in the same place that though no longer explicit the conception must still have been that the Three Rings came from Sauron, both because Boromir asserts this without being contradicted, and because it seems to be implied by 'Certainly they cannot be used by us.' If this is so, there is at least an apparent ambiguity: 'they cannot be used by us', but 'from them the Elvenkings have derived much power' – though in 'they cannot be used by us' Elrond is evidently speaking expressly of their use for war. But any ambiguity there might be is now swept away by Galadriel's assertion: *nothing* that was Sauron's can be made use of: from which it must follow that the Three Rings of the Elves were of other origin.

A page found wholly isolated from other manuscripts of *The Lord of the Rings* carries more developed drafting for Galadriel's refusal of the Ring. This page had been used already for other writing, on the subject of the origin of the Rings of Power; but I have no doubt at all that the two elements (the one in places written over and intermingled with the other) belong to the same time. This other text consists of several distinct openings to a speech, each in turn abandoned – a speech that I think was intended for Elrond at the Council in Rivendell, since the following very faint pencilling can be made out on this page: ' "Nay," said Elrond, "that is not wholly true. The rings were made by the Elves of the West, and taken from them by the Enemy..." '

The first of these openings reads thus, printed exactly as it stands:

In Ancient Days, the Rings of Power were made long ago in the lands beyond the Sea. It is said that they were first contrived by Fëanor, the greatest of all the makers among the Elves. His purpose was not evil, yet in   it was the Great Enemy   But they were stolen by the Great Enemy and brought to Middle-earth. Three Rings he made, the Rings of Earth, Sea and Sky.

This was at once replaced by:

In Ancient Days, before he turned wholly to evil, Sauron the Great, who is now the Dark Lord that some call the Necromancer, made and contrived many things of wonder. He made Rings of Power

Then follows, written out anew, the opening sentence of the first version; and then:

In Ancient Days the Great Enemy came to the lands beyond the Sea; but his evil purpose was for a time hidden, even from the rulers of the world, and the Elves learned many things of him, for his knowledge was very great and his thoughts strange and wonderful.
   In those days the Rings of Power were made. It is said that they were fashioned first by Fëanor the greatest of all the makers among the Elves of the West, whose skill surpassed that of all folk that are or have been. The skill was his but the thought was the Enemy's. Three Rings he made, the Rings of Earth, Sea and Sky. But secretly the Enemy made One Ring, the Ruling Ring, which controlled all the others. And when the Enemy fled across the Sea and came to Middle-earth, he stole the Rings and brought them away. And others he made like to them, and yet false.
   And many others he made of lesser powers, and the elves wore them and became powerful and proud

Breaking off here, my father began once more: 'In Ancient Days the Great Enemy and Sauron his servant came'; and at this point, I think, he definitively abandoned the conception.

These extraordinary vestiges show him revolving the mode by

which he should withdraw the Three Rings of the Elves from inherent evil and derivation from the Enemy. For a fleeting moment their making was set in the remote ages of Valinor and attributed to Fëanor, though inspired by Morgoth: cf. the *Quenta Silmarillion*, V.228, §49, 'Most fair of all was Morgoth to the Elves, and he aided them in many works, if they would let him.... the Gnomes took delight in the many things of hidden knowledge that he could reveal to them.' And Morgoth stole the Rings of Fëanor, as he stole the Silmarils.

The fair copy manuscript of 'Chapter XVIII, Lothlórien' (p. 235) continued on without break, following the primary draft, into the account of the arrival of the Company in Caras Galadon and the story of Galadriel's Mirror. My father's decision to divide the long chapter into two seems however to have been made at the point where Galadriel silently searched the minds of each member of the Company in turn;[29] and it had certainly been taken by an early stage in the writing of 'Farewell to Lórien' (p. 272). The new chapter (XIX) was given the title 'Galadriel', which I have adopted here; and it advances in a single stride almost to the text of FR for most of its length, though there remain some notable passages in which the final form in 'The Mirror of Galadriel' was not achieved.

When the Company came to the city of the Galadrim, Haldir said: 'Welcome to Caras Galadon, the city of Angle' (cf. p. 245 and note 1), which was changed in the act of writing to 'Welcome to Caras Galadon, the city of Lothlórien'; continuing 'where dwell the Lord Arafain and Galadriel the Lady of the Elves'. Since the present text is self-evidently the successor of the text (written over the original draft, see p. 245 and note 3) in which *Keleborn* and *Galadriel* first appear, *Arafain* must have been a fleeting substitution for *Keleborn*, which was immediately restored, and is the name as written throughout the remainder of the manuscript. The journey round the circuit of the walls of Caras Galadon seems to have been differently conceived from its representation in the earliest version, to judge by the little sketch inserted into the manuscript (see note 2), from which it appears that the Company, coming from the north, would pass down the western side – as they did in FR (p. 368). Here, on the other hand, the city climbed 'like a green cloud upon their right', and the gates of the city 'faced eastward'.

Both Galadriel and Keleborn still have long white hair (pp. 233, 246), though this was early changed to make Galadriel's hair golden. As in the rewritten portion of the first draft, 'Aragorn' is greeted by Keleborn as 'Ingold, son of Ingrim' (p. 246 and note 6), and Ingold is his name in the text as written at subsequent occurrences in the chapter.[30] Keleborn speaks the same words to him as in the first draft: 'Your name was known to me before, though never yet in all your wanderings have you sought my house'; and no greeting to Legolas is yet reported, as it is in FR, where he is named 'son of Thranduil'.

In Keleborn's opening words to the Company he says here: 'Your number should be nine: so said the messages. Can we have mistaken them? They were faint and hard to read, for Elrond is far away, and darkness gathers between us: even in this year it has grown deeper.' Galadriel then intervenes: 'Nay, there was no mistake...' (see note 7). But most notably, it is here that the history and significance of the Balrog of Moria first appears (see pp. 185–6, and p. 247 and note 11). The passage in the present version is as follows:

Ingold then recounted all that had happened upon the pass of Caradras, and in the days that followed; and he spoke of Balin and his book, and the fight in the Chamber of Mazarbul, and the fire, and the narrow bridge, and the coming of the Balrog. 'At least, that name did Legolas give to it,' said Ingold. 'I do not know what it was, save that it was both dark and fiery, and was terrible and strong.'

'It was a Balrog,' said Legolas: 'of all elf-banes the most deadly, save the One who sits in the Dark Tower.'

'A Balrog!' said Keleborn. 'Your news becomes ever more grievous. Not since the Days of Flight have I heard that one of those fell things was loose. That one slept beneath Caradras we feared. The Dwarves have never told me the tale of those days, yet we believe that it was a Balrog that they aroused long ago when they probed too deep beneath the mountains.'

'Indeed I saw upon the bridge that which haunts our darkest dreams, I saw Durin's Bane,' said Gimli in a low voice, and terror was in his eyes.

'Alas!' said Keleborn. 'Had I known that the Dwarves had stirred up this evil in Moria again, I would have forbidden you to pass the northern borders, you and all that went with you....'

The remainder of this passage is virtually as in FR (p. 371). – Galadriel's words following 'But we will not here speak more openly of it' were at first retained exactly from the first draft (pp. 247–8), but were changed immediately to read thus:

'... The Lord and Lady of the Galadrim are accounted wise beyond the measure even of the Elves of Middle-earth, and of all who have not passed beyond the Seas. For we have dwelt here since the mountains were reared and the sun was young. Was it not I that summoned the White Council? And if my designs had not gone amiss, it would have been governed by Gandalf the

Grey; and then mayhap things would have gone otherwise. But even now there is hope left. . . .'[31]

The account of the thoughts and sensations of the members of the Company as Galadriel looked at each in turn at first followed closely the text of the original draft (p. 248), but this was changed, probably at once, to the form in FR (pp. 372–3), with however these differences: whereas in the first version 'none blenched' beneath her gaze, and in FR 'none save Legolas and Aragorn could long endure her glance', here 'none of them could long endure her glance' (changed subsequently to 'none of the hobbits'); and their feelings are thus described: 'It seemed that each of them had had a similar experience, and had felt that he was offered a choice between a shadow full of fear and something he greatly desired, that lay clear before his mind lit with an alluring light.' Boromir's remarks on the subject and Ingold's reply here run:

'To me it seemed exceedingly strange,' said Boromir, 'and I do not feel too sure of this elvish lady. Maybe it was only a test, and she sought to read our thoughts for her amusement; but almost I should have said that she was tempting us, and offering us what she had the power to give. It need not be said that I refused to listen, since the gift was not offered to all alike. The Men of Minas-Tirith at least are true to their friends.' But what he thought the Lady had offered him Boromir did not tell.

'Well, whatever you may think of the Lady,' said Ingold, 'she was a friend of Gandalf, it seems. Though this was one of his secrets that he did not tell me. Tonight I shall sleep without fear for the first time since we left Rivendell . . .'

Nothing is said yet of Frodo's experience.[32]

A curious detail arises here, in that in the conversation of the Company in their pavilion near the fountain, before they began to discuss the encounter with Galadriel, 'they talked of their night before in the tree-tops'. At this stage in the evolution of the narrative they met the northbound Elves at Cerin Amroth, and had their blindfolds removed, on the same day as they left Nimrodel (see pp. 233, 235); the whole journey to Caras Galadon thus took a single day, and so it was indeed 'the night before' that they passed in the tree-tops. In FR (p. 364) the journey was extended, and they passed the first night after leaving Nimrodel in the woods: 'Then they rested and slept without fear upon the ground; for their guides would not permit them to unbind their eyes, and they could not climb.' In the light of this, the passage in FR (pp. 372–3) required revision that it did not receive: the words 'the travellers talked of their night before in the tree-tops' survive from the present version, as does Aragorn's 'But tonight I shall sleep without fear for the first time since I left Rivendell.'

The remainder of the chapter in this manuscript is very close indeed to FR. The Company 'remained many days in Lothlórien, so far as they could tell or remember', where FR has 'some days'; but the meeting with Galadriel was now on the last evening spent there, not 'on the evening of the third day' (p. 251).[33] At first my father followed the original draft of Galadriel's reply to Frodo's questions 'What shall we look for, and what shall we see?' (*ibid*.), then changed it to read: 'None can tell, who do not know fully the mind of the beholder. The Mirror will show things that were, and things that are, and things that yet may be. But which it is that he sees, even the wisest cannot always tell. Do you wish to look?' This was further developed to the text of FR in an inserted rider that I think belongs to the time of the writing of the manuscript.

On the back of this inserted page is the following, struck out:

In Ancient Days Sauron the Great contrived many things of wonder. For a time his purpose was not turned wholly to evil, or was concealed; and he went much among the Elves of Middle-earth and knew their secret counsels; and they learned many things of him, for his knowledge was very great. In those days the Rings of Power were made by elven-smiths, but Sauron was present at their making: his was the thought and theirs the skill; for these Rings (he said) would give the Elves of Middle-earth power and wisdom like that of the Elves of the West. [*Struck out as soon as written:* They made many rings, but One and Three and Seven and Nine were rings of special potency. The One only did Sauron take as his reward]; but he cheated them. [*Struck out as soon as written:* For knowing the secret of the rings he] The Elves made many rings at his bidding: Three, Seven and Nine of special potency, and others of lesser virtue. But knowing the secret of their making, secretly Sauron made One Ring, the Ruling Ring that governed all the rest, and their power was bound up with it, to last only so long as it too should last. And as soon as he had made it and set it upon his hand, the Elves found that he was master of all that they had wrought; and they were filled with fear and anger. Then Sauron sought to seize all the Rings, for he saw that the Elves would not lightly submit to him. But the Elves fled and hid themselves, and the Three Rings they saved; and these Sauron could not find because the Elves concealed them, and never again used them while Sauron's mastery endured. War and enmity has never ceased between Sauron and the Elves since those days.

It seems to have been on this page (in view of the rejected words 'The One only did Sauron take as his reward') that the final conception of the relation of the Rings of Power to Sauron emerged, at least in this essential: the Rings of Power were made by the Elven-smiths under the guidance of Sauron, but he made the One in secret to govern all the rest. (This idea had indeed been approached in one of the passages given on p. 255, but there it had been Fëanor himself who made the Rings of Power, and Morgoth who made the Ruling Ring in secret.) It is not said in the passage just cited that Sauron had no part in the making of the Three, which were unsullied by his hand, although this is very clearly implied in the original draft of Galadriel's refusal of Frodo's offer of the One (p. 254).

As with the earlier passages on this subject, I do not think it was written for inclusion in 'Galadriel', but its association with this chapter is again not accidental: for here the questions of the relation of the Three to the One, and the nature of the Three, were at last – through the showing forth of the Ring of Earth on Galadriel's finger – brought to the point where they must necessarily be answered. Ultimately, this passage foreshadows that in *Of the Rings of Power* in *The Silmarillion* (pp. 287–8); my father at this stage probably intended it for 'The Council of Elrond' (cf. p. 255).

Sam's visions in the Mirror, Galadriel's response to his outburst, and Frodo's visions of the wizard and of Bilbo proceed almost word for word as in FR; but the further scenes that appeared to Frodo follow the draft given in note 21, without the mysterious 'vast figure of a man' leaning on a tree. Gollum is no longer seen (p. 252); and the vision of the Eye reaches the form in FR, as does all that follows, with these differences. The white stone in Galadriel's ring is not mentioned; and as in the original text she still calls it 'the Ring of Earth.' In response to Frodo's offer to her of the One Ring Galadriel laughed 'with a sudden clear laugh of pure merriment': 'pure' was struck out early, and afterwards 'of merriment'. And as my father first wrote her words she said: 'And now at last it comes, the final probe.'[34]

A further text of this chapter may be mentioned here. This is an unfinished typescript of the fair copy manuscript just described. Some early emendations made to the manuscript were taken up, but there is no variation whatsoever in the phrasing (always a clear sign that a text was not made by my father). I have noticed (p. 256 and note 30) that in the manuscript Aragorn was 'Ingold' throughout, changed at one occurrence to 'Aragorn' and at another to 'Elfstone', but at the other three left unchanged. The typescript has 'Ingold' at all occurrences except at that where in the manuscript the name was changed to 'Elfstone'. From this I judge that it belongs to the period we have reached, i.e. before 'Aragorn' was restored (see pp. 277–8). But this typescript stops at the bottom of its sixth page, at the words *The air was cool and soft, as if it were* (FR p. 374); and the text is continued to the end of the chapter in a very carefully written manuscript that I made when I was seventeen, beginning at the head of 'page 7' with the words that follow: *early spring, yet they felt about them the deep and thoughtful quiet of winter* (it is thus obvious that my manuscript simply took up from the point where the typescript stopped). The text in my copy shows no further development from my father's manuscript: thus Galadriel's ring remains the Ring of Earth, and she still laughs 'with a sudden clear laugh of merriment'. At the end of it I wrote the date: 4 August 1942.

Whatever the date of the typewritten part of this composite text, my continuation of it in manuscript was certainly made well after my father had completed work on the 'Lothlórien' story. He himself declared, many years later, that he reached Lothlórien and the Great River late in 1941, and it will be seen subsequently that he was writing 'The Breaking of the Fellowship' and 'The Departure of Boromir' in the middle of the winter of that year (p. 379).

NOTES

1   My father first wrote here 'Welcome to Nelennas', immediately striking out *Nelennas* and substituting *Caras Galadon* (which here first appears), and continuing 'the city of Nelennas which [?mayhap] in your tongue is called Angle'. This seems to show that *Nelennas* was very briefly the name of the city, as I have suggested (p. 242 note 39) is the case in the plot-notes given on p. 233: 'They journey to Nelennas'. But the alteration changes the meaning of *Nelennas* back to the 'Gore' or 'Angle', replacing *Nelen* (see p. 231 and note 34).

2   A little rough diagram set in the body of the text shows a circular figure shaped like one ring of a coil, with a very substantial overlap between the ends of the line: the external opening (the entrance into Caras Galadon through the walls) is on the left side of the figure, and the internal opening (the opening from the 'lane' into the city) is at the bottom (i.e. the walls overlap for a full quarter of the circuit or more).

There is no mention of how they passed through the gates (contrast FR p. 368). My father actually wrote here: 'They saw ... the elves on guard at the gate they saw no folk on guard', etc., striking no words out.

3   This is the first appearance of Celeborn and Galadriel. Just visible in the underlying pencilled text are other names: *Tar* and *Finduilas* struck out, and then *Aran* and *Rhien*. *Rhien* is perhaps to be equated with *Rían* (the name of Tuor's mother); cf. the *Etymologies*, V.383, stem RIG: '*Rhian* name of a woman, = "crown-gift", *ríg-anna*'. See notes 5 and 9.

4   The first occurrence of *Halldir* (*sic*) for *Hathaldir*; a few lines further on the name is spelt *Haldir* and so remains. *Haldir* was the original name for this Elf; see p. 240 note 28. In the underlying text the superseded name *Hathaldir* can be seen.

5   This passage (from 'The roof was a pale gold') was retained (i.e. not overwritten in ink or erased) from the original pencilled text, and here reappear (after the words 'side by side') the names *Aran* and *Rhien* (see note 3), subsequently struck out. On the white hair of Galadriel cf. the plot-notes given on p. 233.

6   *Ingold son of Ingrim* for Aragorn replaced *Elfstone* (see p. 239 note 23), since that name can be made out in the pencilled text beneath. At his last appearance in this manuscript (p. 232) he was still *Aragorn*; and it is thus here that *Elfstone* first appears *ab initio* (as also does *Ingold* in the secondary text).

7   Written in here is the following, apparently of the same time but disconnected from the narrative:

    'Nay, there was no mistake,' said Galadriel, speaking for the first time. Her voice was deeper but clear and musical / clear and musical but deep, and seemed to carry knowledge that was too deep for mirth.

    This depends on something said by Keleborn, of which however there is no trace in this manuscript; see p. 257.

8   See p. 227 and note 29.

9   In the underlying pencilled text *Aran* was changed here, as my father wrote, to *Galdaran*; and at the head of the page are written the names *Galdaran* and *Galdrin* (perhaps miswritten for *Galdrien*, see pp. 249–50).

10   On the survival of Balrogs from the Elder Days see V.336, §16.

11   Parts of the underlying pencilled text of this passage can be made out, and the purport of Keleborn's words was very much the same – except that it was Keleborn (Galdaran) himself, not Galadriel, who raised a doubt:

    'A Balrog,' said [Aran >] Galdaran. 'Of them I have not heard since the Elder Days ... had hidden in Mordor but of them naught has been seen since the fall of Thangorodrim. I doubt much if this Balrog has ... and I fear rather ... Orodruin in Mordor by Sauron. Yet who knows what lies hid at the roots of the ancient hills...'

    At the bottom of the page is a variant, added to the revised text but belonging to the same time, in which it is Galadriel who expresses the opinion previously given to Keleborn, and more decisively:

    'No Balrog has lain hid in the Misty Mountains since the fall of Thangorodrim,' said Galadriel. 'If truly one was there, as is told, then it is come from Orodruin, the Mountain of Fire, and was sent by the Lord whom we do not name in this land.'

In FR, of course, the view expressed here by Keleborn or Galadriel that the Balrog, sent from Mordor, had entered Moria not long since ('*it is come* from Orodruin') has no place. In LR the Balrog of Moria came from Thangorodrim at the end of the First Age, and 'had lain hidden at the foundations of the earth since the coming of the Host of the West' (see pp. 142–3).

I have suggested (p. 186) that although a Balrog appears in the original sketch of the Moria story, the connection with the flight of the Dwarves from Moria had not yet been made. The present passage is the chief evidence for this. It is true that in the version in the main text Galadriel is less positive than Keleborn, but in the subsequent variant she utters an emphatic denial that a Balrog could have 'lain hid in the Misty Mountains since the fall of Thangorodrim' (not that anybody present had suggested that it did). This must have been my father's view, since it would be strange indeed to introduce the Lord and Lady of Lothlórien, 'accounted wise beyond the measure of the Elves of Middle-earth', in the immediate expression of an erroneous opinion.

12   The phrases 'The lord and lady of Lothlórien are accounted wise *beyond the measure of the Elves of Middle-earth*' and 'For we have dwelt here *since the Mountains were reared and the Sun was young*' strongly suggest that my father conceived them to be Elves of Valinor, exiled Noldor who did not return at the end of the First Age. The Noldor came to Middle-earth in exile at the time of the making of the Sun and the Hiding of Valinor, when the Mountains of the West were 'raised to sheer and dreadful height' (V.242). Afterwards, when my father returned to *The Silmarillion* again, Galadriel entered the legends of the First Age as the daughter of Finarfin and sister of Finrod Felagund.

13   The first word in this sentence could be 'Nor' or 'Now', but must in fact be 'Now' since it is followed by 'we will', not 'will we'. But in FR Galadriel says 'I will not give you counsel', and her explanation of why she will not is almost word for word the same as what she says here. I think therefore that my father must have changed his mind concerning Galadriel's speech as he wrote, but failed to alter her opening words.

14   A scribble at the foot of the page advances Boromir's words towards the form in FR (p. 373): 'she was tempting me, and offered something that she had the power to give. It need not be said that I refused to listen.' Cf. p. 258.

15   A first suggestion of Keleborn's offer to Legolas and Gimli appears in the plot-notes on p. 233. The last two sentences of Keleborn's speech and the first part of Gimli's reply were subsequently used in Glóin's conversation with Frodo at Rivendell (FR p. 241): 'Frodo learned that Grimbeorn the Old, son of Beorn, was now the lord of many sturdy men, and to their land

between the Mountains and Mirkwood neither orc nor wolf dared to go. "Indeed," said Glóin, "if it were not for the Beornings the passage from Dale to Rivendell would long ago have become impossible." '

16   The biscuit factory of Sandyman & Son (p. 216).

17   This is the first appearance of the name *Mithrandir* (see V.345).

18   Scribbled notes at this point direct that Merry and Pippin should speak of Gandalf, and that they should speak of the 'temptation of Galadriel'; there is also a reference to the 'Song of Frodo and Sam' (FR pp. 374–5). A page of rough workings for the song is found with these papers, though without any narrative framework. The first and third verses were almost in final form; the second at this time read:

> *When morning on the Hill was bright*
> *across the stream he rode again;*
> *beside our hearth he sat that night*
> *and merry was the firelight then.*

The second verse in FR, *From Wilderland to Western shore*, was added in, apparently to stand between verses 2 and 3. The fourth verse ran:

> *A shining sword in deadly hand,*
> *a hooded pilgrim on the road,*
> *a mountain-fire above the land,*
> *a back that bent beneath the load.*

The fifth verse had virtually reached the form in FR; the sixth read:

> *Of Moria, of Khazaddûm*
> *all folk shall ever sadly tell*
> *and now shall name it Gandalf's tomb*
> *where hope into the Shadow fell.*

19   The meeting with Galadriel was altered at the time of writing to the form given. At first my father did not say that it was the *evening* of the third day, and when they came to 'a green hollow over which there was no roof or trees' the sun, which was in the south, looked down into it; cf. the outline given on p. 249; 'Mirror is of silver filled with fountain water in sun'.

     A note in the margin directs that Sam should also be present, and another reads: 'Answer to remarks of Sam and Frodo that these elves seem simple woodland folk, skilled, but not specially magical' (cf. FR pp. 376–7).

20   At this point the following was entered disconnectedly in the manuscript: 'Frodo (Sam?) had been heard to say to Elfstone: Elves seem quiet, and ordinary. Have they magic as is reported?' Cf. note 19.

21   Against this passage my father wrote in the margin: *Bilbo.* In an isolated draft developing this passage the vision of Bilbo in his room at Rivendell (FR p. 379) is found almost as in the final

form. In this draft the vision of 'a fortress with high stone walls and seven towers' is followed by 'a vast figure of a man who seemed to be standing leaning on a tree that was only up to his breast'; this was placed in brackets. This is followed by 'a great river flowing through a populous city' (as in FR), and then by the vision of the Sea and the dark ship, as in the primary text.

22 Cf. the outline of the visions in the Mirror given on p. 250: 'Sees Gollum?'

23 It is notable that in this earliest form of the story the visions that Frodo sees in the Mirror have no reference to Sauron, yet Galadriel at once speaks of him, and the contest of their minds, introducing thus her revelation that she is the keeper of the Ring of Earth. In FR (p. 380) it is because Galadriel knows that Frodo has seen the Eye that she at once speaks to him of the Dark Lord, and the showing of her Ring is directly related to his vision: 'it cannot be hidden from the Ring-bearer, and one who has seen the Eye.'

24 For 'the Ring of Earth' see VI.260, 269, 319.

25 Cf. the isolated note concerning the fading of the power of the Elf-rings if the One Ring were destroyed, p. 237.

26 The word could be equally well read as 'shall' or 'should'; 'should' in the next manuscript of the chapter (and in FR).

27 Cf. pp. 115, 162. In FR Sam says here that 'Elrond knew what he was about when he wanted to send Mr. Merry back'; earlier (FR p. 289) Elrond had said that he had thought to send both Merry and Pippin back to the Shire, but after Gandalf's support for their inclusion in the Company he expressed doubt specifically concerning Pippin.

28 In the outline given on p. 249 'They dwell 15 days in Caras Galadon'. Starting from 15 December as the date of arrival in Lothlórien, even though that seems to be two days out (see p. 215 note 1), and seeing that in the original story it was only a single day's journey from the night spent on the flet near the falls of Nimrodel to the arrival in Caras Galadon at nightfall, the date of departure can be reckoned to be 1 January.

29 Up to this point the pagination is doubled, e.g. 'XVIII.34 / XIX.8'; from this point only that of 'XIX' is given.

30 At three occurrences *Ingold* was never changed; at one it was changed afterwards to *Elfstone*, and at one to *Aragorn*. See pp. 277–8.

31 An addition to the manuscript after the words 'For we have dwelt here since the mountains were reared and the sun was young' reads: 'And I have dwelt here with him since the days of dawn, when I passed over the seas with Melian of Valinor; and ever together we have fought the long defeat.' This was not taken up into the following typescript text (p. 260), though it was entered

onto it in manuscript, and no doubt belongs to a later time. For the coming of Melian to Middle-earth in a very remote age of the world see IV.264, V.111.

32 There are pencilled additions to the manuscript after the words 'But what he thought the Lady had offered him Boromir did not tell': 'Here insert what Frodo thought?' and 'Neither did Frodo. Whether it had been a temptation, or a revealing to himself of the way of escape from his task that he had already secretly considered, he could not tell. But now that the thought had been made plain he could not forget it.' Against this my father wrote: '(rather so:) And as for Frodo, he would not speak, though Boromir pressed him with questions. "She held you long in her gaze, Ringbearer," he said. "Yes," said Frodo, "but I will say no more than this: to me no choice was given." He drooped and laid his head upon his knees.'

Frodo's reply to Boromir was then struck out, with the note: 'No! for this does not fit with the scene at the Mirror', and the following substituted: ' "Yes," said Frodo, "but whatever came into my mind then, I will keep there" ' (as in FR, p. 373).

None of this appears in the following typescript text (though the two latter versions were written onto it in turn), and as with the passage cited in note 31 must be accounted a later revision. But what is hinted at in the words 'the way of escape from his task that he had already secretly considered'? My father meant, I think, that Frodo, under Galadriel's gaze, pondered the thought of surrendering the Ruling Ring to her (cf. the passage cited on p. 254).

33 Of Frodo's song of Gandalf it is said: 'yet when he wished to repeat it to Sam only snatches remained that said little of what he had meant.' At this point there is a large space on the manuscript page and a pencilled note: 'Insert Frodo's Song?' The verses are found on a page of the familiar examination script, headed 'Frodo's Song', and were evidently written before this point in the manuscript was reached. For the earliest form of the song see note 18. The song has now 8 verses, since both *When morning on the Hill was bright* and *From Wilderland to Western shore* are included, and the last verse in FR *He stood upon the bridge alone* here appears as the penultimate (with the fourth line *the cloak of grey is cast aside*), the final verse being the same as in the earliest version, *Of Moria, of Khazad-dûm*.

34 '*Eärendil*, the Evening Star' is spelt thus, not *Eärendel* (see p. 290 note 22). – In Frodo's question 'why cannot I see all the others' (FR p. 381) 'I' should be italicized; and in Sam's reply to Galadriel's question at the end of the chapter 'Did you see my ring?' he should say 'I saw a star through your fingers', not 'finger'.

XIV
FAREWELL TO LÓRIEN

In the earliest materials for this chapter (without title) my father did not complete a continuous primary text, but (as it might be described) continually took two steps forward and one step back. He halted abruptly, even at mid-sentence, at certain points in the narrative, and returned to revise what he had written, often more than once; the result is a great deal of near-repetition and a very complex sequence. On the other hand, much (though by no means all) of this drafting is written in ink in a quick but clear and orderly hand on good paper (the 'August 1940' examination script being now virtually exhausted).

The reason for this situation is clear. The first consecutive text of the chapter, a well-written 'fair copy' manuscript, stands in very close relation to the draft materials. By this time it had become my father's method to begin making a fair copy before a new stretch of the narrative had proceeded very far: it has been seen in 'The Bridge of Khazad-dûm' (p. 202) and in 'Lothlórien' (pp. 221–2 and note 14) that drafting and fair copy to some extent overlapped. This was the case here also (thus the extracts from Keleborn's description of the Great River given on pp. 282–3 were drafts for the text found in the fair copy, and they immediately preceded that point in the writing of that text), but to a much more marked degree: for in this case, as I think, the fair copy was built up in stages, as the different sections of draft were completed.

Before turning to the original text, or texts, of this chapter, however, I give first some very difficult pencilled outlines, which I will call (a), (b) and (c). I take (a) to be the first since in it the name *Toll-ondren*, which occurs also in the others, is seen at the point of emergence. The pencil is now faint to the point of vanishing, and the first lines (as far as 'the Bridges of Osgiliath'), which were written before and apparently disconnectedly from the following portion, are partly illegible.

(a)

The travellers must choose which side of Anduin [?to be on] at [?Naith] Lórien. River is narrow but... at Stone Hills.[1] Not possible to cross without a boat until the Bridges of Osgiliath.

Keleborn says they must [?journey] in the morning. Though his people do not often go outside borders he will send them by *boat* as far as [*struck out: Toll-ondu Toll-onnui*] *Toll-ondren* the Great Carrock.[2] The east bank is perilous to elves. River winds among the Border Hills [*struck out: Duil*] *Emyn Rain*.[3] There they must decide because the Wetwang *Palath Nenui*[4] lies before them and to reach Minas Tirith they must go west round and across [*added:* along hills and then across] Entwash. But to go the other way they must cross Dead Marshes.

(b)

This outline is also extremely faint. It takes up towards the end of the narrative in this chapter and extends beyond it, but was written at an early stage in the development of the story, since the presence of Elves accompanying the travellers is mentioned, and this element was soon abandoned.

This is the Naith or Angle.[5] Calendil or the Green Spit.
[*Struck out:* Nelen] Calennel[6]
We are come before you to make all ready, said the Lady Galadriel, and now at last we must bid you farewell. Here you are come at last to the end of our realm, to Calendil, the green-spit tongue. Green-tine.[7] Three boats await you with rowers.
They get into the boats. Elv[en] archers in one behind and before. Company 2 in first, Ingold, Boromir. Hobbits in middle. Legolas, Gimli behind.
Parting gifts.
Warning against Entwash (Ogodrûth) and Fangorn[8] – not necessary to Boromir and Ingold, but probably Gandalf did not tell them all.
Blessing of Galadriel on Frodo.
Song of Farewell of Elves.
Swift passing down the River.
Description of the [?Green Ravines].
Tollondren.
Scene with Boromir and loss of Frodo.
          End of Chapter.

In this outline the names *Galadriel* and *Ingold* were written *ab initio*.

(c)

This third outline, again in very faint pencil, belongs with the others; a further section was added to it, but not I think after any significant interval.

Argument in pavilion at night.

They postpone decision until they reach Tolondren the Great Carrock.

They sail in [*number changed between* 2, 3, 4, *final figure probably* 3] boats. 1 filled with bowmen before and after.

Farewell of Galadriel.

They pass into the Rhain hills[9] where river winds in deep ravines.

A few arrows from East.

Elves give travellers special food and grey cloaks and hoods.

They say farewell at Tol Ondren and leave travellers [*struck out:* a boat > 2 small boats].

The Company lands and goes up into Rhain Hills for a safe place. The debate. Then comes Boromir's attempt at seizing Ring and Frodo's flight.

Arrows from East shore as they pass down river?

The Company lands on Tollondren. Then debate. Frodo (and Sam) want to go on with the Quest and get it over. Boromir against it (vehemently?). They beg Elves to wait while they decide. They cross to East bank and go up into Green Hills (or Emyn Rhain?) to look around.

The journey by boat down Anduin enters in outline *(a)* (see p. 213); in *(b)* the 'scene with Boromir and loss of Frodo' is removed from 'Angle' (see pp. 207–8, 213) and takes place after the journey down the river, while in *(c)* it occurs in the 'Rhain Hills'.

The geography of these regions was coming into being. My father knew at this stage that the Great River wound in ravines (the 'Green Ravines' doubtfully read in outline *(b)*?) through a range of hills (Stone Hills; Emyn Rhain, Rhain Hills, Border Hills; Green Hills – which were not merely alternative names, as will be seen in the next chapter); and that there was a great rock or tall island (the Great Carrock; *Tolondren*, variously spelt) in the midst of Anduin. This was associated with the hills, since the Company lands on the island and goes up into Emyn Rhain or into the Green Hills. In the added section of *(c)* they cross the river to do so. The Wetwang now appears, obviously if not explicitly associated with the confluence of Anduin and Entwash (or *Ogodrûth*), flowing out of Fangorn (p. 210).

I turn now to the earliest narrative texts of 'Farewell to Lórien', in which indications are found that the fair copy manuscript of 'Galadriel' was already in existence (notes 10 and 21). The opening portion of the chapter, in which the Company came before Keleborn and Galadriel on the eve of departure and then returned to their pavilion to debate their course, is extant in several different versions. The earliest of them begins clearly but soon descends to my father's roughest script; it was written in ink over a faint pencilled text some of which can be read (see note 12).

(i)

That night[10] the Company was summoned again to the chamber of Keleborn, and the Lord and Lady of the Galadrim looked upon their faces. After a silence Keleborn spoke to them.

'Now is the time,' he said, 'when those who wish to continue the Quest must harden themselves to depart. And now is the time for those to say farewell to the Company who feel that they have gone as far as they have the strength to go. All that do not wish to go forward may remain here until there is a chance for them to return to their own homes.[11] For we stand now on the edge of doom; and ere long things will grow better, or will grow so evil that all must fight and fall where they stand. There will be no homes to seek, save the long home of those that go down in battle. Here you may abide the oncoming of the hour till the ways of the world lie open again, or we summon you to help us in the last stand of Lórien.'[12]

'They are all resolved to go forward,' said Galadriel.

'As for me,' said Boromir, 'my way home lies onward.'

'That is true,' said Keleborn. 'But are all the Company going with you to Minas Tirith?'

'We have not decided that yet,' said Ingold.

'But you must do so soon,' said Keleborn. 'For after you leave Lothlórien the River cannot easily be crossed again until you come to Ondor,[13] if indeed the passage of the river in the South is not held by the Enemy. Now the way to Minas Tirith lies on this side of the River, on the West bank, but the straight way of the Quest lies upon the other, upon the East bank. You should choose before you go.'

'If they take my advice it will be the west side,' said Boromir, 'but I am not the leader.'

'It shall be as you choose. But as you seem still in doubt, and do not maybe wish to hasten your choice, this is what I will do. It will speed your journey somewhat, and show you my good will – for I do not send my people often and only at [?great] need beyond my borders. I will furnish you with boats which we use upon the rivers. Some of my folk shall go with you as far as the Green Hills, where the river winds deep among [?wooded] slopes. But beyond the Toll-ondren, the isle that is there amid the river flood, they shall not go. Even so far there are perils for Elves upon the East bank; beyond that it is not safe for any to go by water.'

The words of Keleborn lightened their hearts a little that were heavy with the thought of departure. They took leave of the Lord and Lady and went back to their pavilion. Legolas was with them. They debated long but they came to no decision. Ingold was evidently torn between two things. His own plan and desire was to have gone to Minas Tirith; but now that Gandalf was lost he felt that he could not abandon Frodo if he could not be persuaded to come. To the others there was little choice, for they knew nothing of the ... of the land in the South. Boromir said little but kept his eyes ever fixed on Frodo as if he waited for his decision. At length he spoke. 'If you are to *destroy the Ring*,' he said, 'then there is little use in arms, and Minas Tirith cannot help you greatly. But if you wish to *destroy the Lord*, then there is little use in going without force into his domain. That is how it seems to me.'

Here this text ends.

(ii)

The next version is a fair copy of (i) so far as it went, and follows it closely, improving the wording but introducing few significant changes; but it extends further into the chapter.

Keleborn now speaks with greater certainty of the crossings of Osgiliath: 'it is said that the Enemy holds the passages [> bridges].' Elves of Lórien shall go with the Company 'as far as the Green Hills where the river winds among deep ravines'; here *Rhain* is written in pencil over *Green*. 'There is a wooded island there, Toll-ondren, amid the branching waters. There at last in the midst of the stream you must decide your courses, left or right.' Above *(Toll-)ondren* is written in pencil *Galen?*, i.e. *Tol Galen*: another use of a name from the legends of the Elder Days (the Green Isle in the river Adurant in Ossiriand, home of Beren and Lúthien after their return, and a further instance of an island amid a river's 'branching waters' – from which indeed the *Adurant* took its name, V.268).

In the part of this version that extends beyond the point reached in (i) the text of FR (pp. 385–6) is closely approached. Boromir now breaks off at the words 'and no sense in throwing away...', finishing his sentence lamely after a pause with 'no sense in throwing lives away, I mean.' And as in FR Ingold was deep in his thoughts and made no sign at this, while Merry and Pippin were already asleep.

The passage describing the bringing of the Elvish cakes and Gimli's delight at discovering that they were not *cram* is at once almost exactly as in FR, the only difference being that the words 'But we call it *lembas* or waybread' do not appear. The description of the cloaks is however much briefer than in FR – and there is no mention of the leaf-shaped brooches that fastened them.

For each member of the Company they had provided a grey hood and cloak made according to his size of the light but warm silken stuff that the Galadrim used.

'There is no magic woven in these cloaks,' they said, 'but they should serve you well. They are light to wear, and at need warm enough and cool enough in turn...'

Later, my father would not have the Elves introduce the idea of 'magic' cloaks, and it is Pippin who uses the word, which the leader of the Elves finds hard to interpret. The remainder of the passage is as in FR, except just at the end: 'We have never before clad strangers in the garb of our own people, certainly never a dwarf.' With these words the second text stops abruptly.

(iii)

The next text, going back once more to the beginning of the chapter, carries the number XX, showing that the story of Galadriel's Mirror had been separated off, as XIX 'Galadriel', from XVIII 'Lothlórien' (see p. 256). This manuscript rapidly becomes very complex through a process of what might be called 'overlapping false starts'. The form in FR is now very closely approached as far as the point where Keleborn says 'I see that you have not decided this matter' (cf. FR p. 383). It is to be noted that *Ingold* was changed subsequently, at both occurrences in the opening dialogue, first to *Elfstone* and then to *Trotter* (see pp. 277–8). Keleborn now says: 'And are not the bridges of Osgiliath broken down, and the passages of the river held now by the Enemy since his late assault?'[14] But from the point mentioned the story is developed thus:

'I see that you have not decided this matter, nor yet made any plan,' said Keleborn. 'It is not my part to choose for you, but I will do what I can to help you. Are there any among you that can manage boats upon a strong river?'

Boromir laughed. 'I was born between the mountains and the sea, on the borders of the Land of Seven Streams,'[15] he said, 'and the Great River flows through Ondor.'

'I have journeyed by boat on many rivers,' said Ingold;[16] 'and Legolas here is from the elf-folk of Mirkwood who use both rafts and boats on the Forest River. One at least of the hobbits is of the riverside folk that live on the banks of Baranduin. The rest can at least sit still. They have all now passed through such perils that I do not think a journey by boat would seem so terrible as once it might.'

'That is well,' said Keleborn. 'Then I will furnish you with two small boats. They must be small and light, for if you go far by river there are places where you will have to carry your craft: there are the falls of Rhain where the River runs out of the ravines in the Green Hills,[17] and other places where no boat can pass. [*The following struck out as soon as written:* This I will do to show you my good will. Two Elves shall guide you for a short way, but far abroad I cannot permit my folk to stray in these evil days. But when you leave the River, as you must whichever way you go at the last, I ask only that you should not destroy my boats save only to keep them from the orcs, and that you should draw them ashore and] In this way your journey will be made less toilsome for a while, though perhaps not less perilous. How far you can go by water who now can tell? And the gift of boats will not decide your purpose: it may postpone your choice, yet at the last you must leave the River and go either east or west.'

Ingold thanked Keleborn many times in the name of all the Company. The offer of the boats comforted him much, and indeed it cheered most of the travellers. Their hearts were heavy with the thought of leaving Lothlórien, but now for a while the toils of the road at least would be lessened, though the dangers doubtless would remain. Sam only felt a little alarm. In spite of all the perils he had now passed through

(iv)

Here the third text breaks off, and all from 'Are there any among you that can manage boats upon a strong river?' was rejected, and begun again; the narrative now becoming close to the form in FR: 'There are some at least among you that can handle boats: Legolas, whose folk go on rafts and boats on the Forest River; and Boromir of Ondor, and Ingold [> Elfstone] the traveller.' The Elves to accompany them down the River have now gone; and *the falls of Rhain* 'where the River runs out of the ravines in the Green Hills' become *the Falls of Rosfein* (with the same comment).

After Ingold (> Elfstone > Trotter) had thanked Keleborn, and after the account of the lightened hearts of all the travellers,[18] the new text continues with Keleborn's words 'All shall be prepared for you and await you before noon tomorrow at the haven' (FR p. 384); but whereas in texts (i) and (ii) – as in FR – Keleborn's offer of boats is

followed by the withdrawal of the Company to their pavilion, and
there is no mention of gifts, this new version has Galadriel say: 'Good
night, fair guests! But before you go I have here parting gifts which I
beg you to take, and remember the Galadrim and their Lord and
Lady.' The outline *(b)* on p. 268, obviously earlier than the stage now
reached since there is mention in it of Elves going with the Company in
boats, placed the Parting Gifts at the time of the final departure down
the River, and this must have been my father's original intention,
which he now temporarily changed. In this version (iv) there now
follows the recital of the gifts to each member of the Company.

Galadriel's gift to Ingold (the name not here changed) is the sheath
that had been made to fit his sword, which is called *Branding*:[19]
overlaid with silver and with runes of gold declaring the name of the
sword and its owner. Nothing more is said, and there is no mention of
the great green stone (FR p. 391). Boromir's belt of gold, the silver
belts for Merry and Pippin, and the bow of the Galadrim given to
Legolas, appear and are described in the same words as in FR.
Galadriel's gift to Sam and her words to him are almost exactly as in
FR. The box containing earth from her garden was 'unadorned save
for a single flowering rune upon the lid' ('a single silver rune,' FR). On
the manuscript page my father drew an Old English G-rune ('X') in the
form of two flowering branches crossed one upon the other:[20]

The word 'flowering' was later crossed out, and another, purely
formal elaboration of the rune was drawn at the head of the next page:

The gift to Gimli differs, however, from his gift in FR, and differs in the most remarkable way.

'And what gift would a dwarf ask of Elves?' said the Lady to Gimli.

'None, Lady,' answered Gimli. 'It is enough for me to have seen the Lady of the Galadrim and known her graciousness. I will treasure the memory of her words at our first meeting.'[21]

[*Rejected, but not struck out, as soon as written:* 'Hear, all you Elves!' said the Lady, turning to those about her. 'And say not that dwarves are all rough and ungracious, grasping at gifts and / I have heard it said that dwarves are openhanded – to receive, and count their words – when they give thanks'] 'It is well that those about me should hear your fair words,' said Galadriel, 'and may they never again say that dwarves are grasping and ungracious. Let this small token be given as a sign that goodwill may be remade between dwarves and elves, if better days should come.' She put her hand to her throat and unclasped a brooch, and gave it to Gimli. On it was an emerald of deep green set in gold. 'I will set it near my heart,' he said, bowing to the floor, 'and Elfstone shall be a name of honour in my [?kin] for ever, and like a leaf [?amid] . . . gold.'

Once again the text was stopped short, before Frodo's gift was reached. Beneath the last words my father wrote: *Elfstone Elfhelm*, and then:

'Hail, Elfstone,' she said. 'It is a fair name that merits a gift to match.'

It was clearly at this point that 'the Elfstone' first emerged, as a green gem set in a brooch worn by Galadriel and given as a parting gift to Gimli; and it seems equally plain that my father immediately adopted it (or more accurately, re-adopted it) as the true name of Trotter. To this question I will return in a moment.

(v)

He now started again from Keleborn's words 'All shall be prepared for you and await you at the haven before noon tomorrow' (p. 273), and repeated what he had written of the gifts to Boromir, Merry, Pippin, and Sam, but omitting Ingold; and now Gimli's request and gift (a strand of Galadriel's hair) are told word for word as they appear in FR (pp. 392–3), the sole difference being that at the end, after 'and yet over you gold shall have no dominion', Galadriel said: 'Dark are the waters of Kheledzâram, yet there maybe you shall one day see a light.' The phial in which was caught the light of Eärendel's star,[22] her gift to Frodo, now appears, and this passage also is almost word for word as in FR.

It looks as if Ingold's gift was omitted inadvertently; or else my father may have briefly intended to make it the last. There are four versions describing it, the final one being a rider marked for insertion into the text at the beginning of the gift-giving.

It has been seen that the Elfstone was at first the gift to Gimli, and that Gimli in accepting it took it also as a name; but that the moment he had set this down my father wrote: ' "Hail, Elfstone," she said. "It is a fair name that merits a gift to match" '; and this is obviously addressed to Trotter. The variant versions of the description of Galadriel's gift to the leader of the Company are developed from this; and the pages on which they stand are covered with names: *Elfstone, Elfstone son of Elfhelm, Elfstan, Eledon, Aragorn, Eldakar, Eldamir, Qendemir.* There is no need to cite these successive variants except in their opening sentences, until the last, which I give in full.

(1) 'Eledon!' she said to Trotter. 'Elfstone you are named; it is a fair name, and my gift shall match it.' (She then gives him a green gem.)

(2) 'Elfstone,' she said. 'It is a fair name...' (as in 1, except that here she unclasps the gem from her throat).

(3) 'Here is the gift of Keleborn to the leader of the Company,' she said to Trotter...' (continuing as in the final version, 4).

(4) (The version inserted into the text)

'Here is the gift of Keleborn to the leader of your Company,' she said to Elfstone [> Trotter], and gave him a sheath that had been made to fit his sword. It was overlaid with a tracery of flowers and leaves wrought of silver and gold, and on it were set in runes formed of many gems the name Branding and the lineage of the sword. 'The blade that is drawn from this sheath shall not be stained or broken even in defeat,' she said. 'Elfstone is your name, Eldamir in the language of your fathers of old, and it is a fair name. I will add this gift of my own to match it.'[23] She put her hand to her throat and unclasped from a fine chain a gem that hung before her breast. It was a stone of clear green set in a band of silver. 'All growing things that you look at through this,' she said, 'you will see as they were in their youth and in their spring. It is a gift that blends joys and sorrow; yet many things that now appear loathly shall seem otherwise to you hereafter.'

The seeming conundrum presented by the bewildering movements in the names which replaced 'Aragorn' in this phase of the work must now be confronted.

For all the apparently contradictory changes, whereby *Aragorn* becomes *Elfstone* but *Elfstone* also becomes *Aragorn*, and *Elfstone* becomes *Ingold* but *Ingold* also becomes *Elfstone*, it is in fact perfectly clear that the first change was from *Aragorn* to *Elfstone*. This took place in the course of the writing of the original draft of the long 'Lothlórien' chapter (see p. 262 note 6) and in the fair copy (p. 236). That this is so is confirmed and explained by a note on the 'August 1940' examination script:

> NB. Since Aragorn [> Trotter] is a *man* and the common speech (especially of mortals) is represented by English, then he must not have an Elvish name. Change to *Elfstone* son of *Elfhelm*.

Beside this are written other names, *Elf-friend*, *Elfspear*, *Elfmere*. It was now that *Aragorn* (or *Trotter*) was changed to *Elfstone* in earlier chapters;[24] but at this stage the name 'Elf-*stone*' will not have had any particular significance or association.

That *Ingold* was a replacement of *Elfstone* is shown by its appearance *ab initio* (i.e. not as a correction of an earlier name) in the overwritten part of the original draft of the 'Lothlórien' story, where *Elfstone* can be read in the primary pencilled text beneath (p. 262 note 6). This change is the subject of another note written on the same paper as the first:

> Instead of Aragorn son of Kelegorn *and* instead of the later variant Elfstone son of Elfhelm use *Ingold son of Ingrim*; since Trotter is a *man* he should not have a Gnome-elvish name like Aragorn.[25] The *Ing-* element here can represent the 'West'.

Some texts, therefore, call him *Ingold* from the first; and at the same time *Ingold* replaced (in principle) *Elfstone* in texts already extant at this time.

When my father wrote the first version of the Parting Gifts passage (p. 275) the gift of Galadriel to Gimli of the green gem set in gold was totally unforeseen, as was Gimli's thereupon taking the name *Elfstone* to be 'a name of honour' in his kin. At that very moment a sudden new possibility and connection emerged. Trotter had been for a while *Elfstone* – a name chosen for linguistic reasons; that had been rejected and replaced by *Ingold*; but now it turned out that *Elfstone* was after all the right name. The Elfstone was the Lady's gift to him, not to Gimli; and in giving it to him she made a play on his name.

The next step, therefore, and principal ˙cause of the apparent confusion, was a *reversion* from the short-lived *Ingold* to *Elfstone*, and the chain of changes now becomes:

Aragorn (or *Trotter*) > *Elfstone* > *Ingold* > *Elfstone*

The further emendation of this new *Elfstone* to *Trotter* (pp. 272–3, 276) does not necessarily mean that *Elfstone* had been abandoned again as his real name, but rather that my father now wished to make his name *Trotter* for general use in the immediate narrative (thus he is *Trotter* throughout the fair copy manuscript of 'Farewell to Lórien', see p. 293). Ultimately *Aragorn* returned; and thus the circular series is completed:

Aragorn (or *Trotter*) > *Elfstone* > *Ingold* > *Elfstone* (> *Trotter*) > *Aragorn*

This series appears in more or less fragmentary form in the manuscripts (cf. p. 244 note 52) for various reasons, but largely because my father carried out the corrections to the extant texts at each stage rather haphazardly. In some cases only parts of the series are found because in these cases the succession of changes was already more or less advanced; in some cases the expected change is not made because the text was rejected before the occasion for it arose (note 16). Running through and crossing this is the name *Trotter*, which might be changed or retained according to my father's changing view of when it should be employed.

Afterwards, of course, when Galadriel gave Aragorn the Elfstone she *conferred* on him the name 'that was foretold' for him (FR p. 391); Aragorn became *Elessar, the Elfstone* in that hour. On the history and properties of the Elfstone or Elessar see *Unfinished Tales* pp. 248 ff.; cf. especially 'For it is said that those who looked through this stone saw things that were withered or burned healed again or as they were in the grace of their youth.' In FR nothing is said of the properties of the stone.

This text (v) continues – since the gift-giving took place on the last night, in the chamber of Keleborn and Galadriel – with a further version of the debate of the Company, and the gifts next morning of elven-cloaks and food for the journey. The text of FR is further approached in many details of wording; but of Trotter's thoughts on the question of what they should do now this is said:

Elfstone [> Trotter] was himself divided in mind. His own plan and desire had been to go with Boromir, and with his sword help to deliver Ondor. For he had believed that the message of the dreams was a summons, and that there in Minas Tirith he would become a great lord, and maybe would set up again the throne of Elendil's line, and defend the West against assault. But in Moria he had taken on himself Gandalf's burden...

The remainder of the debate is now virtually as in FR (p. 385), the only difference being that the sentence 'He [Boromir] had said something like this at the Council, but then he had accepted the correction of Elrond' is here absent. The passage concerning the cloaks remains the same as in the previous draft (p. 272), except that the

Elves now add that 'All who see you clad thus will know that you are friends of the Galadrim', and the words 'certainly never a dwarf' are omitted. Thus there is still no mention of the detail, afterwards important, that each cloak was fastened with a leaf-shaped brooch. But the sentence previously absent (p. 271), 'But we call it *lembas* or waybread', now appears.

(vi)

For the next part of the chapter, from 'After their morning meal they said farewell to the lawn by the fountain' (FR p. 386), the form of the text changes, though the actual writing was clearly continuous with what precedes. There was first a draft in very faint pencil which went as far as the Elves' warning about the handling of the boats, and then became an outline of the further course of the narrative:

> They were arranged thus. Elfstone and Frodo and Sam in one, Boromir and Merry and Pippin in another, and in a third Legolas and Gimli (... dwarf become more friendly).[26] The last boat being more lightly burdened with passengers took more of the packs. They are steered and driven by broad-bladed paddles. They practise on advice of Elves and though they will only be going downstream practise going up the Silverlode.
>
> Thus they meet the Lord and Lady in their *swan-shaped* barge. Curved neck, and jewelled eyes, and half-raised wings. They take a meal on the grass and then a last farewell. Here comes in advice of Keleborn and last farewell of Galadriel.
>
> Frodo looks back and sees in the westering sun upon the haven a tall, slender, and sad figure with an upraised hand. Last sight of the Ring of Earth. (He never saw it again?)
>
> Song of Galadriel.

On top of the pencilled draft my father wrote a new text in ink, so that virtually all – except the outline just given, which was left intact – was obliterated. He then continued this new text, which soon became very rough and petered out at Keleborn's invitation to eat with them. Since this was in turn overtaken by a further version which followed it closely so far as it went, nothing is lost by turning at once to that.

(vii)

This text is in soft pencil on large and now very battered sheets, but legible. The story as told in FR appears fully formed, even to much of its wording, and I shall not give it in full; there are however many interesting features of names and geography.

With Haldir, returned from the 'northern fences' and acting as guide to the Company from Caras Galadon, his brother Orofin came also. It

is said that 'Haldir brought news': ' "There are strange things happening away back there," he said. "We do not know the meaning of them.
But the Dimrill Dale is full of clouds of smoke and vapour..." ' (see
note 11).

The Tongue is thus described (cf. FR p. 387):

The lawn ran out into a narrow tongue of green between bright
margins: on the right and west glittered the narrower and
swifter waters of the Silverlode, and on the left and east ran the
broader greener waters of the Great River. On the far banks the
woodlands still marched southwards as far as they could see,
but beyond the Naith or Angle (as the elves called this green
sward) and upon the east side of the Great River all the boughs
were bare. No mallorn-trees grew there.[27]

On 'Naith or Angle' as a name of the Tongue see note 5. This sentence
was corrected, probably at once, to: 'but beyond the Tongue (*Lamben*
the elves called this green sward)'; then the words '*Lamben* the elves
called this green sward' were in turn crossed out. On Elvish names of
the Tongue see p. 268 and note 6.

The passage in FR concerning the ropes and Sam's interest in
rope-making is wholly absent, just as his realisation too late that he
has no rope before leaving Rivendell (p. 165) and his bemoaning that
he has none in Moria (p. 183) are also lacking.[28] The old text reads
here:

Three small grey boats had already been prepared for the
travellers, and in these the elves stowed their goods.

'You must take care,' they said. 'The boats are light-built, and
they will be more deeply laden than they should be, when you
go aboard. It would be wise if you accustomed yourselves to
getting in and out here, where there is a landing-place, before
you set off downstream.'

In the first draft (vi) of this passage Trotter is here called *Elfstone*,
and it is said that 'Trotter led them up the Silverlode'; in this second
version (vii) he is *Eldamir* at both occurrences, replaced (at the time of
writing) by *Trotter*. *Eldamir* ('Elfstone') appears in Galadriel's address
to him at the time of her parting gifts (p. 276); as will be seen shortly,
my father was on the point of removing the gift-giving from the
evening before their departure to their final farewell on the Tongue,
and this apart from any other consideration would probably explain
his removing *Eldamir* at this point in the story.

A curious detail in the description of the swan-boat was subsequently removed:

Two elves, clad in white, steered it with black paddles so

contrived that the blades folded back, as a swan's foot does, when they were thrust forward in the water.

It may be that my father saw this as too much of a 'contrivance', too much a matter of ingenious carpentry. – There is no suggestion that Galadriel's song on the swan-boat, though it is referred to in the same words as in FR, was or would be reported.

Where FR has 'There in the last end of Egladil upon the green grass' (see note 5), this earliest version had 'There in the green Angle', changed to 'There in the Tongue of Lórien'; this was a change made at the time of composition. The description of Galadriel as Frodo saw her then is almost exactly as in FR; but as my father wrote it there was included in it a notable phrase which he (then or later) struck out:

She seemed no longer perilous or terrible, nor full of hidden power; but elven-fair she seemed beyond desire of heart. Already she appeared to him (since her refusal in the garden)[29] as by men of later days elves at times are seen: present, and yet remote, a living vision of that which has already passed far down the streams of time.

I cite in full the text of Keleborn's advice to the Company:

As they ate and drank, sitting upon the grass, Keleborn spoke to them again of their journey, and lifting his hand he pointed south to the woods beyond the Tongue. 'As you go down the water,' he said, 'you will find that for a while the trees march on. For of old the Forest of Lórien was far greater [added: than the small realm which we still maintain between the rivers].[30] Even yet evil comes seldom under the trees that remain [added: from ancient days]. But you will find that at length the trees will fail, and then the river will carry you through a bare and barren country / before it flows [replaced by: winding among the Border Hills before it falls down] into the sluggish region of Nindalf. The Wetwang men call it, a marshy land where the streams are tortuous and much divided: there the Entwash River flows in from the West. Beyond that are [struck out: Emyn Rhain the Border Hills and] the Nomenlands, dreary Uvanwaith that lies before the passes of Mordor. When the trees fail, you should travel only by dusk and dark and even then with watchfulness. The arrows of the orcs are bitter and fly straight. Whether you will journey on by river after the falls I do not know. But beyond the Entwash it may be that [Ingold >] Elfstone[31] and Boromir know the lands well enough to need no counsel. If you decide to go west to Minas Tirith, you will do best to leave the river where the isle of Toll-ondren stands in the stream above the falls of Rosfein and cross the Entwash above the marshes. But you will be wise not to go far up that stream, or to risk becoming entangled in the Forest of Fangorn. But that warning I need hardly give to a man of Minas Tirith.'

'Indeed we have heard of Fangorn in Minas Tirith,' said Boromir. 'But what I have heard seem to me for the most part old wives' tales, such as are told to our children. For all that lies north of Rohan seems now to us so far away that fancy can wander freely there. Of old Fangorn lay upon the borders [of the realm of Anárion >] of our realm; but it is now many lives of men since any of us visited it to prove or disprove the legends that have survived. I have not myself been there. When I was sent out as a messenger – being chosen as one hardy and used to mountain-paths, I went round by the south about the Black Mountains and up the Greyflood – or the Seventh River as we call it.[32] A long and weary journey [*struck out:* but not at that time yet one of great peril, other than from thirst and hunger]. Four hundred leagues I reckoned it, and it took me many months, for I lost my horses at the crossing of the Greyflood at Tharbad.[33] After that journey, and the road I have so far travelled with this Company, I do not much doubt that I shall find a way through Rohan, and Fangorn too, if need be.'

'Then I will say no more,' said Keleborn. 'But do not wholly forget the old wives' tales!'

Then follows: 'Remove the gift scene and place it at this point just before drink of farewell.'

On an isolated page are two further versions of Keleborn's description of the Great River, immediately preparatory to the passage in the fair copy manuscript, and both beginning in mid-sentence. The first of these was at once replaced by the second and need only be cited in its opening sentences:[34]

(i) [For of old the Forest of Lórien] was greater than it now is, and even yet evil comes seldom under the trees upon the shores of the River. But after some nine leagues you will be brought to a bare and barren country of heath and stone, and the river will wind in deep ravines until it divides about the tall island of Tolondren....

(ii) [you will find that] the trees will fail, and you will come to a barren country. There the river flows in stony vales among high moors, until it comes to the tall island of Tolondren. About the rocky shores of the isle it casts its arms, and then falls with noise and smoke over the cataracts of Rhosfein [*written above in pencil:* Dant-ruin] down into the Nindalf – the Wetwang as it is called in your speech. That is a wide region of sluggish fen, where the stream becomes tortuous and much divided; there the Entwash river flows in by many mouths from the West. Beyond, on this side of the Great River, lies Rohan. On the further side are the bleak hills of Sarn-gebir [*in version (i)* Sarn > Sern Gebir]. The wind blows from the East there, for they look out over the Dead Marshes and the Nomenlands [*in version (i)* the Nomen-lands (of Uvanwaith)] to the passes of Mordor: Kirith Ungol.

This passage in its variant forms is the fullest account of the geography of these regions yet encountered, and I postpone discussion of it, in relation to the earliest map of *The Lord of the Rings*, to the next chapter.

Despite his direction to bring in the gift scene 'just before the drink of farewell' (p. 282) my father now changed his mind, and introduced the cup of parting here, in the same place as in FR (pp. 390–1), and in the same words, except that Galadriel first said 'though the hour of shadow has come in its appointed time', and then 'though shadows long foretold approach', before her words in FR were reached: 'though night must follow noon, and already our evening draweth nigh.' After 'Then she called to each in turn' my father directed: 'Here take in gift-scene (in short or longer form).' The 'short form' of the scene is found under the heading 'If the gift-scene is cut out, or down, it might run thus:'

To each of the guests she gave a small brooch shaped like a golden flower with three leaves of jewelled green. 'This shall be in remembrance of Lothlórien,' she said, 'and all elves that see these shall know that you are friends. For you two,' she said, turning to Frodo and Sam, 'I have also small gifts of my own in remembrance of our last meeting. To you, little gardener and lover of trees, I will give this, though it may seem little to look on. She beckoned to Sam and laid in his hand (. . . so to end of Sam . . .)
'And for you, Frodo, I have prepared this,' she said . . .

(The last part of this text is written thus in the original.)

(viii)

The conclusion of the chapter in its earliest extant form is written in ink in clear script with little hesitation in the phrasing, and closely approaches FR (despite very many small differences in the actual words). The feeling of the Company as the River bore them away from Lórien is expressed thus (and is the first suggestion of the idea that

Lórien existed in a mode of Time distinct from that of the world beyond its borders, unless it is present in Keleborn's words on p. 249):

Lórien was slipping backward like a green vessel masted with trees sailing to forgotten shores, while they were cast again on the grey never-halting water of time.

Galadriel's song heard in the distance as the boats slipped down Anduin is not recorded; indeed there is a clear suggestion that when he first wrote this concluding passage my father did not intend that it should be (although the words 'Song of Galadriel' in the outline on p. 279 perhaps suggest otherwise):

But she sang in [the ancient elvish tongue >] some ancient hidden tongue, and he heard not the words. [*Added:* The music was fair but it bore no heart's ease.] Then suddenly the river swept round a bend and the banks rose upon either side. They saw her never more. Turning now their faces to their journey they faced the sun ...

The initial workings for Galadriel's songs were nonetheless found with the earliest manuscripts of this chapter, both her song upon the swan-boat (of which there is also a finished text) and *Namarië*. The completed form of the first reads:

I sang of leaves, of leaves of gold, and leaves of gold there grew:
Of wind I sang, a wind there came and in the branches blew.
Beyond the Sun, beyond the Moon, the foam was on the Sea,
And by the strand of Tirion there grew a golden Tree.
Beneath the stars of Evereve in Eldamar it shone,[35]
In Eldamar beside the walls of Elven Tirion.
But far away and far away beyond the Shadow-meres
Now long the golden leaves have grown upon the branching
    years.
And Lórien, O Lórien! the river flows away
And leaves are falling in the stream, and leaves are borne away;
O Lórien, too long I dwell upon this Hither Shore
And in a fading crown I twine the golden elanor.
But if a ship I now should sing, what ship would come to me,
What ship would bear me ever back across so wide a sea?

Pencilled changes bring the song in all points to the form in FR. My father was working at the same time on the Elvish song, which had reached this form:

> *Ai! laurie lantar lassi sūrinen*
> *inyalemīne rāmar aldaron*

inyali ettulielle turme mārien
anduniesse la mīruvōrion
Varda telūmen falmar kīrien
laurealassion ōmar mailinon.

Elentāri Vardan Oiolossëan
Tintallen māli rāmar ortelūmenen
arkandavā-le qantamalle tūlier
e falmalillon morne sindanōrie
no mīrinoite kallasilya Valimar.

I have mentioned earlier (p. 266) the very close relationship between the writing of the foregoing drafts and the writing of the fair copy manuscript; and the result of this mode of composition is that there is very little that need be said about the new text (numbered XX but without title: 'Farewell to Lórien' was pencilled in later).

In Keleborn's words to the Company on the last evening (see p. 273) he still speaks of 'the great falls of Rosfein, where the River runs out of the ravines among the Green Hills', but this was changed, before the manuscript was completed, to 'where the River thunders down from Sarn-gebir'. His parting advice at the Tongue on the following day naturally scarcely differs from the text (pp. 282–3) which was written for this place in the fair copy (note 34); but 'the cataracts of Rhosfein' become 'the cataracts of Dant-ruinel' (*Dant-ruin* is pencilled over *Rhosfein* in the draft text), and at the end of the passage Keleborn says, not 'to the passes of Mordor: Kirith Ungol', but 'to Kirith Ungol, and the gates of Mordor'.

Pencilled alterations to the passage in the fair copy manuscript changed *Tolondren* to *Eregon*, then to *Brandor*, then to *the Tindrock that we call Tol Brandor*; and *Dant-ruinel* to *Rauros* (with marginal notes *Rauros* = 'Rush-rain' or 'Roar-rain'). At this time *Rosfein* in Keleborn's earlier speech was changed to *Rauros*.[36]

The much fuller account in FR (p. 386) of the elven-cloaks provided for the members of the Company (see p. 272) was added in, probably not much later (see p. 343 and note 35), and the words of the Elves 'There is no magic woven in these cloaks' removed with the introduction of Merry's question (Pippin's in FR) 'Are these garments magical?' The leaf-brooches were a further and subsequent addition (see p. 398).

When Haldir reappeared to act as their guide from Caras Galadon (now without his brother Orofin) he said, just as in the draft for this passage, 'There are strange things happening away back there. We do not know what is the meaning of them' (see pp. 279–80). This was subsequently struck out on the fair copy, but then marked *Stet*; this was in turn struck out, and Haldir's words do not appear in the following text of the chapter or in FR (p. 387). It is very hard to see why my father removed them, and why he hesitated back and forth before finally doing so. Apparently as a comment on this, he pencilled a note on the manuscript: 'This won't do – if Lórien is timeless, for then *nothing* will have happened since they entered.' I can only interpret this to mean that within Lórien the Company existed in a different Time – with its mornings and evenings and passing days – while in the world outside Lórien no time passed: they had left that 'external' Time, and would return to it at the same moment as they left it. This question is further discussed later (pp. 367–9). But it does not seem to me to explain why only Haldir's opening words were removed. His announcement, which was allowed to stand, that the Dimrill Dale was full of smoke and that there were noises in the earth, merely explains what the 'strange things' were which the Elves did not understand; and these 'strange things' had obviously only begun *since* the Company entered the Golden Wood.

As in the draft (p. 281) the words of Galadriel's song on the swan-boat are not reported, but my father subsequently put a mark of insertion on the manuscript, with the word 'Song'. On the completed text of her song found with the draft papers and given on p. 284 he then wrote 'Galadriel's Song for XX.8', this being the number of the page in the present manuscript. Similarly there is no suggestion that Galadriel's parting song ('in some ancient tongue of the West, from beyond the margin of the world') should be given, though 'he heard not the words' was changed on the manuscript to 'he did not understand the words', as in FR; but here again my father subsequently pencilled a mark of insertion and the word 'Song' in the margin.

'They saw her never more' of the draft (p. 284) becomes now 'Never again did Frodo see the Lady Galadriel', where in FR it is said 'To that fair land Frodo never came again.'

The following outline is found on a small, isolated scrap of paper. The only evidence of date that I can see is the fact that 'Sam's casket' (i.e. his gift from Galadriel) is referred to, and it therefore followed the present chapter. But this seems as good a place as any to give it, in relation to the end of the major outline which I have called 'The Story Foreseen from Moria' on p. 212.

The Three Rings are to be *freed*, *not* destroyed by the destruction of the One. Sauron cannot arise again in person, only work through men. But Lórien is saved, and Rivendell, and the Havens – until they grow weary, and until Men (of the East) 'eat up the world'. Then Galadriel and Elrond will sail away. But Frodo saves the Rings.

Frodo saves the Shire; and Merry and Pippin become important.

Sackville-Bagginses are chucked out (become pot-boys at Bree).

Sam's casket restores Trees.

When old, Sam and Frodo set sail to island of West and [*sic*]   Bilbo finishes the story. Out of gratitude the Elves adopt them and give them an island.

At the head of the page is written: 'Saruman becomes a wandering conjuror and trickster'.

NOTES

1   The Stone Hills are named in the outlines given on pp. 233 and 250. The last word in the illegible phrase preceding 'at Stone Hills' might possibly be 'drop', which taken with the note in the outline on p. 233 that the 'parting of ways' would take place 'at Stonehills' might suggest that this was a first hint of the great falls in Anduin.

2   The word *Carrock* is very indistinct; it occurs again in outline *(c)*, but is there equally so. Yet I think that this is what it must certainly be, especially since it seems very suitable: for Tolondren was the origin of Tol Brandir, and thus the 'Great Carrock' would answer to Beorn's 'Little Carrock' or 'Lesser Carrock', itself also rising amid the waters of Anduin but far to the North; *ondren* being no doubt a derivative of the stem GOND 'stone' (*Etymologies*, V.359).

3   With the rejected word *Duil* cf. *Duil Rewinion*, name of the Hills of the Hunters (west of the river Narog) on the first *Silmarillion* map, IV.225. – *Emyn Rain* is subsequently spelt *Rhain* (see note 9); cf. the *Etymologies*, V.383, stem REG, Noldorin *rhein, rhain* 'border', also *Minas rhain* (Minas Tirith) p. 116.

4   This is the first occurrence of the *Wetwang*. The second word in the Elvish name *Palath Nenui* is slightly uncertain, but seems probable. Cf. the *Etymologies*, V.380, stem PAL, Noldorin *palath* 'surface'; also *palath* 'iris', VI.432, VII.101. *Palath Nen[ui]* occurs also on the First Map (see pp. 299, 308).

5   The word *Naith* 'Angle' (see the Etymologies, V.387, stem SNAS, Noldorin *naith* 'gore') seems in the context of this outline to be a name for the 'green spit' or 'Tongue' where the Company embarked from Lórien on their journey down Anduin (cf. also *Naith Lórien* in outline *(a)*); and subsequently (p. 280) this is expressly stated: 'The Naith or Angle (as the elves called this green sward)'.

The name *Angle* is variously used. In the earliest mention of the Lórien story, p. 207, the Company 'journey *to Angle* between Anduin and Blackroot. *There they remain long*'; and '*at Angle* they debate what is to be done.' Since this was written before the actual story of Lothlórien had been begun, the precise wording cannot perhaps be pressed; and in the original text of the first

'Lothlórien' chapter the meaning seems entirely unambiguous. As soon as they had crossed the Blackroot Hathaldir told them that they had 'entered the Gore, Nelen we call it, which lies in the angle between Blackroot and Anduin' (p. 231), and he told Gimli (*ibid.*) that in the north there were 'hidden defences and guards *across the open arms of the Angle between the rivers*'. The other references in that text do not contradict the obvious conclusion from these two passages, that whatever the extent of the woods of Lothlórien may have been, the Angle or Gore (*Bennas, Nelen, Nelennas*) was 'the heart of Lórien' (see p. 243 note 46), Lórien-between-the-Rivers, the base of the triangle being the eaves of the forest in the North.

Thus 'Naith or Angle' in this outline, and again in the text of the present chapter, referring expressly to the 'Tongue' (the apex of the triangle), represents either a changed meaning of *Angle*, or else perhaps the use of the English word to signify both the large triangle ('Lórien-between-the-Rivers') and the very small triangle (the Tongue) that was the apex of the other.

On the other hand, in the fair copy manuscript of 'Lothlórien' the distinction is between *Narthas* 'the Gore', the larger region, and *Nelen* 'the Angle', the region in the south where the Elves dwelt (see p. 236). I doubt that any clearly correct and consecutive formulation can be reached amid such fluidity.

In FR (p. 361) 'the Naith of Lórien, or the Gore' is the large triangle, entered after passage of the Silverlode; and in the same passage Haldir speaks of the dwellings of the Elves *down in Egladil, in the Angle between the waters*. *Egladil* occurs once again in FR, p. 389: 'There in the last end of Egladil upon the green grass the parting feast was held.' Robert Foster, in *The Complete Guide to Middle-earth*, defines *Naith* as 'That part of Lórien between Celebrant and Anduin', adding: 'The Naith included Egladil but was of greater extent'; and he defines *Egladil* as 'The heart of Lórien, the area between Anduin and Celebrant near their confluence. Called in Westron the Angle.'

6 *Nelen* (with changed application) and *Calennel* were presumably other possible names, beside *Naith* (see note 5) and *Calendil*, of the 'green spit' or 'Tongue', for which in FR no Elvish name is given.

7 *Green-tine*: translation of *Calendil*; Old English *tind* (cf. the *Tindrock*, Tol Brandir), later *tine*, spike, prong, tooth of a fork; now probably known chiefly of the branches of a deer's horn. Cf. *Silvertine*, one of the Mountains of Moria (*Celebdil*).

8 Cf. the outline on p. 250: the Company is told to 'beware of Fangorn Forest upon the Ogodrûth or Entwash'.

9 In the original text of the chapter the word is clearly spelt *Rhain*, while *Rain* is clear in outline *(a)*. In this outline *(c)* it seems to be

Rhein at the first occurrence, with *Rhain* written above, but *Rhan* at the second and third; but the writing is very unclear and I read *Rhain* here also.

10 The showing of the Mirror now took place on the last evening in Lothlórien: see p. 259. Very probably the fair copy manuscript of 'Galadriel' was now in existence.

11 Obviously written at the same time as the rest of the text on the page is a disconnected passage that seems best placed here:

> At present that is not possible. Westward the servants of Sauron are far abroad and are ... the land ... the Baranduin and the Greyflood. Northward there are strange things happening which we do [not] understand clearly. The Dimrill [Dale] is filled with ash and smoke, and the mountains are troubled. You, Gimli and Legolas, would find it hard to make your way back even with a great company.
>
> 'What of the Beornings?' said Gimli.
>
> 'I do not know,' said Keleborn. 'They are far away. But I do not think you could now reach them'

The illegible passage could possibly be read (assuming rejection of the word 'are') as 'and have taken over the land between the Baranduin and the Greyflood.' See further note 12. – A part of Keleborn's speech here was afterwards given to Haldir, returned from the northern borders of Lórien to guide the Company from Caras Galadon: pp. 280, 285–6.

12 With this speech of Keleborn's compare that in the last chapter (pp. 248–9) which was marked for transference to the beginning of this. That passage was indeed quite different, in that Keleborn seemed almost to assume that Gimli and Legolas at least would not continue the Quest, and offered them both the hospitality of Lórien, while also advising Gimli that he might be able to make his way back through the land of the Beornings. Now (quite closely approaching the text of FR, p. 383) he offers a generalised invitation to remain to any of the Company who wish. But from what can be read of the underlying pencilled text it is seen that my father at first retained the passage transferred from the previous chapter in much the same form. The passage given in note 11 shows a change of mind: Gimli and Legolas would stand little chance if they tried to return.

13 The form *Ondor* (as written *ab initio*) occurs in the fifth version of 'The Council of Elrond' (p. 144 and note 6).

14 In a rejected form of this passage Keleborn takes up Ingold's remark that he doubted whether even Gandalf had had any clear plan:

> 'Maybe,' said Keleborn. 'Yet he knew that he would have to choose between East and West ere long. For the Great River lies between Mordor and Minas Tirith, and he knew, as do you

Men at least of this Company, that it cannot be crossed on foot, and that the bridges of Osgiliath are broken down or in the hands of the Enemy since the late assault.'

15 On 'the Land of Seven Streams' see p. 177 and pp. 310–12.

16 Here and again below ('Ingold thanked Keleborn many times') *Ingold* was not changed to *Elfstone* because the passage was rejected before my father decided to abandon the name *Ingold* (see pp. 277–8).

17 This is the first mention of the great falls in Anduin (apart from a very doubtful hint of their existence referred to in note 1).

18 As the text was written Sam's attitude to the boats was different from what it had been in the previous version (where he felt 'a little alarm') and from what it is in FR:

> Even Sam felt no alarm. Not long ago crossing a river by a ferry had seemed to him an adventure, but since then he had made too many weary marches and passed through too many dangers to worry about a journey in a light boat and the peril of drowning.

This was subsequently changed to the passage in FR.

19 The name of the Sword of Elendil reforged, *Branding*, was first devised here, and then written into 'The Ring Goes South' at the time of the reforging in Rivendell: 'and Elfstone gave it a new name and called it *Branding*' (p. 165). *Branding* is obviously an 'English' name (Old English *brand* 'sword'), and consorts with the names *Ingold*, *Elfstone*: see my father's notes on this subject cited on p. 277.

20 The drawing, in pencil, is now very faint. I have reinforced the drawing on a photocopy, and the reproduction is based on this.

21 In the original account of the first meeting of the Company with the Lord and Lady of the Galadrim (pp. 246 ff.) Galadriel addresses no words to Gimli. These first appear in the fair copy manuscript of 'Galadriel', where she says just as in FR (p. 371) 'Dark is the water of Kheled-zâram, and cold are the springs of Kibil-nâla...': a further indication that that text was already in existence.

22 Although *Eärendil* appears in the fair copy manuscript of 'Galadriel' (p. 266 note 34), *Eärendel* is the spelling here, both in the draft and in the fair copy. In my copies of these chapters made in 1942 I wrote *Eärendil* in Chapter XIX and *Eärendel* in Chapter XX.

23 The meaning of Galadriel's words to Trotter is plainly that *Elfstone* was his real name. The fact that the final version of the passage begins ' "Here is the gift of Keleborn to the leader of your Company," she said to Elfstone' – before the green gem, the Elfstone, has been mentioned – is decisive.

24 This change has often been remarked in earlier parts of this book.

The first examples of *Aragorn* > *Elfstone* are p. 80 note 17 (at Bree) and pp. 146 ff. (the fifth version of 'The Council of Elrond'). It was carried through the fair copy manuscripts of 'The Ring Goes South' (p. 165; including *Trotter* > *Elfstone*), and of the two 'Moria' chapters (pp. 176, 204, the change here being always *Trotter* > *Elfstone*).

25 With the statement in both these notes that Trotter's real name must not be 'Elvish' or 'Gnome-elvish' ('like Aragorn') contrast LR Appendix F ('Of Men'): 'The Dúnedain alone of all races of Men knew and spoke an Elvish tongue; for their forefathers had learned the Sindarin tongue, and this they handed on to their children as a matter of lore, changing little with the passing of the years', together with the footnote to this passage: 'Most of the names of the other men and women of the Dúnedain [i.e. those whose names were not Quenya], such as *Aragorn*, *Denethor*, *Gilraen* are of Sindarin form...'

26 In the first draft following this outline it is said of Gimli and Legolas that they 'had grown more and more friendly during their stay in Lothlórien'; in the following version (vii) that they 'had grown strangely friendly of late'. In FR they 'had now become fast friends'. – The complement of each boat is now as in FR, and not as in outline *(b)* to this chapter (p. 268), although there already Legolas and Gimli were placed together in the third boat.

27 In the fair copy manuscript of 'Farewell to Lórien' the text here is:

> On the further shores the woodlands still marched on south-wards, as far as eye could see; but beyond the Tongue and upon the east side of the River all the boughs were bare. No mallorn-trees grew there.

The intended meaning seems clear: on the west bank beyond the confluence of Silverlode and Anduin, and all along the east bank of Anduin, there was still forest, but the trees not being mallorns they were leafless. So Keleborn says that as they go down the River they will find that 'the trees will fail', and they will come to a barren country. In the following manuscript, which I made (undated, but clearly following on my copy of 'Galadriel' dated 4 August 1942, p. 261), the sentence reads 'all the *banks* were bare'. This, I think, must have been a mere error (as also was 'the eye could see' for 'eye could see', retained in FR), since (in relation to 'the woodlands still marched on southwards') it is obviously a less well-chosen and somewhat ambiguous word: 'bare banks' suggests treeless banks, not wooded banks in winter.

Probably in order to correct this, but without consulting the earlier manuscript and so not seeing that it was an error, my father at some stage changed 'further shores' to 'further western shores' on my copy, but this still gives a confused picture. The text in FR (p. 387) removes the reference to the west shores of Anduin altogether, but retains the 'bare banks', which must therefore be interpreted as 'wooded banks in winter'.

28 In the earliest draft for the scene in the first 'Lothlórien' chapter in which the Company encounters the Elvish scouts near the falls of Nimrodel (p. 239 note 26) the lowest boughs of the trees 'were above the reach of Boromir's arms; but they had rope with them. Casting an end about a bough of the greatest of the trees Legolas ... climbed into the darkness.'

29 There is no more than the briefest outline sketch of Galadriel's 'refusal in the garden' in the original 'Lothlórien' chapter (p. 254), whereas in the fair copy the scene is fully formed (p. 260).

30 This reference to the once far greater extent of the Forest of Lothlórien is not found in FR (see note 34). Perhaps to be compared is *Unfinished Tales*, p. 236: 'the Nandorin realm of Lórinand [Lórien] ... was peopled by those Elves who forsook the Great Journey of the Eldar from Cuiviénen and settled in the woods of the Vale of Anduin; and it extended into the forests on both sides of the Great River, including the region where afterwards was Dol Guldur.'

31 *Ingold* here can only have been a slip for *Elfstone*.

32 The *Seventh River* has been mentioned in the fifth version of 'The Council of Elrond', p. 149. See pp. 310–12.

33 *Tharbad* has been named in the second version of 'The Ring Goes South', p. 164 and note 8.

34 These passages were actually written when the fair copy had reached this point. In the fair copy a page ends with the words 'you will find that for a while the trees march on. For of old the Forest of Lórien'. It was at this point that my father wrote the first of these passages, which was in fact simply the top of the next page of the fair copy. Deciding however to cut out the reference to the once much greater extent of Lothlórien, he struck out these words at the bottom of the preceding page in the fair copy, and wrote the second draft given here.

35 In the original workings the fourth line was *And by the mere of Tirion there grew the golden tree*. Another version of the fifth line was *Beneath the Hill of Ilmarin lies Aelinuial* – Aelinuial 'Lakes of Twilight' being the name of the region of great pools at the confluence of the rivers Aros and Sirion in Beleriand; cf. *the Shadow-meres* in the seventh line. In Bilbo's song at Rivendell occur the lines

> beneath the hill of Ilmarin
> where glimmer in a valley sheer
> the lights of Elven Tirion
> the city on the Shadowmere

and also *From Evereven's lofty hills* (see pp. 93, 98; FR pp. 247–8).

36 Boromir's words 'I have not myself been there' (referring to Fangorn), p. 282, were changed to 'I have not myself ever crossed Rohan.'

Additional Notes on the name Elfstone

A puzzling detail in the fair copy manuscript of this chapter is that while Trotter is referred to as *Trotter* throughout the narrative (see pp. 277–8), on the two occasions where he is named by Keleborn the name is *Ingold*. According to the explanation advanced on pp. 277–8 he should now, if called by his true name, be *Elfstone*. Moreover when we come to the scene of the Parting Gifts in this manuscript Galadriel's words to Trotter remain exactly as in the draft text on p. 276 ('Elfstone is your name ... and it is a fair name. I will add this gift of my own to match it'). How then can Keleborn call him *Ingold*?

The answer, I feel sure, is (as I have suggested, p. 267) that the fair copy manuscript itself grew in close relation to the drafts, where the names were not stable; and that it was not carefully revised in this point. In the first case, near the beginning of the chapter, where in the draft text Keleborn names 'Boromir of Ondor and Ingold the traveller' among those of the Company accustomed to boats, *Ingold* was changed subsequently to *Elfstone* (p. 273), but in the fair copy 'Ingold the traveller' remained unchanged. In the second case also, towards the end of the chapter, where in the draft Keleborn says 'it may be that Ingold and Boromir know the lands well enough to need no counsel' – which can only have been a casual inadvertence, note 31 – *Ingold* was corrected to *Elfstone* in the draft but not in the fair copy.

Later, my father corrected the second *Ingold* on the fair copy to *Aragorn* but did not notice the first. Without knowledge of the earlier texts this hasty and incomplete revision of names can produce incomprehensible tangles later on, when amanuenses such as myself simply followed what they saw before them: so in the next text of this chapter, a manuscript that I made (note 27), I wrote *Ingold* at the first occurrence and *Aragorn* at the second.

Galadriel's words at the gift-giving, *Elfstone is your name, Eldamir in the language of your fathers of old, and it is a fair name*, were struck out on the fair copy, with the curious result that in the manuscript that I wrote in 1942 Galadriel says: 'The blade that is drawn from this sheath shall not be stained or broken even in defeat. I will add this gift of my own to match it.' Later on, my father wrote on his fair copy manuscript (but not on the one that I made), against the description of Galadriel's gift and her words concerning it (retained exactly from the draft on p. 276): *Make this the reason for his taking the name Elfstone*; and after the words 'yet many things that now appear loathly will appear otherwise to you hereafter' he wrote in: 'And

[Eldamir >] Elessar shall be a name for you hereafter, Elfstone in [the tongues of common speech >] your speech. Long may it be remembered.'

XV

THE FIRST MAP
OF THE LORD OF THE RINGS

Of the various small-scale maps of the western regions of Middle-earth that my father made, one is very easily seen to be the earliest; and I have no doubt at all that this was not only the earliest of the maps that are extant, but was in fact the first one that he made (other than the hasty sketches of particular regions published in Vol. VI).

This 'First Map' is a strange, battered, fascinating, extremely complicated and highly characteristic document. To gain understanding of it, its construction must first be described. It consists of a number of pages glued together and on to backing sheets, with a substantial new section of the map glued over an earlier part, and small new sections on top of that. The glue that my father used to stick down the large new portion was strong, and the sheets cannot be separated; moreover through constant folding the paper has cracked and broken apart along the folds, which are distinct from the actual joins of the map-sections. It was thus difficult to work out how the whole was built up; but I am confident that the following account is correct. In this account I refer to the figure 'Construction of the Original Map of The Lord of the Rings' on p. 297. This is a diagram and not a map, but I have inserted a few major features (the sea-coast, Anduin, Mirkwood, the rough outlines of the mountainous regions) as a guide.

The original element in the map consisted of two pages glued together along their vertical edges, and is the big rectangle framed in the figure by a black and white line and lettered A. East of the vertical line of squares numbered 22 it extended for a further three lines, but these were left blank.

A new section (made up of three portions glued together) extended the original map to North and West. (I say 'new section', since the paper is slightly different, and it was obviously added to what was already in existence.) This section is marked B on the figure and framed in double lines. It extends north of what is shown on the figure by five more horizontal lines of squares (A–E, 1–17).

As already mentioned, a third section, marked C on the figure and framed in double lines (squares O–W, 9–19), was superimposed on a part of the original map 'A', obliterating almost all of its southern half.

This new section 'C' extends further south than did 'A', by three horizontal lines of squares (U–W, 9–19). Fortunately, a good part of this section has no backing paper, and by shining a bright light through it it has been possible to make out certain names and geographical features on the 'lost', southern half of 'A'. This is a difficult and confusing operation, and the results are very incomplete, but they are quite sufficient to show the essentials of what lies beneath 'C'. All that I can make out after long peering is shown on the map numbered III^A (p. 308).

The small rectangle lettered D on the figure and framed in dots was replaced over and over again, and is by far the most complex part of the map, as the region covered is also crucial in the story: from the Gap of Rohan and Isengard to Rauros and the mouths of Entwash.

The original element in the First Map

The First Map was my father's working map for a good while, and thus as it stood when he left it – as it stands now – it represents an evolution, rather than a fixed state of the geography. Determination of the sequence in which the map was built up does not, of course, demonstrate that names or features on 'A' are necessarily earlier than names or features on 'B' or 'C', since when 'A' + 'B' + 'C' were in being the map was a single entity. There are, however, certain clues to relative dating. The earliest layer of names is recognisable from the style of lettering, and also to some extent from the fact that my father at that stage used red ink for certain names, chiefly in the case of alternatives (as for example *Loudwater* in black ink, *Bruinen* beside it in red). On the directly visible part of 'A', virtually all of which is shown on Map II (p. 305), all the names are 'original' with the exception of the following: *Torfirion (Westermanton)*; *North Downs*, *Fornobel (Northbury)*; *Forodwaith (Northerland)*; *Enedwaith (Middlemarch)*; *Caradras*; *Nimrodel, Silverlode*; *Mirkwood the Great*, *Southern Mirkwood, Rhovanion*; *Rhosgobel, Dol Dúghul* (but *Dol Dúgol* in red ink, struck out, on M 15–16 is original); *Bardings*; *Sea of Rhûnaer* and *Rhûn*. Notable is the case of *Silverlode*: here the original name was *Redway*, struck out and changed in the same script to *Blackroot*, and this change is very precisely documented in the second version of 'The Ring Goes South', p. 166.

In this 'original layer' of names are a few others which I have not included in the redrawn map (II) since I could not find room for them without unnecessarily confusing it, the scale being so small: these are *Chetwood, Midgewater, Forest River, Woodmen, Wood Elves, Dale*. *F.I.* (so written in the original) on the Road east of Bree stands for *Forsaken Inn*. On the *River Rushdown (Rhimdad)* cf. V.384, VI.205, where the form is *Rhimdath* (also *Rhibdath*).

Three of the original names were changed, and I have entered the

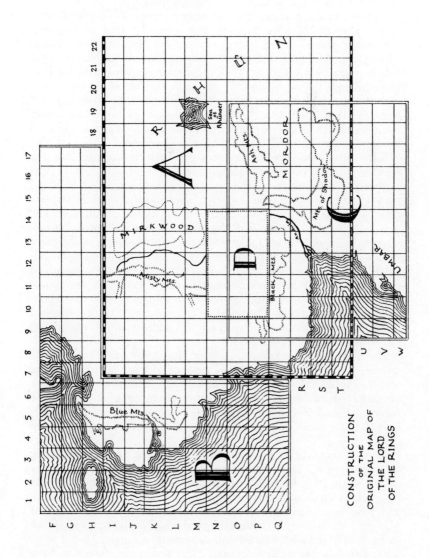

CONSTRUCTION
OF THE
ORIGINAL MAP OF
THE LORD
OF THE RINGS

later form. These are the river *Isen*, first written *Iren* on P 8 (Old English, 'iron', which varied with *Isen*); *Andrath* on L 8, where the original form is unclear since a broken fold of the map runs through it, but seems to have been *Amrath* (as in a draft for a portion of the chapter 'Many Meetings', see pp. 69–70 and note 7); and *Anduin* (M–N 13, Maps II and IVᴬ), first written *Andon* (see p. 299).

Of geographical features, most of what is represented on the directly visible part of 'A' goes back to the beginning, and of course a substantial part of that was derived from the Map of Wilderland in *The Hobbit*. Elements that are not 'original' are the highlands in the North-west of Map II (I 8–9, J 7–8); the markings representing the Iron Hills (though the name itself is original); the Sea of Rhûnaer, the mountainous region to the South-west of it, the river flowing into it from the Iron Hills, and the lower course of the (unnamed) River Running, which as the map was first made scarcely extended beyond the eastern edge of the Wilderland Map in *The Hobbit*.

Some other geographical features are slightly doubtful, but the western arm of the Misty Mountains across squares I 10–11 was probably a subsequent addition, and the vast region of highland between Mirkwood and the Sea of Rhûnaer, together with the streams flowing from it into the Dead Marshes (N 16), almost certainly so. The original siting of the name *Dol Dúgol* (M 15; see p. 296) probably had nothing to do with these highlands (at the first occurrence of the name on p. 178 Gandalf speaks of Sauron's 'older and lesser dwelling at Dol-Dúgol in Southern Mirkwood'): faint traces of green colour suggest to me that originally Mirkwood extended much further to the South-east, covering L 15 and a good part of M–N 15–16, and that this region of the forest was erased. The hills that emerge onto N 15 from the area which I have left blank on Map II are also additional: this region will be discussed later in this chapter.

The river Isen is a bit doubtful, since though the name as originally written (*R. Iren*, see above) clearly belongs with the primary layer of names, the coastline as drawn had no river-mouth opposite the off-shore island on P 7, and a pencilled indentation was made subsequently. The same is true of the unnamed river (afterwards *Lefnui*) to the south of Isen, whose mouth was drawn in on R 8 (Map III).

On the part of the original map 'A' that is obliterated by the sticking on of portion 'C' some names and features can be seen, as already described (p. 296; Map IIIᴬ). It is clear that at that stage relatively little was entered on the map. Those in black ink can be readily seen, and I do not think that there were any others beyond *Land of Mor-dor*, *Minas Morgol* (with *Ithil* in red ink), *Osgiliath*, *Minas Tirith* (with *Anor* in red ink), *Blackroot* > *Silverlode* (see under Map II on p. 306), *Tolfalas*, *Bay of Belfalas*, and *Ethir-andon* (as it seems to have been written, before being changed to *-anduin*, as on the northern part of 'A'). *Dead Marshes* is in red ink; other names seem to have been entered in red chalk (*Land of Ond*) or pencil. The actual sites of Minas Morgol and the Dark Tower cannot be seen, nor can the last two letters of *Palath Nen[ui]* (on which see p. 268 and note 4); and the mountain-chains are extremely hard to make out. The bits of the mountains of Mordor in the North-west that I have been able to distinguish with certainty suggest however a disposition essentially the same as that in 'C'. The occurrence of *Dol [?Amroth]* at this stage is notable.

It is thus clear that, whenever the First Map was actually begun, it had reached the stage seen in the original 'layer' of portion 'A' before the time we have now reached in the texts, and also that much of that layer belongs to this period of the work: many of these original names on the map emerge first in the texts given in this book – for example *Sarn Ford* (p. 9), *Entish Land* (p. 10), *Mitheithel* (p. 14), *Bruinen* (p. 14), *Minas Tirith* (p. 115), *Minas Morgol* (p. 116), *Minas Anor, Minas Ithil* (p. 119), *Bay of Belfalas* (p. 119), *Tharbad* (p. 164), etc. *Andon* (*Ethir-andon*) was a form preceding *Anduin* which never occurred in the texts: *Anduin* appears in the fifth version of 'The Council of Elrond' where the name *Sirvinya* 'New Sirion' appears in the third (pp. 119, 144).

The 1943 Map

In 1943 (see *Letters* nos. 74 and 98) I made a large elaborate map in pencil and coloured chalks, companion to a similar one of the Shire (see VI.107, 200). It was the First Map that I had in front of me when I made it. My map is thus of historical value in showing what the state of the First Map was at that time – especially in respect of names, for though I was as faithful to the courses of rivers and coasts as I have attempted to be 45 years later, I used pictorial forms for the mountains and hills, which are less precise.[1]

The redrawn maps in this book

In *Unfinished Tales* I referred (pp. 13–14) to my father's maps of *The Lord of the Rings* as 'sketch-maps'; but this was an ill-chosen word, and in respect of the First Map a serious misnomer. All parts of the First Map were made with great care and delicacy until a late stage of correction, and it has an exceedingly 'Elvish' and archaic air. The difficulties of interpretation do not arise from any roughness in the original execution, but in part from subsequent alteration in very small space, and in part from its present condition: it is wrinkled, creased, and broken from constant use, so that connections are lost, and many names and markings added in pencil are so blurred and faint as to be almost invisible. My father made a good deal of use of pencil and coloured chalks: mountain-chains are shaded in grey, rivers (for the most part) represented in blue chalk, marshland and woodland in shades of green (Mirkwood is conveyed by little curved marks in green chalk, suggestive of treetops); and this colouring is rubbed and faded (it is often very difficult to be sure of the courses of rivers). In regions where the development of the story caused substantial alteration in the geography, notably where the hills and mountains were much changed and overlaid by new representations, there are so many lines and strokes and dots that it is impossible to feel certain what my father intended, or even to make out what there is on the paper.[2]

Inevitably, the attempt to redraw the map involves more than merely copying (and since it must be represented in black and white, different symbolisation, notably of wooded regions, must to some extent be used, or else dispensed with); to redraw is in such a case to interpret. My redrawings are therefore to an extent simpler, less subtle, and more decisive in detail, than the original, and of course uniform in appearance, since they have all been made at one time and with the same pens. These maps are therefore quite insufficient in themselves as a substitute for the original, and the discussion of the redrawn maps is an integral part of my attempt to present this remarkable document.

The major question to resolve, however, arose from the fact that this map was a continuous development, evolving in terms of, and reacting upon, the narrative it accompanied. To redraw it involved a decision on what to include and what to exclude. But to attempt to limit its content to the names and features that might be supposed to have been present at a particular time (in terms of the narrative) would involve a host of complexities and dubious or arbitrary decisions. It was clearly far better to represent the map in a developed form; and except in the case of Map III^A (where a large part of the original map 'A' was early abandoned) and of maps IV^{A-E} (where there are six successive and distinct versions) I have therefore taken my 1943 map as a conveniently fixed and definite terminus, though not without a number of exceptions. It is to be understood throughout the following discussion that everything on my redrawn versions in this book appears in that form on the 1943 map unless something is said to the contrary. Many of the subsequent alterations made to the First Map or to the 1943 map or to both are however mentioned.

The map-squares of the original are of 2 centimetre side (on my 1943 map the squares were enlarged to 4 centimetres). No scale is given; but a later and much rougher map, also ruled in squares of this size, gives 2 centimetres = 100 miles, and this was clearly the scale of the First Map also.

Maps I and I^A

Map I, with the extreme North and North-east on I^A, gives virtually the whole of the added portion 'B' (see the figure on p. 297): thus 'B' extends from A to H, 1–17, and from I to Q, 1–6 and a portion of 7. The section marked off on the right-hand side of Map I is the left-hand side of the original portion 'A', and this is duplicated on Map II.

This portion 'B' received no emendation whatsoever after its first drawing except in one minor point. The great highlands (afterwards called the Hills of Evendim) between the river Lune and the North Downs certainly belong with the rest of 'B', and were extended into square J 7 of 'A', already in existence; and the North Downs were entered on 'A' at the same time (for the place-names see under Map II).

This is the only map that shows the far northern coast, and the vast bay shaped like a human head and face (E–G 7–9, on map I^A). In view of Appendix A (I. iii) to *The Lord of the Rings*, where there is a reference to 'the great cape of Forochel that shuts off to the north-west the immense bay of that name', it is clear that this bay is 'the Icebay of Forochel' (see *Unfinished Tales* p. 13 and footnote) – although on a subsequent map of my father's the much smaller southern bay (H 6–7) is very clearly labelled and limited 'the Icebay of Forochel', as it is on my map published with *The Lord of the Rings*[3]. No names are given in this region on the First Map, but subsequently my father pencilled in *North Sea* across G 4–5, and this I entered on my 1943 map, though inadvertently omitted on Map I.

On the islands of *Tol Fuin* and *Himling* see p. 124 and note 18. – The 'sea-lines' are not present in the original, but they are marked on parts 'A' and 'C' and I have therefore extended them throughout. – I cannot explain the wavy line that extends roughly parallel to the coast from H 4 to K 3[4].

It will be seen on Map I that the distinction between the North and South Havens (here *Forlorn* and *Harlorn* for later *Forlond* and *Harlond*), situated in bays of the Gulf of Lune, and *Mithlond*, the Grey Havens, at the head of the gulf, was already present (but see p. 423).

With this first representation of Ered Luin, the Blue Mountains, in the context of *The Lord of the Rings* cf. the revision of the end of *The Fall of Númenor* cited on pp. 122–3. Very notable is the appearance of *Belegost* (L 5), which is marked on the 1943 map also, but on no subsequent one. The Dwarf-cities of the Blue Mountains were not originally marked on the second *Silmarillion map* (V.409, 411), but were put in roughly later: Belegost being situated on the eastern side of the mountains somewhat north of Mount Dolmed and the pass by which the Dwarf-road crossed them. Cf. *Unfinished Tales* p. 235:

There were and always remained some Dwarves on the eastern side of Ered Lindon, where the very ancient mansions of Nogrod and

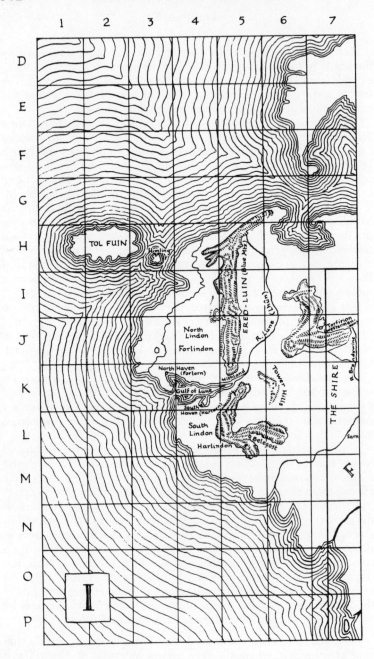

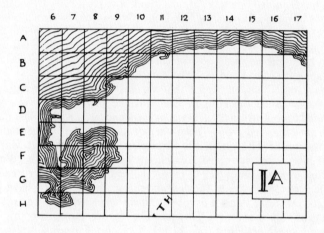

Belegost had been – not far from Nenuial; but they had transferred most of their strength to Khazad-dûm.

The White Towers on the Tower Hills are represented by three dots in a line (K 6). – The letter F on square M 7 of Map I and the letters ITH on square H 11 of Map I^A belong to *Forodwaith*, on which see under Map II.

Map II

This redrawing, as will be seen by comparison with the diagram on p. 297, covers almost all the still directly visible part of 'A', the only areas not included being the almost blank squares I–T 20 eastwards and Q–T 7–8 in the South-west, which is mostly sea (and is shown on Map III). It also covers the two top lines of squares of the superimposed portion 'C' (O–P 9–19), and the rectangle 'D', which is here left blank apart from the continuation of certain names. On the left Map II overlaps with Map I and at the bottom with Map III.

I have noted under Map I that the eastern end of the highlands afterwards called the Hills of Evendim and the North Downs were extended onto portion 'A' (I 8–9, J 7–8) when 'B' was added. The names *Torfirion* (changed from *Tarkilmar*) or *Westermanton* occur in the fifth version of 'The Council of Elrond', p. 144; on the First Map my father afterwards scribbled *Annúminas* here, but *Torfirion (Westermanton)* appears on my 1943 map. The name originally written here on the First Map was in fact *Fornobel*, but this seems to have been changed at once, and *Fornobel (Northbury)* written against the habitation on the North Downs. The earlier name for this was *Osforod, the Northburg* (pp. 120–1, 129), but *Fornobel* appears by emendation in the fifth version of 'The Council of Elrond' (p. 147). Here my father scribbled in the later name *Fornost*, but the 1943 map still has *Fornobel (Northbury)*.

Most of the names and features on the 'A' part of Map II are original, and have been commented on already (p. 296). On the significance of *Greyflood or Seventh River* see pp. 310–12. *Gwathlo* is certainly an original name, though it has not appeared in any text.

The various additions made to 'A' (listed on p. 296) were made in the same spidery lettering and very fine lines characteristic of the superimposed section 'C'. The name *Enedwaith (Middlemarch)* was written across 'A' and 'C' after 'C' had been stuck on, and *Forod-(waith) (Northerland)* belongs with it (though -*waith* was a further and rougher addition). *Enedwaith* here denotes a much greater region than it afterwards became (the lands between Greyflood and Isen): the original conception, it is seen, was of a great 'triad', *Forodwaith* or *Northerland*, bounded on the South-east by the Greyflood, *Enedwaith* or *Middlemarch* between Greyflood and Anduin, and *Haradwaith* or

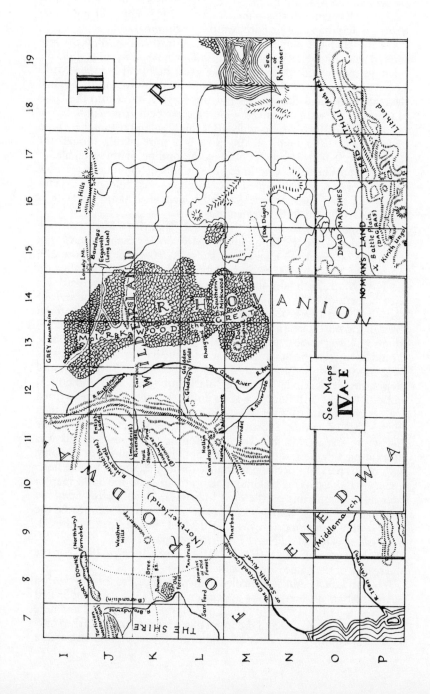

Sutherland (on Map III) bounded on the North-west by Anduin (or by the river Harnen). All this remains on the 1943 map, but my father wrote on that map against Forodwaith: *(or Eriador).*

On the changed names *Iren* > *Isen*, *Amrath* (?) > *Andrath* (not entered at all on the 1943 map), and *Andon* > *Anduin*, see p. 298.

I have mentioned (p. 298) that the great highland between Mirkwood and the Sea of Rhûnaer was almost certainly not an original element of 'A', and the streams flowing down from it into the Dead Marshes (N 16) were continued with the same pen-strokes onto 'C' (O 16), which had already been added. (Of this highland region there is no trace on my 1943 map: all this area is a pure blank, though the streams on N 16 are shown.) Within the outline of these highlands pencilled markings showing lines of high hills or mountains are now extremely faint, and disrupted by a large cracked fold that extends across the map through line M; and a pencilled name on M 16 is illegible save for the initial element *East.* . . .

The name *Mirrormere* (L 11) is original. The Misty Mountains are not named, nor are the Mountains of Moria other than *Caradras* (an addition); on the 1943 map appears also *Kelebras* (p. 174 note 21), but not the third peak (*Fanuiras*). Afterwards my father pencilled on the First Map the final names *Celebdil* and *Fanuidol* (so spelt). As already mentioned (p. 296) *Silverlode* was a correction (in the style of portion 'C') of *Blackroot*, itself replacing *Redway*; and the southern river *Blackroot* appears on the hidden portion of 'A' (Map III^A) – where however it also was changed to *Silverlode*! The change here should have been the other way about: for the names of the two rivers were transposed, the northern 'Blackroot' becoming 'Silverlode', and the southern 'Silverlode' becoming 'Blackroot' (see p. 177 and note 1, and p. 241 note 36). But there is no doubt that the first name written against the southern river was *Blackroot*, and that this was then changed to *Silverlode*. Subsequently my father struck out *Silverlode* and wrote *stet* against *Blackroot*: I suppose therefore that this was either a passing hesitation, when he thought for a moment of going back on his previous decision to change the names, or else a mere slip.

Entish Land (J 11) is original, but is absent from the 1943 map; a later note against this on the First Map says: 'Alter *Entish Lands* to [*Trollfells* > *Bergrisland* >] *Ettenmoor*'. This would seem to be the place where *Ettenmoor(s)* was first devised, but see p. 65 note 32. *Bergrisland* is from Old Norse *berg-risi* 'hill-giant'.

On the two sites of *Dol Dúgol* (*Dol Dúghul*) see p. 298. For the emergence of the name *Rhosgobel* see p. 164.

Against *Lonely Mt.* is pencilled *Dolereb*, and also *Erebor* with a query (neither of these names appear on the 1943 map). *Erebor* first occurs in the fifth version of 'The Council of Elrond', p. 142 and note 2. The Grey Mountains and the Iron Hills were originally marked only as names, but my father afterwards drew in the latter, and also rather vague pencillings to show a mountainous region to west and south-west of the Sea of Rhûnaer; these features are shown on the 1943 map, as also are the river flowing from the Iron Hills and the eastward extension of the River Running to join it (K 16–17), though on the 1943 map the River Running is very much the major stream and that from the Iron Hills a slender tributary. *Rhûn* was an addition in the 'C' style. The name *Rhûnaer* (i.e. 'Eastern Sea'), also an addition to 'A' (as was the Sea itself), is unclear on the First Map on account of a crack in the paper, but is confirmed by its appearance on the 1943 map and on a later map of my father's, where, though the Sea itself is not included, there is a direction that the River Running flows into the *Sea of Rhûnaer*. On the map published in *The Lord of the Rings*, it is the *Sea of Rhûn*, and there are three references to the *Sea of Rhûn* in Appendix A (see also p. 333 in the next chapter). The forest bordering the Sea of Rhûnaer (L 19) extends on the First Map round the north-eastern point of the Sea and down its eastern shore (L–M 20), and against it my father pencilled *Neldoreth*; no name for the forest is marked on the 1943 map, which ends at the same point eastwards as does Map II in this book.[5] The island in the Sea is coloured green on the First Map, and on the 1943 map is marked as wooded.

The name *Bardings* on J 15 was a pencilled addition that appears on the 1943 map; the pencilled addition of *Eotheod* on I 12, however, does not (on the regions where the Éothéod dwelt, at first between the Carrock and the Gladden Fields and afterwards in the region of the source-streams of Anduin, Greylin and Langwell, see *Unfinished Tales* pp. 288, 295).

For features marked on the south-east corner of Map II, O–P 15–19, see under Map III.

Maps III[A] and III

The line of squares P 7–19 overlaps with Map II. Map III contains no portion of the original map 'A' except for the two lines of squares on the left, P–T 7–8, where the river (afterwards Lefnui) on Q 8–9, P 9 seems certainly a later addition. Map III[A] shows the names and geographical features of the original map 'A' that I can make out through the overlay (pp. 298–9). Granting the difficulty of seeing what was there, it is clear, I think, that when this part of 'A' was made the story itself had not advanced into these regions, and only a few names and features were entered. Comparison of Maps III[A] and III will show that in the second version Ethir Anduin was moved south and east, becoming a vast delta, and the course of Anduin was entirely changed, flowing in a great eastward bend between Nindalf and the Mouths, whereas originally its course was almost in a straight line south-south-west. Concomitantly with this, Minas Tirith and Osgiliath were moved

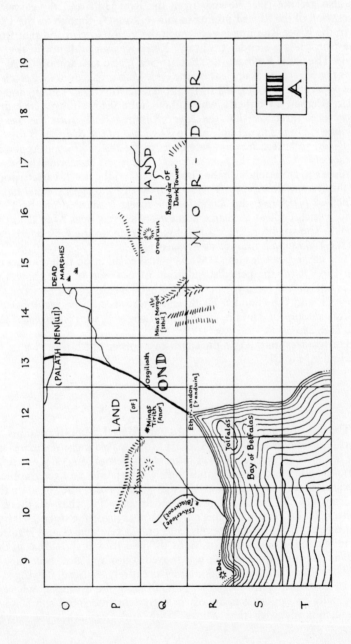

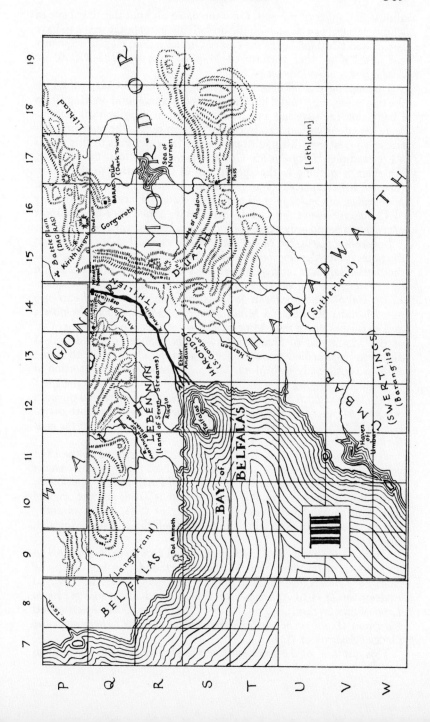

almost 200 miles to the east. Only the name and not the actual site of Minas Morgol can be seen on the underlying map, but it seems to have been a good deal further to the east of Osgiliath than was subsequently the case.[6] On other features of Map III[A] see pp. 298–9, and on *Blackroot > Silverlode* see p. 306.

Turning to the superimposed portion 'C' of the First Map (of which the uppermost horizontal line of squares O 9–19 is found on Map II), as I have said the lettering and representation of geographical features were here done with an exceptionally fine pen-nib; at the same time it is scarcely possible to distinguish earlier and later elements by this means – for example, *Harondor (S. Gondor)* is obviously later than *Ondor*, but there is nothing in the appearance of the lettering to show this. (*Ondor* here replaces *Ond* of the underlying map; for the first appearance of *Ondor* in the *Lord of the Rings* papers see p. 144.) My 1943 map is however effectively identical with the First Map in almost every feature, and only a few points need to be specially noticed here.

I postpone discussion of the *Dead Marshes* and *No Man's Land* to the notes on the development of Map IV. The original name *Dagras* of the Battle Plain was replaced in pencil by *Dagorlad*, which appears on the 1943 map but is omitted on the redrawing through lack of space. *Kirith Ungol* still appears in 1943 as the name of the chief entrance into Mordor, but I placed *Minas Morgul* (Q 15) further to the north, and so further north than Minas Tirith – very near to the northern tip of the Mountains of Shadow (P 15). This change complied with a direction by pencilled arrow on the First Map (where incidentally the name was originally spelt *Minas Morgol*, as on the overlaid portion of 'A' beneath). Among several changes that my father made to the 1943 map in these regions he replaced Minas Morgul in its original position on Q 15. Another was the addition of *Ephel* to *Duath* on both maps. For the significance of the two small circles on either side of the *n* of *Kirith Ungol* on P 15 see p. 349 note 41.

The *Nargil Pass* (S 17) is clearly represented and lettered on the 1943 map, whereas on the First Map it was scribbled in very hastily and is hardly legible (but apparently reads *Narghil Pass*). *Mount Mindolluin* was similarly added in roughly between Minas Tirith and the original mountain shown in the north-east corner of Q 13, but is carefully shown on mine (see note 1); the name is left off the redrawing through lack of space.

On the 1943 map only, my father moved *Dol Amroth* from R 9 to R 11 (south of the mouth of the river Morthond); on both maps he changed *Belfalas* to *Anfalas*; on the First Map only, he changed *Anarion* on Q 14 to *Anórien*, and altered *Land of Seven Streams* to *Land of Five Streams*; and on the 1943 map he struck out *Anarion* and *Lebennin (Land of Seven Streams)* and re-entered *Lebennin* in the place of *Anarion* on Q 14.

This question of the southern rivers is very curious. In the original

draft of Gandalf's story of his adventures to the Council of Elrond
(p. 132) Radagast told him that he would scarcely come to Saruman's
abode 'before the Nine cross the Seven Rivers', which in the next
version (p. 149) becomes 'before the Nine have crossed the seventh
river'. In 'the Lord of Moria' (p. 177) Boromir advises that the
Company should 'take the road to my land that I followed on my way
hither: *through Rohan and the country of Seven Streams*. Or we could
go on far into the South and come at length round the Black
Mountains, and crossing the rivers Isen and Silverlode [> Blackroot]
enter Ond from the regions nigh the sea.' I have remarked there that
this can only mean that the Company would pass through 'the country
of Seven Streams' if they went to Minas Tirith by way of Rohan, north
of the Black Mountains. On the other hand, in 'Farewell to Lórien'
(p. 282) Boromir on his journey to Rivendell 'went round by the south
about the Black Mountains and up the Greyflood – or the Seventh
River as we call it.' And earlier in the same chapter (p. 272) he says
that he was born 'between the mountains and the sea, on the borders
of the Land of Seven Streams.'

The naming of Greyflood *the Seventh River* is an original element of
the oldest portion 'A' of the First Map, and is surely to be associated
with *the Land of Seven Streams*, especially in view of the change in the
drafts of Gandalf's tale to the Council of Elrond, cited above, from
'the Seven Rivers' to 'the seventh river'. But what then were these
rivers? I am certain that there is no river save Blackroot (with a
tributary) west of Ethir Anduin on the hidden part of 'A' (Map III[A]).
Even if Anduin itself is counted, and the tributary of Blackroot, and if
the unnamed river (later Lefnui) is supposed a very early addition, Isen
is the fifth and Greyflood the sixth. I have not been able to find any
solution to this puzzle.

With the replacement portion 'C' the nature of the puzzle changes.
Lebennin (Land of Seven Streams) is a small region, and it is notable
that seven rivers are indeed shown here (Map III, Q–R 11–14):
Morthond and an unnamed tributary; Ringlo and an unnamed
tributary; an unnamed river that enters Anduin above the Mouths;
and an unnamed river entering Anduin further up its course (R 14),
formed of two tributaries one of which flows from Minas Tirith.[7] But
Greyflood, some 450 miles to the north-west of the most westerly of
these seven streams, remains *the Seventh River*.[8] A further twist to the
problem arises from the fact that *Lebennin* does not in any case mean
'Seven Streams', but 'Five Streams'. The original Quenya word for
'five' was *lemin* (I.246); and in the *Etymologies* (V.368) are found the
Quenya word *lempe* 'five' and the Noldorin word *lheben* (cf. Q. *lepse*,
N. *lhebed*, 'finger'). *Ossiriand* was the Land of Seven Rivers (cf. the
Etymologies, V.379, Quenya *otso*, Noldorin *odog* 'seven'). As noted
above, my father afterwards changed 'Seven' to 'Five' on the First
Map, and in *The Lord of the Rings* the name *Lebennin* means 'Five

Streams': cf. *The Return of the King* V.1 (p. 22), 'fair Lebennin with its five swift streams'.

A later map of my father's does not solve these problems, but carries a note that is very interesting in this connection. When this map was made *Lebennin* had been moved to its final position. The note reads:

Rivers of Gondor
Anduin
   From East
Ithilduin or *Duin Morghul*
Poros   Boundary
   From West
Ereg   First
Sirith
Lameduin   (of Lamedon) with tributaries   } The 5 rivers
   Serni (E.) and *Kelos* (W.)   } of Lebennin
Ringlo, Kiril, Morthond and *Calenhir* that
   all flow into Cobas Haven
Lhefneg   Fifth
In counting only the mouths are counted: *Ereg* 1, *Sirith* 2, *Lameduin* 3, *Morthond* 4, *Lhefneg* 5, *Isen* 6, *Gwathlo* 7

Thus in relation to the final geography of the region:

— *Ereg* (the unnamed river on the First Map flowing into Anduin on R 14) became *Erui*.
— *Sirith* (the unnamed river on the First Map flowing into Anduin on R 13) remained.
— *Lameduin* here has tributaries *Serni* and *Kelos*, which evidently constitute Lameduin from their confluence. On the First Map Lameduin is *Ringlo*, with unnamed tributaries. In the final form Lameduin became *Gilrain*, with its tributary *Serni*, while *Kelos* was transferred to become a tributary of Sirith.[9]
— Of the four rivers *Ringlo, Kiril, Morthond*, and *Calenhir* 'that all flow into Cobas Haven' the first three only are named on this map; but though the *Calenhir* is not, it is shown as an unnamed river, most westerly of the four, flowing eastwards from Pinnath Gelin. These four rivers join together not far from the coast, and flow (as *Morthond*, according to the list of river-mouths above) into the sea in the bay north of Dol Amroth, which is named *Cobas Haven*.[10] In the final geography this configuration remains, although *Calenhir* is lost.
— *Lhefneg* became *Lefnui*.
— *Isen* remained.
— *Gwathlo* or *Greyflood* is on this map given an alternative name *Odotheg*, changed to *Odothui* (i.e. 'seventh').

For the first appearance in the texts of the *Mountains of Shadow* and the *Valley of Gorgoroth* see p. 144; cf. also the *Gap of Gorgoroth*, p. 208. *Kirith Ungol* ('the passes of Mordor') appears in 'Farewell to Lórien', p. 283. For *Lithlad* ('Plain of Ash') see pp. 208, 213, and for the first occurrence of *Orodruin* p. 28. *Lothlann* (U 17–18) was apparently an original name on portion 'C' of the First Map, but it was struck out; whether it appeared on the 1943 map cannot be said, for the bottom right-hand corner of that map was torn off. *Lothlann* ('wide and empty') derives from *The Silmarillion*: see the Index to Vol. V.

On *Haradwaith (Sutherland)* see pp. 304, 306. The name *Swertings* appears in *The Two Towers*, IV.3 (p. 255), where Sam speaks of 'the big folk down away in the Sunlands. Swertings we call 'em in our tales.' *Barangils* is found later as a name in Gondor for the men of the Harad.

Maps IV^A to IVE

We come now to what is by far the most complex part of the First Map, the rectangle of fifteen squares (N–P 10–14) lettered 'D' on the figure on p. 297, and left blank on Map II. This section was redrawn and replaced many times.

IV^A

In Map IV^A the uppermost line of squares N 10–14 is part of the original 'A' portion of the First Map, whereas lines O and P are part of the superimposed portion 'C'; but I believe that most of the features and names shown on the line N were added in after portion 'C' had been glued on, and that there is no need to trouble with this distinction. The little that can be seen (and very little seems to have been marked in) on lines O and P of the original 'A' portion is shown on Map III^A, where the line of Anduin below Palath Nenui (Wetwang) was entirely different (see p. 307).

The vertical line of squares N–P 15 on the right-hand side of Map IV^A is repeated from Map II, and is merely added to make the conjunction easier to follow (it includes also the remainder of the name *Border Hills*, which was later struck out). The shaded area on N–P 10–11 is invisible owing to a later pasted overlay (see under Map IV^D below).

I think it is certain that the hills marked *Green Hills* and those marked *Emyn Rhain (Border Hills)* were put in at the same time, at the making of portion 'C'; but I do not think that they were named at once. This matter is rather complex, but it reveals, as I believe, an interesting aspect of the relation between my father's narrative writing and his maps. I set out first the various statements made in the earliest texts of the chapter 'Farewell to Lórien' about the country through which the Anduin flowed south of Lothlórien.

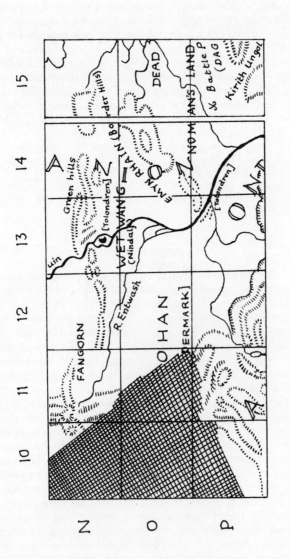

- (i) The River *winds among the Border Hills, Emyn Rain.* They must decide their course there, *because the Wetwang lies before them* (p. 268).
- (ii) They pass into *the Rhain Hills where the River winds in deep ravines* (p. 269).
- (iii) The Company lands (on Tolondren, the island in Anduin) and *goes up into the Rhain Hills* (p. 269).
- (iv) The Company lands on Tolondren. . . . They cross to the East bank and *go up into the Green Hills (or Emyn Rhain?)* (p. 269).
- (v) Elves of Lórien shall go with the Company *as far as the Green Hills where the River winds among deep ravines* (with *Rhain* written above *Green*) (p. 271).
- (vi) Keleborn speaks of *the falls of Rhain where the River runs out of the ravines in the Green Hills* (p. 273).
- (vii) Keleborn says that the River will pass through *a bare and barren country before it flows into the sluggish region of Nindalf,* where the Entwash flows in. *Beyond that are Emyn Rhain the Border Hills . . .* The Company should leave the River *where the isle of Tolondren stands in the stream above the falls of Rosfein* and cross the Entwash above the marshes (pp. 281–2).

(Here the Border Hills are displaced southwards, *beyond* Tolondren and the Nindalf. Keleborn's words were rewritten to say:)

- (viii) the River will pass through *a bare and barren country, winding among the Border Hills before it falls down into the sluggish region of Nindalf* (p. 281).

There is clearly a doubt or confusion here as to the Green Hills and the Border Hills, and different views of how the Border Hills relate to Tolondren, the falls, and the Nindalf or Wetwang. I do not think that any definite conclusion can be drawn from these texts taken by themselves, but from the Map IV^A I believe that the development can be tolerably well understood.

The line of hills extending on either side of Anduin (N 12–14), and the hills rising to east and south-east of these (N–O 14–15), were drawn in at the same time and in the same style, characteristic of portion 'C', with outlining in short strokes. The lettering, I feel sure, was put in subsequently. My belief is that these ranges were a datum already provided, illustrating my father's words in his letter to Naomi Mitchison of 25 April 1954 (*Letters* no. 144): 'I wisely started with a map, *and made the story fit*'; and that the confusing statements in the earliest 'Farewell to Lórien' papers show him moving towards a satisfactory relation between the evolving narrative, his vision of the lands about Anduin in these regions, and what was drawn on the map (i.e. these ranges of hills).

At one stage he decided that the hills should be the Green Hills and the Border Hills respectively. He wrote in these names, and at the same time extended the latter (more roughly, and with dotted outlines) southwest, so as to embrace both sides of Anduin (O 14, P 13–14). This perhaps illustrates Keleborn's words in extract (vii) above, where the Border Hills are south of Tolondren and the Nindalf. But in the margin of the First Map he noted: 'Place [?Tolondren a little more south] and *combine Green Hills with Border Hills*, and make Nindalf or Wetwang all round mouths of Entwash.' The last remark probably refers to the curious feature seen on Map IV^A, that the Wetwang lies distinctly northward of the mouths; that concerning Tolondren is no doubt reflected in the striking out of the name on N 13 and its reintroduction in a more southerly position (P 13, at the confluence with Anduin of a stream flowing in from the Black Mountains), where it was again struck out. This bit of the map had clearly become in need of redrawing.

It may be noted incidentally that the stream from the Black Mountains rises in an oval lake on P 11; and it seems perfectly clear that the Morthond rises in this lake also: see Map III, Q 11.

Map IV^B

What now happened to the geography is clear. In the extract (viii) above Keleborn says that the River will pass through 'a bare and barren country, winding among the Border Hills before it falls down into the sluggish region of Nindalf.' In the draft (ii) given on p. 282 he says that 'the trees will fail, and you will come to a barren country. There the river flows in stony vales among high moors, until it comes to the tall island of Tolondren' (largely preserved in FR, p. 389). Thus the *Brown Lands* emerge, in place of the original Green Hills, on Map IV^B, which is a detached slip of 9 squares that was never pasted in. Here Tolondren (but no longer so named) is definitively in the more southerly position, and in relation to this the course of Entwash is greatly changed, bending in a great southward sweep, *so that the Wetwang is still south of Tolondren and the falls* (here called *Dant Ruinel*, this name being struck out: *Rauros* was later added in pencil).[11] In fact, the new course of Entwash partly takes over that of the unnamed river in IV^A, flowing in from the Black Mountains (P 12–13). The southwestward extension of the Emyn Rhain, lightly entered on IV^A, is now called *Sarn Gebir* and strongly reinforced (cf. Keleborn's reference to 'the bleak hills of Sarn-gebir', p. 283), but this was done very coarsely, clearly after the little slip was first drawn; on account of the heavy lines marking these hills other markings are difficult to interpret, but it can be seen that there is now a large lake (coloured blue), and a large island in the lake named the *Isle of*

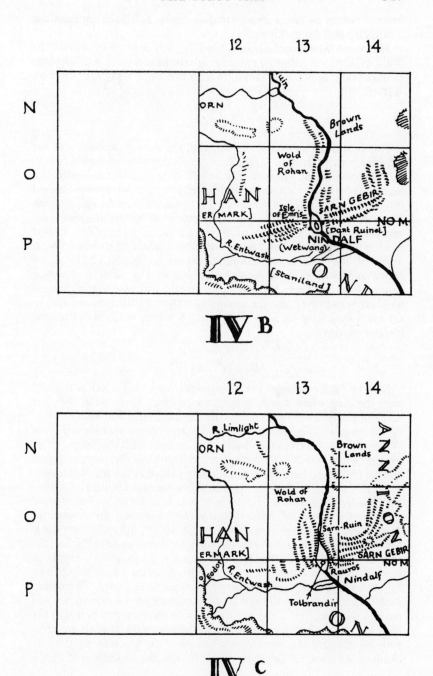

IV B

IV C

Emris,[12] while on either shore are dark spots, no doubt representing Amon Hen and Amon Lhaw.

The name *[Staniland]* beneath *Ond(or)* was entered in pencil. The Wold of Rohan is coloured green, as are the hills on N 12–13. The river Limlight now appears (N 12–13), though the name was only pencilled in later.

Map IV^C

This is another detached slip showing the same 9 squares and not differing greatly from IV^B, save in the representation of Sarn Gebir to the west of Anduin, where the line of hills now runs North-South. The names *Tolbrandir*,[13] *Rauros*, and *River Limlight* were now entered (the latter two added in pencil on IV^B), and the rapids, called *Sarn-Ruin*, north of the lake. In pencil the names *Westemnet*, *Eastemnet*, and the *Entwade*, not included in the redrawing, were added. G was written before *Ondor*, and an arrow moved *Wold cf Rohan* to N 12, north of the hills (again coloured green) on N 12–13. The name *(Rhov)annion* is spelt thus, with doubled *n*. The name *Eodor* was entered in pencil on P 12, but struck through, and (apparently) moved westwards onto P 11 (the six squares N–P 10–11 at this time existing in the form they have on Map IV^A, where however much is obliterated by later overlay).

Maps IV^D and IVE

Map IV^D is a section of twelve squares (N–P 10–13) which was glued onto the map when it was in the state represented by Map IV^A, but here the glue has only adhered on the left-hand side, and thus much of IV^A is revealed. The vertical line of squares N–P 14 was cut off from IV^C, and IV^D was drawn to join (more or less) with this strip. Then, the four squares O–P 10–11 were overlaid by yet another superimposed section (IVE), and here the corresponding part of IV^D is totally hidden.

On IV^D pencilled changes made to IV^C were now included: *Gondor* for *Ondor*, the *Entwade*, *Eastemnet* and *Westemnet*, and the movement of the *Wold of Rohan* northwards. The two great loops in Anduin on N 13 (afterwards called the North and South Undeeps: see *Unfinished Tales* p. 260 and Index, entry *Undeeps*) appear,[14] while the course of Limlight is changed. No name is given to the rapids in Anduin – *Sarn* is not written to join with *Ruin* on the strip cut from IV^C; *Sarn Gebir* was written here subsequently in pencil. The names *Anarion* on Q 14 (Map III) and *Ithilien* opposite on the eastern bank of Anduin were entered at the same time as *Anarion* on P 13 here. On the First Map my father changed *Anarion* to *Anórien* on Q 14; on my 1943 map he changed *Anarion* to *Anórien* on P 13, whereas on Q 14 he changed *Anarion* to *Lebennin* (p. 310). On the western side of the

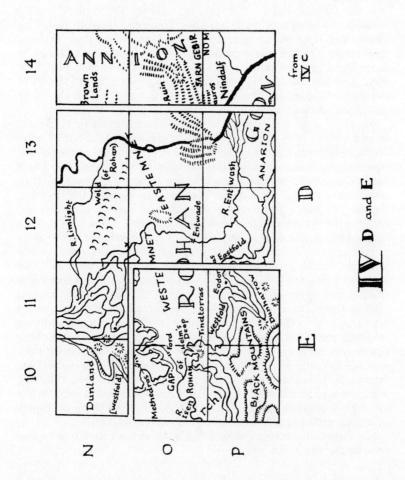

The following labels appear on the map:

ANN

ION

Brown
Lands

SARN GEBIR
NOM

Auin

Taros
Nindalf

GON

from
IV c

R. Limlight

Wold (of Rohan)

(of Rohan)

WNET
EASTE MNET

R O H A N

G
ANARION

Entwade

R. Entwash

Eastfold

WESTE

Dunland

[Westfold]

Methedras
GAP
OF
R.
Isen ROHAN
Helm's
Deep

Tindtorras

Westfold
Eodor
Dunharrow

A Ch

BLACK MOUNTAINS

IV D and E

14   13   12   11   10

D   E

N   O   P

Misty Mountains *Dunland* was entered (N 10), and against the vale to the south was written *Westfold*, which was struck through.

It seems that when map IVE was glued on much of the adjoining region on IV^D was rather coarsely overdrawn, and this is a very difficult part to interpret and to represent; but as this part of the geography has not yet been reached in the texts I shall not consider it here. The westward extension of the Black Mountains on P 8–9 (Map III) belongs with this.[15] Map IVE is the first representation of Isengard and the Gap of Rohan that can be reached, IV^A and IV^D being invisible. Here appear *Helm's Deep*, *Tindtorras* (earlier name for *Thrihyrne*), the *Ford of Isen*, *Dunharrow*, and *Methedras*. *Eodoras* appears on P 11 (see above under Map IV^C); *Eastfold* appears to be represented by a dot, which may however be no more than a mark on the paper; and *Westfold* is pencilled in along the northern foothills of the Black Mountains. The letters *rch* on O–P 10 continue the name *Middlemarch* (see Map II).

On IV^{D-E} (but not on the 1943 map) certain roads or tracks are shown which I have not inserted on the redrawing. At about 12 miles NNW of Eodoras there is a road-meeting: one road goes to the Ford of Isen, keeping near to the foothills but running across the outer limits of the Westfold Vale; another goes north-east to the Entwade and then north along the east bank of Entwash, passing between the river and the downs; and a third runs south-east and east to Minas Tirith, crossing the streams that flow down into Entwash.

The 1943 map is here anomalous and I cannot relate it to the series of replacements made to the First Map. My map was obviously made when the First Map had reached its present state (i.e. when IV^D had been stuck on, and IVE on top of a part of that), for it agrees in every feature and name in its representation of the Gap of Rohan and Helm's Deep; Dunland, Methedras, Tindtorras, Dunharrow, etc. all appear. On the other hand, the courses of Anduin and Limlight on N 12–13 are very distinctly as on Map IV^C. Seeing that the course of the Entwash in the square below (O 12) is carefully represented in the later form of IV^D, this is inexplicable, except on the assumption that the courses of Anduin and Limlight on N 12–13 (introducing the Undeeps) were changed after the 1943 map had been made; but I cannot detect any sign of alteration or erasure on IV^D. On the 1943 map the rapids in Anduin are named *Sarn Ruin*, and the hills *Sarn Gebir*.

My father afterwards changed *Black Mountains* to *White Mountains* on the 1943 map (only).

No Man's Land and the Dead Marshes

In 'Farewell to Lórien' (p. 281) Keleborn says that beyond the Wetwang are *the Nomenlands, dreary Uvanwaith that lies before the passes of Mordor*; and in a subsequent draft of the passage (p. 283) he

speaks of the bleak hills of Sarn-gebir, where the wind blows from the
East, *for they look out over the Dead Marshes and the Nomenlands to
the passes of Mordor: Kirith Ungol*. With the later names *Emyn Muil*
and *Cirith Gorgor*, this was retained in FR (p. 390): 'On the further
side are the bleak hills of the Emyn Muil. The wind blows from the East
there, for they look out over the Dead Marshes and the Noman-lands
to Cirith Gorgor and the black gates of Mordor.' This is the land
described in *The Two Towers*, IV.2 (p. 238):

> The air was now clearer and colder, and though still far off, the
> walls of Mordor were no longer a cloudy menace on the edge of
> sight, but as grim black towers they frowned across a dismal waste.
> The marshes were at an end, dying away into dead peats and wide
> flats of dry cracked mud. The land ahead rose in long shallow
> slopes, barren and pitiless, towards the desert that lay at Sauron's
> gate.

And when Sam and Frodo at last approached the Black Gate (*ibid.*
p. 239):

> Frodo looked round in horror. Dreadful as the Dead Marshes had
> been, and the arid moors of the Noman-lands [*First Edition*: of
> Nomen's land], more loathsome far was the country that the
> crawling day now slowly unveiled to his shrinking eyes.

It will be seen that when the mouths of Entwash and the Wetwang
were moved south (Maps IV^B, IV^C) 'No Man's Land' lay between the
Wetwang and the Dead Marshes. My 1943 map is in complete agreement with this. On my father's later maps, when the geographical
relations in this region had shifted somewhat, the Wetwang and the
Dead Marshes are continuous, and no map later than that of 1943
shows *No Man's Land* (*Noman-lands, Nomenlands, Nomen's Land*).
From these passages in *The Two Towers*, however, it is plain that this
region of 'long shallow slopes, barren and pitiless', of 'arid moors',
that succeeded the marshes still lay between Frodo and Sam and the
pass into Mordor (see the large-scale map of Gondor and Mordor
accompanying *The Return of the King*).

After this demanding journey across the First Map we can return to
the lands themselves, and in the next chapter follow the fortunes of
(unexpectedly, as it may seem) Sam and Frodo.

NOTES

1   A note of my father's about this map is extant:
    This map was made before the story was complete. It is
    incomplete and much is missed out.
       Chief errors are in Gondor and Mordor. The White Moun-

tains are not in accord with the story. Lebennin should be Belfalas. Mindolluin should be immediately behind Minas Tirith, and the distance across the vale of Anduin *much* reduced, so that Minas Tirith is close to Osgiliath and Osgiliath closer to Minas Morgul. Kirith Ungol is misplaced.

2 The style in which natural features were represented varied. In particular, my father when drawing the Black Mountains surrounded them with a fine continuous line (whereas for the Mountains of Shadow and Ered Lithui he used small strokes to define the foothills), and this can be very confusing in relation to the similar lines representing streams falling from the mountains (see note 7). To make my redrawing as clear as possible, I have substituted lines of dots or small strokes in representing the foothills of the Black Mountains (see note 15).

3 On the revised map first published in *Unfinished Tales* an arrow directs that the name *Icebay of Forochel* applies to the great bay of which the southern bay is only a small part.

4 In the absence of 'sea-lines' the inner line could itself be taken to be the coast; but on my 1943 map the coastline follows the outer line on the First Map (and neither the inner wavy line nor the small circular area are present). This no doubt followed my father's instruction.

5 For another use of *Neldoreth*, from the legends of the First Age, in *The Lord of the Rings* see VI.384.

6 The three cities were still relatively far apart on the redrawn portion 'C' of the First Map, repeated on the 1943 map; see note 1.

7 That this river flowed from Minas Tirith is not perfectly clear on the First Map, owing to a difficulty in distinguishing between the fine lines that mark the outer contours of the mountains and those that mark streams (see note 2); but on my 1943 map it is shown very clearly as flowing out of the city (and I have so redrawn it on Map III).

8 This is still the case not only on the 1943 map but also on a later map of my father's (p. 312).

9 This is a convenient place to notice that the redrawn version of the LR map first published in *Unfinished Tales* contains an error, in that I showed Sirith as the western arm and Celos, its tributary, as the eastern, whereas it should be the reverse (as it is on the large-scale map of Mordor, Gondor, and Rohan in *The Return of the King*).

10 *Cobas Haven*: cf. *Kópas Alqaluntë* in *The Book of Lost Tales* (I.257 and Index). In the *Etymologies* (V.364–5) Quenya *kópa* 'harbour, bay' was given under the stem KOP, but this entry was replaced by a stem KHOP, whence Quenya *hópa*, Noldorin *hobas*, as in *Alfobas* = *Alqualondë*.

11 For *Dant-ruin, Dant-ruinel,* and *Rauros* see pp. 283, 285.

12 This name can in fact only be made out in the light of the appearance of the *Isle of Emris* in a time-scheme of this period (see p. 367), where it was changed to *Eregon,* and that to *Tolbrandir.* On the fair copy manuscript of 'Farewell to Lórien' *Tolondren* was changed to *Eregon* (p. 285).

13 For earlier forms *Brandor, Tol Brandor* see p. 285.

14 The divided course of Anduin on O 13 is very clear on the map.

15 I have represented the extension of the Black Mountains on P 8–9 with dots and strokes to make it consistent with the representation of mountains elsewhere on Map III (see note 2); in the original the contours are shown by continuous lines, as on Map IVE.

XVI

THE STORY FORESEEN FROM
LÓRIEN

(i)

The Scattering of the Company

It seems certain that *before* my father wrote the conclusion of
'Farewell to Lórien' – that is, from the point where the Company
returned to the hythe and departed down the Great River – he began
to write a new and very substantial outline of the way ahead. The
opening pages of this outline are complex, and at the beginning the
text was much altered, though it is clear that my father was changing
the embryonic story as he wrote and that the layers of the text belong
together. The notes are here again an essential part of the elucidation.

At the head of the text he wrote, in a second stage, 'XXI', then
changed it to 'XX continued' and after the opening words 'The
Company sets off from Tongue' wrote in 'XXI'. On the arrangement
of chapters in this outline see pp. 329–30.[1]

The Company sets off from Tongue.
They are attacked with arrows.[2]
They come to [*struck out:* Stony] Stoneait [*struck out:*
Tolharn] Tollernen[3] [*added:* sheersided except on North where
there [is] a little shingle beach. It rises to a high brown hill,
higher than the low brown hills on either bank. They land and
camp on the island]. Debate whether to go East or West. Frodo
feels it in his heart that he should go East and crosses over with
Sam to east shore and climbs a hill, and looks out south-east
towards the Gates of Mordor. He tells Sam that he wishes to be
alone for a while and bids him go back [and] guard the boat on
which they had crossed from the Island. Meanwhile Boromir
taking another boat crossed over. He hides his boat in bushes.
[*This passage changed to read:* Debate whether to go East or
West. Frodo feels it in his heart that he should go East and
climbs the tall hill in the midst of the island. Sam goes with him
but near the top Frodo says to him that he is going to sit on hill
top alone and bids him wait for him. Frodo sits alone and looks

out towards Mordor over Sarn Gebir and Nomen's land.[4]
Meanwhile Boromir has crept away from Company and
climbed hill from west side.]

As Frodo is sitting alone on hill top, Boromir comes suddenly
up and stands looking at him. Frodo is suddenly aware as if
some unfriendly thing is looking at him behind. He turns and
sees only Boromir smiling with a friendly face.

'I feared for you,' said Boromir, 'with only little Sam. It is ill
to be alone on the east side of the River.[5] Also my heart is
heavy, and I wished to talk a while with you. Where there are so
many all speech becomes a debate without end in the conflict of
doubting wills.'

'My heart too is heavy,' said Frodo, 'for I feel that here
doubts must be resolved; and I foresee the breaking up of our
fair company, and that is a grief to me.'

'Many griefs have we had,' said Boromir, and fell silent.
There was no sound; only the cold rustle of the chill East wind
in the withered heather. Frodo shivered.

Suddenly Boromir spoke again.

'It is a small thing that lies so heavy on our hearts, and
confuses our purposes,' said Boromir. [Here include conversation written above and bring down to Boromir's attempt to
seize the Ring.]

This last sentence was written continuously with the preceding text.
The conversation referred to is found on two pages of the 'August
1940' examination paper, written in pencil so faint and rapid that my
father went over it more clearly in ink, although, so far as the
underlying text can be made out, he followed it almost exactly. This
obviously preceded the new outline into which it is inserted, and was a
development from the scene in the previous Plot ('The Story Foreseen
from Moria') given on p. 208, where the debate, Boromir's intervention,
and Frodo's flight wearing the Ring all take place 'at Angle': here the
scene is set 'at the Stone Hills, whence Eredwethion[6] can be glimpsed'
(these words being visible in the underlying text also). In the notes
given on p. 233 the 'parting of the ways' took place 'at Stonehills'; in
the outlines for 'Farewell to Lórien' (pp. 268–9) the debate and the
'scene with Boromir' follow the landing on Tolondren and the ascent
into the Green Hills, or the Emyn Rhain.

Conversation of Boromir and Frodo at the Stone Hills,
whence Eredwethion can be glimpsed like a smudge of grey,
and behind it a vague cloud lit beneath occasionally by a fitful
glow.

'It is a small thing from which we suffer so much woe,' said Boromir. 'I have seen it but once for an instant, in the house of Elrond. Could I not have a sight of it again?'

Frodo looked up. His heart went suddenly cold. He caught a curious gleam in Boromir's eye, though his face otherwise was friendly and smiling as of old.

'It is best to let it lie hid,' he answered.

'As you will. I care not,' said Boromir. 'Yet I will confess that it is of the Ring that I wish to speak. (Yet hidden or revealed I would wish now to speak to you of the Ring?) ... [*sic*]

Boromir says that Elrond etc. are all foolish. 'It is mad not to use the power and methods of the Enemy: ruthless, fearless. Many elves, half-elves, and wizards might be corrupted by it – but not so a true Man. Those who deal in magic will use it for hidden Power. Each to his kind. You, Frodo, for instance, being a hobbit and desiring peace: you use it for invisibility. Look what a warrior could do! Think what I – or Aragorn, if you will – could do! How he would fare among the enemy and drive the Black Riders! It would give power of command.

'And yet Elrond tells us not only to throw it away and destroy it – that is understandable (though not to my mind wise since I have pondered on it by night on our journey). But what a way – walk into the enemy's net and offer him every chance of re-capturing it!'

Frodo is obdurate.

'Come at least to Minas-tirith!' said Boromir. He laid his hand on Frodo's shoulder in friendly fashion, but Frodo felt his arm tremble as if with suppressed excitement. Frodo stepped away and stood further off.

'Why are you so unfriendly?' said Boromir. 'I am a valiant man and true,' he said. 'And I give you my *word* that I would not keep it – would not, that is I should say, if you would lend it to me. Just to make trial!'

'No! No!' said Frodo. [*Added:* 'It is mine alone by fate to bear.']

Boromir gets more angry, and so more incautious (or actually evil purpose now only begins to grow in him). 'You are *foolish!*' he cried. 'Doing yourself to death and ruining our cause. Yet the Ring is not yours, save by chance. It might as well have been Aragorn's – or mine. Give it to me! Then you will be rid of it, and of all responsibility. You would be free' (cunningly) 'You can lay the blame on me, if you will, saying that I was too strong and took it by force. For I *am* too strong for you, Frodo,' he said. And now an ugly look had come suddenly over his fair and pleasant face. He got to his feet and sprang at Frodo.

Frodo could do nothing else. He slipped the Ring on, and vanished among the rocks. Boromir cursed, and groped among the rocks. Then suddenly the fit left him, and he wept.

'What folly possessed me!' he said. 'Come back, Frodo!' he called. 'Frodo! Evil came into my heart, but I have put it away.'

But Frodo was now frightened, and he hid until Boromir went back to camp. Standing on rocks he saw nothing about him but a grey formless mist, and far away (yet black and clear and hard) the Mountains of Mordor: the fire seemed very red. Fell voices in air. Feels Eye searching, and though it does not find him, he feels its attention is suddenly arrested (by himself).[7]

Here the inserted text ends and the new Plot continues:

Then Frodo took counsel with himself, and he perceived that the evil of the Ring was already at work even among the Company. (Also its evil was again on him, since he had put it on again.) He said to himself: this is laid on me. I am the Ringbearer and none can help me. I will not emperil the other hobbits or any of my companions. I will depart alone.

He slips away unseen and coming to the boats takes one and crosses over to the East.

Boromir is now himself frightened and though (half) repenting his own greed for the Ring the curse has not wholly left him. He ponders what tale he shall tell to the others. Hastening back to the River he comes upon Sam, who anxious at Frodo's long absence is coming to the hill-top to find him.

'Where is my master?' says Sam.

'I left him on the hill-top,' said Boromir, but something wild and odd in his face caused Sam sudden fear. 'What have you done with him?' 'I have done nothing,' said Boromir. 'It is what he has done himself: he has put on the ring and vanished!'

'Thank goodness the island is not large,' said Sam in great alarm, but he thought also to himself: 'And what made him do that, I should like to know. What mischief has this great fool been up to?' Without another word to Boromir he ran back to the camp to find Trotter. 'Master Frodo has disappeared!' he cried.

Consternation. The hunt. Some scour the island. But Sam discovers the fact that a boat is missing. Has Frodo gone East or

West? Trotter decides that they cannot hope to recapture Frodo against his will, but they must *follow* him if they can. Which way?

[Or make Island inaccessible: steep shores. Black birds circle high above its tall cliffs and central summit. Distant noise of the falls of Dantruinel.[8] They camp on *west* shore. Hence when Frodo is lost they all go after him. Thus Pippin and Merry get separated.[9] Sam sits alone and so discovers missing boat. He takes another and goes after Frodo.] [*Against this bracketed passage is written* Yes.]

It is clear that my father at once accepted his suggestion in this last passage that the Company camped on the west bank, not on the island in the river, because that passage contains the words 'Sam ... discovers missing boat. He takes another and goes after Frodo', and this, as will be seen in a moment, is a necessary element in the story that follows.

Boromir is for West. In any case he says he is afraid – the Ring will fall now almost certainly into the Enemy's hands. 'This madness was set [in] him for that purpose.'[10] He wishes to get now to Minas-Tirith as quick as possible. Sam goes West [*read* East], others East [*read* West].

Sam picks up trail of Frodo.[11] How? He finds boat knocking against the bank.[12] A little further he finds a scrap of grey stuff on a bramble – a great bramble tract has to be crossed. Very soon Sam discovered that he was lost in a pathless listening land. But he felt sure his master would steer towards the Fiery Mt. Away on his right the falls roared. He climbed down into the Wetwang. Daylight fell. Slept in tree. Heard Gollum at foot and tried to track *him*, thinking he was after Frodo. But Sam is not clever enough for Gollum, who is soon aware of him and turns and discovers him. He confesses to Gollum that he is trying to find Frodo.

Gollum laughs. 'Then his luck is better than he deserves, yes,' said Gollum, 'for Gollum has been following him: Gollum can see footprints where he can't see nothings, no!'

Gollum was so intent on the trail – muttering to himself 'Footsteps, Gollum sees them, and he smells them: Gollum is wary' – that he did not seem aware of Sam's (relatively) clumsy efforts at stalking the stalker.[13]

It was near the evening of the second day when Frodo, every sense keyed up, became suddenly aware of footfalls. He puts on the ring, but Gollum comes up and circles near. To Frodo's great surprise Sam appears. To the equal surprise of Sam and Gollum Frodo suddenly takes off ring and stands before them.

Gollum is the most surprised: for between Frodo and Sam he is overmatched. He cringes: for as Ringbearer Frodo has a power over him (though he is really an object of great hatred). Gollum pleads for forgiveness, and promises help, and having nowhere else to turn Frodo accepts. Gollum says he will lead them over the Dead Marshes to Kirith Ungol.[14] (Chuckling to himself to think that that is just the way he would wish them to go.)

Here ends Chapter.

At this stage my father was following the previous Plot (p. 208): 'At point where Sam, Frodo and Gollum meet return to others – for whose adventures see later. But they should be told at this point.' He now decided, I think, that not even so much of the story of Frodo and Sam east of Anduin should yet be told, and he bracketed all that follows from 'Sam picks up trail of Frodo', writing against it 'Put in later chapter. XXIV' (subsequently altering XXIV to XXV: see p. 330).[15] At the same time he struck out 'Here ends Chapter' and went on with the story of the other members of the Company.

Dismay of the hunt at finding no trace of Frodo. Boromir, Legolas, Gimli, Trotter return to camp, only to find now that Sam also is missing, and Pippin and Merry as well.

Trotter is overwhelmed with grief, thinking that he has failed in his charge as Gandalf's successor. He imagines that the hobbits are all together; and waits in camp until the morning.[16]

In the morning no sign is found of them. The Company is now broken. Trotter sees nothing for it but to go south to Minas-Tirith with Boromir. But Legolas and Gimli have no further heart for the Quest, and feel that already too many leagues are between them and their homes. They go north again: Legolas meaning to join the Elves of Lothlórien for a while, Gimli hoping to get back to the Mountain.[17]

Here ends Chapter XX.

('Chapter XX' was subsequently changed to 'XXI', and the numbers of the chapter synopses that follow were also altered, as will be explained in a moment.)

XXI   What happened to Gimli and Legolas. They meet Gandalf?

XXII   What happened to Merry and Pippin. They are lost – led astray by echoes – in the hunt, and wander away up the Entwash River and come to Fangorn. Here they meet with Giant Fangorn or Tree-beard. He takes them to Minas Tirith.

XXIII   What happened in Minas Tirith. Siege by Sauron and Saruman. Treachery of Boromir. Sudden arrival of Gandalf – now become *a white wizard*. Treebeard raises the siege. Enemy driven over the Anduin. Horsemen of Rohan come to assistance.

XXIV   What happened to Frodo and Sam.

Comparison with the previous Plot (pp. 210–11) will show that these synopses repeat, much more briefly, what was set out there, and show no further development. At this juncture my father made various alterations of chapter-structure in the plot-sketch. At the beginning, as already noted (p. 324), he indicated that 'The Company sets off from Tongue' should form the conclusion of Chapter XX ('Farewell to Lórien'), while all that follows should constitute XXI (apart from the story of Sam's tracking of Frodo and the encounter with Gollum, which would be placed in a later chapter, as already decided: p. 329). The brief synopses just given were now renumbered and slightly reordered: XXII (Merry and Pippin); XXIII (Gimli and Legolas); XXIV (Minas Tirith); XXV (Frodo and Sam).[18]

(ii) *Mordor*

While my father seems never to have doubted that after the breaking of the Company the 'western' stories must be followed, the 'eastern' story of Frodo and Sam was bursting into life and expression; and he now at once went on with the outline of that story from the point where he had left it (p. 329), noting: 'XXV: continuation after part above.'

They sleep in pairs, so that one is always awake with Gollum.[19]

Gollum all the while is scheming to betray Frodo. He leads them cleverly over the Dead Marshes. There are dead green faces in the stagnant pools; and the dry reeds hiss like snakes. Frodo feels the strength of the searching eye as they proceed.

At night Sam keeps watch, only pretending to be asleep. He hears Gollum muttering to himself, words of hatred for Frodo and lust for the Ring.

The three companions now approach Kirith Ungol, the dreadful ravine which leads into Gorgoroth. Kirith Ungol means Spider Glen: there dwelt great spiders, greater than those

of Mirkwood, such as were once of old in the land of Elves and
Men in the West that is now under sea, such as Beren fought in
the dark cañons of the Mountains of Terror above Doriath.
Already Gollum knew these creatures well. He slips away. The
spiders come and weave their nets over Frodo while Sam sleeps:
sting Frodo. Sam wakes, and sees Frodo lying pale as death –
greenish: reminding him of the faces in the pools of the marshes.
He cannot rouse or wake him.[20]

The idea suddenly comes to Sam to carry on the work, and he
felt for the Ring. He could not unclasp it, nor cut the chain, but
he drew the chain over Frodo's head. As he did so he fancied he
felt a tremor (sigh or shudder) pass through the body; but when
he paused he could not feel any heart-beat. Sam put the Ring
round his own neck.

[Suddenly the Orc-guard of the Pass, guided by Gollum,
comes upon them. Sam takes Galadriel's present to Frodo – the
phial of light. Sam slips on the Ring, and attempts to fight
unseen to defend Frodo's body; but gets knocked down and
nearly trampled to death. The Orcs rejoicing pick up Frodo and
bear him away, after searching in vain (but only a short while)
for 'the other hobbit' reported by Gollum.]

This last paragraph, which I have bracketed, was struck through
with a direction to replace it by the following much longer passage on
a separate page. It is clear, however, that this replacement was not
written significantly later.[21]

Then he sat and made a *Lament for Frodo*. After that he put
away his tears and thought what he could do. He could not
leave his dear master lying in the wild for the fell beasts and
carrion birds; and he thought he would try and build a cairn of
stones about him. 'The silver mail of mithril rings shall be his
winding-sheet,' he said. 'But I will lay the phial of Lady
Galadriel upon his breast, and Sting shall be at his side.'

He laid Frodo upon his back and crossed his arms on his
breast and set Sting at his side. And as he drew out the phial it
blazed with light. It lit Frodo's face and it looked now pale but
beautiful, fair with [an] elvish beauty as of one long past the
shadows. 'Farewell, Frodo,' said Sam; and his tears fell on
Frodo's hands.

[But] at that moment there was a sound of strong footfalls
climbing towards the rock shelf. Harsh calls and cries echoed in
the rocks. Orcs were coming, evidently guided to the spot.

'Curse that Gollum,' said Sam. 'I might have known we had not seen the last of him. These are some of his friends.'

Sam had no time to lose. Certainly no time to hide or cover his master's body. Not knowing what else to do he slipped on the Ring, and then he took also the phial so that the foul Orcs should not get it, and girded Sting about his own waist. And waited. He had not long to wait.

In the gloom first came Gollum sniffing out the scent, and behind him came the black orcs: fifty or more it seemed. With a cry they rushed upon Frodo. Sam tried to put up a fight unseen, but even as he was about to draw Sting he was run down and trampled by the rush of the Orcs. All the breath was knocked out of his body. [*Added in pencil:* Courage failed him.] In great glee the Orcs seized Frodo and lifted him.

'There was another, yes,' whined Gollum. 'Where is he, then?' said the Orcs. 'Somewheres nigh. Gollum feels him, Gollum sniffs him.'

'Well, you find him, sniveller,' said the Orc-chief. 'He can't go far without getting into trouble. We've got what we want. Ringbearer! Ringbearer!' They shouted in joy. 'Make haste. Make haste. Send one swift to Baraddur to the Great One. But we cannot wait here – we must [get] back to our guard post. Bear the prisoner to Minas Morgul.' [*Added in pencil:* Gollum runs behind wailing that the Precious is not there.]

Here the replacement text ends.

Even as they do so, Frodo seems to awake, and gives a loud cry, but they gag him. Sam is torn between joy at learning he is alive and horror at seeing him carried off by Orcs. Sam tries to follow, but they go very speedily. The Ring seems to grow in power in this region: he sees clearly in the dark, and seems to understand the orcs' speech. [He fears what may happen if he meets a Ringwraith – the Ring does not confer courage: poor Sam trembles all the time.][22] Sam gathers that they are going to Minas Morgul: since they are not allowed to leave their post – but a messenger has at once been despatched to announce to the Dark Lord the capture of Ringbearer, and to bring back his orders.[23] 'The Mighty One has great business afoot,' says one. 'All that has gone before is but a skirmish compared with the war that is about to be kindled. Fine days, fine days! Blood on blade and fire on hill, smoke in sky and tears on earth. Merry weather, my friends, to bring in a real New Year!'

The Orcs go so fast that Sam soon gets weary and falls behind; but he plods on behind in the direction of Minas Morgul, remembering as much as he could of the maps. The path led up into the mountains – the north horn of the Mountains of Shadow that sundered the ashen vale of Gorgoroth from the valley of the Great River. Sam looking out saw all the plain alive with armies, horse and foot, black plumes, red and black banners. Countless hosts of the wild peoples of Rhûn, and the evil folk of Harad, were pouring out of Kirith Ungol to war. Smoke and dust afar off suggested that away in the East more were coming. [In truth they were – far beyond Sam's eyesight the armies rode and marched: the Dark Lord had determined to strike. From beyond the Inland Sea of Rhûn[24] up the rivers east of Mirkwood, round the towers of Dol Dúghul they poured through fen and forest to the banks of the Great River. Lothlórien was lapped in flame. From the Misty Mountains, from Moria – Khazaddûm and many hidden caves poured the orcs to meet them; from Harad and from Mordor they came against Ondor, and sought the walls of Minas-Tirith; and out from Isengard, seeing the war-beacons afar off blazing in Mordor, came the traitor Saruman with many wolves.][25]

Sam comes so close behind that he sees from below the orc-host entering the gates of the City[26] [*struck out:* – and they have not time to despoil Frodo].

At last Sam saw before him the walled city that had once been the City of the Sun [> Moon]: Minas Anor [> Ithil] in the days of old (Elendil).[27] Amidst it stood a tall tower – from afar off it looked beautiful. But Sam passed into the city and saw that all was defiled: and on every stone and corner were carved figures and faces and signs of horror. Such a dread ran through all the streets that he could hardly drag his legs or force himself along.

'Where in all this devilish hole have they put my poor master,' thought Sam. He feels drawn to the Tall Tower. He wanders up a seemingly endless winding stair, windowless; shrinks into foul-smelling recess[es] when snarling Orcs go up or down. At the top are four locked doors, North, South, East, West. Which is it? And anyway how can he get in: all are locked.

Suddenly Sam took courage and did a thing of daring – the longing for his master was stronger than all other thoughts. He sat on the ground and began to sing. 'Troll-song' – or some other Hobbit song – or possibly part of the Elves' song *O Elbereth*. (Yes).

Cries of anger are heard and guards come from stairs above
and from below. 'Stop his mouth – the foul hound' cry the Orcs.
'Would that the message would return from the Great One, and
we could begin our Questioning [or take him to Baraddur. He
he! They have a pretty way there. There is One who will soon
find out where the little cheat has hid his Ring.][28] Stop his
mouth.' 'Careful!' cried the captain, 'do not use too much
strength ere word comes from the Great One.' By this trick Sam
found the door, for an Orc unlocked the East door and went
inside with a whip. 'Hold your foul tongue,' he said, as Sam
heard the whip crack.

Swift as lightning Sam slipped inside. He longed to stab the
Orc but wisely restrained himself. In the light of [the torch >]
the small East window he saw Frodo lying on the bare stone –
his arms over his face [?guarding] from the whip blow. Muttering the orc went out and closed the door.

Frodo groaned and turned over uncovering his face – still pale
from the poison. 'Why do dreams cheat me?' he said. 'I thought
I heard a voice singing the song of Elbereth!'

'You were not dreaming!' said Sam. 'It is me, master.' He
drew off the Ring.

But Frodo felt a great hatred well up in his heart. Before him
there stood a small orc, bowlegged, leering at him out of a
gloating face. It reminded him faintly of some one he had once
known and loved – or hated. He stood up. 'Thief!' he cried.
'Give it to me.'

Sam was greatly taken aback: and stepped away, so sudden
and grim was his master's face. 'The poor dear is still
mithered,'[29] he thought.

'Surely, Master Frodo. I have come behind as quick as I could
just for to give it you.' And with that he gave the ring into
Frodo's snatching hand, and took the chain from about his
neck. [Only for two days had he been Ringbearer, yet he felt a
curious regret as it left him.][30]

'Sam!' cried Frodo. 'Sam! my dear old Sam. How did you
come here? I thought' – and then he leant upon Sam and wept
long. 'I thought,' he said again at last. 'Well never mind. I
thought I was lost and that they had taken the Ring and all was
in ruin. How did you get it – tell me.'

'Not by thieving,' said Sam with an effort at a smile. 'Or not
exactly. I took it when I thought you were gone, Master. Yes, I
thought you were dead for certain away back in that Kirith

place, with those crawling horrors. That was a black hour, Master Frodo, but it seemed to me that Sam had got to carry on – if he could.' Then he told the tale of the attack and how he had followed. 'And it is in a place called Minas Morgul that we are,' he said, 'and not for a small mercy in the Dark Tower itself, leastways not yet. But Minas whatever it be: we have got to get out quick. And how, I don't see.'

They talked it over long in whispering voices. 'The Ring won't cover two,' said Sam; 'and I think you won't want to part from it again. Anyhow the Ring is yours, master,' said Sam. 'Once out of here you can get away fairly easy, so long as none of the Ring-wraiths or Black Riders turn up, or something worse. There is some nasty eyes in this town, or the pricking of my skin is merely the shivers of a cold coming on. My advice to you is to leg it as quick as may be.'

'And you?' said Frodo.

'O, me,' said Sam. 'That can't be helped. I may find a way out, or I may not. Anyway I have done the job I came to do.'

'Not yet, I think,' said Frodo. 'Not yet. I do not think that we part here, dear friend.'

'Well then, master, tell me how.'

'Let me think,' said Frodo. 'I have a plan,' he said at last. 'A risk, but it may work. Have you still got your sword?'

'I have,' said Sam, 'and Sting too, and your glass of light. I was a-going to lay them by you under the stones,' he stammered, 'when the murdering Orcs came on us. I thought you were dead – until you cried out as they gripped you.'

Frodo smiled and took back his treasures. He drew Sting half from its sheath and the pale blue light of it flickered from the blade. 'Not surprising,' he said, 'that Sting should shine in Minas Morgul! Well now, Sam, get away over there – where you will be behind the door when it opens. Draw your sword. I will lie on the floor as I was. Then you can start your song again – and that should bring in an orc soon enough. Let us hope it is not many more than one.'

'But the whips, master, the murdering hounds will fetch you one for me, and I cannot abide it.'

'You won't have to abide it if you are quick with your sword,' said Frodo. 'But you need not worry! They have not had time to search me – not that Orcs dare touch the Ring that is for none less than servants of the Ring or for Sauron himself. They made sure that I had no sword and flung me on the floor. So I have still my mithril-coat. That lash you heard as you came in was laid well across my side and back – but I don't think you would find any weal.'

Sam was much relieved. 'Very well, what's the idea, Mr. Frodo?' he asked.

'You must do your best to kill the Orc that comes in,' said Frodo. 'If there is more than one I must leap up and help, and maybe we shall have to try and fight our way out. But to get someone to come in seems our only way of getting out.'

Frodo now began again to sing O Elbereth (a few lines). With an oath the door was flung open and in strode the orc-captain, cracking his lash. 'Lie quiet, you dog,' he shouted, and raised his whip. But even as he did so, Sam leapt from behind the door and stabbed at his throat. He fell with a gurgle. Frodo sprang up, pushed the door gently to, and crouched waiting for any other orc that might come. The sound of harsh voices far off up the further stairs came to them, but no other sounds.

'Now's our chance,' said Frodo. 'Get into his gear as quick as you can.' Swiftly they stripped the orc, peeling off his coat of black scale-like mail, unbuckling his sword, and unslinging the small round shield at his back. The black iron cap was too large for Sam (for orcs have large heads for their size), but he slipped on the mail. It hung a little loose and long. He cast the black hooded cloak about him, took the whip and scimitar, and slung the red shield. Then they dragged the body behind the door and crept out. Frodo went first.

It was dark outside when the door was shut again. Frodo took out the glass of light. They hurried down the stairs. Halfway down they met someone coming up with a torch. Frodo slipped on his Ring and drew aside; but Sam went on to meet the goblin. They brushed into one another and the goblin spoke in his harsh tongue; but Sam answered only with an angry snarl. That seemed satisfactory. Sam was evidently mistaken for someone important. The goblin drew aside to let him pass, and they hastened on. [*Struck out:* They did not guess that it was the messenger returning from Baraddur!]

Now they issued from the Loathly Tower. Evening was falling: away in the West over the valley of the Anduin there was some light. Far away loomed the Black Mountains and the tower of Minas Tirith, had they known. But in the East the sky was dark, with black and lowering clouds that seemed almost to rest upon the land. An uneasy twilight lay in the shadowy streets. Shrill cries came as it were from underground, strange shapes flitted by or peered out of alley[s] and holes in the [?gaping] houses; there were [??dispirited] voices and faint echoes of monotonous and unhappy song. All the carven faces leered, and their eyes glowed with a fire at great depth.

The hobbits shuddered as they hurried on. Feet seemed to follow them, and they turned many corners, but they never threw them off. Rustling and pattering on the stones they came doggedly after them.

They came to the gates. The main gates were closed; but a small door was still open. Sentinels stood on either side, and at the opening stood an armed warder, gazing out into the gathering dusk. The Orcs were waiting for the messenger from Baraddur.

'Stay here,' whispered Frodo, drawing Sam into a shadow of a pillar just before the gate. 'While I wear the Ring I can understand much of their speech, or of the thought behind it – I don't know which. If I cry out come at a run, and get through the door if you can.'

[*The following was struck out probably as soon as written:* He went forward. The guard at the open door was grumbling. 'One would have thought we had caught no more than a stray elf,' he said. 'Is [?the] Ringbearer [*written above:* Thief] of no matter to them at the Dark Tower now? One would have thought He would have sent a Rider at least. Not even the war that is now set afoot can surely have lessened the worth of the One Treasure.'

Suddenly Frodo stabbed with Sting. The warder fell. But Frodo leant against the door lest a guard should thrust it to and called out. The sentinels sprang up. Sam came running, but at first they took him for a goblin running up to help. He smote one down before they were aware of his enmity and sprang through the door]

'Nay,' said Sam, 'that won't do. If we have a fight at the gate it won't be much use getting through. We'll have the whole wasps' nest a-buzzing after us before we have gone many yards: and they know these nasty mountains as well as I mind me of Bagend. Swagger is the only hope, Mr. Frodo, begging your pardon.'

'Very well, my good Sam,' said Frodo, 'try swagger.'

Feeling as little like 'swagger' as ever in his life, Sam walked as unconcernedly as he could manage into the shadow of the dark gateway. The sentinels on either side looked at him and did not move. He came beside the warder and looked out. The warder started and looked at him angrily.

Frodo came behind warily. He saw the orc's hand go to the hilt of his scimitar. 'Who are you and who do you think you are pushing,' said he. 'Am I in charge of the gate or not?' Sam tried the trick again. He snarled angrily and stepped out of the gate. But the trick did not work so well a second time. The warder sprang after him and grabbed at his cloak. 'Closing time is [? by *read* past by?] half an hour,' he said, 'and you know that. No one but the Lord's messengers are allowed in or out, and you know that well enough. If I have any more trouble I shall report you to the Captain [*struck out:* of Morgul].' Sam prepared to give battle. He turned to face the warder gripping his hilt and swung round his shield. It was a red shield, and in the midst was painted a single black eye. The warder fell back nimbly. 'Your pardon,' he said, 'O Captain of Morgul. I did not recognize you. I only did my duty as I thought.' Sam, guessing something of what had occurred, snarled again and waved his hand as if in dismissal and walked away down the path into the dusk. The warder stared after him shaking his head. He stood blocking the door so that Frodo could not pass.

Sam had now disappeared on the downward track, and still Frodo waited hoping for a chance to slip out without a fight, before the door was closed. Suddenly there was a loud boom. Dong Dong Dong. A big bell was ringing in the Loathly Tower: the alarm was sounded. Frodo heard distant cries. Soon he could hear voices calling: 'Close the gates. Bar the door. Watch the walls. The Bearer has escaped from the Tower.'

The warder seized the door and began to close it. Feet came running. Frodo took the only chance. Stooping he seized the warder's legs and threw him down and sprang out. As he ran he heard loud shouts and oaths. 'But the Captain is lying dead and stripped in the Tower, I tell you,' he heard. 'Take that for a fool. You have let the bearer escape. Take that for a fool.' There was a blow and a cry. Orcs came pouring out of the gate, and still the bell tolled.

Suddenly dark overhead a black shape appeared flying low out of the east: a great bird it seemed, like an eagle or more like a vulture. The orcs halted chattering shrilly: but Frodo did not wait. He guessed that some urgent message concerning himself had come from the Dark Tower.

Here the text in ink ends, but is followed by a few pencilled notes:

Finds Sam

They escape – and as they are actually making *towards* Mordor this delays hunt which goes towards the Anduin North and West.

End of Chapter XXV

Gorgoroth

How Frodo came to the Fiery Mountain. See sketch (b) (c).

This last is a reference to the pages of the previous Plot, in this book pp. 208–9, from 'The Gap of Gorgoroth not far from Fire Mountain' to 'hurls himself and Gollum into the gulf?'

All this story of the escape from Minas Morgul was developed from the brief words of the earlier Plot (p. 209):

> Sam ... passes into Morgol and finds Frodo. Frodo feels hatred of Sam and sees him as an orc. But suddenly the orc speaks and holds out Ring and says: Take it. Then Frodo sees it is Sam. They creep out. ... Sam dresses up like an orc.

There can be no doubt whatsoever that the text just given, beginning as an outline in the present tense and sliding almost imperceptibly into full narrative, was the actual emergence on paper of what ultimately became 'The Tower of Cirith Ungol' in *The Return of the King* (VI.1). It was written very fast (though surprisingly legibly), with virtually no correction made on grounds of suitability of phrasing, and gives an impression of uninterrupted composition, perhaps even at one sitting. Being written at this stage,[31] its relation to the ultimate form of the story in 'The Tower of Cirith Ungol' is much more remote than has been the case anywhere else, and although certain new elements (not present in the previous Plot) now enter and would be preserved – notably Sam's song, instrumental in his discovery of where Frodo was – the story would be radically refashioned in every point, in geography, in motives, in the structure of events, so as to become almost a new conception.

Some further development seems in fact to have taken place quite soon. Found with this text are some other papers, themselves all of the same time, but entirely distinct in appearance and mode of writing. Here the story of Frodo and Sam is roughly outlined further, and the escape from Minas Morgul is reconsidered and rewritten. I think that this further material belongs in fact to the same or much the same time as the primary text. There are various pointers to this. The suggestion found here that 'it could be Merry and Pippin that had adventure in Minas Morgul if Treebeard is cut out' shows that the fully formed narrative had not at any rate advanced beyond the Breaking of the Fellowship; and the chapter is still referred to as 'XXV', which carries the same implication (i.e. my father was still assuming the chapters 'XXI–XXIV' as outlined on pp. 329–30 and had not yet embarked on the writing of the 'western' adventures).

The text is written fairly legibly in ink, but towards the end becomes a pencilled scribble, here and there formidably difficult to make out.

Ch. XXV

Minas Morgul must be made more horrible. The usual 'goblin' stuff is not good enough here.

The Gate shaped like a gaping mouth with teeth and a window like an eye on each side. As Sam passes through he feels a horrible shudder.[32] There are two silent shapes sitting on either side as sentinels.

Substitute something of the following sort for p. [337].

The main outer gates were now closed. But a small door in the middle of one was open. (It faced south.) The tunnelled Gate-house was dark as night and the pale skylight showed up as a small patch at the end of a tunnel. As Sam and Frodo crept closer they saw or guessed the great ominous shape of the Sentinels on either side: still sitting soundless and unmoved: but from them there seemed to issue a nameless threat.

'Stay here!' whispered Frodo drawing Sam into the shadow of a wall not far from the gate. 'While I wear the Ring, I can understand much of the speech of the enemies, or of the thought behind their speech: I don't know which. I will go forward, and try and find out something. If I call out, come at a run: and get through the door if you can.'

'Nay!' said Sam, 'that won't do. If we have a fight at the gate, we might as well or better stay inside. We'd have the whole wasps' nest, orcs and bogeys and all, buzzing after us, before we'd gone a dozen yards: and they know these horrible mountains as well as I mind me of Bag-End. Swagger is the only hope, Mr. Frodo, begging your pardon.'

'Very well, my good Sam,' said Frodo, 'try swagger!'

Feeling as little like 'swagger' as ever in his life, Sam walked forward, as bold and unconcerned as he could manage to look, all shaking at the knees as he was, and with a queer tightening of his breath. Each step forward became more difficult. It was as if some will denying the passage was drawn like invisible ropes across his path. He felt the pressure of unseen eyes. It seemed an age before he passed under the gloom of the gate's arch, and he felt tired as if he had been swimming against a strong tide. The

Sentinels sat there: dark and still. They did not move their clawlike hands laid on their knees, they did not move their shrouded heads [*struck out:* staring stiffly] in which no faces could be seen; but Sam felt a sudden prickle in his skin, he sensed that they were alive and suddenly alert. As he came between them he seemed to shrink [and] shrivel, naked as an insect crawling to its hole under the eyes of gigantic birds. He came to the open door: just outside the path ran to a flight of stairs leading to the downward road. Only one step and he would be out – but he could not pass: it was as if the air before him had become stiff. He had to summon up his strength and his will. Like lead he lifted his foot and forced it slowly bit by bit over the threshold, on either side he felt the darkness leer and grin at him. Slowly he pressed his foot down, down. It touched the step outside: and then something seemed to snap. He stood fixed. He thought he heard a cry, but whether just beside him, or far away in some remote watchful tower he could not tell. There was a sudden clash of iron. An Orc ran out from the guard-room.

Frodo creeping warily behind was now also under the archway. He heard the guard cry out in harsh tones. 'Ho there: who are you, and what do you think you are doing?' He laid hold of Sam's cloak. Sam snarled angrily, but the trick did not work so well a second time. The guard held him. 'Closing-time is past, half an hour ago,' he growled. 'No one but the Lord's messengers are allowed in or out, and you know that. The door awaits the bringer of word from Baraddur, but it is not for any other.'

Of all this Sam understood only that he was forbidden to pass. He could not move forward: so he stepped suddenly back stepping on the feet of the Orc behind. Frodo saw the guard's hand go to the hilt of his scimitar. 'Hey, who are you stamping on?' said he. Sam prepared for battle. He turned, etc. as before.

[*Struck out:* An alternative would be to make the gate impassable. The alarm is sounded. The City is aroused. The Vulture (Black Rider) arrives in the main square. Frodo at once knows that Ring is useless. He feels almost discovered. Messenger says Ring is still in the town: he feels it.]

Alternative account.

Make light fade in the window as Sam and Frodo talk in the

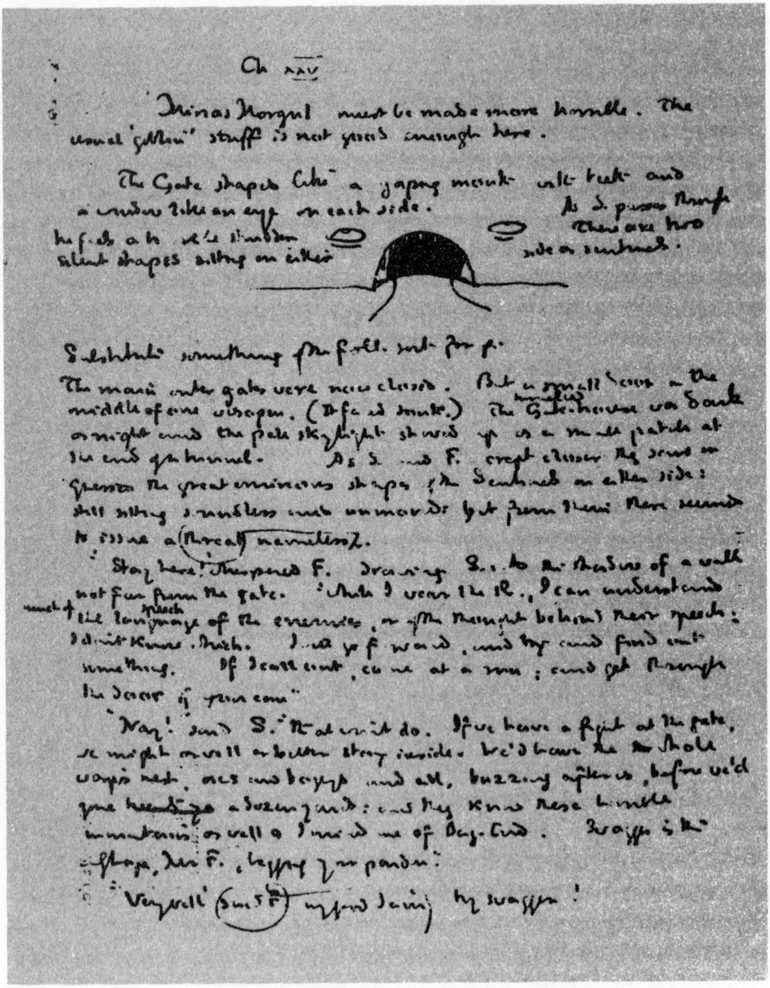

Sketch for the Gate of Minas Morgul.

Loathly Tower. They try the trick of getting an orc to open the door as twilight deepens. *No dressing up.* They creep out into the town. Something warns Frodo *not* to use the Ring. The elf-hoods prove better in the City of Sorcery than the Ring – the two hobbits (aided by some grace of Galadriel that went with the garments) pass along the streets like mist. The gate is closed – the sentinels described: three a side.[33]

The walls are high and if it were possible to get onto them unseen – it is not: the few ascents are guarded – they could not get down. They are trapped.

A cry from a watch tower. The waning moon rises in East. A dark shape flying out of the East, a black speck against clouds. Vulture bearing a Ringwraith settles in main square. The Ringwraith has come to take Frodo back to the Dark Tower. At that moment *boom*, the alarm is sounded from Loathly Tower. Ringwraith says Ring has not left City: he feels it. Hunt in town. Hairbreadth escape of hobbits. In spite of the Ringwraith a host of orcs assemble to scour mountains (? Frodo and Sam trap two orcs in an alley and take their cloaks and gear. ?) Pass out in rear of the company. Describe the reluctant feeling, and moveless sentinels. Even as they pass the sentinels stir: and give a fell, horrible, far-off cry. The moon is suddenly clouded. A fierce cold wind from East. Rain? The hobbits fling themselves flat among the rocks. Orcs pass over them. Hunt misses them because they go *towards* Mordor. The hunt goes West and North.

Now go on to describe the journey to Fiery Mountain. Footsteps come after them. Gollum has picked up trail.

Frodo and Sam journey by night down the slopes of Duath out into the dreadful waste of Gorgoroth.[34]

[The grey cloaks of Lothlórien must be made more magical and efficacious. 'Are these garments magical?' asks Frodo. 'We do not know what you mean by magical,' said they. 'They have virtues: for they are elvish.' They were green and grey: their property is to blend perfectly with all *natural* surroundings: leaves, boughs, grass, water, stone. Unless a full light of sun was on them, and the wearer was moving or set against the sky, they were not invisible, but *unnoticeable*.][35]

Far away they saw the underside of the Mountains stained red with the glow of Amarthon [*written above:* Dolamarth]: Mount Doom: the Mountain of Fire.[36] There is a constant rumble of thunder. Frodo feels the Eye. They come down a long ravine opening onto Gorgoroth beyond the south-east end of Kirith Ungol: it is end of road from Barad-dûr to Morgul.[37] Great hideous cavern[38] pillars. They peer [?out ?about] in the grey day over Gorgoroth. Mount Doom is smoking and burning to left. Black cloud lies over Baraddur. Millions of birds – [?led by vultures]: plain seems crawling with insects – a great host assembled – all sweeping out towards Kirith. By evening all plain is silent and empty. Cinders fall on plain. Moon rises late. Very dark. They begin the perilous crossing. Rustle of following feet. Journey all night.

Distances are rather too large – it would be eased if Orcs took Frodo to [?East] Guard Tower of R... – Loath and Grim [*written above:* Fell and Dire]. They could then see easier the host and would not have to cross Kirith Ungol.[39]

[*Struck out:* It could be Merry and Pippin that had adventure in Minas Morgul if Treebeard is cut out.][40]

From Dire-castle Gorgos (and Nargos) it would be only 70 miles. They could creep round edge of Eredlithui.[41]

Sam must fall out somehow. Stumble and break leg: thinks it is a crack in ground – really Gollum. [?Makes ?Make] Frodo go on alone.

Frodo toils up Mount Doom. Earth quakes, the ground is hot. There is a narrow path winding up. Three fissures. Near summit there is Sauron's Fire-well. An opening in side of mountain leads into a chamber the floor of which is split asunder by a cleft.[42]

Frodo turns and looks North-west, sees the dust of battle. Faint sound of horn. This is Windbeam the Horn of Elendil blown only in extremity.[43]

Birds circle over. Feet behind.

It is then at night before ascent of Mount Doom that Frodo sees the lone eye, like a window that does not move and yet searches in Baraddur.

Description of Baraddur seen afar.

I give here the latter part of a time-scheme of this period which covers the events of this outline plot. For the chronological structure in this scheme see p. 367 ('scheme I').

Dec. 25   Reach Tolbrandir in evening.
    26   Flight of Frodo.
Jan. 3   Gollum slips away.
    5   Frodo, Sam [*struck out:* and Gollum] reach Kirith Ungol.
    6   Frodo captured.
    8   Sam rescues Frodo in [Minas Morgul >] Gorgos.

9   Sam and Frodo journey in Duath.
10   Sam and Frodo see host in Gorgoroth and lie hid.
    [*These two entries changed to read:* Jan. 9, 10, 11 Sam
    and Frodo journey in Eredlithui (see hosts going to war).]
12, 13   Ascent of Mount Doom.
14   [?Horns] . . . Fall of Mordor.
15   Victory and return to Minas Tirith.
    [*Added:* Jan. 25 Reach Minas Tirith. Jan. 26 Great Feast.]

Notable points in this time-scheme are the corroboration of the statement in the text that Sam had been Ringbearer for two days (see p. 334 and note 30); the change in the place of Frodo's imprisonment from Minas Morgul to Gorgos (see p. 344 and notes 39, 41); and the mention of the great feast that followed the victory (cf. p. 212).

NOTES

1   On the back of the first page of this outline are some rough workings for revision of *The Lay of Aotrou and Itroun*, which was completed in its original form in 1930. This stray page perhaps shows my father turning to it again at this time. It was ultimately published in greatly revised form, to which these workings were moving, in 1945.

2   Cf. the outline *(c)* for 'Farewell to Lórien', p. 269: 'Arrows from East shore as they pass down river?'

3   *Tolharn* and *Tollernen* were passing replacements of *Tolondren*. Subsequently *Stoneait* (*ait* 'islet', = *eyot*) and *Tollernen* were struck out in pencil (all other changes in the opening section being made in ink) and replaced by *Eregon* (= *Stone pinnacle*). On *Eregon* see p. 323 note 12.

4   Sarn Gebir and Nomen's land (Nomenlands) emerged in the course of the writing of 'Farewell to Lórien' (pp. 281, 283).

5   *It is ill to be alone on the east side of the River*: this was left unchanged when the text immediately preceding was altered to the story that Frodo and Sam did not cross to the east bank but climbed the hill on the island where they camped. – In the outline *(c)* to 'Farewell to Lórien' (p. 269) it is told that 'They' crossed to the east bank and went up into the hills 'to look around', where 'They' may be the whole Company or Frodo and Sam only.

6   *Eredwethion* 'Mountains of Shadow' is derived from *The Silmarillion*.

7   With this scene compare the previous Plot (p. 208):
    Boromir takes Frodo apart and talks to him. Begs to see Ring again. Evil enters into his heart and he tries to daunt Frodo and

then to take it by force. Frodo is obliged to slip it on to escape him. (What does he see then – cloud all round him getting nearer and many fell voices in air?)

In that Plot there is no mention of the Eye – but cf. the much earlier outline dated August 1939 (VI.381): 'Horrible feeling of an Eye searching for him'.

8   On the name *Dantruinel* for Rauros see pp. 285, 316.

9   It seems very likely that the reason for shifting the place where the Company camped to the west bank of the river and making the island inaccessible was to allow Merry and Pippin to become separated and lost – a development that had already been conceived in the previous Plot (see note 16).

10 I take these words, set in inverted commas, to be Boromir's, referring deceitfully to Frodo's having put on the Ring.

11 The account of Sam's tracking of Frodo that follows is developed from that in the previous Plot (p. 208):

The search. Sam is lost. He tries to track Frodo and comes on Gollum. He follows Gollum and Gollum leads him to Frodo.

Frodo hears following feet. And flies. But Sam comes up too to his surprise. The two are too much for Gollum. Gollum is *daunted* by Frodo – who has a power over him as Ring-bearer....

Gollum pleads for forgiveness and feigns reform. They make him lead them through the Dead Marshes.

12 Sam is now on the east side of Anduin, and the boat 'knocking against the bank' is the boat in which Frodo has crossed.

13 This paragraph ('Gollum was so intent on the trail...') evidently replaced the story that preceded, although that was not struck out.

14 Kirith Ungol was at this time the name of the great pass leading into Mordor in the North-west (pp. 283, 285, and Map III on p. 309).

15 At some time later my father struck it all out and wrote in pencil:

Steep place where Frodo has to climb a precipice. Sam goes first so that if Frodo falls he will knock Sam down first. They see Gollum come down by moonlight *like a fly*.

This is where the story in *The Two Towers* (IV.1, 'The Taming of Smeagol', p. 219) first appears.

16 Cf. the previous Plot, p. 210. It is seen from the synopsis that immediately follows (pp. 329–30) of the chapter telling what happened to Merry and Pippin that my father had still no idea that anything more untoward had happened to them.

17 This passage remains virtually unchanged in substance from the previous Plot (p. 211).

18 At a later stage my father pencilled in various developments to Chapters XXII and XXIII (as renumbered). The synopsis of the

former he altered thus: 'Black orcs of Misty Mountains capture
Merry and Pippin, bear them to Isengard. But the orcs are
attacked by the Rohiroth on borders of Fangorn, and in the
confusion Merry and Pippin escape unnoticed.' Also added here
was 'Trotter is led astray by [?finding] orc-prints. He follows the
orcs believing Frodo, Sam, etc. captured. He meets Gandalf.' To
'What happened to Gimli and Legolas' he added: 'Went with
Trotter to rescue Merry and Pippin.'

19 Noted beside this sentence: s G – f asleep. f G – s asleep. s f – G
asleep.

20 The origin of this passage is seen in the earlier Plot (p. 209):
'There is a ravine, a spiders' glen, they have to pass at entrance to
Gorgoroth. Gollum gets spiders to put spell of sleep on Frodo.
Sam drives them off. But cannot wake him.' Kirith Ungol was not
yet its name when that was written: there is mention in that
outline of the Gap of Gorgoroth, clearly the pass leading into
Mordor (pp. 208, 213), but the words 'a ravine they have to pass'
perhaps suggest that the 'spiders' glen' led off the Gap. In the
present Plot, however, Kirith Ungol, ravine of spiders, is the pass
itself.

21 It was no doubt put in when the story had gone somewhat past
this point, since it is avowedly narrative in form and not outline
(present tense).

22 This sentence is enclosed in square brackets in the original.

23 At the top of the page is written: 'All Sauron's folk, however,
know that if Ringbearer is taken he is to be guarded as their life,
but otherwise to be untouched and undespoiled, and brought
intact to the Lord.' This was struck out.

24 On the Sea of Rhûn or Rhûnaer see p. 307.

25 This passage is enclosed in square brackets in the original.

26 For the site of Minas Morgul see Map III on p. 309. The Orcs
appear to have come from there, in view of 'Sam gathers that they
are going to Minas Morgul: since they are not allowed to leave
their post'; and 'the path led up into the mountains' suggests that
the way to Minas Morgul was by a track leading upwards out of
Kirith Ungol; hence Sam sees 'from below' the Orcs entering the
City.

27 Unless my father had decided to restore the original conception of
Minas *Anor* in the East becoming Minas Morgul, and Minas *Ithil*
in the West becoming Minas Tirith, which seems exceedingly
improbable, this can only be a momentary confusion. But it
occurs again: p. 366 note 19.

28 This passage is enclosed in square brackets in the original.

29 *mithered*: 'confused, bewildered'. My father often used this
English dialect word, though as I recollect always in the form
moithered; but *mithered* is recorded from Staffordshire and

Warwickshire and the neighbouring counties of the English midlands.

30   This sentence is enclosed in square brackets in the original. Two days seems a very long time to have elapsed since Sam took the Ring from Frodo in Kirith Ungol, and is by no means suggested in the narrative; on the other hand, on Map III (p. 309) Minas Morgul was at least 30 miles from the eastern edge of the Mountains of Shadow at Kirith Ungol. See also the time scheme on pp. 344–5.

31   It should be emphasized that the fact of its being written at this stage in the history of *The Lord of the Rings*, and not later, is clear and certain.

32   This refers of course to Sam's entry into Minas Morgul, alone.

33   Cf. 'The Tower of Cirith Ungol' in *The Return of the King*, p. 178: 'They were like great figures seated upon thrones. Each had three joined bodies, and three heads facing outward, and inward, and across the gateway. The heads had vulture-faces, and on their great knees were laid clawlike hands.' – A little diagrammatic sketch is included in the manuscript at this point:

34   *Duath* (replacing *Eredwethion*, p. 325) is the name of the Mountains of Shadow on the First Map and on my map made in 1943; my father added *Ephel* before *Duath* on both maps subsequently (pp. 309–10). – The sentence was changed in pencil to read: 'Frodo and Sam journey by night among the slopes and ravines N. of Duath towards the dreadful waste of Gorgoroth.'

35   The brackets are in the original. This notable passage is the origin of the much enlarged description of the cloaks of Lothlórien which first appears as an addition to the fair copy of 'Farewell to Lórien' (p. 285), though expressed in a wholly different way. The question 'Are these garments magical?', here asked by Frodo, was then given to Merry, and finally (FR p. 386) to Pippin ('Are these magic cloaks?').

36   The first devising of an elvish name for Mount Doom (later *Amon Amarth*).

37   My father first wrote here: 'They come down a long ravine opening on Kirith Un(gol)', striking out this name at once and writing instead 'opening onto Gorgoroth', etc. It is hard to be sure, but it seems likely that he saw a path climbing up to Minas Morgul out of Kirith Ungol (the pass into Mordor), by which Frodo was taken, and another more southerly approach, a road running westwards from the Dark Tower and climbing to Minas

Morgul by the 'long ravine' down which Sam and Frodo made
their escape (see Map III, p. 309).

38 This word is clearly written *cavern*, not *carven*.

39 This short paragraph is very hard to read and not easy to interpret, but at least it is clear that here is the first suggestion of a
doubt that it was to Minas Morgul that Frodo was taken. The
word I have given as *East* begins *Ea* but does not look at all like
East; yet that seems appropriate to the sense (see further note 41).
The name of the tower might be *Rame* or *Raine*, among other
possibilities. The words 'They would not have to cross Kirith
Ungol' are at first sight puzzling, since it has just been said that
they emerged from the long ravine 'beyond the south-east end of
Kirith Ungol'; but I think that my father meant that they would
not have to cross the open plain between the Mountains of
Shadow and the Ash Mountains (Ered Lithui), whether this be
called Kirith Ungol or Gorgoroth at that point.

40 See p. 339; and for an earlier suggestion that Merry and Pippin
might find themselves in Mordor see p. 211.

41 On the First Map there are two small circles on either side of
Kirith Ungol (on my redrawing, square P 15 on Map II, p. 305).
These reappear on my 1943 map as two small towers. On neither
map are they named; but it seems clear that they represent a
western and an eastern guard tower – presumably the Nargos
and Gorgos named here (cf. 'There are Orc guard-towers on
either side of Gorgoroth', p. 208). The words 'From Dire-castle
Gorgos (and Nargos) it would be only 70 miles' mean, I think,
'From the eastern tower Gorgos (and for the matter of that from
the western tower Nargos also) it was only 70 miles to Mount
Doom.'

42 The three fissures and Sauron's well of fire appear in the earlier
Plot (p. 209), but this is the first glimpse of the Sammath Naur.

43 *Windbeam*: if this name occurs elsewhere in my father's writings
I have not found it, except in the Last Letter of Father Christmas,
where he calls it the Great Horn, and says that he has not had to
blow it for over four hundred years (cf. 'only in extremity' here)
and that its sound carries as far as the North Wind blows. (Cf.
Old English *bēme* (*bēam*) 'trumpet'.)

XVII
THE GREAT RIVER

It has been seen (pp. 324, 330) that having written an outline of the story from the departure from Lórien to the 'Scattering of the Company' at 'Tollernen' my father decided that the first element in the outline, 'The Company sets off from Tongue', should in fact form the conclusion to Chapter XX ('Farewell to Lórien'), and XXI should take up with 'They are attacked with arrows'.

As I have mentioned (p. 283), the original draft for the last section of 'Farewell to Lórien' (i.e. 'The Company sets off from Tongue') was written in ink in a clear script with little hesitation. That draft section ends with the words 'End of Ch. XX', showing that the chapter-arrangement just referred to had already been devised. The character-istic very pale ink used for this section was also used for the text 'The Story Foreseen from Lórien' and for the first part of the new chapter XXI: the three texts have a strong general likeness, and were obviously written at the same time.

The draft of the last section of 'Farewell to Lórien' ends halfway down a page, and is followed by 'XXI: The Scattering of the Company'; at this stage my father assumed that the narrative outlined on pp. 324–8, 329 (i.e. excluding the story of Sam's tracking of Frodo) would constitute a single chapter. For the journey down the River to 'Tollernen' he had set down no more in the way of event than 'They are attacked with arrows.' I give now the opening draft of the new chapter as it was first written.[1]

Sam woke him. He was lying in a bed of blankets and furs under tall grey-stemmed trees near the river bank. The grey of morning was dim among the bare branches. Gimli was busy with a small fire near at hand. He had slept the first night of their river journey away. They started again before the day was broad. Not that most of the Company were eager to hurry southwards: they were content that the decision which they must make when they came to Rauros and the Isle of Eregon[2] lay yet some days ahead, and still less did they wish to run swiftly into the perils that certainly lay beyond, whatever course they took, but Trotter felt that the time was urgent and that willing or not they should hasten forward.

As the second day of their voyage wore on the lands changed slowly: trees thinned and then failed: on the East bank to their left, long formless slopes stretched up and away towards the sky; brown they looked as if a fire had passed over them, leaving no living thing of green; an unfriendly waste without even a withered tree or a bold stone to break the emptiness. They were come to the Brown Lands, the Withered Wold that lay in a vast desolation between Dol Dúghul in Southern Mirkwood and the hills of Sarn-Gebir: what pestilence of war or fell deed of the Lord of Mordor had so blasted all that region they did not know.[3] Upon the west bank to their right the land was treeless and quite flat, but green: there were forests of reeds of great height in places that shut out the view as the little boats went rustling by along their fluttering borders: the great withered flowering heads bent in the light cold airs hissing softly and waving like funeral plumes. Here and there in open spaces they could see across the wide rolling meads hills far away, or on the edge of sight a dark line where still the southernmost phalanx of the Misty Mountains marched.

'You are looking out across the great pastures of Rohan, the Riddermark, land of the Horsemasters,' said Trotter; 'but in these evil days they do not dwell nigh the river or ride often to its shores. Anduin is wide, yet the orc-bows will with ease shoot an arrow across the stream.'

The hobbits looked from bank to bank uneasily. If before the trees had seemed hostile, as if harbouring secret dangers, now they felt that they were too naked: afloat in little open boats in the midst of wide bare land, on a river that was the boundary of war. As they went on the feeling of insecurity grew upon them. The river broadened and grew shallow: bleak stony beaches lay upon the east, there were gravel shoals in the water and they had to steer carefully. The Brownlands rose into bleak wolds over which flowed a chill air from the East. Upon the other side the meads had become low rolling downs of grey grass, a land of fen and tussock. They shivered thinking of the lawns and fountains, the clear sun and gentle rain of Lothlórien: there was little speech and no laughter among them. Each was busy with his own thoughts. Sam had long since made up his mind that though boats were maybe not as dangerous as he had been brought up to believe, they were far more uncomfortable. He was cramped and miserable, having nothing to do but stare at the winter lands crawling by and the dark grey water, for the

Company used the paddles mainly for steering, and in any case they would not have trusted Sam with a paddle. Merry and Pippin in the middle boat were ill at ease. [*Added and then struck out:* Merry was at the stern, facing Sam and steering.] Boromir sat muttering to himself, sometimes biting his nails as if some restlessness or doubt consumed him. Often Pippin who sat in the prow, looking back, caught a queer gleam in his eye when he peered forward gazing at the boat in front where Frodo sat.

So the time passed until the end of the sixth [> seventh] day. The banks were still bare, but on both sides on the slopes above them bushes were scattered, behind and further south ridges with twisted fir-trees could be glimpsed: they were drawing near the grey hill country of Sarn-Gebir: the southern border of Wilderland, beyond which lay the Nomanland and the foul marshes that lay for many leagues before the passes of Mordor. High in the air there were flocks of dark birds. Trotter looked at them with disquiet.

'I fear we have been too slow and overbold,' he said. 'Maybe we have come too far by day, and ere this we should have taken to journeying between dusk and dawn and lain hidden in the day.'

He stayed his boat with his paddle, and when the others came up he spoke to them, counselling that they should go on into the night, and put off their rest until night was old and dawn was at hand. 'And if we make another two or three leagues,' said he, 'we shall come, if I am right in my memories, to Sarn Gebir, where the river begins to run in deep channels: there maybe we shall find better shelter and more secrecy.'

Already twilight was about them. The hobbits at any rate had been hoping soon for the warmth of a fire to their cold feet, and the feel of solid earth beneath them. But there seemed no place in that houseless country which invited them to halt; and a cold drowsiness was on them, numbing thought. They made no answer, yes or no. Trotter drove his paddle in the water and led them on again. [*Added:* The stars leapt out above. The sky [was] clear and cold. It was nearly night when][4] Just ahead there loomed up rocks in the midst of the stream, nearer to the west bank. To the east there was a wider channel, and that way they turned: but they found the current swift. In the dusk they could see pale foam and water beating against the rocks upon the right hand.

'This is an evil time of day to pass through such a dangerous

reach,' said Boromir. 'Hey Trotter,' he cried, cupping his hands
and calling above the noise of the waters to the boat ahead – it
was already too dark to see whether it was far or near. 'Hey!' he
called. 'Not this way tonight!'

'No indeed,' said Trotter, and they saw that he had turned his
boat and had come back almost alongside without their seeing
him. 'No: I did not know we had come so far yet: the Anduin
flows faster than I reckoned. The rapids of Pensarn[5] are ahead.
They are not very long nor very fierce, yet too dangerous to
venture on in the dark for those who know the Great River little
or only from tales. See,' he said, 'the current has flung us right
over to the east shore: in a little we shall be on the shoals. Let us
turn and go back to the western side, above the rocks.'

Even as he spoke there was a twanging, and arrows whistled
over and among them. One smote Frodo between the shoulders
but fell back, foiled by the hidden coat of mail; another passed
through Trotter's hair; and a third stood fast in the gunwale of
the middle boat close by Merry's hand.

'To the west bank!' shouted Boromir and Trotter together.
They leaned forward straining at the paddles – even Sam now
took a hand, but it was not so easy. The current was flowing
strong. Each one expected at any minute to feel the sting of a
blackfeathered orc-arrow. But it was now grown very dark,
dark even for the keen night-eyes of goblins; goblins were on the
bank, they did not doubt. When they had come into midstream
as far as they could judge, and out of the swirl of waters running
into the narrow channel, Legolas laid down his paddle, and
lifting the bow he had brought from Lórien strung it, and
turned, peering back into the gloom. Across the water there
came shrill cries; but he could see nothing. The enemy were
shooting wildly now and few arrows came near the boats: it was
grown very dark: there was not even a grey glimmer on the face
of the river, only here and there the broken twinkle reflecting a
misty star.

As he gazed into the blackness away east the clouds broke
and the white rind of the new moon appeared riding slowly up
the sky; [but its faint light did little to illumine the further
shore.][6] Sam looked up at it in wonder.[7] Even as he did so a
dark shape, like a cloud yet not a cloud, low and ominous, for a
moment shut off the thin crescent and winged its way towards
them, until it appeared as a great winged shape black against the
dark heaven.[8] Fierce voices greeted it from across the water.

Frodo felt a sudden chill about his heart, and a cold like the memory of an old wound in his shoulder: he crouched down in the boat.

Suddenly the great bow of Legolas sang. He heard an arrow whistle / whine. He looked up. The winged shape swerved: there was a harsh croaking cry and it seemed to fall, vanishing down into the darkness of the eastern shore; the sky seemed clean again. They heard a tumult as of many voices murmuring and lamenting [*written above:* cursing], and then silence. No more arrows came towards them.

'Praised be the bow of Galadriel and the keen eye of Legolas!' said Gimli. 'That was a mighty shot in the dark.'

'But what it hit who can say,' said Boromir.

'I cannot,' said Gimli. 'Yet I liked that shape as little as the shadow of the Balrog of Moria.'

'It was not a Balrog,' said Frodo, still shivering. 'I think it was . . .' He did not finish.

'You think what?' asked Boromir quickly.

'I do not know,' said Frodo. 'Whatever it was its fall seems to have dismayed the enemy.'

'So it seems,' said Trotter. 'Yet where they are, and how many, or what they will do next, we do not know. This night must be watchful!'

At last the boats were brought to the western bank again. Here they moored them close inshore. They did not lie on the land that night, but remained in the boats with weapons close to hand. One sat alert and vigilant watching either bank while the other [? *read* others] dozed uneasily.

Sam[9] looked at the moon again, slipping down now swiftly to the horizon. 'It is very strange,' he murmured drowzily. 'The moon I suppose does not change his courses in Wilderland? Then I must be wrong in my reckoning. If you remember, the old moon was at its end as we lay on the flet up in that tree.[10] Well now I can't remember how long we were in that country: it was certainly three nights, and I seem to remember a good many more – but I am certain sure it was not a month. Yet here we are: seven days from Lórien and up pops a New Moon. Why, anyone would think we had come straight from Nimrodel without stopping a night or seeing Caras Galadon. Funny it seems.'

'And that Sam is probably about the truth of it,' said Trotter.

'Whether we were in the past or the future or in a time that does
not pass, I cannot say: but not I think till Silverlode bore us back
to Anduin did we return to the stream of time that flows
through mortal lands to the Great Sea. At least, so I guess: but
maybe I dream and talk nonsense. Yet do either of you
remember seeing any moon in Lórien, old or young? I remember
only stars by night and sun by day.'[11]

The text, becoming ragged at the end, now peters out in pencilled
notes for its continuation:

In morning Trotter and Legolas go forward to find path. They
lie hid among rocks all day and at evening laboriously cart their
boats to end of the rapids. (Hear the sound as they pass.) No
sign on far shore. Below rapids stream is soon quiet and deep
again – but less broad. They creep along the west bank by night.
They pass into the gullies of Sarn Gebir. Pinewoods. About
dawn on 10th day come to Eregon [later > Tol Brandor or -ir]
and hear roar and [?foam] of Rauros. Inaccessible isle high
peak many birds.[12]

In the journey down Anduin at this stage the chronology differed by
one day from that in FR, for the attack at the head of the rapids took
place at the end of the seventh day (p. 352), not of the eighth (FR pp.
400–1), and much detail remained to be changed or added: notably
the incident of Gollum, the 'log with eyes', was absent. This story was
written on a separate sheet while the drafting of the chapter was still in
progress, and was immediately achieved in the final form at almost all
points. Some of the Company were sleeping that night on the eyot and
some in the boats; and after Frodo had seen Gollum's eyes and had put
his hand on the hilt of Sting the original text continues:

Immediately they [the eyes] went out, and there was a soft
splash and a dark shape shot away downstream into the night.
Nothing else occurred, until the first grey of dawn peeped in the
East. Trotter awoke on the eyot and came down to the boats.
But Frodo now knew that Sam had not been deceived; and also
that he must warn Trotter.
'So you know about our little footpad, do you? . . .

Primary drafting from the point reached (the discussion of Time in
Lórien) is of an extreme roughness, some of it scribbled faintly
between the lines of the candidates' writing on examination scripts,
and it is not entirely complete and consecutive. In this case the fair
copy manuscript, following immediately on the primary drafting, is

the first complete text, and it is most convenient to turn now to this manuscript.

In this version Chapter XXI bore a succession of titles, all of them pencilled in subsequently: 'Southward'; 'The Company is Scattered'; 'Sarn Gebir'; 'Breaking of the Fellowship'; and finally 'The Great River' – this last not struck out, and obviously arising when my father had decided that his original ideas for XXI had so expanded as to require two chapters to fulfil the narrative. As usual, in point of expression the fair copy advances very largely to the form in FR, although a good deal of change in respect of the actual narrative had still to come.

To the original opening of the chapter (p. 350) my father made the following alteration and addition on the manuscript of the draft:

Sam woke him. He was lying in a bed of blankets and furs under tall grey-stemmed trees near the bank of the Great River, in a corner of quiet woodland where a small stream (the Limlight) flowed in from the western mountains.

This is the first mention of the Limlight in the texts. In the fair copy the chapter opens:

Frodo was roused by Sam. He found that he was lying, well wrapped, under tall grey-skinned trees in a quiet corner of the woodlands. [Beside them a stream ran down from the western mountains far away and joined the Great River close by their camp] on the western bank of the Great River Anduin.

The sentence I have bracketed was struck out as soon as written. That their first night camp on the journey down the River was beside the inflow of Limlight agrees with maps IV^B and IV^C (p. 317), where the Limlight, here first shown, joins Anduin not far south of Silverlode (see Map II, square M 12); on map IV^D the confluence is much further south (p. 319).

Where the draft has 'Rauros and the Isle of Eregon' (p. 350) the new text has 'Rauros and the Isle' (changed later to 'the Tindrock Isle', as in FR). Trotter's policy of letting them drift with the stream as they wished appears; but the chronology remains here as in the draft: 'Nonetheless they saw no sign of any[13] enemy that day. The dull grey hours passed without event. As this second day of their voyage wore on, the lands changed slowly...' The 'Withered Wold' of the draft becomes 'the withered wolds' (and was then struck out). The flight of the black swans is still absent.

Trotter now speaks of the latitude and climate, the Bay of Belfalas, and their distance from the Shire – but here he first said 'I doubt if you are much more than sixty leagues south of the Sarn Ford at the southern end of your Shire', this being changed at once to the reading of FR; and he says that 'ere long we shall come to the mouth of the Limlight' (see above),[14] defining the Limlight, as in FR, as the north boundary of Rohan. But he says here 'Of old all that lay between Limlight and Entwash belonged to the Horsemasters' (FR: 'all that lay between Limlight and the White Mountains belonged to the Rohirrim').

In the next part of the chapter (after the episode of Gollum in the river) the story advances to the form in FR, but it was still at the end of the seventh day of the journey, not of the eighth, that they came to the rapids, and there is no mention at this point of the weather, or of the New Moon, which in FR (p. 400) was first seen on the seventh night. Though the bird-haunted cliffs of Sarn Gebir and the flocks of birds circling high above are described in the same words as in FR (p. 401) there is no mention of the eagle seen far off in the western sky. Following the mention of the birds, the new version continues thus:

Trotter had glanced often at them doubtfully, wondering if Gollum had been up to some mischief. But now it was dark: the East was overcast, but in the West many stars were shining.

After they had been paddling for about an hour, Trotter told Sam to lie forward in the boat and keep a sharp look-out ahead. 'We shall soon come to the gates of Sarn-Gebir,' he said; 'and the river is difficult and dangerous there, if I remember rightly. It runs in deep swift channels under overhanging cliffs, and there are many rocks and eyots in the stream. But I do not know these reaches, for I have never journeyed by water in these parts before. We must halt early tonight, if we can, and go on by daylight.'

It was close on midnight, and they had been drifting for a while, resting after a long spell of paddling, when suddenly Sam cried out.

After Boromir's shouted remonstrance ('This is a bad time of day to shoot the rapids!') Trotter, struggling to back and turn his boat, said to Frodo: 'I am out of my reckoning. I didn't know we had come so far. We must have passed the gates of Sarn-Gebir in the dark. The Rapids of Pensarn must be just ahead' (the last two sentences were crossed out, probably immediately). There is no indication here of what 'the gates of Sarn-Gebir' might be (see p. 359).

The attack by Orcs from the east bank, and the struggle to get the boats back to the west bank, follows the draft pretty closely, with some changed or added detail: an arrow passed through Trotter's hood, not his hair; Frodo 'lurched forward with a cry'. The weather is changed from the obscure statements in the draft (note 6): the clouds in the east mentioned earlier had now almost entirely covered the sky, and so 'it was very dark, dark even for the night-eyes of orcs' as they paddled the boats back. The same is said of the New Moon 'riding slowly up the sky' in 'a sudden break in the cloud-cover away in the East' as in the draft (see note 7); here it is seen 'passing behind dark isles of cloud and out into black pools of night.' In FR (p. 401) it had set hours before.

Sam's remarks about Time in Lothlórien remain almost exactly as in the draft (p. 354), as does Trotter's reply (in FR given to Frodo), except that he now says (as does Frodo in FR): 'In that land, maybe, we were in some time that elsewhere has long gone by.' Then Frodo speaks:

'The power of the Lady was on us,' said Frodo. 'There are days and nights and seasons in Lothlórien; but while she holds the ring, the world grows no older in her realm.'

'That should not have been said,' muttered Trotter, half rising and looking towards the other boats; 'not outside Lórien, not even to me.'[15]

The warm and foggy morning that succeeded the night of the attack and the argument between Aragorn and Boromir about the course to follow were roughly sketched in initial drafting, where the conversation proceeds thus:

'I do not see why we should pass the rapids or follow this cursed River any further,' said Boromir. 'If Pensarn lies before us, then we can abandon these cockles and strike westward, and so come round the east shoulders of Sarn-Gebir and cross the Entwash into my own land of Ondor.'

'We can, if we make for Minas Tirith,' said Trotter. 'But that is not yet agreed. And even so such a course is perhaps more perilous than it seems. The land is flat and shelterless south and east [read west] of Sarn-Gebir, and the [?first] ford over Entwash is a great way west.[16] Since the Enemy took ... Osgiliath that land may be full of foes: what do we know of events of late in Rohan or in Ondor?'

'Yet here the Enemy marches all along the east bank,' said Boromir. 'And when you come to Rauros what will you do? You must then either turn back hitherward, or cross the hills of Gebir and land in the marshes, and still have the Entwash to cross.'

'The River is at least a path that cannot be missed. In the vale of Entwash fog is a mortal peril. I would not abandon the boats until we must,' said Trotter. 'And I have a fancy that in some high place above the Falls we may be able to see some sign that shall direct us.'

That a 'high place' would be the scene of a decisive moment in the unfolding of the story had already been conceived: the summit of the island in the River whence Frodo looked out (p. 324); but there is no suggestion in Trotter's words here that this 'high place' would be an ancient post of the men of Ondor.

In the fair copy manuscript Boromir objects: 'But the Enemy holds the eastern bank. And even if you pass the gates of Gebir, and come unmolested to the Tindrock, what will you do then? Climb down from the hills and land in the marshes?' Here, the 'gates of Gebir' are the later Gates of Argonath; thus the earlier references (p. 357), where Trotter places the 'gates' before the rapids, had already been rejected.

Of Trotter's reply to Boromir's scoffing question there are three forms: a draft text in pencil taking up at this point, and two versions in the fair copy manuscript. The first version in the manuscript has Trotter reply:

'Say rather, climb down from the hills to Rauros-foot and then take boat again, and hope to slip unseen up the mouths of Entwash – if we go to Minas Tirith. Do you choose to forget the ancient path, Boromir, and the high seat upon Tol-Brandir, that were made in the days of Valandil?[17] I at least have a mind to stand in that high place before I decide my course. There maybe we shall see some sign that will direct us.'

This version of Trotter's reply was struck out, and the pencilled draft (which continues on for some distance) seems to have been written at this point. This draft begins:

'No,' said Trotter. 'Do you choose to forget, Boromir, the North Stair, and the high seat upon Tol-Brandir that were made in the days of Isildur? I at least have a mind to stand in that high place again before I decide my course. There maybe we shall see some sign that will guide us. Thence we [may] perhaps descend by the ancient way to Rauros-foot and take again to the water; and those who make for Minas Tirith may slip unseen up the mouths of Entwash.'

Finally, the second version written in the manuscript is as in FR (p. 406), but still with 'in the days of Isildur' for 'in the days of the great kings', and the high seat is still upon the isle – which is here Tol-Brandor for Tol-Brandir of the previous versions. The isle therefore was not inaccessible; and this is puzzling, for the inaccessibility of Tol Brandir is found both in the outline given on p. 328 and in the preliminary draft material for the present chapter (p. 355).

Trotter's words before he and Legolas set off into the fog to find a path take this form (and are very similar in the draft):

'No road was ever made along this bank by the men of Ondor: for even in their great days their realm did not reach beyond Sarn-Gebir, and the high seat upon the Tindrock was their northmost watchtower. Yet there must be some path, or the remains of one; for light boats used to journey out of Wilderland down to Osgiliath; and still did so, until Sauron returned to Mordor.'

'But he has returned,' said Boromir; 'and if you go forward, you are likely to meet some peril, whether you find a path or no.'

The story of the exploration made by Trotter and Legolas, their return, the portage of the boats and baggage, and the departure of the Company next morning, reaches in the fair copy virtually the text of FR, with *Pensarn* for *Sarn Gebir* as the name of the rapids and the *Gates of Sarn-Gebir* for the *Gates of Argonath*. From painfully difficult writing the original description of the Pillars of the Kings can be extracted out of the initial drafting, of which I give the following as an example:

The great pillars seemed to rise up like giants before him as the river whirled him like a leaf towards them. Then he saw that [they] were carved, or had been carved many ages ago, and still preserved through the suns and rains of many forgotten years the likenesses that had been hewn upon them. Upon great pedestals founded in the deep water stood two great kings of stone gazing through blurred eyes northwards. The left hand of each was raised beside his head palm outwards in gesture of [?warning] and refusal: in each right hand there was a sword. On each head there was a crumbling crown and helm. There was still a power in these silent wardens of a long-vanished kingdom.

In the fair copy the text of FR was almost reached, through a good deal of correction as the manuscript was being written.

Trotter's words as they passed through the chasm (' "Fear not!" said a strange voice behind him . . .') are exactly as in FR (p. 409), except in two notable respects: 'In the stern sat Elfstone son of Elfhelm' – a decisive demonstration of the correctness of the view (p. 277) that *Elfstone* had reappeared and supplanted *Ingold*; and 'Under their shadow nought has Eldamir son of Eldakar son of Valandil to fear.'[18] It seems very improbable indeed that some other Valandil is meant and not the son of Isildur: only shortly before Valandil has been named in a draft ('in the days of Valandil', p. 359 and note 17, where the text immediately replacing this has 'in the days of Isildur'), and in the corresponding passage to the present in FR Aragorn calls himself 'son of Arathorn of the House of Valandil Isildur's son'. But if this Valandil is the son of Isildur, then at this stage Trotter/Elfstone/ Aragorn was the great-grandson of Isildur; and what then are we to make of the Pillars of the Kings, carved *many ages ago*, preserved through the suns and rains of *many forgotten years*, the silent wardens of *a long-vanished kingdom*? How can Frodo's amazement at the Council of Elrond that Elrond should remember the array of the Last Alliance ('But I thought the fall of Gilgalad was *many ages ago*', p. 110) be reconciled to a matter of four generations of mortal Men? And Gandalf had said to Frodo at Rivendell (p. 105 note 3) that 'he is Aragorn son of Kelegorn, *descended through many fathers* from Isildur the son of Elendil.' For the moment, at any rate, I can cast no light on this.[19]

After the description of the Pillars of the Kings there is no further initial drafting, and the earliest, or earliest extant, text is the fair copy manuscript, in which the conclusion of the chapter 'The Great River' in FR is very closely approached. Trotter, so called throughout the chapter until he becomes 'Elfstone son of Elfhelm' when they pass the Pillars of the Kings, is called 'Elfstone' when he points to Tol Brandir at the far end of the lake (which is not named): see p. 370. And after 'Behold Tol Brandir!' he says no more than 'Ere the shade of night falls we shall come thither. I hear the endless voice of Rauros calling.' The journey had taken nine days; in FR 'the tenth day of their journey was over.'

In the foregoing account I have attempted to discern the form of the fair copy manuscript as my father first set it down; but the text was heavily worked on, and certainty in distinguishing immediate from subsequent corrections is not possible without close examination of the original papers. This manuscript, as emended and added to, reached in fact almost the form of the final text; yet an object of this history is to try to determine the mode and pace in which the whole structure came into being. Since some error is inevitable, I have erred by assuming, if uncertain, a correction to be 'later' rather than 'immediate'; but that a good deal of the development took place during this present phase of writing is clear. In particular, it is clear that the entire section of the narrative from the end of the Gollum episode to the escape of the Company from the rapids had been rewritten before my father reached 'The Departure of Boromir', because an outline for the opening of that chapter (p. 380) refers to Trotter's having seen an eagle far off from the river 'above the rapids of Sarn Ruin',[20] and this element (previously absent, p. 357) is inseparable from the whole complex of revision at this point in the present chapter.

This revision was carried out on inserted slips, one of which is an Oxford University committee report dated 10 March 1941. This slip provides of course only a *terminus a quo*, and proves no more than that my father was revising this chapter during or after March 1941; while a similar slip, dated 19 February 1941, used for initial drafting at a later point in Chapter XXI (i.e. in the part corresponding to 'The Breaking of the Fellowship' in FR), proves no more. It might be argued that he would scarcely have preserved such reports of committee meetings for use long after, and that these revisions therefore belong to 1941, but this is much too flimsy to support any view of the external dating. See further p. 379.

The next version of the chapter was a manuscript made by myself, presumptively after 4 August 1942, the date that I wrote at the end of my copy of '[The Mirror of] Galadriel' (p. 261). I think that this copy of mine provides exact evidence of the state of this chapter when my father moved on from it to new regions of the story, and I shall now therefore turn to it, noticing first certain names (in the form in which I wrote them, of course, and before subsequent emendation by my father).

Sarn-Gebir remains in my copy, for later *Emyn Muil*; the *Gates of Gebir* or the *Gates of Sarn-Gebir* for the *(Gates of) Argonath*;[21] and *Ondor* for *Gondor*. *Trotter* remains *Trotter*, because my father had not emended it on his manuscript, until the end of the chapter, where the Company passes beneath the Pillars of the Kings, and he is called in the first manuscript 'Elfstone son of Elfhelm': this my father had changed to 'Aragorn son of Arathorn', and my copy follows. On the other hand he did not correct 'Under their shadow nought has Eldamir son of Eldakar son of Valandil to fear', and my copy retains it. This might be thought to be a mere inconsistency of correction on his part; but this is evidently not the case, since on *both* manuscripts he added a further step in the genealogy: 'Eldamir *son of Valatar* son of Eldakar son of Valandil.' Since he did not strike out 'Eldamir son of Eldakar son of Valandil' on my copy, but on the contrary accepted the genealogy and slightly enlarged it, it must be presumed that *Eldamir* beside *Aragorn* was intentional; cf. FR (p. 409): 'Under their shadow Elessar, the Elfstone son of Arathorn ... has nought to dread!', and cf. *Eldamir > Elessar*, p. 294. My father's retention of the genealogy, with the addition of Valatar, is also remarkable in that it shows him still accepting the brief span of generations separating Aragorn from Isildur.

By the criterion of presence or absence in my copy of the chapter the flight of the black swans was added early. The chronology remained as it was, the attack at the rapids taking place on the night of the seventh day; and the references to the New Moon in FR pp. 400–1 are still absent. The New Moon still first appears in the course of the attack, but changed in that the clouds through which it broke were now in the South, and the Moon rode 'across' not 'up' the sky (see pp. 353, 358).

The conversation concerning Time in Lothlórien (p. 358) was developed in several competing and overlapping riders, and when I came to make my copy my father evidently instructed me to set the passage out in variant forms. The opening speeches (Sam's and Trotter's – the latter given in FR to Frodo) remained effectively unchanged – Sam's now ending: 'Why, anyone would think we had come straight on, and never passed no time in the Elvish land at all.'[22] The conversation that follows contains two pairs of alternatives, which I here mark with numbers: 1 to 1 or 2 to 2 being alternatives, and (within 2) 3 to 3 or 4 to 4 being alternatives.

¹ 'The power of the Lady was on us,' said Frodo. 'I do not think that there was no time in her land. There are days and nights and seasons in Lothlórien; and under the Sun all things must wear to an end sooner or later. But slowly indeed does the world wear away in Caras Galadon, where the Lady Galadriel wields the Elven Ring.'¹

² Legolas stirred in his boat. 'Nay, I think that neither of you understand the matter aright,' he said. 'For the Elves the world moves, and it moves both very swift and very slow. Swift, because they themselves change little, and all else fleets by: it is a grief to them. Slow, because they do[23] not count the running years, not for themselves. The passing seasons are but ripples ever repeated in the flowing/endless stream. Yet beneath the Sun all things must wear to an end at last.'

³ 'But Lórien is not as other realms of Elves and Men,' said Frodo. 'The Power of the Lady was upon us. Slow for us there might time have passed, while the world hastened. Or in a little while we could savour much, while the world tarried. The latter was her will. Rich were the hours and slow the wearing of the world in Caras Galadon, where the Lady Galadriel wields the Elven Ring.'³

⁴ 'But Lothlórien is not as other realms of Elves and Men,' said Frodo. 'Rich are the hours, and slow the wearing of the world in Caras Galadon. Wherefore all things there are both unstained and young, and yet aged beyond our count of time. Blended is the might of Youth and Eld in the land of Lórien, where Galadriel wields the Elven Ring.'⁴, ²

'That should not have been said,' muttered Trotter, half rising and looking towards the other boats; 'not outside Lórien, not even to me.'

The night passed silently . . .

At the end of the chapter the lake remains nameless in my copy, first *Kerin-muil* and then *Nen-uinel* being added to both manuscripts; but an addition to my father's manuscript in which Aragorn speaks of Amon Hen and Amon Lhaw was made before my copy was written. This addition is precisely as in FR p. 410, except that both manuscripts have 'In the days of Isildur' for 'In the days of the great kings', and both add after Amon Lhaw '[Larmindon]' and after Amon Hen '[Tirmindon]'.

The original drafting shows that my father included all the narrative to the end of 'The Fellowship of the Ring' as Chapter XXI, and the fair copy manuscript likewise; but it is convenient to interrupt it at the point where the break (present in my copy) between XXI 'The Great River' and XXII 'The Breaking of the Fellowship' was subsequently made.

NOTES

1 Like the companion texts, the last section of 'Farewell to Lórien' and 'The Story Foreseen from Lórien', this was written very legibly for one of my father's initial drafts, and with remarkably little hesitation. I take up small changes made at the time of composition into the text given.

2 This is the first occurrence of *Rauros* in a text *ab initio*. For *Eregon* see p. 345 note 3.

3 I have attempted to set out the evolution of the Brown Lands in relation to the First Map on pp. 313–16. In this passage appears the description of them that survived with very little change into FR (p. 396).

4 It looks as if this addition were made immediately. See note 6.

5 My father wrote here first *Sarn*, then *Pen*, striking them out in turn before arriving at *Pensarn* (cf. the *Etymologies*, stems PEN, SAR, V.380, 385).

6 The brackets are in the original. – The weather described is obscure. Nothing is in fact said in this earliest form of the narrative about the weather during the journey down Anduin until the evening of the seventh day, when the weather was clear and cold, and starlit (but this was an addition); now, not much

later, it was very dark, though the water reflected here and there a misty star. Then, 'as Legolas gazed into the blackness away east the clouds broke.'

7   'Sam looked up at it in wonder': as well he might, seeing 'the white rind of the new moon' rising in the East and 'riding up the sky'. This is strangely paralleled in VI.325, where the moon on the night spent by the hobbits with the Elves in the Woody End was described thus: 'Above the mists away in the East the thin silver rind of the New Moon appeared, and rising swift and clear out of the shadow it swung gleaming in the sky.' In FR (pp. 400–1) the new moon is seen glimmering in the western sky on the evening before the Orc-attack, and on the evening of the attack 'the thin crescent of the Moon had fallen early into the pale sunset.'

As the text was written it was Trotter who 'looked up at it in wonder'. This was changed first to Merry, then to Sam; see note 9.

8   The dark shape 'like a cloud yet not a cloud' that momentarily cut off the moon's light is surely reminiscent of the shadow that passed over the stars as the Company journeyed on from Hollin in 'The Ring Goes South' (VI.421–2), and which Gandalf unconvincingly suggested might be no more than a wisp of cloud. Then too Frodo shivered, as here he 'felt a sudden chill'. As I noted (VI.434), the former incident was retained in FR but never explained: the Winged Nazgûl had not yet crossed the Anduin. But it seems likely to me that the shadow that passed across the stars near Hollin was in fact the first precocious appearance of a Winged Nazgûl.

9   Sam is again (see note 7) changed from Merry, and Merry from Trotter. In fact, the speech was given to Sam before its end was reached, as is seen from ' "And that Sam is probably about the truth of it," said Trotter'; and the transition from one speaker to another is seen in the transition from the very un-Samlike 'The moon I suppose does not change his courses in Wilderland?' to 'up pops a New Moon'.

10   Cf. the original draft of 'Lothlórien', p. 228: 'The last thin rind of the waning moon was gleaming dimly in the leaves.'

11   Cf. the comment on Time in Lórien written on the fair copy manuscript of 'Farewell to Lórien', p. 286; and see further on this matter the 'Note on Time in Lórien' that follows.

12   On the emergence of the idea of the inaccessibility of the island see p. 328.

13   *any enemy* is the correct reading, not *an enemy* (FR p. 396).

14   Sixty leagues (180 miles) south of Sarn Ford agrees well with the more southerly confluence of Limlight and Anduin on Map IV^D (p. 319).

15   Aragorn says this ('not even to me') also in FR (p. 405); but at this stage he had no previous knowledge of Lórien, and presumably had no knowledge until this moment of Galadriel's Ring.

16   No doubt the first reference to the Entwade, which was pencilled in on map IV^C and entered on IV^D (pp. 318–19).

17   Valandil is named as the son of Isildur in texts of 'The Council of Elrond' (pp. 121, 128, 147).

18   For an earlier occurrence of *Eldakar* see p. 276. An isolated scrap (in fact the back of an envelope) has this note:

> *Trotter's names*
> Elessar
> Eldamir (= Elfstone) son of Eldakar (= Elfhelm). Or Eldavel = Elfwold.

On the same envelope is written, in almost identical words, the passage concerning Frodo's thoughts under Galadriel's scrutiny that was added to the fair copy manuscript of 'Galadriel' (p. 266 note 32: 'Neither did Frodo...').

19   On the back of the preceding page in the fair copy manuscript my father scribbled down a first version of Trotter's words (in which no genealogy appears), and it is curious that he wrote here: 'How my heart yearns for Minas Ithil. .ı.', changing *Ithil*, probably at once, to *Anor*: see p. 333 and note 27. – Also noted down here in extreme haste are thoughts for the story immediately to come:

> Frodo on Tol Brandir.
> [?Strong] sight. Sees Minas Tirith and Minas Morgul opposed. Sees Mordor. Sees Gandalf. Suddenly feels the *Eye* and wrenches off the ring and finds himself crying Wait, wait!

20   A passing name for the rapids, replacing *Pensarn*, was *Ruinel*. *Sarn-Ruin* is the name on map IV^C, p. 317. Cf. *Dant-ruin*, *Dant-ruinel*, earlier names of Rauros (p. 285).

21   A passing form which my father entered on both manuscripts before *Argonath* was reached was *Sern Aranath*.

22   When the chronology was changed, with the attack at the head of the rapids taking place on the eighth night, and the New Moon seen far away in the West on the seventh and eighth evenings, Sam's words were expanded (and entered on both manuscripts), though subsequently largely rejected:

> Yesterday evening I saw it, as thin as a nail-paring, and this evening it wasn't much bigger. Now that's just as it should be, if we'd only been in the Elvish land for about a day, or more than a month. Why, anyone would think that time slowed down in there!

23   The phrase as my father wrote it was 'because they *need* not count the running years', but in copying I missed out the word *need*. Looking through my copy, but without consulting his own manuscript, he wrote in *do*; and *do* survives in FR (p. 405).

Note on Time in Lórien

The narrative passages that introduce this question are found on pp. 285–6, 354–5, 358, 363, and in note 22 above. This note is primarily concerned with the various time-schemes that bear on it, but for their understanding it is necessary to consider the chronology a little more widely.

The first time-scheme to be considered here I will call 'I'; for previous references to it see pp. 169, 215 note 1, and 344–5. In its 'Lothlórien' section it obviously belongs with the first drafting of the story, and preceded the emergence of the idea that there was a different Time in the Golden Wood. Here the dates are:

Nov. 24   Leave Rivendell
Dec.   6   Hollin (Full Moon)
         9   Snow on Caradras
        11   Reach Moria
        13   Escape to Lothlórien (Moon's last quarter)
        14   Go to Caras Galadon
        15   Night at Caras Galadon
        16   Mirror of Galadrien
   17–21   Stay in Caras Galadon (Dec. 21 New Moon)

This stands at the foot of a page, but a second page, though in pencil and not in ink, was clearly continuous:

Dec. 22–31   Remain at Caras Galadon, leave with the New Year
               (Dec. 28 Moon's first quarter)

Jan. 1–4   No notes against these dates except Jan. 4 Full Moon.

On the departure of the Company from Lórien on New Year's Day see p. 253 and note 28. But at this point, it seems, the idea of the disparity of time entered; for after Jan. 4 my father wrote: 'Dec. 15 onwards time at Caras does not count, therefore they leave on morning of Dec. 15' (cf. p. 286: 'if Lórien is timeless ... *nothing* will have happened since they entered'). The rest of the scheme is based on this chronology (and has been given on pp. 344–5).

At first the journey down the Great River was only to take two days: 'Dec. 17 Reach Tolondren. Dec. 18 Flight of Frodo. Dec. 19 Frodo meets Sam and Gollum.' This was struck out, with the note: 'Take ten days to reach [Emris > Eregon >] Tolbrandir' (on Emris see pp. 316–18 and note 12). The New Moon that caused Sam to raise the question of Time in Lórien was still on Dec. 21; and they reached Tolbrandir in the evening of Dec. 25.

Another scheme ('II') takes up at Dec. 22, but this is based on a later date of departure from Rivendell: Dec. 25, as in FR. The chronology of FR from Rivendell to Lothlórien was not yet reached, however, for two reasons: first, that the journey to Hollin still took eleven days and not fourteen (pp. 165, 169); and second, that in FR there are two

Yule-days after Foreyule (December) 30 as against Dec. 31 in scheme II. Thus II is two days in advance of FR. The numerical dates in II, when the Company left Rivendell on Dec. 25, soon become identical to those in I, when they left on Nov. 24, simply because November has 30 days but December has 31; thus in I they crossed the Silverlode by the rope-bridge and entered the Gore on Dec. 14, and in II on Jan. 14. At this point the scheme in II reads:

Jan. 14   Over Silverlode
Time ceases
Jan. 15   Leave Lórien

Scheme II continues for some way on this basis before petering out. These therefore are the relations between the former chronology (I), the new (II), and FR:

	I	II	FR
Leave Rivendell	Nov. 24	Dec. 25	Dec. 25
Hollin	Dec. 6	Jan. 6	Jan. 8
Snow on Caradras	Dec. 9	Jan. 9	Jan. 11
Reach Moria	Dec. 11	Jan. 11	Jan. 13
Escape from Moria	Dec. 13	Jan. 13	Jan. 15
Cross Silverlode	Dec. 14	Jan. 14	Jan. 16
Leave Lórien	[Jan. 1 >] Dec. 15	Jan. 15	Feb. 16
Reach Tol Brandir	Dec. 25	Jan. 25	Feb. 25
Flight of Frodo	Dec. 26	Jan. 26	Feb. 26

In II the New Moon was on Jan. 21, just as in I it was on Dec. 21, and against this date in II is also: 'Battle with Orcs?' This was the seventh day of the voyage down Anduin, as in the texts. But it is odd that in both I and II the journey took eleven days, whereas in the texts it took nine (pp. 361–2).

At the foot of the page carrying scheme II my father wrote: 'Does Time cease at Lórien or go on faster? So that it might be Spring or nearly so.' With this cf. p. 363: 'The Power of the Lady was upon us. Slow for us there might time have passed, while the world hastened. Or in a little while we could savour much, while the world tarried. *The latter was her will.*'

Another chronology of far greater elaboration, made after the changes introduced in October 1944 (see p. 406), was still based on the conception that 'exterior' Time ceased in Lórien, for it begins:

Thurs. Jan. 19   Fifth day of voyage
Fri.   20   Sixth day
Sat.   21   Seventh day. Sam observes New Moon and is puzzled.

Lastly, another later scheme of dates begins:

> They spend what seems many days in Lórien, but it is about the same time and date when they leave. [*Added:* In fact, one day later, time moving about 20 times slower (20 days = 1).]

Here the Company again leaves Lórien on Jan. 15, but the chronology of the journey approaches that of FR: 'Sam sees New Moon low in West after sunset' on Jan. 21, but as in FR the attack by Orcs takes place on the night of the eighth day, here Jan. 22; and Tol Brandir is reached at dusk on Jan. 24. Here this scheme ends; but across the page my father afterwards wrote these separate notes:

> Why have any difference of time? Shift the dates a month forward.
> If Lórien time is not different, then no need for Sam to see the Moon.
> Better to have *no* time difference.

A passage in the first manuscript of 'The White Rider' (p. 431) may be mentioned here: Gandalf tells that after his rescue by Gwaihir from the peak above Moria he came to Lothlórien and 'tarried there in the long time which in that land counts for but a brief hour of the world'.

Phases of the Moon

Either while the making of Time-scheme I was in progress or at some later point my father wrote at the head of the first page of it: *Moons are after 1941–2 + 6 days.* He changed this to + *5 days*, and added: *thus Full Moon Jan. 2 is Jan. 7.* The phases of the Moon were entered on scheme I in red pencil, and it is very hard to know whether they belong with its making or were put in later. Many of these dates were much changed, but no discernible relation with the phases of 1941–2 emerges, the dates in the scheme varying between two to six days later. The phases as entered, also in red pencil, on scheme II, when the departure from Rivendell took place on Dec. 25, are however regularly five days later than those of 1941–2, beginning with New Moon on Dec. 23, and then First Quarter on Dec. 30, Full Moon Jan. 7, Last Quarter Jan. 15, New Moon Jan. 21 (against which is written the time: 9.32), First Quarter Jan. 29 (time 6.35), Full Moon Feb. 6. It is possible, therefore, though far from certain, that it was only with scheme II and the decision to postpone the departure from Rivendell by a month that my father decided to pattern the phases precisely on those of 1941–2.

It will be seen shortly (p. 379) that my father was working on 'The Departure of Boromir' in the winter of 1941–2. The postponement of the departure from Rivendell is first seen in an outline for the story following the ride of Gandalf and his companions from Fangorn to Eodoras (p. 434 and note 1; see also pp. 422–3).

XVIII
THE BREAKING OF THE FELLOWSHIP

In the latter part of the original chapter 'XXI' initial drafting and 'fair copy' were a continuous process. Up to the point where Sam broke in on the discussion among the Company beside the river with 'Begging your pardons, but I don't think you understand Mr. Frodo at all' (FR p. 419), the drafting is very rough indeed, with separate passages written in slips and not forming a consecutive narrative, while the 'fair copy' is itself a mass of correction and rewriting in the act of composition. Some passages gave my father great difficulty and he experimented with their ordering and phraseology in many forms. But from that point, and evidently made after the 'fair copy' had reached it, there is a clear primary draft, in which the story just as it is in FR (pp. 419–23) 'wrote itself', on the basis of a preliminary outline; and the fair copy from here onwards can be properly so called. In this manuscript the text of FR was effectively reached throughout, but the division of 'XXI' into two, with a new chapter 'XXII The Breaking of the Fellowship', was not made until after the text had been completed.

At first Trotter is 'Elfstone', not corrected, in both draft and fair copy (see p. 361), but soon becomes 'Trotter', and is then so named throughout.

The draft text begins:

That night they went ashore, and camped upon a green sward beneath the slopes of [*added:* Amon Hen] the western hill. They set a watch, but they saw no sign of any enemy or spy. If Gollum had contrived to follow them, he remained unseen. 'I do not think he would dare the passage of the Gates,' said Elfstone. 'But he may have travelled far over the hills, while we were delayed at Pensarn. By now he knows the country well, and he will guess too much of our divided purposes.[1] For we have with us what he long possessed and it draws him ever towards us. "If they turned west at Pensarn," he will say, "then for a time I can do no more. Sooner or later I shall know, and then Gollum can find a way, even to the walls of Minas-Tirith. But if they did not turn west there is but one end to the river-road: Tol Brandir and Rauros, and the North Stair. There they must go West or East. I will watch upon the East." Likely enough he spied us with his fell eyes far off from the eastern beaches or from some post among the hills.'

The day came like fire and smoke . . .

Amon Hen looks as if it were added immediately, and is probably the first occurrence of the name. An addition to the draft text introduces the nocturnal conversation between Trotter and Frodo and the drawing of Sting to see what its blade would show – a sign that the attack by Orcs had now entered; but here it is Frodo who feels 'some shadow or threat', and it is Frodo who says 'I thought as much. Orcs are near. But how came they across the river? Never have I heard that they came into this region before', with an authoritative tone more characteristic of Trotter. In the fair copy Trotter's surmises about Gollum's intentions were lost, and the opening of the chapter 'The Breaking of the Fellowship' in FR was attained, except that the green lawn beneath Amon Hen was named *Kelufain*, subsequently changed to *Calenbel*.[2]

The description of Tol Brandir as Frodo saw it that morning, already in the primary draft very close to the final form (FR p. 412), with its sides springing sheer out of the running water (where 'no landing place could be seen'), shows that the idea of its inaccessibility was present (see p. 359). The conversation before Frodo departed from the Company alone was very largely achieved at once, but in the fair copy Trotter says: 'My own heart desires to go to Minas-Tirith, but that is for myself and apart from your Quest', this being rejected, probably immediately; and in both texts, in very similar words, he says: 'Very well, Frodo son of Drogo. You shall be alone. But do not let your thoughts be too dark. For after you have chosen you shall not be alone. I will not leave you, should you decide to go to the gates of Baraddur; and there are others of the same mind, I think.' To this Frodo replied, in the fair copy: 'I know, and it does not aid my choice [> it does not help me at all].' The primary draft continues:

The others remained behind near the shore, but Frodo got up and walked away. Sam watched his master with great concern. Then the Company turned again to debating what they could do to aid the Quest, hopeless as it seemed [*struck out:* and whether it were wise to try and end it swiftly or to delay]. Boromir spoke strongly, urging ever the wisdom of strong wills, and weapons, and great plans he drew for alliances, and victories to be, and the overthrow of Mordor.[3]

Sam slipped away unnoticed. 'If orcs are anywhere nigh,' he muttered, 'I am not going to let Mr. Frodo wander about alone. In his frame o' mind he would not see an elephant coming, or he might walk off the edge of a precipice.'

In the meanwhile aimlessly wandering Frodo found that his feet had led him up the slopes of the hill.

The idea that Sam left the Company at this point was evidently very soon abandoned.

The encounter with Boromir on Amon Hen was now developed from the form it had reached in the outline given on pp. 325–7, and with much difficulty the text of FR was achieved. I give here so much as I can puzzle out of the form in which my father first wrote down what Frodo saw when he looked out from Amon Hen wearing the Ring (for the brief suggestions in previous outlines see p. 327 and note 7 and p. 366 note 19): his writing here is at its most difficult, the marks very weak and the pen seeming to float or glide on the paper.

Northward he looked, and the Great River lay like a ribbon beneath him, and the Misty Mountains small and hard as broken teeth. Eastward into wide uncharted lands he looked. West he gazed and saw little horsemen galloping like the wind upon wide green plains, and beyond was the dark tower of [Isengard >] Orthanc in the ring of Isengard.

Southward he looked ..... Ethir Anduin the mighty delta of the Great River, and myriads of seabirds [like a dust of white specks] whirling ... like a white dust, and beneath them a green and silver sea rippling in endless moving lines.

But everywhere he looked he saw signs of war. The Misty Mountains were like anthills to his sight: orcs were [?pouring] out from countless [?holes]. Under the boughs of Mirkwood there was deadly strife. The land of the Beornings was aflame. A cloud was over Dimrilldale / Moria gates. Smoke rose upon the borders of Lórien. [Dol Dúghul] Horsemen galloping wildly on the grass of Rohan, wolves poured forth from Isengard. From the grey southward Havens [or Haven] an endless column of armed men came. Out of the wild East men were moving in endless [?shining] swordmen, [?spearmen], bowmen upon horse; chariots and wains: whole peoples. All the power of the Dark Lord was in motion.

Then as he came back south he saw Minas Tirith. Far and beautiful it was, white-walled, many-towered, high upon its mountain seat strong in the sun: its battlements glittered with steel and its turrets were bright with many banners. .... was Minas Morgul .... its dark walls carven with ... shapes, its great tower like a tooth, its banners black, its gates like evil mouths, and to eastward the Shadow of Death the hopeless

[?gates] of Gorgoroth. Then he saw the .... Mount [Doom >] Dûm: the Hill of Fire and .... Baraddur.

Then suddenly his gaze halted. The [?mists cleared] and he cried aloud in fear. There was an eye in Baraddur. It did not sleep. And suddenly it had become aware of .... There was a fierce eagerness ... [?will] ... It leapt towards him, almost like a finger he felt it [?feeling] for him. In a minute it would nail him down, know just exactly [?to an inch] where he was. Amon Lhaw it touched, it glanced at Tol Brandir – he cast himself from the seat, [?crouching, covering] his head with his grey hood. He was crying out but whether he was saying Never will it get me, never, or Verily I come, I come to you, he could not say. [?Probably] both.

Then as a flash from some other point of power there came ... another thought. Take it off. Take it off. O foolish! Take it off. The two powers strove in him: for a moment perfectly balanced between their ... points he writhed. Suddenly he was aware of himself.

In the complete manuscript that followed the draft, with much further correction and experimentation of phrase as he wrote, my father reached the final form; but the opening description of Frodo in the high seat (for which there is no earlier drafting) in this manuscript is of much interest. As first written, with a good deal of correction in the process, the passage read:

At first he could see little: he seemed to be in a world of mist in which there were only shadows. The Ring was on him. [Then the virtue (*written above:* power) of Amon Hen worked upon him] Then here and there the mists gave way and he saw many things: small and clear as if they were beneath him on a table and yet remote: the world seemed to have shrunk. [*Added:* He heard no sound, seeing only bright images that moved and changed.][4] He looked South and saw below his very feet the Great River curve and bend like a toppling wave and plunge over the falls of Rauros into a foaming pit: the fume rose like smoke and fell like rain lit by a glimmering rainbow of many colours. More remote still beyond the roaring pools were fens and black mountains, many streams winding like shining ribbons. Then the vision changed: nothing but water was below him, a wide rippling plain of silver, and an endless murmur of distant waves upon a shore he could not see.

He looked West and saw horsemen galloping like the wind: their

On beyond the falls his eye wandered, here crossing reed-grown fens, there marking the winding ribbons of swift streams leaping down from small hard black mo(untains).

At this point my father rejected the entire passage from the words 'Then the virtue (power) of Amon Hen worked upon him' and began again:

At first he could see little: he seemed to be in a world of mist in which there were only shadows. The Ring was on him. [*Struck out at once*: But also he sat now upon the seat of Sight which the Men of Númenor had made.] Then here and there the mists gave way and he saw many visions...

The new text then reaches the form in FR (p. 416); Frodo is sitting on 'the seat of Seeing, upon Amon Hen, the Hill of the Eye of the Men of Númenor.'

Frodo 'seemed to be in a world of mist in which there were only shadows. *The Ring was on him. Then the power of Amon Hen worked upon him*': and the mists began to break. Still clearer is the next stage of revision: '... *The Ring was on him. But also* he sat now upon the seat of Sight which the Men of Númenor had made. Then here and there the mists gave way...' Only one interpretation seems possible: the wearing of the Ring *inhibited his sight* – he was in a world of mists and shadows; but nonetheless he was sitting on the Seat of Seeing on the Hill of the Eye, and 'the power of Amon Hen worked upon him.' On the other hand, in the last outline written before this point in the narrative was actually reached, the idea of the 'Seat of Seeing' had not emerged (p. 327): Frodo was 'standing on rocks' in the Stone Hills when Boromir attempted to take the Ring. It is said there that from this place the range of the Mountains of Shadow could be glimpsed 'like a smudge of grey, and behind it a vague cloud lit beneath occasionally by a fitful glow'; but when Frodo put on the Ring 'he saw nothing about him but a grey formless mist, and far away (*yet black and clear and hard*) the Mountains of Mordor: *the fire seemed very red*.' In its origin, then, the peculiar clarity of Frodo's vision on this occasion derived solely from the wearing of the Ring. This question is discussed further on pp. 380–1.

When Frodo came down from the summit of Amon Hen, and putting on the Ring again 'vanished and passed down the hill like a rustle of the wind', the primary draft continues: 'The power of the Ring upon him had been renewed; and maybe it aided his choice, drawing him to Mordor, drawing him to the Shadow, alone.'

There exists a rough outline for the last part of the chapter, where the story turns from Frodo to the Company, sitting where he left them beside the river. This was written in faint pencil, subsequently inked over.

Frodo does not come back in an hour. The hour wears on to two, and the sun is at noon. Trotter gets anxious. He saw Boromir go off, and return. 'Have you seen Frodo?' 'No,' said Boromir, lying with a half truth. 'I looked for him and could not see him.' [*Added:* ? 'Yes,' said Boromir, 'but he ran from me and I could not find him.'] Trotter decides they must search and blames himself for allowing Frodo to go alone. Boromir comes back?

Great agitation, and before Trotter can control them they all run off into the woods. Trotter sends Boromir after Merry and Pippin. He runs himself toward the Hill of Amon Hen followed by Sam. But suddenly Sam stops and claps his head. 'You're a fool, Sam Gamgee. You know quite well what was in Mr. Frodo's mind. He knew he had to go East — that old Gandalf intended it. But he was afraid, and still more afraid of taking anyone with him. ..... He's run away, that's it — and .... boat.'⁵ Sam dashed down the path. The green camp-ground was empty. As he raced across it he gasped. A boat was grinding on the shingle — seemingly all by itself was slipping into the water. It was floating away. With a cry Sam raced to the water-edge and sprang after it. He missed it by a yard and fell into deep water. He went under with a gurgle.

Conversation of Sam and Frodo. They go off together.

At this stage my father was not intending to end the chapter here, and this sketch continues into the story of what became the first chapter of *The Two Towers*, III.1 'The Departure of Boromir'; but I postpone the remainder of it to the next chapter in this book.

The discussion among the members of the Company during Frodo's absence took draft after draft to achieve,⁶ and though the actual content of what was said does not greatly differ from the form in FR (pp. 418–19) it was at first given in part to different speakers (thus in the earlier form it is Trotter who emphasizes, as does Gimli in FR, that on no member of the Company save Frodo was obligation laid).

Notably, there appear in these drafts the phrases found in FR: 'the Lord Denethor and all his men cannot hope to do what Elrond declared to be beyond his power', and 'Boromir will return to Minas Tirith. His father and people need him.' This is where the name *Denethor* first emerged, with only the slightest initial hesitation: my father wrote a B, or perhaps an R, then *Denethor*.⁷ That Boromir was the son of Denethor is clear, and is explicit in the outline given at the beginning of the next chapter; in any case he was named long before as the son of the King of Ond (VI.411).

As I have said, from the point where Sam intervened in the discussion the conclusion of *The Fellowship of the Ring* was virtually achieved at its first drafting and with very little hesitation, and there are only two matters to notice. One concerns the return of Boromir to the Company, where at first he replied to Trotter's question quite differently (cf. the outline on p. 375):

'He has not returned then?' asked Boromir in return.

'No.'

'That's strange. To say the truth I felt anxious about him, and went to seek him.'

'Did you find him?'

Boromir hesitated for an instant. 'I could not see him,' he answered, with half the truth. 'I called him and he did not come.'

'How long ago was that?'

'An hour maybe. Maybe more: I have wandered since. I do not know! I do not know!' He put his head in his hands and said no more.

Trotter looked wonderingly at him.

This was rejected at once and replaced by his account as it stands in FR. – The other passage is that describing Sam's headlong descent down the slopes of Amon Hen:

He came to the edge of the open camping-place[8] where the boats were drawn up out of the water. No one was there. There seemed to be cries and faint hornblasts in the woods behind, but he did not heed them.

Before this was written, my father had already sketched out, in the continuation of the outline of which I have given the first part on p. 375, the story of the Orc-attack and Boromir's death (p. 378). He had now abandoned important elements in his former vision of the course of the story after the disintegration of the Company: the journey of Merry and Pippin up the Entwash, and the evil dealings of Boromir in Ondor (pp. 211–12, 330). So far as written record goes, it was only now that he perceived that Boromir would never return to Minas Tirith.

NOTES

1 I think that Trotter's meaning was: 'he will guess, too, much of our divided purposes.'

2 The fair copy in fact followed the draft in the opening sentences, and the paragraph with which 'The Breaking of the Fellowship' opens in FR, describing the green lawn (*Parth Galen*), was added. As the manuscript was written, the green lawn was not named. See note 8, and p. 382.

3 This sentence was subsequently marked: 'Put this into his talk with Frodo' (cf. FR p. 414).

4 The sentence a little later in this passage, 'an *endless murmur* of distant waves upon a shore he could not see', was not changed when this was added.

5 Written transversely across this part of the text, before the underlying pencil was inked over, and extremely difficult to read, is the following:

   A good arrangement would be for Frodo running down hill to run [?into] orcs attacking Merry and Pippin and Boromir. Boromir is aware of his presence. When Boromir falls Frodo escapes [to *or* (in) the] boat − because Frodo would not leave Merry and Pippin in hands of orcs.

   I do not understand the implication of the last sentence.

6 One of these drafts is written on an Oxford University committee report dated 19 February 1941: see p. 362.

7 In the First Age *Denethor* led the Green-elves over Eredlindon into Ossiriand. On the name see V.188.

8 Replaced in pencil in the fair copy manuscript by 'the lawn of Kelufain': see note 2.

XIX

THE DEPARTURE OF BOROMIR

I mentioned in the last chapter that the outline for the end of the story of 'The Breaking of the Fellowship' (p. 375) in fact continues on into the narrative of the first chapter ('The Departure of Boromir') in *The Two Towers* (henceforward abbreviated as TT).

Horns and sudden cries in the woods. Trotter on the hill becomes aware of trouble. He races down. He finds Boromir under the trees lying dying. 'I tried to take the Ring,' said Boromir. 'I am sorry. I have made what amends I could.' There are at least 20 orcs lying dead near him. Boromir is pierced with arrows and sword-cuts. 'They have gone. The orcs have got them. I do not think they are dead. Go back to Minas Tirith, Elfstone, and help my people. I have done all I could.' He dies. Thus died the heir of the Lord of Minas Tirith. Trotter at a loss. He is found standing perplexed and grief-stricken by Legolas and Gimli (who have driven off a smaller company). Trotter is perplexed. Was Frodo one of the hobbits? In any case ought he to follow and try to rescue? Or go to Minas Tirith? He cannot go in any case without burying Boromir. With help of Legolas and Gimli he carries Boromir's body on a bier of branches and sets it in a boat, and sends it over Rauros.

Trotter now finds that one boat is missing. No orc-prints at camp. Whether hobbit-marks are old or new cannot be made out. But Sam is missing. Trotter sees that either Frodo and Sam, and Merry and Pippin, were together, or Frodo (and Sam?) have gone off. Now little or no hope of finding Frodo in latter case. He with Gimli and Legolas decide to follow Merry and Pippin. 'On Amon Hen I said I might see a sign to guide us! We have found a confusion – but our paths at least are set for us. Come, we will rescue our companions or else we will die after slaying all the orcs we can.'

An addition to this text, certainly of much the same time, reads:

Trotter sees by the shape and arms of the dead orcs that they are northern orcs of the Misty Mountains – from Moria? In fact

they are orcs of Moria that escaped the elves, + others who are
servants of *Saruman*. They report to Saruman that Gandalf is
dead. Their mission is to capture hobbits *including Frodo* and
take them to Isengard. (Saruman is playing a double game and
wants the Ring.)

At the bottom of the page is written:

Does Trotter have any vision on Amon Hen? If he does, let him
see (1) an Eagle coming down. (2) old man, like Frodo [sees] in
mirror. (3) orcs creeping under trees.

While working on the book my father would sometimes 'doodle' by
writing, often in careful or even elaborate script, names or phrases
from a newspaper that lay beside him or on which his paper rested. On
the back of the sheet carrying this outline – an examination script, like
most of the paper he used – he wrote out many such odds and ends, as
'Chinese bombers', 'North Sea convoy'; and among them are 'Muar
River' and 'Japanese attack in Malaya'. It is out of the question, I
think, that these writings on the verso should come from a different
time from the text on the recto. It is certain, therefore, that the time
was now the winter of 1941–2.[1]

This obviously agrees with my father's statement in the Foreword to
the Second Edition of *The Lord of the Rings* that he 'came to
Lothlórien and the Great River late in 1941.' He said that 'almost a
year' had passed since he halted by Balin's tomb in Moria; but I have
argued (VI.461), I think with good reason, that he stopped in fact at
the end of 1939. To maintain this view it must be supposed of course
that something like two years (1940–1) passed between the halt in
Moria and the point we have now reached; but further evidence on the
subject seems to be lacking.

There are two preliminary versions of 'Trotter upon Amon Hen',
the first proceeding directly from the suggestions at the end of the
outline just given.

Trotter sped up the hill. Every now and again he bent to the
ground. Hobbits go light, and their footprints are not easy even
for a ranger to pick up. [Most of the path was stony, or covered
with old leaves still lying thick; but in one place a small spring
crossed it, and here Trotter stooping saw tracks in the moist
earth, and beyond on the stones faint traces. 'I guessed right', he
said. 'When he came to the top he saw...][2] But not far from the
top a small spring crossed the path and in the wet earth he saw
what he was looking for. Quickly he ran forward across the
flagstones and up the steps. 'He has been here,' he said to

himself. 'Not so long ago his wet feet came this way, [and up the steps.] He climbed to the seat. I wonder what he saw?'

Trotter stood up and looked round. The sun seemed to be darkened, or else the eastern clouds were spreading. He could see nothing in that direction. As his glance swept round it stopped. Under the trees he saw orcs crawling stealthily: but how near to Amon Hen he could not guess. Then suddenly far away he saw an eagle, as he had seen it before above Sarn Ruin.[3] It was high in the air, and the land below was dim. Slowly it circled. It was descending. Suddenly it swooped and fell out of the sky and passed below his [?view].

As Trotter gazed the vision changed. Down a long path came an old man, very bent, leaning on a staff. Grey and ragged he seemed, but when the wind tossed his cloak there came a gleam of white, as if beneath his rags he was clad in shining garments. Then the vision faded. There was nothing more to be seen.

At the end of the text, and I think immediately, my father wrote: 'The second vision on Amon Hen is inartistic. Let Trotter be stopped by noise of orcs, and let him see nothing.'

The second version continues on into Trotter's leaping descent from the summit, his discovery of Boromir, and his words with him before he died. Though written here in the roughest fashion the text was scarcely changed afterwards, except in one respect: here (following the instruction at the end of the first version) Trotter does not go up to the high seat at all:

Trotter hesitated. He himself desired to [sit in the Seat of Seeing >] go to the high seat, but time was pressing. As he stood there his quick ears caught sounds in the woodlands below and to his left, away west of the River and camping-place. He stiffened: there were cries, and among them he feared that he could distinguish the harsh voices of orcs; faintly and desperately a horn was blowing.

In the first version the power of the Seat of Seeing upon Amon Hen 'works upon' Trotter indeed, but the visions he sees are isolated scenes, more akin in their nature perhaps to those in the water of Galadriel's Mirror than to the vast panorama of lands and war vouchsafed to Frodo. In the second draft he does not ascend to the high seat, and therefore sees nothing. In the fair copy manuscript that immediately followed he does go up, as in TT, but again sees nothing, save the eagle descending out of the sky: 'the sun seemed darkened, and the world dim and remote.' Why should this be? The utter unlikeness of the experiences of Frodo and of Aragorn in the Seat of Seeing is not explained. I have said (p. 374) that as my father first drafted the account of Frodo's vision it is explicit that it was 'the power of Amon Hen', and not the wearing of the Ring, that accorded it to him; and the first version of Aragorn's ascent to the summit shows this still more clearly (by the very fact that he also saw visions there). The final text of Frodo's vision is less explicit, and if this is associated with the fact that in the final form Aragorn does go up but sees nothing it may suggest a more complex relation between the power of Amon Hen and the power of the Ring, a relation which is not uncovered.

As I have said, the second of the original drafts for 'Trotter on Amon Hen'[4] continues to the death of Boromir, and there are a few details worth mentioning: it is not said (nor is it in the fair copy) that the glade where Boromir died was a mile or more from the camping-place (TT pp. 15, 18); Trotter says 'Thus passes the heir of Denethor, Lord of the T[ower]' ('Lord of the Tower of Guard' in the fair copy, as in TT); and very oddly, Boromir says 'Farewell, Ingold' – which can surely be no more than an unwitting reversion to the former name, instead of 'Elfstone'. In the fair copy, where he is otherwise called 'Trotter' throughout, Boromir says 'Farewell, Aragorn'; and this was probably the first time that the name 'Aragorn' was used again (apart, of course, from later correction at earlier points) after its abandonment.

A full and tolerably legible draft takes up just a little further on, from the coming of Legolas and Gimli to the glade, and there are only very minor differences from TT (pp. 16–17) as far as 'The River of Ondor will take care that no enemy dishonours his bones' (here given to Legolas). At this point in the draft manuscript there is a little hasty sketch, reproduced on p. 383, which indicates a difference (though immediately rejected) from the later story: Legolas alone returned to the camping-place. In the sketch are seen the rill that flowed through the greensward there, and the two remaining boats (the third having been taken by Frodo) moored at the water's edge, with Tol Brandir, and Amon Lhaw beyond; X marks the battle where Boromir died. At the shore is the boat brought back by Legolas, marking the place where Boromir's body was set aboard it.

In the draft text there is no mention of finding the hobbits' 'leaf-bladed' knives (cf. VI.128, FR p. 157), nor of Legolas' search for arrows among the slain; the first is absent from the fair copy also. Then follows:

'These are not orcs of Mordor,' said Trotter. 'Some are from the Misty Mountains, if I know anything of orcs and their [gear >] kinds; maybe they have come all the way from Moria. But what are these? Their gear is not all of goblin-make.' There were several orcs of large stature, armed with short swords, not the curved scimitars usual with goblins, and with great bows greater than their custom. Upon their shields they bore a device Trotter had not seen before: a small white hand in the centre of the black field. Upon the front of their caps was set a rune ᛁ fashioned of some white metal.[5]

'S is for Sauron,' said Gimli. 'That is easy to read.'

'Nay,' said Legolas. 'Sauron does not use the Runes.'

'Neither does he use his right name or permit it to be spelt or spoken,' said Trotter. 'And he does not use white. The orcs of his immediate service bear the sign of the single eye.' He stood for a moment in thought. 'S is for Saruman, I guess,' he said at last. 'There is evil afoot at Isengard, and the West is no longer safe. What is more: I guess that some of our pursuers escaped the vigilance of Lórien or avoided that land, passing through the foothills, and that Saruman also knows now of our journey, and maybe of Gandalf's fall. Whether he is merely working under the command of Mordor, or playing some hand of his own, I cannot guess.'

'Well, we have no time to ponder riddles,' said Gimli.

With this compare the passage added to the outline on pp. 378–9. – Both Legolas and Gimli now went back to the green lawn of the camping-place, which is here named *Kelufain*, corrected to *Forfain*, and that in turn to *Calen-bel* (all these changes being made at the moment of writing),[6] but they returned together in a single boat. Thus whereas in TT, where they brought both the remaining boats, the three companions in the one towed out the other bearing Boromir, and after passing Parth Galen cast it loose, here Legolas took the funeral boat to Calen-bel while Trotter and Gimli returned there on foot. At Calen-bel, 'All three now embarked in the remaining boat, and drew the funeral boat out into the running river.' In the fair copy the final story entered as my father wrote the text.

Apart from this, the account of Boromir's departure is almost word for word as in TT, save that his hair is called 'gold-brown' (so also in the fair copy, changed to 'long brown'; 'dark' in TT), and that it ends:

But in Ondor it was long recorded in song that the elven-boat rode the falls and the foaming pit, and bore him down through Osgiliath, and past the many mouths of Anduin, and out into the Great Sea; and the voices of a thousand seabirds lamented him upon the beaches of Belfalas.

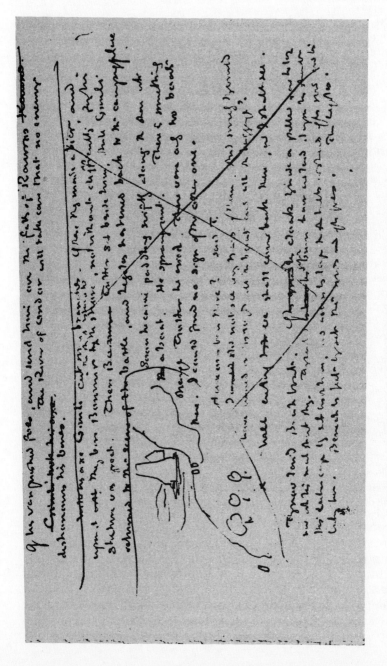

Sketch-plan of the scene of the Breaking of the Fellowship.

There is no suggestion however that any lament was sung for him by his companions; the draft reads here simply:

For a while the three companions remained gazing after him, then silently they turned and drove their boat back against the current to Calen-bel.

'Boromir has taken his road,' said Trotter. 'Now we must swiftly determine our own course. . . .'

The fair copy manuscript is virtually the same. The earliest extant text of the lament for Boromir (*Through Rohan over fen and field*, TT pp. 19–20) was however found with these draft papers, and a finely written text was inserted into the fair copy, with re-writing of the surrounding prose, at some later time. The earliest version is entitled [*Song >*] *Lament of Denethor for Boromir*, and only differs in few and minor points from the form in TT;[7] of rough working there is a page bearing the most primitive sketching of phrases for the lament (including the East Wind, that blows 'past the Tower of the Moon'), and another of rough working for the North Wind (which seems to have been swiftly achieved).

It might seem, from the original title *Lament of Denethor*, that it was at first intended to be indeed the father's own song of grief, and not merely in form: to be brought in at a later point in the story. But against this are the first words on the page of rough working, clearly belonging to the same time: ' "They shall look out from the white tower and listen to the sea," said Trotter in a low voice.' The song is, in any case, Denethor's Lament. The occurrence of 'Trotter' here suggests that it belongs to this time, for before much more of the story was written 'Aragorn' would replace 'Trotter' as the name by which he is generally referred to. Another pointer in the same direction is a line found in the rough working: 'The North Wind blows from Calen-Bel', since in the course of the writing of the fair copy manuscript the name changes from *Calen-bel* to *Calembel* (note 6).[8]

Trotter was at first less certain in his observations and conclusions when he examined the ground at Calen-bel; and he did not think to examine the baggage (nor yet in the fair copy). I cite the next part of the draft text, which here becomes very rough, in full:

'No orcs have been here,' he said at last. 'But otherwise it is not possible to say anything: all our footprints are here, and it is not possible to say whether any of the hobbits' feet have returned since the search for Frodo began. I think, but I cannot be sure, that a boat was dragged to the water at this point,' he said, pointing to the bank close to where the rill from the spring trickled into the river.

'How then do you read the riddle?' asked Gimli.

'I think that Frodo returned from the hill-top wearing the Ring,' said Trotter. 'He may have met Sam, but I think not: Frodo was probably wearing the Ring. I think Sam guessed Frodo's mind: he knew it better from love than we from wisdom; and caught him before he went.'

'But that was ill done, to go and leave us without a word, even if he had seen the orcs and was afraid,' said Gimli.[9]

'No, I think not,' said Trotter. 'I think Sam was right. He did not wish us to go to death in Mordor, and saw no other way to prevent that but by going alone and secretly. No, I think not,' said Trotter. 'He had a   Something happened on the hill to make him fly. I do not know all, but I know this. Boromir tried to take the Ring by force.'

Exclamation of horror from Legolas and Gimli.

'Think not ill of him,' said Trotter. 'He paid manfully and confessed.'

Then follows in pencil:

Don't let Trotter tell of Boromir's misdeed?

They draw up boat. Set out west after orcs. Trotter's plan is to descend from Sarn Gebir into Rohan and try and learn of orcs and *borrow horses*.

Legolas sees Eagle from escarpment, descending.

They meet an old man coming up hill to meet them. Don't recognize him, though there is something familiar. Suspect he is Saruman?

The final story of the reappearance of Gandalf moves a step closer. In the 'Plot' written before Lothlórien was reached (p. 211) it was Gimli and Legolas, on their way back North, who fell in with Gandalf, Aragorn having gone with Boromir to Minas Tirith; and Gandalf then 'hastens south' with them. This was still the story in the subsequent outline (p. 329). Now, the death of Boromir having entered, Trotter, Gimli and Legolas are as in the final story on the trail of Merry and Pippin when they encounter Gandalf returned; but they are to meet him before their journey through Rohan has begun, before they have set foot in the grasslands. The descending eagle that Legolas saw from the escarpment of Sarn Gebir was bearing Gandalf (see p. 396); and it is clear that the eagle that Trotter saw descending to earth as he looked out from the summit of Amon Hen in the original draft (p. 380) was the first appearance of this idea.[10]

In the fair copy the suggestion in this outline that Trotter should not tell Gimli and Legolas what Boromir had done was taken up:

'. . . Something occurred after he left us to make his mind up: he must suddenly have overcome his fear and doubt. I do not think that it was a meeting with orcs.' What he thought it was Trotter did not say. The last words of Boromir he kept ever secret.

This was changed, probably at once, to the dialogue in TT (p. 21), but it is still said of Trotter that 'the last words of Boromir he kept ever secret' ('he long kept secret', TT).

The draft text becomes formed narrative again with words of Trotter's that in TT are given to Legolas: ' "One thing at least is clear," said Trotter. "Frodo is no longer on this side of the River. Only he could or would have taken the boat. As for Sam, he must be either with Merry or Pippin or Frodo, or dead. He would have returned here otherwise ere now." ' Gimli's words that follow, and Trotter's, expounding his decision to follow the Orcs, are much as in TT; and I give the remainder of the draft, which at the end peters out, in full:

They drew up the last boat and carried it to the trees, and laid beside it such of their goods as they did not need and could not carry. Then they struck west. Dusk was already falling.

'Go warily,' said Gimli. 'We are assuming that all the orcs made off after they had slain Boromir and captured Merry and Pippin. But those that attacked Boromir were not the only ones. Legolas and I met some away southwards on the west slopes of Amon Hen. We slew many, creeping on them among the trees: the cloaks of Lórien seem to deceive their sight. But many more may still linger.'

'We have not time for wariness. We will follow the trail from the glade. Well is it that Orcs do not walk like hobbits! No folk, even Men of the cities, make such a trampling, and they slash and hack and beat down growing things as they pass, as if the breaking of things delighted them.

'It is plain to see which way they went – west near to the shore, but not on it, keeping to the trees.'[11]

'But orcs go swiftly,' said Gimli. 'We shall have to run!'

'If my guess is right,' said Trotter, 'and they make for Isengard, they will descend from the hills into Rohan. [*Struck out:* There they will not dare to journey save by night – and I wonder indeed how they cross] Mayhap we can get horses in Rohan,' said Trotter. 'If my guess is right and the orcs are making for Isengard, they will

I interrupt the narrative here because, although my father had no thought of halting, initial drafting from this point is lost (p. 390).

The draft that takes up with the coming of Legolas and Gimli to the glade (p. 381) is numbered on each page 'XXIII', and 'XXIII' continues on through the story of the chase across Rohan; the fair copy likewise begins 'XXIII' at 'Trotter sped on up the hill', with the title 'The Riders of Rohan', though another title apparently underlies this. Although all these were pencilled additions to the manuscripts in ink, I think it very probable that by this time the chapter-divisions of LR had been introduced: XXI 'The Great River' ending after the passage of the Pillars of the Kings and XXII 'The Breaking of the Fellowship' ending at the departure of Frodo and Sam, with XXIII extending all the way from Trotter's ascent of Amon Hen into whatever adventures might befall the three companions from their setting out from Calembel on the trail of the Orcs.

NOTES

1   The Japanese invaded Thailand and N.E. Malaya on 7–8 December 1941. The crossing of the Muar River was on 16 January 1942. This information has been kindly provided by Mr. F. R. Williamson. – Further evidence is provided by the use of the Moon's phases of 1941–2; see p. 369.

2   This passage was placed within square brackets in the original, as also was 'and up the steps' immediately following.

3   On the eagle seen far off on the evening before the Company came to the rapids of Sarn Ruin see pp. 361–2.

4   At the top of the page carrying this text are written many experimental Elvish names: *Llawhen, Amon Tirlaw, Lhawdir, Lasthen, Henlas, Hendlas*, all being struck out save the first and last. I am at a loss to account for these satisfactorily. Since both *Amon Hen* and *Amon Lhaw* appear in primary drafting and outlines that obviously preceded this text, it is perhaps possible that the names already stood on the page before my father used it for the account of Trotter on Amon Hen. If this were so, it might be – since all of them are compounds of elements one of which refers to hearing (*l(h)aw, las(t)*) and the other to sight (*hen(d), tir*) – that they were devised before the eastern and western hills were distinguished as the Hill of Hearing and the Hill of Sight.

5   The Old English S-rune is found also in the fair·copy manuscript, but there with the vertical strokes strongly curved, the upper

curve open to the left, the lower to the right. In that text the caps of the Orcs become 'leathern caps' ('iron helms' TT).

6 The name *Kelufain* for the green lawn below Amon Hen was added to the fair copy of 'The Breaking of the Fellowship', and in one instance changed to *Calenbel* (p. 371 and note 2). In the fair copy of the present chapter the name was *Calenbel* at the first occurrence but subsequently *Calembel* (and once *Cálembel*).

7 The differences are:
Verse 1: line 1 *Through the mountain-pass, through Rohan* >
     Over mountains tall, through Rohan
          5 *over many streams*
Verse 2: 2 *brings*
          4 *Why tarries Boromir the fair? For Boromir I grieve.*
Verse 3: 4 *Where now is Boromir the bold?*
          5 *I heard his horn.*

In every case these readings were replaced in careful script by those in TT. At first only the third verse had the concluding couplet beginning *O Boromir!*; but against this my father wrote: 'Omit? Or put extra couplet onto the other stanzas?' and then provided them, as in the final form. Certain other changes were put in later: see note 8.

8 The text of the Lament inserted into the fair copy is the final form, though here written in short lines. An accompanying page gives 'Alternatives to Song of Boromir', which were not used. These change verse 1 line 3 *tonight?* to *this morn?*, line 4 becoming *Have you seen Boromir the fair or heard his blowing horn?*; and verse 2 line 3 *at eve?* to *tonight?*, line 4 becoming *Where tarries Boromir the tall by moon or by starlight?* Another variant given here was to change verse 2 line 3 *at eve?* to *at morn?*, line 4 becoming *Where dwells now Boromir the fair? What valleys hear his horn?* These changes were pencilled also onto the first text of the song. – In LR *Calembel* is a town in Lamedon ('The Passing of the Grey Company', at end).

9 Cf. the passage given on p. 377 note 5.

10 Both sightings of the eagles survived in TT: Aragorn on Amon Hen still sees one descending, and Legolas sees one from the western escarpment of the Emyn Muil (see pp. 396–7).

11 Though no speaker is named, this speech ('We have not time for wariness') is certainly Trotter's.

XX

THE RIDERS OF ROHAN

A single page of extremely rough notes, headed 'Sketch' and 'XXIII' was written in pencil, and partly inked over.

Dusk. Night. Track less easy to follow. Sarn-Gebir runs North-South.[1] They press on through night. Dawn on ridge – then .... the escarpment. Legolas sees eagle far away. (Fangorn.)[2] Rich vegetation.

They see Black Mountains, 100 miles south. Entwash winding. Find orc trail going up river. Meeting with Rohiroth. They ride to Fangorn and hear news of battle and destruction of orcs and mysterious old man who had discomfited orcs. They hear that *no* captives were rescued. Despair. Old man appears.

[*Added:* XXV and later.] They think he is Saruman. Revelation of Gandalf, and his account of how he escaped. He has become a *white* wizard. 'I forgot most of what I knew.[3] I was badly burned or *well* burned.' They go to Minas Tirith and enter in.

Rest of war in which Gandalf and / on his eagle in white leads assault must be told later – partly a dream of Frodo, partly seen by him (and Sam), and partly heard from orcs. (? Frodo looks out of Tower, while prisoner.)

Minas Tirith defeats Haradwaith. They cross at Osgiliath [*written above:* Elostirion], defeat orcs and Nazgûl. Overthrow Minas Morghul, and drive forward to *Dagorlad* (Battle Plain). They get news that Ringbearer is captured.

Now Treebeard.

Then Frodo again.

In those passages where the original text was inked over the underlying pencil can be largely made out, and it is seen that *Haradwaith* was present: this appears on the First Map, translated *Sutherland*, as the name of the great region south of Mordor and east of the Bay of Belfalas (Map III, p. 309).[4] On the other hand *Nazgûl*, here first met with, was not, and nor was *Dagorlad* (the pencilled text had only Battle Plain); the First Map had *Dagras*, changed to *Dagorlad* (p. 310). *Elostirion* above *Osgiliath* was also an addition when the text was inked over; on this new name see p. 423. – There are other notes on the page which do not relate directly to the foregoing consecutive sketch, but which may be given here.

(1) Greyfax [> Shadowfax]. Halbarad. Horse of Gandalf reappears – sent for from Rivendell. Arrives later. It is 500–600 miles from Rivendell and would take Shadowfax 10–14 days.

The name *Halbarad* was added at the same time as *Greyfax* > *Shadowfax*, and these changes look as if they were made at once. In Gandalf's tale in the fifth version of 'The Council of Elrond' the horse that Gandalf got in Rohan was likewise named *Halbarad* and *Greyfax*, and there *Greyfax* was certainly changed to *Shadowfax* in the act of writing. In that text there is no mention of what happened to Shadowfax after Gandalf reached Rivendell (see p. 152); but an isolated slip of paper has a note on this (together with a passage of initial drafting for 'The King of the Golden Hall'): 'Some account of "Shadowfax" in the house of Elrond must be given and what arrangements were made about him. Or did he just run off after Gandalf got to Rivendell? How did Gandalf summon him?'

(2) Rohiroth are relations of Woodmen and Beornings, old Men of the North. But they speak Gnomish – tongue of Númenor and Ondor, as well as [?common] tongue.
(3) Trotter should *know* Eomer.
(4) Marhad Marhath is 2nd Master. [*Written in margin:* Marhad Marhath Marhelm Marhun Marhyse Marulf][5]
(5) Eowyn Elfsheen daughter of Eomund?

On the back of this page is very rough drafting for the conversation with Eomer (p. 400), but there is also here the note: *Eowyn Elfsheen daughter of Theoden.*

The original manuscript of 'The Riders of Rohan' is a difficult and chaotic document, and its textual history was hard to ascertain. In this chapter (numbered throughout 'XXIII' and without new title, see p. 387), as in those that follow, my father adopted the practice, occasionally found earlier, of *erasing* his primary draft, or substantial portions of it, and writing a new version on the pages where it had stood. In this case the original drafting from the point reached on p. 386 ('If my guess is right and the orcs are making for Isengard, they will') is lost for a long stretch through erasure and the re-use of the pages, though here and there bits of it can be read. The original draft, which I will call 'A', emerges however at the point in the narrative (corresponding to TT p. 29) where Aragorn, Legolas and Gimli approached the low downs to the east of the river Entwash, and continues through the story of the encounter with the Riders; at which point my father abandoned it, realizing that the story as he was telling it was 'not what really happened' (see the letter cited on p. 411). It was now that he returned to the beginning, and began a new text ('B') using the erased pages of A up to the point mentioned. It seems clear

that what survives of A survives because it was written largely in ink
and not in pencil. The structure of the manuscript is thus:

A erased   B written on erased A
A not erased; ends because abandoned
                                                  B continued independently

The textual history of the writing of the chapter is of course simply A
followed by B.

Both ways of presenting the material have their disadvantages, but
after much experimentation it seems to me best to look first at what
remains of A. This I give in full, excepting only one passage.

[Their elven-cloaks faded against the] background, and even in
the clear cool sunlight few but elvish eyes would have seen them
until close at hand as they passed, running or striding tirelessly
with a brief pause every three hours or so.

That evening they reached the low downs. A narrow strip
of moist green land some ten miles wide lay between them and
the river winding in dim thickets of sedge and reed. Here the
Entwash and the line of downs bent due north,[6] and the orc-trail
was plain to see under the lee of the hills. 'These tracks were
made today,' said Trotter. 'The sun was already high before our
enemy passed. We might perhaps have glimpsed them far ahead,
if there had been any rising ground to give us a long view.'

'Yet all the while they draw nearer to the mountains and the
forest, where our hope of aiding our friends will fail,' said
Gimli. Spurred by this thought the companions sped onward
again through the dusk, and far into the night. They were
already half-way along the downs before Trotter called a halt.
The waxing moon was shining bright. 'Look!' he said. 'Even
orcs must pause at times.' Before them lay a wide trampled
circle, and the marks of many small fires could be seen under the
shelter of a low hillock. 'They halted here about noon, I guess,'
said Trotter. 'How long they waited cannot be told, but they are
not now many hours ahead. Would that we need not stay; but
we have covered many a long league since we last slept, and we
shall all need our strength maybe tomorrow, if we come up with
our enemies at last.'

Before dawn the companions took up the hunt again. As soon
as the sun rose and the light grew they climbed the downs and
looked out. Already the dark slopes of the forest of Fangorn
could be seen, and behind, glimmering, the white head of
Methen Amon, the last great peak of the Misty Mountains.[7]
Out of the forest flowed the river to meet them. Legolas looked

round, turning his gaze through west to south. There his keen elf-eyes saw as a shadow on the distant green a dark moving blur.

'There are folk behind as well as in front,' he said, pointing away over the river. Trotter bent his ear to the earth, and there was a silence in the empty fields, only the airs moving in the grass could be heard. 'Riders,' said Trotter rising: 'many horsemen in haste. We cannot escape in this wild bare land. Most likely it is a host of the Rohiroth that have crossed the great ford at Entwade.[8] But what part the Horsemasters are minded to play and which side they serve I do not know. We can but hope for the best.'

The companions hastened on to the end of the downs. Behind them now they could hear the beat of many hooves. Wrapping their cloaks about them they sat upon a green bank close to the orc-trail and waited. The horsemen grew ever nearer, riding like the wind. The cries of clear strong voices came down the following breeze. Suddenly they swept up with a noise like thunder: a long line riding free many abreast, but following the orc-trail, or so it seemed, for the leaders rode bent low, scanning the ground even as they raced. Their horses were of great stature ...

The account of the Riders and their horses, though rougher in expression, is very much as that in TT pp. 33–4, and the description in this original draft of the wheeling horses suddenly halting was never changed – except in the point that 'fifty lances were at rest pointing towards the strangers', where TT has 'a thicket of spears' (Legolas had counted one hundred and five Riders, p. 32).[9] – The conclusion of the primary draft, the conversation between Eomer and Aragorn in its earliest form, ran thus:

'Who are you, and what are you doing in this land?' said the rider, using the common speech of the West, in manner and tone like Boromir and the men of Minas Tirith.

[*Rejected immediately:* 'I am Aragorn Elessar (*written above:* Elfstone) son of Arathorn.][10] 'I am called Trotter. I come out of the North,' he replied, 'and with me are Legolas [*added:* Greenleaf] the Elf and Gimli Glóin's son the Dwarf of Dale. We are hunting orcs. They have taken captive other companions of ours.'

The rider lowered his spear-point and leaped from his horse, and standing surveyed Trotter keenly and not without wonder. At length he spoke again. 'At first I thought you were orcs,' he said, 'but that is not so. Indeed you know little about them, if you go hunting them in this fashion. They are swift and well-armed, and there are very many, it is said. You would be likely to change from hunter to quarry, if you ever caught up with them. But there is something strange about you, Master Trotter.' He bent his clear bright eyes again upon the ranger. 'That is no name for a man that you give. And strange is your raiment – almost it seems as if you had sprung out of the grass. How did you escape our sight?'

'Give me your name, master of horses, and maybe I will give you mine, and other news,' answered Trotter.

'As for that,' said the rider, 'I am Eomer son of Eomund, Third Master of the Riddermark. Eowin the Second Master is ahead.'

'And I am Aragorn Elfstone son of Arathorn Tarkil, the heir of Isildur Elendil's son of Ondor,' said Trotter. 'There are not many among mortal men who know more of orcs. But he that lacks a horse must go on foot, and when need presses no more friends may a man take with him than he has at hand. Yet I am not unarmed.' He cast back his cloak: the elven-sheath glittered and the bright blade of Branding shone like a sudden flame as he swept it out. 'Elendil!' cried Trotter. 'See the sword that was broken and is now remade. As for our raiment, we have passed through Lothlórien,' he said, 'and the favour of the Lady of the Galadrim goes with us. Yet great is our need, as is the need of all the enemies of Sauron in these days. Whom do you serve? Will you not help us? But choose swiftly: both our hunts are delayed.'

'I serve the Father and Master of the Riddermark,' said Eomer. 'There is trouble upon all our borders, and even now within them. Fear which was once a stranger walks among us. Yet we do not serve Sauron. Tribute he seeks to lay on us. But we – we desire only to be free, and to serve no foreign lord. Guests we will welcome, but the unbidden robber will find us swift and hard. Tell me [?briefly] what brings you here.'

Then Trotter in few words told him of the assault on Calenbel and the fall of Boromir. Dismay was plain to see on Eomer's face and many of his men at that news. It seemed that between Rohan and Ondor there was great friendship. Wonder too was in the eyes of the riders when they learned that Aragorn and his two companions had come all the way from Tolbrandir since the evening of the third day back on foot.

'It seems that the name of Trotter was not so ill given,' said Eomer. 'That you speak the truth, if not all the truth, is plain. The men of Rohan speak no lies, but they are not easily deceived. But enough – there is now more need of speed than before. We were hastening only to aid of Eowin, since news came back that the orc-host was large and outnumbered the pursuers, but twenty-five that we first sent. But if there are captives to rescue we must ride faster. There is one spare horse that you can have, Aragorn. The others must make shift to ride behind my two esquires.'

Aragorn leapt upon the back of the great grey horse that was given to him.

Here the primary draft A ends, and as my father broke off he noted:

This complicates things. Trotter etc. should meet Eomer *returning* from battle north of the Downs near forest .... and Eomer should [?deny] any captives.

Trotter learns war has broken out with Saruman [?even] since Gandalf's escape.[11]

From 'Aragorn and his two companions had come all the way from Tolbrandir since the evening of the third day back' the chronology at this stage can be deduced:

Day 1 Death of Boromir. Leave Calenbel; night in Sarn Gebir.
Day 2 First day in plains of Rohan.
Day 3 Second day in plains of Rohan; reach downs in evening.
Day 4 In morning go on to northern end of downs; encounter with Riders.

Despite the radical alteration in the story that now entered (the Riders were returning from battle with the Orcs, not on their way to it) this chronology was retained for a long time.

We come now to the second version 'B'. This text was much worked on subsequently, but I mostly cite it as it was first written, unless a change seems to have been immediate. It was now that my father began to use 'Aragorn' again in place of 'Trotter' as the ordinary name in narrative, though at first he still now and then wrote 'Trotter' out of habit before changing it immediately to 'Aragorn'.

At the point where in TT 'The Departure of Boromir' ends and 'The Riders of Rohan' begins the text reads thus:

'We have no time now for wariness,' said Aragorn. 'Dusk will soon be about us. We must trust to the shadows and our cloaks, and hope for a change of luck.' He hastened forward, hardly pausing in his stride to scan the trail; for it needed little of his skill to find.

'It is well that the orcs do not walk with the care of their captives,' said Legolas, as he leaped lightly behind. 'At least such an enemy is easy to follow. No other folk make such a trampling. Why do they slash and beat down all the growing things as they pass? Does it please them to break plants and saplings that are not even in their way?'

'It seems so,' answered [Trotter >] Aragorn; 'but they go with a great speed for all that. And they do not tire.'

'In both we may prove their equals,' said Gimli. 'But on foot we cannot hope to overtake their start, unless they are hindered.'

'I know it,' said Aragorn; 'yet follow we must, as best we can. And may be that better fortune awaits us if we come down into Rohan. But I do not know what has happened in that land in late years, nor of what mind the Horse-Masters may now be between the traitor Saruman and the threat of Sauron. They have long been friends with the people of Ondor and the lords of Minas Tirith, though they are not akin to them. After the fall of Isildur they came out of the North beyond Mirkwood, and their kinship is rather with the Brandings, the Men of Dale, and with the Beornings of the woods, among whom still may be seen many Men, tall and fair, like the Riders of Rohan. At the least they will not love the Orcs or aid them willingly.'[12]

Dusk deepened. Mist lay behind them among the trees below...

Here in TT the chapter 'The Riders of Rohan' begins, and this earliest extant text is already very close to it in the story of the night spent scrambling on the ridges and in the gullies of *Sern-gebir* (as the name is written at this point) and the discovery of the slain Orcs. The Rohirrim are still the *Rohiroth*, Gondor is *Ondor*, and the White Mountains are the Black Mountains (described in precisely the same words as in TT p. 24, and as there distant 'thirty leagues or more').

Aragorn's verse took this form:

(Aragorn sings a stave)
Ondor! Ondor! Between the Mountains and the Sea
Wind blows, moon rides, and the light upon the Silver Tree
Falls like rain there in gardens of the King of old.
O white walls, towers fair, and many-footed throne of gold!
O Ondor, Ondor! Shall Men behold the Silver Tree
Or West Wind blow again between the Mountain[s] and the Sea?

It can be made out from the erased primary text A that this verse was not present, but only Aragorn's words that precede it. In this earliest form *many-footed throne of gold* was changed, probably very soon, to *wingéd crown and throne of gold* as in TT. These are the first references to the Winged Crown and the White Tree of Gondor.[13]

Then follows (as originally written):

The ridge fell steeply before their feet: twenty fathoms or more it stood above the wide shelf below. Then came the edge of a sheer cliff: the East Wall of Rohan. So ended Sarn Gebir, and the green fields of the Horsemasters rolled against its feet like a grassy sea. Out of the high land fell many freshets and threadlike waterfalls, springing down to feed the wandering Entwash, and carving the grey rock of the escarpment into countless crannies and narrow clefts. For a breathing space the three companions stood, rejoicing in the passing of night, feeling the first warmth of the mounting sun pierce the chill of their limbs.

'Now let us go!' said Aragorn, drawing his eyes of longing away from the south, and looking out west and north to the way that he must go.

'See!' cried Legolas, pointing to the pale sky above the blur where the Forest of Fangorn lay far across the plains. 'See! The eagle is come again. Look! He is high, but he is coming swiftly down. Down he comes! Look!'

'Not even my eyes can see him, my good Legolas,' said Aragorn. 'He must be away upon the very confines of the forest. But I can see something nearer at hand and more urgent...'

On previous references to the descending eagle see p. 385. Subsequently my father pencilled in against this passage:

Eagle should be flying *from* Sarn Gebir, bearing Gandalf from Tolbrandir where he resisted the Eye and saved Frodo? If so substitute the following:

'Look!' said Legolas, pointing up in the pale sky above them. 'There is the eagle again. He is very high. He seems to be flying from Sarn Gebir now back northward. He is going back northward. Look!'

'No, not even my eyes can see him, my good Legolas,' said Aragorn. 'He must be far aloft indeed. I wonder what is his errand, if he is the same bird that we have seen before. But look! I can see something'

This is virtually the text of TT (p. 25); and it is curious to see what its meaning was when it was first written – that Gandalf was passing high above their heads. The eagle was flying to Fangorn (and therefore north-west rather than north), whereas in TT Gandalf explains later to

Legolas (pp. 98–9) that he had sent the eagle, Gwaihir the Windlord, 'to watch the River and gather tidings': Gwaihir had told him of the captivity of Merry and Pippin.[14] Against the suggestion here that the eagle was carrying Gandalf from Tol Brandir 'where he resisted the Eye and saved Frodo' my father wrote N O in large letters; cf. TT p. 99: 'I sat in a high place, and I strove with the Dark Tower; and the Shadow passed.' Nonetheless he preserved the new text.

In TT (pp. 25–6) the three companions followed the Orc-trail north along the escarpment to the ravine where a path descended like a stair, and followed the trail down into the plain. In the present text the story is different:

...a rough path descended like a broad steep stair into the plain. At the top of the ravine Aragorn stopped. There was a shallow pool like a great basin, over the worn lip of which the water spilled: lying at the edge of the basin something glistening caught his eye. He lifted it out and held it up in the light. It looked like the new-opened leaf of a beech-tree, fair and untimely in the winter morning.

'The brooch of an elven-cloak!' cried Legolas and Gimli together, and each with his hand felt for the clasp at his own throat; but none of their brooches were missing.

'Not lightly do the leaves of Lórien fall,' said Aragorn solemnly. 'This clasp did not betray its owner, nor stray by chance. It was cast away: maybe to mark the point where the captors turned from the hills.'

'It may have been stolen by an orc and dropped,' said Gimli.

'True enough,' said Legolas, 'but even so it tells us that one at least of our Company was carried off as Boromir said.'

'It may tell no more than that one of our Company was plundered,' answered Gimli.

Aragorn turned the brooch over. The underside of the leaf was of silver. 'It is freshly marked,' he said. 'With some pin or sharp point it has been scored.[15] See! A hand has scratched on it M ᛉ ᛈ.'

The others looked at the faint letters eagerly. 'They were both alive then so far,' said Gimli. 'That is heartening. We do not pursue in vain. And one at least had a hand free: that is strange and perhaps hopeful.'

'But the Ringbearer was not here,' said Aragorn. 'At least so we may guess. If I have learned anything of these strange hobbits, I would swear that otherwise either Merry or Pippin would have put F first, and F alone if time allowed no more. But the choice is made. We cannot turn back.'

The three companions climbed down the ravine. At its foot they came with a strange suddenness upon the grass of Rohan.

I think that it was here, arising out of this moment in the narrative, that the leaf-brooches of Lórien were conceived; they were then written into the fair copy manuscript of 'Farewell to Lórien' (p. 285). But it is strange that Aragorn should speak as though the brooch was at last a clear if not altogether final evidence that Frodo was not a captive of the Orcs, for in drafting for 'The Departure of Boromir' (p. 386) he had said: 'One thing at least is clear. Frodo is no longer on this side of the River. Only he could or would have taken the boat'; and that he should feel that this evidence called for some reinforcement of the decision to pursue the Orcs. – The postponement of the discovery of Pippin's brooch to its place in TT (p. 26) was introduced not long afterwards in a rider; see p. 408.

The entire account in TT from the debate at nightfall of the first day in the plains of Rohan (27 February: the second day of the chase) to their setting off again on the following morning (pp. 27–9) is lacking here. The text reads thus:

. . . No longer could any sight of them be seen in the level plains.

When night was already far advanced the hunters rested for a while, somewhat less than three hours. Then again they went on, all the next day with scarcely a pause. Often they thanked the folk of Lórien for the gift of *lembas*; for they could eat and find new strength even as they ran.

As the third day [*i.e. of the chase*] wore on they came to long treeless slopes, where the ground was harder and drier and the grass shorter: the land rose, now sinking now swelling up, towards a line of low, smooth downs ahead. To their left the river Entwash wound, a silver thread in the green floor. The dwellings of the Rohiroth were for the most part far away [south >] to the west[16] across the river, under the wooded eaves of the Black Mountains, which were now hidden in mist and cloud. Yet Aragorn wondered often that they saw no sign of beast or man, for the Horsemasters had formerly kept many studs and herds in this eastern region (Eastemnet),[17] and wandered much, living often in camp or tent, even in the winter-time. But all the land was now empty, and there was a silence upon it that did not seem to be the quiet of peace. Through the wide solitude the hunters passed. Their elven-cloaks faded against the background of the green fields . . .

It is at this point that the original text A emerges (p. 391). The new version B, still replacing it but no longer destroying it, advances far towards the final text, and for long stretches is almost identical. The original time-scheme, as set out on p. 394, was retained: the three companions still came to the downs at the end of the third day of the chase (i.e. the second day in the plains of Rohan); Aragorn still asserted that the tracks which they found there had been made that day; and they still went on far into the night, not stopping until they were halfway along the downs, where they found the orc-encampment. In this version, in fact, the Orcs were less far ahead than they were in A: ' "They halted here in the early evening, I guess," said Aragorn.' It was at this point that Aragorn lay on the ground for a long time motionless (cf. TT pp. 28–9; but here it was by moonlight, in the night following 'Day 3' of the chase, not at dawn of 'Day 3' and still far east of the downs).

'The rumour of the earth is dim and confused,' he said. 'Many feet I heard, far away; but it seemed to me also that there were horses, horses galloping, and yet all were going away from us. I wonder what is happening in this land. All seems strange. I distrust the very moonlight. Only the stars are left to steer by, and they are faint and far away. I am weary, as a Ranger should never be on a fresh trail; yet we must go on, we must go on.'

In this version they seem not to have slept at all that night: 'when dawn came they had almost reached the end of the downs'; and 'as the sun rose upon the fourth day of the pursuit, and the light grew, they climbed the last height, a rounded hill standing alone at the north end of the downs' – where in TT (p. 31) they spent the night of the fourth day.[18]

The coming of the Rohiroth now reaches the text of TT,[19] and the only difference to mention is that Legolas, seeing them far away, said: 'There are one hundred save three'; this almost certainly indicates, I think, that three Riders had been lost from an *éored* of 100 horse. But 'one hundred save three' was changed to 'one hundred and five' before the end of the chapter was reached, for Eomer subsequently tells Aragorn that they had lost fifteen men in the battle. (On the constitution of an *éored* see *Unfinished Tales* p. 315.)

The first part of Aragorn's conversation with Eomer in B is actually a third version, for it is written over erased pencil drafting, as far as the point where Gimli explains to Eomer the meaning of the word 'hobbits' (TT p. 37); and here the final form is reached apart from one or two details: *Branding* as the name of Aragorn's sword, *Masters* for *Marshals* of the Mark. It is here that *Theoden son of Thengel* first appears: if some other names preceded these they are lost in the underlying erased text. Theoden is not here called 'King', but 'the First Master'.

For the next portion of the chapter there is some extremely rough drafting, scarcely more than notes, preliminary to the writing of B. In these my father did not see Gandalf as a well-known figure in Rohan, and he still thought that there was another troop of Riders in that region (detached from Eomer's host?):

> The old man who said he had escaped from Orthanc on an eagle! And demanded a horse and got it! Some said he was a wizard. And Shadowfax ... [?came back] only a day ago.
>
> Eomer says some orcs fled towards Wold. Aragorn may meet other Riders: Marhath the Fourth Master [*see p. 390*] is there with a few men. Aragorn wishes to go on. Eomer gives him token to show Marhath. Aragorn pledges his word to return to Theoden and vindicate Eomer. Farewell.

In the part of the B-text developed from these notes the hobbits are called the 'Half-high', not as in TT the 'Halflings': in Gimli's reference to 'the words that troubled Minas Tirith' he says 'They spoke of the Half-high', as in the form of the verse in the fifth version of 'The Council of Elrond' (p. 146).[20] Aragorn's reply to the scoffing question of Eothain 'Are we walking in legends or on the green earth under the daylight?' here takes the form: 'One may do both; and the latter is not always the safer' (added to the manuscript: 'But the green earth is a legend seen under the light of day'). Eomer's remarks about Gandalf, which were achieved in this form through a mass of small changes, now read thus:

> 'Gandalf?' said Eomer. 'We have heard of him. An old man of that name used to appear at times in our land. None knew whence he came or where he went. His coming was ever the herald of strange events. Indeed since his last coming all things have gone amiss. Our trouble with Saruman began from that time. Until then we had counted Saruman our friend, but Gandalf said that evil was afoot in Isengard. Indeed he declared that he had been a prisoner in Orthanc and had escaped. Riding on an eagle! Nonetheless he asked us for a horse! What arts he used I cannot guess, but Theoden gave him one of the *mearas*: the steeds that only the First Master of the Mark may ride; for it is said that [they are descended from the horses which the Men of Westernesse brought over the Great Seas >] their sires came out of the Lost Land over the Great Sea when the Kings of Men came out of the Deeps to Gondor. Shadowfax was the name of that horse. We wondered if evil had befallen the old man; for seven nights ago Shadowfax returned.'[21]

'But Gandalf left Shadowfax far in the North at Rivendell,' said Aragorn. 'Or so I thought.[22] But, alas, however that may be, Gandalf is gone down into the shadows.' Aragorn now told briefly the story of their journey from Moria. To his account of Lórien Eomer listened with amazement. At last Aragorn spoke of the assault of the orcs on Calen-bel, and the fall of Boromir.

Only shortly before in this text the name was still *Ondor*. In view of the fact that it is *Ondor* in the draft and fair copy of 'Treebeard', it may be that the alteration of the sentence about the *mearas*, in which the form *Gondor* appears, was made later. On the actual date of the change *Ondor* > *Gondor* see p. 423.

In the remainder of the conversation with Eomer there are only these differences from the text of TT (pp. 38–41) to notice. There is no suggestion yet of Wormtongue: Eomer does not speak of 'some, close to the king's ear, that speak craven counsels'. He says that there has been war with Saruman 'since the summer' ('for many months', TT); and he remarks of Saruman himself that 'He walks about like an old man, indeed there are some that say Gandalf was only old Saruman in disguise: certainly they are much alike to look on.'[23] In his account of his own present expedition Eomer does not refer to his going without Theoden's leave:

'... I do not know how it all will end. There is battle even now away upon the Westemnet under the shadow of Isengard. Hardly could we be spared. But scouts warned us [> Theoden] of the orc-host coming down out of the East Wall three nights ago: among them they reported some that bore the badges of Saruman. We overtook them yesterday at nightfall, only a little way from the edges of the Forest. We surrounded them, and gave battle at dawn. We lost fifteen of my *eored* and twelve horses, alas!'

On the chronology see the *Note on Chronology* at the end of this chapter. Eomer tells of the Orcs that came in from the East across the Great River, and the Isengard Orcs that came out of the Forest. The story of the finding of Pippin's brooch was still in its former place (p. 397), as is seen from Aragorn's words here: 'Yet our friends are not behind. We had a clear token that they were with the Orcs when they descended into the plain.'[24]

At the end of the conversation Eomer says:

'... But it is hard to be sure of anything among so many marvels. One may pardon Eothain, my squire. The world is all turned strange. Old men upon eagles; and raiment that deceives the eye; and Elves with bows, and folk that have spoken with the

Lady of the Wood, and yet live; and the Sword comes back to
war that was broken ere the Fathers of the Fathers rode into the
Mark! How shall a man judge what to do in such times. It is
against our law to let strangers wander free in our land, and
doubly so at this time of peril. I beg you to come back
honourably with me, and you will not.'

Aragorn in his reply tells (as in TT p. 41) that he had been in Rohan,
and had spoken with Eomund father of Eomer, and with Theoden,
'and with Thengel that was Master before him.' 'None of them would
have desired to force a man to abandon friends whom the orcs had
seized, while hope or even doubt remained.' Eomer relents. He
requests that Aragorn return with the horses over the Entwade to
'... *torras* where Theoden now sits.' This name was changed at once
or very soon to *Meodarn*, *Meduarn* ('Mead-hall'), and then to
'*Winseld* ['Wine-hall'], the high house in Eodor.' *Eodor* (singular,
'fence, enclosure, dwelling') is seen on Map IV^C (p. 317); *Eodoras*
(plural) on Map IV^{D-E} (p. 319). Eothain's surliness at the loan of the
horses is not present. The horses were first given names in Modern
English, that for Aragorn being 'Windmane' and that for Legolas
'Whitelock'; these were changed to the Old English names found in
TT, *Hasofel* ('Grey-coat', cf. *Hasupada*, note 21) and *Arod* ('Swift').

In the last part of the chapter, after the Riders had gone, the story is
for most of its length at once almost as in the final text; but Aragorn's
words about Fangorn, the earliest account of it that my father wrote,[25]
took this form:

'I do not know what fables men have made out of old
knowledge,' said Aragorn. 'And of the truth little is now
known, even to Keleborn. But I have heard tell that in Fangorn,
clinging here on the east side of the last slopes of the Misty
Mountains, the ancient trees have taken refuge that once
marched dark and proud over the wide lands, before even the
first Elves awoke in the world. Between the Baranduin and the
Barrowdowns is another forest of old trees; but it is not as great
as Fangorn. Some say that both are but the last strongholds of
one mighty wood, more vast than Mirkwood the Great, that
held under its dominion all the countries through which now
flow the Greyflood and the Baranduin; others say that Fangorn
is not akin to the Old Forest, and that its secret is of other kind.'

This was rejected at once and replaced by a shorter passage, close to
Aragorn's words in TT (p. 45), though Elrond is not here cited as his
authority: 'Some say the two are akin, the last strongholds of the

mighty woods of the Elder days, in which the Elves strayed, when they first awoke.'

At the end of the chapter, when Gimli was watchman and all was silent, save that the tree rustled and that 'the horses, picketed a little way off, stirred now and again,' the old man appeared; and his apparition and disappearance are told in precisely the same words as in TT, except that he was 'clad in rags', not in a great cloak, and his hat was 'battered', not 'wide-brimmed'. But the chapter ended altogether differently.

There was no trace of him to be found near at hand; and they did not dare to wander far – the moon was hidden in cloud, and the night was very dark. [*Struck out:* The horses remained quiet, and seemed to feel nothing amiss.] ? The horses were restive, straining at their tether-ropes, showing the whites of their eyes. It was a little while before Legolas could quiet them.

For some time the companions discussed this strange event. 'It was Saruman, of that I feel certain,' said Gimli. 'You remember the words of Eomer. He will come back, or bring more trouble upon us. I wish that the morning were not so far off.'

'Well, in the meantime there is nothing we can do,' said Aragorn, 'nothing but to get what rest we can, while we are still allowed to rest. I will watch now for a while, Gimli.'

The night passed slowly, but nothing further happened, in any of their two-hour watches. The old man did not appear again.

While this is no more than a guess, I suspect that when my father wrote this he thought that it was Gandalf, and not Saruman, who stood so briefly in the light of the fire (cf. the outline given on p. 389).[26]

NOTES

1 *Sarn-Gebir runs North-South:* see Map IV^C, pp. 317–18.
2 This means that the eagle was seen in the direction of Fangorn; see p. 396.
3 *I forgot most of what I knew:* cf. TT p. 98.
4 *Haradwaith* is here the name of a people: see p. 434, and cf. *Enedwaith*, rendered 'Middlemarch' on the First Map (Map II, p. 305), but afterwards (while remaining the name of a region) 'Middle-folk.'
5 On *Mar-* and *Eo-* names in Rohan see *Unfinished Tales* p. 311 note 6 and p. 315 note 36. – Names in *Eo-* are not written with an accent at this period.

6 None of the successive variants of this section of the First Map illustrate this.

7 *Methen Amon*: earliest name of *Methedras* – which appears on the First Map (Map IVE, p. 319). For *Methen* see the *Etymologies*, V.373, stem MET: Noldorin *methen* 'end'; and see note 18.

8 This is the first occurrence of the name *Entwade* in the texts: see p. 366, note 16.

9 Aragorn does not (of course) cry out: 'What news from the North, Riders of Rohan?'; it is said only that he 'hailed them in a loud voice.'

10 This is the first occurrence of the name *Arathorn* of Aragorn's father, replacing earlier *Kelegorn* (cf. also *Eldakar* p. 360, *Valatar* p. 362).

11 Gandalf's escape from Orthanc.

12 This passage is found later in TT (p. 33). The reference there to Eorl the Young is here absent; and the *Brandings* of Dale (named from King Brand son of Bain son of Bard) are in TT the *Bardings* (which was added to the First Map, p. 307). See note 19.

13 In a design of my father's for the cover of *The Return of the King* the throne is shown with four feet. This design, in white, gold and green on a black ground shows (as he noted) 'the empty throne awaiting return of the King' with outstretching wings; the Winged Crown; the white-flowering Tree, with seven stars; and dimly seen beyond in the darkness a vision of the fall of Sauron. This design, in simplified form, was used for the cover of the India paper edition of *The Lord of the Rings* published by George Allen and Unwin in 1969.

14 Yet Gandalf had himself been in, or over, those regions, it seems: 'No, I did not find them. There was a darkness over the valleys of the Emyn Muil, and I did not know of their captivity, until the eagle told me.'

15 Altered later to: 'It has been scored with the pin, which is broken off.' – An error in the text of TT may be mentioned here. Aragorn did not say (p. 26) that Pippin was smaller than *the other*' – he would not refer to Merry in such a remote tone – but 'smaller than *the others*', i.e. Merry and Frodo and Sam.

16 *to the west*: subsequently changed back to *to the south*.

17 This is the first occurrence in the texts of the name *Eastemnet*, which is found on the First Map (Map IV^D, p. 319). *Westemnet* occurs later in this text (p. 401).

18 Here, as they looked about them, they saw to their right 'the windy uplands of the Wold of Rohan', and beyond Fangorn the last great peak of the Misty Mountains (first named *Methen Amon*, p. 391 and note 7), *Methendol*, immediately changed to *Methedras*.

19 The passage in which Aragorn tells Gimli what he knows of the

Riders of Rohan (TT p. 33), which had first appeared much earlier in B (p. 395), was transferred subsequently to the place that it occupies in TT on an inserted rider. This retains almost exactly the form in which it was first written, without mention of Eorl the Young, but with *Bardings* for *Brandings*.

20   In the preliminary drafting the Old English form is used: *Halfheah* (*Halfheh*, *Healfheh*).

21   A pencilled rider was inserted into the manuscript later as a substitute for this speech: here the origin of the *mearas* remains the same, but in other respects the text of TT is largely reached: Gandalf (not yet called Greyhame) is murmured by some in Rohan to be a bringer of ill, Theoden is called King, and his anger against Gandalf for taking Shadowfax and the horse's wildness after his return appear. By an addition to the rider Eomer says: 'We know that name, or *Gondelf* as we have it.' *Gondelf* is an 'Anglo-Saxonising' of Norse *Gandalf(r)*. At the foot of the page is written the Old English word *Hasupada* ('Grey-coat'), and it appears from a subsequent typescript text of the chapter that this refers to Gandalf ('Greyhame'): ' "Gandalf!" said Eomer. "We know that name, and the wandering *witega* that claims it. *Hasupada* we call him mostly in our tongue"' (Old English *witega* 'wise man, one who has knowledge').

22   On Shadowfax at Rivendell and after see pp. 390 and 438 note 2.

23   Eomer calls Saruman 'a wizard of great power', changed to 'a wizard and man of craft', and that to 'a wizard and very crafty'. Against the word *wizard* is pencilled *wicca* (Old English, 'wizard', surviving at any rate until recently as *witch*, masculine, not distinct in form from *witch* deriving from the Old English feminine *wicce*).

24   These words are in themselves ambiguous, but what my father intended is shown, I think, by the fact that he afterwards corrected them on the manuscript to 'We had a clear token that one at least was still with the orcs not far from the East Wall.' The original story was still present when he wrote the outline for the next chapter.

25   If the very early images, when Treebeard was a Giant and his forest correspondingly gigantic (VI.382–4, 410), are excepted.

26   Other supports, admittedly slight, for this idea are the statements that the old man was 'clad in rags' (cf. Trotter's vision on Amon Hen, p. 380); that he had a 'battered hat' (cf. Frodo's song in Lórien, FR p. 375: *an old man in a battered hat*); and that 'the horses remained quiet, and seemed to feel nothing amiss.' – It is curious that Aragorn's words in TT, p. 46 (when the old man was certainly Saruman, TT p. 102) 'I marked also that this old man had a hat not a hood' were an addition to the text made long after.

Note on the Chronology

'The Riders of Rohan' is unusual in that the narrative underwent an important change in structure long after it was to all intents and purposes completed.

I set out below the relations between the time-scheme in the second text (B) and that in *The Two Towers*. 'Day 1' is the day of Boromir's death.

	Text B		*The Two Towers*
Day 1	Orcs descend into plains of Rohan at night.	(Feb. 26)	The same
Day 2	Aragorn &c. descend into Rohan in the morning. First day in the plains.	(Feb. 27)	The same
Day 3	Second day in the plains. Aragorn &c. reach the downs in the evening and go on through the night. – Riders overtake Orcs at nightfall.	(Feb. 28)	Aragorn &c. approach downs in the evening and halt for the night. – Riders overtake Orcs at nightfall.
Day 4	Battle of Riders and Orcs at dawn. – Aragorn &c. reach northmost hill of the downs at dawn. Encounter with Riders returning in the morning.	(Feb. 29)	Battle of Riders and Orcs at dawn. – Aragorn &c. reach downs towards noon. Night spent on northmost hill of the downs.
Day 5		(Feb. 30)	Aragorn &c. encounter Riders returning in the morning.

In B, Aragorn, Legolas and Gimli took two days and two nights after their descent from the 'East Wall' to reach the isolated hill at the northern end of the downs where they met the Riders; in TT they took three days and two nights to reach that place, and passed the third night there. In B, they encountered the Riders returning in the morning after the battle at dawn; in TT the meeting was on the following day: the Riders had passed a whole further day and night by the eaves of Fangorn before setting off south again.

This change in the chronology, with very substantial rewriting and reordering (TT pp. 27 ff.) of the existing chapter, was introduced in October 1944. On 12 October my father wrote a letter to me in South Africa in which he said (*Letters* no. 84):

I began trying to write again (I would, on the brink of term!) on

Tuesday, but I struck a most awkward error (one or two days) in the synchronization, v. important at this stage, of movements of Frodo and the others, which has cost labour and thought and will require tiresome small alterations in many chapters...

Four days later he wrote again (*Letters* no. 85):

I have been struggling with the dislocated chronology of the Ring, which has proved most vexatious ... I think I have solved it all at last by small map alterations, and by inserting an extra day's Entmoot, and extra days *into Trotter's chase* and Frodo's journey...

(On the extra day of the Entmoot see p. 419.)

In one point however the text of TT retains an uncorrected vestige of the original story. Éomer tells Aragorn (p. 39) that 'scouts warned me of the orc-host coming down out of the East Wall *three nights ago*,' just as he does in the B text (p. 401). But in B this was said on the morning of Day 4, and the reference is to the night of Day 1; in TT it was said on the morning of Day 5. It was therefore not three nights ago, but four, that the Orcs came down from the Emyn Muil.

In *The Tale of Years* in Appendix B to LR the dates are:

Feb. 26 Éomer hears of the descent of the Orc-band from the Emyn Muil.
Feb. 27 Éomer sets out from Eastfold about midnight to pursue the Orcs.
Feb. 28 Éomer overtakes the Orcs.
Feb. 29 The Rohirrim attack at sunrise and destroy the Orcs.
Feb. 30 Éomer returning to Edoras meets Aragorn.

Thus Éomer's 'three nights ago' in TT cannot be explained by taking it to refer, not to the descent of the Orcs into Rohan, but to his receiving news of it.

XXI
THE URUK-HAI

For this chapter there exists, first, a brief outline as follows:

> Some want to go North. Some say ought to go straight to
> Mordor. The great orcs were ordered to go to Isengard.
> They carry prisoners. Neither of them are the One. They haven't
> got it. Kill 'em. But they're hobbits. Saruman said bring any *hobbit,*
> *alive.* Curse Saruman. Who does he think he is? A good master and
> lord. Man's flesh to eat.
> Fight breaks out. Slain orc falls on top of Pippin with blade
> drawn. Pippin manages to cut wrist bands. Ties cord loosely again.
> Isengarders win. Mordor orcs are killed. They start on. [?Leader]
> called Uglúk [?leaves them]. They rouse Merry, give him drink; cut
> ankle bonds and drive hobbits with whips. Dark night. Pippin
> manages to unclasp brooch unseen.
> They get into plain. Merry and Pippin made to run till they faint
> and fall. Orcs carry them.
> Pippin awakes to hear horsemen. Night.... Terror of orcs. They
> run at great speed. Uglúk refuses to let hobbits be slain or cast aside.
> Horsemen ride up. Uglúk steals off [?from his friends seizing]
> hobbits. But a horseman rides after him. Pippin pulls Merry down
> flat and covers him with cloak, the horseman rides past and spears
> Uglúk. Merry and Pippin fly into forest.

'Uglúk' is here of course the Mordor Orc subsequently called Grishnákh. It is seen that Pippin still drops his brooch before the descent
into the plain (p. 401 and note 24).
  For almost half of this chapter there is no initial drafting extant, and
this is largely because my father again, as in the previous chapter,
wrote a new version in ink over erased drafting in pencil; in addition,
it seems that some initial drafting on separate pages has been lost. As
far, then, as ' "Very well," said Uglúk' (TT p. 54) the earliest extant
text is this second version or fair copy, in which the story as told in
TT was reached almost down to the last detail, with relatively very
little subsequent correction and addition. The manuscript begins
without title, but my father clearly saw it as a new chapter, 'XXIV'.[1] A
title, 'An Orc-raid', was written in later.
  The later story of Pippin's casting aside his brooch after the descent
into the plain had now entered. The Orc-names are all present:

Lugbúrz, Uruk-hai; Uglúk (leader of the Isengarders), *Gríshnák* (so spelt), *Lugdush*. Uglúk does not use the word *Halflings* (TT p. 48), but calls them *hobbits*; he says 'We are the servants of *the old Uthwit* and the White Hand' (cf. TT p. 49), this being Old English *úþwita* 'sage, philosopher, one of great learning'; and he calls the descent into the plain of Rohan 'the Ladder' (changed to 'the Stair': TT p. 50). Gríshnák does not name the Nazgûl (TT p. 49), but says 'The winged one awaits us northward on the east bank'.

At the point where Pippin is given the orc-draught my father wrote a brief outline in the body of the text:

> Uglúk smears Merry's wound. He cries out. Orcs jeer. But torment not the object. Merry recovers.
>
> Orcs become aware of pursuit by horsemen. Merry and Pippin do not know about horsemen; but perceive that orcs are afraid.
>
> Gríshnák brings a small company of Mordor-orcs from the East. Uglúk evidently does not like it. He asks why the Nazgûl has not come to help them. The Nazgûl is not yet permitted to cross River: Sauron is keeping them for the War – and for another purpose.
>
> Gríshnák brings a small company of Mordor-orcs from the East. what a mess you have got into! They fly to the Forest.
>
> When surrounded Gríshnák searches Merry and Pippin and drags them out of ring of horsemen. He is slain, and Merry and Pippin passed over. They run into forest.
>
> Adventure with Treebeard.

From the point where Uglúk sends the 'Northerners' running off towards the Forest (TT p. 54) initial drafting is extant, except for a further passage where my father reverted to the method of erasing it and writing a new version above. This draft text, dashed down in faint pencil and extremely difficult to make out, is astonishingly close to the final form. I give a brief passage in exemplification (TT p. 56), where the draft text is not in fact so close to the final form as it is in some others:

The Forest was drawing near. Already they had passed a few isolated trees. The land was beginning to slope upward, ever more steeply. But this did not stay the orcs, now desperately putting on their last spurt. Looking to one side Pippin saw that riders coming in the East were already level with them, galloping over the plain, the sunset touching their spears and helmets and their pale flowing hair. They were hemming in the orcs driving them along the line of the river. He wondered very much what sort of folk they were. He wished he had learned more in Rivendell, looked at more maps – but then the journey was all in more competent hands, he had not reckoned on being cut off from Gandalf and Trotter – and even Frodo. All he could remember about them was that he [*read* they] had given Gandalf a horse. That [?sounded] well.

If the original drafting where it is extant is characteristic of the parts where it is not, as seems very probable, it can be said this chapter was achieved with far greater facility than any previous part of the story of *The Lord of the Rings.*

The second version of the latter part of the chapter only differs in very minor touches here and there from the final form.[2] The watchfires of the Riders were a later addition to the text; Grishnákh (now so spelt) had evidently had personal experience of Gollum, for he says 'That's what he meanss, iss it?' (cf. TT p. 59); and at the point where the chapter ends in TT this text has only:

There he was slain at last by Eomer the Third Master of Rohan, who dismounted and fought him sword to sword. So ended the raid, and no news of it came ever back either to Mordor or to Isengard.[3]

Neither in the draft nor in the second text did my father stop at this point, but continued on into the following chapter in *The Two Towers,* 'Treebeard'.

NOTES

1   The manuscript is paginated 'XXIV', as also is the draft (with numbers written at the same time as the text).

2   The Orc-names *Snaga* and *Mauhúr* appear already in the preliminary draft.

3   The expansion of the end of the chapter came in with the chronological revision made in October 1944 (see pp. 406–7). In notes on the subject my father said that 'at end of "Uruk-hai" the fight should be made to take longer – chase of stray fugitives, etc.', and that something should be said of the burning of the corpses.

XXII
TREEBEARD

Of 'Giant Treebeard' there have been many mentions in the outlines scattered through the early texts of *The Lord of the Rings*, but there was nothing in any of them to prepare for the reality when he should finally appear. My father said years later (*Letters* no. 180, 14 January 1956):

> I have long ceased to *invent* ... : I wait till I seem to know what really happened. Or till it writes itself. Thus, though I knew for years that Frodo would run into a tree-adventure somewhere far down the Great River, I have no recollection of inventing Ents. I came at last to the point, and wrote the 'Treebeard' chapter without any recollection of previous thought: just as it now is.

This testimony is fully borne out by the original text. 'Treebeard' did indeed very largely 'write itself'.

First, however, there is a page of pencilled notes of much interest but with various puzzling features. I give here this text exactly as it stands, and postpone discussion of it till the end.

> Did first lord of the Elves make Tree-folk in order to or through trying to understand trees?
> Gimli and Legolas to go with Trotter and Boromir. It must be Merry and Pippin who find Gandalf.
> Notes for *Treebeard*.
> In some ways rather stupid. Are the Tree-folk ('Lone-walkers') *hnau* that have gone tree-like, or trees that have become *hnau*?[1] Treebeard might be 'moveless' – but here are some notes [?or] first [?suggestions].
> There are very few left. Not enough room. 'Time was when a fellow could walk and sing all day and hear no more than the echo of his voice in the mountains.'
> Difference between *trolls* – stone inhabited by goblin-spirit, *stone-giants*, and the 'tree-folk'. [*Added in ink:* Ents.]
> Treebeard is anxious for news. He never hears much. But he smells things in the air. Prefers breath from South and West of the Sea. Too much East wind these days. He is bothered about Saruman: a machine-minded man. Fondest of Gandalf. Very upset at news of his fall. Only one of the wizards who understood trees.

Tells how the Horsemasters have ridden away south leaving land empty.

There are only three of us left: myself and Skinbark and Leaflock [*written above in ink:* Fangorn   Fladrib > Fladrif   Finglas]. Saruman has got hold of Skinbark. He went off to Isengard some time ago. Leaflock has gone 'tree-ish'. He seldom comes into the hills: has taken to standing half-asleep all through the summer with the deep grass of the meadows round his knees. Covered with leaves he is. Wakes up a bit in winter. May be somewhere about.

Treebeard offers to take them across Rohan to or towards Minas Tirith. Treebeard smells war.

They see a battle of Wolfriders (Saruman) and the Horsemasters – wild flowing hair and little bows.

How do they meet Gandalf? It should really be *Sam* or Frodo who saw vision in the Mirror of Galadriel.

A possible return of Gandalf would be as an old bent beggar with a battered hat coming to gates of Minas Tirith. He is let in. After, at siege's darkest hour when outer walls have fallen, he throws off cloak and stands up – *white*. He leads sortie. Or he comes with horses of Rohan riding on [*struck out:* Arfaxed] Shadowfax.

Another possibility. Cut out rescue of Frodo by Sam. Let Sam get lost and meet Gandalf, and have adventures getting into Minas Tirith. (But it was Frodo saw vision of Gandalf. Also Sam saw vision of Frodo lying under dark cliff, pale, and of himself on a winding stair.)

The winding stair must be cut in rocks and go up from Gorgoroth to watch-tower. Cut out Minas Morgul.

More roughly scribbled notes were added:

Trotter sends Legolas and Gimli with Boromir to Minas Tirith. He himself wanders looking for the hobbits. He meets Gandalf. He is tempted but forsakes his ambition.

What are Treebeard and Ents to do about Saruman. Seek help of Rohiroth?

It is evident that this page does not belong to the time we have reached in the narrative texts, but to some earlier stage, before the death of Boromir had entered the story. To suppose otherwise would depend, of course, on the assumption that the words 'Gimli and Legolas to go with Trotter and Boromir. It must be Merry and Pippin who find Gandalf' already stood on this page which my father used afterwards for notes on the Ents; but there is nothing in the appearance of the page to suggest it. '*It must be Merry and Pippin* who find Gandalf' suggests the rejection of some earlier idea, and 'How do they meet Gandalf?' later in these notes obviously relates to this. Moreover the notes at the end, in which Boromir is still thought of as going to

Minas Tirith, seem certainly to have been set down after the main text had been written.

In the outline which I have called 'The Story Foreseen from Moria' it was Merry and Pippin who were to encounter Treebeard but Gimli and Legolas who were to meet Gandalf returned (pp. 210–11); and this was repeated in the outline 'The Story Foreseen from Lórien' (pp. 329–30). The reference to the cutting-out of Minas Morgul and the substitution of a watchtower (see on this question p. 344 and note 39) is a reference to the story of Sam and Frodo in 'The Story Foreseen from Lórien'. The death of Boromir entered in an outline for the end of 'The Breaking of the Fellowship', and 'The Departure of Boromir' (pp. 375, 378). On the face of it, then, these notes belong to the time of work on 'The Great River' and 'The Breaking of the Fellowship', and show my father pondering the way ahead after the Company should have been brought to its dismemberment above the falls of Rauros.

The note 'It should really be *Sam* or Frodo who saw vision in the Mirror of Galadriel' – at first sight incomprehensible, since there has never been a suggestion that it was anybody else who looked in the Mirror – is I think to be explained in this way: it would have been clearer if my father had written 'It really *should* be Sam or Frodo...', i.e. the story of the Mirror has been written of Sam and Frodo, and so it should be; it should not be changed. What is the purport of this? I think that my father was changing direction as he wrote – already doubting the rightness of the decision to make it Merry and Pippin who met Gandalf returned; and this seems to have been largely on account of the visions in the Mirror. Hence his suggestion (implying the rejection of the whole story of Sam and Frodo in Mordor as projected in 'The Story Foreseen from Lórien') that Sam should be the one who met Gandalf. Nonetheless he was unwilling to alter the visions seen by Frodo and Sam in the Mirror, to make it Sam who saw Gandalf walking down the long grey road (for that was not 'what really happened'). In the event, of course, Gandalf reappeared to members of the Company who had never looked into the Mirror of Galadriel. Possibly to be connected with this is the vision of Gandalf vouchsafed to Trotter on Amon Hen (pp. 379–80).

The word *Ents* added in ink to the note on the difference between 'trolls' and 'tree-folk' (with its striking definition of 'trolls') was perhaps the first use of it in the new and very particular sense; for its former use in *Entish Lands, Entish Dales* see p. 16 note 14 and p. 65 note 32, and cf. also *Letters* no. 157, 27 November 1954:

> As usually with me they [the Ents] grew rather out of their name, than the other way about. I always felt that something ought to be done about the peculiar Anglo-Saxon word *ent* for a 'giant' or mighty person of long ago – to whom all old works were ascribed.

The textual situation in this chapter is essentially very similar to that in the last, in that there is initial drafting for part of the chapter, but in the rest of it the draft text was erased and the 'fair copy' written over it; and here again, and even more so, the first draft is for the most part extraordinarily close to the final form. My father's words in the letter cited on p. 411, 'just as it now is', must be modified, however, in respect of certain passages where the narrative leaves the immediate experience of Merry and Pippin and touches on wider themes.

The separation of 'Treebeard' as 'Chapter XXV' from XXIV ('The Uruk-hai') was carried out in the course of the writing of the fair copy.

Taking first the part of the chapter for which the original setting down of the story is available, this runs from the beginning of the chapter in TT to 'they were twisted round, gently but irresistibly' (p. 66), and then from '"There is quite a lot going on," said Merry' (p. 69) to Treebeard's denunciation of Saruman (p. 77). The draft, written so fast as to touch on total illegibility if the later text did not generally provide sufficient clues, remained in all essentials of description into TT, and for long stretches the vocabulary and phrasing underwent only the most minor forms of change. As in the last chapter I give a single brief passage to exemplify this (TT p. 73):

No trees grew there. Treebeard strode up with scarcely any slackening of his pace. Then they saw a wide opening. On either side two trees grew like living gate-posts, but there was no gate save their crossing and interwoven branches; and as the Ent approached the trees raised up their boughs and all their leaves rustled and whispered. For they were evergreen trees, and their leaves were dark and polished like the leaves of the holm-oak.

Beyond the trees there was a wide level space, as though the floor of a great hall had been hewn out of the side of the hill. On either side the walls sloped upward until they were fifty feet in height or more and at their feet grew trees: two long lines of trees increasing in size. At the far end the rock wall was sheer, but in it was cut a shallow bay with an arched roof: the only roof save the branches of the trees which overshadowed all the ground save for a broad aisle/path in the middle. A little stream that escaped from the Entwash spring high above and left the main water fell tinkling down the sheer face of the rear wall, pouring like a clear curtain of silver drops in front of the arched bay. It was gathered again in [a] green rock basin, and thence flowed out down the open aisle/path and on to rejoin the Entwash in its journey through the Forest.

All the tiny meticulous changes of word and rhythm that differentiate this from the text of TT were introduced in the writing of the fair copy manuscript.

There are some small particular points worthy of mention in this first part of the chapter. In the fair copy corresponding to TT pp. 66–7 (the passage is lacking in independent draft) Treebeard's height was changed from ten feet to twelve, and then to fourteen; he says that if he had not seen the hobbits before he heard them 'I should have just batted you with my club'; and his ejaculation 'Root and twig!' replaced 'Crack my timbers!'[2]

When Merry (Pippin in the draft) suggested that Treebeard must be getting tired of holding them up (TT p. 69), he replied, both in draft and fair copy: 'Hm, *tired*? *Tired*? What is that. Ah yes, I remember. No, I am not tired'; and later he says when they come to the Ent-house that perhaps they are 'what you call "tired"'.

The first major development from the original text comes with Treebeard's long brooding discourse on Lórien and Fangorn, as he carried Merry and Pippin through the woods (TT pp. 70–2). At first he said:

'... Neither this country nor anything else outside the Golden Wood is what it was when Keleborn was young. *Tauretavárea tumbalemorna Tumbaletaurea landataváre.*[3] That is what they used to say. But we have changed many things.' (He means they have weeded out rotten-hearted trees such as are in the Old Forest.)

This was changed immediately to:

'... Things have changed, but it is still true in places.'

'What do you mean? What is true?' said Pippin.

'I am not sure I know, and I am sure I could not explain to you. But there are no longer any evil trees here (none that are evil according to their kind and light). ...'

Treebeard's remarks about trees awakening, 'getting Entish', and then showing in some cases that they have 'bad hearts', are very much as in TT; but to Pippin's question 'Like the Old Forest, do you mean?' he replies:

'Aye, aye, something like, but not as bad as that. That was already a very bad region even in the days when there was all one wood from here to Lune, and we were called the East End. But something was queer (went wrong) away there: some old sorcery in the Dark Days, I expect. Ah, no: the first woods were more like Lórien, only thicker, stronger, younger. Those were days! Time was when one could walk and sing all day and hear no more than the echo of his own voice in the mountains. And the scent. I used to spend weeks [?months] just breathing.'

In the fair copy this was greatly expanded, but by no means to the text of TT. Here Treebeard begins as in the original draft (with *Mountains of Lune* for *Lune*) as far as 'this was just the East End', but then continues:

'... Things went wrong there in the Dark [> Elder] Days; some old sorcery, I expect [> some old shadow of the Great Dark lay there]. They say that even the Men that came out of the Sea were caught in it, and some of them fell into the Shadow. But that is only a rumour to me. Anyway they have no treeherds there, no one to care for them: it is a long, long time since the Ents walked away from the banks of the Baranduin.'

'What about Tom Bombadil, though?' asked Pippin. 'He lives on the Downs close by. He seems to understand trees.'

'What about whom?' said Treebeard. '*Tombombadil*? *Tombombadil*? So that is what you call him. Oh, he has got a *very* long name. He understands trees, right enough; but he is not an Ent. He is no herdsman. He laughs and does not interfere. He never made anything go wrong, but he never cured anything, either. Why, why, it is all the difference between walking in the fields and trying to keep a garden; between, between passing the time of a day to a sheep on the hillside, or even maybe sitting down and studying sheep till you know what they feel about grass, and being a shepherd. Sheep get like shepherd, and shepherd like sheep, it is said, very slowly. But it is quicker and closer with Ents and trees. Like some Men and their horses and dogs, only quicker and closer even than that. For Ents are more like Elves: less interested in themselves than Men are, better at getting inside; and Ents are more like Men, more changeable than Elves are, quicker at catching the outside; only they do both things better than either: they are steadier, and keep at it. [*Added*: Elves began it of course: waking trees up and teaching them to talk. They always wished to talk to everything. But then the Darkness came, and they passed away over the Sea, or fled into far valleys and hid themselves. The Ents have gone on tree-herding.] Some of my trees can walk, many can talk to me.

'But it was not so, of course, in the beginning. We were like your Tombombadil when we were young. The first woods were more like the woods of Lórien....'

Most of this passage, including all reference to Bombadil, was bracketed for omission,[4] and my father then struck it all out and substituted a new version on a separate page. It is clear that all this revision belongs to the time of the writing of the fair copy manuscript.[5] In this new version the text of TT is all but reached; but Treebeard says this of the Old Forest:

'...I do not doubt that there is some shadow of the Great Darkness lying there still away North; and bad memories are handed down; for that Forest is old, though none of the trees are really old there, not what I call old. But there are hollow dales in this land where [the shadow >] the Darkness has never been lifted....'

Treebeard's song (*In the willow-meads of Tasarinan*) was set down in the draft manuscript in a faint scribble that nonetheless reached without hesitation almost the final form.[6]

When in the draft Treebeard reaches the Ent-house (TT p. 73) he makes no remark about the distance they have come, and in the fair copy he says: 'I have brought you three times twelve leagues or thereabouts, if measurements of that kind hold good in the country of Fangorn', where 'three' was changed to 'seven' before the words were rejected and replaced by his computation in 'Ent-strides'. In the draft he says that the place is named *Fonthill*, changed to *Funtial*, then back to *Fonthill*,[7] and finally 'Part of the name of this place could be called *Wellandhouse* in your language' (*Wellinghall* in the fair copy).

Treebeard *stooped* and lifted the two great vessels onto the table (this my father wrote in the fair copy also before at once striking it out); and he said before he lowered himself onto the bed ('with only the slightest bend at the waist') 'I think better flat'.

The next major development in the evolution of the text comes at this point, when Merry and Pippin tell Treebeard their story. Here the draft reads:

They followed no order for Treebeard would often stop them, and go back again or jump forward. He was only interested in parts of the tale: in their account of the Old Forest, in Rivendell, in Lothlórien, and especially in anything to do with Gandalf, most of all in Saruman. The hobbits were sorry that they could not remember more clearly Gandalf's account of that wizard. Treebeard kept reverting to him.

'Saruman has been here some time, a long time you would call it. Too long I should now say. Very quiet he was to begin with: no trouble to any of us. I used to talk to him. Very eager to listen he was in those days, ready to learn about old days. Many a thing I have told him that he would never have known or guessed otherwise. Never. He never repaid me – never told me anything. And he got more like that: his face more like windows in a stone wall, windows with blinds (shutters inside).

'But now I understand. So he's thinking of becoming a Power,
is he. I have not troubled myself with the great wars: Elves are
not my business, nor Men; and it is with them that wizards are
mostly concerned. They are always worrying about the future.
I don't like worrying about the future. But I shall have to begin,
I see. Mordor seemed a long way, but these orcs! And if
Saruman has started taking them up, I have got trouble right on
my borders. Cutting down trees. Machines, great fires. I won't
stand it. Trees that were my friends. Trees I had known from
nut and acorn. Cut down and left sometimes. Orc-work.

'I have been thinking I should have to do something. But I see
it will be better sooner than later. Men are better than orcs,
especially if the Dark Lord doesn't get at them. But the Rohiroth
and the folk of Ondor if Saruman attacks at the back will soon
be in a [?lonely].... We shall have [?hordes] from the East and
... [?swarm] of orcs all over us. I shall be [?eaten] up – and there
will be nowhere to go. The flood will rise into the pines in the
mountains. I don't think the Elves would find room for me in a
ship. I could not go over sea. I should wither away from my own
soil.

'If you'll come with me we'll go to Isengard! You'll be helping
your own friends.'

With the further words '[?Of] the Ents and Entwives' the initial draft
peters out here; but in these last hastily jotted lines we see the
emergence of a major new idea and new direction. The rôle that
Treebeard was to play in the raising of the siege of Minas Tirith (pp.
211, 330, and cf. p. 412) is gone, and all is suddenly clear: Treebeard's
part is to attack *Saruman*, who dwells on his very borders.

There is very little further initial drafting for this chapter extant;
almost all is lost erased beneath the fair copy text. Rough workings for
the Song of the Ent and the Entwife are found (see p. 421); and there is
also a little scrap which shows my father's first thoughts for the march
on Isengard:

Ents excited. To Isengard!
Hobbits see trees behind. Is Forest moving?
Orc woodcutters come on the Ents. Horrible surprise to find wood
alive. They are destroyed. Ents take shields. They go on to Isengard.
End of Ch. XXV.

But it seems to me most unlikely that those parts of the original
drafting that are lost were any less close to the fair copy than are those
that survive.[8] The text of the fair copy manuscript in the latter part of
the chapter was retained in TT (pp. 75–90) without the smallest

deviation of expression almost throughout its length: Treebeard's thoughts of Saruman and his becoming 'hot', his story of the Entwives, the Entmoot, the time spent with Bregalad, the march of the Ents and Pippin's awareness of the moving groves of trees behind them, to the last words: ' "Night lies over Isengard," said Treebeard.'

Exceptions to this are very few.[9] Against the passage in which Treebeard condemns Saruman this note (it is scarcely in Treebeard's style) is written in the margin (and subsequently struck through): 'It is not perhaps mere chance that *Orthanc* which in Elvish means "a spike of rock" is in the tongue of Rohan "a machine".' With this cf. 'The Road to Isengard' (TT p. 160): 'This was Orthanc, the citadel of Saruman, the name of which had (by design or chance) a twofold meaning; for in the Elvish speech *orthanc* signifies Mount Fang, but in the language of the Mark of old the Cunning Mind.'

The alteration to the text made in 1944, extending the Entmoot by an extra day, has appeared already: see p. 407. Until this change was made the Entmoot ended on the afternoon of the second day (cf. TT pp. 87–8):

Most of the time they sat silent under the shelter of the bank; for the wind was colder, and the clouds closer and greyer; there was little sunshine. There was a feeling of expectancy in the air. They could see that Bregalad was listening, although to them, down in the dell of his Ent-house, the sound of the Ent-voices was faint.

The afternoon came, and the sun, going west towards the mountains, sent out long yellow beams...

At the same time as this was rewritten, my father replaced the Entish words (first appearing in the fair copy manuscript) of the song sung by the Ents as they marched from the Moot past Bregalad's house, but not to the text in TT p. 88.[10]

NOTES

1   The word *hnau* is taken from C. S. Lewis, *Out of the Silent Planet*: on Earth there is only one kind of *hnau*, Men, but on Malacandra there are three totally distinct races that are *hnau*.

2   A pencilled note on the fair copy says that 'Crack my timbers' had been 'queried by Charles Williams'. The same change was made at a later point in the chapter (TT p. 75).

3   This was changed to the form in TT already on the draft manuscript, but with *lómeamor* for *lómeanor*, and this remained uncorrected on the fair copy.

4   It would be interesting to know why Treebeard's knowledge of and estimate of Tom Bombadil was removed. Conceivably, my

father felt that the contrast between Bombadil and the Ents developed here confused the conflict between the Ents and the Entwives; or, it may be, it was precisely this passage that gave rise to the idea of that conflict.

5   This is seen from the fact that the new version was still numbered in 'Chapter XXIV', i.e. 'Treebeard' had not yet been separated off as a new chapter, as was done in the course of the writing of the fair copy (p. 414). Moreover, when later the hobbits told Treebeard their story he was 'enormously interested in everything', and 'everything' included Tom Bombadil.

6   The names in the draft have these differences from those in TT: *Dorthonion* is *Orod Thuin* (preceded by *Orod Thon*), which remained in the fair copy and following typescript, changed later to *Orod-na-Thôn* (see the *Etymologies*, V.392); and for *Aldalómë* appears another name that I cannot certainly read: *His..eluinalda*.

7   The name *Fonthill* is specifically derived from Fonthill in Wiltshire, as is seen from *Funtial*, which is the form of the place-name found in a tenth-century charter. The first element of the name is probably Old English *funta* 'spring', and the second the Celtic word *ial* 'fertile upland region'; but my father no doubt intended it to be taken as if from Old English *hyll* 'hill'.

8   This is supported by the bits of text where the erased draft can to some extent be made out, and by a piece of independent draft revision of a part of the 'Saruman' passage. – The name *Dernslade* (*slade* 'valley, dell, dingle') can be seen in the draft where the fair copy has *Derndingle*.

9   In addition to those mentioned in the text, it may be noted that Treebeard's answer to Pippin's question about the small number of the Ents: 'Have a great many died?' is here briefer: ' "Oh no!" said Treebeard. "But there were only a few to begin with, and we have not much increased. There have been no Entings . . .'

    Among names, *Angrenost* (Isengard) now appears; a blank was left for the Elvish name of the Valley of Saruman, *Nan Gurunír* being added in; and Gondor remains *Ondor* (see p. 401).

10 The original form of the Entish words was thus:
>   Ta-rūta dūm-da dūm-da dūm / ta-rāra dūm-da dūm-da būm /
>   Da-dūda rūm-ta rūm-ta rūm / ta-dāda rūm-ta rūm-ta dūm /

    The Ents were coming: ever nearer and louder rose their song.
>   Ta-būmda romba būmda-romba banda-romba būm-ta būm /
>   Da-dūra dāra lamba būm / ta-lamba dāra rūm-ta rūm!
>   Ta-būm-da-dom / ta-rūm-ta-rom / ta-būm-ta lamba dūm-da-
>   dom //
>   ta-būm / ta-rūm / ta-būm-ta lamba dūm //

This was changed in 1944 to:
>   A! rundamāra-nundarūn tahōra-mundakumbalūn,

tarūna-rūna-rūnarūn tahōra-kumbakumbanūn.
The Ents were coming: ever nearer and louder rose their song:
Tarundaromba-rundaromba mandaromba-mundamūn,
tahūrahāra-lambanūn talambatāra-mundarūn,
    tamunda-rom, tarunda-rom, tamunda-lamba-munda-
    tom.

The Song of the Ent and the Entwife

Rough workings and a first completed draft are extant; in this, verses
1 and 3 are as in the final form.

2   When Spring is in the sprouting corn and flames of green arise,
    When blossom like a living snow upon the orchard lies,
    When earth is warm, and wet with rain, and its smell is in the air,
    I'll linger here, and will not come, because my land is fair.

4   When Summer warms the hanging fruit and burns the berry brown,
    When straw is long and ear is white and harvest comes to town,
    When honey spills and apple swells and days are wealthiest,
    I'll linger here, and will not come, because my land is best.

5   When winter comes and boughs are bare and all the grass is grey,
    When   and starless night o'ertakes the sunless day,
    When storm is wild and trees are felled, then in the bitter rain
    I'll look for thee, and call to thee, I'll come to thee again.

The blank space in this verse is left thus in the original. Verse 6 differs
from the final form only in the first line, with repeated *When Winter
comes, when Winter comes*; and the concluding lines differ only in *the
roads that lead* for *the road that leads*. A preliminary version of the
ending is found, written as prose, thus:

> I'll come back to thee and look for thee again, I'll come to thee and
> comfort thee, and find thee in the rain. We'll walk the land together
> and gather seed and set, and journey to an island where both can
> live again.

XXIII

NOTES ON VARIOUS TOPICS

There are three isolated pages of notes, heterogeneous in content and obviously even on the same page written at different times, but each of which has links to the others. Some of the notes may well be earlier than the time we have reached,[1] others later, but rather than split them up and try to fit them in uncertainly elsewhere it seems best to give them together.

The page that I give first begins with the note 'Wizards = Angels', and this same note is found on the other two pages also. I take it to be the first appearance in written record of this conception, i.e. that the Istari or Wizards were *angeloi*, 'messengers', emissaries from the Lords of the West: see *Unfinished Tales* pp. 388 ff., and especially my father's long discussion in *Letters* no. 156 (4 November 1954). Then follows:

> Gandalf to reappear again. How did he escape? This might never be fully explained. He passed through fire – and became *the* White Wizard. 'I forgot much that I knew, and learned again much that I had forgotten.' *He has thus acquired something of the awe and terrible power of the Ring-wraiths*, only on the good side. Evil things fly from him if he is revealed – when he shines. But he does not as a rule reveal himself.
>
> He should have a trial of strength with Saruman. Could the Balrog of the Bridge be in fact Saruman?
>
> Or better? as in older sketch   Saruman is very affable.

With this compare the initial sketch for 'The Riders of Rohan', p. 389. The extraordinary idea that the Balrog of Moria might be Saruman has appeared in a note written on the back of a page of the fair copy manuscript of 'Lothlórien', p. 236: 'Could not Balrog be Saruman? Make battle on Bridge be between Gandalf and Saruman?' The reference to the 'older sketch' – 'Saruman is very affable' – is to 'The Story Foreseen from Moria', p. 212, where on the homeward journey 'They call at Isengard. Gandalf knocks. Saruman comes out very affable', etc.

The next note on this page records my father's decision to move the whole chronology of the Quest forward by a month:

> Time Scheme. Too much takes place in *winter*. They should

remain longer at Rivendell. This would have additional advantage of allowing Elrond's scouts and messengers far longer *time*. He should discover Black Riders have gone back. Frodo should not start until say Dec. 24th.

It seems likely that 24 December was chosen as being 'numerically' one month later than the existing date, 24 November (p. 169); and that it was changed to 25 December to make the new dates agree 'numerically' with the existing time-structure (since November has 30 days but December 31): see p. 368. I do not understand the statement here that 'he [Elrond] should discover Black Riders have gone back', since the final text of 'The Ring Goes South' had been reached in Gandalf's words 'It is rash to be too sure, yet I think that we may hope now that the Ringwraiths were scattered, and have been obliged to return as best they could to their Master in Mordor, empty and shapeless.'

Another note on this page, not written at the same time, refers to 'Chapter XXIV: Open with conversation of Goblins and their quarrel. How are Merry and Pippin armed?' And the last reads: '*Sarn-gebir* = Grailaw or Graidon Hills'. Both these names mean 'Grey Hill(s)': Old English *hlāw* 'hill', Northern English and Scottish *law*, and Old English *dūn*, Modern English *down*.

The second page contains exact repetitions of notes found on the other pages or in outlines already given, and need not be cited. On the third page the following (only) was written in ink, and seems to be the primary element on the page:

Feb. 9 1942 Geography
Ondor > Gondor
Osgiliath > Elostirion. Ostirion = fort. *Lorn* = haven. *Londe* = gulf.

On the date see p. 379, where I have noted that on the back of an outline for 'The Departure of Boromir' is a clear indication that it was written in the winter of 1941–2. The precise date given here for the change of *Ondor* to *Gondor* is notable; in the fair copy of 'Treebeard' the form was still *Ondor* (see p. 401).

Elostirion was written above *Osgiliath* in the outline for 'The Riders of Rohan' given on p. 389. This change was of course impermanent, but the name *Elostirion* became that of the tallest of the White Towers on Emyn Beraid, in which the *palantír* was set (*Of the Rings of Power*, in *The Silmarillion*, p. 292).[2] – With *lorn* 'haven' cf. *Forlorn* 'North Haven' and *Harlorn* 'South Haven' on the First Map (pp. 301–2), for later *Forlond*, *Harlond*; but on that map appears also *Mithlond*, the Grey Havens (where however it is possible that *Mithlond* actually meant 'Grey Gulf').

The other notes on this page are heterogeneous and not necessarily of the same time. The heading 'Geography' was extended to 'Geography and Language'. Some of these notes are concerned to find a new name for Sarn Gebir: rejected names are *Sern Lamrach*; *Tarn Felin*; *Trandóran*, before (added much later to the page) *Emyn Muil* is reached (for *Muil* see the *Etymologies*, V.374, stem MUY). There are also the English names *Graydon Hills* and *Grailaws*, as on the first page of these notes, and *Hazowland*.[3]

Another group of notes reads:

Language of Shire = modern English
Language of Dale = Norse (used by Dwarves of that region)
Language of Rohan = Old English
'Modern English' is *lingua franca* spoken by all people (except a few secluded folk like Lórien) – but little and ill by orcs.

NOTES

1   It is to be remembered that statements such as 'Gandalf to reappear again' do not by any means imply that this is where the idea first arose: often they are to be taken as reassertions of existing but as yet unachieved ideas.

2   An altogether isolated and undateable note on a slip of paper also evinces dissatisfaction with the name *Osgiliath*. The reverse of the slip carries notes on unconnected matters which my father dated '1940', which may or may not be significant. At the present time, at any rate, I can cast no light on the purport of this note:

   Lord of Rings
      Osgiliath won't do. Name should = New building   'Newbold'
      Town built again   *echain   Ostechain*

   The word 'building' is very unclear, but is assured by 'Newbold', a common English village name meaning 'New building', from Old English *bold* (also *boðl, botl*) closely associated with *byldan*, Modern English *build*. I will add here, incidentally and irrelevantly, that another derivative from the same source is *Nobottle* (Northamptonshire), which my father allowed me to add to my map of the Shire made in 1943 (VI.107, item V) and which remains in that published in *The Lord of the Rings*, although at that time I was under the impression that the name meant that the village was so poor and remote that it did not even possess an inn.

3   *Hazowland* is clearly from the Old English poetic word *hasu* (inflected *hasw-*) 'grey, ashen'; cf. *Hasupada* 'Greycoat', name of Gandalf in Rohan (p. 405 note 21), and *Hasofel* (*Hasufel*) of the same meaning, the horse lent to Aragorn by Eomer.

XXIV

THE WHITE RIDER

For the greater part of this chapter the evolution can be traced very clearly. Initial drafting not erased or overwritten, more developed but discontinuous drafting, and a 'fair copy' that itself underwent constant correction in the act of composition, were a continuous process, and the history of almost every sentence can be followed until near the end of the chapter. This was numbered 'XXVI' from an early stage; a title was added to the 'fair copy' later, first *Sceadufax* in Old English spelling, then 'The White Rider'. The process of composition here was continuous and all of the same time, so that 'first draft', 'second draft', 'fair copy', 'corrections to fair copy' cannot be treated as distinct entities, each complete before the next stage.

An example of this overlapping is seen at once. In the original form of the opening, to Gimli's insistence that the old man who stood by the fire in the night was Saruman, Aragorn replies: 'I wonder. The horses showed no signs of fear.' In the 'fair copy' (more accurately, the first coherent manuscript) this became: ' "I wonder," said Aragorn. "What did he seem to be? An old man? It is strange enough in itself: that an old man should be walking alone by the eaves of Fangorn. Yet the horses showed no signs of fear." ' This obviously belongs with the sentence struck out at the end of 'The Riders of Rohan': 'The horses remained quiet, and seemed to feel nothing amiss', and suggests to my mind that my father believed the old man to be Gandalf (see p. 403 and note 26). Yet in the most 'primitive' drafting further on in the chapter the old man in the night certainly was Saruman (see further pp. 427–8).

The later chronology of the chase across Rohan not being present, of course (see p. 406), Aragorn remarks that the footprints by the riverside 'are a day old'; Gandalf says that the hobbits 'climbed up here yesterday', and that he himself had seen Treebeard 'three days ago': in TT all these are made one day earlier, on account of the extra day added in 1944. At one point, however, the need for correction escaped my father's notice: Legolas' words that the last time he saw the eagle was 'three days ago, above the Emyn Muil' (TT p. 98). This should have been changed to 'four days ago': see the table on p. 406, and cf. *The Tale of Years* in LR: 'February 27   Aragorn reaches the west-cliff at sunrise', and (February having 30 days) 'March 1   Aragorn meets Gandalf the White'.

The story of the first meeting with Gandalf was sketched out in every essential point in the earliest draft. When the three companions saw the old man walking through the wood below them, Gimli's horror of Saruman was at first expressed in more murderous fashion: 'Shoot, Legolas! Draw your bow! Shoot! It is Saruman, or worse. Do not let him speak or bewitch us!' This was retained in the fair copy; and when subsequently it was softened to a demand that Legolas only prepare to shoot, Gimli's following words were retained: 'Why are you waiting? What is the matter with you?' In the earliest draft the wizard wore an 'old hat'; this became a 'battered hat', then a 'wide-brimmed hat' (see p. 403).[1]

The opening of their long conversation proceeds thus in the earliest draft (cf. TT pp. 98–9):

'... At the turn of the Tide. The great storm is coming, but the Tide has turned even at this moment. I have passed through fire and ruin and I have been badly burned, or well burned. But come, tell me now of yourselves. I have seen much in deep places and in high since we parted; I have forgotten much that I knew, and learned again much that I had forgotten.[2] [Some things I can see far off and some close at hand; but not all can I see. *Changed at once to:*] Many things I can see far off but many that are close at hand I cannot see.'

'What do you wish to know?' said Aragorn. 'All that has happened would be a long tale. Will you not first tell us tidings of Merry and Pippin? Did you find them, and are they safe?'

'No, I did not find them,' said Gandalf.[3] 'I was busy with perilous matters, and did not know of their captivity until the eagle told me.'

'The eagle!' said Legolas. 'We have seen an eagle high and far off: the last time was three days ago, above Sarn Gebir.'

'Yes,' said Gandalf, 'that was Gwaewar the Windlord who rescued me from Orthanc. I sent him before me to gather tidings, and to watch the River. His sight is keen, but he cannot see all that passes in wood and valley. But there are some things that I can see unaided. This I may tell you: the Ring has passed beyond my help or the help of any of our original Company. Very nearly it was revealed to the Enemy, but not quite. I had some part in that. For I sat upon the mountains beneath the snows of Methedras and I strove with the Dark Tower, and the shadow passed. Then I was weary: very weary.'

The story that Gandalf was on Tol Brandir when Frodo sat on Amon Hen, and that he was borne across Rohan by the eagle (see p. 396), has been abandoned; Gwaewar (Gwaihir) is now in his later rôle as gatherer of tidings for Gandalf in the region of Anduin. It is not clear at this stage what had happened to Gandalf, and it seems that my father did not for the moment intend to make it so. Is it to be supposed that he made his way south along the mountains and so came to Methedras, where he sat 'beneath the snows and strove with the Dark Tower' while Frodo wore the Ring on Amon Hen? A single isolated and interrupted sentence says 'Gwaewar found me walking in the woods. Of him I'; which surely means that Gandalf came from Methedras into Fangorn, and that Gwaewar having found him he sent the eagle away east 'to watch the River and gather tidings'. This may suggest that the story of his being borne by the eagle to Lothlórien had not yet arisen.

When drafting the chapter my father had at first no thought, it seems, that Gandalf should display to Aragorn, Legolas and Gimli 'a piece of his mind' (TT p. 100) on the hopes and chances of the War. After Gandalf has been told that they think that Sam went with Frodo to Mordor, he says: 'Did he, indeed. It is news to me, but not at all surprising. But now about Merry and Pippin, for I shall not get your tale out of you before I have told you of them.'

It was perhaps at this point that my father set down a short outline for what Gandalf might now say:

Eagle sights orcs and hobbits. Saruman about in the woods. Orc-battle. Treebeard. They are safe, but something is going on. Revolt of trees? But we are called south. War is beginning. They must wait in hope and patience to find Merry and Pippin ... – but their friendship and devotion in following them was rewarded. The Company had done nobly and Gandalf was pleased with them. They ask what had happened to him – he won't tell yet.

It seems that the new course of the conversation ('Now sit by me and tell me the tale of your journey', TT p. 99) was at once introduced, leading to Gandalf's account of the intentions, desires, and fears of the Dark Lord and of Saruman. This was a characteristic development in stages by expansion, refinement of expression, and some re-ordering of its structure, but all the essentials of Gandalf's thought were present from the first drafting. There are however in the earlier stages a number of interesting differences to be recorded.

That Saruman was 'about in the woods' is mentioned in the little outline just given; in the first drafting Gandalf tells (as in TT, p. 101) that 'he could not wait at home and came forth to meet his captives', but that he was too late, the battle was over, and being 'no woodcraftsman' he had misinterpreted what had happened. 'Poor Saruman!' Gandalf adds, 'what a fall for one so wise! I fear that [he started too late to make a success of wickedness >] he started in the race too late. He seems not to have the luck he needs in his new profession. He at least will never sit in the Dark Tower.'

The passage about the Winged Messenger, absent in the draft, appears in the fair copy, where Legolas says that he felled him from the sky 'above Sarn Ruin' (see p. 361 and note 20), and that 'He filled us all with fear, but none so much as Frodo.'

In the first draft Gimli asks: 'That old man. You say Saruman is abroad. Was it you or Saruman that we saw last night?' and Gandalf replies: 'If you saw an old man last night, you certainly did not see me. But as we seem to look so much alike that you wished to make an incurable dent in my hat, I must guess that you saw Saruman [or a vision >] or some wraith of his making. [*Struck out:* I did not know that he lingered here so long.]' Against Gandalf's words my father wrote in the margin: *Vision of Gandalf's thought.* There is clearly an important clue here to the curious ambiguity surrounding the apparition of the night before, if one knew how to interpret it; but these words are not perfectly clear. They obviously represent a new thought: arising perhaps from Gandalf's suggestion that if it was not Saruman himself that they saw it was a 'vision' or 'wraith' that he had made, the apparition is now to emanate from Gandalf himself. But of whom was it a vision? Was it an embodied 'emanation' of Gandalf, proceeding from Gandalf himself, that they saw? 'I look into his unhappy mind and I see his doubt and fear', Gandalf has said; it seems more likely perhaps that through his deep concentration on Saruman he had 'projected' an image of Saruman which the three companions could momentarily see. I have found no other evidence to cast light on this most curious element in the tale; but it may be noted that in a time-scheme deriving from the time of the writing of 'Helm's Deep' and 'The Road to Isengard' my father noted of that night: 'Aragorn and his companions spend night on the battle-field, and see "old man" (Saruman).'

The earliest of several versions of Gandalf's reply to Legolas' question 'Who is Treebeard?' is notable, though extremely difficult to read:

'Ah,' said Gandalf, 'Now you are asking. He is Fangorn, that is Treebeard, Treebeard the Ent: what else shall I call him? The eldest of the old, the King of the Treebeards, the dwellers in the Forest. Stone-old, tree-hale, snail-slow, strong as a growing root. I wish you had met him. Your friends were more fortunate. For they came up here, as Aragorn has [?already] discovered. But no marks of them go down, as he may have discovered and soon would. But here ... marks by [?one] [?of] Treebeard's feet. This was a place, he often came to it when he wished to be alone and look outside the Forest. He has taken the hobbits away.'

'Then they are safe, since you speak well of Treebeard?'

'Safe? Yes, as far as the Ents go. But there is [?terrible] hurry.' Gandalf tells them about Ents. Says it was well that Merry and Pippin [?came there]. They did right to follow. Yet to meet the Ents is not their task. Too late anyway. He looks at sun. 'We have spent all the time allowed to a meeting of parted friends. We must go. We are needed South.'

In a more developed draft Aragorn's response to Gandalf's naming 'the Ents' (TT p. 102) reads:

'The Ents!' exclaimed Aragorn. 'Then there is truth in the ancient legends, [and the names that they use in Rohan have a meaning! The Entwash and the Entmark (for that is how they call the Forest)]

Above *Entmark* is written *Entwood*. – These remarks about the names containing *Ent* were bracketed for rejection at once, since the text continues: 'about the dwellers in the deep forest, and the giant Shepherds of the Trees', as in TT. In one of many draftings for Legolas' words at this point he says: 'I thought that [Fangorn] was the name of the Forest. A strange name for a wood, now I consider it.' The words 'he is the oldest living thing that still walks beneath the sun upon this Middle-earth' appear in the draft, written just so, without any hesitation in reaching them. Of his seeing Treebeard in the woods Gandalf says:

'...I passed him in the forest three days ago; and I do not doubt that he saw me, since the eyes of Treebeard miss little [*written in margin:* and he saw me, indeed he called my name]; but I did not speak, for I had much to think about, and I did not then know that Merry and Pippin had been carried off.'

The text of TT is reached in the fair copy. He says in the draft that 'something is going to happen which has not happened since the Elves awoke'; in the fair copy this becomes 'since the Elves first woke', changed to 'since the Elves were born' ('since the Elder Days', TT p. 103). But when Legolas says 'What is going to happen?' Gandalf replies: 'I do not know. Merry and Pippin do perhaps, by now; but I do not.'

To his words to Aragorn, urging him not to regret his choice 'in the valley of Sarn Gebir', he adds (both in draft and fair copy):

'...Also I say to you that your coming to Minas Tirith will now be very different from what would have been, had you come there alone reporting that Boromir son of the Lord Denethor had fallen, while you lived....'

In the draft text he tells Aragorn that he must go now to Winseld, changed to Eodoras (see p. 402): 'The light of Branding must now be uncovered. There is battle in Rohan and they are hard put to it in the

West, even as the great [?flood] of war comes up from the East.' In the fair copy this becomes: 'There is war in Rohan and it goes ill for the horsemasters': thus again (see p. 401) there is no suggestion of Wormtongue (cf. TT p. 104: 'There is war in Rohan, *and worse evil: it goes ill with Théoden*').

The textual development of the last part of this chapter and its relation to the beginning of the next is complex and doubtful, the manuscript material being very hard to interpret, and I shall not go into the question in any detail. But it is clear that at least half of 'The King of the Golden Hall' had been written before the conclusion of 'The White Rider' approached at all the form it has in *The Two Towers*; for as will be seen (p. 446) Aragorn tells Theoden in Eodoras that Gandalf *had not told them* 'what befell him in Moria'.

How my father ended 'The White Rider' at this stage is not entirely clear to me, but it seems probable that he stopped at Gandalf's words of the Balrog (TT p. 105): 'Name him not!': 'and for a moment it seemed that a cloud of pain passed over his face, and he sat silent, looking old as death.' He would then have begun a new chapter (XXVII) at 'Gandalf now wrapped himself again in his old tattered cloak. They descended quickly from the high shelf...' (TT p. 107).

I cannot say at what precise point my father decided that Gandalf should in fact tell something at least of what had happened to him after his fall from the Bridge of Khazad-dûm, but it must have been in the course of the writing of 'The King of the Golden Hall'. In what is apparently the earliest draft (but written over erased pencil) of Gandalf's story of his escape from Moria[4] the four companions are already riding south from Fangorn when he tells it:

> On the way they ask Gandalf how he escaped. He refuses the full tale – but tells how he passed through fire (and water?) and came to the 'bottom of the world', and there finally overthrew the Balrog, who fled. Gandalf followed up a secret way to Durin's Tower on the summit of the mountains (?of Caradras). There they had a battle – those who beheld it afar thought it was a thunderstorm with lightning. A great rain came down. The Balrog was destroyed, and the tower crumbled and stones blocked the door of the secret way. Gandalf was left on the mountain-top. The eagle Gwaihir rescued him. He went then to Lothlórien. Galadriel arrayed him in white garments before he left. While Gandalf was on mountain top he saw many things – a vision of Mordor etc.

This is the first appearance of the form *Gwaihir* (here apparently first written *Gwaehir*) for earlier *Gwaewar*, which was still the name in the earlier part of this chapter.

A very rough and unfinished draft for the final form and placing of Gandalf's story ('Long I fell, and he fell with me...', TT p. 105) is found. Here Gandalf describes the Balrog, his fire quenched, thus: 'he was a thing of slime, strong as a strangling snake, sleek as ice, pliant as a thong, unbreakable as steel.' Of the 'dark things unguessed' that gnaw the world 'below the deepest delvings of the dwarves' he says: 'Sauron alone may know of them, or one older than he.' And after his words 'I will bring no report to stain the light of day' the text continues:

> '...Little had I guessed the abyss that was spanned by Durin's Bridge.'
>   'Did you not?' said Gimli. 'I could have told you had there been time. No plummet ever found the bottom – indeed none that was ever cast therein was ever recovered.'[5]

The form of Gandalf's story in TT is almost reached in the 'fair copy' manuscript, but there remain some differences. He tells that clutching at the Balrog's heel 'I set my teeth in it like a hunting hound, and tasted venom'; and that Durin's Tower was 'carved in the living rock in the very pinnacle of red Caradras.' This was subsequently changed to 'the living rock [of] Zirakinbar,[6] the pinnacle of the Silverhorn. There upon Kelebras was a lonely window in the snow...' On these names see pp. 174–5, notes 18, 21–2.

Gandalf does not say, as in TT (p. 106), 'Naked I was sent back – for a brief time, until my task is done', but simply 'Naked I returned, and naked I lay upon the mountain-top.'[7] And of his coming thence to Caras Galadon, borne by Gwaihir, he says that he 'found you three days gone', and that he 'tarried there in the long time which in that land counts for but a brief hour of the world' ('in the ageless time of that land', TT): see pp. 368–9.

At this time the messages that he bore from Galadriel to Aragorn and Legolas were very different:

> *Elfstone, Elfstone, bearer of my green stone,*
> *In the south under snow a green stone thou shalt see.*
> *Look well, Elfstone! In the shadow of the dark throne*
> *Then the hour is at hand that long hath awaited thee.*
>
> *Greenleaf, Greenleaf, bearer of the elven-bow,*
> *Far beyond Mirkwood many trees on earth grow.*
> *Thy last shaft when thou hast shot, under strange trees*
>   *shalt thou go!*

The dialogue that follows, between Gimli, Legolas, and Gandalf, is however precisely the same as in TT, p. 107. On the significance of the verse addressed to Aragorn see p. 448.

With the addition of Gandalf's story to this chapter, what was originally the opening of 'The King of the Golden Hall' (from 'Gandalf now wrapped himself again in his old tattered cloak', see p. 430) was incorporated into 'The White Rider', which now ended at Gandalf's words 'Show no weapon, speak no haughty word, I counsel you all, until we are come before Theoden's seat' (TT p. 111). The final form of the story of the departure from Fangorn, the summoning of the horses, the great ride south across the plains with the sight at sunset of smoke rising far off in the Gap of Rohan, and the distant view of Eodoras at sunrise (TT pp. 107–11, where it constitutes the end of the one chapter and the beginning of the next), was achieved almost down to the last detail in the fair copy manuscript.[8] By this time my father had changed the ending of 'The Riders of Rohan' (p. 403) to the form it has in TT, pp. 45–6 ('The horses were gone. They had dragged their pickets and disappeared'), and had changed the beginning of 'The White Rider' similarly to its form in TT, p. 91 (' "Did you hear them, Legolas? Did they sound to you like beasts in terror?" "No," said Legolas. "I heard them clearly. ... I should have guessed that they were beasts wild with some sudden gladness" ').

NOTES

1   A little slip of paper used to draft the moment of recognition of Mithrandir (TT p. 98) was a page from an engagement calendar 'for the week ending Saturday February 22'. February 22 fell on a Saturday in 1941, not in 1942.

2   The forerunner of this phrase appeared in the outline given on p. 389, as also did 'I was badly burned or *well* burned'; cf. also the notes given on p. 422. Gandalf's suggestion that he now 'is' Saruman, in the sense that he is 'Saruman as he should have been', is lacking, but appears in the fair copy as first written.

3   Gandalf's words that follow in TT: 'There was a darkness over the valleys of the Emyn Muil' are absent in the draft, but are found in the fair copy (with *Sarn Gebir* for *the Emyn Muil*).

4   For the earliest notes on Gandalf's escape from Moria see VI.462 and p. 211 in this book.

5   It is interesting to look back to my father's original ideas about the chasm in the passages referred to in note 4: 'probably fall is not as deep as it seemed ... eventually following the subterranean stream in the gulf he found a way out', and 'The gulf was not deep (only a kind of moat and was full of silent water). He followed the channel and got down into the Deeps.'

6   This form *Zirakinbar*, preceding *Zirakzigil*, is found also in an entirely isolated note: '*Barazinbar, Zirakinbar, Udushinbar*', together with a reference to 'Silverhorn and the Horn of Cloud'.

7   Cf. *Letters* no. 156 (4 November 1954): ' "Naked I was sent back – for a brief time, until my task is done." Sent back by whom, and whence? Not by the "gods" whose business is only with this embodied world and its time; for he passed "out of thought and

time". Naked is alas! unclear. It was meant just literally, "un-clothed like a child" (not discarnate), and so ready to receive the white robes of the highest. Galadriel's power is not divine, and his healing in Lórien is meant to be no more than physical healing and refreshment.'

8 Initial drafting is very largely lost through overwriting. – The only points of any significance in which the text of the fair copy differs from that of TT, other than names, are that Theoden is the 'Master of Rohan' and 'lord of the Mark' where in TT he is called 'King' (see p. 444); that Gandalf says to Shadowfax 'Far let us ride now together, ere we part again!' where in TT he says 'and part not in this world again!'; and that 'the mountains of the South' (the Black Mountains) are 'black-tipped and streaked with white', whereas in TT, where they are the White Mountains, they are 'white-tipped and streaked with black': cf. the earlier description in 'The Riders of Rohan' (TT p. 24), where the original text was retained (p. 395), 'rising into peaks of jet, tipped with glimmering snows'.

Among names, *Sarn Gebir* (for *Emyn Muil*), *Winseld*, *Eodoras* are still present. At the end of the chapter, in Gandalf's phrase 'the Horse-masters do not sleep' (TT p. 111), the form *Rohir* (not *Rohiroth*) was written above.

XXV

THE STORY FORESEEN FROM
FANGORN

In this chapter I give two outlines of great interest, for in them my
father discussed the structural problems of the story that he foresaw at
this time. The first one given here was evidently written when 'The
White Rider' had been completed in its earlier form (i.e. without
Gandalf's story of the Balrog, see p. 430); the ride across Rohan and
the distant sight of Eodoras in the morning may or may not have
existed yet, but the question is immaterial.

XXVII
Gandalf, Aragorn, Legolas, Gimli reach Eodoras on the morn-
ing of Jan. 31.[1] (That aft[ernoon] Merry and Pippin go with
Ents to Isengard.)

They enter Theoden's halls. Theoden greets Gandalf dubiously
– as herald of trouble. Shadowfax had been reported coming
from the West through the Gap and fleeing away north.[2] They
feared Gandalf would return. Then Eomer had come riding
back, with strange news concerning Gandalf's fall. 'That,' said
Theoden, 'was too much to hope, it seems; for now Gandalf
returns and worse tidings follow.'

Against this paragraph was written in the margin, at the same time as
the text, 'A messenger from Minas Tirith is present.'

There is a battle on the borders of the West Emnet. An
invasion of Orcs of Saruman had been driven back (not without
loss to the Rohiroth) to the banks of the Isen River. But news
came that orcs were pouring out of Isengard, and that men of
the Middlemarch[3] (whom Saruman had long subjected) were
coming up. 'We cannot hope long to hold the river,' said
Theoden. 'Eomer has gone thither with what men could still be
spared. And now as we are beset in the West, there comes dire
news indeed. The whole of Rhûn the Great, the endless East, is
in motion. Under the command of the Dark Lord of Mordor
they move from the far North even to the South. Minas Tirith is
beset. The fierce dark men of the South, the Haradwaith

(Harwan Silharrows Men of Sunharrowland Men of Harrowland) have come in many ships and fill the Bay of Belfalas, and
[have] taken the isle of Tolfalas. They have passed up the
Anduin in many galleys, and out of Mordor others have crossed
at Elostirion.[4] A tide of war rolls beneath the very walls of
Minas Tirith. They have sent us urgent prayer for help. And we
cannot give it. Yet if Minas Tirith falls then the dark tide will
sweep over us from the East.

Against this passage concerning Minas Tirith was written in the
margin, at the same time as the text, 'Not yet have they heard of
Boromir's fall.' Later, the whole passage from 'And now as we are
beset in the West' to this point was closed off in pencil with the note
'Place after return victorious from Isengard.' Theoden continues:

You come at the end of the days of Rohan. Not long now shall
the hall (which Brego son of Brytta [*changed later in pencil to*
Eorl son of Eofor] built)[5] stand. Fire shall eat up the high seat.
What can you say?'
    Gandalf speaks words of comfort. All that can be done is to
do one deed at a time and go forward and not look back. Let us
assail Saruman and then if fortune is with us turn and face East.
There is a hope. Something may happen in West (he does not
openly name Ents).
    Gandalf begs for the gift of Shadowfax.
    Theoden says Yes – that will at least ensure Gandalf's escape,
when all else fall. Gandalf does not lose temper. He says there
will be no escape for anyone. But he wishes for *gift*, as he will
take Shadowfax into great peril: silver against black.
    The ceremony of gift. Gandalf casts aside grey robe and be-
comes White Rider. He bids Theoden arm, old as he is, and
follow with all left who can bear arms. The rest shall pack and
prepare to flee to the mountains.
    They ride off without rest. Meet messengers reporting death
of the Second Master and the forces of Rohan hemmed almost
in, while the forces of Saruman are continually strengthened.
    Gandalf spurs Shadowfax and spurs into the setting sun.
    By his help and Aragorn the Isengarders are driven back. The
camp of the Rohiroth. *But Isengarders are across the river.*
    In the morning they awake and look out in wonder. A *wood*
stood where none had been, between the Isengarders and the
West. There is clamour and confusion. Vast columns of vapour
are seen rising from Isengard, and the rumour of strange noises

and rumblings. The Isengarders are driven into the river. Those who cross are suddenly assailed by the trees which seem to come to life. Only a few escape fleeing southward to the Black Mountains.

The victorious forces under Eomer and Gandalf ride to the gates of Isengard. They find it a pile of rubble, blocked with a huge wall of stone. On the top of the pile sit Merry and Pippin!

Meeting of Treebeard and Gandalf.

How did the Ents overcome Isengard? They open[ed] sluice gates at North end and blocked the outlet near the Great Gate. First they watched all the night seeing more and more orcs etc. pour out of Isengard. Then they simply broke a way in at North end and spied and found Saruman was left nearly all alone in his tower. They broke the door and stairway to the tower and then withdrew. At North end they let in the River Isen but blocked its outflow. Soon all the floor of the circle was flooded to many feet deep. Then while some kept guard the rest fell on the rear of the battle.

Here comes scene of Saruman being let out of his tower and trying to speak in friendly fashion to Gandalf. 'Ah, my dear Gandalf! I am so pleased to see you; we at least (we wizards) understand one another. These people all seem so unnecessarily angry.[6] What a mess the world is in. Really you and I must consult together – such men as we are needed. Now what about our spheres of influence?'

Gandalf looks at him and laughs. 'Yes, I understand you well enough, Saruman. Give me your staff,' he said in a voice of terrible command. He took it and broke it. 'I am the White Wizard now,' he said. 'Behold you are clad in many colours!' They turn his coat inside out. Gandalf gives him a rough staff. [Added subsequently: Saruman is to go without a staff, and have no wooden thing to lean on by decree of Treebeard.] 'Go Saruman!' he said, 'and beg from the charitable for a day's digging.'[7] [Added subsequently: Or put this toward end of story – in meanwhile give Saruman over to the guard of the Ents. Further addition: Yes.]

[Written in margin at the same time as the text: Better: the ring of Isengard is broken by Ents, but Saruman shuts himself up in Orthanc and cannot be assailed yet for there is no time.]

Another way of telling the story would be to carry on from end of Chapter XXVI and relate the coming of Ents to

Isengard.[8] How they resolved not to break in at first, but came behind the orc-army. Let Merry and Pippin see the orcs driving the men of Rohan back over the River. Ents camp behind them. Then relate the battle from Merry and Pippin's point of view – distant vision of the white rider on a shining horse. They recognize the sword and voice of Aragorn, but do not know who the White Rider is. Gandalf and Treebeard meet after the battle – and then comes the storming of Isengard by Gandalf and the Ents.

Return to Eodoras. Funeral of —— the Second Master[9] [*Added above:* Háma and Theodred]. Feast in Winseld.[10] Eowyn sister of Eomer waits on the guests. Description of her, and of her love for Aragorn.

News comes at the feast or next morning of the siege of Minas Tirith by the Haradwaith.[11] [*Added subsequently:* brought by a dark Gondorian like Boromir.[12] Theoden answers that he does not owe fealty – only to heirs of Elendil. But he will come.] The horsemen of Rohan ride East, with Gandalf, Aragorn, Gimli, Legolas, Merry and Pippin. Gandalf as the White Rider. [*Added subsequently:* Eowyn goes as Amazon.] Vision of Minas Tirith from afar.

In the part of this outline that concerns the immediate story to come, and with which this book ends, it will be seen that while Theoden is unwelcoming and scarcely well-disposed towards Gandalf, he is nothing more than that: of the ugly state of affairs at Eodoras that came in with Wormtongue there is no trace – no hint of the subjugation of Theoden's mind and will, of the disgracing of Eomer, of Gandalf's triumphant display of his power in the hall of Winseld. Eowyn, Eomer's sister, appears, and her love for Aragorn, but not until the funeral feast held in Winseld after the victory.

Judging by the opening of the second outline, this also belongs to about this time.

Order of Tale.
Bring each party to crisis. Ents break off with 'Night lies over Isengard'. End XXVI with far vision of Winseld's golden roof (and sight of the smoke).[13] (Possibly they see men in strange armour riding also from East to Eodoras.)

Now return to Frodo and Sam. Meeting with Gollum. Betrayal by him. Capture of Frodo on *west* side of Kirith Ungol. Frodo imprisoned in tower[14] – because (a) no ring is on him, (b) Sauron is busy with war and it takes time for message to reach him.

Then return to Gandalf and battle of Isen, feast of victory, relief of Minas Tirith, and march of the army of Gandalf towards Dagorlad and gates of Kirith Ungol.

Then return to Frodo. Make him look out onto impenetrable night. Then use phial which has escaped (clutched in his hand or wrapped in rag). By its light he sees the forces of deliverance approach and the dark host go out to meet them.[15] Grieves for Sam – or thinks he has betrayed him too.

The orc-guards come on him and take phial and shutter windows, and he lies in dark and despair.

Where put parley of Sauron and Gandalf? If after capture of Frodo readers will know that Frodo [*written above:* Sauron] has not Ring. [*Added subsequently in two stages:* No, not if you break off with Frodo carried off by Orcs and before Sam rescues him. / Even if Sam's taking of Ring is told,[16] you can make Sam fly among the rocks with Gollum (and orcs) on his trail and his escape seem unlikely.]

Possibly best as originally planned – [?all account] of Gandalf as far as Kirith Ungol – and then return to Sam and Frodo.

Sam rescues Frodo and while battle is joined at mouth of Gorgoroth they fly towards Orodruin.

NOTES

1   The later date of the departure of the Company from Rivendell, 25 December, had now entered (see pp. 422–3): thus 'Day 1' (the day of Boromir's death) in the table on p. 406 was January 26 (see the table on p. 368), and Aragorn, Legolas and Gimli encountered Gandalf in Fangorn on January 30 ('Day 5').

2   In the fifth version of 'The Council of Elrond' (p. 152) Gandalf does not say what happened to Shadowfax, but the isolated note given on p. 390 says that 'some account of Shadowfax in the house of Elrond must be given.' This note asks also, however, 'Or did he just run off after Gandalf got to Rivendell?', and 'How did Gandalf summon him?' In preliminary notes for 'The Riders of Rohan' (p. 390) it is said that 'the horse of Gandalf reappears – sent for from Rivendell'; and in the text of that chapter (pp. 400–1) Eomer tells Aragorn that he had returned seven days before, to which Aragorn replies: 'But Gandalf left Shadowfax far in the North at Rivendell. Or so I thought.' In the present passage Shadowfax had recently come out of the West through

the Gap of Rohan and then gone away north: which surely suggests that he had come from Rivendell and was going north to Fangorn in obedience to a summons from Gandalf mysteriously conveyed to him.

The earliest extant account of Gandalf's summons to Shadow-fax with his three great whistles, and his coming across the plain to the eaves of Fangorn with Arod and Hasofel returning, is already exactly as in TT (see p. 432); and this seems to fit the story in the present text, for Gandalf says to Shadowfax 'It is a long way from Rivendell, my friend; but you are wise and swift, and come at need,' and he says to Legolas 'I bent my thought upon him, bidding him to make haste; for yesterday he was far away in the south of this land.' (On the other hand, Legolas says 'I have not seen his like before', which does not suggest that Shadowfax had been at Rivendell when the Company was there.)

The story in the published LR is extremely difficult to understand. In 'The Council of Elrond' (FR p. 278) Gandalf says: 'It took me nearly fourteen days from Weathertop, for I could not ride among the rocks of the troll-fells, and Shadowfax departed. *I sent him back to his master...*' This was about October 4. The next we hear is in 'The Riders of Rohan', where Eomer still tells Aragorn that Shadowfax had returned 'seven nights ago' (but 'now the horse is wild and will let no man handle him'), to which Aragorn replies: 'Then Shadowfax has found his way alone from the far North; for it was there that he and Gandalf parted.' But it was now February 30, so that on his return nearly five months had elapsed since Gandalf dismissed him at Weathertop! And then, at the end of 'The White Rider' (TT p. 108), there is the passage already cited: 'It is a long way from Rivendell, my friend; but you are wise and swift and come at need.' It is hard to resist the conclusion that the alteration in Gandalf's story to the Council of Elrond was not carried through.

3   *Middlemarch:* Enedwaith, between Greyflood and Anduin; see Maps II and III, pp. 305, 309.

4   Cf. the outline given on p. 389: 'Minas Tirith defeats Harad-waith.' – All these names (*Harwan, Silharrows; Harrowland, Sunharrowland*) are derived from the Old English *Sigelhearwan* 'Ethiopians'. My father's article in two parts entitled *Sigelwara land* (*Medium Ævum* 1 and 3, Dec.1932 and June 1934) studied the etymology and meaning of the name *Sigelhearwan*, and concluded that while the meaning of the first element *Sigel* was certainly 'Sun', that of the second element *hearwan* was not discoverable: 'a symbol ... of that large part of ancient English language and lore which has now vanished beyond recall, *swa hit no wære* [as if it had never been].' With these names cf. *Sunlands, Swertings*, p. 313. – *Tolfalas* appears on the original element of

the First Map (see p. 298, and Map III^A on p. 308). – On *Elostirion* for Osgiliath see p. 423.

5   In LR the father of Eorl was Léod, and Brego was Eorl's son; Brytta was the eleventh King of the Mark, some two and a half centuries after Brego (see LR Appendix A (II)).

6   These remarks of Saruman's, from 'we at least...', were bracketed at the time of writing.

7   This sketch of the 'affable' Saruman and Gandalf's breaking of his staff is derived very closely from 'The Story Foreseen from Moria', p. 212; cf. also p. 422.

8   Chapter XXVI is 'The White Rider'.

9   The Second Master was first called *Marhath* (p. 390; this name was then given to the Fourth Master, p. 400), then *Eowin* (pp. 393–4).

10   For the name of the Golden Hall see p. 402.

11   Thus the passage on pp. 434–5 (in which Theoden in his initial conversation with Gandalf speaks of the attack by the Haradwaith on Minas Tirith) bracketed with the note that it should be placed after the victorious return to Eodoras has already been moved.

12   I have not found an explanation of the conception underlying this. Possibly to be compared are Gandalf's words in *The Return of the King*, Ch. 1 'Minas Tirith', p. 31: 'by some chance the blood of Westernesse runs nearly true in him; as it does in his other son, Faramir, *and yet did not in Boromir* whom he loved best.' But this was written several years later.

13   The smoke seen rising at sunset of the day before in the direction of the Gap of Rohan (p. 432).

14   On the taking of Frodo to a guard-tower (not to Minas Morgul) see p. 344 and note 39, and p. 412.

15   The light of the Phial of Galadriel must be conceived here to be of huge power, a veritable star in the darkness.

16   I do not follow the thought here: for Sam's taking of the Ring must in any case be told before Frodo is carried off by the Orcs.

XXVI
THE KING OF THE GOLDEN HALL

The textual history of this chapter is much the same as that of 'The White Rider': the first coherent and legible manuscript is also in a sense the first extant text of the chapter, because the rough drafts were set down, section by section, as the main manuscript proceeded. In other words, that manuscript was the vehicle of the development of the narrative, and the distinction between 'draft' and 'fair copy' is not at all a distinction between two separate manuscript entities, the one completed as a whole before the other was begun. For almost all of the last third of the chapter, however, there is no independent drafting, for the initial conception in pencil was overwritten in ink.

A substantial part of the chapter was in being in some form before Gandalf's story of the Balrog was added to 'The White Rider' (see p. 430), and the point of separation of 'The King of the Golden Hall' (not so named) from 'The White Rider' was twice changed.[1]

In the earliest stage of the narrative, abandoned before it had gone far, Gandalf (with Gimli) left Aragorn and Legolas before they came to Eodoras:

'Eodoras those courts are called,' said Gandalf, 'and Winseld is that golden hall. There dwells Theoden[2] son of Thengel, lord of the mark of Rohan. We are come with the rising of the day. Now the road lies plain to see before you. Make what speed you may!'

Then suddenly he spoke to Shadowfax, and like an arrow from the bow the great horse sprang forward. Even as they gazed, he was gone: a flash of silver, a wind in the grass, a vision that fled and faded from their sight.

Swiftly they urged their horses in pursuit, but if they had walked upon their feet they would have had as much chance of overtaking him. They had gone only a small part of the way when Legolas exclaimed: 'That was a mighty leap! Shadowfax has sprung across the mountain stream and already he has passed up the hill and vanished from my sight.'

The morning was bright and clear about them, and birds were singing, when Aragorn and Legolas came to the stream; running swiftly down into the plain it bent across their path, turning east to feed the Entwash away to the left in its marshy bed. Here there were many willow-trees, already in this southern land blushing red at the tips of twigs in presage of spring. They found a ford, much trampled upon either bank with the passage of horses, and passed over, and so at length they too rode up along the green road to Eodoras.

At the foot of the hill they passed between seven high green mounds. Already they were starred with small pale flowers, and in the shelter of their western flanks the grass was white with nodding flowers (blossoms) like tiny snowdrops. 'See, Legolas!' said Aragorn, 'we are passing the mounds where the sires of Theoden sleep.' 'Yes,' said Legolas. 'Seven mounds there be, and seven long lives of men it is, since the Rohiroth came hither from the North. Two hundred times and more have the red leaves fallen in Mirkwood in my home since then,[3] and little change does it seem to us. But to them it seems so long ago, that their dwelling in the North is but a memory of song, and their speech is already sundered from their northern kin.'

The companions entered the gates. Horsemen guarded them, and led them to the hall. They dismounted and walked in up the echoing hall. There they saw Theoden the old. Beside him sat Gandalf, and at his feet Gimli the dwarf.

At the foot of the page, where this draft ends, is the note: '? News of the attack on Minas Tirith by Haradwaith in ships'; see pp. 434–5, 437.

It would be interesting to know what thought lay behind this story of the 'divided entry' into Eodoras; but whatever it was, the arrival there and even the entry into Winseld was accomplished, as it appears, without any ceremony, interrogation, or laying aside of arms. There is no suggestion of hostility or even suspicion towards the strangers, and this accords with the first outline given in the last chapter (see p. 437). It will be seen in what follows that the entire conception of the situation at Eodoras arose during the writing of 'The King of the Golden Hall'.

While the story of the divided entry of the four companions was still maintained, however, a strongly 'Beowulfian' reception of Aragorn and Legolas at the gates was at once introduced, in a revised draft.[4]

... they came at last to the wide windswept walls and the gates of Eodoras. There sat men in bright mail upon proud steeds, who spoke to them in a strange tongue.

'Abidath cuman uncuthe! [*Rejected at the time of writing:* Hwæt sindon ge, lathe oththe leofe, the thus seldlice gewerede ridan cwomon to thisse burge gatum? No her inn gan moton ne wædla ne wæpned mon, nefne we his naman witen. Nu ge feorran-cumene gecythath us on ofste: hu hatton ge? hwæt sindon eower ærende to Theoden urum hlaforde?'[5] Aragorn understood these words] asking their names and errand. These words Aragorn understood and answered. 'Aragorn son of Arathorn am I,' he said, 'and with me is Legolas of Mirkwood. These names maybe ye have already heard, and our coming is awaited? But we ask now to see Theoden your lord; for we come in friendship and it may be that our coming

Here this draft tails off. It does not seem that the story that Gandalf with Gimli went ahead on Shadowfax and entered Eodoras first was taken any further. It is curious, however, that when the story was changed my father seems to have forgotten Gimli: he is not named in the encounter with the guard at the gates, there is no mention of his surrendering his axe at the doors of the house, and my father even wrote 'Now the three companions went forward' up Theoden's hall. These references were added in to the 'fair copy' manuscript, and 'three' changed to 'four'; and Gimli appears as the text was written when he strode forward, and was restrained by Gandalf, at Wormtongue's words about Lothlórien (TT p. 118). I do not think that this can have any narrative significance; but it was certainly an odd lapse, and not easy to explain.[6]

The story of the arrival at Eodoras was now revised again. Gandalf is present when the travellers are challenged at the gates, and the guards, crying *Abidath cuman uncuthe*, are rebuked by him for using the tongue of Rohan.[7] The flowers on the mounds (still seven) become *nifredil*, the flowers of Lórien (see note 4, and pp. 233–4); and Aragorn utters the verse *Where now the horse and the rider?*,[8] referring to 'Eorl the Old', changed at once to 'Eorl the Young', 'who rode down out of the North', and to 'his steed Felaróf, father of horses' (TT p. 112). But at this stage Wormtongue had still not emerged, and the suspicion and hostility of the guards evidently proceeded from Theoden's unfortified dislike and distrust of Gandalf;[9] moreover Eomer had not returned to Eodoras since Aragorn, Legolas and Gimli parted from him:

'...Has not Eomer then returned and given warning of our coming?'

'Nay,' said the guard. 'He has not passed these gates. He was turned aside by messengers from Theoden, and went away west to the war without staying. But maybe, if what you say is true, Theoden will have knowledge of it. I will go to my lord and learn his will. But what names shall I report? ...'

With this cf. TT p. 113. – In the original draft for the scene in which the travellers must lay aside their weapons before entering Theoden's house there is a brief description of it:

Before Theoden's hall there was a portico, with pillars made of mighty trees hewn in the upland forests and carved with interlacing figures gilded and painted. The doors also were of wood, carven in the likeness of many beasts and birds with jewelled eyes and golden claws.

It is curious that in the 'fair copy' manuscript, and thence in the final text, there is no description at all of the exterior of the house, and I think that it may have got lost in the complexities of redrafting and reordering of the material.[10]

As they stood in the darkness by the doors of the hall and saw on one of the hangings the figure of the young man on a white horse (TT p. 116) Aragorn said: 'Behold Eorl the Young! Thus he rode out of the North to the Battle of the Field of Gorgoroth.' A very difficult draft preceding this has 'the Battle of Gorgoroth where Sauron was [?overthrown],' making it clear that at this stage my father conceived that Eorl came south to the great battle in which Gil-galad and Elendil were slain and Isildur took the Ring.[11]

In the encounter with Theoden the manuscript evidence is not very easy to interpret, but it seems certain that it was at this point that Wormtongue entered the story; for what is obviously the very earliest description of Theoden, written in the faintest scribble, reads thus:

At the far end of the hall beyond the hearth and facing the doors was a dais with three steps, and in the midst of the dais was a great chair. In the chair sat a man so bent with age that he seemed almost a dwarf. His white hair was [?braided] upon his [?shoulders], his long beard was laid upon his knees. But his eyes burned with a keen light that glinted from afar off. Behind his chair stood two fair women. At his feet upon the steps sat a wizened [struck out: old] figure of a man with a pale wise face. There was a silence.

In the 'fair copy' the text moves close to that of TT (pp. 116–17), and now appears the 'thin golden circlet' worn by Theoden (who is subsequently called 'King' in this manuscript); but he bears on his forehead 'a large green stone' (not the 'single white diamond' of TT: see p. 448), and there were still 'two fair women' standing behind his chair.

But though Wormtongue was present he did not, as the scene was first drafted, intervene, and it is Theoden who speaks of the death of the Second Master of the Mark, here called Eofored,[12] on the west marches of Rohan, and it is Theoden who names Gandalf Láthspell,

Ill-news. Gandalf responds, as in TT, by speaking of the different ways in which a man may come with evil tidings, and it is again Theoden, not Wormtongue, who retorts 'Verily he may, or he may be of a third kind', and who decries the idea that Gandalf had ever brought aid to Rohan: 'Last time it seemed to me that you asked my aid rather, and to get you from my land I astonished all men and myself also by lending you Shadowfax.'[13] At this stage Eomer's story remains as it was: 'Eomer has ridden away thither [to the west marches] with all but the last handful of my horsemen.'

At this point, however, before the conversation had proceeded any further, 'the pale man sitting upon the steps of the dais' began to play a part; for he now took over those parts of Theoden's remarks that are given to him in TT. Yet it is interesting to observe that my father did not introduce him into Theoden's household with the conscious intent that he should play the rôle that he did in fact come to play: for he still says, as Theoden had done, 'Now Eomer has ridden away thither with all but our last handful of horsemen.'[14]

After Gandalf's triumph over Wormtongue (who is not yet given any other name) Theoden is assisted down the hall by the two women, and he says to them: 'Go, Idis, and you too Eowyn sister-daughter!'[15] As they went, the younger of them looked back: 'very fair and slender she seemed. Her face was filled with gentle pity, and her eyes shone with unshed tears. So Aragorn saw her for the first time in the light of day, and after she was gone he stood still, looking at the dark doors and taking little heed of other things.'

Looking out from the porch of his house with Gandalf Theoden says: 'Not long now shall stand the high hall which Brego son of Brytta built' (cf. p. 435 and note 5; TT p. 120 'Brego son of Eorl'); and Gandalf tells him, as in TT, to send for Eomer. It was at this point in the writing of the chapter that there entered the story of the imprisonment of Eomer by the instigation of Wormtongue, who now receives his true name: *Frána* (*Gríma* did not replace this till much later).

In TT when Gandalf spoke to Theoden (p. 121) 'his voice was low and secret, and none save the king heard what he said.' In the early form of the chapter, however, this was not so:

His voice was low and secret, and yet to those beside him keen and clear. Of Sauron he told, and the lady Galadriel, and of Elrond in Rivendell far away, of the Council and the setting forth of the Company of Nine, and all the perils of their road. 'Four only have come thus far,' he said. 'One is lost, Boromir prince of Gondor. Two were captured, but are free. And two have gone upon a dark Quest. Look eastward, Theoden! Into the heart of menace they have gone: two small folk, such as you

in Rohan deem but the matter of children's tales. Yet doom
hangs upon them. Our hope is with them – hope, if we can but
stand meanwhile!'

There are several drafts for this passage preceding that in the fair copy
just given, and in one of these occurs the following:

Of the Council and the setting forth of the Company of Nine. So
he came at last to the Mines of Moria and the Battle upon the
Bridge.

'Then it was not wholly false, the rumour that Eomer
brought,' said Theoden.

'No indeed,' said Aragorn, 'for he did but repeat what I said
to him. And until this time yestermorning we thought that
Gandalf had fallen. Even now he has not said what befell him in
Moria. We would gladly hear.'

'Nay,' said Gandalf. 'The sun is riding towards noon.'

This is clear evidence that my father had reached this point, at least, in
'The King of the Golden Hall' *before* he wrote the conclusion of 'The
White Rider' in its later form: see p. 430.

The passage just given is followed by a brief outline:

Eomer returns. *Wes thu Theoden hal*. He rejoices to see Theoden
so much better; but begs pardon – save only for his advice to ride
west. Says how the day's delay has grieved him.

Gandalf continues tale and holds out a *hope* (of Frodo in the
East). But they must ride west.

Theoden bids them stay and rest. But Gandalf won't stay except
for food ... Theoden has to take heart and send every man west. He
himself is to lead his folk out of Eodoras into the secret refuge[?s] in
the mountains – more defensible if all goes ill.

Eomer asks that Wormtongue should go west too. Shadowfax.
They set out. Gandalf fleets ahead.

As already mentioned, in the last third of the chapter, from the point
where Legolas gazes far off and believes that he can see 'a glint of
white' and 'a tiny tongue of flame' (TT p. 121), there is little further
independent drafting, the manuscript in ink being written over the
original pencilled text. But it is clear that the story as known from *The
Two Towers* of the unmasking of Wormtongue, the rehabilitation of
Eomer, the meal before departure, the gift of Shadowfax, was
achieved almost unhesitatingly.[16] In an important respect, however,
my father at first conceived things differently.

In this first version of 'The King of the Golden Hall' the Second
Master of the Mark, slain in fighting at the River Isen, is Eofored, and

he is not Theoden's son (p. 444 and note 12).[17] On the other hand, in addition to Eowyn (Eomer's sister, p. 437; addressed by Theoden as 'sister-daughter', p. 445), there is another lady in close association with Theoden, Idis – his daughter. All through this part of the chapter she is present, yet never once does she speak. When Gandalf asks Theoden who shall rule his people in his place when he departs to the war, he replies that Eowyn 'shall be lady in my stead'; and Gandalf says 'That is a good choice.' There is no mention of Idis here; yet she was still present, for at the meal before the riding of the host 'there also waiting upon the king were the ladies, Idis his daughter, and Eowyn sister of Eomer.' It was Eowyn who brought the wine, and Idis is again not mentioned; yet Háma still says, in response to Theoden's words that Eomer is the last of the House of Eorl (TT p. 128): 'I said not Eomer. He is not the last. There are Idis your daughter, and Eowyn his sister. They are wise and high-hearted.' But it was at this point that the brief existence of Idis came to an end; for the next words that my father wrote were: 'All love *her*. Let *her* be as lord to the Eorlingas, while we are gone.' All references to Idis were then removed from the manuscript.

I cannot say what function in the narrative my father had in mind for Idis (and it is notable that in the original outline, p. 437, only Eowyn sister of Eomer is mentioned as waiting on the guests at the feast in Winseld after the victory); still less why the daughter of the King (and older than Eowyn, p. 445) should be so silent and so overshadowed by the niece.

The significance of the meeting of Aragorn and Eowyn, on the other hand, was destined to survive, though fundamentally transformed. In this first version, in a passage already cited (p. 445), after she had gone 'he stood still, looking at the dark doors and taking little heed of other things'; at the meal before the departure 'Aragorn was silent, but his eyes followed Eowyn' (struck out); and when she brought the wine to the guests 'Long she looked upon Aragorn, and long he looked upon her' – for which was substituted: 'As she stood before Aragorn she paused suddenly and looked upon him, as if only now had she seen him clearly. He looked down upon her fair face, and their eyes met. For a moment they stood thus, and their hands met as he took the cup from her. "Hail Aragorn son of Arathorn!" she said.' With this contrast the passage that appears in its place in TT (p. 127). And after Theoden's words 'But in [Dunberg >] Dunharrow the people may long defend themselves, and if the battle go ill thither will come all who escape' (TT p. 128) Aragorn says: 'If I live, I will come, Lady Eowyn, and then maybe we will ride together.' Then Eowyn 'smiled and bent her head gravely.'

There is an isolated list of matters 'to be explained before the end', which in view of the first item seems to have been written just about this time. Only one other item is relevant here, but I give the whole list:

Gandalf's escape – put this at the end of XXVI [i.e. 'The White Rider']

What happens to Bill (the pony)? [*Added:* Goes back to Bree and is found by Sam who rides him home.]

Bill Ferney.

Bree and Merry's ponies.

Barnabas Butterbur [*added*: and the ponies).

Galadriel.

Ents. Treebeard. Entwives.

Aragorn weds Eowyn sister of Eomer (who becomes Lord of Rohan) and becomes King of Gondor.

Feast in Gondor. Home Journey. They pass by round Lórien.[18]

But the story of Aragorn and Eowyn would in the event, of course, be quite otherwise; and in another short group of notes, isolated and undateable, this marital alliance of Rohan and Gondor was rejected (and no other was foreseen):

? Cut out the love-story of Aragorn and Eowyn. Aragorn is too old and lordly and grim. Make Eowyn the twin-sister of Eomund, a stern amazon woman.

If so, alter the message of Galadriel (XXVI.17).

Probably Eowyn should die to avenge or save Theoden.

But my father added in a hasty scribble the possibility that Aragorn did indeed love Eowyn, and never wedded after her death.

The reference 'XXVI.17' is to the page in the 'fair copy' manuscript of 'The White Rider' where appears Galadriel's message to Aragorn delivered to him by Gandalf (p. 431):

Elfstone, Elfstone, bearer of my green stone,
In the south under snow a green stone thou shalt see.
Look well, Elfstone! In the shadow of the dark throne
Then the hour is at hand that long hath awaited thee.

The green stone in the south was borne on Theoden's brow (p. 444), beneath his white hair, and it was Eowyn who would stand in the shadow of the dark throne within his hall.

NOTES

1   Beginning originally at 'Gandalf now wrapped himself again in his old tattered cloak' (p. 430; TT p. 107), the opening of 'The King of the Golden Hall' was then moved to 'The morning was bright and clear about them' (pp. 431–2; TT p. 111). The second rearrangement, giving the form in TT, was made after 'The King of the Golden Hall' was completed.

2 Names in *Theod*-, like names in *Eo*- (p. 403 note 5), are not written with an accent at this time.

3 In TT there are sixteen barrows at the foot of the hill of Edoras, and it is 500 years since Eorl the Young came out of the North. See note 11.

4 The flowers on the burial mounds, 'like tiny snowdrops' in the first draft, became in the second 'tiny flowers star-shaped and frail'. And in the second Legolas says: 'Seven mounds I see, and seven long lives of men it is, since the golden hall was built. [*Struck out at once:* And many more lives still since the Rohiroth first passed into this land.]' It seems curious that such awareness of the history of the Riders of Rohan should be attributed to Legolas.

5 'Stay, strangers unknown! Who are ye, friends or foes, that have come thus strangely clad riding to the gates of this town? None may here enter in, neither beggarman nor warrior, if we know not his name. Now, ye comers from afar, declare to us in haste: what are ye called? What is your errand to Theoden our lord?' – My father first used the Old English letter 'thorn' but changed to 'th' as he wrote.

   The passage in *Beowulf* (lines 237–57) in which Beowulf and his companions are accosted by the watchman on the coast of Denmark is very distinctly echoed, as also is the passage in Modern English in TT, p. 113 ('Who are you that come heedless over the plain ...').

6 Conceivably there was some confusion arising from the initial idea that Gandalf with Gimli entered Eodoras in advance of Aragorn and Legolas: Gandalf was introduced into the scenes at the gates and the doors, but Gimli, who would play little explicit part in them, was neglected. 'The *three* companions went forward' is certainly very surprising, since here the scene seems to be expressly visualised without Gimli; but this may have been a mere slip, deriving from the frequent use of 'the three companions' (Aragorn, Legolas, and Gimli) in preceding chapters.

7 One of the guards replies that 'None are welcome here in days of war save only those that come from [*struck out:* Gemenburg] *Heatorras Giemen Minas Tirith*', with *Mundbeorg* written in the margin. These Old English words are *gēmen, gīemen* 'care, heed, watch'; *Hēatorras* 'high towers'; and *Mundbeorg* 'protection-hill', distinct from *Mundburg* in LR. *Mundbeorg* occurs in another draft: 'And I am Aragorn son of Arathorn ... and it is to Mundbeorg that I journey as to my home' (cf. TT p. 113, 'it is to Mundburg that he goes').

8 An echo of the Old English poem known as *The Wanderer*, line 92: *Hwær cwom mearg? Hwær cwom mago?*

9 It is perhaps possible that the 'Beowulfian' reception at the gates

played some part in the increased hostility of Theoden before ever Wormtongue entered the story.

10   Two small details in the scene before the doors may be mentioned. The guards, turning their sword-hilts towards the strangers, cried *Cumath her wilcuman!* This was later changed to *Wesath hale, feorran cumene*, which appears in TT (p. 114) translated, 'Hail, comers from afar!' And Gandalf speaks to Aragorn with an asperity that was afterwards softened (TT p. 115): 'Needless is Theoden's demand, but needless also is your refusal, Aragorn.'

11   In LR the time-span was of course vastly greater: according to the Tale of Years Eorl the Young won the victory of the Field of Celebrant and the Rohirrim settled in Calenardhon (Rohan as a province of Gondor) in the year 2510 of the Third Age, which was that number of years after the overthrow of Sauron by Gilgalad and Elendil. With the statement here cf. the genealogy that Aragorn gives of himself at the passage of the Pillars of the Kings, in which he is only separated from Isildur by three (subsequently four) generations (pp. 360–1).

It is difficult to explain the name 'Battle of the Field of Gorgoroth': on the First Map the Battle Plain (*Dagras*, later *Dagorlad*) is placed where it remained, outside the mountain-fences of Mordor and separated from Gorgoroth by the great pass, then named Kirith Ungol (Map III, p. 309).

12   Eofored is not named as Theoden's son. In the outline for this chapter the Second Master seems to have been slain in the final battle of the River Isen, and his funeral feast was held after the return to Eodoras (pp. 435, 437). His death has now been moved back to the fighting before Gandalf's arrival.

13   Theoden here says that 'only a few days ago men reported to me that Shadowfax had come back out of the West; but none could lay hands on him, for he went away swiftly northwards.' See p. 434 and note 2. This then became 'men reported that Shadowfax had been seen again, running wild through the land'; and finally, as in TT, 'I heard that Shadowfax had come back riderless'.

14   Wormtongue still says that 'to the wonder of us all my lord *lent to you* Shadowfax'. This was subsequently changed to his words in TT: 'my lord bade you choose any horse you would and be gone; and to the wonder of us all you took Shadowfax in your insolence.'

15   In the draft for this passage the reading is 'Go [*struck out:* Eowyn and you too Ælflæd Flæd] Idis and you too Eowyn'. Cf. the Old English poetic word *ides* 'woman, lady'. In early notes Eowyn is 'daughter of Theoden' and 'daughter of Eomund' (p. 390).

16   Even to the names of Theoden's sword, *Herugrim*, and his horse, *Snowmane*: only in the case of Dunharrow was there an earlier

form, *Dunberg*. *Dunharrow* is so named on Map IVE, p. 319.

17   In LR the genealogy is:

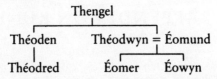

Near the end of the chapter 'Theodred' appears: ' "Behold I go forth," said Theoden. "[*Struck out at once:* Theodred my son] I have no son. I name Eomer my sister-son to be my heir" ' (cf. TT p. 127). On the other hand, in a second version of this passage, Theoden says: 'I have no child. Theodred my brother's son is slain.'

18   To this last item in the list the following was added at some later time:

No. They learn (in Rivendell?) that Nazgûl razed Lórien and Keleborn fled with a remnant to Mirkwood. Galadriel was lost or was hidden. Or shall Lórien be left slowly to fade? Yes. Galadriel parts with Keleborn who elects to stay in the world and [?woods]. She is seen by Frodo in old age, when he and Sam see Galadriel and Bilbo (and Elrond? No – he has one [*written above:* 3?] [*struck out:* age] life of men still to rule in Rivendell).

APPENDIX ON RUNES

It is notable that all references to runes in *The Lord of the Rings* were associated with Gandalf until my father came to the words graved on Balin's tomb in Moria. In *The Hobbit* runic writing is almost entirely associated with Dwarves (who are said, in Chapter III 'A Short Rest', to have invented the runic Moon-letters), but runes had been an element in Middle-earth from a very early stage.* In his letter to G. E. Selby of 14 December 1937, cited in the Foreword to Vol. VI *The Return of the Shadow*, my father said that he preferred his own mythology 'with its consistent nomenclature and organized history' to *The Hobbit*, and spoke with humorous disparagement of 'this rabble of Eddaic-named dwarves out of Völuspá, new-fangled hobbits and gollums (invented in an idle hour) and *Anglo-Saxon runes*.' As will be seen, when he wrote these last words he was thinking of his own runic alphabets, already at that time highly developed, and not in any way particularly associated with the Dwarves, if associated with them at all. It is conceivable, I think, that it was nonetheless Thror's Map, bearing runic writing of great importance in the story of *The Hobbit*, that brought that close association into being (although the Dwarves always remained the inheritors and not the first devisers of the *Angerthas*).

There seems to be relatively little extant writing concerning the runes from the period we have reached in this book, but my father's linguistic papers and work on scripts and alphabets were left in so chaotic a state that it is often impossible to be sure even of a broad and relative dating. A central problem lies, as always in this context, in the existence of two sets of variables. The richly divergent development of scripts, as of speech-sounds, among different peoples was a datum from the start; but the detail of those divergences was subject to unceasing modification in the mind of their deviser. When the papers (almost always undated and often without consecutive pagination) are so disordered that material which may well be separated by decades is jumbled together, the risk is great of false conjunctions and false constructions.

---

* The earliest runic document relating to Middle-earth that I know of is a little slip of paper in my father's early handwriting, headed *Gondolinic Runes*. This gives an alphabet in which the values of the runes are almost totally different from the *Angerthas*, but in which the principles of phonetic organisation in relation to letter-shape are strongly evident.

I give here first two brief texts that seem to me to come most likely from the period shortly before the beginning of *The Lord of the Rings* – more or less contemporary with the *Quenta Silmarillion* and the *Lhammas* given in Vol. V, *The Lost Road and Other Writings*. Both are clear manuscripts in ink, and to both of them my father later added in pencil; I give these additions, though I suspect that they were substantially later. It will be seen that these additions concern the especial importance of Runic writing among the Dwarves, of which no mention is made in these texts as written.

(i)

The Elvish Alphabets

These have three main forms: the alphabets of Rúmil, of Fëanor, and [of] Dairon; also called the Valinorian, Túnian, and Beleriandic letters.

The first two are of Noldorin origin and ultimately related; , the last is distinct and of Ilkorin origin.

The oldest is the *Alphabet of Rúmil*. This is a final cursive elaboration of the oldest letters of the Noldor in Valinor. Only the completion and arrangement of this system was actually due to Rúmil of Túna; its author or authors are now forgotten. Though originating in Túna it is called 'Valinorian' because it was mainly used for writing of Qenya, and was later ousted from use among the Noldor by the alphabet of Fëanor. It is said still to be used by the Lindar of Valinor; but is not in general use among the Qendi.*

The *Alphabet of Fëanor* was partly derived from this, and partly devised afresh to fit a different system of writing (from left to right). Its actual author – in all forms except the later modifications to fit the changed conditions of Noldorin after the Exile, which were made after his death – was Fëanor. He constructed it both as a general phonetic alphabet, and devised special arrangements to fit the characteristics of Qenya, Noldorin, and Telerin. This alphabet is the one generally used for Qenya, and for all purposes by the surviving Qendi.

The so-called *Alphabet of Dairon* was in origin a 'runic' script devised for inscriptions, especially on wood, that originated among the Ilkorins. It is usually said to have arisen in Doriath, and it certainly there developed most completely, even

---

* With this passage cf. the *Lhammas* in Vol. V, pp. 173–4.

producing a written form. But probably its actual invention was due to the Danian elves of Ossiriand (who were ultimately of Noldorin race).* The name 'alphabet of Dairon' is due to the preservation in this script of some fragments of the songs of Dairon, the ill-fated minstrel of King Thingol of Doriath, in the works on the ancient Beleriandic languages by Pengolod the Wise of Gondolin. The Noldor did not use this script much, even in Beleriand, though Pengolod cites cases of inscriptions at Nargothrond and Sirion's mouth that are in Noldorin tongue. [*Added in pencil:* But this runic alphabet spread eastward from Ossiriand to the Dwarves, and was largely used by them.]

(ii)

The 'Alphabet of Dairon'

The Ilkorins of Beleriand devised an alphabet of 'runes', or angular letters used in inscriptions. This became widespread in Beleriand, already before the exile of the Noldor of Valinor, and showed various divergences in forms and uses at different times and places. Its chief elaboration took place in Doriath, where a written form was developed. Owing to the ruin of Beleriand, before the departure of the Noldor to Eressëa, no actual inscription or book in this script is now preserved. Knowledge of it [*changed in pencil to:* no actual Elvish inscription or book in this script was preserved. Knowledge of its use by the Elves] is now preserved only in books in Eressëa – in the works of Pengolod of Gondolin upon the Beleriandic languages, and other similar writings. Pengolod copied and gave extracts from various inscriptions and books that were still extant in his day. Of the books, or written form, his principal source was some fragments of the songs of King Thingol's minstrel Dairon. From this fact is derived the [*struck out:* erroneous] name: Alphabet of Dairon.

The origin of the script is probably to be placed in Ossiriand among the Danian elves, many of whom were incorporated in Doriath after the coming of Morgoth and the fall of their king, Denethor.† The Danian elves were ultimately of Noldorin race, and inventions of this sort were a special aptitude of the

* On the Danian elves or *Danas* see especially V.176, 188–9.
† See the *Quenta Silmarillion* in Vol. V, p. 263.

Noldor.* Moreover a related alphabet was early in use among the eastern branch of the Danians, beyond the Blue Mountains, whence it also spread to Men in those regions, becoming the foundation of the Taliskan *skirditaila* or 'runic series'. [*Added in pencil:* Related alphabets were (> A related alphabet was) also borrowed (from both Men and Elves) by the Dwarves; the western Dwarves early borrowed and adapted the full inscriptional 'Alphabet of Dairon', and most of the inscriptions in this form that survived the Great War in Eriador and elsewhere are of Dwarvish origin, though their language is seldom the secret tongue of the Dwarves.]

This alphabet was not much used by the exiled Noldor, but in certain cases, in the absence of parchment or for carving on wood, or where as at Sirion's mouth they were mingled with Ilkorins, they employed these letters during their exile, and modified their forms or applications to fit their own language. Pengolod gives some examples of this Noldorin usage. [*Added in pencil:* The greatest elaboration was reached in Eregion and Moria, where during the Second Age Elves and Dwarves lived in harmony. This later form was called the 'Runes of Moria', because it remained long in use among the Dwarves, and most of the inscriptions employing it survived in the halls and chambers of Moria.]

With this view of the origin of the name *Alphabet of Dairon* cf. *The Lord of the Rings* Appendix E (II): 'Their richest and most ordered form was known as the Alphabet of Daeron, since in Elvish tradition it was said to have been devised by Daeron, the minstrel and loremaster of King Thingol of Doriath.'

The reference to Taliska (for which see V.179, 191, 196: 'the language of the three houses of Bëor, of Haleth, and of Hador') is very interesting as adumbrating a relationship between the runes of Beleriand and the ancient Germanic runes; cf. V.279 on the 'Indo-European' word *widris* 'wisdom' in the ancient tongue of the people of Bëor. It seems clear that the second element of Taliskan *skirditaila* 'runic series' is to be understood as an ancestral cognate of the word seen in Old English *tæl* (with a sense 'number, reckoning, series'; Old Norse *tal*, etc., and cf. Modern English *tale*, *tell*); the first element may perhaps be connected with the Germanic stem *sker-*, seen in Old Norse *skera* 'cut, carve', Old English *sceran* (Modern English *shear*, cf. ultimately related *shard*, *potsherd*).

Detailed exposition from this time of the ancient Elvish runes seems

* Cf. the *Ainulindalë* in Vol. V, p. 162.

to be restricted to a series of five manuscript pages – which are indeed extremely informative. In style and bearing they seem to me to belong with substantial work on Noldorin phonology that certainly comes from the time not long preceding the start of *The Lord of the Rings*. Since it would be extremely difficult to print these pages as part of the text, and since they would be unclear in facsimile reproduction (and require a lot of unnecessary explanation and annotation), I have rewritten and redrawn them as a series of plates, numbered I to IV, at the end of this Appendix. I have attempted to remain very faithful to the originals, and have only edited them in a few minor points that in no way alter their purport; I have not attempted to smooth away the various inconsistencies of presentation. There are a very few pencilled changes that are ignored. At the head of the first sheet my father wrote: 'All this has been revised and rewritten. See Appendices to *Lord of the Rings*.'

On plate V I reproduce a separate manuscript leaf entitled 'Dwarf-runes for writing English (phonetic)', which I shall refer to in this Appendix as 'E'. This is obviously quite distinct from the other pages, but it will be found that it agrees well on the whole with 'the later Noldorin use' on plate II (referred to subsequently as 'N'), though there is some difference in the application of signs, notably in the nasals and in those representing English *š* (*sh*), *ž* (as in *vision*), *tš* (*ch*), and *dž* (*j* as twice in *judge*), which are either used for different sounds in N or not found there. As will be seen shortly, this page evidently dates from the time of my father's return to the Moria story, as described in this book. Curiously, *kw* (*qu*) is absent from E, and the rune V for *kw* in the Doriath and Noldorin usage is there given to *tš* (*ch*). In E, also, *h* is represented by $<$, but by $>$ in the others.

At the bottom of plate V I have transcribed the runic inscription on Balin's tomb from the end of the original first 'Moria' chapter in Vol. VI (see p. 460 and note 40). As noted there, it was at that point that my father decided to use the Runes of Beleriand in preference to Old English runes, for he first wrote the inscription in the latter but at once wrote it in the former as well – in two forms, which I have marked (i) and (ii). The words *Runes of Dwarves* on the same page (VI.460) no doubt have some significance in this connection; cf. also Gandalf's words in the second version of the chapter ('The Lord of Moria', p. 186): 'These are dwarf-runes, such as they use in the North.' – On the name *Burin* of Balin's father see VI.444.

Version (i) of the tomb-inscription agrees with E (and with N) in every point save one: the use of the rune $>$ for *s* in *son* instead of λ. In E $>$ is used for the vowel [ʌ] (as in English *cup*); while in N it is used for *h*.

Version (ii) agrees with (i) in the *s*-rune, but reverses ō and ŏ in *lord* and *Moria*, and for *l* in *lord* substitutes V for $+$: the former is found in the Doriath and Noldorin use. Here the rune ᛗ is used for the vowel in *son*, where (i) has the unphonetic ∨ (*o*). In E this rune has the value *ai*, in N the value *ae* (later changed in pencil to *ai* in a reversal of the values *ai* and *ae*).

The next (third) version of the tomb-inscription, at the end of the second version ('The Lord of Moria') of the chapter, is hidden by a fourth version pasted over it; but Taum Santoski has been able to read the underlying inscription by lighting the page from the back. With *Fundin* for *Burin* (see VI.444) the runic writing thus recovered is almost as in version (i), with the same use of > for *s*; but very curiously this same rune is used for *o* in both occurrences of the word *of*, although ∨ for *o* appears in *son*, *lord*, and *Moria*. In addition, the Dwarvish words *Balin Fundinul Uzbad Khazaddūmu* are added beneath, the rune for *z* being apparently ⋏ , which is *s* in all the alphabets given here.

The fourth version of the inscription, that pasted over the third, and the fifth, at the end of the typescript text that followed, are identical in all forms; the latter is reproduced on p. 186. So far as the brief text goes, agreement with E is here complete, with *s* represented by ⋏ , *z* represented by ⋏ , and > used for the vowel [ʌ], which here appears in the word *son*, treated phonetically.

On plate VI I have redrawn the runic writing from the two earliest illustrations of a burnt and blackened page from the Book of Mazarbul. These redrawings are intended to show the runes and their relative placing and nothing more. The earliest form (i) is found on the back of the last page of the original 'Moria' chapter (see VI.460, 467). This is the merest sketch, an indication of what might be done in this direction: it was made very hastily, scribbled down, with little attempt at verisimilitude, the illegible parts of the page being represented by rough scribbled strokes (and the number of missing lines in my redrawing is approximate and impressionistic). The right-hand bottom corner is shown as a triangular detached piece, on which only the word *Kazaddūm* is written. The second form (ii) is a much more developed representation of the slashed and discoloured leaf, done in pencil and coloured chalks; here again the bottom corner is shown as torn right off. (The evolution of this page is emblematic in miniature of my father's mode of work: the evolution of the details of shape is progressive and continuous. In this second version there are two holes on the right hand side of the page and a bite out of the top; in the third and fourth versions these remain, but the bottom corner is added back, with a triangular indentation above, continuing into the page as a black line. In the final form, reproduced in *Pictures by J. R. R. Tolkien* no. 23, the central hole is enlarged and moved to the left, but the black line remains where the bottom corner was originally shown as torn off and separate.)

The words of the original sketch have been given in VI.467, but I
repeat them here in phonetic form:

1	Wē drouv aut *the* orks fro[m] .... gard
2	... [f]irst hōl. Wī slū meni ʌndr *the* brait sʌn
3	in *the* deil. Flōi woz kild bai ʌn arou ....
4	Wī did..........
9	Wī ha[v] okjupaid *the* twentifʌrst hōl ov
10	norþ end. Ðer ōr iz..........
11	.... šaft iz..........
12	[B]alin haz set ʌp hiz tšēr in *the* tšeimbr ov Mazar
13	bul......................Balin iz lord ov
14	Moria..........
18	Balin..........
20	Kazaddūm

Here there is close but not complete agreement with E. The s-rune is
ʌ not >, the latter being used for [ʌ], as in E; but there is divergence
in the *w*-rune, which is here ⱴ, to which E gives the value *dž* (*j*) and N
the value *gw*. The short single vertical used in E as abbreviation for *the*
when in the upper position and as a sign for the vowel [ə] when in the
lower position is here used for *the* in the lower position, but in the
upper position for *h* (in *have*, *has*, *his*): in both occurrences of the
word *hall* the stroke stands in the lower position, but this may have
been no more than an inadvertence, for the runes in this sketch were
pencilled very rapidly and several were written erroneously and then
corrected. The rune for the initial consonants [š] in *shaft* and [tš] in
chair, *chamber* also differ in their values from those ascribed to them
in E. The use of the *m*-rune for *v* in *we have occupied* (line 9) can only
be a slip. Lastly, the vowel [ʌ] is employed not only in *under*, *sun*, *up*
but also in *an (arrow)* and in *first* (at the second occurrence).

Comparison with E will show that the second version of the page
from the Book of Mazarbul agrees with it in every point and detail.
The different form of the *l*-rune in *Flōi* (line 4), with the crossing
stroke falling, not rising, to the right, is probably merely accidental (in
the third version the shape is normal at this point).

To this version my father appended a phonetic transcription. In this
he interpreted *oukn* in line 6 as *?broken*, *it* at the end of line 10 as *?its*,
and the word before *helm* in line 17 as *(?sil)vr*, though the last rune is
very clearly *n*, not *r* (in the third version an *r*-rune is written here).

The sequence of development in this much-considered passage was
very probably as follows. The original form of the text that Gandalf
first read out from the Book of Mazarbul seems to have been that of
the earliest drawing of the page itself (plate VI, i). Closely related to it
is the form in the original pencilled narrative of the scene, which can
be largely made out beneath the text written over it in ink (see pp. 191

and 205 note 4). Both forms had *the Orcs* for *Orcs* and Balin's *chair* for Balin's *seat*; but the original narrative text had *we have found truesilver, well-forged*, and *(To)morrow Óin is ... lead ... seek for the upp(er) armoury of the Third Deep*, all of which is absent from the first drawing of the page.

The overwritten text in the first narrative, which is given on p. 191, is effectively the same as the text in the second drawing of the page (plate VI, ii).

The third drawing of the page (which is otherwise very similar to the second, and employs exactly the same runic system) corresponds to the text of the fair copy manuscript of 'The Mines of Moria (ii)' given on pp. 200–1.

It is plain therefore that the first three drawings of this page from the Book of Mazarbul all belong to the same time, and relate step by step to the rewriting of this passage through the original draft and first fair copy of the narrative chapter; and that the runic alphabet set out in E, 'Dwarfrunes for writing English' (plate V), belongs to this time also. But when the fourth version of this page was done the runic values had changed.

The first drawings of the other two pages from the Book of Mazarbul (that written by Ori in Elvish script and the last page of the book, in runes) belong with and were done at the same time as the third drawing of the first page; for the texts see pp. 200–1.

I

Runes of Beleriand

The oldest signs seem to have been the following:-

Series (1) ᚹ . ᛒ . ᛩ . ᛥ . ᛰ . ᚱ . ᛯ . ᛱ .

(2) ᚾ . ᚠ . ᛀ . ᛁ . ᛏ . ᛚ . ᛕ . ᛘ . ᛣ .

(3) ᚴ . ᛆ . ᛁ . ᛄ . ᛉ . ᚴ . ᛇ . ᛈ .

(4) miscellaneous. ᛁ . ᚷ . ᛘ . ᚼ . ᚢ . ᚻ .

The distribution of these signs among the required values differed considerably at different times and in different places, but all varieties agreed on taking Series 1 generally as <u>labials</u> and Series 2 as <u>dentals</u>, while the principles were also usually observed that reversal represented a spirant (ᚹ p ᛩ f) and addition voicing (ᚾ t ᚠ d ᛁ đ).

The chief divergence occurred in the invention and application of later signs. As usual in runes there were no horizontal bars in the original runic form; but it may be noted that most of the runes consisted of a single vertical with a side appendage which was never attached to the bottom (except as a reduplication of one already at the top). Later elaborations developed inverted forms as ᛚ ᚦ and here the application was variable.

The original Doriath order of letters in transcription (phonetic) was as follows: (1) a . i . u . e . o. (2) p. t. k. (3) b. d. g. (4) f. þ. s. X (h). (5) ƀ. ȝ. ʒ. l. r. z. (6) m. n. ɲ. ng. (7) j . w. In this order it was borrowed in Ossiriand, and so in E. Danian and Taliska.

The runes associated with these values were usually :—

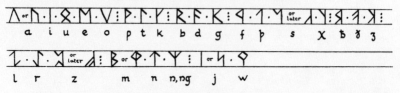

This series was altered by the intrusion of signs for kw etc. (inverted p or k runes being used : ᚦ or ᛚ) ; and the use of signs for vocalic and consonantal diphthongs ; also a differentiation was made between ɲ and ng, h and X, and between ē/e, ō/o (the other long vowels being distinguished later).

The special <u>Doriath</u> long series thus became as follows:—

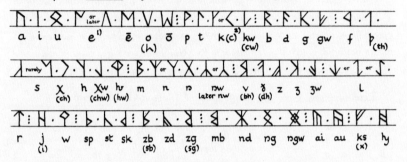

(The values in brackets are normal transcriptions).

Notes. 1) o + o V+V > W; therefore M taken as ∧+∧ = long ē. But also
∧ = inverted V = o; therefore k was also used as o.   2) Normally a spirant is
a reverse; therefore when > was invented as differentiation of Y = X and h,
also < as variant of Y = k, c arose.

The later Noldorin use.

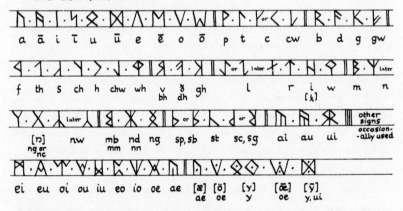

The order was variable. The above order was usual. The only vowel
diphthongs ever counted as fixed letters were ai, au, ui : the rest were
only occasionally used instead of writing with two letters (aj, uj, aw, ow, ei, ej

III

and so on), which was frequently done even with ai, au, ui.

Since later in Noldorin mb, nd became m(m), n(n) confusion arose with ꞵ 8, and both tended to be used indiscriminately, while ✱ dropped out of use except for occasional employment as nn. ng also became ŋ, so two developments occurred: (a) ✗̃ was used = ŋ (transcription ng), and X was used for ŋk (transcription nc); or (b) ✗̃ was dropped and only X used.

The written form, or 'Alphabet of [Pengolod >] Dairon'

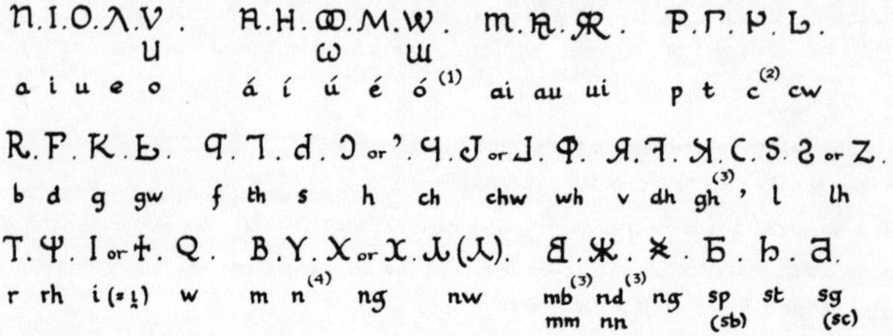
a i u e o
á í ú é ó (1)
ai au ui
p t c (2) cw
or
b d g gw
f th s h ch chw wh v dh gh (3) ' l lh
or
r rh i (= i̯) w
m n (4) ng nw
mb (3) nd (3) ng sp st sg
mm nn (sb) (sc)

Notes. (1) These letters (á í ú é ó) originally longs were variously employed in representations of later Noldorin. (2) Originally C was also employed as a variant; but later it was used as a sign of hiatus between vowels, and especially initially to represent vocalic beginning after loss of Ꙅ (gh from g by mutation). (3) These letters though only employed regularly in Old Noldorin were retained in the alphabet and sometimes in orthography — as Z∩8 = *lamb* pronounced *lăm* (< **lambē*) 'tongue'; but X and ✗̃ became used as mere variant shapes of the same letter. (4) Originally Ψ was used as a variant of Y = n (and ሐ of ⅄ = nw); but later Ψ became used as the sign for initial voiceless r (rh), when the two forms of l became differentiated (as S = l Ƨ or Z = lh).

Other vocalic signs were also often employed but not reckoned as separate letters. Thus ⅄̃ ei = ΛI; A eo = ΛV; ∀ or ꓤ oe = VΛ; and the modifications: V̈ Ẅ = oe monophthong [ö], ʘ, ϖ̈ = y.

The signs Ә z, Ƃ zd, ሐ ngw were no longer retained in the alphabet. Similarly Ɛ (x, ks, hs), H or ℌ = ly were only used in representing foreign words

IV

The smaller and more cursive letters were as follows.

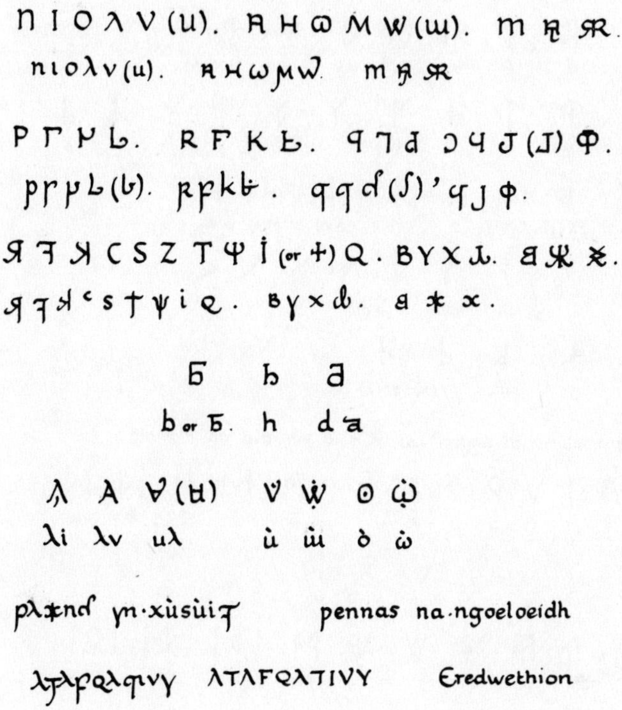
pennas na·ngoeloeidh
Eredwethion

Dwarf runes for writing English (phonetic)

General nasal sign ∧ as R̂ = ᛞ mb but on P̂ = mp

the ' of R and ∫

The earliest forms of the inscription on Balin's tomb in Moria

(i)

RᚢᛏIY · >VYY · Vᚱ : RᚪᛏIY : ᛏVᛏF · Vᚱ : BWᛏIᚾ

(ii)

RᚢᛏIY · >ᛗY · Vᚱ RᚪᛏIY : ᛚWᛏF · Vᚱ BVᛏIᚾ

(i)

VI

'Page of Balin's Book'

```
1
2
3
4
5  . . . . . . . . . . . . . . . . . . . . .
6  . . . . . . . . . . . . . . . . . . . . .
7  . . . . . . . . . . . . . . . . . . . . .
8  . . . . . . . . . . . . . . . . . . . . .
9
10
11
12
13
14
15 . . . . . . . . . . . . . . . . . . . . .
16 . . . . . . . . . . . . . . . . . . . . .
17 . . . . . . . . . . . . . . . . . . . . .
18
19 . . . . . . . . . . . . . . . . . . . . .
20
```

(ii)

'One page of the Book of Moria'

```
1
2
3
4
5
6
7
8
9
10
11 . . . . . . . . . . . . . . . . . . . . .
12
13
14
15
16
17
18
19
20
21
22
23
24
25
```

INDEX

As in the Index to *The Return of the Shadow*, I have slightly reduced
the number of page-references in the case of names that occur very
frequently by using the word *passim* to mean that the name is missing
only from a single page here and there in a long series otherwise
unbroken.

The very large number of names occurring in this book that were
soon rejected and replaced are nearly all given separate cross-
references to a primary name; exceptions are cases where such a name
falls in immediate proximity to the primary name (thus whereas
Dolamarth is entered separately from *Amon Amarth*, *Amarthon* is
not), and certain purely experimental names (such as the rejected
names for *Amon Hen/Amon Lhaw*). Names in *Errantry* are all entered
under *Errantry*.

Names appearing on the redrawn maps, on the reproductions of
pages from texts of *The Lord of the Rings*, and on the manuscript
pages at the end of the *Appendix on Runes*, are not indexed.

Bregalad Quickbeam the Ent. 419

Brego Builder of the Golden Hall. Son of Brytta 435, 445; in LR son of Eorl the Young 440, 445

Bridgefields In the Eastfarthing. 33, 39

Broken Sword, The See *Sword that was Broken.*

Brownhay Rhosgobel, home of Radagast. 164, 173

Brown Lands 316, 351, 364. See *Withered Wold.*

Bruinen, River 17, 59, 65, 296, 299; *Ford of Bruinen* (including references to *the Ford*) 13–14, 16, 57, 61, 70, 113, 137, 172. See *Loudwater.*

Brytta Father of Brego. 435, 445; in LR eleventh King of Rohan 440

Buckland 6, 11, 13, 30–1, 53–5, 68, 72, 135, 249; *Horn-call of Buckland* 54

Bucklebury Ferry (including references to *the Ferry*) 13, 55, 70–1

Budgeford In the Eastfarthing. 33, 39

Bundu-shathûr One of the Mountains of Moria (Cloudyhead). 174; *Shathûr* 174. Earlier name *Udushinbar* 432

Burin (1) Son of Balin. 172, 204. (2) Father of Balin. 456–7

Butterbur, Barnabas 10, 34, 37, 40, 42–9, 51–2, 56, 62–3, 73, 77–8, 132, (134), 152, 448; *Barney* 47; later name *Barliman* 77

Buzundush Dwarvish name of the Blackroot river (= Silverlode). 166–7, 241

Bywater 253

Calacirian The Pass of Light. 98, 101; *Carakilian* 93, 95; *Kalakilya* 95

Calenardhon Rohan as a province of Gondor. 450

Calembel (1) Town in Lamedon. 388. (2) See *Calenbel.*

Calenbel Lawn beneath Amon Hen (afterwards *Parth Galen*). 371, 382, 384, 388, 393–4, 401; *Calembel* 384, 387–8. Earlier names *Kelufain* 371, 377, 382, 388; *Forfain* 382

Calendil, Calennel See *(The) Tongue.*

Calenhir, River In Gondor. 312

Caradras 161, 164, 166, 169–71, 174, 188, 215, 247, 257, 296, 306, 367–8, 430; *Caradhras* 166–8, 174. See *Barazinbar, Red-horn, Ruddyhorn.*

Carakilian See *Calacirian.*

Caras Galadon 233, 235, 242, 245–6, 249–50, 256, 258, 261, 265, 279, 285, 289, 354, 363, 367, 431; *Caras Galadhon* 235; *Caras* 367

Carn Dûm 37

Carpenter, Humphrey Biography 66, 187; in *Letters* 90; *The Ink-lings* 106

Carrock Beorn's 'carrock' 287, 307; *the Great Carrock* (Tolondren) 268–9, 287

Dol Dúgol   Dwelling of the Necromancer in Southern Mirkwood (see 298). 178, 233–4, 242, 244, 296, 298, 306. Replaced by *Dol Dúghul* 244, 296, 306, 333, 351, 372; and that by *Dol Guldur* 292

Dol Guldur   See *Dol Dúgol*.

Dolmed, Mount   In the Blue Mountains. 301

Doriath   110, 124, 331, 453–5; runes of Doriath 456–7

Dorthonion   240, 420. See *Orod-na-Thôn*.

Downs   East of Entwash. 320, 391–2, 394, 398–9, 406. See *Barrow-downs*.

Dragon(s)   28, 170; referring to Smaug 22, 142, 160; *dragon-fire* 28

Dream of the Tower, Frodo's   11, 33–6, 56, 130. See *Western Tower*.

Duath   See *Ephel Dúath*.

Du-finnion   Trotter. 61

Duil Rewinion   Hills of the Hunters. 287

Duin Morghul   Stream in the Morgul Vale (in LR *Morgulduin*). 312. Also named *Ithilduin* 312

Dúnadan, The   (of Aragorn). 83. *Dúnedain* 291. See *Tarkil*.

Dunharrow   320, 447, 450–1. Earlier name *Dunberg* 447, 451

Dunland   167, 320

Durin   141–2, 180, 183–5, 189, 220, 234; *Durin's folk, clan* 143, 156, 246; ~ *axe* 191, 200; ~ *crown* 220; ~ *stone* 203, 219; ~ *tower* 430–1; ~ *bridge* 431

Durin's Bane   143, 185–6, 188–9, 202, 257

Dwarrowdelf   Moria. 166, 173, 183, 186

Dwarves   At Bag End 20–1; of the Blue Mountains 301; of the Lonely Mountain 117, 142, 155, 160, 424; of Moria 142, 156, 164, 166, 175, 179, 181, 183–6, 188, 218, 225, 247, 263, 304, 431, 455; other references 24, 114, 125, 142–3, 152, 158, 160, 162, 170, 181, 212, 227, 231, 257, 275. War of the Dwarves and the Orcs (Goblins) 142–3; *Western Dwarves* 455; *Dwarf-cities, Dwarf-road* 301; *Dwarf-door* (of Moria) 191, *Dwarf-doors* 187; language 117, 181, 185–6, 455; runes of the Dwarves 186, 200, 452–9. See *Seven Rings*.

Dwarvish   174, 191, 241, 455, 457; *dwarfish* 241; *dwarven* 104, the *Dwarven-door* of Moria 178, 204

Eagle(s)   75–6, 116, 130, 134, 139, 151, 389, 400–1; eagle seen far off 357, 361, 379–80, 385, 387–9, 396–7, 403, 425–6. See *Gwaewar*.

Eärendel   91, 95–6, 99, 102, 108, 110, 266, 290; *Eärendil* 95, 103, 266, 290; *Eärendel's star* 276, *the Evening Star* 266; *the Short Lay of Eärendel: Eärendillinwë* 102–3 (development of the 'Rivendell version' of *Errantry*, 90–105).

Eastemnet   318, 398, 404